David Kirby

ALSO BY MICHAEL M. THOMAS

Green Monday

SOMEONE

Simon and Schuster • *New York*

ELSE'S
MONEY

a novel by

Michael M. Thomas

Although human nature and behavior are repeated and replayed, as is history both ancient and modern, the characters, events and institutions herein depicted are fictitious.

Published by Simon and Schuster
A Division of Gulf & Western Corporation
Simon & Schuster Building
Rockefeller Center
1230 Avenue of the Americas
New York, New York 10020
SIMON AND SCHUSTER and colophon are trademarks of Simon & Schuster
Designed by Irving Perkins Associates
Manufactured in the United States of America

10 9 8 7 6 5 4 3 2 1

Library of Congress Cataloging in Publication Data

Thomas, Michael M.
Someone else's money.

I. Title
PS3570.H574S6 1982 813'.54 82-11105

ISBN 0-671-43302-4

For the good times

"As a portion of the world affect to despise the power of money, I must try and show them what it is."

—Charles Dickens, *The Life and Adventures of Nicholas Nickleby*, 1838–1839

"Oh, there is an aristocracy here [in New York], then?" said Martin. "Of what is it composed?"

"Of intelligence, sir," replied the other man; "of intelligence and virtue. And of their necessary consequence in this republic. Dollars, sir."

—Charles Dickens, *Martin Chuzzlewit*, 1843–1844

MORGAN: *"The question of control, in this country at least, is personal; that is, in money."*
COUNSEL: *"How about credit?"*
MORGAN: *"In credit, too."*
COUNSEL: *"Is not credit based primarily upon money or property?"*
MORGAN: *"No, sir, the first thing is character."*
COUNSEL: *"Before money or property?"*
MORGAN: *"Before money or anything else. Money cannot buy it."*

—*Testimony of J. P. Morgan before the Pujo Committee, 1912*

Prologue

Through the branches of the oak tree, the moon shone bright as a Mexican dollar. It glistened wet as water on the moatlike white gravel drive in front of the ranch house. The house, of wood mainly, had been built in the lee of a slight rise in the midst of the black sea of the plains.

Upstairs in the Big House, the sleeping child dreamed that his mother was riding to him across a sunlit field of waving grass. He was five years old. It had been a lovely day; the heat of summer was abating, and the evening brought with it a faint, cool breath that hinted of winter building up hundreds of miles to the north, beyond the Rockies.

He had spent the day playing with the berry-brown sons of the vaqueros, the only other little boys within forty miles. Before supper he had been given a favorite treat, a canter around the yard perched on the silver-inlaid pommel of the saddle of Ildario, the head vaquero. He wished his grandfather and father could have been there to see him, but they had gone off the evening before on a business trip. His sister wasn't there either; she was far away, up North, visiting her grandparents, the ones he wasn't kin to. But his mother had left her piano lesson to come to the porch to watch his triumphant circuit of the yard and had told him how proud he made her. Afterward, he and his mother, and her piano teacher, had had an early supper. When he was taken up to bed, his mother had read to him from his favorite book; it was about Mulberry Street, in a huge city far away, called New York, which his mother talked about sometimes. All sorts of wonderful things happened on Mulberry Street. There were a blue elephant and a wonderful, strange horse, not at all like the ranch ponies. His mother had promised she'd take him to Mulberry Street one day. He wondered if his friend Ildario could come too.

Suddenly a shriek sawed jaggedly through the golden film of his dream. Other noises crowded in: angry shouts; loud reports; shufflings. His room burst alight and he sat up, terrified, unsure whether he was awake or in a dream. He was surprised, and frightened, to see his grandfather standing over him, eyes flaming with rage, a gun in the hand hanging loosely at his side. Why was Granddaddy there? He wasn't supposed to be back. There was no time for the question. His grandfather wrenched him violently out of his bed, causing him to yelp with pain and fright, to break into tears. He was dragged, wailing for Mamma, down the hall toward her room while all around him were the confused sounds of a household being startled into life. A burning smell hung in the air.

His grandfather jerked him through the door. He tried to dig his feet into the floor, to stop whatever was happening to him, knowing instinctively that he wanted no part of whatever was in that room; then he was through the door, and picked up and held by his grandfather, feeling the steel of the revolver hot against his arm, smelling the powder and seeing, so that some part of him would forever retain the sight, two naked bodies on the bed. One was a man, but his face wore a mask of blood so the child didn't recognize him as the piano teacher. But he could see that the other figure, breathing with gulping, ratcheting sobs, trying to say something, was his mother, as he had never seen her, without any clothes on, one hand covering the dark hair at her crotch, the other pressing on her stomach, trying to hold back the blood that was welling through her fingers. She looked at her little son for a long moment, her eyes starting to glaze and a red, foaming bubble at her lips, while he looked back, shivering, the tears and wails choked in his throat by terror. The boy felt himself being shaken violently by his grandfather, being shouted at as if he had done something horrible and wrong:

"See that, Buford! See that! Don't you never trust them New York people! They're whores and thieves, every one of them. Don't you never forget that, boy! Don't you never!"

Then his grandfather went silent and bore him away from the bed and the room. He was carried down the stairs and thrust into the arms of a Mexican woman. He saw his father clinging to the newel post, trembling. His grandfather said something to his father in a voice like a knife. Then he was settled on a warm Mexican bosom, smelling of frijoles and flour, and cajoled with Spanish endearments until he whimpered his way to sleep.

The next day, the house was empty except for the servants. They were all gone: Granddaddy, Mamma, his father. It all seemed part of a terrible nightmare, which started to fade on waking and which, within hours, had drifted back to some recess of his mind beyond recall. So that when, weeks later, his grandfather and father returned and told him his mother wouldn't be coming back, that she had gone away to the angels, he cried briefly and knew he would miss her—but without a glimmer of remembrance of that night. Not then, nor a day later, when his grandfather's revolver, with a dated brass plaque set in its handle, appeared in the case downstairs—among the deeds, maps and old brown photographs which evidenced the history of the ranch and its people—nor for years and years afterward, except as a nightmare.

CHAPTER ONE

In the later seventeenth century, what was now a small square had been the farm of a middle-aged Dutch widow. Vrouw Stoffel was a doughty, self-reliant woman who had settled on Manhattan in 1654, a decade before the English came. Her farm had been located about a half-mile inland to the west and north of Corlaer's Hook and slightly over a mile northeast of the old city wall. It provided her with a small living from the butter, eggs and cream she sold in the town that had sprouted on the tip of the island. The entire operation consisted of a grassy yard where five hens and a rooster scrabbled, separated by the brook from a small rail-fenced garden and a patch of meadow where two Holsteins grazed. It was modest enough material for posterity.

Over the next three centuries, successive invaders—soldiers of the English King, wave after wave of immigrants and, inevitably, politicians, bankers, builders and other rascals growing rich on the irresistible northward sprawl of pavement and building stone—caused the peaceful market garden to be trodden under and asphalted over until nothing remained of its original dimensions and topography. Yet, in the odd way history works things out, Vrouw Stoffel's farm finally found a measure of patchy immortality as Rostval Place, the phonetic corruption and contraction of her name finally settled by the nineteenth century on the pleasant little square that Nicholas Reverey, a slender, agreeable-looking man in his early forties, found himself entering on an early April evening, observing that the square's sparse and blackened trees were finally showing small green evidences that spring had at last arrived.

Unprepossessing as it was, Rostval Place was among the few remnants of what natives of the city like Nick called "the real New York"—to distinguish the Manhattan of sentiment and nostalgia from what the island seemed to him to have become: the hunting ground of real estate sharks, laundered foreign money and flash and voguishness. The small, bare lawn in the middle of the square, surrounding the sooty pedestaled effigy of some long-forgotten politician, was unadorned except for a few benches, scruffy hedges and sad plane trees, sorry monuments to a long-abandoned effort at elegant landscaping. It was surrounded by an iron fence, scrupulously re-blacked every May out of the shallow pockets of the Rostval Place Association; there were two gates into the park, which yielded only to keys issued to members of the Association, as well as the periodic tire irons of muggers and graffito artists. The gates were marked by bronze plaques proclaiming the historical interest and exclusivity of the park, which had once upon a time been an important social nexus for Old New York.

Four blockfronts of town houses made up the square, looking down on the clockwise flow of traffic. On the northern perimeter, Old Groome Street ran eastward from Madison Avenue, a block to the west, through to Third Avenue, beyond which it finally petered out at the foot of a housing development overlooking the East River. Rostval Place was entered from the south by Midden Way, a sorry three-block extension of Fourth Avenue that had once been a broad trolley path meandering north from the financial district. With the years, and the changes in the city's character, most of the length of Midden Way had been smothered by an irruption of tenements and second-class commercial buildings. On the evening Nick turned east of Madison Avenue, the remaining length of Midden Way now consisted of a collection of small enterprises—two delicatessens, an undistinguished liquor store, a dry cleaner, a disconsolately mediocre Italian restaurant and a Chinese takeout place—which eked their livings supplying the less exotic or last-minute needs of the gentry of Rostval Place.

The square had sometime before been declared a historic district, and was thus legally protected from the tax-abated destruction of light, space and movement which was now the city's consuming preoccupation. To a disinterested observer, however, it must have been instantly clear that this exalted status had been conferred more out of sentiment and respect for age and the substantiality of the residents than for architectural or historical distinction. Its four sides were a stew of characteristic Manhattan domestic architecture: four- to six-story houses in every color of brick and stone, dating from the last decade of the eighteenth century to the middle of the twentieth.

Two large structures dominated Rostval Place. They stared at each other like hostile dowagers at a garden party, Nick thought, as he strolled into the square; the simile suited the current social facts of Rostval Place.

By far the more imposing of the two was the Fuller Institute, which now consisted of two substantial buildings of vastly different character flanking the narrow pedestrian walkway that connected the southwest corner of the square with Madison Avenue. The elder, more northerly of the two was a splendid stone mansion, dating from the first years of the century, which had originally been the home and personal temple of Darius Fuller, the iron-and-coal emperor; completed in an era when smart Manhattan still considered anything north of Ninety-sixth Street as "country," it was a grand survivor of an earlier, autocratic age, an implacable personification of a man of great and envied substance. On his death in 1936, the house and its treasures had passed to his only son, Xerxes Fuller, who in turn, in 1940, as part of a tax settlement, had conveyed the mansion and its contents to the Fuller Endowment to be maintained as a museum for the benefit of the citizens of New York City. The original house was now joined, by a hideous umbilical arch sheathed in steel and copper, to a younger sister, the Fuller Annex.

The Annex was a windowless construction of enormous limestone slabs of a pinkish-brown color. Lighted entirely from above, it consisted of a hangarlike, three-storied covered atrium around which a series of small balcony galleries had been cut, burrowing like rabbit warrens into the giant stone trapezoids and parallelograms; they functioned to provide what the architect had described in a *Times* interview as "moments of orgasmic intimacy with the living art." He was a Vietnamese who had fled Saigon a few years earlier and had gotten the commission for the Annex during a brief period of intense, altruistic vogue for Oriental architects. Sympathy soon gave way to scandal, however, when the Annex was finally completed for over $65 million, triple its budgeted cost, a sum that would deplete the Fuller Endowment for at least a decade. Nick had heard rumors in the art world that this had so discouraged his friend Sir Frodo Crisp, the Institute's autocratic Director, that he was considering handing in his resignation and accepting a position in Texas.

Small wonder, thought Nick. Frodo was accustomed to spending up to $10 million a year for the acquisition of Old Master paintings, drawings and prints, rare books and manuscripts or whatever else seemed to his practiced, perceptive eye to meet the Fuller's high standards. From Nick's point of view as an art dealer, the prospective loss of the Fuller as a customer could only hurt. That morning, just for the fun of it, he'd added up his sales to the Fuller during the ten years he'd been in business as a private art dealer: it came to something over $3 million to date, beginning with the Fragonard *Pastorale* from Deely Castle, and concluding with the great Carpaccio drawing of the Crucifixion that he'd finally separated from a wealthy Portuguese collector just months ago.

Poor Frodo, Nick thought. Acquisitions were the Fuller Director's life, his nourishment. Epicene and dictatorial, he was Nick's idea of a model museum director. He lived for the Institute. His connoisseurship was legendary. He had a fair sense of value—and, critically important to any worthwhile dealer, he could make up his mind. He was skillful, sometimes magically so, it seemed, at persuading his trustees to follow his vision. But all the vision and expertise in the world were nothing if the money wasn't there. In the art world as anywhere else where items of value changed hands, money spoke loudest and last. Frodo must now be raging inside. The gossip along Madison Avenue was reporting that the Duke of Sowell's Memling portrait, which Frodo had been chasing for fifteen years and had finally cornered not six weeks earlier, had been returned to the London dealer representing the Duke and was now on its way to Buenos Aires.

There were other reverberations quite outside the art world from the "Fuller Folly," as the *Times*'s architectural critic had described the Annex. It was also being noised about that certain Fuller loyalists, people who could normally be considered among its most dependable supporters, had been so enraged by the Annex's style and cost that they had turned their backs on Hugo Winstead, the well-known, socially ambitious lawyer whose marriage to Xerxes Fuller's only child had, among other things, propelled him to the presidency of the Fuller Endowment. As a result, Winstead had been obliged to take to the streets in a frenzied search for the last few million dollars needed to finish the new building, a quest that had involved sucking up to certain people who were hardly "Fuller quality." Much acid discussion was had over East Side teacups and cocktail tables as to whether the Institute, regarded by many as the unassailable repository of Old Manhattan's most enduring household gods, had sold its soul. On this issue the jury was still out, although Nick himself felt that this very evening, the Tiffany-invitation, black-tie, champagne-and-caviar opening of the new building, might yield an answer. It was, after all, something of a switch for the Fuller to put on a fancy, ostentatious affair like this—a fact that Manhattan's social entrail-readers had not missed. Everyone's eyes, Nick knew, were on the Winsteads' "A" List dinner. Their guest list would speak volumes to the question "Whither the Fuller?"

He paused for a moment to look at the new building, a massive incongruous presence among the discreet facades of Rostval Place; shook his head and continued toward Number 17, the imposing Federal mansion on the southeast corner of the square. As famous an address as there was in the city, it had been the home for over forty years of Nick's host for dinner, Solomon Greschner, the legendary public relations genius. In the dwindling light, Greschner's house seemed to glower at the Institute with fierce, pale eyes. No wonder, he thought. The intimacy that had existed between the Institute and Solomon Greschner had for some years been merely a matter of history, which was ironic, since the Institute itself had really been Sol's idea. It had been Sol who had proposed the benefaction to his client Xerxes Fuller as a neat way out of a tax trap. It was through Sol as much as through anyone that the Fuller had consistently turned up new patrons and supporters, more often than not newcomers to the client roster of Greschner Associates, Public Relations Advisors. It had been Sol who dreamed up The Fuller Associates and The Fuller Council of Fellows, carefully graduated categories of annual giving and social ascendancy which at their peak added close to $1 million a year to the Institute's operating funds. That Sol benefited as much as the Fuller from the relationship irritated many in Old New York. Everyone knew that he was not above using his institutional connections—principally the Fuller, but other prestigious bodies as well—as stepping-stones on the upward climb of the men and women whose social and cultural cravings Sol assuaged, yielding handsome fees to himself and liberal contributions to his favored institutions.

Sol himself had served as a trustee of the Fuller Endowment, until Hugo Winstead, himself an artfully sculpted Greschner success story, had forced him off the board. There were quite a few Winstead types around town, thought Nick. Promising men and women whom Sol, unmistakably motivated by his Socratic notion of himself, had taken up during their early years and guided until their grasp matched their reach. Once they felt themselves secure on pedestals of prominence and success, carpentered as much by Sol's manipulative skills as by their own innate qualities; once they could confidently admire themselves in mirrors glazed and polished by Sol's busy hands; once they had been plucked dexterously by Sol from various messes and scrapes, usually of their own making, and deposited safely on shore; frequently, then, wishing their high estate to be taken by the world as entirely of their own achievement, they would turn away from him. It was not altogether surprising, Nick thought: gratitude was a very uncontemporary emotion, not at all to the taste of this egocentric, selfish age. On the other hand, Nick knew, Sol could be very high-handed and assertive with his clients, to their faces and behind their backs. Sometimes it was as if he himself resented what he was able to do for them. There were few Greschner relationships that did not suffer from a debilitating inner tension. Well, Nick thought thankfully: not my own.

Nick was close enough to the front door of Number 17 to make out the gilded tusks of the heavy brass boar's-head knocker gleaming through the dusk. Well, he thought, I'm not one of the ingrates. Too middle-class, probably. He speculated as to whom Sol would have put together for tonight's big do. People whom Calypso Fuller Winstead would have asked Sol to invite. Hopefully there would be some game to stalk. Nick was loaded for bear; thanks to his friend Johnny Sandler, another dealer, he had been given the best and biggest piece of business in his career. An evening like this could be a really happy hunting ground. He was humming with anticipation as he reached the front steps of Number 17.

Looking north from the delicate small building which stood in a grove of cottonwoods nourished by an underground spring a few hundred yards from the main ranch house, Masako Katagira reflected that the stump of his left arm was a more reliable prophet of oncoming weather than any meteorologist. The sky remained clear, yet the tingling in his severed elbow told him beyond question that unseasonably chill winds were gathering force beyond the horizon. He hoped for his employer's sake that the oncoming storm wouldn't force a fatiguing delay.

Other people might have thought him a strange, incongruous figure—a middle-aged Japanese, severe and compact in his robe, watching the weather from the porch of a Japanese house set down in the Texas Panhandle. After a dozen years, Katagira and the rest of the ranch population took no more than casual notice of each other. And no one else came to the Lazy G.

He was looking forward to his employer's return from the clinic in Minnesota. Earlier in the day he had completed his outline of the "battle plan," as he now called it. He was sure it would work, so simple was it in its essence, so sturdily founded on the basest, hence most reliably predictable aspects of human nature. Getting the details down in summary form had been exacting; several times the adrenal rush of inspiration or the need to think through one or another aspect or angle of the plan had prompted him to get up from his worktable and spend a few minutes at his casting pool until he was back on the track. Only for the last hour had he been able to relax, to study the day's *Wall Street Journal* and the other financial publications which were flown in each day from Dallas, nearly three hundred miles to the southeast. That morning's perusal had brought a smile to his face: yet another much-applauded captain of finance had been discovered by his somnolent board of directors to have brought his company to the brink of insolvency; to have risked the integrity of the business, the commitments of his creditors, the jobs of his employees and the assets of his stockholders in an effort to make himself into a giant of industry. Well, thought Katagira, this was not surprising in a system which saw each rising of the sun not as a new beginning, but as a last chance.

It never did change, Katagira thought. This foolishness was born with capitalism itself. It had been observed by Adam Smith; depicted by Dickens and Trollope and a hundred writers since. To exploit it meant finding what the markets wanted to believe, and what the market-makers wanted for themselves, and dangling that before their eyes. Of feeding them the right euphemisms. Of spiking them on their vanity. The market licked euphemisms like lollipops. Let the big banks indulge their wish to fish in global waters while urban America fell apart; let them assume the oil sheikhs' unconscionable credit and currency risks while small business begged for credit. As long as there were headlines in it for them, puff pieces grandiosely describing the process as "petrodollar recycling," and a deluge of critically unsound banking practice could be justified. Or create storms of newfangled paper: make options, futures, swaps and straddles, all speculatively so mouth-watering as to lure investment money away from the linchpin securities, the stocks and bonds, of a sound capital system based on savings and prudence; merely christen them "financial products" and the further debasement of the investment function became a matter of sound marketing.

Katagira held a skeptical view of the financial world. It was steeped in foolishness, he thought; an idiocy, however, which mercifully suited his purposes; it was a delirium of folly which would make possible the completion of the huge task his employer had set him. It was there for him to exploit and manipulate. "I want to get that sonofabitch," Mr. Gudge had said, referring to Senator Rufus Lassiter (Republican/Independent-Connecticut), the so-called "Senator from Wall Street"; "And Granada too; she's as bad as him," referring to Granada (Mrs. Waldo) Masterman, Gudge's half-sister and the founder and chairwoman of Masterman United Corporation, and a close confidante of Senator Lassiter. "And break as many eggs as you got to."

Mr. Gudge's "eggs," Katagira knew, included Jews, liberals, nigger-lovers, congressmen, federal regulators, Washington, the East, New York and the rest. The avatars of a classic Texas paranoia.

"I got nothing to lose," he had told Katagira, "and we got this much to play with." Katagira didn't have to look at the sheet of paper he was handed; he knew the bottom line well enough. It showed that the net worth, based on a current appraisal of oil and gas assets and book value of the other interests, of Mr. Buford Gudge IV was something over $14 billion. A treasury presumably more than adequate to finance the kind of war that Mr. Gudge had in mind.

So now he had the plan. Finally. It had to begin with Seaco Group, of course. Both Senator Lassiter and Mrs. Masterman were heavily involved there, financially, ideologically and emotionally. And to undermine a big brokerage firm like Seaco Group would create a nice fission pattern throughout the financial markets in general. Which specifically interested Katagira, since he believed that America needed a convulsive, purifying shock at the core of its folly, at the very top of the private sector. Something that would reveal the current heroes of business for puffed-up, public-related human fabrications presented as leaders and statesmen; that would reveal not inspiration and vision in the highest councils, but shortsightedness and narcissism.

His arm twinged; he'd left the lower half of it almost forty years earlier on a slope in Europe. Fighting for a system under which he had suffered the humiliation of internment; for which he then had fought, and then had seen inherited by men content to run down the nation's industrial plant and gamble away its financial integrity. He was tired of watching them chase conceptual butterflies while real work remained undone. He found unacceptable the notion that the economic life of this vast, populous nation might somehow be conducted with no more than lip service to critical political and social connections; mutual admissions of mutual responsibility and interdependence—employer to worker; executive to stockholder; manager to employee; citizen to citizen, have to have-not—which added up to a properly virtuous political and commercial system, which underpinned a truly democratic society. This was what his spiritual mentor Mishima had raged against. Now Katagira would have his chance.

Well, he thought, we shall see. Seaco will be my instrument. And we'll trap Seaco through the bond market.

His stump was beginning to ache. Along the northern horizon a feathery barrier of gray clouds was building up. Hopefully, Gudge would beat the weather.

In his mind, he reviewed the plan again. Katagira was a constant reader. One must always, he reflected, come back to Shakespeare. Hamlet had the right words: "The play's the thing/Wherein I'll catch the conscience of the king."

At about the moment Nick set out for Rostval Place from his house on the Upper East Side, Harvey Bogle, a nationally known real estate and stock-market investor—some would have said "speculator"; others, "corporate raider"—was standing, half-dressed for the evening and not happy, in the living room of his penthouse apartment in the Tennyson Hotel, which he owned. He was studying a marked-up printer's proof of a column which in five days was due to appear in *Pritchett's*, the financial weekly the entire financial community devoured each Monday. The proof was headed "THE BOTTOM LINE/BY ROBERT CREIGHTON." It was the most widely read financial column in Wall Street. It was a primal force in the seismic interplay of gossip and speculation which often underlay the street's more violent or dramatic turns. "Robert Creighton's" true identity was known only to the publisher and managing editor of *Pritchett's*. In fiftieth-floor offices and the better watering places along Hanover Square, it was generally assumed that "Creighton" was a well-placed mole in a major bank or brokerage house, whose ideological aversion to the fun-and-games that made really big money hadn't compromised his nose for news or his ability to read through and behind even the most artistically cooked-up numbers. It was also clear that "Creighton," given the wealth of his information, couldn't be going it entirely alone; for sure, said the boys in the bars, he's got other moles up and down the Street feeding him this dynamite.

Reading the column this evening, Bogle was upset because he was by nature a secretive man who believed that surprise was to financial strategy what presentation was to French cooking: 90 percent. To his discomfort, he found that one of his more promising moves was about to be laid before the readers of *Pritchett's*.

"We hear," the column read,

> that Harvey Bogle, as audacious a pirate as has roamed the seas of finance in recent years, is taking a significant position in Seaco Group (SGS-NYSE), the brokerage and financial-services complex which many hardened Wall Streeters think has gotten a bit fat in the assets and long in the tooth. Smart money has been loading up on Seaco stock, which has moved resoundingly upward in an indifferent market, anticipating more of the hot-and-heavy action that Bogle always seems to create. Uneasy may lie the crown on the head of Homer Seabury, the hyper-Establishment chairman of Seaco Group, who only six months ago took in $15 million of needed new equity money by selling 10% of Seaco's common stock to Masterman United (MUD-NYSE), the half-billion-dollar business empire founded and controlled by Granada Masterman, perhaps the most successful female entrepreneur since the Empress Messalina. MUD thus has built up a 23% stake in Seaco. Some years ago it acquired the 13%

interest in Seaco that was sold by Senator Rufus Lassiter (R/Ind.-Conn.) along with Homer Seabury, a cofounder of Seabury Lassiter and Co., the small, upper-class brokerage that has since grown into Seaco Group. The Senator sold his shares when he abandoned Wall Street for Washington. What Bogle is up to is anyone's guess, although it appears he is moving toward a confrontation with Mrs. Masterman on two fronts: TransNational Entertainment Communications (TEC-NYSE), in which MUD, hoping to tie its enormous in-home personal-services network into TEC's burgeoning cablevision network, has a 9% interest and Bogle something over 15% and reportedly still buying. In any case, things should be popping at Seaco. Granada Masterman is known to be a great admirer of Senator Rufus Lassiter's unquestioned marketing and promotional ability, and it is a fact that the Senator is itching to quit Capitol Hill and get back to Wall Street. Now, with Bogle in the picture, where it all will end at Seaco, as a wiser man than this writer once remarked, knows God.

Bogle's irritation was not tempered by the arrival of his wife in the living room, waving an illustrated tabloid at him.

"Harvey, look at this picture of me in *That Woman!* This one here, talking with Milty Mosker at the Books 'n Bucks Banquet. Harvey, I look like a toadstool in this dress! Here I'm the biggest-selling writer who doesn't do diet in this country and I told Hernando I wanted something that said 'Jane Austen' and he does this to me! How could *That Woman!* print this awful picture? Can't we do something?"

Harvey reflected briefly. Distractions like this he didn't need. Success had transformed Esmé, whom he'd married when they'd graduated from high school, into a real pain in the ass, though he had to admire her success as a novelist.

He looked at the page briefly.

"Honey, you've got twenty million bucks in the bank from that shit you write. Do what I do. If it bugs you, sue; if it really bugs you, buy the goddamn paper. Or call Gratiane. Or Jill. Or that Guinea fag editor over there. You're always telling me they're your asshole buddies. You've got problems, I've got problems. That's what happens in a two-income family."

He chucked the paper onto a sofa and went off to finish dressing.

About fifteen blocks to the north, Homer Seabury, one of the subjects of the *Pritchett's* piece, was mulling the new, unwelcome problem of Harvey Bogle; a friend at the paper had telephoned a preview of Creighton's forthcoming column. Hanging up, Seabury had allowed himself an instant's wry reflection as to why *Pritchett's* even bothered to print a newsstand run: its contents were invariably out and digested by the market well before the ink-wet first press run hit the streets Sunday nights.

He was a large man just on the far side of sixty. A comforting sort: ruddily handsome and ample in the way that those who had dealings with him found reassuring. He looked exactly what he was: decent, reliable, dependable, usefully obtuse. Intellectually absolutely unthreatening; a meat-and-potatoes sort. Incapable of the flights of creative inspiration or the edged competitive keenness which businessmen of his stripe associated, uncomfortably, with poets and reformers, and other unreliable thinkers. As he stood looking into his mirror, Seabury's hand instinctively sought the gold charms hanging from the chain that circumnavigated his spacious dinner vest, fingering the tiny totems of Harvard and the Navy as if by rubbing them he might summon some genie to bail him out of his predicament.

How typical of Bogle to get involved, he thought. Now he had two of them to deal with, Bogle and Granada Masterman, let alone all those young men at the firm who kept pushing him, pushing him, to build and expand. He was sure Bogle wouldn't be in there if Granada hadn't been, and she wouldn't be there if those young men hadn't kept on him so that the business needed more and more capital.

His eye drifted across his dressing room to the large framed photograph, now showing yellow tinges of age under the glass, that sat on the table under the framed diplomas and commendations. Three young officers in 1945, posed proudly on the flight deck of the aircraft carrier, the Brooklyn Bridge in the background like a gateway to all the bright opportunity that ever could come to brave warriors returning home. Rufus Lassiter; Homer Seabury; Hugo Winstead, arms over each other's shoulders.

Then, their alliance had seemed one that would last forever; but Homer had long since learned that "forever" was a word that tripped too easily off the tongues of young men. Hugo, for instance, should have kept him out of Granada's clutches. But it was Hugo who had brought Granada in to buy Rufus out when Rufus went to Washington; and Hugo who had persuaded him to turn again to Granada when they needed more capital.

Had he so totally misjudged Hugo's character? Homer wondered. Had his father, who'd taken Hugo into Seabury and Partners and launched his career? Had Sol, who'd taken Hugo under his wing, and brought him into the orbit of the Fullers, and practically married him to Calypso Fuller? Be fair, he told himself. It had been a two-way street. Seaco Group had made a fair piece of change underwriting the securities of Masterman United. Hugo had brought that business through the door, even ahead of Sol, who had, funnily enough, been the first to know Granada Masterman—not that her acquaintance was any particular pleasure.

He finished knotting his bow tie. Things could be worse. He still personally owned nearly 20 percent of the stock of Seaco Group, which made him the second-largest shareholder, and he was pretty sure he could count on another 20 percent inside the firm and around the Street; so for the moment, he had Granada blocked. He earned close to a million dollars a year in salary and bonus. He had built the firm—heeding the proddings of his younger associates, he acknowledged—by running things the same way he had when he and Rufus were partners and Rufus was always after him to try this, try that. Prudently, cautiously, with a clear eye and a calm hand on the tiller, minding the strength of the balance sheet and the dependability of the cash flow.

To be sure, there were times he wished he were back where they'd started, in three rooms in the old Equitable Building, overlooking Broadway where there were only two things to deal in: stocks and bonds. None of that confounded new paper, all those options and things which he could barely understand. Stocks and bonds; a good meat-and-potatoes business for the meat-and-potatoes man he knew himself to be.

What did they have today at Seaco? Thirty-six offices in ten countries? A firm that never entirely went to sleep; Hong Kong flourished while the wires shut down in Montreal and Atlanta. Four thousand people, give or take a couple of hundred. To Homer Seabury it seemed that the mountain had just pushed up and grown beneath him, thrusting and expanding volcanically, bearing him heavenward with practically no effort or direction from him.

Well, they weren't going to take it from him. He liked being where he was, and his name was on the door; well, at least part of his name. It was a terrible thought—that Granada Masterman might have designs on bringing Rufus in. He and Rufus could never work together. That was for certain.

And now Bogle. It made it head-hurting difficult to sort out. He wished his father were alive.

Seabury shrugged into his dinner jacket. His father was dead, but there was always the next-best thing. If he hurried, he might just have a chance for a few words with Sol Greschner before Sol's other guests arrived.

Nick's good mood had been ignited by the morning papers. He fancied himself a connoisseur of foolishness, and the society column in the *Daily News* had carried a report of a major piece of idiocy. An Arab had given a ball in Paris to celebrate the triumph of OPEC. A quick scan of the names listed by the gossipist reassured Nick that every constituency of international social dreck was adequately represented: Lebanese oil traders; aging Texas debutantes; most shades of sexual deviation; intimates of the White House. In keeping with the times, the party had been held in a department store instead of a ballroom. It was a trend that had severely curtailed Nick's social life, at least that small fraction which he dedicated to big events, like the Fuller opening, which he would be attending that evening. Nick couldn't bring himself to go to parties in stores.

According to the *News*, the pièce de résistance of the evening, an occurrence that in time would elevate the evening to the pantheon of tasteless ostentation, right up there with the Reagan Inaugural, was the unveiling of a giant piñata—designed by a young man who had been voted "Pedé de l'Année" by a jury of his peers—in the shape of a huge oil drum which, on being cracked, disgorged not the expected profusion of luxurious party favors but a score of decrepit Hapsburg and Hohenzollern nobles and such, hired for the evening to symbolize the final conquest of the West by Islam. According to the report, which was written with tongue deep in cheek, in the melee of exiting the piñata an elderly Papal count had tripped over the shinbone of an equally rickety White Russian prince and severely bruised his fibula, in consequence of which he was suing the evening's host for several millions of new francs.

Nick had laughed out loud, shaking his head, and turned to the comics, where he read *Doonesbury* and *Shoe;* having thus restored some balance and rationality to the day, he went to the back of his apartment to dress.

As he had grown older, observation and the pleadings of his considerable intelligence had convinced him that the world was as likely to perish of foolishness as by atomic holocaust, and if the latter, it would be brought on by the former. He watched the caperings and posturings of the so-called captains of the world, of America in particular, with amazement. There seemed so little common sense or common decency around. So much taste when it came to Italian shoes or gold bracelets or money to be made; so little taste when it came to human values. How long, he wondered, could the balloon stay aloft, with all these types nibbling away with the sharp little teeth of self-indulgence?

The skepticism he'd acquired while growing up had somehow stopped short of disenchantment. Nick was, in a very special way, a child of the old middle-class morality; his father had been perhaps the best-known illustrator in America and had pictured over a generation and a half, an imaginary world of middle-class decency, of backyard clotheslines, first haircuts and firehouse parades that much of the country took for its own true image. Those same images had rooted themselves early and permanently in Nick's mind, so that even as he grew in sophistication and sharpness, they continued to assert themselves and acted as a kind of counterweight. Settled in his sense of values was a country with its hair cut a little too short and crudely and its suit fitting slightly awkwardly, which compared altogether favorably with the slick, plastic poseur who'd since taken over. Not that Nick was naive. He knew that bigotry and venality had been as much alive then as now.

Nevertheless, Nick thought, combing his hair and putting his still-uncomfortable reading glasses into his jacket pocket, however much his ideals might take a beating, however much his good wishes for all the rest of the world might go unregarded, he had little enough to complain about. As long as there was art to love and a supply of jesters for amusement, life was bearable.

When he came downstairs just after nine o'clock, he was surprised to learn that he had already had two calls from Johnny Sandler. Urgent, Sandler had said, which surprised Nick, since although they were the best of friends, he and Sandler dealt in fundamentally different types of art to widely divergent types of client. Sandler lived a full dawn-to-dawn calendar going head to head, glassful to glassful with the big new rich who clamored for the dazzling nineteenth- and twentieth-century French paintings that were the specialty of Sandler and Sandler. It was a style of living that often resulted in Johnny's late arrival at his gallery, but it had also produced a skiing lodge in Aspen, sables for Deirdre Sandler and an entire floor in a coveted cooperative building on Fifth Avenue.

Johnny, like Nick, was the happy possessor of a natural eye for artistic quality—and, unlike Nick, a sublime ability to sell it. Hard. His gifts were to some extent inherited—Johnny was the fourth of a distinguished line of New York art dealers—but his flair for salesmanship overwhelmed his aesthetic genes. His energy was legendary. He brought taste and enthusiasm to everything that counted in his line of work, from matching pictures to clients to getting the right tables in the right restaurants to selectively dispensing gossip and keeping equally selective confidences. He was tailored to his calling; they were made for each other.

If there was one aspect that set Johnny apart from the mass of people around the world who were equally capable of spieling a Renoir or a Monet to a shipowner a bare decade off the Piraeus docks, or of getting a good table at Maia's or Dove Sono, it was his ability to handle rich people. Especially people whose millions or billions were as tremblingly fresh and fragile as spring buds. He had a real understanding of the insecurities, anxieties and ambitions of big new money. He automatically empathized with tycoons fearful of being taken for mannerless clods, or with gobbling heirs concerned that the world would perceive them as no more than an extension of their fathers' checkbooks. Sandler mothered these frail-feathered creatures like fledglings, soothing them with friendship and the comfort of $3-million Cézannes; welcoming them as friends.

Nick didn't himself happen to be at ease with the sort of collector who went after pictures simply because he had the money, or thought it was a good investment, or wanted to keep up with whoever or whatever was in fashion. The finer-boned society of museum people and old-line collectors with whom he did most of his business tended to be scholarly and circumspect; they perceived virtues in themselves and their collections other than a string of zeros or personal pride: it had to do with education, connoisseurship, the broad culture on which art historians prided themselves. Of course it took big money to grease the cultural wheel, Nick recognized, so his attitude was mainly a matter of personal prejudice which could be suppressed under certain conditions. Who cared, for instance, where the money came from if a wonderful museum like the Fuller could land a sought-after acquisition that melded perfectly with its collections? A skilled persuader like Frodo, after all, could sell as hard as Johnny Sandler, wheedling money out of some pet-food dynast like a fakir tootling a cobra out of a basket. In such cases, which were rare, dealers like Nick conspired, as it were, with clients like Frodo to seduce the man who was in the room into putting up the cash to buy a painting which he might not entirely understand. Anybody, he often chaffed Sandler, could understand the beautiful coloring and charming, appealing compositions of Impressionist and Post-Impressionist painting. What he didn't admit was that, given his druthers, he'd as soon own a great Cézanne—the blue lakescape in the Courtauld, for example—as the work of any artist he knew.

Off duty, Nick spent as little time as possible with the rich, which accounted for his failure to understand, sympathetically, why wealth had to be such a psychological burden on its possessors. For every rich man he'd encountered who radiated cultivation and quiet confidence in his own judgment, he knew a dozen others who were as suspicious and insecure as Russian bureaucrats. He guessed it had something to do with a fear that their money might in fact be the only justification for their existence; that it might in fact be existence itself. If they lost their money, or someone took some of it from them, it would be like a dreadful, even mortal wound. Only that could explain why they seemed happy only in the company of other big rich, huddled like sheep in a snowstorm, on their yachts, in their resorts and nightclubs, fortresses walled off from the rest of the world by the hideously high cost of entry. Presumably this Big Rich didn't covet the money of that Big Rich, Nick guessed; although judging by the velocity with which they traded off and stole wives and mistresses, he figured that that might be as far as the armistice went.

So Nick held great affection and admiration for Johnny, but he envied him not a bit. The price of Johnny's rise in the world was more than he personally cared to pay. As the years wore on, the Sandlers seemed more and more imprisoned in a world in which only money appeared to matter. Increasingly, their circle seemed to include emotionally late-blooming multimillionaires and their younger, extravagant consorts. Nick found them tiresome: the men tended to be preoccupied with the discovery of sex at fifty-plus; grateful to the shopworn child-brides who breathed new fire into musty loins, they suffered the spending of their millions—at a clip and vulgarity that were frightening—with the uncomprehending grins of retards at an outing.

Nick's late uncle, who had taught political economy at Stanford, had once described the upper crust as "a bunch of crumbs held together by dough." A clever remark which had briefly polluted Nick's point of view, until he saw how totally unacceptable a philosophy it would be for a man who earned his living selling extremely expensive works of art. So Nick had gotten pretty good at subjugating his inherent distaste, although it still pained him that some Arab five years off a camel or some London-tailored guttersnipe a cat's whisker away from jail should be able to take hostage a Dürer drawing or a pretty Boucher. There were some things, he felt, that should be licensed: like the right to own a Rembrandt, drink Château Cheval Blanc and admire Deirdre Sandler.

Johnny, naturally, didn't see it that way. You paid your money; you owned the picture. One man's dollar was as good as any other's. Money was good, and a lot of it was better. In the Sandler world-view, the fun of being a dealer was fifty percent art; fifty percent action.

That they didn't entirely agree about their vocation made no difference to their friendship. They both had too many other important things in common; they were good drinking companions; liked many of the same things; above all, they shared the view that being able to enjoy a painting and talk about it didn't mark a man as a phony or a pillar of gay society.

Given a genuine love and understanding of art, a Rembrandt or a Corot could be discussed with the same involvement and relish as the prospects for the Yankees or Raquel Welch's bosom.

Under Johnny, the growth of Sandler and Sandler had been extraordinary. His radical ideas about what the gallery should sell, and to whom, together with his enthusiasm and drive, had overwhelmed his older partners' exclusive allegiance to the firm's traditional business; they were hurled along by forces which, in the frailty of age and gentility, they were powerless to withstand.

Johnny had grasped that the big new money of the sort he'd watched being made on Wall Street would want art that was easily understood, visual rather than bookish, was more obviously stylish and depicted good, clean, secular subjects in bright colors. He put the gallery on the map by outbidding the trade for a private collection of Pissarro landscapes which he sold for double his cost. He followed this with a daring bid for a group of decent Impressionist and Post-Impressionist pictures: Renoirs, Cézannes, an early Matisse, nice Monets: the good, irreproachable, salable names. Within three years such a covey of French pictures had flown out of Fifty-eighth Street onto the walls of Park Avenue triplexes, flats in Eaton Square, ski chalets in Santa Marta and private islands in the Aegean that Sandler and Sandler could move uptown to the private house on East Seventy-eighth Street. The day he closed on the new building, Johnny Sandler sold his first million-dollar picture, a late Cézanne portrait.

Deirdre Sandler enjoyed the intertwining of their private and professional lives. She understood what put the caviar and Cristal in the refrigerator, so if that determined what they did and whom they saw, so be it. She tolerated the occasional pinch and proposition from the overhearty oilmen and forbore the strange little olive-colored people who smelled of peculiar seasonings and wiped their rear ends on the Pourthault guest towels. The clients crawled all over one another to entertain and spoil the Sandlers. Whenever he decided to make his famous "house calls," to fly around the world to make certain that this "Sandler" Picasso or that "Sandler" Bonnard was where it ought to be, and hadn't been betrayed into some other dealer's hands, Johnny could choose between St. Moritz and Sardinia, depending on the season. A great American success story, Nick thought, reaching for the telephone, and it couldn't have happened to a nicer guy.

Sandler came right onto the line. He had obviously been waiting for Nick to call back.

"Nick, you want to move some canvas?"

"Do I ever! The rent keeps going up."

"I've got something special. When can you get your ass over here?"

Sandler's tone made Nick curious. On the rare occasions when Johnny talked to him about doing something together, it was usually a straight money deal. Prices these days had made it practically impossible for a single dealer to go it alone on a major painting—an important Van Gogh or

Manet, or a major Old Master—unless he had a committed purchaser in the wings. The heavyweight French pictures that were Sandler's specialty were outside Nick's taste and expertise, not to mention his pocketbook. But great Old Masters turned up with decreasing frequency, so it made sense for Nick to bet a piece of his otherwise idle working capital and bank line on paintings for which he might not have specialized knowledge or the right client but Johnny did. Not that his participation didn't mean something, friendship apart. Big pictures had become so expensive that syndications, which famous old-timers like Duveen had despised, were now the rule among otherwise competitive dealers. With money costing 20 percent, it made sense to split up the risk and the profit. It kept certain major collectors from shopping around. With everyone on the same team, it was possible to hold the market in line. Except for Du Cazlet, downtown—the big Belgian dealers who were richer than any of their customers and could afford to go it alone on anything up to the Sistine Ceiling.

"You doing anything for lunch? No? Good; how about coming here around noon to look at something, and then I'll get us a table at Maia's. Take some salt-peter, 'cause you're gonna have a hard-on when you see what I've got." Sandler's cheery vulgarity was a good sign; the hotter the deal, the worse his language.

So Nick had found himself turning into Seventy-eighth Street just before twelve. The town house occupied by Sandler and Sandler was halfway down the block between Madison and Fifth Avenues. It was six stories tall. The bottom two floors were taken up by exhibition space—including a tiny rear room in which old Moses Sandler, Johnny's octogenarian uncle, was tolerantly permitted to hang scholarly little shows of the Hague School landscapes that were his passion. "Dicking around with his cows and windmills" was the way Johnny put it, out of his uncle's hearing. Scattered through five other galleries were ornate French writing tables at which Johnny stationed his staff of assistants: seven young men and women, ex-apprentices at the big auction houses, hired away by Johnny after they had acquired the supercilious air and strange, strangulated diction that now seemed to be a prerequisite for employment in the art world.

The elevator opened on a small foyer, where Johnny's secretary sat amid a forest of filing cabinets, at the head of the broad marble stairs that rose to the third story. The rest of the floor, an area nearly forty feet square, was given over to the proprietor's office. Above, reached by a creaking birdcage elevator imported from London in the interest of atmosphere, were storage rooms for frames and less important paintings, and a small apartment occupied by Raul, the gallery's man-of-all-work. The most valuable works were kept in the basement, which had been converted into a triple-locked, photoelectrically guarded concrete bunker.

Johnny's office was a big, cheerful room, functionally oriented to a southern exposure which flooded the room with sunlight during the critical afternoon hours. Very little important spending was done at Sandler and Sandler before three o'clock. The walls of the office were lined to the ceiling with laddered, glass-fronted bookshelves filled with catalogues and monographs. Sandler's desk stood at the north end of the room; it was an elegant George III partners' desk, usually hidden under a mess of photographs, catalogues and glassine-clad color transparencies, equipped with a thirty-line telephone console and an 11-by-14-inch photograph of his wife and children. At the other end, some thirty feet away, was what Johnny called "my operating room": a comfortable grouping of sofas and soft armchairs picketed at a discreet distance by five or six easels—one of which was said to have belonged to Cézanne. The seating was arranged to get maximum heat and light from the late-afternoon sun. It was here that the clients of Sandler and Sandler first encountered the treasures Johnny had in mind for them. Every dealer had his own way of building up to the moment when a fine work of art was expected to seize forever the heart and soul of the purchaser he had chosen. At Sandler and Sandler, the moment of communion usually followed a long and winy lunch at Chez Maia. Drowsy with Montrachet and mesmerized by the magic and beauty that flowed from Gauguins and Monets on the easels which Raul had drawn close to their chairs, Johnny's guests (he seldom called them "clients" and never anything as vulgar as "customers") succumbed warmly and gratefully to the seductive intimacy of the moment, their sense of rich well-being intensified by Johnny's discreet and modulated patter. And by repeated replenishments of wine from the silver coolers maintained by Raul, natty for the occasion in a white waiter's jacket.

Following the secretary into Sandler's office, Nick was struck as always by the effectiveness of the setup. On this particular morning the office seemed washed in gold. It positively exuded expensiveness.

Sandler turned to greet Nick. He looked well. He seemed to be winning his running battle with those five extra pounds. He was, as always, elegantly turned out, to a point just short of slick. At thirty-six, he was five years younger than Nick.

When Nick came in, Sandler was studying a small picture on an easel before him. In his left hand he held a sheaf of photographs. Two large books—monographs, Nick guessed by their size and heft—lay open on a sofa. He shook Nick's hand.

"Take a look at this. And bad luck on that Florentine picture in Lugano. Grundy's must have done a real number to get it away from you. I hear they're gonna reserve the picture for three-quarters of a million pounds. Lots of luck to them—because a guy I know says old Sanger thinks it may have been painted around 1940 instead of 1490. He's apparently gonna piss all over it in the next *Burlington*." He was referring to an interesting Florentine portrait Nick had bid on in Switzerland and lost to Grundy's, the big auction house, which had promised the owner an exorbitant result if he would put it up for public sale.

"I'm not so sure myself that I didn't miss a bullet there," said Nick. "The picture bothered me. But I got greedy."

It was reassuring to know that Francis Sanger, still, at eighty, the most knowledgeable, instinctive expert on Italian Renaissance painting in the world, also had his doubts. Normally he would have checked with Sanger, who had been his teacher, but he'd been under the gun in Lugano and so he'd gone ahead and made a big offer—which Grundy's had topped.

That was the problem with the business these days. Great Old Masters turned up so seldom that it was almost easier to live with an overoptimistic misjudgment on a painting than to let a possible masterpiece slip through one's fingers. It was a theory that had cost more than one gambling dealer or overeager museum director his serious reputation. Being too anxious to believe was dangerous in any line of work; in art dealing, where experience and judgment—and reputation—counted for everything, it was disastrous.

The "Ghirlandaio" presented the sort of problem that sometimes made Nick wish he had taken the other path—that instead of sitting in a $150 hotel room having to decide whether to bet $800,000 on a hand that didn't feel like a lock, he had elected to remain an academic art historian. It would be a pleasure to be able to sit in a library office, musty with pipe smoke and old tweed, and play solitaire with piles of photographs. To rule on the authenticity of old pictures and the reputations of artists long dead on the basis of secondhand black-and-white and Kodachrome impressions, consigning now this one, now that to the scholarly purgatories of "Attributed to," "School of," "Pupil of," "Circle of," "After."

Having lost the picture to Grundy's, Nick hoped that Sanger was right. It must be thirty years since Sanger could have seen the picture, but the old man's miraculous, confounding memory for every work of art he'd ever seen couldn't be discounted. Francis Sanger remembered it all from frescoes once seen in the naves of obscure churches destroyed in World War I to great masterpieces ornamenting the national museums of a dozen countries.

"Anyway," Johnny continued, "forget Grundy's; this'll cheer you up. When's the last time you saw anything like this?" He drew Nick over to the easel.

On it was a wooden panel perhaps two feet across by a foot high. The paint seemed as fresh as morning, applied in lively, dashing strokes. The work depicted Hercules Slaying the Hydra. Slightly off center, the heavily muscled hero slashed away at a multiheaded dragon, under a sky of palest pink and gray. The scene was framed by fruited trees, barely intimated by brusque little touches of the paint-loaded brush. In the foreground a large dog, a cross between a greyhound and a mastiff, made a brave, barking show. In the background a hilly landscape receded through planes of transparent green and brown to a smoky horizon and the suggestion of an ocean.

The painting was a sketch in oil, an airy, vigorous jotting-down of an idea for a major composition, presumably to be expanded later to the epic scale which suited the subject. Nick's quick but careful examination confirmed that the glistening, bright surface was intact; it showed no trace of inconsistent restoration or repainting. It was as young and unspoiled after three and a half centuries as when it had left its author's workshop.

Nick saw at once that it was by Rubens. The style, that mysterious amalgam of spirit and appearance, was unmistakable. Peter Paul Rubens. Born 1577; died 1640. In every expert's opinion, among the greatest of the painters. Nick happened to like Rubens better than nearly any other artist. He loved the drenching urgency and liveliness, the color and passion, the assurance, the confidence, and beneath the surface, the wellspring-deep humanity with which Rubens invested everything he touched. Other eyes might prefer Raphael's innately classic balance; or Rembrandt's irresistible, probing insights into human nature; or Michelangelo's Olympian furor and tension. At his best, especially in his oil sketches, Rubens was like a great virtuoso playing Beethoven: letting forth a seemingly free-running outpouring of emotion and color so brilliant, so controlled and natural, as to conceal the intelligence, imagination and discipline that hold an audience breathless.

For a minute or so Nick simply devoured the painting, saying nothing; he relished it visually, trying subconsciously to suppress the inevitable rush of art-historical associations: the whens and wheres and whys of his professional apparatus. Unlike many art historians, Nick preferred to look at pictures for pure pleasure. He would liken himself to an alcoholic wine expert; he might know all the vintages and labels, but getting drunk was where the fun was.

Finally, he said "Holy shit!" It was more exhalation than exclamation.

"Good, huh?"

"Jesus Christ, it's unbelievable! As good as anything I've seen. It looks as good as the Whitehall sketch, the one at Yale." That little picture had brought $800,000. "The condition looks perfect. Where's it been? In a salt mine?"

"Something like that. Barry Winters and I got it through a Swiss scout we use to keep an eye on Zurich and Geneva. A guy who watches the obits and the bank vaults. That's how we got onto this. It's come down through one of those Viennese Hapsburg families damn near since it was painted, I guess. The old girl who owned it died last year; she was the end of her line. Lived in Sta. Marta in that fancy hotel of Kratsch's, with ten cats and a nurse. Left everything to them. The picture was in the vault of the cantonal bank in beautiful downtown Sta. Marta. Our guy's thick with the manager and so he heard about it. It turns out it's been there since 1938. She got it out of Austria before the Anschluss. How about that? From there on, it's the usual story. There's an executor. On the take as usual, plus a notary down the valley; we've got him on ice for the time being. Don't ever tell me about the financial morality of the Swiss.

"The nurse wants to sell; buy a condominium; lay in a ten-year supply of cat food; meet some poor Italian count who can appreciate her for her money, marry her and get her into the Skihawk Club so she can eat with the rich folks and get her picture took. This picture's her ticket to society. But here's the best part, old buddy!" He handed Nick the sheaf of photographs.

They were old black-and-whites mounted on heavy, crumbling cardboard; from their appearance Nick judged they had been made well before the Second World War.

There were eleven of them—obvious siblings of the picture on the easel! It was astonishing. At first Nick didn't really grasp its significance; discoveries like this generally sent the eye and intellect into a sort of shock which required a while to regroup. It was a complete cycle. The Twelve Labors of Hercules: The Hydra on the easel, and in the photographs, the rest: The Nemean Lion; The Erymanthian Boar; The Hind of Ceryneia; The Stymphalian Birds; The Augean Stables; The Cretan Bull; The Horses of Diomedes; The Girdle of Hippolyta; The Oxen of Geryon; The Apples of the Hesperides; The Taking of Cerberus.

An entire cycle. The greatest of heroic subjects, painted for an age that had still possessed some sense of heroism, executed in the first flush of inspiration by the most heroic painter of the age, possibly of all time. It was like having the sketches for a secular Sistine Ceiling.

"Jesus Holy Christ," Nick muttered. He went through the photographs again. There wasn't a weak sister in the bunch. Rubens had been a prolific, busy artist, with a large workshop and following, so he had had his indifferent moments; but here his mind and talent had clearly been in his work.

"Can they travel?"

"These pictures come with clean Swiss hands, Nick," said Johnny. "They can leave Zurich anytime. Papers and passport all in order. What I need from you is, what do you think? Are these as good as they look? I'm no Rubens expert, but whoever could paint this knew what the hell he was doing."

He pointed to a passage in the painting on the easel, a smoky juncture where sky and land met in a pale flurry of green and yellow, pink, umber and azure.

"That's as good as Monet." From Johnny Sandler there could be no greater praise.

"You have come up roses, Johnny, absolute roses. These are all autograph, I'd say. Late. Generalized, sketchy—the way all artists tend to work as they grow old, trying to put the ideas down before time runs out. These are probably 1635, 1636, somewhere around there. He did a bunch of mythological subjects for the King of Spain then, but I don't remember a Hercules series. Hell, we can look that up. But don't take me as gospel. Get Marco in. He's putting that big family portrait back together, the one the boys in the Midwest screwed up." Marco Carraccino was the leading restorer in the United States; many people thought he was the equal in technique of the masters whose works he restored.

"Or Karpinski," Nick added. Old Ludwig Karpinski, the head of the Rubens Center in Antwerp. Sixty years dedicated to studying Rubens' personality, artistic handwriting, creative processes. Karpinski could detect the merest passing presence of Rubens on a big canvas on which a half-dozen assistants' hands might have worked.

Nick's eyes returned to the sketch on the easel. Moving closer, he scrutinized its surface, looking for imperfections or inconsistencies on the surface which would betray a restorer's hand. There was nothing obvious to be seen; anything less obvious would come later, when they had the sketch radiographed. Now his pure visual pleasure began to give way to art-historical instincts; his mind surrendered to a Pavlovian gloss of cross-references, associations, comparisons and questions which spread varnish over his first fresh enjoyment of the picture. He was pretty sure about the date, which meant the Spanish connection might hold up. That was something his researcher could dig into. The subject was ideal, he thought, for the first time, letting his mind work like a dealer's. What a combination! Hercules and Rubens were a natural mating of subject and temperament. Hercules, Hercules . . . Nick thought he remembered a couple of oil sketches of Hercules subjects, and a few scattered drawings, but nothing like a complete cycle. He tried to recall the big Rubens show in Antwerp in 1977. There had been a couple of Hercules items there, but nothing like this in completeness and quality.

"If you were me, Nick," Johnny was saying, "how much would you spring for these? I don't handle Old Masters. You do. What would you go for if these walked in the door?"

Nick thought for a minute. Oil sketches by Rubens were not exactly hen's teeth. The definitive catalogue listed nearly five hundred. But an entire series like this was a different ball game. The Whitehall sketch had made $800,000 because of its subject, the Apotheosis of King Charles I, and because there was a specialist collector with unlimited resources interested in the field; yet another sketch, perfectly good but no great shakes, had recently sold privately for about $250,000. There was no hard-and-fast price level. The subject of this series was great. Salable. Hercules presumably still had some meaning for a culture that got most of its popular mythology from gossip magazines. That was a plus. The condition was perfect. Nick quickly concluded the sketches would bring more if sold as a single lot. Which was a switch. The market nowadays was dominated by the "breakers," dealers who pontificated on "sum of the parts" and broke up anything held together by a binding or a frame, from medieval altarpieces to Claude Lorrain notebooks to Audubon folios, selling each individual piece for the cost of the whole. But this was different. These little pictures would be worth more if they were kept together and sold together. Off the top of his head he estimated the cycle might make $5 million at auction. That was what the National Gallery in London had paid for the big early *Samson*. These were, collectively, at the same level of importance, and infinitely more pleasing. And more manageable. Exhibited together they would make a hell of an impact. And a hell of a story; the kind that brought the public in droves.

Start at five million, he thought, and be prepared to go up from there. At auction, five million would theoretically net four point five to the seller, after the house commission. Theoretically, that was. Everybody in the business knew that for something like this, something really important that could pay off in big, newsworthy numbers in the salesroom and a lot of publicity to the auction house, Grundy's and the other big houses would charge no commission to a seller.

It seemed to Nick that he could beat five million net in the private market. There was a lot of big money around that hated the limelight that went with buying pictures in the salesrooms. Money with its hat pulled down over its eyes. Legal money, but shy. Of course, he'd have to scare it up—but for something like this, broke as damn near every museum in America was, there were collectors who could spring for something unique.

Winding up his internal soliloquy, he said, "Johnny, if I was trying to do this on my own, I'd start at five million, assuming my friendly banker would be his advertised friendly self. If it was a syndicate, I'd say five five easy. There's no risk here, except time and the cost of money. What are you guys thinking? Anyway, is this an invitation to your and Barry's party?"

Sandler smiled. "Of course it is. If I buy old pictures, someone else has to do the selling. What do I know from Rubens? And all those guys in museums and deep-thinking collectors think I'm some kind of shlock dealer, anyway. They buy your act, Nick. Now, Barry thinks we should offer four million. You know Barry. He always tries to chisel, unless he's shelling out to feed his fat face or trying to please some chippie. Based on what Rubens has done, and he's always sold big—the good stuff, obviously —I was thinking five myself, or better. There're people out there that'll pop for stuff like this: a couple of hitters out West; a few South Americans; Greeks. And there's always some guy comes out of the woodwork you never heard of. I think we should offer five, and be ready to go up to five five, somewhere around there, give or take ten percent either way. Plus the extras. Then we'll put them out, as a single lot, at seven five. If nothing happens, I bet we can get out pretty close to whole. Shove them into Grundy's ourselves. That's the worst case. You agree? And if we have to, we can break up the set." He took note of Nick's expression. "C'mon, Nick. Don't throw up."

"I won't. And I agree. What are the extras?"

"Our guy in Zurich gets a hundred thousand dollars—in Swiss francs, of course—plus ten percent of the striking price. He's probably getting ten from the sell side too. That's the deal at the auction houses, so it follows that all the other crooks do the same. They figure: Why not us? Anyway, that's for finding, negotiating and taking care of the executor. So our cost is between five point five and six million all in. Okay?"

"Okay. How do you see it shaping up?"

"I'm in for a million. Winters the same. His art fund for a million five. I have you down for a million, more if you want it, although Barry and I would like to throw something Brenner's way. Barry and I owe him for helping us on that Cézanne last summer. The one that went to Baltimore. Say a million for the Good Humor Man. That's five five, and we bank the balance with Martell at the Commerçante in Geneva."

The "Good Humor Man" was Franz Brenner, the biggest dealer in West Germany. He owned a private salt mine lined with his personal collection of nearly two hundred Cézanne watercolors and drawings, as well as refrigerators filled with ice cream, to which he rushed on every rumor of Russian maneuvers, wanting to perish with his eyes full of high-priced beauty and his mouth full of vanilla crunch.

"All right with me. A million's fine. Of course, I've got to clear it with the bank. What's the pecking order on the selling? I'm not all fired up about letting Barry loose on something as good as this. He has this unbelievable ability to crap in his nest. And everyone else's."

Johnny let this go by. Even though there were few big pictures on which he didn't go partners with Winters, he appreciated Nick's concern. Barry stayed up late, drank a lot and talked more. Nick thought that if Winters had been as keen a judge of what he said as he was of what he saw, he would have had no competition as a dealer.

"Not to worry. You get the first ninety days, with another sixty if you're close to a deal. After that, it's Frank's turn for ninety days. Then mine. If we strike out by the end of next January, say, we stick them into Sotheby's for the June sales. From 'a private collection,' naturally. And we pray a lot. But you'd be the main man on this one, Nick. A big Cézanne or a Monet; that'd be something else."

"I understand," Nick said. "Horses for courses—and I've got a couple of good ideas. But no pictures in the papers. And keep that gang of Barry's quiet! I also think there ought to be a bonus per picture if we have to split them up. But that we can do later. Are you sure that fund of Frank's is money good?"

"It's okay," said Johnny, "Barry swears he has a blank check on this one. The rest of the arrangements will be as usual. Money to Martell in Geneva within twenty-four hours of my notifying you that we've got a deal. We'll fly the rest of the pictures in as soon as we can after closing. Barry'll ride shotgun from Zurich. Then the three of us can sit down and make sure we don't try to bag each other's special pigeons. Okay with you?"

The buzzer on the phone console sounded. Johnny picked up the receiver, listened briefly, smiled in a pleased way and instructed, "Tell him to look at the exhibition and I'll be right down. Point him at the Vlaminck." He turned to Nick.

"I'm afraid I'm going to have to bag you on lunch, but a chance for a real turkey shoot just turned up. A very useful Lebanese. He walked in off the street six months ago and bought a lot of crap in our Christmas show—Dalis, Foujitas, fifty-thousand-dollar 'gift items'—a lot of which I took in trade from some Jap that went belly-up last year. I was about to send them to the church fair. So this character strolls in off the street and buys two hundred thousand bucks' worth! For cash on the spot."

"The best kind of customer. Got any good Leroy Neimans for him?"

Sandler chuckled. "Don't talk dirty. This is an *art* gallery. Here." He handed Nick an envelope into which he'd put the photographs of the Rubens sketches. "Run along, now. I guess we'll see you tonight at the Fuller. You going to Greschner's? It figures. How is the old bastard? Anyway, get that research cutie of yours cracking on these."

He stuffed the photographs into an envelope and handed them to Nick, then accompanied him down the stairs to the second floor. He paused at the entrance to Gallery 3, where a squat figure in an electric-pink suit was studying an unpleasant winter landscape which appeared to have been painted with shoe polish. The figure was toting an enormous ostrich-skin shoulder bag.

"That's where he keeps the cash," whispered Johnny, leaving Nick. "He's a great believer in liquidity." Then, loudly: "Ah, Bouzir, what an unexpected pleasure. I've reserved a table at Maia's. Afterward, we can come back and do some serious looking."

As Nick walked out through the brass-gated entrance of Sandler and Sandler, he began to make an agenda of things to be done in connection with the cycle of sketches. First, he'd get Sarah Ruggles, his research assistant, to work up the Rubens literature and draft a brochure. Next, call Marco Carraccino to come and have a look. Better wait until all twelve of the pictures got here. Nick was 99 percent convinced of what they were, but Carraccino could give that vital 1 percent which transformed assurance into certainty. The 1 percent that had steered Nick off the so-called Poussin in the Brooks collection which had turned out to be a school picture.

It didn't concern Nick that he had no specific buyer in mind. Of course, he'd let Frodo have first look, notwithstanding the rumors about the Fuller. It was axiomatic these days that the finest and rarest works still commanded top dollar, which was what they were talking about. It was much less of a struggle to move a great work of art for a million or more than some Fifty-seventh Street piece of crap for five thousand. He knew he had at least a half-dozen big collectors, some individuals and a couple of museums, who would jump at the chance to buy a single Rubens sketch of this quality and period. Most of them were like the Fuller in its present condition, though: out of gas when it came to a $7-million acquisition. Damn, he thought, if they hadn't built that goddamn Annex, Frodo would jump at the pictures —probably on the basis of the one upstairs at Sandler's.

He was exhilarated at being handed this ball to run with. And grateful to Sandler. This was the greatest "discovery" he could remember; certainly the greatest during his career. Well-known or spectacular pictures did come onto the market with some regularity, old friends changing residences, but this was a discovery. Like a new planet. To acquire something like this could create an important collector or collection at one coup. That fact in itself would help the pictures sell.

Hell, the evening itself had to be loaded with prospects. Every art-loving dollar within five thousand miles would turn out for this opening, the fanciest the Fuller had ever thrown. And Sol Greschner's dinner party could be a good place to start prospecting. In or out of favor, Sol never set out place cards for nickel bettors.

By the time he reached the steps of Number 17 that evening, Nick was so pumped up with a sense of possibility that he gave the brass boar's-head knocker a snap that nearly tore it loose.

CHAPTER TWO

It was on an October afternoon in 1922 that Solomon Greschner, then a boy of fifteen, first saw, fell in love with and became determined to possess Number 17 Rostval Place.

He was then working after school for Tatnall's, the fancy tailor's and haberdasher's owned by his uncle and his father. The Greschners had migrated to New York—at the insistence of his grandfather, who had concluded that the New World alone offered an adequate opportunity for wealth and posterity. In later years, when it would serve Sol's interest to project a refugee, tenement childhood, replete with scenes of Ellis Island, he would intimate a background of impoverishment and near-starvation, incessant pogroms and a final, desperate flight from a geographically unspecific Carpathian ghetto barely two steps ahead of the hooves of pursuing Cossacks. The fact was that three generations of Greschners before Sol had lived in perfectly respectable circumstances in the Midlands of England, tailoring clothes for the textile gentry of Yorkshire. Since Sol's vocation was to reshape the lives and characters of other important men, who could begrudge him a little self-indulgence with his own past? After all, he had made millions over five decades inventing public personas for those who could pay, and had the ear of moguls and cardinals, poets and senators. A little self-invention on Sol's part seemed perfectly reasonable.

In 1906, Grandfather Greschner had loaded his wife; his two sons, Moritz and Levi, and Levi's wife, then two months pregnant with Sol, on a medium-class steamer and set off from Liverpool in pursuit of a richer life. A cousin, proprietor of a thriving tailor shop in New York, had died and his widow wished to return to Yorkshire. By mail an arrangement was concluded whereby the widow received a sum of money and the freehold of the Greschners' comfortable house in Leeds and Grandfather Greschner and his family took over the tailoring business and six light and comfortable rooms just off Midden Way, where in due course Solomon Greschner was born.

To his credit, Sol never disclaimed the family trade. "Clothes and reputations come to the same thing," he would tell the profilers who sought him out when he became rich and famous; "it's simply different goods, you see. Suits in one case; in the other, perceptions. Both cut for the man who's made money and wants to be turned out smartly in the eyes of the world." That was his benign, for-publication description of his occupation. Off the record, in his bitter or cynical moments, he was less lordly. "What I do," he'd grumble, "is cobble stilts for midgets."

Sol and the family concern grew on parallel courses. By the time he reached adolescence, Tatnall's was outfitting a significant part of smart New York. Uncle Moritz ran the shop on lower Fifth Avenue; Sol's father, Levi, supervised the loft off Hudson Street where the cutting and sewing were done. Sol preferred the shop. His uncle was a flashy, literate sort, with an elaborate personality, who treated his customers, mostly men active on the stock exchange, as equals, feeding them a mixture of financial shoptalk and risqué asides which they seemed to find intellectually nourishing. Sol watched it all. Often, at the end of the day, Uncle Moritz, helped along by dollops of whiskey from the bottle hidden behind Mr. Morgan's patterns, would review the patrons of the afternoon. This one, he'd explain, had just cornered Central. That one was amalgamating Northern Steel and Western Iron. Another was short fifty thousand shares of National Surety. From time to time, important customers would disappear, carried off to jail or bankruptcy by the risks that men must take, Uncle Moritz explained, if they would become rich in this land of infinite possibilities.

The Greschners lived peacefully and well in their spacious, sunny rooms. Sol was the only child in the house. Well fed and flourishing, he attended the neighborhood public schools, went to temple regularly and, when he was large enough, hurried to the shop in the late afternoons to work as a delivery boy, thirsty for more of the rich life that he observed there and in the houses to which he carried parcels often larger than he was.

It was surely during this time that Sol's own ambition to be rich and grand, largely the latter, formed within him. Certainly it all came together on the afternoon he called at 17 Rostval Place to deliver a package of suits to the Wall Street speculator who lived there.

An English butler with jowls like abalones answered his ring. As he took the parcel from Sol, he asked peremptorily, "Can you mark a suit? Master has gained weight at Saratoga. His evening clothes need altering." Of course Sol could. He had watched his uncle's fitters and his father's cutters often enough, and always carried a piece of chalk and a handful of pins in his pocket. He nodded, beaming up into the butler's vast striped waistcoat, and was led up what seemed like endless flights of marble stairs to "Master's" dressing room. Sol missed nothing as he went. He took in the dining room, with twenty candles set in gilded sconces around the walls, and a mahogany table which looked as large as the Polo Grounds, with an enormous silver ewer in its center; the large square drawing room, draped in heavy magenta velvet, its ornate furniture watched over by slick Boldini portraits. Finally he was shown into a carpeted sanctuary lined with walnut wardrobes. He thought it was the most beautiful place he had ever seen. A chubby, baby-faced man of about forty was struggling to button shut a pair of unyielding evening trousers. He gestured Sol to the work at hand. As he marked the trousers, vest and tailcoat, the master of the house prattled on to the butler about the day's doings on the Stock Exchange, talking loftily of "eighths" and "corners" and "short," in the way negligible men use jargon to simulate knowledge. Sol was not impressed by the arcane vocabulary; he had heard it often enough at Tatnall's to know that a seat on the Stock Exchange was no guarantee of prosperity or importance. His impression was that the man doing the talking was a weightless idiot. All he had was money and what it bought: a fine house; a butler, whose contemptuous expression Sol could see in the mirror, and a suit of clothes being chalked by a kneeling boy. Sol felt he was fitting clothes to a shadow, whose only substance was his fine house, the silver on the table and the purchased deference of his manservant.

When he finished, the man went to his oak bureau and took from it a silver dollar which he gave to Sol. "I need these clothes tomorrow night, no later," he instructed sternly. "For Darius Fuller's waltz evening," he added, as if to emphasize the gravity of the commission.

The butler showed Sol out the way he had come. In the street, Sol paused and looked the house up and down as greedily as a sailor studying a blonde. If a man like that can own a house like this, he thought, why shouldn't I? He strolled east toward the trolley stop, the package of marked clothing under his arm. The silver dollar in his pocket seemed to burn through his shirt, like some enchanted talisman; sixty years later, he would still have it. It symbolized the ambition to own that particular house which had been focused within him, like light through a magnifying glass, a pinpoint of fire slowly spreading. To own a house like that would take a great deal of money. More, he guessed, than even a successful business like Tatnall's could provide. Which meant he would have to earn the money elsewhere.

Now, nearly sixty years later, Sol himself stood in the same dressing room where the tailor's boy had knelt and chalked the trousers of a fat man who talked nonsense. He himself slipped into a custom-made coat held for him by his own butler, a close replica of the dewlapped monolith who had first opened the door of Number 17 to him.

Downstairs he heard the doorbell ring. That would be Homer Seabury. He had sounded pretty frantic when he called. He told his butler to put the early arrival in the library and went about the business of putting the final meticulous touches to his toilet.

A blue norther had forced the Lazy G Falcon to hold near Tulsa for nearly an hour, so that it was after dark before the jet could sweep in over the damp, cold plains to the welcoming lights of the ranch's airstrip. When the boss came slowly down the steps, Stumpy saw that he was badly tired. So he kept his greeting brief, helped the pilots load the bags into the Rolls and kept quiet for the short drive back to the Big House. José came out to greet the car, took the bags and followed the boss into the house. Standing by the pickup, Stumpy watched Gudge's hunched figure pass under the light. Goddamn, he looks beat, he thought. Beat and thin and gray. Shrinking. Like death. He's surer'n hell sicker than he's saying. It made Stumpy sad to see his boss so bad off. They were both Lazy G bred and born and almost the same age. Kitchen gossip had it that Stumpy was old Gudge's bastard. Who knew? All Stumpy knew was that his first awareness of light and life had been of the ranch, and the ranch was all the existence and memories he'd ever had.

He limped back to the Rolls and drove it around behind the Big House to the bunkhouse. He stopped in his little room, took a snort of blackberry brandy and wandered into a big room where a half-dozen Mexican cowboys, all that was left of the hundreds who had patrolled the Lazy G at the turn of the century, lounged in front of a television set. "How is Mr. B?" asked one of them with a concern that touched Stumpy. He never ceased to be surprised that Mexicans could feel the same kind of feudal devotion to the ranch and its ruler that he felt.

"Don't look so good," he said sadly. Then, fearing that he'd laid his sentiments open, he reverted to his role as foreman and ramrod. "Goddammit, ain't you boys got nothing better to do than watch this shit?" On the television screen, fueled by a videotape recorder, three women were approaching the outer limits of pornographic indescribability. He limped back to his room.

Inside the Big House, Buford Gudge IV paused to look at the computer printouts that had been placed on the large table in the front hall. There was one for each day he'd been away. He studied the papers briefly, pursing fleshy lips which seemed too large for his sickness-drained face, folded them and stuck them into his jacket pocket and turned to José.

"Miz Gudge call?"

"Yessir. Said she'd missed you in Minnesota. She was going out. To Mr. Greschner's. Said you could try her there, otherwise she'll call you in the morning. She's in the suite. Asked for the Gulfstream to pick her up Friday at LaGuardia after lunch. Got a lot of packages, she said."

Gudge nodded. "Dinner ready?"

"Yessir. Whenever you want. I'll call Mr. K."

As José went to call Katagira, he saw Gudge stop pensively in front of the lighted glass case that contained the history of the ranch: old deeds, maps, invoices, tailings of barbed wire, core samples. Shards of a hundred years of Gudge history. Just that morning, Stumpy, as he did every month, had oiled and checked out the old revolver which had belonged to Mr. Buford II and which occupied a place of honor in the case. There were stories about that six-gun; but what were stories after so many years?

As was their habit, Gudge and his dinner companion ate in silence, shadowy figures at opposite ends of the dining table which had been fashioned from the staves and floorboards of the chuckwagon that had embarked in 1886 with the first Lazy G herd, a bare hundred head, across the Canadian River northeast to Dodge City. The lighting in the dining room was dim, and the table long enough so that the two men had difficulty making each other out. They ate without a word, the sound of their implements seeming to echo in the gloom like the rattle of bones, while José padded in and out, changing plates, pouring water.

Finally, Gudge put down his knife and fork.

"It's as bad as they figgered. They want me to go up there and get hooked up like an airplane getting gassed up and put a lot of stuff in me and pray. Stuff that makes your hair fall out and your bones shrink. I said the hell with it. If my time's come, my time's come. Besides, I'm kinda interested in our little business; I figger that'll keep me distracted even when it gets bad, which they say won't happen for maybe nine months, maybe a year. That's the sort of time we got. You have it all figgered out?"

"I do. The target has to be a brokerage firm called Seaco Group; you may have heard of it. Mrs. Masterman has close to twenty-five million invested in it through her company. And it's said she's planning to bring in Senator Lassiter to run it. To the discomfiture of the present management. That's presumably the reason the Senator's announced his plans to give up his seat in the Senate."

"Seaco Group? How do we get in their pants without them knowing what we're doing?"

"I have a plan for that. We can discuss it in detail tomorrow. For the moment, let's just say that we'll go fishing on Wall Street. With the right baits and lures. Designed to bring the fish boiling to the surface. Fish called greed, and pride, and opportunism. Fish that feed on themselves and seldom discover it until it's too late."

He put down his chopsticks with a faint click, bade Gudge a low goodnight and faded away, leaving the ruler of the Lazy G alone with his last perfect cube of perfect beef, pondering how much he hated that world up there, worse even than he hated whatever it was that was eating up his blood.

Nick's knock had scarcely sounded when the door swung open. Behind the maid at the peephole loomed the majestic figure of Vosper, Greschner's celebrated butler, the chief operating officer of Number 17.

"Good evening, Vosper. It's nice to see you. I was sorry to hear about your cousin."

He referred to a relative of Vosper's who had been concussed by a falling coconut while serving canapés on a Palm Beach terrace. Vosper was the fifth sprig of his family tree to enter the service of American millionaires in the nearly seventy years since the first Vosper to buttle in America had arrived, won from a bibulous duke in a game of croquet by the chairman of

Ohio Central. As with the Greschners, the emigration had been successful, providing security, fortune and a fair measure of fame in a young nation anxious to accouter itself with every evidence of civility that a good, hard dollar could buy. The Vospers had proved to be sturdy breeders; there were siblings functioning in several states. But only Greschner's butler could be counted a genuine legend.

"Kind of you to inquire, sir. These things will happen at the end of the season. I'm pleased to say he's doing nicely. Of course, he is covered by his employer's company's major-medical plan. You are well, I trust, sir."

"Very well, Vosper. And Mr. Greschner?"

"Off his feed, I fear, sir. He seems to be taking age rather badly. I quite worry about him. He's very lonely. So many fewer people seem to come to call. So many fewer people are alive to call, if the truth be told, sir. And practically none of the old faces. His young men. Only you and Mr. Seabury, really. And Mrs. Winstead once in a while. It's a pity. There's very little seems to interest him. I'm afraid he's becoming bored, and boredom ages a man worse than anything, sir."

"He did sound down to me, the last time I spoke with him. We'll have to think of something to cheer him up." He shook Vosper's hand again. "Don't worry, I'll find my own way, thanks. It's awfully nice to see you looking so trim."

"Thank you, sir. It's the jogging. Confidentially, sir, I'm thinking of trying the marathon next year. Assuming we're all still around, sir."

Nick headed up the staircase. He liked to take a fresh look at the house every time he came. There was something so irreplaceably enhancing about mounting a grand staircase like this; it made a man feel like a real aristocrat, this business of ascending to picture-lined drawing rooms, the clink of crystal and the glow of candles on oak and walnut. On the first landing he paused to look at the big Reynolds portrait of David Garrick as Macbeth. The first time he'd met Sol, his own first visit to this house, he'd arrived just as the picture had been uncrated. With Hermann Zauber, the dealer for whom he had just gone to work and who had sold Sol the picture. That had been when he'd met Frodo Crisp for the first time, too. Crisp had walked over from the Fuller, which he'd joined just over a year earlier after having been the Keeper of Paintings at the Caledonian Museum in Scotland. He'd agreed to supervise the hanging of the Reynolds. He was very close to Sol by then; Greschner had not hesitated to take Crisp under his wing.

Seeing the Reynolds again reminded Nick how fortunate he'd been in his chance acquaintances; how unexpected meetings, usually accompanying his mentor of the moment, had in fact shaped the pattern of his life: with Felix Rothschild he'd met Johnny Sandler and Max Lefcourt and Francis Sanger; with old Zauber, Solomon Greschner and Frodo Crisp. All the luck a man needed. He looked up at Garrick, posed stormily in an outlandish Scottish costume on an Augustan blasted heath, and fancied that the image of the immortal English actor smiled at him.

Continuing up the stairs, he remembered that first lunch at Number 17 as if it had been yesterday. Sol had apologized for the inconvenience, fidgeted nervously while Crisp got the laboring men from the picture movers to position the painting just so and then led his three guests in to lunch. Over a tongue soufflé and a salad, the three older men had swapped anecdotes both vicious and merry about society and the art world while Nick kept his ears open and tried to laugh in the right places. Afterward, Zauber had told him, "Nicholas, you handled yourself quite well. Most young men try to say too much in new company. I think you may do."

On the second floor, the Palladian dining table was turned out as if for royalty. Fresh candles were in the sconces. Nick quickly noted twelve places, set out with Sol's Derby armorial dinner service and his George II silver. The sixteenth-century cassone that served as a sideboard held a battery of old English cut-glass decanters. The place cards weren't out yet, as Nick had known they wouldn't be. Sol didn't countenance table-peekers. To his right, the octagonal room in which Sol screened films was dark; thank God, thought Nick, there would be no movie tonight. Showing movies after dinner had become a preferred form of entertainment these days. For people with no conversation, Nick thought. Who were bored with their guests and very probably with themselves. What the hell was the world coming to? Nick wondered. Parties in stores. Movies after dinner. What could be next?

He mounted to the third floor, climbing the final chute of stairs, which was hung with drawings of great musicians: a crayon by Longhi depicting Vivaldi looking sinister at the organ of San Marco; Bach drawn in a crude, punctilious way by some unknown German; Beethoven glowering at an even less competent Austrian draftsman; a silhouette cutout of Liszt; Ravel smiling in a study by Matisse; perhaps twenty more lining the stairwell to the top. More of Sol's remarkable possessions. The possessions that were as well known as the man himself: the first editions, brass candlesticks, small Renaissance bronzes, Cycladic antiquities, amulets and scarabs, majolica, George I wine cisterns, tapestried stools and benches, marble busts of English writers and statesmen, framed autographs of French writers from Voltaire to Proust, china: Coalport and Spode, export porcelains. An astonishing profusion scattered and grouped throughout the house, but remarkable, really, more for the quantity and range of the cumulation than for the special distinction of any: nothing Sol owned was less than high medium-grade, but nothing was definitive either. It was as if this multitude of objects were as bricks which built a fortress within a fortress, a battlement within which Sol had walled himself up, protected by his objects from the threatening world beyond the walls of Number 17.

Arriving on the third-floor landing, Nick was met by a white-jacketed manservant wanting his drink order. Sol's compact, exuberant figure was striding bouncily across the drawing room, arms outstretched.

"Nicholas, dear boy, how are you? You called this afternoon but I was napping. Sorry. It's awful to grow old. Come in."

Nick embraced his host, then backed off gently, wanting to check Sol out for overt symptoms of depression. But he looked the same as ever. Short, bald, confidently ruddy, his flourishing burnside whiskers perfectly trimmed. The gray eyes on either side of his great beak—Roman to Sol, Semitic to others—were as clear and cynical as ever. He looked fine and hale. He was buttoned up tight in a close-fitting scarlet-piped dinner jacket topped with a vast bow tie into which had been worked, in blue embroidery barely less dark than the black silk of the tie, the emblem of a second-rate London club. As always, however, his customary flush was heightened; he gave every appearance of a nervous host.

At first, that had come as a surprise to Nick; Number 17 housed, on average, two large dinners a week from October through May; entertaining on this scale and degree of excellence would, one would have thought, have become second nature to Sol. Nick's early reaction had been to put Sol's unease down to the tension associated with sustaining perfection. The longer he knew him, however, the clearer it seemed that Sol had never truly become the master of his own house; on occasions like this, when the outside world was admitted with pomp and circumstance, he could seem more like a newly arrived tenant with a long lease offering a housewarming to suspicious neighbors.

"How are you, Sol?" he asked as his host guided him into the paneled drawing room. An unseasonal fire blazed in the hearth. It was probably Nick's favorite room in New York. Filled with bookcases, silver-framed signed photographs of Sol's current favorites and a motley of overstuffed chairs and good heavy English furniture. Over the mantel hung a small Hogarth depicting Dr. Johnson as Socrates. It was Sol's favorite possession, combining his two most adored, most frequently quoted idols; it was a mirror of his aspirations. He would have wished it to have been a self-portrait. As Greschner guided him across the room, Nick took a quick measure of the company. Sol's dinners were invariably "working" occasions; someone or something was being set up, positioned. Nick wondered what it would be tonight.

"I think you know Lucienne and Tarver Melton," Sol said, leading Nick over to a couple perched anxiously on a love seat near the door. Nick shook hands. What in Christ are these people doing here? he thought. He knew the Meltons. They were filler: the human equivalent of the polystyrene flakes in which china came packed. Rich and insipid, inoffensive and colorless enough to fit in anywhere. From Palm Beach to Sta. Marta to Newport, depending on the season, the Meltons filled chairs: they made twelve at dinner, four for bridge, six for a box at the opera. They always arrived at parties early and sat as close as possible to the dining room, keeping an eye on the tables lest the cards inscribed with their names be suddenly removed and they be ushered to the back door.

"And Arden, of course," said Sol. A tall, fortyish woman in a batik caftan rose from her seat and engulfed Nick. Arden Maypole. The famous color-field painter notable also for her frighteningly persevering sexual energy.

"Darling," she said, "how wicked of you not to fetch me. I so wanted you to see my new paintings." Her humid breath in Nick's ear was positively tropical. He backed off.

"And this is Mrs. Buford Gudge," said Sol, bringing Nick face to face with a young woman who had been off behind a sofa, looking closely at a Bonington watercolor of the Grand Canal. "Mrs. Gudge. Mr. Nicholas Reverey, the art dealer."

She was a good-looking young woman, Nick saw, but pretty in a standard all-American way, and a little used around the edges, although he guessed she was still in her early thirties. Very pale, with shoulder-length reddish hair. Around her neck was a necklace of emeralds that would have paid a small city's school bill. Her breasts were winners, pushed up by a white crepe dress spangled with pale green sequins. She had obviously been very carefully put together in expensive trappings designed, Nick suspected, to distract from a personality that would doubtless prove as tough and common as a nail. Her expression seemed to bear this out. Watching her eyes dart around the room, alighting on this object and that, even as she greeted him, Nick thought she looked like a greedy child making up a million-dollar Christmas list; it was sly, discordant note amid the bland, carefully assembled and made-up perfection of her appearance and her features. Nick pegged her as an ex-model on the make. Or a cheerleader. One of those queens of bumper-sticker country whom people like Buford Gudge were popularly assumed to marry; and usually did.

Gudge was a name he recognized. It meant money. Mrs. Gudge herself was rising in society's consciousness. Nick recalled having noticed a couple of small, recent items about her in the gossip columns. Inconspicuous stuff: appearances at selected charity balls and a day at the races with a carefully winnowed Vanderbilt; a Halston showing; polo in Palm Beach. Now she was here.

Of course, he thought, it figured. Another Greschner promotion, that was what she was. The stuff in the papers was just the band tuning up.

She shook his hand warmly. Her grip was tough. Ah, well, he thought, Sol will learn you, honey. In no time you'll be extending a pale, languid arm, hand palm down, available for kissing. Wait until the Europeans get hold of you, thought Nick.

"You know Señor von González?" She gestured to the man next to her, whom Nick had barely noticed. Nick knew who Von González was, although he had never actually met him. These days, you couldn't avoid the Von Gonzálezes, who were inescapable presences in every magazine, paper or broadcast that had to do with how expensively people lived and dressed. This year's couple; or maybe, by now, last year's. Nick wasn't sure. They must be slipping, he thought, to be at Sol's this evening. And Sol must be slipping to have people like them, he reflected wryly. This was clearly the number two dinner party of the evening, ranking well behind the banquet being set uptown by Calypso and Hugo Winstead for Max Lefcourt, whose collection was being exhibited in the new Annex. Anyway, he knew, people like the Von Gonzálezes gave the ache to the old bones of old money, which defined "real society" with astronomical precision, and never confused the fixed stars and true comets with people who came on like fireworks over the river, climbing high and splendidly, popping all their colors and drawing an instant's worth of oohs and aahs before fizzling down. Hugo Winstead might be an arriviste himself, thought Nick, but his Fuller connection made him old money, and no Von Gonzálezes would sit down at his table.

He shook hands. The Massimo von Gonzálezes were an unlikely couple. Thanks to Sol, Nick knew that she had first burst on the scene as the private secretary and, some said, lover of an aging French novelist, a once-renowned Sapphic by then too feeble to do more than pucker her lips. What she had been before that was veiled, although the more vicious gossips claimed she was in fact an Iowa farm girl who had been booted out of the WAC on a morals rap. In the event, Gratiane de Dovre, as she was then known, served the old novelist for several years; her patroness' death brought her little money, but a nice house on the rue du Bac. She was talented, aggressive, plain enough so that other women found her unthreatening, and had a wicked tongue. She'd stayed in Paris until the mid-'60s, then had come to New York on the proceeds from selling the rue du Bac house, and kept herself fed and clothed as she had in Paris, doing this and that—decorating, jewelry designing, public relations for a costume-jewelry firm, which was how she'd first met her husband.

He was in fact born Miguel González. He was the son of an opportunistic Buenos Aires painting contractor of pronounced fascist sympathies. In 1944, with things going badly for the Third Reich, González senior had advised the German Legation that he had an opening in his business in the event the former Herr Schicklgruber might deem it advantageous to take up house painting again. As it turned out, the Führer had been unable to take Señor González up on his generous offer. But in those awful times, the Germans were grateful for any crumbs of affection, and González was duly summoned to the Legation and there given a minor decoration, which never left his body until he died, and the right to add "von" to his name. It was a critical item of young Miguel's baggage when he emigrated to New York. He became Massimo soon after he discovered that far too many people whose company and favors he craved thought he was a Puerto Rican.

He and Gratiane discovered that they shared a thirst for publicity. She had the ambition and intelligence necessary to bring it off, but she needed another pair of hands. He had just the equipment she was looking for in a partner: sallow, slick good looks not quite greasy enough to give offense, a classic homosexual talent for making up to older women and no personal convictions on any subject apart from clothes and dinner. He also had a gift for saying what he was told to say and for doing what he was told to do.

She pushed him hard, but he never complained—not after she reminded him sternly, "Do it my way, my little love, or you'll end up teaching the fox-trot to blue-haired old ladies on cruise ships." Through influential friends, her husband was recommended as a fashion editor to the crabby misanthrope who published *That Woman!*, which was then a garment-trade paper read principally by furriers. The timing was perfect. America was just entering that period of weirdly imitative life-styling which would end with otherwise sensible people going around covered in other people's initials. *That Woman!* took off, thanks to the clever assistants Gratiane rounded up for Massimo to put the right words under his by-line.

Massimo now called the fashion tune for New York. In his role as Things Editor of *That Woman!*, his word was life-style law. "Massimo von González went up the Sinai of stylishness and brought down the tablets," wrote the gushing journalism-school bloom dispatched by *Time* to report on the extraordinary phenomenon of the Von Gonzálezes.

He had come to be known as "The Pope of Life-Style." The nickname dated from the year that he declared the religious look to be "InStyle," so that wimples blossomed on the heads of smart women and sweetish sacramental wine chased Pouilly Fumé from stylish Manhattan and Lake Forest lunch tables. Tiffany representatives had swept through Rome and bought up every cross and pectoral to be found in the Vatican City. Nick recalled the craze: his phone had rung off the hook with requests from interior decorators looking for inexpensive religious pictures that didn't show people being hacked to pieces or hanging from crosses. In due course the fad had expired, but not before a promising climber from Houston, rendered invulnerable to the Heimlich Maneuver by her Joan of Arc armor, had choked to death on a sacramental wafer at a "Come as You Were Martyred" party.

Nick slid his hand into Von González' lubricated grasp and withdrew it quickly. He returned to Caryn Gudge and was starting to say something when a large, feathered shape interposed itself and encircled the startled Mrs. Gudge with an embrace like a boa constrictor's.

"Darleeng Carine . . ." It was Gratiane. "So nice to see you zis evening." She turned to her husband, ignoring Nick. "I've choost come in weeth the Bogles. Darling, eet's eempossible to deal with zat man. So cheap. Hello!" She rounded on Nick, smiled at him with the microsecond's condescension of one who has time only for the powerful, rich and gifted, and brushed past toward Arden Maypole, managing somehow simultaneously to kiss the air by Massimo's cheek, flourish her marabou stole and hiss back over her shoulder to her husband, "We have a crisis Sunday night! Henry's weekend parole ends at nine and no one else will want to leave that early!"

Once again, Nick's knowledge of the road maps and rosters of smart society allowed him to understand. The Von González "Sunday potlucks" were famous, especially now that fascism, in various phases, was back in political fashion. Their country-style Park Avenue kitchen welcomed the public elite of the moment—out-of-office politicians, discredited former cabinet officers, corporate bigwigs free on bail and writers and artists more notable for interviews than for accomplishment, all of whom had successfully converted the perquisites and privileges of political, financial and cultural stewardship into six- to seven-figure incomes. They gathered around the ten-place butcher-block table and were fed whatever was currently a la mode, from cassoulet to couscous, and lied to one another about their book advances and the degree of their friendship with Mrs. Astor. The one unbreakable rule of the evening was that all the guests had to leave together, so that no one could have a head start telephoning an account of the evening's goings-on to his or her favorite columnist. In a spirit of fair play, Gratiane and Massimo agreed to wait a half-hour after their guests had departed before picking up the direct lines that connected them to the heavyweight gossipists of the *New York Post* and the *Daily News*.

Harvey and Esmé Bogle were names more interesting to Nick. He turned to examine the couple who had entered the room behind Gratiane. They were not, on balance, a prepossessing pair. Esmé Bogle was a small, blond, fiftyish woman, who was stubby all over: puglike face under choppy curls, stout short arms and porky little trotters peeking from beneath a silver-gilt skirt. Hers was an astonishing success story. With her husband away much of the time, supervising his investment empire, she had turned in idleness to writing a first novel, *Salon*, portrayed, in a style an unkind critic had described as "emphysematous," the rich psychosexual life of the staff and customers of a high-priced Manhattan hairdressing parlor. A leading women's magazine had serialized it under a banner heralding its "thrilling gynecological verisimilitude." The book had sold three hundred thousand copies in hardcover, earned $2.2 million on its paperback sale and been made into a television series which outpulled *Dallas* in the ratings. Her second novel had done even better. Her new book, still in the writing, had garnered advances aggregating close to $5 million. Although the specifics of the plot were still a matter of speculation, the dam of secrecy at Coronet Books had been sufficiently pierced so that it was a matter of fairly common knowledge that the "new megaBogle" was about the life and fortunes of a beautiful female proctologist and her marriage to one of England's belted earls.

Her husband was also in his fifties. He was short as well, perhaps half a foot taller than his wife. Nick was interested in Bogle. Not simply because he was thought to be worth close to a billion dollars. The largest part in real estate, spread across the United States; but big stock-market positions too, and heavy investments in hard-rock mining and in leasing. A finger in a great many important pies. He was reputed to be bold and persistent; hard to scare off: the sort of man the Old School financial types rumbled about in the club chairs as "a raider." To his admirers, mostly people who'd made money following him into deals and takeovers, straightforward, clear-thinking and plainspoken: "the perfect capitalist." To his detractors, mostly fat-bottomed executives whom Bogle had run off the cuddy corporate pastures in which they grazed like indolent cattle, a first-class, government Choice, blue-ribbon, grade-A shit: "makes me ashamed to be an American." To everyone, recognized as having a taste for blood in his deals. None of which really interested Nick except as background. What was important was that Bogle was believed, on the authority of no less a source than Sol, to have an incipient interest in collecting art.

Nick looked him over. Bogle's appearance belied his reputation as a gutter fighter. He was obviously no clod-featured, cigar-chewing ham-fist in a thousand-dollar suit. There was nothing crude about him. If anyone had asked him the key to his success, he would have replied that he'd made a lot of money off so-called sharp guys who believed in the proposition that inherited money was dumb money. By the time they woke up to the realization that they had grievously underestimated him, Bogle usually had their wallets in his trophy case.

Looking at Bogle, Nick wondered how that sort of man could put up with a load of crap like Gratiane von González, who had been given the decorating commission at the newly built Esmé Palace. Probably doing it for the wife, Nick guessed. These women were drawn like iron filings to a tastemaker like Mme. von González. That hotel was going to look like something. In an interview with the *Times*, she had announced the theme of her decor as "the reindustrialization of America, which is so so important to us each, but particularly the little people like our little vegetable-and-fruit man in Bridgehampton, who is the backbone of America but especially in the matter of decent broccoli."

Responding to a high sign from Sol, he crossed the room with his host to be introduced to the Bogles. "Get to know him, and the Gudge girl," the older man said quietly. "There's business to be done there." Nick exchanged perfunctory greetings with Esmé, who was then borne away by Sol to greet another couple who had just entered the room, and stood with her husband, both men waiting for fresh champagne.

Bogle looked at him appraisingly. That stare, thought Nick, could cut a sequoia in half. "Who are these funny-looking people?" he asked in a reasonable, matter-of-fact way. "The big French one I know. She's a new friend of Esmé's. She's doing the lobby of my new hotel. In machinery—says it's the theme of the times. Can you believe it? Today they delivered forklifts and lathes to put around the atrium instead of trees! Fifty of them. Got any idea what that stuff costs? Tomorrow, she tells me, she's got a dozen of those industrial robots the Japs build Toyotas with. Says they can serve hors d'oeuvre at the buffet. I think these people are absolutely bananas, you ask me, but my wife, the famous novelist and talk-show star, tells me it's the height of fashion. You go in for fashion, Mr. Reverey?"

"Only when it starts to hurt."

"Keep it that way." He gave Nick a thin smile. Affability was clearly not his long suit. "Greschner tells me you are the guy to talk to about pictures. . . . Oh, shit."

Nick followed Bogle's pale, fierce gaze. A heavy, distinguished-looking man was bearing down on them. Nick felt Bogle balance himself like a fighter anticipating the bell.

"Hello, Homer. This must be pretty big-time if you're here." Again the matter-of-factness which just skirted rudeness. He made the introductions.

"Mr. Reverey, Mr. Seabury. Mr. Seabury, Mr. Reverey. You two know each other?" They'd met at Sol's a number of times before. Nick and Seabury nodded to each other.

"It's very nice to see you, Harvey." Homer Seabury spoke in a genial voice which betrayed no special feeling about Bogle. There was nothing in his manner that could have suggested to Nick or to anyone else in the room, except Greschner, who was in on the game, that there was anything going on between them.

"Nice to see you too, Homer. You look pretty good. I'd think you'd get pretty tired, especially at your age, chasing so hard after Merrill Lynch and Bache. Not to mention keeping Winstead away from the office pussy."

"Oh, not so much, Harvey. After all, the game's worth the candle." Seabury was affable. The man's self-conscious bonhomie irritated Nick, who was unhappy anyway at being interrupted. Irritated him and made him uneasy. He began to feel that there was something serious in the air between these two.

"Especially now," Seabury continued pompously, "with an administration in Washington that really understands business. A free market, that's the thing, Harvey. Stand or fall on your own ability. None of this bailing out firms that can't cut the competitive mustard. It's good to have those knee-jerk-liberal hand-me-outers back in the think tanks where they belong." Seabury rocked on the balls of his feet and beamed. He seemed mightily pleased with the vigorousness of his declaration. Bogle said nothing for a few seconds.

"Maybe so," said Bogle, thoughtfully. "How're you getting along with Granada, Homer?"

"Surprising you should ask, Harvey. Actually quite well, really." Another rumbling chuckle.

"She gonna bring Lassiter back to rain on your parade?"

The beam on Seabury's face lost some of its radiance. The chuckle came a little harder.

"Oh, I'd doubt that, Harvey. Really I would."

"She's a brute, Granada is. I've known her a long time. We all went to high school together, you know. Her and Esmé and me. She didn't have a pot to piss in then. We used to give her my sister's old clothes. She got tough then. C'mon, Homer, 'fess up. Granada's on your ass? And Lassiter? He's a real class-A prick, but I don't have to tell you that, Homer."

"I'd say you're being a little harsh, Harvey. We were partners, after all, Rufus and I. And he is married to my sister. Now, of course, I find his politics a little, well, shall we say a little too pragmatic. Of course, now that he's regained his senses—economically, I mean—he's ever so much more palatable."

"I doubt you'll say that if you come in one Monday morning and that sonofabitch is sitting at your desk giving orders."

That stung, Nick saw. Lassiter was a sore subject with a lot of people. Sent to the Senate by the wealthy suburban voters of Connecticut, he'd jumped all over the political lot in his two and a half terms. For most of his career he'd never been a Vietnam-style liberal. Infuriating his constituents, who nevertheless returned him twice more, because he was at least their sort. Then their faith had been confirmed. Two years earlier, Lassiter had completely changed course; it was as if he'd smelled the new conservative tide, so he went with the flow. Characteristically, he turned a nice profit on it. He had combined the laissez-faire, love-the-rich economics and the neo-Calvinist, neo-McCarthyist religiosity of the new order. His book *Moral Money* had been a best seller. A second, *God and Gold,* had just gone to the printer. The hands that had fed Rufus Lassiter and helped him on his way were scarred with the marks of his teeth. Of course, Nick remembered: it had been Senator Lassiter who had put Mrs. Gudge's husband through the wringer at those televised hearings. Lassiter at his righteous, finger-pointing worst; Gudge reduced to a stuttering mediocrity. It had been a sorry spectacle on all counts.

"Oh, I doubt that'll happen, Harvey. After all, I've got twenty percent of the shares myself. And good friends among our institutional holders."

"Maybe. Personally, Homer, I never saw an institutional stockholder that wasn't a complete whore. And neither did you, my friend; neither did you."

"Well, we'll just have to see what happens, won't we, Harvey?"

"That we will just have to do, Homer. Would you excuse Mr. Reverey and me for a second? Nice to see you."

"Umm, yes, Harvey. Nice to see you. And you too, Mr. Reverey." Seabury fastened on an avenue of graceful escape. "Ah, I see the Tarver Meltons are with us tonight. I must say hello. I'll see you both later. Umm yes, Harvey. Mr. Reverey." He took Nick's hand in both of his for an instant, then rumbled off across the room to the sofa where the Meltons sat, quivering like marmosets.

Bogle turned back to Nick.

"Not a bad guy, Homer. But out of his depth. He's likely to hit the panic button. I can't say I blame him, poor bastard. He's got a pretty good company there—slow, but safe. But that Granada's a real cunt, and Lassiter's worse. So Homer's running scared, and scared guys make mistakes. Big mistakes. And they also make a lot of money for people who see how scared they are. Two things really get you in trouble, Reverey: panic and believing it when someone who wants something tells you how smart you are—especially if that someone is yourself."

They were interrupted by the call to dinner. As Esmé came up to take her husband's arm, he said to Nick, who was preparing to square off with Arden Maypole, "Maybe after dinner we can talk a little more? I want to learn a couple of things. Look for me later. I'd like to have a little talk."

As they formed up for the ritual procession one flight down to the dining room, Nick was interested to note that Sol's right arm, the arm of honor, was occupied by Caryn Gudge. It confirmed his earlier conclusion that Sol was on a job again, which was something to be thankful about. A good assignment might change his mood. Sol then stepped off, and Nick, stiffening to keep Arden Maypole's arm from investigating his inner leg, followed the Bogles down the stairs; behind him came Homer Seabury and his lady, and then, last, came the Meltons, smiling happily, finally certain of a place at table and something to eat.

If, in his imaginary autobiography, Solomon Greschner could have fixed the moment at which he became open to the thought of turning his vocation inside out, so that instead of building people up, as he had done for sixty years, he might rather enjoy tearing some of them down, he would very probably have settled on this dinner party. When, at some point, he would look it up in his records, it would turn out to have been the 4,024th dinner he had given at Number 17 since he had bought it in 1937. Of itself, an unmemorable fact, he thought: not a milestone like a ballplayer's three-thousandth base hit, or the thousand and three women Don Giovanni had seduced in Spain, or any of the other statistical high points of Western culture. Nor, as he looked around the table, was the company that evening so distinctive one way or the other as to inspire a fervid change of heart.

On the whole, it was a mediocre group, gathered here purely because Calypso had asked him to do it for her. Oh, Nick was always fine, always a treat, and Bogle was interesting. But after all, until very recently the table at Number 17 had been set only for the brightest and most intriguing names. The chair in which an overbred cretin like Tarver Melton now sat, scarfing down caviar-stuffed blinis as if there were no more sturgeon left in the Caspian Sea, had cushioned Einstein, Greta Garbo and Willie Mays, and three generations of Rockefellers. To his immediate left, where Homer Seabury's wife dithered away about beagles to his unhearing ear, the wife of the Japanese Ambassador had whispered to him—it was Thanksgiving, 1941—that it would make sense to sell out any Hawaiian investments in his portfolio. He had done so silently, and gone short Castle and Cooke in the bargain; without remorse at having profited from foreknowledge of Pearl Harbor. It was axiomatic that nothing said at Solomon Greschner's table left the house unless through the host himself. Other people's eagerness for indiscretion was the price they paid for access to a brilliant company and extraordinary food. That was the rule of the house; it was slavishly obeyed by guests who wanted to return, and enforced by their host, whose Buddha-like omniscience was so pervasive that more than one departing first-time guest, overtaken by the wine, champagne, and brandy, had tried to rub Sol's stomach for good luck.

One man who had never dined here was Morgan Seabury, Homer's father. "It won't do for us to be seen together, Solomon," Seabury had said, trying to be kind. "Not good for you; not good for me. We're different worlds. To work well together we must keep them separate. If you want—

if it's useful to you—you can always say I'm coming to dine and set a place for me, but I'll not turn up." In Sol's mind, that place was empty still, even though, by chance, Seabury's son sat in it tonight.

The dinner tonight incorporated the customary splendors of the four-thousand-odd that had preceded it. In the kitchen, Ferdinand had performed his usual sorcery. Wild rice pancakes sprinkled with the last of the Oestrava caviar which came from the Russian Ambassador, followed by fingers of stir-fried gray sole and Arkansas catfish. Then the special steaks which had been flown in by Caryn Gudge, accompanied by a mélange of the same vegetables—turnips, new potatoes and fiddleheads—that Ferdinand's researches at the Historical Society had unearthed as having very likely been raised by the Dutch widow whose garden once had grown where Number 17 now stood. Sol's food was as important as his guest list in making his invitations nonregrettable. His guests arrived knowing that they were there to be used, were being served up themselves. So what? He gave better than he got, Sol did, and he had done so for most of the fifty years he had been in the business. Now, looking around the table again, he saw no reason to think otherwise.

Ah, well, Sol thought, there was still enough going on of the old business to pay him to keep his hand in. But so many of his humane illusions had fled, and nothing had appeared to replace them, that the motions he still went through, magically effective though they might seem to the few people who sought him out for help, no longer did much for him. Sighing, with a violence that for a moment shut even Mrs. Seabury up, he nodded to Vosper, hovering behind him with a linen-wrapped magnum of Meursault, and let the game go on.

Four places down the table, between Caryn Gudge and Arden Maypole, Nick was doing his best to catalogue for Mrs. Gudge the artifacts of the house and the evening while struggling to wrest free of the under-table advances of the lady painter, who seemed to have been poleaxed by the champagne and powerful white Burgundy. Mrs. Gudge operated without pretense, he noted. She was there to learn. Halfway through the blinis, she had produced a small leather notebook, into which, lips slightly moving as she wrote, she entered the details of the dinner with a gold pencil. She had loose, oval schoolgirl handwriting, Nick saw, completely out of scale with the chic little pages on which she recorded each course and its wine.

As Vosper circled the table, now pouring red wine into the company's glasses, she paused in her accounting to turn to Nick and said, "This better be real good wine. You're going to taste steak like you never tasted it. These are from our Los Rojos steers. That means 'the Red Ones' in Spanish. It's a special Lazy G breed. The Lazy G—that's my husband's ranch in the Panhandle. We don't raise much beef anymore; just prize bulls for the sales in Dalhart. But Buford—that's my husband, although most folks call him Bubber, but not to his face 'cause it's a nickname he just hates—has Stumpy—that's our foreman—pick out a few choice steers—all grass-fed, none of those chemicals, butchered up just for us, all lean meat; Buford's been away a whole lot the last few months, so when Mr. Greschner asked me here, the least I could do was get into the locker and bring a few up with me on the Gulfstream, which is the plane I like to use 'cause you can stand up in the potty. We also have a Lear and a Falcon, that's Buford's favorite, but I get along better in the big plane. He's a real gentleman, Mr. Greschner is, isn't he? I mean, being Jewish and all? Now, what's *this* wine called?"

For the third time, Nick's raised eyebrows brought Vosper over.

"Can we see the bottle, Vosper?"

"Of course, sir." Vosper brought a silver wine basket from the sideboard and showed Nick the label. "It's the last of the '59 Cheval Blanc, sir." He turned the label to Caryn Gudge, who set to work with her gold pencil, her free hand steadying the bottle in the flickering candlelight. "Mr. Greschner was sad to see how little we had left, sir," Vosper said, lowering his voice to that near-subaural pitch which only great butlers possess, and which only experienced diners-out can hear, "but then he said who cared, considering how little time he has left himself. Try to cheer him up, sir."

Nick looked up the table at Sol, on the face of it beamingly attentive to a conversation being animatedly conducted across his bow by Mrs. Seabury and Gratiane von González. He was endeavoring to read Sol's mind behind the fixed, genial expression when a moist breath in his ear shut him off.

"Listen, Nick," murmured Arden Maypole, "let's leave right after dinner. I've got a limo downstairs. Come on up to the studio. Goddammit, you never look at my goddamn pictures. I've got three pictures hanging in the goddamn Metropolitan Museum, so you can goddamn well come and take a look."

She placed her hand on his thigh and started it north. He cut her off just short of the danger zone. Ever polite, he muttered, "Maybe after the Fuller. But Arden, you know I've got to make an appearance. It's my business." He turned back to Caryn Gudge, who was passing the remainder of her steak to Tarver Melton, chatting brightly about the Red Cross Ball in Monte Carlo. When he shifted back to his other side, he saw thankfully that Arden, head plumped down in her hands, was trying to converse with Harvey Bogle. As he looked over at Bogle, whom he hadn't really thought about during dinner, Nick suddenly remembered Johnny Sandler, and the Rubens sketches, and that Bogle wanted a word with him. Maybe . . . The threads of the evening momentarily drew together. No, he said to himself, are you crazy? The guy doesn't own one picture, for all you know, and you're thinking of starting him off at a quick seven million. Yet . . . it was a thought. He glanced at the end of the table, but with his mind on his business, he didn't see the bleakness behind the smiling facade of Sol's expression. Introduce Rubens to Bogle, he thought. Crazy. Ridiculous. Another drink needed to restore its reality. Nick placed a finger on the rim of his empty glass and Vosper came gliding across the floor, smooth and perfect as ever, to fill it with the last of the wine.

CHAPTER THREE

A man should at least be allowed to live to fifty, Gudge thought. It would be close to see if he made it, the way the doctors talked. He was sitting alone in the dark in his upstairs bedroom, gazing out the window, its curtains faintly ruffled by a scant night wind blowing through a moonless night. He supposed he was the fourth Gudge to do so: to sit in the dark looking over a domain that stretched to the horizon. In another few years, on a day the doctors had told him he wouldn't live to see, the Gudges would have been on this land a hundred years. His great-granddaddy, Buford I, as the books and newspapers called him when they periodically wrote up the Gudge family like royalty, had bought the first land in 1885. Bought it with money borrowed from a bank in Scotland. Bubber had been to Scotland; Gudge Aberdeen, Ltd., was partners with Mobil and Marathon on a little field out in the North Sea: nothing too big, just a round hundred and twenty-five thousand barrels a day. He'd liked Scotland a whole lot; the people up there were his sort—straightforward, tough, close-mouthed, impatient of strangers.

By the turn of the century, the ranch had swelled to over a million acres looking east and south, about fifty miles from Amarillo at its closest point, its westernmost extremity running for a spell along the Canadian River. A big ranch, although nothing like the three-million-acre XIT up north along the New Mexico border; it was enclosed by fifteen hundred miles of barbed-wire fencing which caged a hundred-odd thousand head of cattle, Herefords and Durham and Angus, watched over by close to a hundred vaqueros. That was the ranch at its peak—when cattle ruled, and the summer sun was sometimes blotted out by the dust raised by the great herds being driven north to the Colorado grasslands or the slaughterhouses of Kansas. That was all ancient history now, of course; as remote as the ziggurats of Babylon; a time preserved in the yellowing sepias and scratchy documents downstairs in the glass case.

By the time Bubber was born, in late 1932, the ranch had shrunk down to a couple of hundred thousand acres running a sparse ten thousand head.

What had once seemed an army of vaqueros had dwindled to barely a score; now the ranch occupied just over ninety thousand acres, since they'd sold off the farthest reaches, fallow fields enclosed by rusting wire hanging from rotted posts, to small operators foolish enough to think a man could survive by running cattle.

Shrinking the ranch had been Granddaddy's doing. He was the dominant figure in its history—as he had tended for eighty years to be in the life or history of anyone or anything he came up against. He'd taken over the ranch when he'd just turned fifteen. He was born unsentimental. Best of all he liked shooting; until the day he died, a week after his eightieth birthday, he spent a part of every day patrolling the ranch with shotgun, .30-30 carbine and revolver, blowing to perdition anything that moved and didn't wear the Lazy G brand: coyotes, rabbits, hawks, crows, rattlers, migrating wildfowl. It was said he'd killed a couple of rustlers in his time. And of course, whenever the help gathered in the shadows or out with the cattle, there was the other thing to talk about.

History didn't interest Granddaddy. The legends of Coronado crossing this land in search of the golden city of Gran Quivira were so much bunk to him. It was just acres and acres of dirt and grass and money to be made. Let the professors down in Lubbock puff on about the Llano Estacado, the vast "staked plains" which had once been the province of the great Spanish ranching kingdoms. He had an idea in his mind; the Lazy G was an abstraction to him, but a perdurable one. A symbol under which he gathered whatever it took to make the place immortal.

He quickly dispensed with the necessaries. He married a daughter of one of the vaqueros and she gave him a son, Buford II, Bubber's father, in 1908. He looked around for something better than cattle and found it in oil. The ranch already had a nice little income from some Oklahoma acreage which Buford I had won in the last of the big federal lotteries. Granddaddy decided to parlay it. Piece by piece, section by section, he sold off Lazy G grazing land to people who still believed in King Cattle and put the money into the oil business. Of course, he was lucky. The land he kept, on the advice of some young geologists from the University of Oklahoma, impinged on the Panhandle gas field. By 1921, when the gas boom began in earnest, he was drilling a dozen wells on his own land. From there it was into East Texas and the Permian, where, in the late 1920s, the Lupita Gudge No. 3 roared in at three thousand barrels a day, delineating the great Gudge field, still pumping twenty thousand barrels a day into Bubber's pocket after fifty years.

Bubber's granddaddy had neither use nor time for the emotional amenities and courtesies of family life. Buford III became a grandmamma's boy. Abashed, sulky and full of book fantasies, fairy-tale stuff which he got from his grandmother, and only seventeen years younger than his father, Buford III came to sense himself and his father as rival siblings as much as parent and child.

The life was hard on the ranch's queen mother. Mrs. Buford I was a city girl, from Edinburgh, who had met and married her husband when he had journeyed to Scotland to negotiate the financing of the original Lazy G. Her husband's Englishness had sustained her on the prairies. Now, with her son abrasive and withdrawn, by day preferring the company of the ranch hands and giving his evenings to his ledgers, leaving her to the company of a Mexican daughter-in-law who scarcely spoke English, life on the ranch became intolerable. Under the surface, she felt that her son's decision to sell off the land of which her husband had been so proud and for which he had held out such plans was a very measured betrayal of his heritage.

Finally, one day, the dowager Mrs. Gudge left the Lazy G for good, having come to an arrangement with her son for a generous check to be deposited monthly with the Fulton Trust Company in New York. She took Buford III with her. Her grandson was then seventeen; a studious, quiet young man still terrified of his profane and distant young father. At his grandmother's insistence, a series of imported tutors had been grudgingly permitted on the ranch to bring the boy up to a decent level of proficiency in his studies. Buford II smoldered at the sound of all the fancy talk and locked himself in his office and spent his days there, with the telephone and the ranch-house telegraph, making oil deals, building and dismantling his empire—or on his long, hateful forays, his pistol on his hip, into the plains in search of dumb victims.

That his son went off with the grandmother to New York didn't bother him. There would be time enough to break Buford III. The boy's future was the Lazy G—it was that simple—as the ranch would in time be the future for the boy's own son when he came along. No question. No argument.

Buford III and his grandmother settled into a comfortable apartment off Lexington Avenue. She was quickly gathered into a pleasant circle of widows and matrons who attended the opera and one another's teas in winter and, in the appropriate season, made genteel cultural excursions to the capitals of Europe. Buford III enrolled at Columbia. He was interested in writing; he met people who could talk; his eyes were opened to a world that illuminated the life back on the ranch with a light that seemed to him to glare like the fires of Hell.

In the spring of his senior year, he was summoned back to the Lazy G to stand behind his father as his Mexican mother, dead of influenza, was buried amid the reproachful mourning of her relatives. His father's eyes were dry as flint; looking at the knotty figure before him, Buford III suddenly felt a chill, as if some fearful presence had passed between him and the sun.

It was the future.

Afterward, in the ranch house, his father had sat him down and looked at him coldly.

"Now your college's about over, you'll be coming back here."

It was a statement of fact.

"Well, Daddy, I—"

"You better get yourself a wife. If you want, you do it yourself. Otherwise we got plenty down here so I'll pick one out. Vasquez's got him a pretty cute daughter, although I ain't got much use for no more Mexicans in the family. Probably find you something over in Amarillo or Borger."

"Daddy, I'd kind of like to stay in New York."

His father's eyes froze over. "Maybe so. But you're not going to. You're gonna come back here and take up what you're supposed to be. Which is this place, boy. This place is what you are, just like it's me, and it was my daddy before, and it's gonna be your boy afterward. I'm giving you a fair deal, boy. You pick you a wife up there if you want; get good stock; it's a son we want. Let me tell you something, boy. You been fancy-foolin' up there long enough, you and Mamma. I'll give you six months. Then I'll come get you. I'll come get you and tie you tight with a riata and ship you back here in a boxcar. And don't you figure you can run away from me, boy. I got a long shadow. Wherever you go to run from me, there won't be no sunshine."

Then he'd gotten up and gone into his office, leaving his son to contemplate the certainty that his father would do exactly what he said he would.

So Buford III went back to New York, and in July he returned with a bride. And a stepdaughter: his new wife's two-year-old daughter, Granada.

He had married the daughter of a stockbroker who had been wiped out in the crash of the previous October and had fled to Europe. She was blond and beautiful, in the way of Eastern girls from expensive private schools. She had a kind of inner toughness which Buford III must have thought might help him endure his father. She had made and terminated a miserable forced marriage which had given her the child.

Deep in his heart Buford III probably knew what his father's reaction to the little girl would be. Perhaps later he came to realize that another person's life couldn't be used to slap an opponent's face, like a duelist's glove.

In the event, they were married quietly and after a two-day train ride came to the Lazy G on a perfect July morning, when the sky was alive with high clouds driven like yachts before the wind, and the grass rippled like a sea which stretched beyond the limits of vision. The little girl followed two days later with her nurse.

The stepchild arrived at the ranch to find herself in the center of an emotional fire storm. Buford II was in an ice-cold rage at his son for what he had done. Night after night, behind the doors of his office, he raged at his son for despoiling the Lazy G with a soiled bride and what he charitably called "a bastard little she-bitch."

"Bad enough you got to go where another man's already left his tracks, boy, but then you think you got the right to come here and walk them tracks all over this house. No different than walking them all over my heart and your granddaddy's honor, boy. Now, I don't know what she thinks, boy, that bitch whore wife of yours; what she came here to get; but the Lazy G is Gudge, and pure Gudge. Ours, boy. Our blood. Our guts. Our flesh, boy."

It went on that way for a couple of weeks. Until his father's malevolent vocabulary was exhausted and a translucent veil of hatred settled in his eyes. He took his meals in his room and, night and day, paced the surrounding grasslands, presumably trying to purge himself of the imploding rage he felt, expending his venomous exhalations into the broad plains air.

Despite it all, the new Mrs. Buford III managed, even prospered. She liked the outdoors; could spend hours on horseback; gave affection and confidence to her husband. She avoided her father-in-law when she could and seemed to pay no attention to his glaring silences when she couldn't. If the ostracism he so obviously wanted her to feel cast her down, she didn't show it. Her daughter was too young to understand everything that was going on; like most children, she had a strong sense of what and a merciful innocence of why. She was large for her age; a genial, awkward girl with big, plain features who would surely never be a beauty, but would thankfully never be worse than plain. Her mother protected her. The Mexican women nuzzled her and gave her flan and caramel. She was like a jolly vapor on the edges of the storm that was gathering in the Big House.

In October 1932, Buford Gudge IV was born in the Big House after an easy labor. From the instant of his birth, it was apparent his granddaddy wanted to take him over, but somehow his mother drew a second strength from his arrival and began actively to oppose her father-in-law. She let her hatred of him simmer to the surface. Interposing herself between her husband and his father, she crossed swords with him. The baby was her surety. He was an easy, open baby who twinkled at the sight of his mother. Although she couldn't keep his grandfather away from him, she tried never to leave them alone together, even after the training in "man's work" began. When little Buford IV was stuck up on a pony for the first time, barely three years old, she insisted on accompanying him around the corral. When the child was four, his grandfather took advantage of an unguarded moment to lead the little boy around behind the bunkhouse, where he placed the baby's chubby finger on the trigger of his old Colt Navy Model .44 and caused the child to fire it. The report hurt the baby's ears and sent him wailing to his mother. That night words of a new ferocity were exchanged in the ranch house; upstairs, later, she rounded for the first time on her husband for his spinelessness and turned her back to him in bed forever.

The next day she was calmer. The fight appeared to have settled a mantle of ice on angry feelings. Life on the ranch, though frostier, returned to its old pace. The baby was starting to talk; she made sure either she or her daughter was always close to him. It was at that time that Buford IV first became known as "Bubber"—a nickname his half-sister laughingly contrived from his childish efforts to say "brother." His efforts to get it out made Granada giggle first, and then laugh and point, and finally, with the infinite capacity of children for unthinking cruelty, run to the kitchen to fetch her cronies, who joined their gold-tooth grins to hers without the slightest idea of what was going on. The nickname stuck; even his father started to call him by it, so Bubber he remained to this day.

His mother turned contemplative. She had a piano installed in the parlor of the Big House. Twice a week a young man from Borger, like herself an expatriate forced by fortune to dwell among the savages, came over to give her lessons. He was a nice, soft-spoken man, who played the piano poorly but was deeply serious about music. So was she. Hour after hour she filled the downstairs with the bittersweet cheerfulness of Schubert and the deep languor of Chopin. Immured in his office, her father-in-law tried to shut out the hated noise and burned with ire.

Then, suddenly one morning, she was gone. Forever. There was from that moment a tumult in the child's mind, like crashing waves keeping the foundering lifeboat from reaching the shore, that left him only tormenting hints of a night's horror. Later, she would return to him as a bloody, terrifying apparition, a stock figure of his repertory of nightmares. Later, also, he would realize, without having learned, that his nightmare was a mental photograph of something real and awful.

But when his grandfather and father returned days later, saying only that his mother had been taken by the angels, it was all too much to understand, and he took up his life as a man among men. His father acted funny, of course; took to his room among bottles and made little sense. But now Granddaddy had Bubber all to himself and the life they lived! Granada, of course, didn't come back. Not until a long time later, after Buford II and Buford III were both dead. She was going to stay up East with her grandparents, he was told; it was better that way, he was told. And he agreed. After the way she had teased and pointed at him, who wanted old fat her around?

Buford III died in 1951. Bubber stood beside his granddaddy on a cold gun-metal morning while the few remaining vaqueros wheeled by the grave, sombreros at their sides in the traditional salute to the dead. Then there were just the two of them, Bubber and Granddaddy. And then just he, incubating enough confusion and hatred for a dozen lifetimes.

A faint, brisk tremor stirred the bedroom curtains. Gudge shifted. The Lazy G wasn't really a ranch anymore. It was sulfur mines in Arizona, and banks here and there, and manganese nodules on the Pacific floor and the spoutings of radio and television evangelists over Gudge-owned stations. The fifteen hundred miles of barbed wire that had defined the ranch in 1900 had given way to an electronic spiderweb tying together everything marked with the Lazy G, from Dubai to Del Rio. All flowing into this house where he sat; all flowing in to him.

He wondered how Caryn was getting on in New York. Maybe she'd run into Granada, which would be something to see. Caryn was going to be his best revenge on Granada and her fancy ways, no matter what Katagira had thought up.

He rose and went back to his bed, knowing that he would like as not lie there sleepless, eyes staring up, trying to hold off the slumber that inevitably these days brought the nightmares. Maybe, he wondered, I should have asked those fancy Minnesota doctors if they had anything for being afraid.

After coffee, it was time for the Greschner party to make its way across the Rostval Place to the Fuller. Sol led the way, between Caryn Gudge and Gratiane von González; the rest of the party trooped behind in an irregular file. The square was jammed with honking limousines, edging angrily around its perimeter to the main entrance of the Institute. Prominent among the quacking procession was a mauve Rolls-Royce which Nick recognized. It belonged to Granada Masterman, which meant that Sol's party would arrive at the steps of the Institute just about simultaneously with the Winstead group, which could make for amusing viewing. Possibly Mesdames Gudge and Masterman would meet.

Mrs. Masterman had been Solomon Greschner's greatest social creation, his most complete and triumphant invention. She had appeared in New York from Dallas, where her business had gotten its real momentum, and the money had been made that could buy her the society she wanted and the identity she craved. Sol had done it. He had made the right introductions, called in the right due bills, pulled and teased and wheedled and saw that she spent her money scientifically, to establish her as a patroness, a hostess and a lady. That she was neither generous nor welcoming nor gentle had been no obstacle. And then, when Sol had brought her within a hairbreadth of the most coveted trophy "publiciety" had to offer, a seat on the Board of Trustees of the Fuller Endowment, she'd dumped him. The puppet had cut its strings. Pinocchio had turned on Gepetto. Granada was not yet on the Fuller Board, but with the lock she had on Hugo Winstead, who was her personal attorney—thanks to Sol—and counsel and director of Masterman United—thanks to Sol—as well as the club she held over Homer Seabury with her big stockholding in Seaco—thanks to Lassiter and Winstead—it could only be a matter of months. If she could make it, Granada would have passed over to the other side of the river, the safe shore where old money and immutable respectability dwelt. The word in art circles was that she'd come up with two million for the new building. If she would make it five, the sum Winstead had in mind and the amount needed to pay off the last construction loan, the seat was hers.

Was Sol now trying to repeat the act with Caryn Gudge? Nick wondered. Very likely, he concluded. What a wonderful prospect!

His mischievous musings were interrupted by Harvey Bogle, who came up beside him.

"Maybe we can talk for a minute without being interrupted. Where does Greschner get these people? You see that Melton woman go after the caviar? They should've set out a trowel at her place. How come this big deal anyway? I didn't think the Fuller went in for this sort of society crap. I always liked the low-key way they worked."

"They didn't use to," Nick said. "The world's changing."

"And, as they said when Ty Cobb quit, not for the better, either. Anyway, let me tell you what's on my mind."

"Shoot."

"I've been looking at pictures. Thinking about starting a collection. I was in London a few months ago and I had nothing to do and this woman who runs our office over there said to me would I like to see the Wallace Collection. So why not, and away we go. And I was knocked out! I mean, I grew up in Port Chester, you know, so I went to the Met and maybe the Frick a few times, but I guess the time wasn't right, or I wasn't—it doesn't matter. I think there's a right time for everything. There're gonna be years what you want to do is buy real estate. Other times you want to do nothing but kick ass. Now, all of a sudden, pictures interest me. Stuff like in the Wallace Collection, pictures you can think about and read up on. Study; get to know them. The other stuff, the Impressionist pictures these Spic decorators wet their pants about, doesn't turn me on. It's pretty, but it's just not my thing."

"Are you thinking of important collecting?" Nick felt a slight adrenal prickling.

"Maybe. I don't know. That's what I wanted to talk to you about. I've been doing a hell of a lot of reading. There can't be a hell of a lot of great stuff left, and I don't want to buy seconds. I mean, I could go pretty good, but I can't butt heads with the Getty, say. They've got nine hundred million goddamn dollars."

"Well . . ." Nick tried to sound casual. "There're still some fine things around. Not like there used to be. But that's what they said twenty years ago and twenty years before that. There's room. Look at Norton Simon's collection."

"There's room if you're smart and quick and have the money and the best advice. Which is where you come in. Say I buy a building in Fort Worth; I have the best guy down there look it over. Or a factory that makes widgets. I find the best widget guy around. I believe in experts. Real experts, I mean; not some bullshit management consultant six months out of business school. Guys with money of their own on the line who know what they're talking about. Guys who've done it. So I asked around, including Greschner, and the name that keeps coming up in New York is yours."

"That's flattering, Mr. Bogle. There are other good people. Agnew and Creel in London. Thaw, Newhouse here in town, to name two."

"You as good as they are?"

"Well, I don't think I'm much worse. We all have our moments."

"You rich?"

"Nowhere near it."

"Good incentive. You like making money?"

"Enough, yes. Piling it up doesn't turn me on. I don't like sitting in the cheap seats, but that doesn't mean I want to own the goddamn ball park. It depends on the psychic rate of return. Big doesn't mean much to me. The thing is, you see, I really like what I do. I happen to love works of art."

"That's what they tell me." They were almost at the entrance to the Institute. Nick was startled to see flashguns popping and a crowd of photographers on the sidewalk. Things really had changed around the Fuller.

"Look," Bogle said, winding up, "I'd like to continue this. Come and have a drink at my place. Next week?"

Nick would have preferred to have the first meeting on his own ground, but what the hell. Bogle was still up in the air. There'd be time enough to pull the good stuff out of the closets. While he reached for his datebook, he ran through his inventory, thinking what he could start with. The trouble was, the museum-quality stuff he had was sparse in the first place and was either reserved or wrong to start a collection with. The Cranach *Venus*? Probably too ugly; Cranach was an acquired taste. The little Dou interior? Possible. Not the Poussin modello of the Martyrdom of Saint Agnes, or the Magnasco. The former too grisly; the latter too weird. He didn't allow himself to think it—but the Rubens sketches were right up the alley, and they constituted a collection in themselves. But as he'd had to say to himself at dinner: you just didn't tee up a brand-new collector with a $7-million pop.

"How about Wednesday next week? Six o'clock. I live on top of the Tennyson."

They fixed the date and Bogle strode off to collect his wife, who had gone on ahead with the Seaburys. Happily, Nick had lost Arden Maypole in the melee.

He halted on the sidewalk to watch the purple Rolls draw up. The reporters and photographers rushed to form an alley as the chauffeur danced around the car to open the rear door. Overhead spotlights rotated across the sky. What a ridiculous circus, he thought.

The first to alight was a tall, perfect-looking man of about sixty, with collar-ad features, wavy gray hair and an imperious manner that seemed to clear a space around him: Hugo Winstead, senior partner of Seabury, Winstead and Corcoran; president of the Fuller Institute and the Fuller Endowment. He handed down a large woman as tall as he, draped in tie-dyed ermine; the plainness of her large features was emphasized by her chignon, its fat glitter-dusted plaits heaped like a sleeping python underneath a jeweled tiara. She had a grim, suspicious mouth that suggested abiding, specific bitterness; her unblinking eyes seemed fixed in an expression of permanent astonishment. He scanned the crowd as if checking it for assassins. Nick could never look at Granada Masterman without thinking of Frodo Crisp's description of her: "a vast, plain woman of indeterminate age with an inexplicable capacity for vengeance."

He also knew that she had no real interest in art—or in the Institute, for that matter—except if she could wear it as she wore her tiara. He'd gotten the word from Sandler, who had mistakenly figured Granada for a sure thing. After a lot of expensive lunches, and having her to one of his number one dinner parties, he'd given up. He couldn't get her to buy even one of the pasteurized Renoirs that were a staple of his business. Sandler had described her aesthetic sensibility as "terminal."

She paused on the sidewalk. Nick saw her glare and followed her eyes to where Sol stood arm in arm with Caryn Gudge. For an instant, she settled her gaze on Sol as if she would laser him into a melted puddle on the marble. She paused briefly and importantly for the photographers and fashion reporters, then gathered her skirt and swept into the Institute, followed by Winstead and the rest of the car's company: a nervous slender woman, as pallid as the white stone of the Annex, with green eyes set in a face that would have been beautiful if its expression hadn't been so anxious—Calypso Winstead, Darius Fuller's granddaughter—and, last to descend, with a gingerly dignity that seemed to set him apart, a small white-haired man, with cheerful, wrinkled features topping a precise little mustache; he stopped on the curb, leaning lightly on a silver-knobbed walking stick, smiling as he surveyed the commotion with obvious amusement. When he saw Nick edging through the crowd toward him, his smile widened.

"Hullo, Nicholas. I was hoping to see you here. How are you, dear boy?" They embraced. As always, Max smelled vaguely of violets; the same cologne from the shop in Curzon Street he'd used for seventy years.

"Max."

"Give me your arm, Nicholas. Sad, but at eighty even a short flight of stairs looks like the Matterhorn. My goodness, isn't that extravagant?" He tapped his cane on a brass plaque affixed to a pilaster. Cut into it was

APRIL 10–JUNE 30
THE LEFCOURT COLLECTION

"No less than you deserve, Max." They mounted the stairs, the old man light as dust on Nick's arm, Bogle close behind them. "I was sick to hear that Frank couldn't make the trip."

"Poor boy. He wanted so badly to come. But we've had a bitter winter in Florence and he caught a touch of cold. I couldn't let him get on an airplane, and there are no decent ships from Genoa or Naples—or anywhere else, I expect. I just can't risk Frank, you know, Nicholas. We have so little time left together as it is. It makes me sad to think about it, but there you are."

Francis Sanger and Maximilian Lefcourt had lived together for more than fifty years in the villa Max's father had built above Florence at the beginning of the century. Nick himself had spent two years there, studying with Sanger, the greatest expert on Italian painting in the world. Max Lefcourt's collection, built up over fifty years, was devoted solely to paintings by Italian artists or artists working in Italy; it was a celebration of Italy and the Italian spirit. Cynics would claim it had been assembled by Lefcourt's money plus Sanger's eye. In fact, it was a true collaboration. They had started with the small, choice collection, including a Raphael, a Pinturicchio and a fine Parmagianino, that had been in the Florentine villa, La Pergola, which Max had inherited from his father on the eve of the Great Depression. The collection had been their passion, an obsession as consuming as their feelings for each other and the overarching attachment they felt for Italy in general and their small corner of Tuscany in particular.

They mounted the steps slowly. No one seemed to take notice of Lefcourt. Inside they could hear the babble of voices and see the constant flaring of the photoflashes.

"Now, now, Max, you two will outlast the rest of us." Max Lefcourt was indeed nearing eighty; Francis Sanger was at least three or four years older. Time would be chiming in their heads. Nick shifted gears.

"Are you here for a while?"

"Until the weather changes in Tuscany. I should guess three weeks or so at bottom. Of course, I'll want to go to Washington for a few days. But you can't just pop me on and off airplanes like a schoolboy. Not at my delicate age. You must come and have a glass with me. They've put me up at the most extraordinary hotel. It's called the Esmé Castle. Have you seen it, Nicholas?"

"No. Not yet."

"It's not a bad hotel, really, as newer hotels go. My room is perfectly agreeable and in surprising good taste, by any standards. But the public rooms appear to be furnished with tractors. Ah, there's Frodo."

They were well inside the mansion now. Approaching was the angular, bobbing figure of Sir Frodo Crisp. He took Max Lefcourt from Nick and dispensed the civilities like an archbishop blessing a cathedralful of penitents.

"How are you, Nicholas? Nice to see you, dear boy. Now, come along, Max. First I'm afraid you'll have to shake hands with that awful grinning man over there; he's the architect. The collection looks wonderful. It's so nice to see it with enough light for a change. Do you know, Max, they're really pretty good. Ah, well, once more into the breach." Crisp saw Winstead approaching. "Noblesse oblige, Max. How was dinner? Pretty ghastly, I expect. I begged off. Last-minute hanging, you know. The food's always unspeakable at the Winsteads'. Poor Hugo. He's come a long way but not quite far enough, I fear."

Winstead had now joined them. Nick made his excuses; as he detached himself, he heard Crisp say "Ah, Hugo. Come right along now and meet the Italian Consul General. He's the dreariest man from Naples, but he was really most helpful in arranging things. You know, Max, one got the feeling the Italians didn't want to let these go. They seemed to think we might take them hostage."

Bantering, he led the guest of honor and Winstead off toward a knot of people.

Frodo could get away with this sort of impertinence with Hugo because he had Calypso Winstead's ear and affection. She was, after all, "the" Fuller. And ferociously loyal to the Institute of which Frodo was as valuable an asset as any painting or drawing on its walls or manuscript on its shelves. Calypso might hang back as Winstead made his grand, condescending progress through life, but she was the class part of the act and everyone knew it. For all Hugo's practiced, prideful suavity and polish, Nick thought the man still came up short; he was a jackal passing as a greyhound, most people knew that, and the impersonation didn't quite come off. Nick had always suspected Hugo might come apart under pressure, but who could know? He was one of life's lucky ones. Still, it was a mystery how Calypso could stay with him. He guessed that she had feelings as easily welted and blistered as her milky skin.

He found Bogle at the bar.

"How about a walk around?" He took a glass of champagne.

"Let's go."

As they turned from the bar, they found Caryn Gudge standing alone, looking perplexed. Sol had somehow gotten away.

"Lost, Mrs. Gudge?"

"Just a little girl in the big city, Mr. Reverey."

"You've met Mr. Bogle, I think?"

"Yes, indeed. I just love your wife's book, Mr. Bogle. She really does know about life." Bogle took a deep sip of his wine and made no comment.

"Well, Mrs. Gudge, Mr. Bogle and I were just going off to look at the new building and the Lefcourt pictures. Would you like to join us?"

"I sure would." She smiled and linked her arms through theirs, and the three of them set off for the archway leading to the Annex.

As they made their way through the crowd, Nick's misgivings about the turn the Institute had taken intensified. This was the sort of crowd you got uptown, at the Met or the Modern. Middle-aged dragons in diamonds and velvet boogying among the sarcophagi. Fibrous pansies in flowered tuxedos. The reigning basilisks of fashion, each with a retinue of desperately clever young men.

Dodging a man outfitted in white tie and a tailcoat that appeared to be sewn from beige pigskin, half-hearing Caryn Gudge chatting with Bogle, Nick reflected that an occasion like this epitomized one of his few real quarrels with Solomon Greschner.

Sol was as responsible as anyone for starting these packaged shows, which brought together, fused, the interests and ambitions of his several spheres of influence and self-interest. It had begun with the Eskimo Show ten years before, which had exemplified Sol's matchless gift for bringing people together symbiotically. As it happened, his Eminence the Cardinal was patron of a series of missionary schools in the Arctic. As it happened, one of Sol's clients, a pharmaceutical company, was in hot water in South America, having maimed a thousand children with a defective batch of anti-rickets vaccine. From every pulpit in Bolivia, priests were howling for the expropriation of the Yankee devils' business, a subsidiary with extraordinarily high profit margins unencumbered by such unbusinesslike considerations as lab safety procedures, clinical testing and the other regulatory persiflage which inhibited business conducted within the United States itself. Somehow, Sol started a roundelay of the right words' being spoken in the right ears. Somehow, under the sponsorship of his client, an exhibition of Eskimo Children's Art found its way into the Natural History Museums of New York and Chicago. Somehow, leading carvers in Yellowknife were commissioned to produce a fifteen-foot totem pole topped with an image of his Eminence the Cardinal. And somehow from Rome issued the encyclical *Casus Accidibunt*—"Accidents Will Happen"—pleading the cause of early commercial exploitation of scientific research. It was a miracle.

The trouble was, as Nick saw it, it had started a landslide. He had no problem with the gentrification of corporate bigwigs by transforming them into patrons of high culture. The money had to come from somewhere. But Bulgarian gold? Russian costume? Photographs from old copies of *Vogue*? Nineteenth-century German paintings of surpassing mediocrity? Prepackaged pap with fancy catalogues and champagne openings. Sometimes he wished he could be angry about it. But it was just stupid, no more than that. Stupidity underwritten by corporate dollars that seemed to belong to no one in particular, so who cared?

They descended the archway into the atrium of the Annex. As he looked around, Nick's first reaction was that it had the facile impressiveness of any new space that was big and overdramatized by trick lighting; it reminded him of the Houston museum. He doubted it would wear well.

"Isn't it wonderful?" said Caryn.

"It's pretty dramatic" was Nick's measured response.

"You suppose they've got any idea what it's gonna cost to light this place?" said Bogle. "They must have ten thousand watts up there."

In the center of the atrium floor, screens had been set up on which the few really large paintings in the collection had been hung. Dead ahead was the big Titian, *The Kiss of Judas*, which Nick considered the finest Venetian painting still in private hands. Off to the right, he caught a glimpse of a large, darkly lit painting of a striking young woman holding a lantern whose light, shining upward, disclosed sightless, milky eyes: the *Saint Lucy* by Caravaggio, one of the few paintings added to the Lefcourt Collection after World War II.

As they proceeded into the atrium, once again finding themselves in a chinking babble of people largely ignoring the extraordinary works of art among which they milled, they were approached by a rosy young woman in a long-sleeved, high-necked gown; over her bosom a gothic *M* had been stitched in gold into the purple fabric. She presented them with thick paperbound volumes bearing a reproduction of the Carpaccio *Saint Augustine* which was one of the glories of the collection and—as Nick well knew—

perhaps the favorite of all in the eyes of Max and Frank. They saw in the small painting a summing-up of what they valued most in early Renaissance painting: tenderness, a feeling for the countryside, an emotive calm in the heart of what must have been the stormiest of ages, a certain irresistible naiveté; the world being seen with fresh eyes. Nick flipped through his catalogue; he knew that Frodo had been knocking himself out for the better part of a year preparing it; the production of the book did him credit. It must have cost a bundle: checking the acknowledgments page, he read that the catalogue had been "published through the generosity of an anonymous friend of the Fuller Institute." Granada Masterman?

Bogle had turned his attention from the economics of the Annex' lighting system.

"Jesus!" he exclaimed.

He wasn't cursing Con Edison. Nick saw that he had fixed on the Titian, which dominated the room, rich and dark and infinitely moving. Titian's late, intense colorism had captured the tragic irony of the scene. Seeing it again, Nick recalled Frank's description of the painting in his *Three Great Venetians: Titian, Tintoretto, Veronese:* "Color seems to be the essence, the sole essence, of the reality of the encounter between Christ and his betrayer, which is sublime and yet deeply human. The drama itself is mute: it happens in the souls of those who represent it and of those who behold it." As they moved toward the picture, Nick saw with pleasure that its unspeaking drama had utterly engaged Harvey Bogle.

"This is a real nice book," said Caryn Gudge.

"Isn't it?" Behind her he saw Sol separate from a knot of people and make for them. "Tell me, Mrs. Gudge, you must know everything about the women's world. That girl who gave us the catalogues. She was wearing some kind of uniform. What was it?"

Her expression darkened briefly.

"She's one of those Masterwomen. You know, that big door-to-door and home-party deal." She didn't want to say more, and in any case, Sol was now upon them. Mrs. Masterman's hand again, thought Nick. She was making a big push.

"Mrs. Gudge—you got away from me," Sol said, feigning reproof. "I want you to meet some people. You might as well come too, Nicholas." Nick looked around. Bogle was already moving from the Titian toward the Caravaggio as if on an invisible wire.

Nick followed obediently. He wasn't going to knock himself out dodging among the crowd to look at a collection that he knew as well as his own family, if not better. If he counted the time spent with and among Max's paintings, and the emotional and intellectual byplay that had gone on about and with them over the years, he'd have to say the Lefcourt Collection *was*, in a way, his family. Anyway, he was here tonight to work the room. He'd already made a date with Frodo for Monday, when the Fuller would be closed, to come in and have a solitary wander. Then would be the time to remake old acquaintances and discover new perceptions, some transforming, others minor—the shadow of a drapery fold; the curl of a leaf; a tiny castle never before noticed on a haze-hidden hillside. That was what was wonderful about all great paintings. The renewal, the familiar passages seen as if for the first time. Not to mention the steadfast privacy of the relationship. Unlike human friends, who got sick, needed money, betrayed confidences, stole lovers, works of art remained ever fresh and ever constant; again and again they gave back the bloom of first meeting.

The group to which Greschner led them struck Nick as pretty much what he'd expect to find at an opening like this. A couple of names he half-recognized. A young couple to whom, on Sol's introduction, he'd sold a crayon drawing by Boucher last year. A pudgy man who had something to do with metals trading, Nick thought, and a great deal to do with cocaine, Nick had heard. The last hand he shook belonged to a handsome, slender young woman. He couldn't remember having seen her before; nor, he was suddenly aware, had such a wave of total interest swept over him in a very long time. Releasing her hand, he looked at her closely. Her hair was dark, the color of sable. She was fresh and insouciant-looking; her eyes—greenish brown—struck him as amused, clever, capable of finding humor in the grayest cloud. Her defects, if that was what they were, were no less compelling: a nose too pointed and prominent, perhaps; lips oddly full in a face built of such refined precise angles and planes. Class with guts, he thought.

"I'm sorry," he said in truth. "I was dazzled. By the lights. So I didn't get your name. Mine's Nicholas Reverey."

"Jill Newman. Shall we shake hands again?"

"Why not?"

An oily, suspicious-looking man standing beside her had escaped Nick's notice. Jill Newman gestured an introduction.

"Do you know each other? Dr. Sartorian; Mr. Reverey." They shook hands. Nick liked her voice: it was accentless, a shade hoarse. There was something familiar about her. Of course. She reminded him of Carole Lombard; Carole Lombard, over whom he'd sighed for a dozen nights running at a Brattle Street movie theater, until common sense and the passage of time had swept that passion into the limbo of unattainability. Class with guts; beauty with spunk.

Nick was nothing if not romantic about himself. Now, suddenly, he imagined that he had been searching for this sort of woman for years; in an instant, as he stood there smiling at her, he drummed up an entire scenario: a quest—that was it. But the machinery of reason was working. Whoa there, sirrah, said the voice of being forty years old.

"How about a drink?" he asked her. The group around her seemed to have melted away. He saw, in the distance, Sol steering Caryn Gudge artfully around the room.

He got champagne for them and they moved away from the crowded bar, looking instinctively for some pocket of relative calm. As they crossed the room, he noticed her calmly acknowledge one person after another. She was measured about it, though. A frantic wave from a beaming, shadow-chinned man in a ruffled blue shirt drew a nod and a pleasant smile. To a beaky vulture of a woman who accosted them, all elbows and cricks, and blew air kisses madly, she smiled and gave a comforting pat. Nick liked the way she handled herself. Her progress wasn't regal, wasn't condescending; there was something about the way these people approached her that said unmistakably she had something they coveted. It was equally clear that whatever it was in her they coveted was not critically important to her.

She didn't introduce him.

"You don't want to know these people," she said when they had found an empty table and sat down. She looked at him very directly.

"You're the art dealer, aren't you? Sol Greschner's said some very nice things about you."

"He's a great old friend, Sol. I hate to think how I might have turned out if it hadn't been for him. Who are you?"

"Oh, I'm kind of a journalist."

"Really? What kind of a kind?"

"Free-lance stuff. This and that. Here and there." She paused and lowered her eyes for a second; then she looked back up at him, smiling, but with a touch of embarrassment. "Oh, hell, you'll find out sooner or later. I write a society column. For a paper called *That Woman!*"

"I don't believe it. I read *That Woman!* every week. I don't want to sound like a smartass, but it's the funniest paper in America. What a riot! Don't tell me you're Gilberte? 'The Party Line'?"

"You do sound a little like a smartass, but that's okay. Honest, at least. Yes, I am Gilberte. On Fridays only."

Nick was genuinely surprised. This beautiful—well, striking—obviously intelligent woman wrote the society gush—who went where with whom and wore what—that was a staple of each week's *That Woman!*? He grinned at her.

"Explanations are obviously in order, but we'll leave those to another day. Tell me something. Are you really a Gilberte? Is that where it comes from? Proust?"

"I am and it is. Every family has its own curse. Proust was ours. My father was a nut on Proust. He was—is, but he's retired now—a professor of Romance Literature; first at Columbia; then, when he got on a big fresh-air kick, at the University of Montana. Salubrious Missoula. I grew up there. Anyway, back to Proust. I have two sisters: Albertine and Odette; a brother: Marcel, naturally; the terrier was named Swann and the lake house near Kalispell had a sign that said 'Balbec.' We had Proust in about twenty French editions, and everything else you can think of from German to Hungarian."

"Fascinating. How'd you get into this racket?"

She laughed. "It's a long story. I'd have to think how to tell it, anyway. So that's for another day, as you said."

"I assume you're working tonight?"

"More or less. It's all under control. All these rich women have got their own P.R. people anyway. I've known for a week what everybody was going to wear and who was going to whose dinner. And what they were going to eat. Food's very big this year, Mr. Reverey."

"Nicholas. Or Nick."

"Nicholas." He was pleased; she'd made the right choice. He thought himself most attractive as "Nicholas."

"What do you do when you're not manning the social battlements?"

"What normal folks do, I suspect. Stay at home; read; take care of things —I have a daughter. Go to movies. Listen to music. And you?"

Nick ignored the question. "Do you like pictures?"

"I like them. I don't know a great deal about them. I do know what I like, if that's not being too trite." She smiled. He believed she was extending him an invitation, very tentative, to something important.

"It's not. It's ninety percent of it." Suddenly he wanted very badly to be her guide to the Lefcourt Collection; to impress her with his obvious intimacy with these marvelous things. "Shall we go take a look? See if we can find something that strikes your fancy?"

"I'd love that." She got up. She was wearing a long black dress with a modest neckline, under a short jacket with a high collar; the jacket appeared to be worked in jet and sequins. No jewelry, Nick noticed. She looked as austere and elegant as a Spanish duchess in a Velásquez portrait; like the stunning portrait in the Wallace Collection, except that Jill was slender and finer-featured. He thought she was absolutely wonderful.

They mounted the ramp leading to the ascending ring of galleries which encircled the atrium halfway up its six-story height. Looking over the mezzanine rail, Nick thought the building a hybrid of the Guggenheim Museum and any of a dozen Hyatt hotels. They entered the first small gallery, screened from the bright central cone by curtain walls of translucent green marble. That was borrowed from the Beinecke Library at Yale, Nick guessed. This place was an architectural catchall. Turning to the gallery itself, he was dismayed to see that the department-store lighting tricks made fashionable by the Met had taken hold here. The pictures were hung on rich fabrics—in this gallery deep maroon—and were picked out by tightly focused spotlights. These pictures had been painted in daylight. To display them like jewelry was a mistake.

Jill paused at the third painting on the wall. The little Giovanni di Paolo *Garden of Paradise*. A Sienese picture not of much significance when it came to adding up the art-historical scorecard, but the kind of engaging painting that could win a heart or brighten the gloomiest day.

"It's sweet, isn't it?" She pointed to the highly stylized castle the artist had painted in the center background; it was obviously an imaginative variation on the towers of his native city. "I'm crazy about Italy. I've only been once. One of those schoolgirl tours. Twenty cities in twenty days. I jumped ship in Venice when the tour was getting ready to move on to Austria. I couldn't abandon it."

"Can we leave for Venice now?" He smiled. "No, seriously, I'm not very good about talking about Italy. It makes me want to cry for love."

"That's nice."

They moved along, not saying much unless there was something to be said. Once he made her stop and pointed out the interesting juxtaposition of a spare, direct Uccello portrait of a handsome, hawklike condottiere with a lyrical little Fra Angelico *Flight into Egypt*.

"The two sides of the Renaissance," he said. "Painted about the same time. Look at the peace of this landscape in the Angelico. Tend your vineyards; go about your business. And wake up the next morning and here's this guy"—he pointed to the Uccello portrait—"banging on the gates with his private army. The great thing about Italy is, it has an imaginary hold which no other country's ever had on me. For me, it's the hills, and the language, and the fact the Italians eat about fifty times better than the French, and Max's pictures, and Easter in Sicily and the color of the roofs along Lago Maggiore. A big composite of about forty trillion impressions that blocks out the facts: the smog, and industrial zones, and the terrorism and poverty. It's probably all a great big lie I've invented for myself—but I'll stick with it." He was surprised at the passion with which he said this.

"I know what you mean. Have you always been crazy about art?"

"My old man was an artist. Then I got lucky. I met the right people. Happened to be in the right places. Now I can't live without it."

There were about a hundred questions he wanted to ask her. But not now. Not in this noisy place. They continued their leisurely tour. She didn't dawdle, he was pleased to see. When something particularly appealed to her, like the little Tiepolo sketch for the *salone* of the Palazzo Bragadin, she stopped; took a close, careful look; and moved on. That was his own style.

As they made their way, he became conscious that an intimacy seemed to have grown between them. He was no longer conscious of the clamor and the crowd; she didn't seem to be either. It was as if they were guarding each other's flanks against the enemy out there; as if they were in a Bell jar, feeling the cautious, tremulous electricity of first acquaintance flow back and forth.

Then they had finished their passage through the nautilus and were back in the atrium. It seemed even more crowded.

"I guess I have to do some work now," she said. "It's been a pleasure. As a matter of fact, it's been more than that."

"For me too. Shall we have dinner sometime? Soon?"

"Dinner sometime would be nice. Sometime. Why don't we start with lunch? We could both take a long look in the daylight that way. Sunday?" Her cautiousness surprised him; after all, she was a public figure, wasn't she, who trafficked in the lives and activities of other people. For an instant there, he'd forgotten what she did for a living.

"Sunday'd be just fine." He got her address and phone number.

"Well . . ." He didn't know quite what to do. To pump her hand vigorously would be too foolish; to kiss her cheek too familiar. Man of the world, he thought, sarcastically. "Well . . . I'll see you Sunday." He reached out and touched the back of her hand fleetingly.

She smiled. "I can't wait. Goodbye."

When she was lost in the crowd, he looked around. Bogle had vanished. Nothing more for him here. He started to make his way out, stopping briefly to say hello to the Sandlers and to a former director of the Met who was working the crowd passing out publicity leaflets for his latest nonfiction novel. He wanted to say thanks to Sol, so he kept looking around as he went.

He found his host in the main hall of the original Fuller mansion, still with Caryn Gudge, to whom he had evidently given a guided tour of the old building and its treasures. They had been joined by Homer Seabury, who towered beamishly above them like a lighthouse of affable propriety. As he said his good-nights, Nick noticed that Caryn Gudge's catalogue had been cruelly folded back on its spine and that the pages he could see were marked with heavy green checks.

She followed his glance and giggled.

"My pencil ran out of lead, so I had to use my eyeliner."

Nick chuckled back, trying to keep any false geniality out of his voice.

"Nothing wrong with that. I always mark catalogues myself. That way I can remind myself what really turned me on."

She looked at him as if he'd said something really foolish.

"Oh, goodness me, this sure isn't for reminding. I just checked off the ones Buford's gonna buy me. 'Course, it'd be easier if he just bought the whole thing. Either way, it's easier if you order by the numbers."

Solomon Greschner stayed up long after he had seen his last guest into a taxi. Upstairs in his study, he sent Vosper off to bed and settled into the tapestried wing chair by the now-dead fire.

His head was full of goblins. The evening had been a real trial; once it would have been a revel. Putting on the old debonair front each day was as suffocating as those rubber masks that kids now wore at Halloween. He was tired of the business—such of it as he still had. In his day, it had been personal; a man's touch and connections were what mattered. Now it was all advertising, like practically everything else in the commercial world an affair for dull conventional men in hideous three-piece suits. The old sense of power was gone. His own power and the legitimate power of the men he'd dealt with. He'd probably been pretty rough with some of them, he recognized. That was probably why so many of them didn't come around anymore; didn't send him their sons for guidance. They couldn't stand to admit to anyone, least of all themselves, how much they owed Solomon Greschner for what they had become, for who they were, for how often he'd rescued them.

So where was he now? Stuck with the likes of Caryn Gudge. A tart from the backcountry whose husband bought her Solomon Greschner the way he bought her a sable coat or a week at Maine Chance. Not that he wouldn't deliver professionally. But it made him feel like an item-planter.

Of course, it was a way of getting back at Granada for turning on him. It still made him sick to think of it. She'd been the best horse he'd ever had; she could have been President, she was that smart and that determined. Once.

Ah, the world had changed. The old institutions on which you were brought up to rely, the banks, the newspapers, the great corporations, had been gnawed down to the bone by the ravenous egocentricity of the men who got to run them.

It was a hell of a way to end a life. Here he'd anticipated spending these yellow-leafed years as a magus, an oracle, a combination of Socrates and Nero Wolfe, dispensing miraculous insights and solutions to an avid congregation of the powerful and the influential. He would have transcended public relations, transcended what lofty men had thought of him and his vocation. A philosopher-king enthroned in his palace on Rostval Place, among his priceless treasures, receiving a supplicant world. That was what he'd intended.

Instead it seemed more and more likely that the baggage he'd packed for posterity was empty. His credentials for immortality were mediocre. Not a wrack to leave behind: no heir, no family, no monument except the great house.

Now it was painfully clear to him that he had counted on a fantasy that would never be, and that all he might end with was an old man's bitter, wishful ruminations alone in a house grand enough for a regiment. Secure on pedestals he had carved for them, his creations looked down on him. How he'd like to crack a pedestal or two, he thought angrily.

He sat by the dying fire for most of the night. Pondering roads not taken and turns he wished he'd avoided. He could stand anything except being what he saw himself as now: an ineffectual, discarded old man.

At the moment Sol rose to go to bed, Buford Gudge was waking from his own recurrent nightmare, crossing his bedroom to sit again by the night-blanked window looking across the prairie. It was a sad parallel, these two lonely men surveying their great domains, terminal cases fifteen hundred miles apart, suffering from the same grievances; railing in their souls against a world that should have done better by them.

CHAPTER FOUR

For more than three decades, Solomon Greschner had spent most of his Saturday mornings on a grand tour of the Upper East Side. He usually began by visiting a number of antiquarian booksellers in the Forties, adding to his collection of first editions; from there he worked his leisurely way north, looking in on a drawings dealer here, an auction gallery there, examining bronzes, manuscripts, antique brasses, until he finally fetched up in the grillroom of the Tennyson, the old London-style hotel on Madison Avenue in the mid-Seventies, where a corner booth was permanently reserved for him. His zigzag northward pasha's progress had become as regular a part of New York weekend life as a Sunday-night quarrel. So much so that men who had need of Sol's ear would frequently waylay him en route.

By and large, however, his weekends were entirely his own. His clients would have fled town: the corporate types to their châteaux in Greenwich, Morristown and Lake Forest; the social white hopes to Palm Beach, Southampton and Litchfield. Although he was never short of weekend invitations, Sol hated the country. He never liked leaving New York, and did so on any regular basis only for his two annual, ritual visits abroad: to London, in late June, for "the season," and to the Swiss resort of Sta. Marta, in early October, for the rejuvenative air, the quiet Swiss countryside and the russet splendor of the Alps in autumn. Sta. Marta was Sol's sole concession to the possibilities of nature. Occasionally, if a particular New York February proved unendurably bitter, he would negotiate an invitation to a warmer venue, selecting one of a half-dozen possibilities among the Palm Beach villas and island retreats owned by clients. On the whole, though, the chronicles maintained by the would-be biographers lurking amid moldering piles of notes and clippings on the Greschner career showed remarkably few sojourns away from Number 17.

This particular Saturday, two days after the opening of the Fuller Annex, he rose at eight and arrayed himself in a fashion suited to a sunny but still-blustery April morning. He picked at the eggs, muffins and newspapers which Vosper had set out in the study, and precisely at ten o'clock as always, strolled out the door and into his old gray Bentley to be driven the thirty blocks uptown to his starting point. The streets were always relatively quiet this early on Saturday: the city was pulling itself together after another rambunctious Friday night. Modern life got itself started later and later, he reflected, remembering the days when men still went to Wall Street on Saturdays; small wonder, he thought next, with so little to get out of bed for. The trip, which on a weekday would have consumed the better part of an enervating, honking half-hour, was accomplished in ten minutes, so that Furlough, the dealer in modern first editions who was Sol's first stop, had scarcely unlocked his shop when Sol arrived on his doorstep.

He spent more than an hour at Furlough's, nosing through cartons of new arrivals, dispensing advice, deploring the decimation of the good booksellers of Manhattan and finally choosing for himself a nice inscribed copy of an early book by Robert Lowell, a poet he much esteemed.

"*Lord Weary's Castle.* A wonderful title, Furlough."

Sol thumbed through the book, looking for a favorite. "Ah, I've always liked the end of this poem." He recited from memory as much as read from the opened page: " 'September twenty-second, Sir, the bough/Cracks with the unpicked apples, and at dawn/The small-mouth bass breaks water, gorged with spawn.' " Furlough smiled.

"A wonderful evocation of the calmness of nature. None of the infernal busyness of men. The sort of thing I go to the Alps for. It's worth thinking about, Furlough. No, don't wrap it; it'll fit in the pocket of my coat. Lord Weary, that's what I am, Furlough; Lord Weary."

Furlough, a tall, bespectacled man who retailed books, not philosophy, showed his customer to the door and watched the stocky, ulstered figure head jauntily for Madison Avenue. An hour of Sol's demanding patronage was a tiring way to sell a $200 book.

Sol next visited Volkswart, the dealer who specialized in old theatrical drawings, who had nothing of interest, having been cleaned out of his last Bibiena earlier in the week by a Düsseldorf collector; next to the English pharmacy for some patent medicine and a cologne; then to the Italian hat-and-shoe repairman who blocked the Lock bowlers which were as integral a part of Sol's image as his muttonchop whiskers and high-buttoned suits. Then, after inspecting and deciding against a pair of sixteenth-century brass candlesticks and purchasing a yellow rose for his buttonhole and shipping a case of champagne to an old client, he turned toward Park Avenue, checking his repeater watch, measuring each step precisely to ensure that he would fetch up at the door of Nicholas Reverey's maisonette, as he had announced he would, precisely at twelve-thirty.

He and Nick lunched at least one Saturday each month. They had been doing so for ten years, since Sol had urged Nick to take over Hermann Zauber's private dealership and helped him finance it. Old Zauber had been a secretive, brilliant autocrat who stored Corots and Botticellis in the linen closets of his unprepossessing East Side apartment. Difficult as Zauber had been, Nick had felt a real affection for him. When he had gone to work at Zauber's, recommended by Felix Rothschild, who had finally given up trying to convert Nick into an academic art historian or a museum type, he had soon found that Zauber's ill-mannered Prussian habits were more than compensated for by the old man's willingness to impart his encyclopedic knowledge of pictures and the art world. Zauber had offered a priceless training, compressing into months what a young man would have taken years to learn in the big galleries. Nick's office was an unused maid's room; he arrived each morning at eight-thirty to deal with the mail and to continue with whatever project Zauber had assigned him, projects that ranged from trekking over to the Frick Art Reference Library to nail down the iconography of a German panel to trying to find out whether a well-known museum curator was in fact on the take from this or that of Zauber's competitors. Zauber had a first-rate library of his own. The old man spent about $3 a year on clothes, but the book budget ran to the tens of thousands and the food budget was even larger. Nick never again ate as well as when he was in Zauber's employ. When the old man stumped into one of the city's great restaurants, proprietors and captains rushed to attend him with the same enthusiasm they normally reserved for Rockefellers.

When there was no client to be given lunch at Maia's or Dove Sono, Zauber and Nick would eat in the apartment, dining on fat sandwiches of brown bread, hard cheese and Westphalian ham prepared by the purse-lipped Valkyrie who had watched over Zauber since his wife's death fifteen years earlier. Nick relished these lunches. The old man would deliver himself of reminiscences or speculations, always personal and generally scabrous, about Duveen, Heinemann, Thaw, Acquavella and the other legendary connoisseur-dealers with whom he had competed for forty years. The only outsiders ever invited in for sandwiches were Sol: "a fair eye for drawings, but vot an eye for millionaires"; Frodo Crisp: "the only museum man in New York who is not a fool, a charlatan and a thief—even if he is a poof"; Felix Rothschild, whenever he came down from Boston: "Professor Rothschild knows something about Italian paintings and everything about Italian girls." Zauber would smack his thick lips and blow like a small whale at the thought of Rothschild's legendary record as a charmer who had once seduced an entire seminar on Piero della Francesca.

Apart from his appreciation of Nick's undeniable flair for paintings, Zauber was deeply interested in what he was convinced was Nick's richly variegated erotic life. He had to know the details of every one of Nick's dates. The next morning it was always: "Vell, vas she any good? Vot happened? Did you screw her?" He was death on homosexuals. Only Frodo Crisp escaped the lash. Poor Francis Sanger, whom Nick regarded as a model of scholarship and taste, and whose fifty-year liaison with Max Lefcourt was as tenderly moving an instance of true and lasting devotion as

Nick could conceive, was libeled on an hourly basis as a poseur, a pederast, a sodomite, a liar. Zauber's vituperation was self-centered: Sanger had once published a "Titian" that was about to be sold to Washington by Zauber as a Palma Vecchio, costing the old man several hundred thousand dollars.

When the old man suddenly dropped dead, Sol encouraged Nick to take over Zauber's business. He arranged for bank loans to pay off the tax due on the inventory and for Nick to acquire the library.

Sol believed in the art business. "Don't listen to the old men. There's more money going to be made in the world in the next dozen years than ever before. Paper money will be a glut on the market. People will want things. Objects. Pictures, jewelry, furniture."

Nick was hesitant. This was a huge step Sol was proposing. Nick was very young, still in his early thirties. He knew his eye was good; he knew all of Zauber's sources and clients personally. That was on his side. But the competition was brutal—ranging from the big galleries like Du Cazlet and Wildenstein, which had unlimited resources, to the dozen or so good private dealers who collectively added up to a generation's worth of connections and experience. Rumbling in the bushes were the big auction houses. Sotheby's had established itself on Madison Avenue with the timely acquisition of Parke Bernet; now it was rumored that both Christie's and Grundy's were pricing choice Manhattan real estate.

On the other hand, Sandler'd made it in the Impressionist field, where the competition played really rough, and so had the Desmond Gallery in London, and others. And what the hell else could he do: become another slick young man at Du Cazlet or prance around the Frick prattling about Vermeer? So he listened to Sol, who would not be turned aside. For a nimble, talented man who could handle people, there was always a prosperous living to be made, Sol asserted night after night, in any business that required real expertise. This wasn't a whore's business like investment banking, he said; you'd need more than a suit and polished shoes. Look at the profession which he, Solomon Greschner, had virtually invented. He rode roughshod over Nick's half-convinced demurrals, demolishing arguments against and building up the younger man's confidence. Nick had a little money, a legacy from his father, but he didn't have the two and a half million it would take to buy Zauber's inventory, let alone another quarter-million for the premises Sol had chosen for him, a maisonette between Park and Madison, in the heart of the uptown art district just then beginning to flower.

The idea had become too appealing to let go, however. He did some figuring. He knew that Zauber had targeted the Pieter de Hooch *Street in Haarlem* for a West Coast collector who was intent on building up a major Dutch collection and that the Dorset Museum would surely go for the pair of Canalettos. That would be over $600,000 right there. With a profit of close to $250,000. He wasn't sentimental about the older items the way Zauber was. Cleveland had been hounding the old man to sell them his little Memling portrait for close to a decade. Nick thought they could pay at least $500,000; it would be on the books at less than a third of that. And he could sell Du Cazlet a half-interest in the big Claude Lorrain *View of the Villa Medici with Nessus and Dejanira* for another $350,000. Du Cazlet considered it a matter of divine right that all important French paintings executed before 1800 be sold through its own house, a conviction it was quite prepared to support with cold cash. Claude had been dead for three centuries, but Du Cazlet nevertheless considered itself his exclusive dealer. So Nick was looking at realizing close to a million off the bat, and would still retain three Rembrandt drawings; a major Tiepolo whose pendant was in Vienna; the *View of Sylt by Night* by Caspar David Friedrich and a dozen other things, including a Ribera *Crucifixion* which Zauber had been incubating to grow up to be a million-dollar picture. It was a good inventory to start with.

So, with an introduction from Sol, he went to see Smithers Ward at the American Surety Trust. When he left the bank he had a $2.5-million credit line, a mortgage to buy the maisonette and the assurance of additional credit to buy inventory. Needless to say, Smithers Ward, ever a model of civility and discretion, did not disclose that Sol had offered to cosign any note of Nick's.

Given the importance Sol attached to Rostval Place, it didn't surprise Nick that Sol made a flap about his having just exactly the right premises. To Sol's credit, the maisonette, which Sol had known for years, had worked out perfectly for Nick. It had been owned by a Greschner client, a well-known investment banker, who used it to house, for consecutive brief periods, a succession of young ladies, some of whom he'd met at the famous monthly Cavalier dinners which Sol attended every so often. Spirit notwithstanding, the gentleman's flesh was no longer willing, and the maisonette was available at a decent price. Nick bought it.

Nick had once asked Sol about those dinners. There had always been rumors, particularly when he was at the apogee of his reputation, that Sol's success had been based on his ability to procure women for his clients.

When questioned by Nick, who was careful to be as amiable and offhanded as possible, Sol had been very sharp.

"That's crap, Nicholas. The fact of the matter is that I spend most of my time getting these men out of, not into, the clutches of unscrupulous women, or repairing errors of moral or amatory judgment, not encouraging them."

Nick believed him. He'd heard Sol's story often enough. How he'd gotten into a good thing selling the house seats he was given by the actors and agents who patronized Tatnall's. How one night he'd traded a pair of seats to *The Band Wagon* for a meal at Jack's, where he met the man who owned the Brixton Hotel, then a popular meeting place on East Thirty-second Street. He'd talked the man into giving him a chance to put the Brixton on the uptown map; then, in turn, he'd talked some of Tatnall's better-known theatrical customers into making the Brixton their New York base, making sure they got a good rate. He swapped his house seats to the hot shows on Broadway for mentions of the Brixton and its new, smart clientele in widely read columns in the *Sun* and the *Herald*. His client was delighted; soon Sol was out of the tailoring business and into an office off the Brixton lobby, with $40 a week plus expenses.

He kept his eye on traffic in the hotel lobby, sure that greater opportunities would present themselves. Sure enough, the moment came when Sol could leap the invisible hurdle to greatness. Acting on cheek and inspiration one afternoon, he sent a magnum of champagne upstairs to the suite where R. Livingston Gordon, a tribune of good society and chairman of American Surety Trust Company, was relaxing with an ingenue. Accompanying the wine was a brief letter outlining some thoughts Sol had as to how the bank, then under press siege for a series of poorly timed tenement foreclosures, might dress up its public image. Gordon greeted the arrival of the tributary wine with mixed feelings. Pleasant as it was to have his eminence acknowledged, he was disconcerted that the young man downstairs would so openly display that he knew who Gordon was and, without doubt, what he was at the moment doing. When he read the letter, however, his interest was piqued. He was a man who knew his priorities. He sent for Sol, banished the ingenue with the promise of the Worth frock she fancied and settled into a meaningful conversation with Sol.

Ensconced shortly afterward as public affairs consultant to American Surety, Sol moved swiftly to initiate and consolidate remunerative connections with corporate and financial America. His client list grew to include much of what was abiding, profitable and not noxiously corrupt in U.S. capitalism. By 1936, his income exceeded $200,000 a year. He was now remaking images and giving advice. That fall, with a loan from American Surety, he bought 17 Rostval Place. The house suited the man he had become.

It was at about this time that he began to "do society." Perhaps he imagined that by hanging new stars in the social firmament, he might himself someday be twinkling there. Whatever the reason, he threw himself into this side of his business with an intensity and creativity exceeding that which he'd given his corporate clients. Soon, Greschner Associates' society business was a substantial contributor. Even as he busied himself with his corporate and social clients, he saw a day coming when culture would be the dominant currency with which social ambition would be able to purchase satisfaction. It was simply a process of elimination. Money could buy almost anything: houses, horses, lovers, even friends. In other words, the list of things money couldn't buy was shrinking. There had to be other goals, beyond things unattainable, golden intangibles. Exclusive almost beyond price. Except if the door be opened by the singular Greschner magic.

Which was what the Fuller Institute came to be for him. Thanks to his friend Gordon the banker, and later, Gordon's friend and attorney Morgan

Seabury, Sol had done some work for Fuller Iron and Coke. He had become friendly with Xerxes Fuller; their houses, after all, overlooked each other from opposite corners of Rostval Place. In 1940, Fuller was facing a considerable tax levy. Inspired by Duveen's persuasion of Andrew Mellon to transform his collection into the core of the National Gallery, Greschner proposed that Xerxes Fuller make over the Fuller mansion, in which he then still lived, and his father's art and book collection, together with a sufficient endowment, as a private museum for the benefit of the City of New York. To keep the administration of the Fuller Institute, which Sol proposed that the collections and the mansion that would house them be collectively renamed, out of the hands of municipal incompetents and scalliwags, a Deed of Settlement establishing the Fuller Endowment was drawn up by Morgan Seabury. It vested all powers with respect to the governance and maintenance of the Institute in a board of five trustees, which would automatically include any surviving direct descendants of Darius Fuller or, if there were none, the president of the family investment corporation—at that time Xerxes Fuller himself. The family trustees alone would have the power to elect new trustees or to make any changes with respect to the qualification of trustees. The deed named Solomon Greschner as an elected trustee.

Xerxes Fuller had a six-year-old daughter, Calypso, who often crossed the square to Number 17. She was the last of the line to that time, the only Fuller of her generation. Xerxes Fuller's only brother had died in infancy; Calypso's mother had died shortly after her birth. Sol was her honorary godfather; she called him "Uncle." When his own son was born, Calypso Fuller came nearly every day to play with the new baby, Moritz, whom she nicknamed Mickey. In 1942, it was to Number 17 that she came, hoarse and weeping, with the telegram that told of her father's death in the flames of the B-17 he was ferrying to England.

Sol himself saw the war through from the Navy public information office on Worth Street. He saw an opportunity in the young heroes for whom he was orchestrating acclaim and exposure. Some among them would surely become men of importance after the war. He kept his eyes open.

Thus, on the night of V-J Day, while sailors and dogfaces clawed runs in the white stockings of nurses caught in the frenzy of Times Square, Number 17 Rostval Place celebrated the end of war and the arrival of the atomic age with a champagne dinner for three young officers whose ship had been lost at Leyte Gulf: Morgan Seabury's son, Homer, and his shipmates Hugo Winstead and Rufus Lassiter, bosom comrades whom the pure chances of war had brought together.

In the euphoria of the moment, it was one for all and all for one, and Sol would be their guide and patron. The prospect was giddying. Like so many friendships forged in war, however, they had nothing root-deep in common. Seabury was a Manhattan aristocrat: right father, right school, right college, right church; somewhere in his future were the right wife and the right address, all as a matter of course. Lassiter was more questionable goods. Like Seabury, from the East Side, but a crucial few blocks closer to the river; Public School 6 instead of Regency for Boys; a practicing Catholic; father an anesthetist at St. Vincent's. Winstead was from nowhere. Some small Midwestern town he was loath to talk about. A state-college education —he was two years older than the others—and a law degree from the same school. But those differences didn't matter that night or for some considerable time afterward; theirs was a common, shining future; they had fought the good fight, been decorated and celebrated by a grateful nation, and now, with Sol's promised help as only their due, they were on their way to triumph in the unbloody battles of love and work.

Morgan Seabury had insisted that Homer and his friends call on Sol. He might himself refuse to dine at Number 17, and not invite Greschner to lunch at his clubs, but he was convinced that there was no one better equipped than Sol to give Homer and his friends useful ideas about their future. Sol knew he was being used, but in the shadings of New York life, that was the way it worked. Nor did he for an instant doubt that he himself could use Morgan Seabury.

The end of the war marked the beginning of Sol's halcyon period, the quarter-century when he was publicly conceived to be an intimate of the innermost circles of power and influence in Manhattan. Mistakenly perhaps, he also saw himself in that role. As he approached his zenith in fame and public estimation, the high-soaring eagle he had become was starting to lose altitude. But that would also come later. Even now, as he came up to Nick's door, he wasn't quite certain how it had happened.

He rang Nick's bell. When the door opened, Nick's face was not an uplifting sight for a Saturday morning.

"Good morning, Nicholas; you look perfectly dreadful."

Nick shook his head like a wet dog.

"Please say nothing. The merest treble rings like an anvil. I won't be a minute. Just let me get a tie. Is it cold out?"

Sol had confirmed Nick's waking suspicion that if his appearance matched his inward physical state, he looked really awful. He'd hoped the bleary face that had stared at him sullenly from his bathroom mirror was an illusion. Actually, he'd forgotten until just an hour before that he was due to lunch with Sol.

The previous evening he'd dined with friends and gone with them to a club, where he found the Sandlers and some people from Buenos Aires, who had all then insisted on gathering him up and heading for a famous West Side discotheque, where the unnecessary, deadly extra bottle of champagne had been ordered. Nick's last conscious recollection of his watch had been that it read 2:00 in the morning: a bad hour for lonely men in cities. Then the fog building in his head had blotted everything sensible out. He didn't think of himself as a cocksman, but every now and then, usually at the end of a long, pointless, overbibulous evening like the one before, something would get loose in his system like an ape in the streets. The ape had been on the town last night: one minute he was drinking champagne with Johnny Sandler; the next he was looking at his watch, which said 6:30, and trying to figure out where the hell he was. He was on a bed, fully dressed. Gradually, shapes in the surrounding room came clear: canvases, an easel. Arden Maypole was sleeping peacefully beside him.

Feeling like a housebreaker, he'd slipped out of bed and left as stealthily as he could, not daring to think of the recriminative phone calls and importunings this little adventure would initiate.

He walked slowly down Park Avenue in the half-dawn, his residual intoxication making his head whistle and buzz. His penitential progress was unwelcomely punctuated by the phutting footfalls of early joggers. Reaching his home at last, he'd fumbled the locks open, reset the alarms and staggered upstairs to fall asleep.

His nerves were jangling like a chorus of harpsichords. The quart of grapefruit juice hadn't really cut the hangover, nor had the three Tabs, nor the roustabout-sized breakfast he'd managed to cook.

"Hurry, Nicholas," Sol called from downstairs. "We're meeting Frodo at one-fifteen and I must stop in at Grundy's on the way."

Nick groaned and shrugged into his jacket.

"Coming," he said.

When José came in to say that *Lazy G One*, the Gulfstream bringing Caryn Gudge home from New York, was on approach vector, Bubber Gudge was settled in front of the eighty-inch Sony projection screen, watching another rerun of his appearance four years earlier before the Select Committee on Illegal Overseas Payments, Senator Lassiter presiding. He'd run the tape forward to the worst part. To flagellate himself with his own ineptness and Lassiter's obvious cruelty. It brought up a throat-filling anger that anesthetized him against any second thoughts. The first forty minutes of his appearance had been painful enough. He'd been summoned to explain a $175,000 payment to the air-force commandant of an African nation in which a Lazy G unit had been contract-drilling for the national oil company. Despite the cadre of lawyers he'd brought with him, Lassiter had asked him a lot of questions in ways that no one could have answered without twisting the appearance of things and the way it had really been. Lassiter wanted to know a lot of details about the Lazy G. The Gudge interests embraced almost two dozen major entities in twenty nations. He had people in the field who did the adding and subtracting, who ran each rig, managed each plant and metered each pound, barrel and cubic foot of mineral production in their area. That was what they were paid to do. Only he and Katagira knew the whole picture, thanks to Katagira's information center downstairs, and he preferred to keep Katagira out of the spotlight. Lassiter had managed the hearing to make it seem as if Bubber should be personally accountable for each molecule of the Lazy G, however remote. The fact was that the Lazy G was too complicated a business structure to be easily explained to a panel of glib Eastern politicians out to make political capital by picking on the so-called richest man in the country. For most of the hearing, Bubber and his lawyers had fumbled with their papers, trying to make unconnected statistics appear relevant to each other in order just to get it over with.

Bubber had had no illusions about the outcome of the hearing. His money made him an easy target for folks like these. Politicians and journalists, especially, never asked the right questions. His nervous vexation made him stutter. At least twice he'd lost his patience with his lawyers, grumbling sourly on camera the way he did if his people dropped a wrench down the casing of a $4-million well. Meanwhile Senator Lassiter glowered and smirked for his national television audience.

Finally, when the Senator had exhausted the inventory of innuendo-loaded, intentionally ambiguous questions fed him by his eager young staff, Bubber had been given his turn. Lassiter had been harrying him about the $175,000 that Buford Producing Company N.V. had paid the African general to get special clearance to land a chartered L-1011 in order to get three drilling crews out of the way of an erupting tribal war.

"Well, Mr. Gudge," Lassiter had hectored, flashing the bright teeth that were his trademark, "you knew perfectly well when you made this payment that such bribes to foreign government officials, assuming there was any good reason to make them, would have had to be cleared with the Federal Reserve Board, the Department of Energy and the Congressional Subcommittee on Overt Operations?"

Bubber's touring company of lawyers pressed around him, seeking his ear. He waved them off. Katagira had prepared him for this.

"Yessir. We know all about compliance. But we had a hundred thirty-two men out there, a revolution starting and them folks talking about barbecuing three real good drilling crews. I mean, they was saying it was the fault of this government's foreign policy, which my people have nothing to do with, except they vote, and I figgered I had to get them out. Naturally, I asked my lawyers—there's ten of 'em here, Senator, and fifty-three more in Dallas, New York, London and places I can't remember—how long it would take to get them clearances you're speaking of, and when they told me maybe six to eight years, and I've got good people I sent out there who look like they're gonna get killed within forty-eight hours tops. I just had to figure I'd get them out of there best way I could. Those are my people, Senator. They count on me just as I count on them." He'd sounded more plaintive than he'd intended.

"The best way you could, eh, Mr. Gudge?" Lassiter grinned at the cameras, sharing his private suspicions with the enormous television audience.

"I don't suppose I have to remind you this is a nation of laws—not men. Not that you seemed to respect that. Didn't it occur to you, sir, when you flew to Africa on your infamous mission, a mission to a regime whose human-rights record is not to the satisfaction of this country, that you were defying the edicts of this Administration and the last three Congresses?"

"Well, sir, I didn't really think about it. I mean, our 1011 was up there circling around, and the general, sir, was sitting there with his hand out. I mean, you know, I just reached down and paid him."

"Paid him?"

"Yessir, in traveler's checks."

"Traveler's checks? One hundred seventy-five thousand dollars in traveler's checks?"

"Yessir. I never leave home without 'em." ("LAUGHTER" reported the Congressional Record.)

"Mr. Gudge, are you suggesting to this committee that you were carrying one hundred seventy-five thousand dollars in traveler's checks?"

"Well, actually a little bit more. I didn't know how much was gonna be have to be paid. These people like that, well, they ain't like us, you know, Senator; you never know how much they're gonna want, what with inflation and all." (LAUGHTER)

"Mr. Gudge, I don't know what you mean. Your attitude is both curious and contemptible. At least, I find it so, and I'm sure my colleagues concur. This nation is in a depression, sir. Don't you realize that your pocket money greatly exceeds the investment capital of many Americans?"

"Well, sir, that may be. I don't know a whole lot about other folks' money. Except my granddaddy told me once that a fellow who knows exactly what he's worth probably isn't worth a whole lot." (LAUGHTER)

Lassiter looked for a long moment into the camera, improvising an expression both smug and mournful. He laid his pencil slowly beside his note pad, as if he were putting down the tablets of sacred law.

"Mr. Gudge, you make me ashamed to be an American." He seemed to be brushing and combing his patriotism. It would be the high point of his now-forsaken liberalism.

It should have been a noble moment for Bubber. Onscreen, he saw himself reach for the statement that Katagira had drafted for him; he saw himself wipe his thick glasses, and look up and down the table of interrogators, just the way Katagira had rehearsed him and they had practiced it.

"Senator Lassiter, Senators," the sheet before him read, "I'd just like to make a real brief statement. I'm speaking for Lazy G Enterprises, Lacy G Communications, Lazy G Financial and Security, Lazy G Offshore Company, Panhandle Service and Supply Inc., First Panhandle Banking Company, Gudge Oil and Gas Inc., Gudge Energy Partners, Agrigudge Inc., Gudge Contract Builders, Southwest Houston Gudge Associates, Panhandle Seismic and Swabbing Inc., North Texas Wireline Inc., Gaz Gudge S.A., Compagnie Gudge d'Afrique, Gudge Nordsee N.V., Western Australia Ranching Properties Ltd., Buford Producing Company, Buford Producing Company N.V., Petróleos Gudge, Petróleos Bufor de Argentina, Bufour Partners, Bufour Associates and Gudge and Gudge."

It was a long list, but in practice he had gotten through it without tripping up too bad, even on some of the weird foreign names.

"These are my companies. I own them. We have—I have"—he had seen Katagira's words before him and heard them in his mind—"pretty near ten thousand people working around the world. In lots of places where folks think different than we do. Our people, my people, take our money figuring we're behind them. I wouldn't do it no other way. They don't count on you, Senator, no more than they vote for you—'course, we've only got twenty people in Connecticut. We don't break no reasonable laws. We pay every tax there is. In twenty-three countries, Senator. And Senator, we will do whatever is necessary to protect our folks wherever we send 'em. So long as we can pay the price. As long as we don't break any local laws, which we look to the locals to tell us about, Senator. Nobody's going to say that someone dies for the Lazy G 'cause the Lazy G was cheap. And Senator, nobody works for us who works for the CIA or the FBI or any of them other fancy initials. Not the best day you ever saw. The only secrets we got are our own. That's our deal with Gudge folks, Senator, no more and no less."

It was a good speech, except it didn't come out the way it was on paper. Flustered, perspiring torrents under the television lights, he saw himself stumble and stammer, starting with a list of companies he knew as well as his own name, now, under pressure, as unfamiliar to him as Deuteronomy, losing the simple, direct phrases in which Katagira had schooled him. He watched himself turn into a fumbling, foundering self-conscious mess. Halfway through, he flat ran out of gas—just stopped, blinking and confused, wishing Katagira was there. In his soaking palms, the type on the paper blurred like watercolor.

That's when Lassiter had really started in.

"Mr. Gudge, I think this committee has seen, and the American people will see as these hearings are broadcast and rebroadcast, that you represent a face of capitalism which is beyond unacceptable, which is despicable. Illiterate. Treacherous. Lawbreaking. Exploitative. All in the interest of profit. You have willfully violated this nation's policy, Mr. Gudge, traduced its noblest traditions. In pursuit of profit. Energy profit, sir. Profit earned on the back and brow of every honest workingman in this land, every man who has to heat a house or drive to work. You must hold this nation, your nation, in great contempt, Mr. Gudge, to treat as you have, callously and contemptuously, with men whose policies are not the policies of this nation.

"There are many of us, sir," Lassiter had wound up, "who have felt for some time that a potentially hostile concentration of economic power is being formed on these very shores, as unregarding of the national well-being as any combination of foreign oil producers. I think your actions demonstrate that, sir. We have our own OPEC here, in the U.S.A. Mr. Gudge, and you are it! Corrupt, greedy, un-American!"

There had been vigorous applause from Lassiter's claque; the Senators to his left and right had reached over to shake his hand.

Rewatching, he felt first horror and then hatred. Katagira, afterward, had tried to console him, but he knew how bad he'd done. How much disgrace he'd heaped on the Lazy G. The punishment was nothing. He was cited for contempt of Congress, and made to pay a fine of $250,000 and promise not to do something he'd never done anyway.

What was money compared with that awfulness? Being stood up on the TV and whipped like a boy with his pants down in a room full of people. On the flight back to the ranch, and for months afterward, he was unable to think clearly, so occluded was his mind with hatred of Senator Lassiter. Even when the doctors told him about the cancer, he felt that it was just as if a little piece of the big hatred had broken off and gotten lodged in his blood somewheres. Ingrained hatreds schooled like sharks in the dark waves of his subconscious. He saw Lassiter as part of something that threatened everything. Lassiter was the East, Big Government, New York—Wall Street. One of them that was out to get him. His hatred metastasized into a consuming urge for revenge, a tidal wave that would suck under Lassiter and all the rest of them. To hit them with the same abandon, the same carelessness with which they'd chopped his insides into dog meat.

The cancer made it easier. The commitment could be entire; well, almost —he'd chop out a little piece for Caryn; make sure she was taken care of. That was when he called Katagira in; told him what he wanted; told him he was willing to bet all his chips; told him to figure it out.

He heaved himself out of his chair, grunting like the fat man he'd been once. The thing inside him made him feel kitten-weak. He and Katagira had spent a long day together. Reviewing all the Lazy G holdings. It was tiring, he thought, and why not? Planning the financial destruction of enemies as big as his was long, detailed work.

He picked his Stetson off the hall table. Even though he didn't feel much pain, he was tired all the time. Stumpy was waiting in the driveway with the Rolls. Caryn liked to be met by a Rolls wherever she landed. Bubber climbed into the front seat and signaled to Stumpy to get rolling.

At his casting pond, Katagira watched the jet pass overhead and heard the automobile slide down the graveled drive.

Returning to his task, he drew back the light bamboo rod, keeping the loop of the tapered line tucked loosely under the stump of his right arm. Accelerated by the flexible rod tip, the line twitched back and forth in the still air, bellying, acquiring momentum, until finally he drove the axis of the rod through the top of an imaginary clock centered on his left shoulder. The line floated out, making a serpentine in the breathless afternoon, driving the fly at the end of the leader in a soft crescent to its target on the pond's surface while the rest of the line whispered weightlessly down behind.

The pond was the only extravagance he had asked of his employer in their years together.

A slight riffle in the water just beyond the fly drew his attention. He prepared himself. The pond's surface seemed to snap open and shut; he felt a sudden unmistakable pressure on the rod's tip. He brought it up sharply, tautening the line. It was difficult for a one-armed man to strike a fish. It made the contest equal.

The trout was on. He played it to the edge of the pond; he was using an automatic reel, which was cheating, he knew, but there was no other way. Now that the fish was on, it was only a matter of time. He let his thoughts stray.

He was happy for his employer that the wife was returning, much as he disliked her. She reminded him of the trout in his pond; completely a creature of appetite and instinct. At least, therefore, she was predictable and thus, in a funny way, trustworthy. He didn't sympathize with Gudge's worship of her, but it was not his business to question it. From time to time, during an idle moment, he might ponder the relationship of the Gudges; invariably he came to the conclusion that Mrs. Gudge had a purely sexual hold on her husband. A familiar story: the dry-hearted, lonely millionaire —in Gudge's case, billionaire—isolated from the world by wealth or work, suddenly being given overwhelming sexual pleasure and believing the unfamiliar sensation in his groin to be the definitive stirring of true love. A tale repeated a dozen times a year in a state like Texas, where men invested their libidos in business, and that made them vulnerable.

He was Gudge's man. As it happened, he was philosophically entirely in accord with the current objective. He knew that for Gudge it was essentially a matter of revenge; for Katagira, who was prone to clothe the events of life with heightened significance, it was a more profound business, more moral: an act of purification, of justification, of regeneration.

Now it seemed to Katagira that the dozen years that he had been with Gudge, since they'd met at the Permian Basin Technology Exposition, where Katagira had been representing a Japanese firm trying to break into oil-field electronics, had been in fact a preparation for this. Gudge's offer had been a welcome chance for him to withdraw from a busy world he found morally and intellectually intolerable. Although he knew Gudge sometimes carelessly referred to him as "my Jap," he was as American as the Lazy G. Born in San Francisco; incarcerated with the other Nisei in 1942; released to serve with the 442nd Regimental Combat Team, the Japanese-American unit; wounded in Europe; with the Army of Occupation in Japan as a civilian interpreter. His history traversed two worlds. He had seen Hiroshima, which had turned him against America and led him to seek his fortune and peace of mind in Japan. He had watched Japan degenerate into a nation of bustling, bowing technocrats, watched the ancient refinements and values buried in the intellectual sludge of absolute commercialism. He had become an ardent follower of Mishima, but he hated violence. So he had turned from Japan, which no longer seemed capable of producing any worthwhile philosophy, literature or art, back to America, where at least there were dreams. He had worked on the Ginza and on Wall Street. He had a degree in economics from the University of Tokyo and a law degree from the University of Texas.

The law degree had been Gudge's idea. When they met, Gudge had been the proprietor of the universe of the Lazy G for five years, but he was already launched on his scheme to make that universe a cosmos and law unto itself. A multibillion-dollar complex capable of supporting and financing itself with minimal recourse to the outside world. That way the only people he would have to see would be his people. The mistrustfulness his grandfather had worked so hard to implant had developed into an obsession with privacy—as if to permit other eyes to see any significant part of the Lazy G's workings would be an unforgivable breach of his compact with the past: a sin punishable by nightmare.

Gudge and Katagira were made for each other; they empathized a mutual reclusiveness, a quality Gudge had sensed so strongly and found so comforting in the other man that he'd offered him a job on the spot. Together over ten years they had built the Lazy G into the type of system Gudge wanted. It financed itself with its own cash flow and through its own banks. It insured itself through its Bermuda company. It drilled its own wells onshore and off with its own rigs. It did its own wire-line work; its own cementing; when a Gudge well needed fracturing, a Gudge service crew handled the job.

The only people who knew the whole picture were Gudge and Katagira. Around the world, there were Gudge people familiar with pieces of the global photograph; in Houston, New York, London and Djakarta there were division managers who knew somewhat more. But only on the ranch itself, in the information center downstairs, which Katagira had planned and seen installed and kept refining and expanding, could all the strands be gathered up and the tapestry seen whole.

Bubber was not content simply to be able to oversee all the pieces of his universe from the Big House; he wanted to be able to control them from there. Without leaving the ranch, he wanted to effect, instantly, whatever moves his evolving business strategy and worldwide tax considerations dictated. To shift a corporate domicile; file on a lease; buy, sell or transfer an asset in the least time-consuming, most cost-effective fashion possible. So he had sent Katagira to law school in Austin, bringing him back to the ranch every evening by jet. Now the ranch house's computers and facsimile transmitters were wired into a battery of legal data services and computerized law libraries, as well as a score of major law firms around the world. The Lazy G created its own substantive documentation. Its outside lawyers were used mainly for local, line-level details, becoming involved with the bigger picture only as messengers, carrying papers to the courthouse.

The ranch life suited Katagira. It gave him the solitude to ponder and synthesize the two cultural streams that conflated in him. He saw his life as priestly: ascetic and contemplative, very much into the Shinto tradition of his ancestors. On the table by his sleeping mat were piled a stack of books out of which, during his decade on the ranch, he had constructed an intellectual ideal of America: De Tocqueville; Thoreau; Emerson; *The Federalist*; Jefferson. Japan or America—in either case it seemed to him that the decay he saw on television or read about in the flood of newspapers and magazines that Stumpy brought over every afternoon was due to a turning away from old values. Sitting at night in the house that Gudge had built for him, a replica of a royal suite in the Katsura Palace near Kyoto, he had convinced himself that some sort of purgative, cleansing shock was needed. Some trauma near the heart of the nation's decadence. Something short of war that would with its flames illuminate the corruption of values, the foolishness, the debasement. He was therefore emotionally and intellectually susceptible when Gudge had told him what he wanted to do—even if, as he had now worked it out, the price of the operation was to be the Lazy G itself.

A good-looking airplane for a good-looking woman, Bubber thought, watching the Gulfstream lance down through the midday sunlight and settle on the landing strip. That airplane and Caryn were his proudest possessions outside the Lazy G. It made him happy to maintain them; see them gleaming and polished. Of course, he said, kicking himself mentally as he watched the plane pivot at the end of the runway and start to taxi back toward the hangar where he was waiting, Caryn was the real treasure. She looked so good, especially when she was all dressed up, and she wasn't hardly grumpy except during her monthlies. And she loved him, and showed it. He was so truly happy she was back that he even forgot his illness.

Wasn't it a funny coincidence that he'd found both a wife and his most trusted associate ten years apart at the technology show in Odessa, Texas? His heart had dropped through the soles of his boots when he first saw her passing out specification flyers at a pump-company booth. He always claimed that he saw her first and fell in love right on the spot; so did she. Probability was on her side. To a pretty girl aching to get out of a dreary life, any man with possibilities had to be tried. It was likely that Caryn had seen him and recognized him instantly; it is certain that she threw him her best look at the precise instant when, for some reason never to be fully understood, his heart was unguarded. It wasn't the first time she'd thrown that look of hers, nor was it a glance that for most men would have launched a dinghy, let alone a thousand ships, although she was a very good-looking woman; but Buford Gudge IV was brought up by the side of her booth like he was harpooned, nearly gasping with sensations he'd never felt before and asking her bashfully if she'd maybe like to have a steak when she got off.

By eight-thirty they were back in his motel. He didn't even know how or why they got there, so fogged was he with feelings utterly new to him and beyond his governance. There, until the small hours, Caryn did to Bubber Gudge what she had done so often before, to Southwest pilots, reporters from the Dallas and Houston papers, Cowboy quarterbacks on the banquet circuit, anyone who looked like there was the remotest chance of a ticket out of Odessa and a place to stay, just for a few days, until she got on her feet, when she got wherever they were going. This time it worked. Nothing like this had ever happened to the man over whom she bent, her long auburn hair brushing his heaving stomach. He'd only ever loved one woman—not this way, for sure—and she'd been taken out of his life by a .44-caliber Soft Point. Given that, and the fact that what he did on the Lazy G had never prepared him for a woman who was making him feel like he was going to fly right up through the ceiling and out into the night sky, it was understandable that he confused the tumult down there with what poets might call the real thing. He just knew he was feeling something he'd never felt before, which, for all he knew, was love.

For Caryn, it was her second and—as far as she knew—last chance to make it. But what a chance! She'd scented it once before, that smell of escape. When she was just out of high school, fresh-complexioned, with breasts that'd had the football captain begging to touch them the very night before the AAAA championship game with Permian High School across town, she'd won the "Miss Downhole Tool" contest, an unfortunately named competition sponsored by a local oil-field-supply firm. No sooner had the gilt-paper crown been placed on her head than she'd been offered a job by Tipco, the Houston conglomerate that was famous for recruiting every backwoods beauty queen in Texas and Louisiana. Tipco had brought her to its Houston headquarters and stationed her as a receptionist on the eighth floor of its black-glass building on Milam Street. Caryn had shared an apartment with three other girls out on the North Loop, gone to the Lamar Hotel on Wednesday afternoons with the sweet old man who was chairman of Tipco's finance committee, and Friday and Saturday nights chased muscle in the Post Oak bars. But Mamma'd got sick and she'd had to come back to Odessa, and by the time Mamma'd finally gone to the angels there were tiny lines at the corners of Caryn's eyes and a Miss Pleasanton or Miss Three-Prong Packer at her old desk in Houston. She was still good-looking, but she was no longer young, by Texas standards; most of the men didn't look seriously at you the next morning if they thought you was over twenty-one.

But Bubber did. By six in the morning, worn out yet begging for more, he sent her back to her place to get her suitcase, enjoining her to keep her mouth shut. At seven-thirty his plane was wheels-up out of Midland Regional bound for the Lazy G. By noon a judge had driven down to the ranch from the county seat, and by twelve-thirty, Caryn, a twenty-seven-year-old ex–beauty queen, was the wife of a man whose income during the ten-minute ceremony was greater than the value of the biggest house in Odessa. Katagira and Stumpy had stood witness. Afterward, the few vaqueros still left on the Lazy G wheeled by the porch on horseback to salute the bridal couple; Caryn and her new husband had then gone back into the house, where she repeated the erotic specialties that had won his heart. At four, he left for Venezuela in a daze of moist and unbelieving fulfillment, and by four-fifteen she was on the phone to the couture department of Neiman-Marcus in Dallas. By four-thirty she had spent more than $60,000. By four-fifty the Lear was on its way to Love Field to bring back the clothes and a fitter.

That had been two years ago. Two years: a long honeymoon memorialized with $3 million worth of Paris dresses, of jewels fit for a rani and shoes from the hide of calves more numerous than those that fed on the grasslands of the ranch. A royal ransom sufficient for most people—but not to Caryn. What was the point of all she had if there wasn't a suitable stage on which to parade it? Without knowing the word, let alone how to spell it, she dreamed of a coronation—a celebration appropriate to the possibilities of being Mrs. Buford Gudge IV. A magazine dream. Something that money could buy. That she wanted it was justification enough for her husband. He told Katagira to fix it up.

Nick accompanied Sol up Park Avenue quietly. The slight nip in the air wasn't enough to clear his head. He dreaded lunch; a glass of anything stronger than water and he would float away. He was still half-loaded and trying not to show it, trying to appear sensible and thoughtful in spite of an impulse to babble and laugh and assert himself. Alone, with a hangover like this Nick was sulky and desperate; in company, the world seemed pebble-shiny and clamoring with voices demanding to be shut out with his own bright chatter.

They turned east at Seventy-fifth Street.

At Lexington, they paused for a light. To Nick, the streets seemed unfairly crowded; he felt like a ball maneuvering delicately among duckpins.

"Nice party the other night," Sol said.

"Very."

"Attractive, that Caryn Gudge, didn't you think?"

"Very pretty. Not quite there yet, though."

"Give her time, Nicholas, give her time. Great possibilities that lady has. Great."

"Who knows?"

They crossed and walked toward Third, interrupted by a man who darted out of his wine store and buttonholed Sol on the subject of the 1978 vintage. While Greschner chatted, Nick took great gulps of the air. It didn't help.

"Saw you spending a lot of time with Jill Newman, Nicholas. What'd you think?"

"Frankly, I thought she was terrific." Had his head been clear, Nick would have been less obvious in his enthusiasm; he liked to downplay his feelings. "Where've you been keeping her?" He sounded strangely aggressive to Sol. "What's she doing writing gossip, anyway? That scummy business. One of your house organs? What's the story?"

Sol put up a mild hand.

"Nicholas, don't be so assertive."

Nick subsided. The city seemed to have concentrated all its honking and buzzing in his ears. A void had been interposed between his eyes and his brain; it was as if every one of his senses had been banished duncelike to a separate corner of an enormous room.

"She's very unusual, Jill." Sol marched ahead, speaking to the city at large. "Very unusual. She was an accountant, you know. Has a gift for numbers. I've known her since she first came to New York. Funny thing, I knew her father years ago. Silly old boy; taught at Columbia; a great Proust expert. Lectured at the Fuller once. Anyway, since you ask, I'm very fond of Jill. She was a friend of my son, Moritz. More than a friend, I suppose, although I never knew her that much then. You know how it was between Moritz and me."

Nick knew. Sol and his son, Mickey, had hated each other. Right up to the day Mickey Greschner'd been snatched by a riptide while he was showing off in the Nantucket surf.

"When I met her she was with an accounting firm," Sol continued. "She wanted to do something else. Wanted to make more money. She asked me for help, so I did what I could. That was after Moritz died. She had wonderful taste, so I recommended her to *That Woman!* As an assistant to the old girl who used to cover the fashion openings. A good job for a young, attractive girl willing to work. Better than selling cooperative apartments, for example. She's done wonderfully there—although, no, to your rude question, she's not one of mine. Oh, once in a while she'll indulge this old man's whim and help me out. With a photograph or a mention of a gown. She was wonderful when I represented Granada, for example. How'd you get on, anyway? I think she's been pretty badly bruised, poor child."

"I liked her a lot. She mentioned a daughter. Who was she married to?"

"Somebody out West. That's where she comes from. Ah, here we are."

They entered the glass-and-concrete pavilion that was the Manhattan headquarters of Grundy's, the third-largest and most rapidly growing of the big London-based auction houses.

Sol led the way up the cylindrical staircase.

"I won't be a minute. There's a Queen Anne estate table coming up that wants looking at. The people at Partridge tell me it hasn't got a patch on mine."

Ah, Sol, Nick thought, you never change, you poor, sad, blessed man. This was one of Sol's real kicks in life: comparing what he had with something someone else owned. Sol's possessions—his furniture, books, silver, porcelain—were owned by him in competition with the rest of the world. A visit to a salesroom, the point of which was, for most people, to look at something they were thinking of buying, was for Sol an event of reaffirmation. An opportunity to confirm that this or that of his possessions was superior in quality or value to what the man down the street owned: an endorsement of the tables, statuettes or drawings that were the confirmations, given his wifeless, childless existence, of Sol's sense of his merit and significance.

At the top of the stairs they parted company. Grundy's furniture man accosted Sol and led him into the main showroom. Attention was always paid to Sol by the auction houses. They were keen students of the actuarial tables; Sol was well past seventy; deference was an easy earnest of their interest in someday selling off Number 17 and its contents. Nick strolled through the smaller galleries.

Finally, he wandered into the main showroom, where he found Sol talking with the Decorative Arts curator of the Met.

"It's not a bad table, James." Sol was saying, gesturing benevolently, "but not quite up to mine, I think you'll agree."

He turned away.

"Time to go, Nicholas. Mustn't keep Frodo waiting. I regret to say he's bringing another of his young men. How he gets away with it I'm sure I don't know."

Nick started for the stairs. Over his shoulder he said, "Oh come on, Sol. Frodo's the best in the business. His friends are his friends—just as long as he keeps them out of sight of Hugo Winstead." Both men knew that Winstead hated homosexuals.

Walking the last three blocks up Madison Avenue, Sol scowled at the chrome storefronts that had replaced the niched and corniced stone of happier days.

"Ungrateful as I may appear, being of good immigrant stock myself, I must nonetheless say, Nicholas, that this city was a damn sight better off when our new arrivals got off the boat without a pot to pee in, instead of a letter of credit from the Vatican Bank. Look at that, for God's sake. The city's going to the dogs."

He pointed at a window in which two Lucite mannequins, of indeterminate gender, appeared to be consummating a perverse coupling witnessed by a parliament of shoes and scarves.

Then they found themselves under the Tennyson's welcoming canopy and Sol's sunny mood returned. Even Nick, who had been preoccupied with getting one foot properly in front of the other, felt better.

The Tennyson was the most esteemed hotel address in Manhattan—a distinction that had survived even its acquisition by Harvey Bogle from its third-generation owners. It had been plunked down on upper Madison Avenue in 1915, an unlikely pile of red London stone relocated from Sloane Street to the hubbub of New York by its first proprietor, who thought that a magnified version of the Connaught Hotel would do well on the far side of the Atlantic. His estimate was premature. The Tennyson clung to life for almost eighty years as a residential hotel favored by genteel old ladies and humble visiting country cousins parked there by their grand Park Avenue relations.

Harvey Bogle had bought the Tennyson in 1971, on the eve of Madison Avenue's commercial explosion. When, after having attacked the transaction for five unrelenting weeks, the *Times* finally sent its architecture critic to interview Bogle on his plans for the building, the new owner had badly bruised the preconceptions of the paper by stating that he intended to keep the Tennyson more or less intact, "because it looks good as it is, where it is." Bogle himself had moved into the proprietor's apartment on the eighteenth floor and was still there. He had refurbished the building top to bottom; he had hired away the chef of the Connaught to give the hotel's grillroom the best menu on the Upper East Side; and he had hired Sol Greschner to make the world aware that the grillroom was the most fashionable eating place in Manhattan and the hotel's ninety-seven rooms and suites the most coveted and possibly most expensive in the world. The customary Greschner magic, which had after all first been perfected on a hotel job, had worked as well as ever. Harvey Bogle, a careful if not a close man with a dollar, had never begrudged a penny of the $215,000 in fees he paid Greschner Associates to get the job done. He had even granted Sol squatter's rights on a prime corner booth in the grillroom, to which Sol and Nick were now bowed by a backward-stepping captain.

"I see Frodo's beat us here," said Sol, not at all pleased to see also that the early arrivals were already well into a bottle of the 1964 Pol Roger which the Tennyson kept aside exclusively for him.

"Ah, Sol, there you are." Frodo rose, urging to his feet a sullen young man in a rumpled tweed jacket and a collarless shirt. The boy had a surly, sleepy face with a mouth so weak it threatened to slide right off his chin and down his chest. "And Nicholas too. My dear boy, what is the matter? You are positively gillish gray. This is Ralph. Say hello, Ralph, to very good friends of mine, Mr. Solomon Greschner and Mr. Nicholas Reverey. Mr. Reverey is an art dealer—but a very good one. Mr. Greschner is a genius. Ralph is a painter; aren't you, my dear? Well, shall we sit down? Sol, my dear boy, this champagne is a marvel. Ho, captain, another bottle!" Nick observed that Crisp's hands were shaking; Friday nights were obviously tough all over town.

"Do you know, Sol," continued Crisp, made expansive and queenish by the wine and the protective familiar company, "I think that last Thursday's little go-round was one of our better efforts. I do wish Ralph could have been there, don't you, Ralph? He's very artistic, Ralph is. I got him from a dear, dear friend, and if he doesn't smile and behave like a human being I will send him back."

Nick was familiar with Frodo's quicksilver bitchiness. He studied Ralph across the table. He recognized the type. A young Englishman, of no particular background or ability, with absolutely no moral sense. There must be five hundred Ralphs around New York these days, Nick thought. Five times five hundred. A sign of the times? Poor Frodo: a boy like Ralph would screw a woman, another man or a snake with equal ardor, so long as there was a good time attached, and plenty of free booze and dope. Nick pitied Frodo Crisp for the agony of his condition. Brilliant as he was, and for all the prestige that went with the directorship of the great museum, he had an ape of his own that also could get loose in the streets, a potentially life-wrecking itch that had to be scratched. Nick knew a lot of gay men who held sensitive jobs, but who had managed to find less masochistic solutions. Poor Frodo indeed. There would always be Ralphs in his life. That was his curse.

His thoughts returned to the table. Sol had taken over, ignoring Ralph's existence. A captain hovered. Nick ordered a beer. It was the minimum possible insult to his delicate condition.

"Now, Frodo, before we get down to cases, who's here today?"

Smart New Yorkers lunched where their mood, the season, and *That Woman!* instructed them to dine. Last year it had been Mortimer's, Quo Vadis and Le Plaisir. This year Massimo von González was pushing Dove Sono, because he was in love with the wine steward; Chez Maia, because that was where the art crowd went and everyone knew that art was In; and, back for a triumphal revival, the Tennyson grillroom, a recommendation not unconnected to the fact that his wife was decorating Bogle's new hotel. For the past five years, the grillroom had done a capacity business with people who liked food and admired Harvey Bogle for retaining the quaint English system that banished the cocktail crowd to the lobby, sparing lingering diners the glares from the bar that were so unpleasing an aspect of New York restaurant culture. And of course there were those whose continued patronage represented a silent vote supporting what liberal newspaper columnists clucked about as "the Tennyson apartheid." Arabs—of any type—were not welcome at the Tennyson. Bogle himself had caused a vein to pop in the forehead of the *Post*'s leading bleeding heart when, in an interview, he suggested that he was doing his bit for a Middle Eastern settlement: "The Jews can come here and the Arabs can join the Trails Club in Palm Beach. That way every rich person's got a place to call his own."

"No one worth catting about," Frodo answered. "Most of them are out in their ghastly pink and green houses in Southampton trying to forget who they really are. Isn't that awful woman over there in the straw hat the gorgon that writes about food for *That Woman!*? Speaking of which, Sol, what are we going to do about *That Woman!*? I simply cannot endure one more view of or hear one more word about or by those Von González people. And thank you, by the way, for having them to dine. Granada Masterman absolutely bullied Calypso into making sure they had a decent dinner to go to; you know how Hugo's sucking up to Calypso. Anyway, I was talking to young Jill Newman last night at the Mastermans'—such an attractive young lady; and Nicholas, don't you think for a moment I didn't see you sniffing around. Much too good for you, Nicholas, I think—although you can be rather good value at times. What have you been up to these days, anyway? You haven't shown me anything lately, and I hear that the Cleveland people have been busying in and out of your shop like roaches. Not that we could afford it, if it comes to that. That ghastly building. Does anyone know what the weather's like in Fort Worth? No, I wasn't cut out to be a cowboy. In any case, I was talking with Jill before dinner—I mean, Solomon, where do these people get their ideas about food?—and she told me, absolutely off the top of her head, of course, that she thought you were okay, which is possible, and then she broke my heart by telling me that foolish little Mr. von González is worth so much to her paper that they're paying him a hundred and fifty thousand a year."

He sniffed malevolently.

Nick saw Frodo's companion's eyebrows rise. A sum of this magnitude was worth Ralph's attention. He interrupted his pouting study of the menu and started to say something. Doubtless to ask for Von Gonzalez' phone number, thought Nick; but Sol cut him off.

"*That Woman!* performs a very useful social service, Frodo, which you know very well. Rich people like both reading about being rich and reading about themselves. A forum is needed which is not generally available to the less privileged. *That Woman!* is such a forum. As for Nicholas' being attentive to Miss Newman, who among us can quarrel with that? She is a very appealing woman, and extremely bright. She was once quite a good friend of my late son Moritz, as you know, Frodo. He was a ladies' man—so he often told me. Her association with him can only be put down to a lamentable, temporary lapse in taste and judgment; one which she has not since repeated, at least not to my knowledge. I know her only professionally; we have done each other favors . . ."

"Favors?" asked Nick.

"Just so. As I was telling you, before you wandered off at Grundy's. A bit of news here, a helpful notice there. But that needn't concern you, Nicholas. Keep your mind on your business. I placed you at that dinner very carefully and with considerable intent. If I were a young man making my way selling pictures, very expensive pictures, I should pay a great deal of attention to that pretty Mrs. Gudge. I think she could be stimulated to take a great interest in art. She is ambitious. Which is useful. She has a rich and, I am told, a loving husband. A very loving husband. Now, that is vital, wouldn't you say, Frodo?"

"Indeed it is. Shall we eat?" Frodo turned to Ralph. "How does the calf's liver strike you, my dear? It should go well with that '71 Corton I know Sol has hidden away belowstairs." Then to Sol, beaming, "I quite agree with you about Mrs. Gudge. It will take time, though, and a great deal of persuasion."

"Oh, I wouldn't think so," said Nick. "She showed me her catalogue at the end of the evening. She'd checked off the things she was going to get her husband to buy for her. I didn't see the whole list, but the page I saw had been marked for a couple of Max Lefcourt's pleasanter bonbons: the Carpaccio and the bigger Raphael."

"Odd," said Frodo. "The smaller Raphael is much finer. That's the one I'd pick. I've never really warmed to the large one. A tired picture, don't you know."

"From the little I know of Mrs. Gudge," said Nick, "I'd guess she'd checked both of them. Raphael's a name they must know even out in Dallas or wherever she comes from. Where is it, Sol?"

"Amarillo. Although she's from Odessa, Nicholas. One of the twin jewels of West Texas. You must remember such things, young man, if you're going to do well with Mrs. Gudge." Greschner sounded like an ambitious Dickensian father sermonizing over the Sunday mutton about the Duke's second daughter. "I think I'll have the veal chop, Frodo, as long as we're drinking my best wine. Nicholas?"

Nicholas ordered a chicken paillard, a small salad and a second beer. A big, heady Burgundy like the Corton would kill him.

Over lunch, Sol, who never did more than pick at his food, resumed while the others ate.

"I'd be very attentive to Mrs. Gudge too, Frodo, were I in your shoes. I think the Gudges have great promise. And more money than God. And you know I like my friends—may I call them that for delicacy's sake—to develop a healthy interest in the Fuller. To do less would not be neighborly. If I were you, Frodo, I'd have her to lunch. Perhaps with Winstead. I can see Mr. Winstead finding Mrs. Gudge to be of considerable interest." He grinned at Frodo; Nick caught the allusion to Winstead's satyriasis.

Sol talked through most of the rest of lunch, interrupted only when Ralph, having been given a small packet by Frodo, left to go to the lavatory, from which he returned just as Sol was initialing the check. Sol had been at his most Socratic, illuminating and defining the world he saw through his own distorted lenses, going on about Mrs. Gudge, whom he painted as a prospective patroness of the arts on a scale to rival Maria de' Medici or Eleonora Gonzaga. Smiling, his mind still uncentered, Nick listened as Sol confused reality with the fantasized notions of people created by his enthusiasm and imagination. From the other side of the table, Frodo seemed to have retreated behind a smile as fixed and protective as a bulletproof pane.

Outside the marquee, the afternoon was blinding after the leather-and-mahogany nocturne of the grillroom. As they were taking leave of each other, Frodo suddenly looked very crossly at Greschner.

"Solomon. I have something I must take up with you. You know there is one seat vacant on our board of trustees. You know that the odds-on favorite right now is Mrs. Masterman. You know that because you made her the favorite. Later, of course, the two of you fell out. But by that time the impetus was strong. Too strong. She has become a friend of Mrs. Winstead's, to the extent that poor Calypso has any real friends at all. At least, they are together a great deal. You know that thanks to your marriagebroking, Hugo Winstead is now Mrs. Masterman's attorney, is the counsel to Masterman Enterprises and is now, I believe, a director of Masterman Enterprises, as well as being chairman of my board of trustees, thanks to his marriage to Mrs. Winstead.

"All of this is due to you. I have no knowledge of the circumstances of your quarrel with Mrs. Masterman. I cannot blame you. She is the sort of woman whom I most despise. She has no love of art. She buys no paintings. That she is not now on my Board is only thanks to a happy series of actuarial accidents. She has given slightly more than nine hundred thousand dollars for the wretched new building—in installments, mind you—which is hardly the two million dollars reported in the *Times*; but the *Times* seldom gets its sums right, and that is, anyway, always the way it is because people like you make it that way and who am I, a beggar in the streets, thanks to that ridiculous building, to set the record straight? Now—and Sol, I know you so well—now you are entering a new horse, Mrs. Gudge, in this race, and tempting me because Mrs. Gudge might buy pictures and Mrs. Masterman won't, and you know I need pictures to live!" Crisp was practically shrieking.

Nick had watched Frodo's outburst building over lunch, helped along by the Corton and by two Calvados with coffee. Alcohol always greased the skids of unhappiness. He saw Sol try to deflect Crisp's excited torrent by gesturing for a quieter tone and raising his eyes toward Ralph, but it was hopeless.

"Don't mind Ralph, Sol. He has one thing I like and it isn't his brain. Just let me finish. You are making mischief, Sol. You know that in the end Calypso Winstead has the sole electing vote, thanks to the terms of the settlement, and that she will listen to me. Or to you. To one of the two of us, at least—and if I know you, you've dealt with that already. You have created a little war, Sol, and put it all on my head. You gave me Mrs. Masterman, Sol, and now you're putting up Mrs. Gudge, her despised sister-in-law, Sol, against her, and I will have to choose, if it comes to that. I am well past sixty, Sol. My museum has no money; two of my five trustees are philistines forced on Calypso by her husband to build up his legal practice. We are friends, but you have had a great deal to do with what has happened. You've never said so, but I have a feeling that you may have had something to do with promoting this new building. It's your sort of thing, Sol. Be that as it may, my life has turned to rubbish, Sol. Rubbish. No money for pictures. People like Ralph for amusement. Excuse me, my dear, don't look so pouty. And Mrs. Masterman to suffer to pay for cement. I love you, Sol, and I suppose I owe you my career, but to submit me to this, now, Sol, is very wicked—and very cruel."

Crisp turned away. He was wearing the pink tweed Inverness cape that was his trademark. Nick watched the cranelike figure, cape skirts aswirl like a Tiepolo cloud, pick its way up Madison Avenue. He turned back to Sol.

"That was pretty rough. Especially on top of a hangover. What the hell is going on with you and Frodo? Is Mrs. Gudge for real?"

"Mrs. Gudge, Nicholas, is for real. Don't you understand? The way the world has become, money is the only dependable reality. Her husband is a multibillionaire. Do you know what that is, Nicholas? A billion dollars? He could buy the Fuller a dozen times over; no, fifty times. He could write out a check for the entire contents of the Metropolitan Museum, with the Frick for dessert. That's money, Nicholas. Real money. That's power, and she looks to me to help her, and I look to you. Just think about that!"

He departed north, leaving Nick, still fluff-headed, to ponder it all for a moment and then to take himself home to bed, a spy novel, an evening alone and a series of three Alka-Seltzers. Only as he drained the last fizzing glass did he remember that he'd intended to probe Sol about Harvey Bogle.

It was never comfortable when the three of them ate together. Bubber knew that Caryn and Katagira didn't like each other; but he needed them both and wanted them around, and it was his money that supported them; so they sat and ate mainly in silence. From time to time, Katagira would inquire politely about Mrs. Gudge's trip to New York. It made Caryn uneasy. The Jap seemed to know a lot more than she did about New York and Greschner and the Fuller Gallery; the questions he asked said he did. She wasn't going to be pressed by this Jap, and she could see her husband wasn't really interested, as tired as he was, so she ducked answering. Besides, you didn't talk family business in front of the help; and Katagira was help—that was what Buford had promised her. Even if she couldn't fire him the way she had that sloppy Mexican girl.

Afterward, Katagira went back to his house and she and Gudge sat in the den and watched a tape of Super Bowl VI. She waited for her moment; then, when her instincts said the time was right, the propitious moment had arrived, she rose from the sofa and lifted her evening skirt, moving to place herself between Bubber and the big videotape screen on which Duane Thomas was going in for six against the Dolphins.

She had nothing on underneath. She saw his eyes go immediately to her crotch, to the thatch of red hair that was the banner of her domination of him. She stayed out of the sun, keeping her skin white as polished marble, to dramatize the brilliant auburn patch between her legs. She fancied it was as brilliant as a sunset over snowfields. It transfixed Bubber. She'd seen that the first time, back in that motel outside Odessa, when she'd taken off her clothes and realized that she was probably the only naked woman he'd ever seen—at least, the way he carried on. She saw the wetness in his eyes, and reached over gently to remove his glasses. Then she brought his face in between her thighs, letting him nurse there; he made small, weeping noises. After a time, she knelt and unzipped him, and took him in her mouth until he was hard enough to penetrate her. She lowered herself on him, watching him look down the length of his torso, seeing his eyes fix on the bright patch of hair where they conjoined. It never took long. Afterward, she pressed his face to her stomach, pillowing him against what she imagined were small concerns.

She didn't know he was dying. He'd never told her.

So it would be unfair to think her callous when she pushed his head back, looked down at him with the casual yearning of a child planning its birthday party and said, "Honey, what I really want is some real good pictures. Old pictures! All the best big houses up East are full of pictures. And honey, I've seen the ones I want. I want them more than anything in the world."

CHAPTER FIVE

When Nick awoke Sunday, his head was finally clear of Friday's disaster and life again seemed possible. Outside, pigeons were cooing. Seven o'clock on a gently sunny April Sunday: a rare time, entirely his own; it would be some hours before the claims and prospective calamities of the coming week would begin to assert themselves. All over New York, Nick knew, there were people for whom even these pleasingly unindentured hours quickly filled up with tension and trepidation, who wasted in apprehension the prosperity of an unencumbered morning; unlike his friend Sandler, Nick did not wear his nerve endings on his sleeve; he didn't fear solitude; a blank page or an unallocated hour in his appointment book didn't terrify him. He shuffled over to close the window, half-consciously taking a satisfied inventory of his bedroom walls and was pleased to see that the chevron of sky above the building across the street was a bright, fearless blue.

Nick washed and dressed; he was not one for sitting around unshaven. As he went downstairs to start the coffee water boiling and fetch the papers from the doorstep, he delightedly reminded himself that he was due to pick up Jill Newman at a quarter to one. He carried the papers into his small kitchen, dumping half the Sunday weight of the *Times* in the trashcan—the sections of it he ignored out of pure indifference: Real Estate, the Classifieds, special flyers for supermarkets and Korean industry. As always, he went first to the Business section to get it out of the way. His own trade required that he keep generally informed about the economy and whatever trends and items might bear on his clients. At the lower left of the front page he recognized a photograph of Harvey Bogle, heading an article which bore the title "BOGLE BUYS IN: WHAT NOW FOR SEACO?"

Standing at the kitchen counter while the coffee water heated, he drank a glass of grapefruit juice and read the piece.

> The thirty-ninth floor at 62 Water Street Plaza, home of the plush executive offices of Seaco Group, the nation's fourth-largest brokerage firm [the story

read], was in a state of turmoil Friday following the announcement just after the opening of trading Friday morning that Harvey Bogle, the real estate and industrial investor, would be filing a Section 13-D statement with the Securities and Exchange disclosing his ownership of 11% of the common stock of Seaco Group, following his purchase Thursday at the close of two major institutional blocks of the firm's shares.

The kettle started to wail. Nick poured out his coffee and took the paper into the front sitting room. As he switched on the reading light by the sofa, he noted approvingly that the little Cranach on the near wall was holding up just as well as he'd guessed it would when he discovered it six months ago, hiding under a thick coat of discolored varnish in an antiques shop a few paces from the Louvre. He returned to the paper.

Homer Seabury, the patrician chairman of Seaco Group, who has overseen the firm's dramatic expansion of the last two decades, from its relatively modest beginnings as Seabury, Lassiter Company, an old-school brokerage house serving a clientele drawn mainly from carriage-trade Manhattan, into a nationwide financial-services organization exceeded in size only by Merrill Lynch, E. F. Hutton and Bache, was unavailable for comment on the new development, although he was understood to be meeting with members of his top management. In any event, there is little doubt that Bogle's announcement was welcomed with open arms at Seaco Group, which is regarded by many as the last bastion of old values and old school ties among Wall Street's Big Four.

Harvey Bogle was also unavailable. Whether his acquisition of a substantial interest in Seaco will prove to be the prelude to the sort of management shaking-up with which he has been identified in the past, and which he is currently attempting at TransNational Entertainment Communications, remains to be seen. There is some feeling on Wall Street that Seaco lacks the creativity and momentum of its competitors. Certainly the firm does not appear to have exploited what most observers concede to be the most conservative capital base in the financial community in the same venturesome fashion as its competitors; although Seaco has effected a significant, aggressive improvement in its bond trading and corporate finance capabilities, principally by bringing in highly regarded younger executives from other firms, seasoned Wall Street observers feel the firm lacks impetus in such critical profit and business-generation centers as commodities margin lending, futures speculation, residential real estate brokerage, credit card mortgage lending, cancer insurance and the other innovative, "wave of the future" financial products in which its more inventive competitors have staked out major market shares. Only last month, for example, one large firm confirmed a long-rumored program for twenty-four-hour utilization of its many brokerage offices around the country by converting them after the close of trading into family counseling and group therapy centers.

Most observers expect a confrontation between Bogle, 55, and Seabury, 61, sometime next week. Before trading in Seaco was halted at 10:23 A.M. Friday, speculators had bid Seaco to $14.75, up $1.25 from Thursday's close. Assuming that Bogle holds approximately 1,000,000 of the approximately 13.5 million shares of Seaco outstanding, Friday's activity yielded him a paper profit of well over $1,000,000. Paper profits, however, are not generally thought to be Mr. Bogle's interest.

Because of the personalities involved, Nick read the story with more than ordinary interest. Judging from the last paragraphs, Bogle presumably had acquired his Seaco stock just hours before he, Nick, had stood with Bogle and Seabury at Greschner's dinner. And nothing had been said by either man that implied an awareness of where he or the other stood. A pretty tough game, Nick thought—just as close-mouthed and edge-seeking as his own, and for much bigger bucks. By his own rough calculations, Bogle must have at least $10,000,000, possibly more, tied up in Seaco. He liked that size bet; it would take a man with chips that big not to whistle in disbelief if and when he got around to talking price on the Rubenses.

He finished the story, which ended with a rehash of Bogle's recent deals, Seaco's current activities and the interesting fact, which Nick hadn't known, that Masterman United was already a 23-percent owner of Seaco stock. Bogle and Granada going head to head, Nick thought. An appetizing prospect for a man with a sense of mischief.

Enough of business. He let the section drop to the floor and picked up the sports section. For a moment, his mind drifted to Jill Newman—which made him feel like hearing music, something with a long, reaching line. He shuffled through his records; he thought Bellini would do nicely. He put Callas singing *I Puritani* on the turntable and settled back to the paper. When the great, soaring quartet at the end of the first act began, he leaned back, feeling as if he were bathing in the soprano's extraordinary, smoky voice. "*O vieni al tempio, fedele Arturo/Eterna fede—mio ben ti giuro* . . ." Eternal faith. He felt very romantic, very poetical. You're overreaching yourself, he thought, and, as the baritone and basso joined Callas, returned to his *Times*.

An hour later, when he had finished all that concerned him in the papers and had eaten a second croissant and drunk a third cup of coffee, and feeling himself content and quite satisfactory, he let his eyes roam around the sitting room. It was one of the three downstairs rooms in which he conducted 90 percent of his business. The maisonette had been formed by a joining together of the small corner apartments on the bottom two floors of a very good Park Avenue apartment building, with a separate entrance on the side street. To the left of the entrance hall was a large room occupied by Nick's secretary and by Sarah Ruggles, his research assistant. It was hung with the nineteenth-century Italian drawings. He was fond of collecting currently unfashionable schools, but it was getting harder and harder. The *ottocento* drawings were following on the heels of Barbizon landscapes, Neapolitan history paintings, Victorian watercolors and most recently, American pastorales: landscape drawings and watercolors by Kensett, Heade and Inness which depicted a dreamy light-bathed world free of traffic, pornography and smog. These were diversions for Nick. By and large it was perfectly understandable to him why history, before the market turned frenzied, had let these sink into deserved obscurity. They were works for which "pleasant" was the operative description; never "great"—or very seldom so.

But the voracious art market, always after new collecting fashions to promote, willing to overesteem in order to create new merchandise for its depleted counters, had seen to it that even these modest trifles had been priced out of proportion.

Across the hall from the office was the pale russet sitting room in which he sat. It had been furnished for comfort. Over the fireplace a tranquil Inness oil, of Sunday picnickers in the Roman *campana*, offset the hoarse Park Avenue traffic. A Watteau drawing and a Braque collage were hung on the fireplace walls, facing an early Riminese gold-leaf panel of *The Madonna in Glory* and a very free and exuberant landscape by Gainsborough hanging on either side of the door from the hall. The dark leather chairs and chesterfield sofa were fugitives from a famous London house which had been exiled into storage from Rostval Place in the course of Sol's relentless trading up of his own environment. They had been Sol's house presents, along with the respectably worn Persian carpet underneath. Through a door to the rear, the shelves that lined all four walls of his working library could be seen. The small window which opened on to the building's courtyard was now blocked over by shelves, so that the room gave the impression of an intimate sealed chamber—an atmosphere suitable for the hundreds of tall volumes that were arranged around the room—monographs on individual artists from Altdorfer to Zurbarán, along with a dozen shelves of general studies and encyclopedias. The only furniture in the room was a round table, two indifferent chairs and a velvet-covered picture stand. Nick never made much of a fuss when he showed pictures in the library. The books gave the necessary flavor to the occasion. Sometimes it seemed to Nick that the titles flew off the spines on the shelves and hung in the air like hummingbirds, turning the unpretentious room into an enchanted aviary alive with the past. It worked its magic on museum curators and visiting art historians, for whom the printed word or the comparative photographs were as central to artistic enjoyment as the color or form of an original.

The balance of the ground floor was devoted to air-conditioned storage space. Upstairs was where Nick lived. There were two large bedrooms with baths, a study, and a small third bedroom with an oversized closet, which Nick used as a small, working gallery in which were hung the most recent arrivals. He never showed pictures to clients there. On a large oak desk would be stacked the books and notes he and Sarah used in building up a brochure on a given work. On a smaller table lay the ultraviolet light he used to scan pictures for obvious restorations; more complex or troublesome scientific problems of condition, always a paramount consideration in the Old Master field, were resolved across town by the sophisticated electronic and radiographic equipment of Marco Carraccino's laboratory, not to mention the unique properties of the restorer's own genius. The room was painted dark gray, a color Nick happened to think worked well with most schools of painting. It would be to this room that the Rubens cycle would go on its arrival.

Sarah Ruggles had left a pile of books on the library worktable. Nick looked in vain for the two fat volumes of the definitive catalogue of Rubens' oil sketches. It was probably home in bed with Sarah, along with a mélange of yellow pads, color transparencies and slide viewers, a dozen or so other books. Sarah fancied herself a cross between Bernard Berenson and Colette, an imaginative, diligent student who believed that working in bed somehow improved the result. Nick knew from experience that there was no hurrying Sarah Ruggles, impatient though he might be for whatever she could dig up. "Dig" was hardly the word, he thought. Great researchers like Sarah used nine parts imagination and one part file work. They had a lively relationship with their subject; it was scarcely the sort of gray-haired, steel-spectacled dogwork that outsiders believed research to be. He picked up an old book, the pages starting to fall from the stained red binding. Oldenbourg's 1921 *Art Classics* volume of Rubens' paintings, now outdated by subsequent discoveries and the refinement of judgment as opinion and experience accumulated. In the index he found only three pictures listed as depicting Hercules subjects: in Leningrad, Dresden and Madrid. He turned to them; they were not remotely similar.

He replaced the book. There would be plenty of time to hunt up everything relevant, to compose the splendid brochures that he envisioned for the cycle. Although Sandler had indicated that the pictures might arrive on the morrow, Nick knew better. These days, everything took longer than anticipated. Eager as he was to see the rest of the sketches, and to get going, there was no point in becoming overheated. Besides, there was Jill Newman to consider. He was interested—although he had certain misgivings about her career. An intensely private person himself—most of the time—he felt a pricking at the thought that she spent her days invading—well, *exploring*—other people's privacy. Of course, he knew, that was what a lot of those people wanted, what they invited, craved. He'd just have to see; but for the moment, he was interested. Would she find him interesting?

Briefly, he considered his assets and liabilities. Assets: an extensive knowledge of European paintings and drawings. An inventory of same worth perhaps $4 million at market. A little over $1 million in the bank and at his broker's. A home for which some Arab would pay at least $3 million. A fluent knowledge of Italian; good French, better reading than spoken; the same for German; a smattering of Spanish. A dozen intimate and dependable friends of all ages. A general familiarity with English and European literature and music. The patronage and support of rich and important clients. Two loyal associates. A library. A reliable list of attractive women to spoil and bed of an evening. A loving disposition. That was about it. On the liability side: two million dollars owed to American Surety, or Transtate National Bank, as it now called itself. A stack of unpaid bills shoved into his top dresser drawer. No family to speak of. No loved one to be worshipped and sheltered. A consequent oversupply of lonely nights, even in the midst of company. A future without predictable passion or poetry. Very little enthusiasm for money and economics in a world that now appeared to think of nothing else.

On balance, a nice situation. In terms of the tangibles, well enough off. In terms of the spirit, solid, if dented, like very old furniture. For an instant, he stared up at the ceiling, wishing that its blank white surface would miraculously be replaced by a fantastic Tiepolo celebrating ancient naughty gods. Stop feeling lost, he muttered to the room at large as he reached for the spy story on the floor where his weary fingers had let it fall; stop feeling sorry and relax. In two hours you're having lunch with a beautiful, intelligent woman you intend to impress.

A half-sentient analyst peering into Nick's mind would have seen at once that here was a man all set up to fall in love. Loaded with gifts and no one to give them to.

Katagira and Bubber had worked most of Saturday morning. About eleven, Gudge had gotten tired. Then Mrs. Gudge had returned from her ride and that was the end of Saturday's work. Katagira had been happy to retire from the table and go back to his house, to work on his bonsai and, after a light supper which José left on a tray, to go over his notes. As was his habit these days, after praying to his ancestors, he read De Tocqueville for a half-hour before turning out the light.

He knew the book so well—it was almost forty years since he had first opened it—that even a random look into its pages would set his memory going:

> In the United States fortunes are lost and regained without difficulty; the country is boundless and its resources inexhaustible. The people have all the wants and cravings of a growing creature; and, whatever be their efforts, they are always surrounded by more than they can appropriate. It is not the ruin of a few individuals, which may be soon repaired, but the inactivity and sloth of the community at large that would be fatal to such a people.

Katagira, who was not in the least a humorous man, chuckled out of admiration at the Frenchman's insight. De Tocqueville had written this in 1835, when he was not yet thirty.

These days, Katagira often found himself talking to his household deities as if they were guests in his house. Well, Monsieur de Tocqueville, he thought, we'll see what we can do about the general sloth. Gudge had put the tools at his disposal to create something like a thunderstorm—a crackling, lightning-flashed hour that would seem, afterward, to have washed the murk and dirt from a sky now as clear as Creation. Katagira believed America was suffering from an infection, a painful but not invulnerable virus which had situated itself in the places from which the nation, public and private, was governed. He proposed to cure the patient with the virus itself. There would be convulsions and fever; some might pronounce the situation critical. But the patient would awaken—weakened by the ordeal, but sounder in limb and spirit. And, the way he had worked it out, Rufus Lassiter and Granada Masterman and that whole smug world of theirs, which his employer feared and hated, would have been hurt to the point of impotence.

As he had come to know Gudge, Katagira had seen how estranged from life the man was. Personal matters were not discussed between them, yet Katagira was convinced that Gudge secretly, perhaps unknowingly, hated his past. Still, the man was irrevocably alloyed with the Lazy G, and all that it meant and that it had been. The ranch and he were bonded as one flesh, which was why he hated Granada so: when she had induced her half-brother to turn over to her a small fraction of the ranch's property, she had not only caused him to betray a sacred trust, to earn his grandfather's eternal glare from beyond the grave; she had also tricked him into slicing off a bleeding chunk of his own body. That, Katagira saw, was how the man felt. The wound could be cauterized, the spiteful ghost pacified, by a vengeful exchange of flesh for flesh; and to these people, flesh meant money.

Well, it was Gudge's to dispose of, if that was his desire. A final victory over the past, perhaps. A gesture of scorn for a future that Gudge wouldn't live to see. How American, Katagira thought. The strangeness of what the country had become, even in his lifetime, was something he often pondered at night on his porch, watching the stars burn in skies as black as sables, or during his morning walks, with the air freshened by a wind blowing down across the tip of Oklahoma from the Colorado foothills and the grass making an endless, undulant vista. Americans fought both their past and their destiny: fathers struggled with sons and those sons with fathers and with their own sons; corporate presidents annulled their predecessors and begrudged their successors. It struck Katagira that Americans, already notorious for a self-defeating shortness of perspective, treated history like an unwelcome old relative, to be pensioned off if someone else could be found to bear, or at least share, the expense. It was a wasteful set of mind unknown in Japanese culture, this denial of both the dead and the uncrowned and unborn and pretense that nothing mattered but today and what today could touch. In Japan, time intermeshed; it was accepted that past and future were intimate to the present; that all levels of life interlocked; that the job and the man flowed together; that security had its price, productivity, and productivity its reward, security. How ironic, he thought, that this nation which had grown and flourished and defended itself and the world thanks to the mutual concern of its citizens, their sense of teamwork, their near-automatic acceptance of the other man's flank, needs and dignity, should be seen to have lost most of that in less than two decades. That was not the point toward which his household gods, Jefferson, De Tocqueville and the rest, had struggled; it wasn't for this that the whitened bone of his forearm now lay plowed under the bank of a stream near Cervaro.

His convictions had been reinforced by his years on the ranch. It had been a simple, comfortable life. The Panhandle retained a powerful sense of the worth and richness of the land, of the toughness it took to make life work. Katagira had walked the length and width of the ranch, often when a hot spell had baked and parched the earth like a pot shattered in a kiln. He had passed by gas wells and smelled the sourness in the air. Seen creeks swollen to man-swallowing force by a sudden rainstorm and fence posts tossed like needles by a tornado. All of this had enriched his feeling for the land and brought up in him, like a swell of distant music, the conviction that this was the heart of the country, the last redoubt sheltering the tattered principles that had midwived this splendid nation. Somewhat as Gudge did, but more self-consciously, he began to compare the tough, laconic men who worked the cattle or the drilling rigs with the chattering me-firsters of Washington and Wall Street.

That study had solved a question which had perplexed him when he had first come to the ranch. At a time when, by his lights, America needed to draw together, region seemed opposed to region, class to class, industry to industry. Here was this great nation, formed and fused in a spirit of interdependent community, which had stood against kings and emperors and kaisers, split up and fractionated by greed and resentment. The old sections, which had underwritten the nation's growth, resented the new and wealthy, the bumptious, ungrateful lands of the Sun Belt, which in turn despised those Northern brethren for their manners, their decrepitude and —above all, Katagira supposed—their pedigree. If patriotism should be the last refuge of scoundrels, he calculated, genealogy must be the last safe house for paupers. In the end, he saw, it didn't matter; it was all so much grist for his mill.

So he was prepared morally when Gudge had told him what he wanted. His heart was in his work, and his tactical advantages were considerable.

First, the Lazy G was a closed, private system. Time and rumor, more than anything else, had convinced the outside world that Gudges were enormously rich, but the conviction, Katagira knew, was based on an accumulation of suppositions and half-facts. It was fairly well established what the Lazy G embraced: the location and acreage count of its oil and gas leases; the production accruing to operations, like the North Sea, in which it was partnered with others; the names of its owned or controlled banks; the wattage and call signs of its broadcasting properties. A rough guess could have been made of the number of vehicles registered to the oil-well service companies. It was possible to make a count of the offshore rigs registered under flags of convenience. But that was where the guessing exhausted reasonable supposition. Apart from the reports the Gudge banks made to the regulation authorities with respect to their own assets, there were no figures available to the public on what the Lazy G empire was worth. Guesses ranged from $3 billion to $20 billion; in terms of hard facts, there was as much to be said for one end of the scale of conjecture as for the other. And the system had deliberately been made leakproof. The Lazy G maintained its own inventory of expertise: its own petroleum engineers, troubleshooters, regional accountants. It kept their exposure fractionated; the Tyler office knew East Texas; the Houma office knew Louisiana; the Djakarta office knew Borneo and West Irian. The decisions were made at the Big House, where the overall picture was guarded in Katagira's computers; the offices in the field followed orders and developed opportunities. The ranch passed out the working capital needed by its many satellites and was the sole judge of the results.

Which was the second factor underpinning Katagira's scheme, for within the orbit of the Lazy G itself, only Gudge and he had both an accurate count of the trees and knew the size of the forest. Gudge wanted it that way. So Katagira had created the information center that was the heart of the system. An automated office and data complex housed in the enlarged, remodeled basement of the Big House: computers, facsimile transmitters, printers and electronic reproducers, word processors and signature machines, interconnected into a single controllable system, fed by telex, long line and satellite with megabytes of information generated daily around the world, capable not only of massaging and manipulating data but of rearranging the structure of the system itself. The computers contained the entire legal structure of the Lazy G, the particularities of every one of its thousand legal entities, each shade and crosshatching of domicile, tax status, subsidiary ownership.

Katagira believed this to be his greatest accomplishment for Gudge. It had taken a year and a fee of $2 million for a team from MIT and the Harvard Business School to develop the program. Now, however, from the basement Katagira, by himself, could prepare all the relevant documentation to reincorporate a subsidiary, sell a rig or create and execute a service contract. While at any given time there might be several hundred legal *maîtres* and solicitors working around the world on local matters for various Lazy G units, there were none near its heart.

This suited Gudge just fine. He hated lawyers. Katagira, with his Texas law degree, was all the house counsel he needed; the machines in the basement, interfaced with four legal-data libraries, were all the law firm he needed. Katagira, less vehement, sympathized. While he didn't affect to despise lawyers or the legal profession, its prevalence in American business life had simply astonished him. He doubted the value of its prolixity; its cost he found appalling, particularly measured against what was received. Of every dozen corporate lawyers he met, perhaps two held any interest as persons. It wasn't this way in Japan. There were relatively few lawyers in Japan, where litigation was as demeaning commercially as taking bankruptcy, an occasion for absolute disgrace—or suicide. Perhaps, he had wondered, it was because in Japan everyone felt as if he had a stake, was a part, of the common enterprise. In America, one sued into and settled out of corporate treasuries, using anonymous, unbranded money that belonged to silent stockholders out there somewhere, fenced beyond the horizon seen from the tinted windows of executive office suites; owners, perhaps, but, because invisible and silent, owners in theory only.

So the machines kept track of the Lazy G's global arithmetic, updating the status of its twelve thousand accounting units, with digital codes representing items as diverse as revenue runs from one North Sea production platform and the entire financial operations of Panhandle Wireline Service's Overthrust Division, which employed a hundred trucks and four hundred people in the Rockies. Katagira spent at least two hours a day in the basement, watching the system grind out the daily status report and evaluation. The machines automatically directed the Lazy G's cash accounts. A series of interfaces with the Gudge-controlled banks kept the ranch's surplus cash, never much more than $300 or $400 million a day over and above the working balances for payroll, inventory and local taxes which the regional units maintained, in high-yielding short-term deposits at seventy-five banks, mostly unaffiliated, in the United States and Asia. Another $100 million, in round figures, was in hard metal: $30 million in gold in the concealed bunker out on the ranch's south section, which only Gudge, Katagira and Stumpy knew about; $6 million of columbium in a Rotterdam warehouse; $25 million in silver in Wilmington; $11 million in uncut stones—diamonds, rubies, emeralds—in a safety deposit box in Mexico City and so on.

In this room, without assistance, Katagira could execute and complete any transaction that suited the Lazy G's objectives or purposes. The machines could fabricate and certify legal or financial documentation. Thus he could produce and sign off on the financial statements of Indonesian or Arizona subsidiaries; make sales or transfers of leases covering thousands of acres in Texas or Wyoming; move the ranch's liquidity into and out of ninety-four clearinghouse accounts in seventeen countries. Each transaction would be appropriately, legally, signed, stamped, counted, bound and ribboned. The room represented the absolute state of the art in modern data and information technology.

The third and last great advantage which Katagira felt he enjoyed was that, apart from liquid assets, the Gudge interest owned no paper. The family was notorious for avoiding paper: no stocks, bonds, options or the rest. No identifiable investment profile. So when the time came for Gudge to make his messianic appearance on Wall Street, as was Katagira's intention, he would come as a stranger—although surely the most sought-after caller in the financial community's history. The paper merchants would slaver for a piece of the Gudge action. Association with Gudge, the way Katagira envisioned it, would be the prize of the day, the week, the month, the year. Of course, it must all in the end come down to greed, in its various colorings and disguises. Greed would stimulate imprudence, which would be justified as exposure based on trust, an ill-founded, self-serving assurance of the other man's honor and good intentions that would set the skyscrapers trembling.

The tools were thus at hand. It had been Katagira's task to figure out how to employ them. Which he believed he had done when he sat down on Sunday morning to go over the plan with his employer.

It was a sunny, hot morning when they got started. Hot enough, and suddenly so, to make the wet chill of the last month seem like a dim figment of a dream. Mrs. Gudge had gone off riding with Stumpy on the half-million-dollar cutting horse that Bubber had bought for her down in Denton. The two men sat at a table shaded by the ancient oak tree that had appeared to the first Buford Gudge as a divine sign for the location of the frame-and-adobe dwelling that in time would become the Big House. Bubber was in his shirt sleeves; Katagira, in the light cotton kimono which was his customary dress on the ranch; his few Hong Kong suits were used only for his regular monthly visits to Dallas and Houston for sushi and a whore. Bubber looked worse than at any time since Katagira had known him. The pallor brought on by his illness had been made more sickly yet by the strain of the sexual adventures through which Caryn had led him the previous evening. Not that he could do too much himself, as sick as he was, but it sure got him all fired up when she fooled with herself and walked around with no clothes. Love hadn't made quite enough of a fool of him to permit him to deceive himself that he was Caryn's first man, or even her fiftieth, but it had convinced him that he would be her last—so long as he could keep her happy by getting her the things she wanted. How lucky he was, he thought, to be able to possess her for money. To lay at her feet the gifts she wanted. Even those pictures she talked about. Belonged to some Italian or someone. Well, he'd get Greschner to help on that. Greschner knew about things like art. Maybe they could talk about it next week when he visited up there. Damn, he was letting his mind wander; with all these medicines, he found he had to pay closer attention.

Katagira had noticed Gudge's drifting concentration. He would have to go very deliberately. He watched Gudge's gaze drift across the field beyond the corral, tracing the trail that Mrs. Gudge and Stumpy had cantered along. When Gudge's eyes were once again turned to him, he began:

"We must start with credibility. In our case, the market's estimate of your wealth—even though no one in the outside world has more than the most hopeful guess as to the size of our assets; but they have fifty years of suppositions in their heads. And the fact that your family has shunned Wall Street for your entire history. That will make you entirely special when you suddenly appear as a potential investor in precisely the kind of paper you have always disdained. Wall Street likes to believe in itself, that its money-making magic must in the end entice even the most skeptical outsider. You will show yourself as receptive, after all these years, for nicely enumerated reasons, to their siren song. You'll be the Pied Piper. The man of respect. The big money that buys them the dream they've sold themselves. Are you with me?"

"I'm sort of following you," Gudge said.

"Let me be specific. I've spent enough time around Wall Street to know that there are always holes in the dike looking for large thumbs to plug them. Seaco Group is one. Through sheer luck, of course—but luck's something we'll accept. Mrs. Masterman has roughly twenty-five million, a good part of that sum borrowed at high rates, invested in Seaco. From what I read and hear, she has plans to integrate the brokerage business, managed by Senator Lassiter, whom she intends to install as chief executive, when the time is right, with her existing business, which is selling women—comforted or reassured by the company of the other women who participate in her home selling activities—products ranging from cosmetics to stocks and bonds. Like Avon Products. Or Tupperware. But Seaco is currently managed by the man who was its founder. Cofounder, actually, with Senator Lassiter. He'll resist Mrs. Masterman and the Senator. Out of pride, stubbornness and the desire to hang on to something he believes to be legitimately his. He can't bear the thought of someone else nursing his child. He's used to what he has. The thought that someone else might take it from him is intolerable, no matter how much money might be there for his stockholders, or for him. His mentality is invested in his position to the point of blindness, because he has no life outside of Seaco and suspects—probably rightly so—that new control will send him packing. Packing at a handsome severance, to be sure; several hundred thousand a year in consulting fees is usually the way it happens. But understand: Mr. Homer Seabury, the head of Seaco, like most other highly paid executives, knows that if he's dismissed in a change of command, he becomes an outcast. My guess is that he's suspicious—rightfully, perhaps—of his own competence. After all, the greatest effort of his life has been expended in getting to the top, and staying there, not in the immortality of his business. If Mrs. Masterman takes over, and installs her own people—Senator Lassiter, for example—where can Seabury go? The world of possibilities, such as they are, is filled with other men no less determined than Seabury to hang on to the prominence for which they've struggled and strained, no matter what and whom it costs."

He watched Gudge digest the notion. He'd expected as much. Gudge was an owner. His own money was on the line. Always had been. He wasn't used to the idea of other interests; he had no stockholders; his executives lived and died professionally by answering to the numbers developed at the Lazy G. He had a simplistic view of answerability: he hired and fired because it was his money at risk, not someone else's. The idea of faceless, distant, complaisant stockholders was something to read about in *Fortune*, curiously, but not to experience in real life.

It was important to keep Gudge engaged. Katagira shifted the thrust of his argument.

"Today, the fact is that face value counts for more than ever before. Let me explain. In the old days, if a man came to you and said he had a thousand dollars, you could ask to see it and he would bring his gold or coins and you could count them. Or his land in fee or under lease. If you were a banker, a man's face and talk were his credit.

"That's no longer true today, except in certain banks in this part of the world. For the most part, all that exists to prove the existence of wealth is an electrical impulse which a computer translates into a string of digits. The computer simply gives its word that so-and-so-many dollars are in an account. The computer makes deposits, transfers and withdrawals, issues credits and verifies balances. But it has no judgment or instinct. It cannot tell who is wicked or who is honest. That is its calamity.

"Now, it is well known that you, who are said to be the richest man in America, have never invested a penny in stocks or bonds, or any of the other instruments which the financial entrepreneurs have created to get and keep their hands on the nation's savings. How is it known that you are wealthy? The answer is that in truth it is not. Our computers contain estimates of the oil and gas reserves of our producing companies, but neither you nor I, nor the engineers who prepared the regional reserve reports, know that the oil and gas is there. Know it for certain—although scientific methods make it at least a fifty–fifty proposition. Yet you could walk into any of the largest banks in the world, because you are who you are, with a file of computer runs containing figures on reserves you claim to have, and borrow several hundred million dollars. The banks would hire their own engineers, who would study the stacks of paper which our engineers furnish them on flow rates, structures and the rest, and their own lawyers, who would accept our ownership of oil and gas leases and drilling rights documented and verified by our own computer room.

"It is all so much paper. It looks very convincing, do you see. All those numbers, those reams and boxes of documents will be hastily looked over by young, tired and bored accountants and attorneys for banks eager to lend us money because you are known to be rich. In the end, you see, it always comes to a question of trust, of credibility at the very top. Not that the documents don't help. We can exploit that credibility; the men who manage the markets have time after time been willing to take enormous risks—in silver, say—to accommodate the man they "know" is rich and who has a thirst for action. Action which looks prestigious, and is obviously highly profitable in one way or another."

He saw that Bubber was beginning to tire. Even at his hardiest, he had never been much for abstract thinking. Katagira, on the other hand, tended to dwell on the theoretical aspect of things; he was as much interested in the broader issues underlying the formulation of a complex strategy as in the practical, operational details of its execution. The plan he had formed for Gudge incorporated years of reflection on the American character. Its strengths, he believed, were as much in its philosophy and sociology as in whatever technical ingenuity it incorporated. But there was no point in exhausting Gudge with such matters. He paused while Gudge tugged a small pill bottle out of his trouser pocket and swallowed a handful of vari-colored capsules. Even the slight task of unscrewing the top was clearly draining.

"I don't want to bore you with a lot of theory," he continued diplomatically. "Nor with the small, practical details of execution, except as they involve you directly. For the most part you can leave the execution to me and the machines downstairs. After it gets going, it will mainly be a matter of bookkeeping. It is important now, given your health, that you devote your energy to Mrs. Gudge or whatever else you find enjoyable."

It was essential to involve Gudge personally. Katagira would have liked to deliver a Socratic discourse on the world as he saw it. He flattered himself that he'd developed a complicated, insightful view of the economic culture that was worth explaining at length. This might, would, be his swan song, he knew. But it needed Gudge's money and Gudge's involvement to make it work, and Gudge was a tired, sick man whose small energy needed to be husbanded.

"Seaco will be the lever," he said. "Homer Seabury's anxiety about his position will be the fulcrum. Which means we must find a way to enlist that anxiety, to make it our chattel, our tool."

For the next ten minutes he laid his logic before Gudge. The way to turn Seaco into their instrument would be to come to Homer Seabury's rescue, to deliver him from Mrs. Masterman's predatory intentions. Katagira had long since recognized as a cardinal principle of American corporate culture that any risk or tactic was justified in the effort to save a chief executive's job. He intended to entrap Seabury on this principle.

He would proceed obliquely. He had at one point considered the possibility of making a public tender for Masterman United; although Mrs. Masterman owned 33 percent of MUD, a tender offer for control of her company, at a handsome premium over its current market value, would still add up to less than $200 million, or about half the Lazy G's cash float. Not a lot of money. In the way these things worked out, however, such an approach would be crude and limited. An invitation to lawsuits, publicity, regulatory condemnation; worse, it would sacrifice the leverage which, deployed differently, the same $200 million could command. Leverage, the use of other people's capital, was the name of the game these days; not to exploit it, Katagira felt, would be a criminal abuse of his responsibility to Gudge.

"I propose we exploit the bond market," he said. "As the vehicle which will tie us to Seaco. The bond market today is a disaster. And has been for a long time, which means that the investment community, of which Seaco is a leader, is absolutely panting for the possibility of recovery. It's like a dog drooling over an empty dish. We'll feed it—or so it will seem. Then we'll go to work."

He talked for twenty minutes, watching Gudge carefully. From where they stood, he explained, no long-term bond that had been sold since the war, a period of nearly forty years, stood at its issue price. An investor who'd bought every outstanding AT&T bond when it first was offered had a loss in each of his twenty-odd purchases. Most of those investors, now, were institutions: banks, pension funds, insurance companies. By and large, the bond portfolios had been relegated to young people, while the senior men were out having fun in venture capital. Which meant there was a vast constituency of hope out there. Potential believers waiting for a bond-market messiah. And Washington waited in the wings. The President insisted that the failure of the investment community to pay 15 percent for twenty-year obligations when 18 percent was being paid for overnight money was a breach of faith with his idealized economics. The stage was set.

"We will begin with the bond market. Your money going into what is generally agreed is a desert will create waves of optimism. We'll use Seaco as our broker. Mr. Seabury, in particular. It will all flow from there."

He sounded confident, and he was. History was on his side: long lines of fact arrayed like dragoons, ready to gallop against papier-mâché redoubts. A strategy perfectly suited to a culture that saw every new day not as a beginning, but as a last chance.

Gudge looked at him. This is one smart Jap, he thought. The numbers didn't bother him, not the way Katagira explained them. Nor that it would destroy the Lazy G. Any way he looked at it, the nightmares would soon be over, forever.

A halloo from the field across the rail fence brought them back from their reverie. Caryn was cantering toward them. She was wearing a new couturier cowgirl outfit. Her hair floated behind her, under a designer sombrero. Bubber looked at her lovingly with eyes made watery by his medication. In the bright sunlight, she appeared to his blinking vision like a figure in a dream; he felt that he had seen this very scene before, had known the sight of a beautiful woman riding across this field, calling to him.

Nick strolled west through the carnival Central Park became once the weather turned warm. He was curious about the West Side; he supposed and hoped that it was a bastion of the old sense of neighborhood that once had characterized most of Manhattan. His old East Side haunts had long since yielded; where once a stationery store, his after-school hangout, had offered egg creams, pink rubber balls and a dozen daily papers, indistinguishable Koreans with carved grins sold bok choy, Bibb lettuce and passion fruit.

Crossing just south of the band shell, he was jolted out of his abstractedness by a near-collision with a mantislike black man attempting an entrechat on roller skates. His mind turned to Jill. Apart from the little Sol had told him, he knew nothing about her. Normally, he would have been better informed, would have done a little more research. Women were a risky proposition in the best of circumstances. First dates were like stepping onto the beach of an unexplored continent. The landing party might be driven off in a shower of arrows before a flag could be planted. Or a beachhead might be established; fires lit; sorties sent into the interior, to sound out the natives, allay their mistrust with trinkets and implements. Later explorations, perhaps an attempt at settlement, might prove the land barren or inhospitable. Then there would be nothing to do but retreat, weigh anchor and sail off, retaining only memories of strange, wondrous sights and markings. Or—the fantasy of all explorers—the party might be welcomed, draped in cloaks of peacock feathers and crowned with ivory and borne on gilded barges up smooth dark rivers into the heart of the country. Who could foresee?

It had been a long time since he'd been seriously in love. The last time had been with the spoiled daughter of a Wall Street magnate and had lasted for five years. Fragile and crazy, she had jerked him back and forth between polarities of manic infatuation and despairing exasperation. They had tried living together for a while—her place, then his place; they took a shack in Amagansett—but couldn't get their roots into each other. She went back to her former boyfriend, then left him and came back to Nick. Left Nick again. Nick was paralyzed by her; seeing this, Zauber had sent him to London to bid on a Castagno portrait for the Fuller, thinking that what his young protégé needed was a bracing dose of reality. When he got back—without the picture, which had been blocked for export by the National Gallery—he was free of her, he thought. He found her waiting in his apartment. Then there were three more years of fits and starts. She became pregnant; they were going to marry; she got an abortion. Finally, worn out with each other, their romance stripped to a husk of shopworn recriminations and useless memories, they had parted for good.

That had been a long time ago. Since then, Nick had been resting, getting his breath back.

He had decided to take Jill downtown to Bert's, just north of Greenwich Village. It was a reliable place, bright and spacious, its tables set thoughtfully far apart. Sunday was not a day to be crowded. Sunday's nerve ends were close to the surface. Bert's food was safe. Nick knew enough not to risk a first date on Szechuan food or *cuisine nouvelle*. Jill didn't strike him as trendy, in spite of what she did for a living—and again he wondered how he was going to handle *that*.

Well, he felt good. The long sleep and leisurely, solitary morning had restored the rhythm of his life. He was in a very good frame of mind when he left the park and crossed Central Park West.

His ring was answered by a small girl. About ten years old, Nick guessed. She had a very serious little face.

"Hello, I'm Nicholas Reverey."

"I'm Jenny." A perfunctory but nicely executed curtsy.

"Well, it's nice to meet you. How are you."

"Fine."

The child led him into a pleasant, sunny living room which looked across to the Sheep Meadow. It was furnished simply, for comfort if not for much money, and with a merciful lack of chic. After looking out the window briefly, Nick settled on the sofa. Jenny took a seat on the hassock on the other side of the coffee table.

"My mother said to tell you she'll be ready in about ten minutes."

"Wonderful. How old are you, Jenny?" He launched the routine he used with strange or unexpected children.

"Ten. Almost ten and a half."

"Where do you go to school?"

"At Morgan, across the park."

"How do you like it."

"Fine."

"Hello." Jill came out, even prettier than Nick had remembered. She was so much to his taste visually that he felt embarrassed to look at her so intently. He had meanwhile learned from Jenny that her father was dead, that she took piano and gymnastic lessons, that her hamster was named Gudget and that by and large the condition of her world and all that it encompassed was "fine."

"Get your coat, darling." Jill sounded careful. Nick recognized the tone. The protective mother exposing her child to another new man, another knight errant not yet made sure of. "Where are we having lunch, Nicholas? I've got to get Jenny to a friend's on East Sixty-fourth."

"No problem. I've made a reservation at Bert's. Downtown. We can zip across the park, drop Jenny wherever she pleases and be on our own merry way."

Jenny disembarked in front of a very imposing town house between Park and Lexington with instructions to be ready at five. It was a perfectly fair, if not very subtle, way of telling Nick that he had exactly four hours in which to make an impression.

In the cab, Jill said, "She's sweet, isn't she? She's my best friend."

"I wish I had one like her. A friend, I mean."

"Never married, Nicholas?"

"Unlucky in love. Is Bert's okay?"

"It'll do fine."

They were on the early side, so the restaurant wasn't yet packed. About half the tables were taken, and to Nick it seemed that at each was someone who knew or courted Jill.

When they had ordered drinks, he said, "Do you always have all these people waving at you? An occupational hazard?"

"Does it bother you? Don't let it. It's a phony thing. Celebrity seems to come cheap these days, and anyway, half those people are press agents. They probably think you're one too. But don't give it a thought, really. It isn't worth it."

"Jill!" They were interrupted by the oily man Nick recognized from the Fuller opening.

"Hello, Victor. Nicholas, you know Dr. Sartorian. Victor, this is Mr. Reverey."

"Mr. Reverey." He gave Nick a throwaway simper. "Jill, darling, I have something so exciting for you. Will I see you tonight?"

"Tonight?"

"At Gratiane's, darling. She's got Grisha and Zbig and Mischa and Zog. The Polish evening, darling, the Polish evening. We must do what we can!"

"Not for me, Victor. Sunday is Mother's Night Home for me." She turned to Nick and smiled. "And every other night I can manage."

"Well, then I'll call you tomorrow, darling. Ciao." He danced away.

"Who, in God's name, is that? He was hanging around you the other night. Should I know who he is?"

"His name is Victor Sartorian. The Society Shrink—or the Park Avenue Pusher, depending on what sort of therapy you require. Freud; cocaine; uppers, downers. He's dexterous with them all. A deceptive fellow. You'd think he was gay, the way he prances about, but one hears he's a great one with the ladies. If that couch of his could talk . . ."

"How can you bear having to spend time with people like that?"

"I was afraid that would come up. It's not my favorite subject or my best angle. It bothers you, doesn't it?"

"I'd be a liar if I didn't say it gives me pause. I don't know why, really. As you say, most of these people want it."

"They seem to." She looked closely at him. "It really does bother you, doesn't it?"

He felt like a dope, to be so transparent. What conceivable right had he to put her through a wringer?

"I guess it does. It just seems, well, like it gives you a proxy on someone else's life. I don't give proxies."

"Nor do I. Let me ask you. Do you read my column? Closely?"

"I see it."

"That's no answer, but we'll let it go. I realize that what I'm going to say may sound like angels dancing on the head of a pin, but you'd better realize that you're not the only one who has to live with what I do."

"I don't have to live with it." Not yet, he thought.

"Well, your mournful, intent look makes it seem that way. Anyway, the answer in a nutshell is that it pays well—I don't know if you've looked at tuitions or rents lately—which is one thing, and I keep it as clean as I possibly can; which, if you'd read it closely lately, is very clean indeed."

Nick felt caught, which made him contentious.

"How so?"

"I write only about clothes and jewels and parties that I'm asked to write about. Sure, I don't like dishing this stuff out while half the country's on relief, but the only people who read it don't care anyway. You may gather I'm not very proud of my audience, and I'm not. Look, Nicholas, it's what I do. I don't think it's great, but it pays well enough—I can't sit around and write delicate ladies' novels with titles like *Fierce Porcelain;* I can't afford to—and I can't take a full-time job, a man's job . . ."

"Why not?"

"Jenny. This lets me stay home with her. Anyway, what I do is what I do, no more, no less. I don't think gossip's great. But who wore what dress somehow seems more—well—decent than who's been sleeping with whom. Although I get a lot of that—which I just bury unprinted. I don't make a big thing of it. No quotations at the head of each column from Shaw or Oscar Wilde to inveigle people into mistaking me for an intellectual. That's really all I can say."

And what could he say? Bread alone might not do the trick in life, but it was necessary. What had Berenson said? That he'd sold his expertise to support his scholarship; that Spinoza had polished lenses to buy time to think. How could he argue; who was he to argue? Besides, he sensed that there was so much more of her to explore.

He grinned—bested—and spread his palms upward.

"You've made your point. I can't think there are many noble occupations left in this world, anyway. And you've got the White House on your side; all they seem to care about is clothes and menus."

She laughed, marking a turning. It was clear the line of conversation needed deflecting.

"I do draw the line somewhere." A mysterious statement.

"Jill!" Another interruption, this time by a graying young man with anxious eyes and a grin like that of a chimpanzee in the ape house in Central Park. Jill didn't bother to introduce him. The intruder gibbered on for a minute or two, talking pretentiously about the world-shakers he claimed to know, and the resorts he'd visited, and then left as abruptly as he had come.

"Now," said Nick, "there comes a time when decency must prevail! What, in God's name, was that?"

"That was Mati. He's one of us in the gossip tribe. He writes chitchat for a Paris weekly. Hasn't got a brain in his head and can't write a straight sentence. All he craves is to be taken seriously. It's so pathetic it's really quite sweet, in its way."

"You meet some wonderful people in your world, don't you? That guy belongs in a zoo. Actually, I want to get off this gossip thing too. Sol tells me you're a whiz with numbers."

"Quick is all. I can multiply, divide, add and subtract in my head. It's just something I was born with. I did free-lance work for an accounting firm once; helping out on rich people's tax returns. I hated it. I haven't got much of a head for business."

"Who were you married to? Sol said you were a widow."

"You must have put poor Sol through the wringer about me. I was married to a man named Bobby Manship. He may have been at Harvard around your time."

"Who said I went to Harvard?"

She smiled slyly. "Dear, dear Nick, surely you know that Sol's got more than one side to his mouth."

"That's another point for you."

"Anyway, Bobby and I were living in Denver. He was trying to get started in the oil business, and then one morning, while we were having coffee, he just opened the window and jumped out. I was carrying Jenny at the time; it's a miracle I didn't lose her."

"Why'd he jump?"

"The same old answer. Money. His trustee wouldn't give him what he needed. That trustee, incidentally, grew up to be Hugo Winstead, the one who was queening it all over the Fuller last Thursday."

"I barely know him. He's supposed to be an awful S.O.B."

"He is. But he's got a wonderful woman—and a saint—for a wife."

"What next?"

"Well, I came back to New York after Jenny was born; I couldn't go back to Missoula, although they wanted me to, and I fell in with Mickey Greschner, so I met Sol and then one thing led to another. I'm surprised we've never met, although Sol and I are, frankly, more friends at a distance."

"Sol likes to keep his treasures in separate compartments. How about some food?" He wanted to avoid talking about Mickey Greschner, the son Sol hated and for whom Nick was perhaps a surrogate.

They ordered. When she resumed, he could see that her mention of Mickey Greschner had caused a rush of memory. It surprised him, although he was pleased to be offered her confidences.

"Mickey was an emotional scavenger, Nick. One of that type that hangs around waiting for new widows and divorcées to fall off the branch. He picked me up, got me a little drunk, took me to his place, made me cry and got me into his bed. I know now—I should've known then—all he wanted was notches on his gun; it still smarts when I think of it. I've learned since then. I watch out for the gun-notchers. Mickey was one. Winstead's one. Sartorian's one. Are you?"

"I don't think so. Honest Injun." He tried to make it light.

"Only time will tell. Anyway, Mickey's dead. So's Bobby. I'm bad luck, Nicholas. Sure you don't want to get up and leave?"

"You must be crazy."

"It's debatable which of us is. Now: it's your turn. I'm famished—for food and poetry—so tell me about Italy, about Florence. Make me dream a little while I eat."

So he told her of his two luminous years in Florence, living at La Pergola helping with the preparation of *Quattrocento Rambles*, Sanger's summation of a lifetime's love and study of Italian painting. Of the days spent in Max Lefcourt's old wing-fendered Citroën, creepingly solving the narrow cobbled streets of a score of hill towns; about peering along a flashlight beam at frescoes high in the ruined choirs of old churches; of tea with ancient countesses with transparent skin who talked softly of D'Annunzio; of Arezzo, Rimini, Lucca, Lovere, and a hundred other towns. But above all, he talked about Florence. About late afternoons in the Piazza Repubblica, with a brass quartet honking in the hot afternoon, reading the *International Herald Tribune* to catch up on the Red Sox; about dark winter days, when the Arno flowed scummy under a veneer of ice and the light was as gray-green as olives; about driving across the city with Lefcourt and Sanger to pay a courtesy call on I Tatti, Berenson's old villa, now attached to Harvard, and afterward stopping for an early pasta supper at the little restaurant in the Casa di Dante and Sanger telling scoundrelly anecdotes about Berenson, who had sold his great and esteemed name for money and how maybe, seeing what Berenson had done for Italian painting and what I Tatti represented, it had been worth it. About the first tasting of young Chianti each year. About the girl who lived above the leather shop in the Via delle Caldaie, near Sto. Spirito, Brunelleschi's perfect church. About being twenty-eight years old in Florence, fancy-free, with a little bit of money and a soul full of Dante and Botticelli and odd bits of songs from San Remo played by a squally little band.

He watched her savor his descriptions, turning his words into images on a screen inside her head. To his surprise, he found her reaction made his own telling of the past more vivid for himself.

As they drank their coffee, she said, "How about a walk? If you get the check and we start now, we ought to be able to make it uptown by five to pick up Jenny."

"How about a taxi instead and come and look at some pictures at my place? No seductive moves planned, I promise. That's fifty blocks of walking you're talking about. And that bottle of Corvo has made me woozy."

"I'd like to walk." She closed the subject.

More than the wine had him woozy. There was something else going on, that emanated from her. It had been coming on him. He wanted to stay close to her. She wasn't like anyone he'd known. He looked at her and nodded.

"If you insist. You are responsible if I die."

They walked uptown, passing through Rostval Place. Sol's house loomed dark and seemingly uninhabited, although they both guessed Sol was in there somewhere; the steps of the Fuller were lively with sight-seers. Then through Gramercy Park and up along Lexington Avenue until they finally found themselves before the house where they had left Jenny. It was two minutes to five.

"Thank you, Nicholas. Don't look so sad. I want to see you again. Yes, I do. And don't seem so surprised. I told you that I'm a slow worker. But look at it this way. You know quite a lot about me now. You have all my information. I have to know I can trust a man with that before I can trust him with me."

She leaned forward and kissed his cheek. It was like the touch of a butterfly's wing, and felt as hot as an ingot.

As he headed up Park Avenue, Nick pondered the afternoon: her beauty, her intelligence—and her contradictions. She was still strangely vulnerable for a veteran of the kind of domestic carnage she'd seen and suffered. He'd have to watch for that; he knew enough of women to be aware that vulnerability of that kind never quite went away. It lurked, waiting, and if you did something to bring it forth, it burst upon you, shrieking, dagger raised.

But that thought passed in the headiness he felt. Young and romantic: that was what he was. He'd ask her to call him Nick.

The rest of the Von Gonzálezes' guests were downstairs in the kitchen. Over lasagne, the disgraced former Secretary was explaining to the genial columnist from *The Nation* why it had been necessary to starve black children in Detroit in order to rebuild the working capital of Arab-owned corporate farms in the Midwest by subsidizing grain sales to Russia and Cuba. Gratiane buzzed around, shuffling plates, making certain of a proper balance between socially significant conversation and praise for her food and chintz.

Victor Sartorian had caught the high sign from Massimo and followed his host, who was clearly *in extremis*, upstairs to the master bedroom. He found Massimo sitting on the edge of the flatbed press that Gratiane had converted into the Von Gonzálezes' bower of what passed for bliss.

"Victor, darling, I simply must have a shot. Such a week. Do be a dear and give me a little trip to paradise. I've got a teeny-weeny late date. Oh, such a week, such a life!"

Sartorian reached into his pigskin shoulder bag and took out a small bottle, three-quarters full of a poisonous-looking orange liquid, and a disposable syringe.

"Of course, dear boy. Nothing like a touch of Victor's Vaccine."

He drew some of the liquid into the hypodermic. It was his own mixture, combining vegetable proteins, so he said; a little cocaine; a healthy charge of Dexedrine and a soupçon of muscle relaxant. It was his universal remedy, producing a leaping feeling of well-being, intense sexual energy and, which some patients found to be a most helpful side effect, a sensitization and expansion of the sphincter. He administered the dose to his patient's right buttock.

"Ouch!" came the girlish exclamation. "Oh, Daddy, that stings so. Be a good Daddy and kiss it well."

Sartorian, whose loose construction of his Hippocratic oath had made him a millionaire and the confidant of the famous, was only too happy to oblige.

Jill and Jenny had watched a Disney picture, eating a pizza off trays in front of the television set. Now she declared bedtime; washed the plates while Jenny got into her nightgown; shared her daughter's prayers; cooed over Gudget, who was spinning happily away on his treadmill, and kissed her daughter good night. She left the light on in the hallway and went back to her study, a converted laundry room off the kitchen. She unlocked the door and flipped on the light.

The room contained a desk with a big Remington Noiseless typewriter, a cheap wooden bookcase with a cassette player on top of it and, in the corner, a Lexitron word processor which was wired directly to the typesetting computer at the Union City plant of the company that published *Pritchett's*, the financial weekly. The cathode-ray screen slowly came alight, a line of print along its upper edge signaling that it was ready. She took a minicassette from the small recorder attached to the unlisted telephone on the worktable, which was littered with financial journals, Wall Street newsletters and brokerage reports and corporate prospectuses and statements. She snapped the cassette into a small transcribing unit, put her feet up on the table and listened, occasionally making notes on a yellow legal pad. The voice that came from the cassette belonged unmistakably to Solomon Greschner.

She played it through twice, drawing lines and arrows between notations on her pad, frequently adding a brief note. When she had finished she picked up another cassette and played it. This time her own voice came to her—a week's worth of notes to herself. Finally, she picked up one of the prospectuses on the desk and studied it. The pages had been underlined; on the financial statements she had circled a number of items.

She heard the second tape through twice, making more written notes and turning once or twice to the prospectus. She turned off the transcriber, tore off a fresh sheet from the yellow pad and made an outline. After a few minutes' further reflection, she settled in front of the word processor, and typed:

> THE BOTTOM LINE/by Robert Creighton . . . This column has been advised that North Kansas Gas Producing Company, which has had its troubles raising money for its projected pipeline from Ardmore to Wichita, may have found a helping hand at the Certified Guaranty Bank thanks to the timely intervention of a friendly director of both concerns. The $200,000 question is, will next year's North Kansas proxy statement reveal the fee paid to this worthy fiduciary for persuading the Certified to take on this very shaky loan? . . . Fans of creative accounting are advised to consult the prospectus for the forthcoming offering of Mismer Hermeneutics, due next week at what spies tell us will be a very fancy price-earnings ratio. Fancier, we think, if one scrutinizes the company's financial statements. To this student, at least, the year-to-year growth of the amount carried as "Deferred Development" suggests that Mismer has been hemorrhaging cash at about twice the rate indicated by its reported profits. . . .

It took her an hour to finish. She ran the text through twice on the machine making a few small changes, watching the cursor dance across the screen, altering paragraphs to get it right. When she was satisfied, she tapped a key and listened while the machine made the scraping noises that indicated her text was on the way to Union City.

She crossed the small room and sat down at the manual typewriter. She riffled through a notebook, rolled a sheet of paper into the machine and started to type with the relentless assurance of a legal secretary.

"THE PARTY LINE/by Gilberte . . ." she typed.

> Thanks to the generosity of GRANADA MASTERMAN, in a ravishing sequined number by Ernesto, le tout New York turned out Thursday evening for the opening of the Fuller Institute's shining new Annex. Among those seen in the glittering crowd, which included everyone who is IN, and a few OUTS who bribed an invitation to the year's best party, were CALYPSO and HUGO WINSTEAD . . . he's the razor-smart lawyer who heads the Fuller board; she's the last living FULLER . . . and ARDEN MAYPOLE, everyone's nominee for the greatest painter in New York; the TARVER MELTONS . . .

It took her another half-hour to finish two pages. No changes were necessary. She clipped the pages together, put them on top of the typewriter and crossed back to the word processor. The CONFIRM GOOD COPY motto glowed eerie green from the screen. She turned off the machine and the lights and locked the door behind her.

After a hot bath, she went to bed. As always, her last thought before dropping off was a prayer of vengeance on the head of Hugo Winstead. Except that it was interrupted, for just another flash, sharp and quick as a pinpoint, of pleasure, as she remembered her lunch with Nick. She knew he was bothered by Gilberte's vocation. What rational, sensitive person wouldn't be? She was herself. She found herself thinking the forbidden thought, wishing she could tell him about Creighton. Creighton was the ethical counterweight to Gilberte. Hidden behind Gilberte's fluttering skirts and bubble-headed gabble, Creighton let her live with herself.

CHAPTER SIX

Making certain that everything was as it should be at the table set for six, where Mrs. Masterman regularly held court at lunch each Tuesday, Luigi, the proprietor of Dove Sono, reflected with pride on his success. He looked around the gilt and pale gray velvet dining room. He was one of the lucky ones—to have been able to persist in a fickle, faddish city like New York, depending for his living on anxiously modish people fearful about putting a foot wrong; of being seen—or worse, publicly recorded—in a place the arbiters had ruled to be no longer smart or in fashion.

Thankfully, the restaurant seemed to have settled down into an ongoing love affair with the kind of crowd for which a restaurant owner made a dozen rosaries. He had been lucky to have Mr. Greschner, whom he had always taken care of when he was a captain at a restaurant down the street, as an early patron of Dove Sono. Greschner, along with some other old customers, had helped fill the place in the early days. And Greschner had made certain that the market became aware, and was kept aware, of Luigi and his restaurant. Greschner had brought in that pretty Mrs. Newman who wrote the column that all these women read. She was very good about mentioning the restaurant and, unlike some others, didn't think that a mention in her column gave her the automatic right to use the restaurant like a free, private cafeteria. Of course, on the few occasions she had come in—with her daughter for dinner before a film, in the early evening when, apart from one or two elderly couples, there was no one in the restaurant—Luigi always tried to pick up her check, but she would never let him. At least, she kept the pâté and the bottle of champagne he sent at Christmas and on her birthday. Luigi was sensibly suspicious of saints in a secular world. He knew how expensive his restaurant was. Luigi's prices had bought a house in Sands Point, a Mercedes and a mink for Mrs. Luigi and a prep-school education for his son.

Greschner's advice had been sound: "Just keep arrogance out of the dining room and turmoil out of the kitchen, and you'll find your niche,

Luigi. Concentrate on the women at lunch and the men at dinner. The idle women with rich husbands who travel are the best. You'll often get them for two meals a day, and they have absolutely no idea of money. Certain people should be permitted charge accounts. I'll send you a list. Add ten percent to their monthly bill to cover the cost of money; they can be a little slow in paying, sometimes."

Greschner had sent him a list which Luigi was astute enough to recognize as the current roster of Greschner clients. But Luigi was also grateful to have been included so immediately in the Greschner apparatus. Some people might have wondered at the importance of a man like Greschner, would have quarreled with the value system that had produced him. But Luigi didn't make automobiles or pour steel. He sold 15 cents' worth of spaghetti mixed with 80 cents' worth of blanched vegetables and olives for $14 a portion as Pasta Petrarca, but after he figured in labor, laundry, breakage and rent on approximately twenty-five hundred choice square feet of Upper East Side real estate, he still had to look to the bar and wine list for his profit.

"Luigi!"

He was jolted from his musings by Mrs. Masterman's Panzer-like arrival.

"Mrs. Masterman." He led her to the table. She was invariably the first to arrive. He signaled his barman to mix up a Negroni; having studied Mrs. Masterman over the last half-dozen years, he'd concluded that her unobserved cocktail was a confidence-builder, a little something to suppress her natural, shy awkwardness. She was a powerful woman, he knew. He'd read much about her in the papers. She didn't wear her influence shyly—or easily.

"Ah, the flowers look quite nice, Luigi. And so do you. Very handsome." From a smallish purple tote she took six small, cubical packages wrapped in glossy paper the same color as the tote; she placed one at each plate. Including her own, Luigi noted. As always. It was a strange habit.

"Fresh for you, Mrs. Masterman. The flowers I mean, of course, naturally." He chuckled; if she found anything to smile at in his little joke, she didn't show it. She had little humor and less small talk, Luigi thought, although he'd observed that she talked mostly about small things and even smaller people. Clothes and parties. In most ways, though, she was what his adopted country called "all business." Pleasure was like a business to her, he thought; a matter of planning, financing and systematization. On Mondays, Luigi knew, she ate with her operating executives in her private dining room on the forty-eighth floor of the Amalgamated Tower and reviewed her business; those lunches were catered in weekly rotation by Dove Sono and five other Manhattan restaurants. Wednesday mornings were spent at one of the half-dozen advertising agencies that handled the constellation of Masterman accounts, so Mrs. Masterman was generally given lunch afterward at one of the places, like the Four Seasons, that did a media business. Thursday was the weekly Masterwoman recruitment-and-welcome lunch in the company cafeteria at the New Jersey training center. On Friday, Luigi would put up a picnic, which the lavender Rolls-Royce would pick up at eleven forty-five exactly; it would be consumed by Mrs. Masterman—and whatever number of weekend guests her personal-affairs secretary had specified—in the course of either the two-hour drive to her Southampton summer house or the three-hour flight in the lavender Gulfstream II to West Palm Beach.

He had no doubt that the rest of her schedule was equally rigid. She needed the backbone it gave her life. That, and the assurance that her hours would be filled with company. She could exist no other way. Granada Masterman would no longer expose herself to long, solitary stretches waiting for the break that would give her intelligence and ambition full play. To fulfill the mission set for her by her dreams, she needed money. It could come only from the Lazy G. That was what her grandparents had drilled into her, when they were still alive and she still lived with them in the dreary fake-Tudor house in Pelham and was working at Bloomingdale's in Stamford. She would have felt that way, even without urging, anyhow. Not even the memory of her stone-souled stepgrandfather, who had glowered at her as if she were something obscene, could take anything away from her memories of the spaciousness of the ranch, the ponies, the hot sun, the companionship of the Mexican women in the compound, the sun-washed cleanliness of the air she'd felt when she was briefly a Gudge. Of her mother. Murdered, she'd guessed, but way too late for her to do more than she had; murdered, as had been hinted at in that one letter she'd had from Bubber's father before he'd died.

The worst part after that had been when Esmé, who'd been her best friend through grade school and Pelham High, had married Harvey Bogle, who was a rich boy from Port Chester, and moved away with him to Manhattan. One day they'd been equals. The next, it seemed, Esmé had a new mink-paw coat and a Park Avenue address and Granada was making $75 a week selling cosmetics.

For thirteen years she had worked steadily and hard, moving from cosmetics into clothes so that she no longer had to cater to shop people like herself. Her suburban customers came to depend on the big woman with the comforting, unchallenging plainness, who possessed fashion instincts unexpected in that sort of person. It was a gift of sorts, and so she was accorded the condescending sympathy which provincial female society reserves for those sisters unlucky enough to lose their money or misguided enough not to have made it, found it or married it. She became part of that substructure of presumptive "ladies" who used their taste or ability to ice the cake of the wealthy: the saleswomen in smart shops; the party planners and invitation addressers, and the other gray figures hovering in the background of visible society. It was decent, genteel work, but it did more to lock in her bitterness than the affronts and oversights which might have been her lot in more bumptious surroundings. Wounded more by the kindness of women than by the cruelty of men—and there were few enough of those, God knew, for a woman like Granada in a place like Stamford, where she now lived in two furnished rooms, her principal company the flickering screen of the television set, hanging on, waiting for the day the papers would bring the news that she knew must someday come.

Finally, in mid-1971, at the newsstand on her way to the bus stop, she had seen a one-column headline in a lower corner of the front page: "RICHEST TEXAN DEAD AT 76." The story below the picture of Buford Gudge II said nothing that was new to Granada. She'd been keeping up on the Gudges, on her days off, at the New York Public Library. As she expected, the story reported that Buford Gudge IV—her half-brother, Bubber—was now the sole proprietor of interests and assets thought to aggregate several billion dollars. There was a picture of Bubber on an inside page, squinting dimly into the camera while attending what appeared to be a livestock show.

She had no idea what sort of man Bubber had become. Her only memory was of a jolly baby who'd been fun to tease. The time had come for her to try to claim something to which she felt entitled. To be compensated for her mother and her soured childhood and youth. No more than that.

She slept on it. The next morning she called in to tell the store she'd be out for a couple of days, dug into her savings and flew to Amarillo. In her purse, creased and hand-stained but still legible, was the letter from her stepfather. It was her only card. She rented a car and drove north on Route 287, crossing the Canadian River and on into Moore County, using the road map and taking the faster way around Lake Meredith, until she turned east on Route 152 at Dumas. She drove carefully, plotting and replotting her strategy, formulating her pleading. Finally, she turned into the narrow road that led to the front gates of the Lazy G. To her misgiving, memory didn't rush upon her as she approached the ranch, which surprised her, so proprietary had her memories of the place become. But it was as she vaguely remembered it. The plains spread wide, topped with rises like the crests of waves; there seemed to be fewer cattle than she had expected; the sightline from the highway was broken periodically by evidences of the presence of industrial man: oil derricks; pumping stations; power lines.

She drove in through the gates. Abreast of an airstrip on which three planes were parked, she passed a small caravan of Cadillacs, including an undertaker's hearse, making for the highway. Those would be the family's few contacts with the outside world. Perhaps the president of the Amarillo bank that had sent the monthly checks to her grandparents until she turned eighteen.

She pulled into the gravel circle in front of the Main House. Now everything seemed, suddenly, to have a throbbing immediacy. It had been twenty-odd years since she'd seen any of it, yet it was all as fresh as the moment. The big oak off to one side of the house looked sturdier than ever. Was the family . . . ?

Her ring had been answered by a squat little cowpoke. He was obviously mystified at finding a woman on the doorstep.

She didn't give him a chance to say no.

"Would you please tell Mr. Gudge—Mr. Buford Gudge IV, that is—that his sister, Granada Masterman, is here to pay her respects and condolences." The look she gave Stumpy was hotter by at least ten degrees than the expression she used on straying customers discovered in Lord and Taylor in the course of one of her fashion reconnaissances. Stumpy looked as if a skewer had been hurled through his brain. Mumbling about seeing about it, he closed the door in her face.

He returned in ten minutes.

"He ain't seein' anyone. Least'v all you. He ain't got no sister. That's what he said to tell you. You better get goin', lady. You got no place here, ma'am. You ain't kin here no longer. You just gonna get in all kinds of trouble."

She wasn't surprised. She would have guessed that decades of his grandfather's companionship and guidance would have dried up Bubber's human feelings. She sighed and reached into her purse, taking out a folded sheet of paper. It was a photocopy of the letter Bubber's father had written her months before he'd died.

"Show him this. Tell him I just want to talk a little. Just the two of us. Brother and sister." Stumpy disappeared again behind the closed door.

She went back to her car and waited.

A half-hour later the front door opened again and Bubber came out, crossing hesitantly toward her, tailed from a few yards by Stumpy, who now had a revolver tucked in his belt. His appearance surprised her. Tall as he was—close to six feet four, she knew from her newspaper reading—and obviously heavy, he just didn't seem very substantial, as if the bones were loose under his skin. His face looked puffy and uncertain; that could be grief, she expected, although on this ranch, that kind of caring emotion had always been in short supply. Mostly, she thought, Bubber looked scared. Nervous at being out alone in the world without his grandfather. Well, that was not her problem.

He put his hands on the windowsill and leaned toward her.

"How you doin', Gran?"

"I'm all right, Buford. It hasn't been easy; you can probably see that, looking at me." She had no illusions. She was a plain, unfeminine woman, with little sex appeal or softness. Her strength and the focus of her feeling about herself was in her brain.

"What d'you want from me, Gran? We took good care of you, you got to say that. And didn't have to, neither. And what's *this* about?" He thrust toward her the piece of paper she'd given Stumpy.

"That's a letter your father wrote me, Buford. About our mother. Our poor, dead mother that neither of us was given much of a chance to know. How'd she die, anyway? Until this letter came, I always thought it was disease down in Mexico. Diphtheria, I think they told my grandparents. Now this letter says maybe something else happened."

"So what's that prove, anyway? What d'you want from us? Granddaddy always said watch out for you Eastern people. Guess he was right—not that it matters anymore. What d'you want?"

"What I want, Buford, is to be in business for myself. I'm good at business, but I can't wait on people anymore. I'm thirty-seven years old. I don't have a college degree. I'm not much to look at. Nobody loves me; I'm not very lovable, I know. I'm ambitious. I want to have some money, some fine things of my own. I'm tired of watching fine things walk out on someone else's back; tired of wanting, wanting, wanting. I'm jealous, Buford. Envious. I admit it."

She could see he wasn't moved.

"You want some money—ain't that it?"

"Money, yes; but enough to start a business of my own with. I've got an idea or two. Or maybe some little business you already own, something I can build on. You've got so much, Buford, and I *am* your sister."

"You ain't nothing. Why don't you go on back East? We'll send you a check, Gran. Couple thousand a month? More? First of every month, regular?"

"No, Buford. I'm at the end of this rope. I want something I own. Capital or a business; but I must have it."

"How come you waited till now? Scared of Granddaddy?"

"Yes. Just like you."

"So, say we don't give you nothing?"

"Then I take the letter to the Public Safety Commission. And the sheriff. And the newspapers. And some lawyers in Dallas. I don't know what good it'll do, but it'll raise a commotion and keep you busy. And create lots of publicity. You Gudges don't like that."

She had made her point.

"I'll be back." He turned from the car.

She sat there another hour, while the heat of the day abated and the shadow of the oak became a finger of darkness trailing over the hood. Finally he came out holding a bunch of papers; Stumpy followed him closely.

"You know, Gran, we just can't do this all superlegal. I'm damned if I'm goin' to have a bunch of lawyers pissin' over the Lazy G. We got this little bitty mud company down in East Texas. Came with a rig business we bought. It's over near Athens. Supposed to be a good man running it. You can keep him on." He looked down at a pad on which were some hastily scribbled figures. "Got assets of 'bout two million dollars. Net worth 'bout a million and a half. Had a cash flow last year 'bout two hundred, two hundred twenty thousand. That's my best offer."

She nodded.

He passed over a single stock certificate and a receipt, which she signed.

"That's it, then?" She looked at him, feeling strangely untriumphant.

He looked back at her with what she now had come to know to be total, raging, resentful hatred, as if she had forced him to commit some obscene, perverse act.

"Nobody ever stole anything from us here before, Gran, or took unless we first decided to get rid of it, no matter how big it was; if it has our brand on it, it's ours. I feel like you just drove up here and cut a piece off me." His voice was uncertain under the pressure of his humiliation. This wasn't a few head of cattle rustled out of some far pasture, or a wrench lifted off the floor of a rig. This was a piece of things. It bled.

Only then, seeing him so moved, did she allow herself a smile of accomplishment.

He read it as a sneer of triumph. Watching her pass out the gates, he thought, Granddaddy'd kill me if he could. Only one day into the grave and already the ranch was getting bitten up. The thought of his grandfather made Bubber shiver.

Now, long years later, Granada sat daydreaming in a restaurant where a plate of lettuce and tomatoes cost $10. She was a multimillionairess. The guiding spirit of Masterman United, the $400-million publicly quoted company that she had built on the foundation she'd snatched away from the Lazy G. She was quality now; a figure inescapably present at anything where exclusivity was a function of price. A great lady. She wondered if her success had changed her. She guessed not: more it was a matter of liberating virtues and attributes she'd always possessed, of letting the golden glow shine through.

"Mrs. Masterman?" Luigi was back. "Miss Newman is here." He showed Jill to a chair.

"My dear," said Granada. A broad smile illuminated her heavy features as she extended a large hand garlanded with rings. "My dear." Granada felt like a reptile stirring in the sun, the first stirrings of hunger pricking its lassitude.

Nick's morning had been full of Rubens. At eight-thirty, Sandler had called to relay a message that the cycle was theirs. The deal had closed in Zurich that morning while they were still asleep. Barry Winters was flying in with the sketches the next Friday. The packing cases were being built and four first-class seats reserved for Winters and the crates. Brink's had been put on notice to coordinate with Customs at JFK to rendezvous with Winters and shepherd the paintings into Manhattan. It was agreed that they would be brought directly to Nick's premises.

"Barry'll miss the goddamn plane, of course," guessed Johnny, "or meet some stewardess, and the pictures'll spend the weekend in the vaults at the Crédit Suisse, giving the seller time to change his mind."

"Be still, my heart," begged Nick.

Before he could get to Sarah, who had intimated some pretty exciting stuff on the cycle in the few words they had had before she lost him to the telephone, he had to spend a half-hour with a young woman from Grundy's, the third of the Big Three auction firms, who had come to discuss the corporate art-investment program they were starting. She was a tightly reined number with a stick up her rear, who made art sound about as exciting as life insurance. She hadn't blinked or smiled when he politely suggested that the Grundy's program struck him as pretty farfetched. He felt the same way about all these proliferating "programs." He ushered the young woman to the door with a promise to think it over.

By the time he finished with her and talking to his banker and double-checking with Brink's and TWA, Sarah Ruggles looked about ready to expire with impatience. He bought time for two more phone calls with the promise of lunch at Maia's.

She had been with him two years, but he'd never looked at Sarah closely. He took her to be of a piece with her careful, closely reasoned synopses of the meaning and history of the works of art that he passed by her. That after hours she had never fewer than three men on the hook and led a full, richly carnal private existence would have stunned him. At work she chose to present a blond, bespectacled weediness which suited her work. The only display of her inner mysteries was a sharp tongue which not even Nick was spared.

At last instructing his secretary to hold the phones, Nick followed Sarah into the book room. She had already pinned the photographs, arranged in the narrative order of the Labors, beginning with the Strangling of the Nemean Lion and concluding with the Abduction of Cerberus, to a door-sized corkboard panel which leaned against one wall of bookshelves. On the round table she had organized two neat piles of books.

"Begin at the beginning," he instructed.

"I shall. You might as well sit down. This'll take a little while. Now let me just get these books open."

While she bustled, he looked over the photographs against the wall. Even in black-and-white, the quality of the pictures sang through their compositional force and dexterity. It was impossible to tell much about color and condition, but the freedom of the composition, the musical exuberance written over each of them was captivatingly, unmistakably Rubens. He tried, quickly, to choose an early favorite among them. Something about the depiction of the Theft of the Oxen of Geryon engaged his eye. He got up and went over for a closer look. Rubens had woven all the critical elements of the tale into a composition that had absolute pictorial integrity. The hero was leading a small herd of bellowing oxen down a hill which ran on a right–left diagonal down to a sparkling narrow beach on which the bowl of the sun, in which Hercules had traversed the earth, was grounded. The shore swept around in a crescent at whose far tip two mountains, the Pillars of Hercules, were faintly indicated, their airy outlines broken by clouds. The composition was balanced by a large tree in the extreme left foreground under which lay the bodies of Geryon, his dog and his herdsman, all killed by Hercules in the execution of his theft.

"If you will get your nose away from the pictures, which you know are merely incidental to the art historian's view, I'll report what I have learned, which is little, and what I've surmised, which is a great deal and really very interesting," announced Sarah. Nick sat down.

"I have been able to find only five extant works that tie up with these iconographically. And a sixth which may have something to do with them.

"I won't go into all the Hercules subjects around. There are fourteen Hercules subjects listed in the catalogue of the oil sketches. As you might expect, a muscular painter like Rubens did a lot with the Hercules myth.

"The Labors offered Rubens a chance to show how much of a virtuoso he could be. They're full of interesting symbolic possibilities, and geographical references, and fantasy, and a lot of other allusive baggage which has to be worked into a visual whole. And these certainly show him at his best!

"They aren't, strictly speaking, sketches, unlike two very vaguely related Hercules subjects in England. These're *modelli* for his assistants to work from; they're very finished and detailed. Stylistically, on the basis of these not-very-good photographs, they appear consistent with the work of around 1635–1640. A good deal of that was done for the King of Spain, on commission from Philip IV's brother, who was the regent of what is now essentially Belgium and was then a dominion of Spain.

"Now, it happens that this period, 1635–1640, was a time of great building activity by Philip IV. He began with the palace of the Buen Retiro in Madrid, his state palace, a setting in which every stone and mirror—and work of art, needless to say—celebrated the king's power and glory.

"Philip IV had become an avid collector and patron—turned on to painting by Rubens, in fact, who was in Madrid for quite a long time in 1628–1629. He gave major commissions for the Buen Retiro, pictures that are now in the Prado in Madrid. The best-known was probably Velásquez' *Surrender of Breda.* But included in the Buen Retiro commission was a series of Labors of Hercules by Zurbarán. Do you remember them? Here." She opened a book and pointed.

Nick had forgotten that Zurbarán, a painter whose work he relished for its intensely projected, almost mystical spirituality, had done a Hercules series. The instant he saw the photographs his memory quickened. Of course he remembered them. They were puzzling; the subject seemed as unsuited to Zurbarán's talent and vision as it was suited to Rubens. His Hercules seemed stiff, awkward, attenuated: unmythic.

"Now, to change direction for a minute, at the same time he was building the Buen Retiro, Philip IV was also fixing up his hunting lodge, the Torre de la Parada, about ten miles outside Madrid. You might describe it as a seventeenth-century version of Camp David. The lodge was going to be decorated with an enormous number of paintings, mostly of mythological scenes taken from Ovid's *Metamorphoses,* the standard source on Greek and Roman mythology in those days.

"Rubens was given the lion's share of these commissions. He had the connections. The state art for the state palace, the Buen Retiro, was, not surprisingly, commissioned from the Spanish court painters. The Torre de la Parada was a different matter. A private business, apart from artistic politics. It was a huge job, measured in sheer numbers. How many paintings Rubens was paid to supply is up in the air, but it must have run well over a hundred. Of course, these were to be big pictures; Rubens would conceive them, prepare the master sketches—*modelli* like these—and then turn the work over to his assistants; Snyders for animals, one of the Brueghels for flowers and so on. In any case, it does seem that the commissions may have included a number of Hercules subjects."

She gestured him to the table.

"Now come here and look at these photographs in this catalogue. As far as I can see, there are six oil sketches that relate to our pictures. First, the two in London: *Atlas Supporting the Heavens* and *Hercules Slaying the Hydra.* These are very loose and free-form, but close enough.

"Now, there are four more sketches that ought to be folded into all of this." Sarah turned the pages, as Nick looked.

She closed the fat volume.

"Now let's pull it all together. In a nutshell, what I'm thinking is that what we have here is a Labors of Hercules cycle for Philip IV's hunting lodge. The subject's right; the style's right. They may not all have been turned into large paintings, or if they were, the large pictures were lost or destroyed. And listen to this." She picked a book from the table, turned to a marked page and quoted: " 'One of the most vexing problems about the decoration of the Torre . . . is posed by the common, but largely unsubstantiated, assumption that the hunting lodge contained a series of works illustrating the life or labors of Hercules.' It doesn't seem perplexing to me, Nicholas. Rubens was very competitive, as he shows in his letters. Can't you imagine how he'd have liked to show up Zurbarán's 'official' treatment of the subject in the Buen Retiro?"

It was a beguiling idea, and it made sense the way Sarah spun it out. She sat back with her hands flat on her thighs, obviously pleased. Nick grinned at her.

"Sarah, you have redeemed the intellectual honor of Radcliffe. You deserve the best meal Maia can cook. Shall we?"

He patted her rear end in a comradely fashion and gave her his arm. If that part of him which dealt with such matters hadn't been in the process of being overcome by Jill Newman, he doubtless would have noticed that hers was everything a behind should be.

Granada Masterman's Tuesday regulars were all in place by one o'clock. Besides Jill and the hostess, there were Esmé Bogle, Gratiane von

González and Calypso Fuller Winstead. The sixth chair at the table was usually filled, at Granada's command, by one of several ambiguously sexed gentlemen whose principal occupation was to keep the girls amused. On this particular Tuesday, Dr. Victor Sartorian was perched on one of Luigi's creakily delicate gilded chairs. Jill, who considered her presence a matter of professional necessity, thought they resembled a bunch of overaged schoolgirls giggling together in a soda-fountain booth. It pleased her to be an outsider, there to report to Granada what was In and Out, and to harvest whatever tidbits might serve the interests of her column; of course, it was all material for the Dickens-Thackeray-Eliot–scaled novel being shaped in her head, the book that would someday illuminate the visible and invisible social fabric of wealthy America. To earn her invitations, Jill made sure to mention these lunches not less than once every five or six weeks in her column. That seemed to suffice minimally; Granada, Esmé and Gratiane fed on publicity of any kind. They seemed to need her tiny, infrequent certifications of their importance. They were all three self-made women, ladies only to the extent that their ample purses could buy the right accouterments, each about as delicate and sensitive as a hammer. Calypso Winstead was different. She endured these lunches, Jill thought, for the sake of her Institute; she had been urged into friendship with Granada by her husband, on the pretense that a large potential donation was at hand. Poor Calypso, Jill thought. As if being the last Fuller weren't problem enough, given her almost religious dedication to the Institute which enshrined her father's sacred memory, Calypso had been persuaded, by Sol Greschner, principally, to marry Hugo Winstead. His interest in himself was supreme; his drive to assert his importance and influence, especially with women, was legendary. He was a tomcat, Jill knew, reputedly able to produce a dance-floor erection on demand, always with seduction in mind. Jill had heard rumors of a secret Greenwich Village apartment and shooting or golfing excursions to so-called distant places where the game was in fact bagged in Westchester motel rooms. Poor Calypso.

You had to admire the other three, she had told herself. Each self-made; each having risen above mediocrity or worse. Gratiane was obvious. Esmé, out of boredom, had begun to write down the fantasies that came to her under the hair dryer where she'd spent most of the early years of her marriage to Harvey Bogle, who was always out chasing his next billion. Unfortunately, Esmé was starting to take herself seriously. Her readers craved the mixture of brand names, startling sexual descriptions and thinly disguised power gossip she fed them; they licked their lips guessing at the realities behind the flimsy masks her characters wore. Her reading public cared little for grammar, pleasure in the language, characterization or point of view. They would probably desert Esmé, Jill guessed, were she to stir gobbets of attitude and comment into the relentless alternation of names and copulation, copulation and names, that had earned her millions.

Granada was the real story. An authentic combination of genius and luck. Luck: to discover that her drilling mud had a miraculous effect on female skin. Genius: to exploit it. Black Gold had been the first Masterman cosmetics line, from which had flowed all the rest. Then, the big step forward: the development of the Masterwoman concept. First, makeup sold door to door, and now, dreams peddled at home parties. Her own past had taught Granada how imprisoned most middle-class women still were, incarcerated in their dreary existences, indentured to cleaning and car pools and junk-food nights in front of the TV. To them, as she conceived it, the Masterwoman, with her unguents for the skin and, later, her balm for the spirit, must appear as a violet angel come to offer salvation from desperation. Twelve years ago, she had moved to Dallas and started with the first class of a dozen Masterwomen, housewives themselves, holding parties in Richardson at which the Black Gold line was demonstrated. Now she had twelve thousand Masterwomen in the field, fifteen hundred more in training and another nine hundred in department stores and shopping centers.

Over this time, the concept had never truly departed its original objective: to liberate the housewife, without embarrassment, in her home or in the company of others demographically like herself, from her psychological chains. "*The Tupperware of the soul*," as an irreverent reporter at *Forbes* put it: Masterwoman home parties embraced self-help and self-realization in every form ranging from weight loss to alpha-wave control, tied naturally with the party-concluding display and sale of a coordinated line of products.

Granada had divined that middle-class women would dare things in small, friendly groups that they would never do by themselves or in public. The demand for products, tangible and intangible, swelled of its own momentum. The eleventh edition of the *Mastermanual*, which would live in makeup history as "the immortal eleventh," contained more than eight hundred pages. The products catalogue enjoyed a commensurate expansion. At the end of weekly Sexual Realization Mastersessions, from Belle Haven to Sausalito, otherwise staid suburban matrons pushed and tore at each other for the right to purchase red satin teddies with nipple cutouts and six-cell vibrators.

The most successful Masterproduct on the market had been Born Again Balm, a dermatological cure-all with a cocaine base. Every tube and vial carried the stamp of approval of the Moral Majority and the legend "BY APPOINTMENT TO THE FIRST LADY"—the first of the new Executive Warrants the White House was granting to favored purveyors. MUD had made a $50,000 contribution to the East Room *Toile de Jouy* fund. The unguent was marketed under the slogan "For Skin as Pure as a Christian Heart." It had done over $12 million at retail in the two weeks following its introduction—a satisfactory figure that, sadly, had done little to dispel the appetite-wrecking gloom which the appearance of Caryn Gudge on her social horizon had laid on Granada Masterman.

Her mood was not helped by Sartorian's opening gambit. By custom, the lone male at the Masterman Tuesdays was expected to open the serious conversation with some bit of choice gossip. Sartorian waited until his ladies had stopped cooing over the Battersea-boxed lip glosses with the pictures of the First Couple that had been at their places.

"What an attractive woman that Mrs. Gudge is," he declared, after the opening chitchat around the table had subsided. "And such emeralds. Did you see them, Calypso? They were quite green." Sartorian knew what he was doing. Living dangerously was his thing, his appeal. He knew who Caryn Gudge was and where she connected with Granada Masterman, but it was a name that would best come from him, known as he was for his wickedness. He also knew that Granada Masterman's emeralds were better, and that he could depend on Gratiane von González to pounce on that, and set the balance wheel turning. He and Señora von González each collected $150,000 a year from Masterman United, as psychiatric consultant and styling adviser respectively. They had long since learned how to work together.

"Oh, Victor, 'ow could you say this thing?" Gratiane—right on cue. "Such a vulgar little woman. Her jewels are glass compared with yours, darling Granada." A less flexible age might have found this statement hypocritical. Caryn Gudge had that morning been invited to dine at the Von Gonzálezes' the following Sunday night, when Gratiane knew Granada would be in Palm Beach. Gratiane could count zeros as well as the next woman; it was easier when there were a lot of them, nevertheless, a bird in the hand . . . "Big, ugly green glass, her stones; nothing, just nothing!" She patted Granada consolingly with her voice.

Granada did the best she could to grin broadly. Ever since Victor had sent her to that plastic surgeon of his in Acapulco for "just a little tuck, sweetie, such a nice birthday present for Waldo to find on the next pillow, uummm, loveyducks?" she'd had trouble making her mouth behave. And she thought she looked a little bug-eyed, although fortunately a lot of people put that down to businesslike toughness.

"Well, she does make a new figure, doesn't she? A little common and no manners, I heard. I had her looked into, you know. She's just a vulgar little cheerleader or something from some terrible place in Texas. It's not surprising. The Gudges have never had any taste. Who brought her to the Fuller? Greschner? The man's poison."

There wasn't a person at the table who didn't owe Sol Greschner a great deal herself, nor one who didn't know how responsible he'd been for the lordly eminence Granada now occupied. Nevertheless, each head except that of Jill, who did no business with Granada, nodded vigorous agreement.

Jill had a question. There was a lot of curiosity around as to how the Born Again line would impact MUD's bottom line. She was really asking the question for her alter ego; Creighton would be very much interested.

"That new BAB line must be selling like crazy, Granada. I know *That Woman!*'s carrying a big co-op ad with Saks in the paper next Friday—and someone said they saw Garbo buying a tube at Boyd's. I have to admit I took a teensy little flyer on your stock last week. I hope I didn't do anything illegal. I mean, we're all so nervous what with Marvin Terrace's son getting indicted for selling pirated videocassettes of the studio's new releases. Anyway, I took a peek at the paper just before coming over. Do you realize MUD is selling at nineteen? Why, Granada, you must be worth trillions!"

Granada smiled. "You did very well to buy, dear. At the rate it's selling, BAB alone could add fifteen percent to our profits. We're all very excited at MUD. Actually, dear, the stock was quoted at nineteen and a quarter when I left the office."

"Jill, you women just surprise me, the way you know all about figures and stocks. I can't even balance my checkbook," said Victor Sartorian naively; for lack of something better to do, he'd executed a six-way graduated Ginnie Mae hedge in three currencies over the restaurant pay phone before joining the ladies. "I'll bet you have one of those pocket computers everyone carries around, Jill. Maybe you ought to come over and help my secretary with our books. They're a disaster."

Plenty of reason for Granada to grin, thought Jill: Mrs. Masterman owned more than 3 million shares of MUD as of the last proxy statement, worth some $57 million. A long way from two furnished rooms in Stamford to 40 percent of a company the market valued at close to $150 million.

The conversation turned to the Terrace scandal, and carried the group through the Poached Turnips Gran Conte and halfway through the Caracollo di Tuberi Misti. Jill picked miserably at the mélange of boiled potatoes, parsnips, carrots and rutabaga, even though she knew that root vegetables had been declared the In Food of the Year by *That Woman!* Anyway, Granada's Tuesday lunch group ate the flesh of no living thing except, by proxy, that of rivals and enemies.

Poor Marvin Terrace, went the lament around the table. He and his wife, Melly, were regulars in the Masterman–Winstead–Von González set. Terrace himself had been an obscure banker whom a set of curious chances had propelled to the chairmanship of TransNational Entertainment and Communications (TEC), the Hollywood film and cable-television conglomerate. Granada was on his board of directors and Terrace on hers. Masterman United owned 9.3 percent of TEC's voting stock. Jill had guessed that Granada had designs on TEC for its cable business, which would be a natural tie-in with the Masterwoman home-party network; just as Granada was obviously looking at Homer Seabury's Seaco to provide Masterwomanhood with a line of financial products. It looked now as if Granada wouldn't get either without a fight from Harvey Bogle. Bogle had filed reports showing that his ownership of TEC now amounted to nearly 16 percent. And he owned a good-sized block of Seaco. TEC was the kind of company people like Harvey went after, Jill knew. It was rich in assets, including an undervalued film library and studio real estate; owned and operated a number of major cable franchises and was run by a man who shivered inside his skin with fear that the world would someday discover how stupid and shallow he really was. Poor Marvin, Jill thought: he was such a pompous simp. And his wife was such a climber. And his son had been caught pirating prints of new films just a month before he was due to marry the only daughter of the richest grandee in Spain. Poor Marvin. He and Melly Terrace had hoped to sleep in the Escorial; now it looked like Sing Sing.

Bogle vs. Masterman. A championship set-to, the way Jill saw it. In the last six months, the company had borrowed $45 million from its banks to make two major investments: $30 million in TEC and $15 million in Seaco Group. Not a lot of money compared with MUD's market value, but cash money. A great ongoing story for Creighton.

"We must all just stand behind Marvin and Melly," Granada declared. "This is a very difficult time for the Terraces. I know they'd appreciate a Mailgram from us."

"Oh, Granada. Such good ideas always. Why not send it from here? Just right now?" Gratiane signaled to Luigi for paper. "Now, Esmé, our literary celebrity"—there were giggles all around—"why don't you compose it?" The next five minutes were spent finding just the right words to tell the Terraces that the Dove Sono crowd was foursquare behind them in their hour of tribulation. Everyone agreed that Esmé had found just the right words. So talented, Esmé.

This was a good item for Gilberte, thought Jill. The lead formed in her mind: "In Crowd hangs tough . . ."

The most marginal literary allusion turned Esmé on like a faucet. She began to draw on her apparently endless supply of Merv Griffin and Johnny Carson stories. Then she brought the table up to date on her new book: "I and Balzac . . ." she began. Jill turned her attention off.

Coffee came. Sartorian conspiratorially repeated his invitation to Jill to help him with his accounts.

"Oh, Victor, I'd love to, but frankly, I'm so out of practice I can hardly do my own. How's business? Have you anything interesting for me?"

He told her an anecdote which, if she had printed it, would have broken the heart of a poor shell of a woman whom Sartorian had long since enmeshed in amphetamine chains.

What a foolish, transparent man. As Jill wondered if the tales of his sexual athleticism could possibly be true, Granada signaled for attention. From beside her chair, she brought up a thick, unbound block of printed sheets.

"I thought you'd all like to see the proofs of the sixteenth edition of the *Mastermanual*. It's just off the presses. Brand-clean. Please don't look at my picture in the front—it's so awful. Here, pass it around."

She turned to Calypso Winstead, who was, as always, seated on her right.

"I must say, Cal, I was hoping to hear from Hugo after our perfectly wonderful party at the Fuller. He and I had such an interesting talk."

Calypso Winstead replied in the voice that fawns would have if fawns could speak. It was scarcely louder than the drift of leaves in the wind.

"Oh, I know Hugo will call, Granada. It was so generous of you to support the building and to underwrite the champagne and the flowers. I'm sure the trustees will want to do something official to mark it."

The proof had worked its way around the table to Jill. Putting something like this into her hands was like giving the other team your playbook on the eve of the Superbowl. She looked quickly through it, noting in passing that the list of Masterbooks—Granada's personal selection of inspirational reading, which consisted of works by economic and political troglodytes, how-to manuals by psychosemantic self-help and diet shamans and breathless glamour chases like Esmé's novels—now included two recent best-sellers: *Nuancing the Nukes: A Caveated World Policy*, by the recently confirmed Secretary of State, and *Moral Money* by Senator Rufus Lassiter, who was Granada's political guru. On the bottom of the page someone had scribbled "*Fr Mkt Pov*," which Jill took to refer to *Poverty and the Free Market*, a work currently all the rage in Washington for its convoluted assertion of the theological and genetic inevitability of poverty, especially among people who couldn't get jobs. Jill had been able to stomach barely a dozen pages. She wasn't able to tune into the politics of the rich.

She flipped the proof sheets casually, looking for some clue that suggested real news. Granada shared the belief of most self-made women that the female company she kept and tried to dominate consisted of airheads. Jill's skipping perusal indicated that there was nothing dramatically new planned in the product area, certainly nothing on the scale of Born Again Balm, which she'd spotted in last year's proofs a year ago. It had been "Robert Creighton's" market scoop of the year, sending MUD to $14 from $8, where it had been languishing in the market's belief that the Masterlady had finally lost her touch.

Esmé was clamoring now for the sheaf of proofs, obviously impatient to see if she was still a Masterbook, so Jill didn't quite get to the page near the back headed "The Mastermoney Concept." She passed it on and started to chat with Calypso Fuller, who hadn't said a word. Jill liked her, although she often asked herself if there mustn't be something terribly wrong with any woman, even one so ladylike and intelligent, who could marry and live with Hugo Winstead. And seem to serve him with such devotion.

Calypso was saying something about the Institute when Jill caught sight of Luigi leading a tall, now familiar figure to a table. Nick looked very appealing, with his brown straight hair shaking as he smiled and nodded with Luigi, who stood by Nick's table. Jill knew without being able to hear that the two men were talking in fluent, familiar Italian. She liked what she had seen of Nick's manner with people. He seemed at home with himself; if the usual male hauntings and confusions were flapping around in his head, they hadn't appeared yet; what was nice was that he didn't talk about money and, better still, he didn't appear to care how much anybody else had. Jill was sick of money. As a subject. As a way of life.

A tall, bespectacled girl sat down with Nick. Jill looked right past the glasses and the heavy, untrendy skirt and the blouse that might have been fashionable in high school in 1958 and saw, to her chagrin, that what was underneath was the right goods.

It quite ruined her lunch. Irritation with other women seemed to be the order of the day at the Masterman table.

Fortunately, Luigi, who could always be counted on in a pinch, let her escape through the back way after coffee. She was sure Nick hadn't seen her. She hoped. Her cheeks felt scarlet with jealousy for which she could feel no rational justification.

CHAPTER SEVEN

As Vosper helped him into his jacket, Greschner considered whether Gudge, who was coming to lunch, would be the wealthiest man ever to have dined at Number 17. Tweaking into symmetry the ends of the yellow silk butterfly at his throat, he remembered that Andrew Mellon had been brought to the house by Duveen a few years before the war. Mellon was in the middle of his tax case with the government, and Duveen had thought a dose of the Greschner magic might help cure the scabrous image that had been built up by the press. In the end, however, Mellon had resolved his difficulties by founding the National Gallery. Greschner guessed that Mellon had probably been the richest, adjusting for inflation, but in terms of the sheer size of the pile, Gudge looked like a clear winner.

He had never seen Gudge in the flesh; the few photographs in his files didn't suggest much about the man's aspect. Nor, really, did the confused disaster of the tape of Gudge's seated appearance before the Lassiter Committee. They had spoken on the telephone, of course. Three months earlier, Gudge had telephoned him, on the introduction of a downtown banker, to discuss Sol's handling his wife's public relations.

Gudge had been straightforward.

"Mr. Greschner, I got a wife who wants to be society. She's run all her traps in Texas; there isn't a party in Amarillo or River Oaks or Dallas that she hasn't been to. Gold and Silver; Idyllwild; The Museum Ball; you name it. Enough parties for ten women in ten lifetimes. Not enough for Mrs. Gudge, though."

Sol wondered about Mrs. Gudge. She was probably one of those country girls on the make, he guessed. An ex–stewardess or travel-agency girl or stockbroker. New York was full of them; and Beverly Hills, Monte Carlo, Palm Beach and any place where "society" was strictly defined by money. New York in particular seemed to be full of them. Girls who lay in wait along the path of life for men like Gudge; men for whom, when their crypto-erotic urge for money-making abated, or the sturdy, predictable caresses of the wife tried and true no longer thrilled, the high breasts and the oral sex and the soft fingers in the groin would be an enslaving revelation. Sol had been called upon to deal with at least a dozen. Either to pay them off or to make ladies of them.

"May I ask how long you and Mrs. Gudge have been married?"

"Little over two years."

That was about par. These ladies needed a year or two to solidify their positions. Implant themselves under the skin like tropical parasites carrying lifelong infections. It took a year or two to deal with the husband's old, perhaps threatening loyalties and connections, using the witchcraft of the first rosy sexual rapture to fracture old friendships; to erect a psychological and financial bulwark against the disapproval of old friends. During this period there would be little visibility. Then would come the breakout. First in the husband's home territory, the social enclaves where his clout importance would ensure that the better doors in town would be opened by the reluctant wives of his bankers and attorneys and brokers. That usually proved diverting for a while; but then, if really big money was involved, all roads led to Manhattan and from there, for those whose striving knew no bounds, to the ballrooms of Monte Carlo and the chalets of Sta. Marta.

To do that required expert guidance. Required Solomon Greschner. It was not prideful work, he admitted, but it had its amusing moments. Mrs. Gudge sounded like a classic case. He agreed over the telephone to take her on.

They had talked for several minutes longer, in the course of which Gudge added a dimension to the matter that Sol had not foreseen.

"There's a woman up your way, Mr. Greschner, Mrs. Masterman; Mrs. Granada Masterman. You probably know her. She's supposed to be real big in New York society. We used to be kin. Had the same mother, but she's dead now, and so's Granada—for all I care. She's become a real social lady, Granada has, I hear which you had something to do with, everyone reckons, so I figure you can do as much for Mrs. Gudge if what it takes is money. I got to figure, then, that if folks start making a fuss over Mrs. Gudge it'll like to kill Granada. Which I wouldn't exactly mind, Mr. Greschner, if you get my meaning."

Greschner did, and could put an immediate price to it. Two days later, an officer of his bank telephoned to say that $50,000 had been wired into the account of Greschner Associates by an Amarillo bank. The next day Caryn Gudge presented herself at Rostval Place. She was about what he'd expected: her looks were more striking, which was a plus, yet he could also see she might be aggressive to the point of coarseness. She clearly knew what she wanted. Two years of intense study of *That Woman!* had armed her with a remarkable arsenal of brand names and Ins and Outs. She knew the right people for hair, face, hands, feet and skin. She knew all there seemed to be to know about the mandated necessaries of the outer woman. She had ideas, some out of date, as to whom she should associate with. She should start in Paris with the collections, he told her. He wrote out a list of Paris connections. Europe was always for sale, so a secure beginning could be made there. Then, to begin her conditioning for her infiltration of the home front, which dictated a constant calmness of spirit, medicated, if necessary, and, for any contender under the age of sixty, a figure kept lissome as a flame, he called Victor Sartorian and made an appointment.

When she left, he made a series of telephone calls to Paris, to concierges and counts, all members of his network, to make sure that the troops were properly arrayed for Mrs. Gudge's arrival. Apart from a ball the Rothschilds were giving at Ferrières, there didn't seem to be anything uncrackable. He called Gratiane von González. He finished up with a last call—to Jill Newman.

"Jill? How are you? How's the child? Good. Do you need anything? Well, you know you have only to call. Listen, my sweet, we have a new comet about to flame over our tawdry horizon. Yes. Oh, yes, naturally I've got her started with Victor. Don't sound so sarcastic. The lady's name is Mrs. Buford Gudge IV. That's right. B—as in 'billions.' The one they call Bubber. Anyway, a little backgrounding by Gilberte would be most welcome. I've got her fixed up to attend the Spastic Revels next week. At the Bosco Wimpelmans' table; they'd kill for a mention by Gilberte, so help me out on this one, okay? As a sidelight, you might be amused to know that Mrs. Gudge is, technically, the half-sister-in-law of our great and admired friend Granada. Yes, yes. No, you can look it up. Now I've got one little thing for your pal Creighton."

Now Gudge was coming to call on business. He must have been pleased with Sol's work so far on his wife's case. Even Sol was pleased. To have secured an invitation to serve as co-chairperson of next October's Blue Ball, after only a couple of months in the field, was a real triumph for Caryn Gudge, and had cost only the $100,000 it took to underwrite the function. Sartorian had done well to plant the idea of Mrs. Gudge in the ear of the patient whose husband was president of the Prostate Foundation. Gilberte's glowing detailing of Mrs. Gudge's triumphal progress through Paris, including the largest one-time bill ever run up at each of four couture houses, hadn't hurt. The more he saw of her, the more Sol was convinced that Caryn Gudge was an idea whose time had come. You had only to look at Washington to know that the age of the cheap rich had finally arrived. Well, she was possibly cheaper and certainly richer than any of them. In a way it was too bad he didn't work Washington, He could have been starting her toward an ambassadorship.

That would fix Granada, he thought. Beat her once and forever at her own game. In the old days, when he had still felt real power within his grasp, he had had great plans for Granada. He would make her President; she had what it took: Eleanor Roosevelt's looks and FDR's balls and cunning. But she had opted for society—and when Sol had remonstrated with her, too vigorously perhaps, she had terminated his contract. Of course, he'd been rough with her; the stakes had merited it. But not rough enough to justify the abandonment of his great objective for Granada. Now, through Caryn Gudge, he would earn some measure of retribution.

Sol finished buttoning up his coat. He looked himself over in the mirror. His suit was an ocher affair, cuffed at sleeve and ankle, with striking red checks. He knew there were people who found his clothes outrageous. But they gave him an unmistakable visual presence which stuck in people's minds like a dart. In his business, the accouterments counted: the suits, the whiskers and, above everything, the house.

The intercom on his dressing table buzzed. Vosper announced that his guests were here. Guests? Now, that was surprising; he had expected Gudge to be alone. He told Vosper to show them into the library.

When Sol came downstairs, Gudge was looking out the window at the trees in the square.

"Mr. Gudge?"

"Mr. Greschner." Gudge turned. His appearance surprised Sol, who had been expecting a big, bluff man. Gudge seemed pale and physically askew; he was tall, but his skin seemed loose on him and his eyes lacked fire.

"It's real good to meet you, Mr. Greschner. This here's Mr. Katagira."

Turning, Sol looked into the face of a Japanese wearing a well-cut brown suit with a pinned left sleeve. The planes and coloring of his face suggested Mongol blood. It was the sort of sinister, expressionless face that Sol had looked for during the war when casting anti-Japanese propaganda films.

"How do you do, sir?" The man's grip was secure, his voice relaxed. He didn't bow. "Mr. Katagira's my chief legal adviser and chief financial officer," Gudge explained. "He keeps an eye on things for me. Set up our systems—all that. Actually, Mr. Katagira's the one who suggested I talk to you about Mrs. Gudge."

"Well, I'm very pleased to meet both of you, at last. I must say Mrs. Gudge seems to be having a very good time. Don't you find it so, Mr. Gudge? But that's neither here nor there for purposes of this visit, I gather. How may I be of assistance?"

Gudge settled wearily into an armchair across from Sol. Katagira took the opposite end of the sofa from Greschner.

"Why'n't you bring him down to date, Mr. Katagira?"

"As you wish." Katagira smiled at Sol. "Mr. Greschner, you may or may not be aware that the financial policy of Mr. Gudge's family enterprise, which those of us fortunate enough to be involved with it know generically as the Lazy G, has historically been to avoid investment in anything the family does not control outright. Specifically shares and other publicly traded instruments: bonds, notes, even obligations of the United States Government. The policy was laid down by Mr. Gudge's grandfather, a man of very strong opinions. I believe his thinking was crystallized by an unfortunate experience in the 1929 collapse, when several hundred thousand dollars of Lazy G capital were lost. Since that time, we have had no contact with Wall Street or its institutions."

Katagira spoke with the deliberate formality customary to educated foreigners, but his English was accentless. Sol speculated that he might be a Nisei.

"Times change, however, Mr. Greschner. The world is a greatly different place than it was even a decade ago. The Lazy G has grown vastly larger than it was when Mr. Gudge assumed control, and so have its requirements. I won't bore you with figures, Mr. Greschner, even though I am quite sure you are as capable as I of understanding them, but suffice it to say that although the Lazy G generates an enormous cash flow, the funding needed to exploit all the opportunities which Mr. Gudge might pursue could at some point exceed its internal resources. To date, I am happy to say, that has not been the case. But it might be.

"Moreover, investment opportunities change, and it would be foolish for us to insulate ourselves from genuine opportunities for the sake of a policy which may have outlived its prudent purpose. We have, we believe, identified such an opportunity where, if we utilize our resources skillfully and effectively, the potential profit would be"—Katagira looked significantly at Gudge, as if for confirmation that he could make the momentous disclosure —"well into the billions. That sort of possibility is, we think, worth our scrutiny—and we have scrutinized it."

He paused. Gudge was looking up at the ceiling. Sol wondered where this was leading. Not even J. Paul Getty could have spoken so relaxedly of this kind of money.

"If we are to do this, however, we will require expert assistance. Expert, and creative. Which has led us to consider the possibility of forming a mutually advantageous connection with a leading Wall Street house. On which matter we would look to you for guidance, Mr. Greschner."

Again he paused for an instant and smiled at Sol, in a way that seemed like a surety of his respect.

"You are a man who is known to be acutely sensitive to human nature, Mr. Greschner. Wise in the ways of the world, shall I say? It is unlikely you would have achieved such recognition and success in your chosen vocation were you not. You will appreciate, therefore, that Mr. Gudge is apprehensive about taking even the most tentative step on the public stage. Which a large-scale involvement must entail—and large, Mr. Greschner, is the only scale we know at the Lazy G. The family has valued its privacy as dearly as any of its assets. As you doubtless know, Mr. Gudge has had a very painful experience of the limelight. Some years ago, at the hands of Senator Lassiter. Which is why we believed it would be sensible to consult you. I might add, Mr. Greschner, that your efforts in behalf of Mrs. Gudge, who, it is fair to say—is it not, Mr. Gudge?—has her husband's ear, have been very impressive. That has certainly been a factor in Mr. Gudge's decision to speak with you on this matter."

Sol felt an invigorating surge of self-esteem. It momentarily occurred to him that Caryn Gudge might have been a stalking horse, a test of the capacity and discretion he might bring to a much more important engagement. If he rightly judged Katagira's drift, he was about to be asked to recommend how Gudge might form a Wall Street relationship, which in a way would mean orchestrating the emergence of Buford Gudge from his chrysalis of total secretiveness. It was surely the biggest opportunity he had ever been offered. A climax that could transform what in his mind had degenerated into a mere career into the great life he had envisioned. Guiding the Lazy G to an investment banker would have very pleasant tangible side effects. The man who had the Gudge business to direct could translate it into very palpable rewards.

"May I ask why Mr. Gudge is interested in doing things right now, Mr. Katagira? You alluded to the fact that you are still self-financing and will be, I gather, for the foreseeable future. The investment climate has been mediocre and unfathomable for some time and shows little prospect of changing. Do you yourselves perceive a change, a trend, that makes it desirable to act now, at the cost of taking on some degree of public visibility? I do know that a great many businessmen seem very optimistic about the new Administration. They look at the President and see what a great American writer called 'the comforting proximity of millionaires.' "

"Mr. Gudge has no politics, Mr. Greschner. Apart from an expedient contribution here and there, the Lazy G takes no identifiable political position. I will be candid. We do see a great investment opportunity, an enormous opportunity, in the long-term-bond market. The senseless, undisciplined credit policies of the last decade, of both the government and the large banks, may be abating. We believe the anti-inflationary policies now in effect can only bring down interest rates. Materially so, Mr. Greschner. I am not talking of a small adjustment. Mr. Gudge is convinced that long-term rates will be cut almost in half over the next year. He is prepared to back that conviction with his capital and his credit. Why not? It is his money—not, as seems generally the case today, someone else's."

"To do that, you realize, Mr. Katagira, on the scale I judge you to suggest, might require letting an outsider take a peek at your books—or at least a page or two?"

"I think we recognize we may have been too isolationist at the Lazy G, Mr. Greschner. Few visitors have come. Which means that relatively few outside ideas have penetrated—except the technological, of course, since Mr. Gudge has an abiding interest in technology. Let us say that we see possible great advantages to be gained by moving closer to the outside world, even at the cost of raising a corner of the veil. To permit a glimpse at our books, as you put it."

He smiled coolly at Greschner. There would be no problem about the books, he knew. Even if anyone asked to look into them—which he doubted, so convinced was he of the magnetism of Gudge's suspected fortune. But if anyone did, what he would see would be a complete fabrication. An imaginary, fictitious Lazy G concocted by his information center. All based, of course, on the actualities of the operating units, but subtly altered, switched, rearranged and redomiciled, into an operational, legal and financial fiction. A forgery of the Lazy G conceived in his own mind and given verisimilitude by his computers. It had been done before. At Equity Funding, for example, which he'd studied carefully, and OPM, highly speculative stocks had been promoted and kept afloat by falsifications taken on faith by investment and financial institutions. What he contemplated was nothing new: only many, many times larger.

Moreover, his strategy eliminated the possibility of premature discovery. There would be no chagrined insiders to bear the truth to the outside world. Above all, the point of the exercise would not be to make money; that was the real difference. He had conceived a many-faceted strategy, which would be apparent in its horrific, ironic whole only when it was too late, when the spreading ripples had surged into waves, when the pebble he'd dropped into the pond was finally seen to be a boulder.

Over an early lunch, the talk turned desultory and difficult. Sol would have liked to plumb Katagira deeper. He sensed they shared a taste for the sort of enlightened, gentlemanly philosophy, Johnsonian, Emersonian, that Sol fancied himself to embrace in his own life and character. He was especially pleased to see that Vosper, having taken notice of the Japanese guest's disability, had caused the planned menu to be altered. Instead of the entrecôte, which Greschner had ordered on the assumption that it would suit Gudge's Texas palate, soup was followed by quenelles of sole, much more manageable with the ivory chopsticks that Katagira, pleasantly surprised, found at his place when the three men came into the dining room.

There seemed to be something on Gudge's mind, as he toyed with his quenelles—he would later describe them to his wife as "some sort of fishburgers"—and stared either at his plate or at the ceiling. Finally, over a raspberry soufflé, which he demolished like a small boy, he came out with it.

"Mr. Greschner, I guess you know about art and all. This house sure has a lot of pretty things. I mean, if a man wanted to buy some art, you could tell him where to go."

"I can certainly try, Mr. Gudge. I like to think I know my way around the art world. What have you got in mind?"

"Well, when Mrs. Gudge was up here last week, she saw some pictures she'd like for me to get for her. Fact was, it was after that dinner of yours she told me all about. She said these were just real great pictures, and she has her heart set on them. I don't have to say, I generally try to keep Mrs. Gudge happy."

Greschner laughed. "Oh, my goodness, Mr. Gudge. She must be referring to the Lefcourt Collection, which is on exhibit at the Fuller Institute. The two large buildings across the way. It's perhaps the most famous private collection in the world. It's here on loan from the villa in Florence where it hangs permanently and to which it will return when the exhibition's over.

I'm afraid that none of the pictures are for sale, although I'm sure Lord Lefcourt, whom I don't really know, would be deeply flattered at your interest. But as for buying them, I'm afraid that's not likely to be possible, Mr. Gudge."

He saw that Gudge did not share his amusement.

"Mr. Greschner, anything can be bought. At some price or in some way. That's a rule of my granddaddy's."

"Perhaps you're right, Mr. Gudge." Sol did some quick thinking. No point in risking this lucrative, potent relationship by dismissing even so fatuous a thought as this. "It's certainly worth exploring." He would get Nick to handle it. Nick could probably divert Mrs. Gudge's attention elsewhere, and turn a handsome profit in the bargain. "Tell me, sir—I believe you said you'd be staying in New York a day or so more. Could you come here to lunch again tomorrow? I'll introduce you to someone who can tell you all about the Lefcourt pictures."

Following lunch, Katagira wished to discuss some further details with Greschner; he was leaving that evening to return to Texas. As Sol showed Gudge to his car, he saw that the sunny spring morning had turned into a forbidding gray afternoon. Across the way he saw a taxi pull up in front of the Fuller and discharge a passenger who looked, even from the back and from fifty yards, thanks to the weary slope of her shoulders, beaten down. It was, of course, Calypso Fuller; on her way, he knew, to her ritual lunch with Frodo Crisp before the monthly Trustees' Meeting.

Returning upstairs, he found Katagira admiring the Hogarth over the fireplace.

"Are you fond of Augustan England, Mr. Katagira?"

"To the extent it fathered the spirit of independence of this nation, yes."

He took a seat across from Greschner and looked at him intently.

"Anything that can be done to assist Mr. Gudge to get those paintings will be greatly appreciated. Mr. Gudge worships his wife."

Greschner heard what Katagira said; he also heard what the Japanese left unsaid. He could well imagine that Katagira and Caryn Gudge were hardly soulmates. There must be days when Gudge felt himself pulled nearly apart by his determined companions.

They talked broadly for the next hour about Wall Street, economic policy, the condition of the financial markets and the range of Sol's experience and expertise in that area. Katagira scarcely paid attention to the details. He was trying to get the measure of Sol. He sensed the man's resentfulness against individuals and institutions close to the very center of the system that Katagira himself proposed to disrupt. There were depths of rancor in Greschner, he felt, which at the right time could be drawn upon to be turned to the Lazy G's account. Katagira was under no illusions about the intellectual worth of vindictiveness; but it could be a useful source of inspiration, given just the right circumstances—of the sort he intended to manufacture.

Listening to Greschner, he briefly considered taking him into his confidence about the whole scheme. He was stayed, however, by a sense of Greschner's egotism. He had heard that Greschner was inclined to boast of his contributions to his clients' success. That could prove problematical. Better to let events acquire a certain momentum of their own, he said to himself; then we may take another look.

Sol watched Katagira's taxi make its way out of Rostval Place. It was an unseasonably chilly afternoon, but his exhilaration warmed him. A good afternoon for reading and dozing. But first he would call Nick and tell him to cancel whatever luncheon plans he had for tomorrow. And he would get onto Homer Seabury tomorrow; Homer would be across the way at the Fuller this afternoon. This could save Homer, Sol thought, mentally calculating the value to himself of another man's salvation. As he hurried inside, a small egg of a man framed by the austere massiveness of the entryway, he wondered whether he should have invited Mrs. Gudge to lunch tomorrow. On reflection, he thought not. He might have to reverse gears on his idea of stirring Caryn Gudge and Nick together. Now that he had whale-size fish to fry. In his own estimate of his strengths, foremost, he felt, throughout his life and career, had been an instinctive gift for letting well enough alone. It was an estimate with which few others who knew him would have agreed.

"Goodbye, my love," said Hugo Winstead to the young, pretty Seabury, Winstead associate, who leaned to plant a last adoring kiss as she slipped into her mushroom-shaped down coat. "I'll see you tomorrow at the office. And perhaps we can lunch again next week." He beamed with a knowing, urbane salaciousness that made her ankles quiver.

He closed the door slowly and checked his watch. Right on time. It never would do for him to ask a lady to hasten her rerobing and her departure so that he could keep to his magnificent, important schedule.

The clock in the kitchenette read 1:43. Plenty of time. The meeting at the Fuller began at two-thirty. Time enough to scrape the mozzarella and tomato shreds from the plates, wrap up the leftover prosciutto from Balducci's to keep in the refrigerator until next week's assignation and get everything, including the wine-stained glasses, into the dishwasher. He moved around the studio efficiently, putting the place in order. He left a note and $25 for the woman who cleaned up on Friday mornings in preparation for the following week's encounters.

The light that poured in through the slatted wooden shades had turned to dishwater gray. Good timing, he thought, standing naked by the window, looking down on Waverly Place, watching the unfamiliar street life of Greenwich Village bustle below.

Gradually his mind refocused on the business at hand. There was now an empty seat at the oaken table where Darius Fuller had once dined alone to the accompaniment of countertenors singing Gesualdo madrigals; that meant that a decision about a new trustee had to be faced. Granada Masterman was, of course, the likeliest candidate. She had made a healthy contribution to the completion of the Annex, although nothing like the sum that people were guessing, and, in the bargain, had covered a large part of the extraordinary expense of bringing the Lefcourt Collection to Rostval Place. And the opening gala.

But was that enough? From someone like Granada? What a nuisance it was. He wished, but for no more than a moment, that he had never met Granada. She never let up in her social demands. He wished he'd never accepted her invitation to join the board of Masterman United. He wished that he had never taken her business a long time ago—when Sol Greschner had arranged for him to meet her as he had requested. She didn't let him forget, ever, how much MUD had paid Seabury, Winstead. As far as that went, he thought, distracted by recollections of the active, joyous thighs of the young lady who had just departed, he would have been better off never to have met Sol Greschner. And never to have met Calypso Fuller through Sol. Never to have listened to Sol's advice about ideal marriage—"the conjoining of fresh ability and established influence." Foolish, he thought; but then he recognized that he was talking to himself about Hugo Winstead Now and Hugo Winstead Then, and everything settled back into the right balance: the perspective from which he could properly appreciate the prominence and prosperity all these despised relationships had brought to Hugo Winstead.

Figures frolicked in his mind. Last year, MUD had paid Seabury, Winstead nearly $1.5 million in fees. Next to the bank and Seaco, it had been the biggest number the firm had billed out. Even larger than the TransNational fees. The bank, which funneled all its loan agreements to the firm, paid for by the borrowers, was the biggest; that was an old Morgan Seabury relationship. Next came Seaco, with all its underwriting and SEC business. His old Navy buddy Homer Seabury had been good for nearly $2 million last year. And of course, he'd been the peacemaker when Granada had bought into Seaco. It was all very confusing. He was on both boards, and when Granada had informed him of her intention to extend her control of Seaco—something about wanting the Masterwoman concept to extend into housewives' investments—he'd had to be pretty nimble. Not that nimbleness didn't have its value. The comptroller at Seabury, Winstead had told him that the hourly billings on his work lighting the peace pipe between MUD and Seaco would come close to $600,000. He'd done it alone, too. Greschner was out of the MUD picture, thank God; mention his once-revered name to Granada and she turned into something out of a Grimm fairy tale. As long as Granada was not on the Fuller Board, he was sure of her. Once she was elected, who could know but that she would discover new ambitions, perhaps better served by others than Seabury, Winstead and Corcoran.

The problem wouldn't go away. Himself and Seabury on the Fuller

Board, thanks to Greschner—well, himself thanks to Calypso, but via Sol —and Granada pushing hard. Pushing hard and complicating things with her big position in Seaco. Although that might be a blessing, since it meant a conflict of interest with Homer. A good excuse for delaying any decision on the Board seat; for doing nothing. And there was always his wife. Calypso had her standards. She was old New York, and she didn't entirely approve of Granada, even though her devotion to the Fuller obliged her to be nice as long as there was some hope of a really major Masterman benefaction. As complicated as it might be, he thought, with everyone connected in different ways to everyone else, the striving and the besieged, there was still the fact that Calypso was the Settlement Trustee, with the only elective vote. He was certain that she still believed in him, and that she would do what he advised. How awfully helpful it was that women now treated each other like men, didn't trust each other. But the fast track was still tough, he thought. After a while, after running as fast and adeptly as possible, there was a point where it came down to praying the pursuers would wear out, and fall.

It made him tired just to keep everything in his head, let alone go through day after day holding it together. Picking up his undershorts from the floor, he crossed to the large mirror on the wall parallel to the bed. When he pushed one of the mounting brackets down, a center section edged free like a cabinet. Behind it was a videotape camera mounted on top of a recorder. The installation had been made by a detective agency the firm used in its marital practice. He switched the cassette around, pressed the right switches, crossed back to the television set across from the bed and turned it on. Settling on the edge of the bed, undershorts hanging loosely from a hand resting on his thigh, he watched a clear picture dispossess the confused flickerings on the screen.

He watched himself embrace the girl, whom he'd maneuvered as precisely as if there'd been chalk marks on the bed, and watched his hand slide down her leg and up and under her skirt. Watched her shrug out of her clothes. He'd been right as rain about the quality of her breasts when he'd interviewed her. He looked at himself and was pleased. Hard as a college boy, he thought approvingly. A twenty-year-old cock on a sixty-year-old body. The figures on the screen sank down on the bed; as always, he'd carefully managed to pose the action so that the camera got everything. Watching was more exciting than doing, thought Hugo Winstead, Ladies' Man.

Fifteen minutes later, confidence renewed, he closed the mirror. Noting the young woman's name and the date on the cassette label, he shoved it into the metal cabinet which he kept locked in the closet. It was getting crowded. He rearranged the clothes hanging over it to hide it from view, and shut the door.

Downstairs, he peered right and left down the street, making sure of the coast, and then walked rapidly to University Place, where he caught a cab.

At Twenty-fifth Street he saw that his car was waiting, as ordered, outside the Madison Avenue entrance to New York Life. With the fatigued dignity of a man who had spent the last three hours discussing indentures with demanding clients, he climbed into the back seat and instructed the driver to take him to the Fuller Institute.

With a low gasp, the patient on the couch began to thrash, punctuating her throes with scarcely coherent, obscene moans. The vibrator buzzed angrily on the floor where she had dropped it. With a final outburst she lapsed into a panting silence. Dr. Sartorian reached over to the table at his side, plucked a Handi-Wipe and cleaned himself. He picked up the vibrator and shut it off.

"Darling," he said, "that's really quite a fantasy." And so it had been. Worth every second of the $200 rich women paid him to listen to an hour of their agonies. Normally he would have lowered himself onto the couch beside her for direct therapy, but she was having her period, and Sartorian, a fastidious man, had a full schedule of other patients to treat.

"I'll see you Tuesday," he said, watching her pull on a $2,000 dress. "Try these in the meantime, love. I suppose I'll see you at the Meltons'." He smiled at her.

"Oh, Victor," she said, "do you suppose it's really my father?"

"It always is." He handed her a plastic vial in which tablets of Quaalude and Percodan were packed like aspirin. "And"—adding a small envelope of silver foil—"here's a touch of fun. A soupçon of the sweet white powder."

She left by the stairs. Sartorian sometimes liked his patients to encounter each other in the waiting room; it promoted a sort of jealousy among these craving women which could be a powerful stimulus. Thank God for husbands and fathers, Sartorian thought. He arranged a fresh paper towel at the head of his couch and rose to open the downstairs door to his next patient.

"Hi." Caryn Gudge looked very beautiful today, he thought. Very tempting. He took her coat and hung it over the back of the chair at his desk.

She posed briefly on the edge of the couch.

"You sure this is what I ought to be doing, Dr. Sartorian? Lying down like this?"

" 'Victor,' dear." Whenever he could, Sartorian liked to expedite the process of transference. "It's the only way, Mrs. Gudge. Believe me. From our talks together, it's clear that you're dealing with an anxiety neurosis. I find it to be a common occurrence among a number of my patients, although each one tries to deal with it in her own way. It's not easy to be married to an extremely wealthy man. Those of us who have made something of a specialty of the neuroses and psychoses of money understand that. The pressures can produce hysteria. The only way to handle it is analysis—which means, as we discussed last time, you have to lie down to talk about it."

She arranged herself coquettishly on his couch. Offhandedly, Sartorian wondered whether there were any psychoanalysts in Texas. It was not, he assumed, the state of the Union most given to introspective self-evaluation.

Once down, she had talked. And talked. She had described a life in small Texas towns that Sartorian didn't know; cheerleading, and tight sweaters, and doing it in the back of cars over to the drive-in, and the time in Houston, and a father who lived on beer to get away from a mother who scolded and screamed, and a first, pregnant marriage in Odessa with a miscarriage that followed right away, and what it was like to wear tight velvet shorts at valve shows and get felt up by the buyers from the supply houses, and about Bubber Gudge, and how sometimes he could get it up to love her and most times now he couldn't 'cause he seemed sorta weak, but who cared, rich and loving as he was, 'cause she loved him too anyway; how she was sick of rayon underwear and crazy about silk, and how being able to spend all this money was the best thing ever. The words tumbled out of her like jackstraws.

She talked about New York, and the big new apartment, and how she was going to get her husband to buy her everything—'cause if you owned everything, everyone knew you were something, the way she figured it. Then she talked more about her husband, telling what he had told her about his life and, especially, his mother, giving Sartorian something to think about.

"What we'll work on," he said, "is this business of your husband's mother. It's clear that's his problem. And it affects you, because he quite rightly sees you, since you're beautiful and intelligent, as his fantasy of her. What he gives you he's really also giving his mother. You'll have to get used to not being his mother, if you're going to enjoy being his wife."

Sartorian smiled. It was as nice a syllogism as he'd put together in recent sessions.

"Do you think he sees his mother? In dreams, for example? Most men do; I see mine all the time. Does he say 'Mamma' when he touches you? Does he say she was beautiful—like you? Does he seem to want you to be like her?"

"Uh-huh. And sometimes he screams when he's asleep. You know, I hear him all the way over in my room. Or he gets silly-looking. He's got this Jap, see, and they're always talking about the old days. And there's this old gun, right downstairs in the front hall in a glass case, which he gets up and goes to look at, sometimes right in the middle of the night when he can't sleep. I mean that's why I can't stand it sometimes down there, y'know, 'cause there's all these ghosts; I mean like there was these ghosts just everywhere we are and his mamma's one of them, and his granddaddy too."

Sartorian took all of this in. It was his job. He looked up from the pad on the arm of his chair in which he had written the few basic facts of Caryn Gudge's life. Looking at his watch, he saw that the session was running overtime. Time to break.

"Well, there's a great deal to discuss." Staring down the long line of the couch, he admired her: ankles as slender as longbows; skirt gathering around her knees in unplanned ripples; breasts drifting heavily sidewise.

"I'm afraid the hour is up. I'll give you something to keep you going. Very good session, Mrs. Gudge; I think we'll do very well together. It's a rare pleasure to have so intelligent and sensitive a patient. Here." He handed over a small vial of brightly colored capsules.

Caryn had never spouted off like this before. The act of confession was exciting. No man had ever called her intelligent, but she expected that was just 'cause now she could be seen for what she really always had been. Now that she had a chance to be a lady. She felt wet and wicked. Rising from the couch, she crossed to the desk to pick up her black sable coat. Sartorian said something, but she didn't quite catch it. She examined herself in the mirror. Her hair looked fine. She was seized with an impulse. Her back still to him, so he couldn't see, she opened her coat, hiked up her skirt and whirled like a chorus girl, seeking to astonish him with the refulgent orange bristle at her crotch, pressed leaf-flat against her belly by her panty hose. As far as surprises went, it was a dead heat. To her own amazement, she saw that the doctor had risen from his chair; his trousers and drawers were puddled around his ankles and he was sticking out like a regular Lazy G stud bull, as ready for her as any man had ever been, and bigger. Well, at least as big as that tool pusher back in Odessa, and that had been a long, long time ago. The sight made her right weak in her knees and she sank slowly toward him. Fortunately, Dr. Sartorian had arranged things so that his next hour was free.

With as incestuously connected a small group as the Fuller Board, such decisions as needed to be taken at its meetings were usually worked out well before the trustees sat down at the table at which, so the dealer who sold it to Darius Fuller had claimed, Charles I had supped his last meal and written his last letters before going out to face the executioner. The mood in that cell in the Tower of London couldn't have been any less jolly than that which, this day, confronted Hugo Winstead as he called the meeting to order. There were decisions to be made—but this time it had proved impossible for him to arrange a preordained consensus. The decisions would actually have to be discussed and concluded at the meeting itself.

Now there were only four trustees. The Agreement of Settlement specified five, although it was silent as to the period which might elapse between the passing of one and the election of his successor. The three faces at which Hugo grinned were those of his wife, who as Settlement Trustee held the sole power of election; Homer Seabury, who had succeeded his father on the Board, and Marvin Terrace, the chairman of TransNational Entertainment Corporation, a major client of Hugo's firm, whom Hugo had caused to be elected as a gesture to everything that was "new" by the

Fuller's traditional standards. New money; the new politics of the Sunbelt and Washington; new values; the new corporate culture. TransNational might be in the entertainment business, and that, after all, could be said to smack suitably of creativity, which was deemed, generally, to be a good thing, but Marvin Terrace himself was as pompous and protective of his own interests as the stuffiest Pine Street trust lawyer, and *that* accorded with Winstead's view of the Board.

Winstead had argued that Marvin would give the Fuller access to the philanthropic resources of corporate America. Not that they'd ever go in for the bread and circuses that had become the order of the day at the Met. The Fuller didn't draw that kind of crowd; only the Michelangelo drawings and, now, the Lefcourt Collection "looked to have legs," as one of Terrace's colleagues at the studio might have put it. It would be nice to have a little help.

Winstead began the meeting in his usual crisp, assured fashion, getting the formalities out of the way; moving right to the important business. He liked to show that he had little time for persiflage.

"I think we'd better begin by authorizing me to draft resolutions of appreciation to Mrs. Masterman and Mr. Bogle for their recent generosity with respect to the Annex building fund, and for underwriting the festivities and documentation of last Thursday's, ah, highly successful opening."

"Shouldn't we also do something for Max Lefcourt?" asked Calypso Winstead.

Her husband regarded her with the patience of a parent responding to a child who has asked a perfectly respectable question at not quite the right moment.

"I think, dear, we can deal with that at our May meeting, which will be the last before we break for the summer. You might be thinking of an appropriate gift. Something from Steuben, perhaps." Steuben was to Winstead's aesthetics as Phidias to Pericles. "Why don't you and Frodo make up a little *ad hoc* committee to come up with something?"

"Now we have really only two items on the agenda, which is why I didn't trouble Frodo's office to send out any preparatory memoranda. The first is to summarize our financial situation. Unfortunately, we're in the middle of our fiscal year, and my figures are a little rough, so I'll ask you to bear with me.

"When I spoke with Certified this morning, they informed me that our endowment stood at $98 million and change as of the first of the month. That's a bit down from last year. It was, I think, around $121 million a year ago. Of course, we did take out $14 million of unrestricted capital for the Annex. It's producing approximately $10 million of current income, but unfortunately, that's beyond us; as you know, the terms of the Agreement of Settlement oblige this Board to limit the annual budget of the Institute to seven percent of the average value of the endowment during any twelve-month period. Without going into the rights and wrongs and whys and wherefores of this limitation, or quarreling with the foresightedness or lack thereof on the part of Calypso's father, that is the way it is. Your father drew up the Agreement, Homer. It is an admirable piece of legal draftsmanship and is, therefore, ironclad.

"What this means is that, barring a significant increase in the value of our investment portfolio, which regrettably contains a substantial holding in fixed-income bonds bought many years ago when the financial order seemed more secure, there is approximately $7 million of annual income available to support the operations of the Institute.

"Heretofore, that has permitted us to live luxuriously and well. Even with the recent rate of inflation, our relatively modest operating structure has been an asset. We are still able to carry on our basic operations for an annual expenditure of around $900,000—which covers Frodo and his small staff, their benefits, and the custodianship, maintenance and energy costs of this building. The Annex, which will require ten additional guards and maintenance personnel, is expected to add $547,000 to that amount, meaning an operating budget of $1,500,000 against a projected income of $7 million.

"Normally, that would produce a surplus of about $5.5 million for exhibitions, publication and the acquisition of objects. To this we have normally added the $750,000, in round figures, given annually by the Fellows and the Associates, and another $50,000 from sales of publications, gift items and the like. Basically, that has been the extent of our financial reach. Where our grasp, in terms of objects we have wished to acquire, has lagged our reach, we have either been able to arrange suitable terms of payment with art dealers or other sellers, as was the case with the Bernini altar upstairs, where you will recall there was some question about its export permit from Italy and our connections were helpful in keeping M. du Cazlet out of a Roman prison; or for limited benefactions, like Harvey Bogle's $50,000 for the Keats manuscript, to make up the difference. It has not been necessary to go for significant outside money—until recently, of course—and by not having to do so, we have been able to preserve the integrity, shall I say, of this Board and of the institution with which it is entrusted."

"There is no point in going over the history of the Annex. I believe we were fortunate to have obtained a $40-million mortgage on extremely favorable terms, thanks to the efforts of Seaco Group's real estate–financing subsidiary. That mortgage, however, calls for annual payments of interest and principal totaling $5.6 million. For the next twenty-five years. It takes no arithmetical genius to see that, between our expenses and the fixed payments we have incurred with respect to the Annex, there is very little left. Factoring for inflation, which a prudent man must do, there is—in fact—nothing left! Barring, of course, a substantial increase in the value of our endowment funds."

He paused to let this sink in.

"Now," he concluded "it is inconceivable that the Institute can continue on this footing. For one thing, I think we now risk losing Frodo, possibly to one of those places in Texas or California that have a lot of money to spend buying things. We all know what Frodo has meant to us. Second, in the Annex, we have a splendid facility—and very little prospect of filling it, on either a permanent or a temporary basis, without new resources. We can hold out a hand to Washington or City Hall, but I think the present political climate is not the most salubrious for that. We can go after corporate help, and that is something that Homer, Marvin and I will explore. And we do have one seat vacant on the Board. That could be worth a great deal!"

He opened the meeting to a general discussion which ranged fitfully back and forth for the next hour. It kept coming back to the question of a new trustee. As much as the three men tried to deflect the issue with schemes such as a corporate campaign, an admission charge, a subvention from the city, Calypso kept returning to the possibility of filling the vacated seat. It was clear that her dedication to the institution which bore her family name exceeded all other considerations.

"I don't understand why we shouldn't consider either Harvey Bogle or Granada Masterman for the seat, Hugo. She's very rich; I heard her income is millions! She likes the Institute. Hugo, you know she gave you money without blinking when you asked her to. She knows everybody and she has a big corporation, and talks about Washington contacts, everybody knows that she and Rufus Lassiter are this close!" She held up a small, freckled hand with index and forefinger tightly pressed together. As always, her voice was mild and pallid. "And Harvey gave even more! Including the land for the Institute. And, what was it, $2 million for the building?"

This question also did not please Winstead. He frowned.

"I really don't think it's appropriate to discuss Bogle at this time, in any case. First, I don't know if he's our sort. His election might put off certain of our better corporate prospects. Secondly, and I'm sure that as a woman you couldn't possibly be aware of this, Calypso, but Bogle's causing difficulties for both Homer and Marvin. His presence would hardly make for harmony."

Thank God for Hugo, thought Homer Seabury. Calypso was still so damn naive, even though she was now in her fifties. Hugo had done a good job keeping her in the dark over the thirty-five years of their marriage. They had gotten married in 1946, a month after Calypso's twenty-first birthday. Their first meeting, then their courtship and marriage in the Church of the Incarnation had been chaperoned and articulated by Sol Greschner, Seabury recalled. He and Greschner and Rufus Lassiter, all still friends then, had stood up for Winstead. Calypso had been attended by an old aunt, long since dead for all Homer knew, and two school friends.

By marrying Hugo, who was older, Homer and the rest of their set had assumed that Calypso had gotten the imitation father she had thought she wanted in a husband. Certainly Hugo had taken over her life as sternly and completely as any Victorian parent. She appeared to know nothing of money, business, intrigue, Hugo's manifold adulteries, his acrobatic professional life. Hugo fashioned their schedule; met with her trustees; guided her on the Fuller Board and enshrouded her hermetically in a life that suited and promoted him. As far as Seabury knew, the extent of her independent contacts with the world outside was her weekly lunches with Frodo Crisp and her passing involvement in Granada Masterman's orbit.

"And," Winstead was saying, "Granada's in somewhat the same position vis-à-vis our two friends here. I don't think she'd do either; at least, not for the moment. Why don't we seek a compromise? Do nothing."

Ah, thought Seabury, he's got us out of it. Homer recognized the true objective of the skillfully administered board of directors: do nothing. Avoid the issue if possible, and if not, avoid the decision. Difficult situations, experience taught, sorted themselves out one way or another if left to their own devices. That was the principle on which the free market and a stable corporate oligarchy depended. Well done, Hugo, he breathed gratefully.

The compromise they agreed on was to postpone consideration of another trustee until the May meeting.

Winstead had a concluding suggestion.

"In the meantime, may I suggest that Calypso invite Mrs. Masterman to become Chairperson of the Council of Fellows? I'm sure I can prevail on the present chairman to step aside in the larger interests of the Institute. I also think, Calypso, that you can persuade Mrs. Masterman, with whose impatience we're all familiar, that our inaction at this time at filling the seat is only due to a decent respect for the recently deceased. I wouldn't worry about Bogle. He'll understand. People like that always do."

Homer, departing, reflected that the tangle of connections and interrelating, sometimes conflicting interests on the Board typified what those damn liberal journalists called "the invisible government." Well, he was proud to be part of it. The way the world had gone the last twenty years, there were few enough anchors to windward for people of their sort, few enough pilings to cling to in battering seas. They had to keep it that way. It was crucial to maintain that sticky, protective web. Keep its strands and turnings beyond the understanding of the heathen; keep them aware that to be outside it was social perdition, which was worse than impoverishment.

He stopped at the information desk and telephoned across the square; Greschner was in and invited him to walk over. Homer was in a fix, and old Sol sometimes gave pretty good advice. Even if he wasn't what he once was.

After Winstead left, Calypso sat alone for a minute in the Trustees' Room, looking alternately at the portraits of her grandfather, tough and buttoned-up, and her father, fresh and spirited in his RAF uniform, which hung at opposite ends of the blond-paneled room. The discussion had bothered her. Through it all, Hugo had treated the Annex, that hateful, bankrupting excrescence for which he was responsible, as if it were a *fait accompli* with which he had really only a most casual connection. But it *was* Hugo who had pushed through the idea three years ago, when the places now filled by Seabury and Terrace were occupied by two frail old men. And had insisted on pushing forward with it, when it became clear that its $25-million budget was too low by almost $40 million, and even after Harvey Bogle had offered to take it over, bail out the Institute and convert it into a low-rise condominium. It was not lost on Calypso that the Vietnamese architect Hugo commissioned was a favorite of Granada's; he had designed the Dallas headquarters of Masterman United. The Fuller commission authenticated his work as art—pumping up the cultural pretensions of the MUD Building down in Texas.

The whole Annex affair had started just after Hugo's firm began doing legal work for MUD. No one on the Fuller Board, she remembered, had even suggested the possibility that one fact was related to the other. As always, she had kept silent. Her apparent meekness served her well, she believed. Especially when dealing with a bully like Hugo. She knew a great deal more than all those men surmised; it was just that her portion of her father's bravura was kept within, like a lively flame lighting walls of a cave. She knew about Hugo and his apartment in Greenwich Village and his girls. Poor man. He suffered from those most blinding afflictions, ambition and vanity. He needed to poke himself triumphantly at every skirt that came along to confirm his potency. For which she was thankful.

That was one of the few intelligent things Sartorian had told her in the year she'd gone to him. Victor was another one: like Hugo, a predator. He'd trade in another man's secrets as the price of buying a body. His lubriciousness was nauseating; an hour with him was like a bath in sludge. But he talked—just the way Hugo did—as if he thought she barely understood, and it really didn't matter, since most of the time men like that were really talking to themselves, confident of womankind's opacity to the so-called real world. Like the Frenchmen and Germans who blabbered away in New York elevators, confident that in this misguided and *arriviste* nation, no one could possibly understand their subtle, sophisticated language.

It really didn't matter. What was important was the things that Hugo and Victor, and the others, didn't know about. Such as the investment course she took at The New School on Wednesday mornings. Or her serious, pleasant teas every other week with Jill Newman. Or that for the last few years, on every possible alternate Tuesday, she took a taxi to an obscure restaurant in Chelsea where she had a light lunch with Harvey Bogle, and learned about life.

When the elevator stopped on the top floor of the Tennyson, a houseman in the hotel's uniform was waiting for Nick.

"Please come in, Mr. Reverey. Mr. Bogle is on the telephone. He shouldn't be long. Would you like a drink?"

Nick took a Scotch-and-water. It had been one of those days. He followed the houseman into what was easily one of the worst-furnished living rooms he could recall seeing. Nothing quite matched. The juxtapositions were unfortunate: gilded imitation French fauteuils pushed up against glass-and-steel side tables from some High Tech decorator. The room memorialized, he saw quickly, each recent stage of the celebrated Von González taste. The only common denominator seemed to be expensiveness. A lot of it might have been cheap-looking, thought Nick, but it had cost a bundle. In a way, it reminded him of what he'd read of Esmé Bogle's fiction: glossy, full of received ideas of style and taste, yet with enough evidence of the proprietress' lace-curtain commonness, gewgaw on top of gewgaw—Boehm bird figurines, Ispanky statuettes, athletic figures made from bent and twisted steel and copper wire—punctuating the dreadful ensemble like commas.

Out of professional habit, Nick began to work the walls. The paintings were of a piece with the room. What he called "Fifty-seventh Street/Palm Beach Crap" Ersatz impressionists and splashy Mediterranean scenes. Palette knives should be licensed like handguns, he thought, examining a *View of Saint Tropez* that seemed to have been vomited onto the canvas. Picture by picture he moved around the room. Somebody had the Bogles' number, he saw. They had one of each: the kids with big, sad eyes; three different gloppy paintings of ballerinas by three different artists; a bad realistic seascape, *Rounding the Point*; another picture, labeled *Clowns*, that seemed to have been painted with a trowel; a primitive of *Apple Day at Granny's Farm*. Practically no commercial, mediocre genre was unrepresented. Then, at the end, next to the door that led into a dining room which Nick scarcely dared to enter for fear of perishing in a maelstrom of false Art Deco and distressed furniture, he found a perfectly acceptable Monet of a child playing with a hoop in the Tuileries. It was an early picture, signed and dated 1873. Very nice, he thought, bending to examine the picture below; it was a very decent Fantin-Latour of roses and anemones, in a dully gleaming brass bowl; he recognized it.

Somebody was doing something right to buy these, he thought.

"These're not too bad, huh?" said Harvey Bogle behind him. Nick turned to find him extending a glass of whisky. "Have a seat. The rest of this stuff is shit." He gestured toward the room at large.

He spoke as a material witness, but not an accomplice, to a crime.

"Esmé bought the rest of this stuff. She likes to go to those galleries where they give you a plastic glass of cheap booze and you stand around with two hundred other overdressed assholes oohing and aahing at pictures of kids with bug-eyes painted by a fag in a velvet suit."

Again Bogle gestured toward the room with his glass. "Awful, isn't it?—but it makes Esmé happy. More of her buddy, that Von González woman. She calls it 'Harem Eclectic,' and I call it bullshit. Like those forklifts and cutting tables down at the Castle. Sometimes, I can't figure it; I mean, Esmé's smart; she writes *books*, which is something, whether you like them or not; yet she falls for this crap. Sorry to make you wait. I was talking to my lawyer, which is what most businessmen spend their time doing. Trying to avoid getting the shaft. You own any stock? Here! Look at this crap!"

Admitting to a few modest stockholdings, Nick took the newspaper Bogle thrust at him. It was headlined, "ILLINOIS OIL TO OFFER $2.4 BILLION FOR ZINC COMPANY."

While Nick puzzled out the story, Bogle left the room, muttering. He reappeared an instant later with a red folder containing a few sheets of paper.

"Read this." He handed Nick the torn-off cover of a copy of *Business Week* dated early the preceding fall. It was a photograph of two bespectacled men in vested suits; by their appearance, they might have been court stenographers or insurance adjusters; it bore the legend "A CHALLENGE FOR ILLINOIS OIL: $2 BILLION IN THE BANK/WHAT TO DO?" The cover story was attached. Nick glanced at it briefly before Bogle slipped another paper on top.

It was a letter on Bogle's stationery to the chief executive officer of Illinois Oil Company:

> Dear Sir:
>
> I am the registered and beneficial owner of 35,963 shares of common stock of Illinois Oil Company.
>
> I have read with interest the recent article in Business Week describing the efforts of you and your management, and doubtless your accountants, management consultants, attorneys and investment bankers, as well as many unacknowledged but eager finders and middlemen, to find a progressive way to spend the windfall which our company has accumulated as a result of our North Slope oil production.
>
> Unless I am incorrect, that money, over and above its application to the company's indebtedness, properly belongs to the owners of the company, namely its stockholders, with whose capital, including the proceeds of a public stock offering of $75 million, the Alaskan oil reserves were financed. May I suggest for your consideration, therefore, the possibility of distributing the company's excess cash to its shareholders on the most equitable and least costly tax basis.

The letter was signed by Bogle in a small, neat script that struck Nick as strangely precise for a man of such a flamboyant business style.

"This is what I got back," said Bogle, showing Nick a letter on the Illinois Oil letterhead; it consisted of a few lines thanking Bogle for his interest and assuring him that "Your Management" continued to seek constructive opportunities for "Our Company." It was signed by the Vice-President for Stockholder Relations.

"Piss on them," said Bogle. "I'm going into court tomorrow in Springfield to get an injunction. I tell you, Reverey, it is tough to be a businessman these days with jerks like this crapping in the community nest. They cry to Uncle Sam to decontrol oil because they need the money to plow back into the ground, and when they get what they want they go running off to buy someone else's paper. I've got two buildings on the West Side where the oil bill went up ten percent a month this winter, and if it doesn't stop my tenants are going to torch me, and I'm not talking about a bunch of spades and Puerto Ricans, but a lot of solid, middle-class professional folks, who don't understand why their rent should keep climbing and they should have to start pricing ranch houses two hours out of town so that Illinois Oil can use two billion dollars to pay sixty dollars a share for a piece of shit that sold for thirty dollars last week. And you can bet your ass that there are some Illinois Oil stockholders out there, moms and pops, who could use a rise in the dividend to pay their own fuel bills which these guys pay by voting themselves raises; I don't understand why, if "my" company—"my" company, my ass—has a couple of big ones to play with, it gets handed to the stockholders of Kesco Zinc instead of to me. And why Kesco stock, which was selling at thirty dollars, is now at sixty dollars thanks to that, while their Illinois stock is down four and a half points because Wall Street, like me, thinks this is the dumbest deal, financially, industrially and politically, that they've seen in a coon's age.

"You and I are sort of the same, Reverey. Independent businessmen. We do whatever we do with our own money and our own judgment. Take our chances. And we are getting fucked over by these jerks in big banks and big companies running around like a Chinese fire drill while Hopalong Cassidy in the White House gives 'em the high sign. They have discovered life's greatest secret: if you're going to take a chance, or you want to be a big deal, make sure you use someone else's money. That way, it doesn't hurt if you come up short."

Bogle dropped the folder disgustedly on the table.

"Sorry about the sermon. I used to spend ninety percent of my time making money and ten percent trying to hang on to it. Now it's the other way around. What a waste of energy! Which is why I wanted to talk to you."

Nick was curious. But he liked to open slowly.

"Is Mrs. Bogle here?"

"Esmé? Hell, no. She's off taping. She's always taping. I tell you, Reverey, there's nothing like a middle-aged woman who turns into a celebrity. Especially if she writes a book that sells about fifteen trillion copies—to people that really want to read wine labels and Halston and whether it's true that society women have no hair under their arms and a lot on their pussies or maybe it's the other way around, and does So-and-so, hidden under an assumed name which everybody can guess, really have to put cocaine on his dick to get it up? Esmé doesn't see it that way, though. She is a writer. With social insights that important critics like Merv Griffin and Rona Barrett are ass-over-teakettle eager to hear. And if she doubts it for a second, don't you think there's a crowd of fags ten deep to tell her how smart she is? Not that I really mind. I never watch TV and I don't read crap. I'm used to Esmé and we work things out.

"We got married right out of high school and suddenly Esmé was rich. Women who are suddenly rich tend to do one or several of four things: shop, have babies, get a job or screw around. The first three are better than having your old lady find self-realization with some South American with a dick like King Kong. Babies were out. I don't like kids and I don't think she does. Anyway, her books are her kids now. Esmé hates shopping. Hated shopping, rather. I'm not so sure anymore. So it had to be a job. But as Mrs. Harvey Bogle, she'd gone uptown, so it had to be something pretty good. So I did what every rich man in this city with any kind of a woman problem has done for fifty years. I went to see Sol Greschner."

"Sol?" Nick saw no reason to conceal his surprise.

"I'll tell you one thing, Reverey; nobody in this city understands more about the relationship of women to money than old Sol. Including that shrink with the loose zipper, Sartorian. There're a lot of ungrateful pricks around New York, mostly people Sol invented, who are trying to forget the fact that he jerked their strings once upon a time, but the fact is, he's got a lot of the answers: still. Anyway, Sol thought it over, and said why doesn't Esmé write a book? She knows all these people and must have seen or heard about all kinds of stuff in the hotel. And you sure as hell don't have to write English anymore to get a best-seller. Just keep it juicy and make sure she spells 'Gucci' with two *c*'s. That's the art of fiction writing today.

"So I bought her an IBM typewriter and a Xerox and a lot of paper and cut her loose. Sol was right. Esmé had a great memory and could write about merchandise. And what else did she need for a best-seller? English? And when she was ready, Sol took over and got her an agent and handled the P.R., although Sol hates to work the talk-show circuit. And away she went. Esmé Bogle, Novelist. As the man says: ain't it the shits?"

Bogle laughed. He offered Nick another drink. As he was pouring it, he said, "Women're funny. How's that girl you were talking to the other night? Jill Newman. Esmé's always talking about her; thinks she hung the goddamn moon, although how any smart woman can write the kind of shit she does—you ever read that crap in *That Woman!*?—I don't know. Anyway, she's got an ass like Angie Dickinson, and that can't be anything but good. You know her long?"

"First time I met her."

"Well, good luck. Anyway, Reverey, you know Greschner's a great admirer of yours. Talks about you like a son. That's important. He can still help. Anyway, what do you think about the pictures? Not the crap—the two little French ones."

"Nice. It seems to me I've seen them before. In pretty good company." Nick had identified the flower piece as one of Johnny Sandler's original cache of Fantin-Latours. The Monet had been hanging on the wall of the Desmond Gallery when he'd gone to London last June for the Cummings sale.

"You may have. I bought them last Christmas at Sandler and Sandler.

Through my secretary. No names. That's a nice show they put up. Do they do one every year?"

"About one in three or four," Nick replied, smiling inside. The Sandler and Sandler Christmas Show was a rotating event—one year in Caracas; the next on Old Bond Street; then Zurich perhaps, or Lausanne, and then back to New York—appearing under a different gallery's auspices in each city: a way by which a tight cadre of friendly dealers could pool their more attractive unsold pictures by topflight names which looked all the better for the company they were keeping.

"Anyway," said Bogle, "Sol tells me you're the best in town on Old Masters. And that show the other night at the Fuller flipped me out. It was like getting laid for the first time. You know why? Because there was something to learn after the first thrill had gone."

Nick listened closely as Bogle defined the terms of his enthusiasm for the kinds of pictures that were in the Lefcourt Collection. At Sol's dinner, Bogle had given every indication of being an intelligent man, but there was nothing about his demeanor or his speech that suggested he was an innately sensitive one. Yet as he described the sort of pleasure that the Lefcourt paintings had aroused in him, and the shape of his individual taste became clear, Nick saw that Bogle took more than a visceral pleasure from paintings; more than a gut kick from a visually pleasing arrangement of shapes and colors, and scenes and objects that were familiar parts of recognizable life: mountains, flowers, strollers on the rue de Rivoli.

Bogle seemed to have an instinctive sense for a painting's historical character, its place in time and history; this involved meanings beyond form pure and simple, the meanings which led the mind inside the skin of a work that was centuries old. It wasn't just scholarship: names, dates and iconography. Nick had argued that point often enough with Johnny Sandler. But a fourteenth-century painting had to be perceived differently from an Impressionist picture.

Bogle produced the Lefcourt catalogue.

"I liked these as much as any of them," he declared, skipping through the pages, and pointing at several. Nick was interested that Bogle had singled out some of his own favorites. The Domenico Veneziano *Saint Jerome*, with a story wilderness landscape that Frank Sanger had once described over an evening's Chianti as "the awakening of modern man to the picturesque; it's the first romantic picture"; the Leonardo sketches of a now-lost *Virgin and Child with a Swan*: a half-dozen scribbled ink drawings on a single sheet, theme and variations by a genius; the Lotto *Allegory of Penitence*, a mysterious little picture executed well after the turn of the sixteenth century, when the Renaissance was all but over, but which was as forceful a statement of a cruel, magical religion as anything painted centuries before, when the mind of Europe was convulsed by the Black Death. And the small Botticelli *Nativity*, which was a pair with the *Annunciation* uptown in the Lehman Collection.

He led Nick into a small, sparsely furnished study. It was more like him than the overstuffed, overdecorated living room.

"Just wanted to show you I was doing my homework." On a desk were stacked some books; Nick saw the eight volumes of Berenson's *Italian Painters*, Sanger's *Tuscan Painting from Giotto to Bronzino*, a couple of Felix Rothschild's monographs and several good general guides.

They went back into the living room and had another drink.

"You know, I'd like to collect pictures, Reverey; like the ones in Lefcourt's collection. But most of the stuff on that level is all wrapped up, I guess."

"Most of it, sadly. But things come up. Pictures disappear, then resurface. Things that have been in a family for centuries suddenly have to be sold. As the wealth shifts, so does the art. There are still opportunities."

"I don't know a hell of a lot about art. Yet. But I think I can pick out a good picture, and the rest I can learn by myself, or—if it's like anything else in the world—I can buy good advice. But I don't see any point in trying to collect anything but the best. If I can afford it, of course. I can go pretty good, but nothing like the husband of that girl that was at Greschner's the other night. Gudge. He wouldn't think my net worth was enough to buy cigarettes. But I could go head to head with most anyone else who wants to spend some real money. I've got this foundation I formed about twenty years ago. When I was just getting started. It owns a couple of buildings in San Antonio and Los Angeles, shopping centers here and there around the country, the equity and a second mortgage on the Castle. I let the rentals pile up and shorted the bond market and winged it in a couple of long-shot speculations that paid off about a hundred to one. The kind of crazy things that only work out if you're playing with money that otherwise would go to Uncle Sam. I let the foundation go partners with me once in a while when I pick up a block of stocks to scare the shit out of some half-assed management which will throw a lot of their stockholders' money at me to save their jobs. It's very well-paid tweaking. I'm doing a little number now on Homer Seabury and a real jerk on the Coast.

"Anyway, I'm about to turn the buildings over to a bunch of Kuwaitis for a ton of money. The dough is there. It'll work out to maybe a hundred and a quarter, hundred fifty million. Enough for openers.

"But I want to collect well. Not just dump a few hundred grand here and there for something pretty good to dress up the walls. And I don't have to buy for investment, or because I'm nigger-rich like Sandler's customers and think that owning a picture and getting a good table downstairs comes to the same thing. I don't want to crash the museum crowd, either, although I can't speak for Esmé. That's for ugly women with wallets for twats like Granada Masterman. I did help out the Fuller on the new building, but that's because I'm a bull on New York and a place like the Fuller brings in the paying customers. I've got two hotels, don't forget, and a third on the architect's sketch pad. Seeing those pictures the other night kind of made my mind up for me. These days anyone with brass balls and a line of credit can make pretty good money, so a lot of the thrill of that chase is gone. But paintings like Lefcourt's got are a real trip. That's a game I think I'd like to play—or at least kibitz a while to get a feel for it. So keep me in mind."

Nick needed no prompting. He had arrived knowing that he had been invited to talk about art. But he had guessed that Bogle's enthusiasm for the Lefcourt Collection might have been one of those freaks of nature, like otherwise retarded children who blurt out calculus or hexameters. He could see that Bogle was more than that. He could be a real collector.

"One other thing," Bogle said. "I don't give a shit about art being an investment. Stocks are for investment; art is for seeing. I want you to understand that from the go-off. Okay?"

Nick did. He smiled understandingly. "I've got something coming in the next few weeks worth looking at. I've never seen anything like it. I'll have to ask seven figures, but it's the most important situation I've ever been involved in. And of course, in the meantime, come and look at some of my other things. It'll give you a feel for the market." Like any good dealer, Nick didn't talk specifics or price without the work of art's being present. But it didn't hurt to let the virus loose in the bloodstream.

They had yet another drink, and Nick accepted Bogle's invitation for dinner. Explaining that he never ate anything except breakfast in his own joints, and then only in the privacy of his apartment, he led Nick out onto Madison Avenue and whistled down a cab. Nick was surprised. He had figured Bogle for a twenty-foot twenty-four-hour limousine. Wrong again.

They went to a private club over near the East River. Over steaks and a bottle of Beaujolais, and then another, they swapped stories, becoming friends, although Bogle still called him "Reverey" and Nick called Bogle "Mr." He told Nick how he had given the Fuller the land under the Annex, "which wasn't worth a shit commercially," and then had offered to buy them out when it was clear that the building was way over budget. "How you can give a job like that to some gook, I don't understand." But the Fuller trustees, "pissing away forty million dollars for prestige," had declined. Nick told Bogle about himself and his first dealings and the first forgery he had gotten stuck with. Then Bogle told Nick about his background. Another bottle of Beaujolais was brought, and they discovered that what they both really shared was a roots-deep devotion to New York. The most important patriotism there was, they agreed.

The place began to fill up. The language in the club shifted from English to Italian, Spanish and Farsi. The sound of the music, loud as it was, seemed to be subdued by snorts and sniffs from every table. Looking over the wispy young men and greasy young women, Bogle wondered what the hell the town was coming to.

Nick saw a familiar figure moving through the smoke, being led to a table which *That Woman!* would have classified as OUT. It was Caryn Gudge. She was followed by a tall, shambling man who seemed to blink his way along behind her. He was clearly uneasy at being in such a place, surrounded by such people.

Nick stood up and said hello as they passed his table. The tall man was introduced as Caryn's husband. His clothes looked loose and uncomfortable. He didn't seem to catch Nick's name. At Bogle's invitation, the Gudges joined them. Nick noticed, halfway curious, that Bogle seemed transfixed by Gudge, and paid only cursory attention to Caryn, who was looking pretty spectacular. During dinner, Bogle hadn't missed a jutting nipple or a single flouncing buttock, and Caryn Gudge was showing plenty of both. The irresistible attraction of big money, guessed Nick, even for other big money. Within minutes, Gudge and Bogle were deep in a discussion of the price of gas.

"First thing's made Buford look halfway happy tonight," Caryn said to Nick. "Let's dance." She gyrated out onto the tiny dance floor.

They were out there twenty minutes. For the first ten, while Nick tried to emulate what he believed was disco rhythm, Caryn shouted to him over the piercing music that they'd dined at Dove Sono, where they'd seen real celebrities like Woody Allen and G. Gordon Liddy, and that Mr. Greschner had fixed it up for them to come here to the club and wasn't it great and how she was going to join. For the next ten minutes, the music slowed to the wailing of an Italian singer with a voice like Spanish fly. Caryn put her head next to Nick's ear.

"My husband doesn't like to get out much. Do you?"

She had all the moves, Nick felt. She was shoving it right in there, and getting some crucial rotation too. He was tempted to slide his hands down on her bottom and pull her closer.

Jesus, he thought, this is not a good idea.

"Uh, look, I think we better sit down." He felt like a sixteen-year-old. Back at the table, Gudge and Bogle were smiling, both made comfortable by the familiar vocabulary of profit. Nick felt Caryn's knee pressing under the table. Stay no longer, *umfundis,* he said to himself. Stay no longer. He got up and made his good-nights. His path to the door was not altogether steady. For a lot of reasons, he thought, as he flung himself gratefully into the night.

"Now, here's the picture," the young man said. "Competitively, we're on our ass relative to the guys in the black hats, Merrill and Hutton in particular, which is why our marketing consultants came up with this Home Options idea. I think it is definitively the hottest new financial product the Street has seen in a long time, and it's all exclusively ours. We move now—and big—and we'll kick Merrill and Hutton right in the nuts."

"Home Options?" asked Homer Seabury, incredulously.

"Correct. We start making a market where people can buy and sell options on the houses where they live. It's a gut product; hits 'em where they live, you might say." He chuckled wickedly before continuing.

"Look, say you own a hundred-thousand-dollar house. It's mortgaged up to the ass. You need dough, but there's nothing left on your Visa card or MasterCharge, and American Express likes to get paid on time. So, with this plan, you sell an option on your house, say, for a year, for, say, twenty thousand. Through us. Now you got twenty thousand dollars to piss away. Which we can help you invest. At the end of a year, the guy who bought the option, he gets to buy your house for a hundred thousand. Or maybe he's sold it to someone else. Anyhow, he exercises, you get a hundred thousand dollars and out you go. Or you pay him what he wants and you stay, if you don't want to move. The agency cooked up a great slogan: 'Pay to Stay or Move Away.' Get it? 'Pay to Stay or Move Away.' And we do the same thing on the sell side. End of a year, the guy gets to put his house to you. Of course, this way, he buys the option from us. Betting that real estate'll go down. And we get in the middle. Make a market; even out our positions short and long."

Homer looked at him with amazement. Make a market in people's own houses? Their homes?

"It's got everything we look for in a financial product. Good tax picture. Ton of leverage. It's where it's at; shit, everybody's sweating real estate. Tie-ins: homeowner insurance on optioned houses; huge secondary market out there in niggers wanting to crack good neighborhoods; credit balances; new customers. We can go to ninety-percent margin. Shit, it'll be like the old days in Orange County. Sixth, seventh mortgages. We can do funds and institutional packages; get into foreclosure pools. Dynamite!"

Homer shook his head. These monthly Financial Product Planning sessions were becoming less and less comprehensible to him. He looked at the young man doing the talking. He was twenty-six years old. Two years out of the B-School. Six months out of the management-consulting firm from which Homer had been persuaded to hire him. He'd never seen war; never had a real job, the kind in which people—fellow employees, customers, suppliers—were something more than numbers; probably never had a home of his own.

It made Homer's head ache. He was richly pleased when his secretary interrupted the meeting to whisper that Mr. Greschner was on the telephone with something so urgent it couldn't wait.

CHAPTER EIGHT

The six-foot French windows overlooking Rostval Place had been opened to admit a morning as soft as cotton. Sol approved of the day. Overnight, it seemed, the trees in the little park had acquired a full summer's cover. Spring in the city, he thought, had it all over the changing of seasons in the country. There was real drama in the appearance of bright leaves against the grim stone landscape of Manhattan. Springtime in New York. He loved it. It charged into the slush-enchained city with the exuberance of a parade of boisterous young people bursting into a stolid banking hall, scattering the dull clerks of winter. From his unseen post, concealed by the softly stirring curtains, he beamed affectionately at a young woman letting herself and her baby carriage into the square. He felt very kingly and benevolent.

Summer seemed also to have arrived in his own head and heart. The appearance of the Gudges in his life had signaled a rebirth. Mrs. Gudge was just another tramp on the make, a *parvenue* with a lot of money who would soon discover, as had her sisters before her through all time, that the glittering world she yearned to crack was not worth cracking. But Gudge was interesting. There was something wrong with the man. He appeared too loose under his skin. And he moved delicately. Sol wondered if he was ill.

As for the Japanese, he was the thinker. Sol's own sort. Contemplative, oracular, deliberately mysterious. The kind of man Sol saw himself to be: revealing only the corners, the shadowed edges, of the large issues and great matters he manipulated. A man who kept the whole picture to himself. And what a picture! They were talking about bringing the Gudge fortune into contact with the outside world, of forming a Wall Street connection—and of doing it all through him. He had already tipped Homer off that something big was in the wind. "Brush up your dress suit," he'd told Homer; "you'll want to be looking your best."

That he would hand Gudge over to Seaco went without saying. Homer needed a leg up, what with Bogle in the game now and Mrs. Masterman under the spell of Rufus Lassiter. In a way, Sol saw with enjoyment, if he played it right, this could even pit Seabury and Gudge against Lassiter and Granada Masterman; old fires of hatred and recrimination could be re-torched—and he would be the man with the match. It was a prospect that gave him great pleasure.

Homer had been the only loyal one. Of the three of them, Hugo, Rufus and Homer, Sol's instinct from the very first meeting had been that only Seabury had the capacity for enduring loyalty. Rufus and Hugo were the smart ones—and the driven ones.

Winstead wanted respectability. He was an insecure climber, for all his obvious brains and his movie-star good looks. Sol had initially trusted Winstead less than the others—Winstead could be devious. By contrast, Rufus Lassiter's opportunism and ambition were transparent. The man craved center stage. It was difficult to judge whether Rufus wanted power or whether he simply wanted visibility; the two might have been confused in his mind. Homer Seabury had what depth of character there was among the three but lacked the slickness or subtlety or intelligence of his comrades. He was no manipulator, nor did he have the grinning, confidence-breeding salesmanship of Rufus. Homer was stolid, serious and dependable: virtues handed down from earlier times, virtues still esteemed in the years just after the war. The other two were confidence men, for whom postwar America was a little slow and guarded, but for whom the '60s, when they zapped onstage, seemed to have been specially designed. They were on the make in a world which, in time, became ready to be made. Amid the general festivity of V-J Day, Sol had seen that Homer was the nice guy of the three, used to being chaffed about by his ambitious, tough young chums, and available to be used by them. He wondered whether to say something to Hugo; but there was nothing that could rightly be said, among the candles and champagne, no warning that could have been discreetly uttered in Homer Seabury's ear. They were boon companions, those three; their friendship had been annealed in the fire of battle; there was no cautioning any of them that evening, as they set their feet along a path dusted with primrose blossoms.

Hugo had been taken on as an associate by Morgan Seabury's law firm. Homer and Rufus had gone to the Street—Homer as a security analyst with an old-line firm; Rufus as a stock salesman for Merrill Lynch, Pierce, Fenner and Beane. They were called back briefly for Korea—Hugo had managed to miss it—and when they came out again in 1953, they started Seabury Lassiter and Company, the compact predecessor of the now-sprawling Seaco Group.

By then they were also brothers-in-law, Rufus having married Homer's sister. Bound by marriage and the success of their fledgling firm, it seemed that they were joined forever.

The opposite qualities the two friends brought to their enterprise served it well, at first. Rufus was dashing, glib, all flair and flash; Homer was diligent, methodical, longsighted and bothered inside by envy of his partner, who was not only as bright and public as neon, but kissed with luck in the bargain. For a time—for as long, in fact, as the partnership lasted—it was known behind Broad Street menus or in knowledgeable asides on Hanover Square as "Pluck and Luck." Poor plucky Homer, the Street said: he'll knock himself out for a fraction one way or the other, a few basis points right or wrong. Lucky Rufus will get up, still drunk from the night before, take on a bond position that Jay Gould wouldn't touch, and Stalin dies and the bond market goes up a hundred basis points. Pluck and Luck. Cruel and apt: the way nicknames tend to be.

But it worked. Not long after Seabury Lassiter and Company opened its doors, Wall Street took off on an upward run which lasted close to twenty years. It got around that the firm's investment customers were making a bundle on Seabury's stock-picking and Lassiter's speculative genius. The daily knock at their door of new business became a steady, musical, enriching thrumming. Other smart guys were encouraged to join the original partners, and Seabury Lassiter grew and grew. Even Rufus Lassiter's departure in 1969, to join the new Administration as Deputy Secretary of Commerce, barely slowed its growth. By 1971, toward the end of the Seven Fat Years, when Rufus Lassiter was appointed by the Governor of Connecticut to fill the unexpired five years of a vacated Senate term, Seaco Group, as it was by then named, employed eight hundred people in a dozen offices and had a total capital of $30 million. Ten years later, with fourteen months left in Senator Rufus Lassiter's lame-duck second term, Seaco had thirty-six offices in the United States and nine foreign countries, employed close to four thousand people and had a total stockholders' capital of $175 million. But the firm was no longer right in the middle of the action, as it always had been when Rufus Lassiter had been on the scene: egging on, needling, bullying his conservative brother-in-law to get with the party, to dance with each new girl who appeared.

Seaco was still an old-line securities firm. It handled customer accounts; managed money; ran mutual funds; took major dealer positions, inventorying stocks and bonds for its own account, but only as a service, a modestly risky accommodation for valued institutional customers looking to clean up positions. Seaco brokers rode the crest of a securities research effort that was the best on the Street. Seaco's selective, personalized corporate-finance staff was considered qualitatively to be close to first-rate, certainly capable of rising to the occasion. But compared with its competitors, Seaco was like an old gray lady. Seaco brokers sold no tax shelters, no butterfly straddles; they pumped no options, no T-bill futures, no unrated commercial paper; its traders—those who valued the relative calm and stayed—slept of nights; customers could not buy insurance or a new house or write a check with a Seaco account. Seaco did not offer MasterCharge or Visa. Hotshot venture capitalists did not approach Seaco to raise capital for them. Takeover and buy-out artists and raiders did not choose Seaco to front for them; embattled managers, like Marvin Terrace, spent their stockholder's money to hire other guns to rescue them.

The impeccable reputation for professionalism and probity which Homer Seabury had so carefully built up—and which Solomon Greschner and Associates had so creatively caused to be circulated and recognized—was deemed by the Street at large to be a wonderful asset—for the nineteenth century. Sensitive to the criticism that his stewardship had been stodgy, Homer had recently been prevailed upon to get more with the times. At the urging of his senior associates, and his counsel, Hugo Winstead, he had taken Seaco public. The shares offered years earlier at $13 stood today at $14, although Seaco was now earning at twice the earlier rate. As a matter of opportunity, he had hired away from a competing firm, *en bloc*, a gutsy, much-talked-about Bond Trading Unit run by a young man whose daring had made him the talk of the Hanover Square drinking crowd.

His largest public stockholder, and most vociferous critic, was Masterman United. When MUD bought out Lassiter, Seabury had thought nothing of it. It was a family affair, as he saw it. Sol Greschner had introduced him to Granada Masterman, and Seaco had handled her first public offering, so she was a Seaco client. Hugo Winstead had endorsed the idea.

It never occurred to Seabury that Lassiter might turn on him, or Winstead equivocate to the point of betrayal. What sensitivity Homer had developed to life's many treacheries was slow in coming. He was a decent man with short hair who wore laces in his shoes and a watch chain across his vest throughout the blabby, hairy, self-expressive decades that followed the Eisenhower years. Whatever vestigial inclination he might have had toward me-firstism was mantled over with ideologies so out of date they appeared ridiculous to the noisy, recognizably postadolescent world of '60s and '70s Wall Street. Only now, Sol knew, was Homer beginning to discover that no one and nothing out there was to be trusted, least of all his cherished values: there wasn't any team; there weren't any team players left.

Well, Sol found himself thinking, perhaps Gudge's infinitely deep pocket can bail Homer out.

These ruminations were interrupted by the murmur of a limousine pulling up at his front door. He watched Buford Gudge ease himself uncomfortably out of the car and straighten up on the curb, seeming to twitch and shrug, as if to rattle his bones into place beneath the loose coat of skin and muscle. Looking beyond Gudge, Sol saw Nick entering Rostval Place from the west. Nick's posture was a good barometer of his mood; today Sol could see from his tall younger friend's jaunty bearing—he was walking like a whistle—that all was right in Nick's world. He felt a surge of fondness for Nick. Nick was intelligent, civilized and born with the right passport; like Morgan Seabury, the kind of man whom Sol wished, to distraction, that he himself could have been. Sol wondered whether there could be something going on between Nick and Jill. Hopefully not, he thought, leaving the window to go downstairs; that could be complicating. He made a note to inquire, gently.

Then he thought again of Seaco; this Gudge thing could open it all up for Homer. It was a cheering notion; it had been a long time since Sol had been able to move and shake.

That morning, Katagira had risen before dawn. He had come to adopt Panhandle hours; like policemen in Dumas, ranch hands on the High Plains, bankers in Borger, machinists in Pampa, he was accustomed to arriving at work with the sun.

It was already warm. He walked toward the Big House, eager to return to his task, to watch his machines create yet another chapter in the Lazy G fiction he was preparing. This morning he would reorganize the Overthrust leases; this afternoon he could begin finalizing the service operations.

Gratiane seemed overjoyed to see Caryn Gudge.

"Darling Carine. So beautiful you're looking. Come sit down here, you beautiful child." She drew the young woman down beside her on the banquette and made wet, kissy noises in the air by Caryn's ear. "Your first time at Maia? No—I don't believe it. Well, we must introduce you. It's so important, a good table at Maia. Says so much about who you are."

Madame von González waved beckoningly to a large, dark-haired woman, who made her way stolidly among the tables of the teeming restaurant to where Gratiane and Caryn were sitting.

"Darling." There was another damp fusillade of kisses. Gratiane bobbed right and left: "Darling Maia, may I present my dearest new friend Madame Gudge. From Tex-ass."

Then to Caryn: "Maia is my dearest, oldest friend. Such a beauty, Maia." Gratiane puckered her lips and made more noises.

Caryn knew enough by now to recognize that this was what society women did in restaurants. The idea of Maia as a beauty struck her as strange. The woman looked as common as goat guts. It made no mind. She felt like she was walkin' through tall cotton, as her daddy used to say, being here with these people in this place at this table. It all looked just like it had in *That Woman!*. She felt prickly with excitement.

Gratiane and Maia were talking about some party the night before. Or maybe some book—Caryn couldn't make out which, except that everything was "clever" or "well done."

Maia said something in a foreign language—French, Caryn guessed; all those languages sounded like French to her West Texas ear, and wasn't French what all the people in *That Woman!* spoke?—and Gratiane smiled dazzlingly and nodded vigorously. Then, in a cloud of more kisses, Maia departed.

"I told Maia to make sure to take good care of you forever, from now, darling. Now tell me. What"—she emphasized the word—"what have you been up to?"

Caryn told her about shopping, and buying jewelry, and the new apartment in the Esmé Castle, and dinner at Dove Sono the night before and going to that club and meeting Mr. Bogle and that nice-looking boy who sold art and about going to see Dr. Sartorian, just like Mr. Greschner had suggested, and how helpful he was. Of course, she didn't feel right about telling Gratiane, even though she was one of her best friends, that she had done some fooling around with Dr. Sartorian. Something clanging in the back of Caryn's head stopped her just short of this confession; something which admonished that if there was no honor among thieves, there was less among whores—not that those were the words she might have chosen herself.

Which acutely disappointed Gratiane. She was pretty sure that Victor Sartorian would have tried something with a juicy baby like this one the first time out. Ah, well, she thought, I'll wheedle it out of one or the other of them in time.

". . . and then," Caryn was saying, "Buford and me're going to go visit that Mr. Reverey and look at some pictures. Buford and I're thinking of buying a whole bunch of those Lefcourt pictures. There's a few with naked women that might not go so good on the ranch, but I really like all of them. Mr. Reverey's going to help us."

"Ah, yes, Nicholas. So clever, don't you think, darling? He had a little, tiny drawings show last year. So well done." She hated Nicholas Reverey; he never seemed to know who she was. Nevertheless, this is real news, she thought. Poor darling Granada; she'll soil her knickers when she hears the Gudges are looking at pictures. It must be true. Gratiane calculated that Greschner was aiming this little tart at the Fuller. Maybe not say anything to Granada, after all. Keep a little hedge.

"Darling, I'm absolutely famished. Shall we eat? Can I help you with the menu? Maia's new *carte* is so frightfully clever and so wonderfully well done. A combination of peasant food and *nouveau cuisine de luxe*, you know?"

It struck Caryn that society people like Granada conversed almost entirely in questions. She made a mental note to learn how.

Taking Caryn's wide-eyed silence for assent, Gratiane ordered them Chicken-fried Truffles, Salade de Collard Greens et Rosepetals, Filet de Chinese Carp aux Six Catsups and Caviar Sorbet.

"And for wine, I think a bottle of Château Baise-Francesca. It's all the rage this year, darling. Such a forward little wine—trying so awfully hard to please. I think you'll love it."

Caryn ate thoughtfully while Gratiane chattered on, punctuating her voluble exposition only with frantic wavings and long-distance lip-smackings as one table emptied or another was filled. Twice she was interrupted as people came up to the table. One was a chubby, sparkling man named

"Beppy" or "Peppy" who wore four wristwatches and told the most awful story about a former President. The second was called something like "Mister Mike"; he had a natty mustache and his fingers were stained a bright orange.

"The number one coiffeur in New York," Gratiane confided as he left. "He dyes the Governor's hair and his wife's mustache."

Caryn had just died and gone to heaven. She was right up there in the clouds, getting to know all these people just like they were folks. This wasn't like River Oaks in Houston, or Highland Park. She'd taken their best shot. They were Niggertown compared with this. She hoped she didn't seem too quiet, too unappreciative. She was just struck as dumb as she had been that one time at the drive-in when the big Caddy pulled in and it was Conway Twitty right there in the front seat.

The food did puzzle her. The fried whatevers looked like number two. She didn't know whether it was right for folks to eat flowers, and there wasn't hardly enough of the fish to get a fork to, and she surely had never eaten pale gray ice cream before, and the wine was kind of yellow-green and sour enough to make her nose pucker, which she hoped Gratiane wouldn't notice, even though she saw Gratiane's own nose make like it smelled something dirty when she sipped the wine.

"Delicious, eh? Now something special." Gratiane snapped her fingers and a waiter with right cute little buns twinkling under his tight flannels brought two demitasse cups of hot water with three dark beans resting on each saucer.

"The speciality of the house. Expresso Reverso. It's hot lemon juice and water; you dip the coffee beans in it and chew them. So clever." She fixed Caryn with a broad smile, like a lioness contemplating an antelope haunch, and began to munch determinedly. "Darling, now I think we should talk, just girl to girl. It's such a big city and so much to know and learn. I'm sure there are some things you worry about knowing. I just want to be helpful. And one other thing, of course: Massimo, my husband—he's the editor of *That Woman!*—he wants you to consider being a story for them. Now tell me about your apartment for a start, darling. Who's doing it for you?"

Caryn chewed the beans diligently, thinking they tasted like paving grit. She guessed this was what people meant when they said being rich was sometimes difficult.

Well, no mind; she choked the beans down and plunged happily into a description of the apartment.

When, forty-five minutes later, Gratiane got up to powder her nose, she had acquired, in no particular order of pecuniary or moral consequence, the story of Caryn Gudge's early life, a summary of the poor little thing's ambitions, a glimpse of wealth of an extent that boggled even Gratiane's unlimitedly blasé standards and an appointment to meet the next morning at the Design Building to start in on her commission to decorate the Gudges' apartment. She sat in the stall pondering these developments until a scrape on the floor made her look down. A face mirror with two thin lines of white powder and half a straw had been passed under the partition from the adjacent stall.

"Maia, you darling." Gratiane made a heavy *moue*-sound. "How clever of you. You beautiful girl."

Outside, she arranged for the bill to be sent to Mrs. Buford Gudge IV at the Esmé Castle, reserved a table for the following day and made her way back to where Caryn Gudge was sitting, transfixed by the excitement and glamour and fast-talking confusion of it all.

"Well, darling, the day never ends for a busy working girl." Gratiane's head felt as clear as an Arctic dawn; the space behind her eyes was as deep and mysterious as an ice cavern. Thank God for the sweet white powder.

"Shouldn't we get the check or something?"

"Oh, darling. That's the beauty of Maia. Here they never present you with the check if they know you. So clever." And like a great locomotive she rumbled through the dining room and out the exit, with Caryn chugging dutifully behind.

The other Gudge lunch that day in Manhattan had been less fashionable, perhaps, but in its way no less interesting and adventurous to certain of its participants. In spite of himself, Nick had been fascinated by Gudge.

Not that the man himself was truly interesting. Not in the terms of flair or wit or magnetism by which New York—by which Nick—measured its own. Gudge was painfully uncertain in his speech: not inarticulate—there was nothing crude or fumbling about his choice of words—but each sentence came so effortfully, as if quarried up from the pits of his mind. He was a plain man. Central Casting would have sent along a fat, porcine clod in a $50 suit and a *Grand Ole Opry* accent. Gudge was almost as tall as Nick; his eyes were clear, if tired; not the rat-red squinting pinholes of an overfed tabloid billionaire. His dark brown hair was pruned within a fraction of a brush cut. His suit was neither here nor there—an expensive ready-made of the sort favored by Sun Belt tycoons who thought that hand tailoring was a mark of faggotry. The texture and patina of his skin hinted at days in the sun, yet Nick's acute perception of shade and tint responded to something under the surface that suggested decay and mold.

For a while, as Gudge talked about the oil business and New York and the other baited topics into which he was guided by Sol, Nick imagined that the man's fascination was simply a matter of who he was, of the very vastness of the incarnate wealth sitting on Sol's right hand talking deliberately in an unmistakable Texas country accent about Saudi Arabia and Wyoming and the Strategic Oil Reserve. Yet, Nick felt, Gudge was no hick. Gradually, Nick got a handle on what it was about Gudge that was absorbing: the man was so sad. So sad it struck Nick that Gudge might not ever have experienced a totally happy moment. It wasn't that Gudge gave off a baleful gloom or a sour disaffection with the state of the world. What Nick saw was nothing transitory. It was in Gudge like his bones.

Only twice during lunch did Gudge brighten, or seem to; on two occasions when Sol mentioned his wife. Nick remembered Sol's remark about Caryn Gudge, and the pelvic pressure of the night before, and thought cynically that Mr. Buford Gudge IV was hopelessly out of his depth with that woman.

Sol snapped him back to attention.

"Nicholas, I've asked you here because Mr. Gudge, who is a good, if new, friend, has something in mind with which you can perhaps be helpful." He looked at Gudge. "Would you like to explain it, Buford—or shall I carry on?"

Gudge turned his pale, sad eyes to Nick.

"My wife's seen some pictures she'd like me to buy for her. Mr. Greschner here said you were the best fella around in this kind of business, Mr. Reverey. Kind of like my land men."

"Land men?"

"That's what we call the fellow who assembles the drilling leases for us. On the quiet. So's every bucktooth farmer or slant driller don't know what we're doing. Up here you folks call it discreet. Well, Caryn's seen these pictures and Mr. Greschner indicates it won't be easy buying them for her, but I never saw a deal there wasn't a way, some way, to make, one way or t'other if the money was right. And I'm a cash buyer."

Nick looked to Sol for clarification. Sol seemed to gather himself; when he spoke, it was in a calm, logical voice.

"Nicholas, Mr. Gudge is interested in acquiring the Lefcourt Collection. Not for himself, mind you. For his wife. And, possibly, down the line, for the Fuller—as a gift in his wife's name. I have discussed the matter with both Mr. and Mrs. Gudge and have apprised them of the difficulty—indeed, the likely impossibility—of carrying out their wish. Nevertheless, they wish to explore the matter as fully as possible. Which is why I have invited you to consult with Mr. Gudge."

Why, Sol, you wily old too-clever-by-half sonofabitch, thought Nick. It was Sol's oldest trick: always let someone else bring the bad news; let someone else reveal the impossibility of this or that scheme. A key part of the Greschner Effect. Sol never reached into rabbitless hats. That was for his cast of supernumeraries, like Nick. Apprentices who hadn't quite mastered the potions and spells.

There was no point in remonstrating. Or laughing. No one got rich laughing at the whims of billionaires.

"Wow," Nick said, "that's a tough one." He wanted to sound like Tom Swift, capable of fashioning an F-15 out of a couple of rubber bands and an egg carton. Playing for time while he figured out how to dump the Lefcourt problem back into Sol's lap and still keep on Gudge's positive side.

"What do you know about the Lefcourt Collection, Mr. Gudge?"

"Nothin'."

"Well, maybe after lunch, if you've got some time, we can walk over to the Fuller Institute and have a look at it. There's nothing like it in the world—not in private hands, anyway; and I'd include the Thyssen Collection and Chatsworth and the Duke of Sutherland's collection in that estimate."

He explained to Gudge about the history of the collection. How in the early '20s Max Lefcourt had inherited several million pounds, when the pound was worth $10, and a famous Florentine villa from his father, the fifth Baron Lefcourt. The money came from tea plantations in Ceylon and Assam, from tin mines in Bolivia, from a small stake in the Mexican Eagle Oil Company; a typical Victorian inheritance, based on the broad reach of empire. He could see that "empire" was a word Gudge understood.

Lefcourt had also inherited a few fine paintings—mostly Florentine: notably the *Birth of the Virgin* by Gentile da Fabriano; the two little *Scenes from the Life of Saint Luke* by Ugolino; the Castagno *Portrait of Sirio dello Circo* and the small Raphael Madonna. Later, Lefcourt had met Francis Sanger, an American a few years older who was rapidly making a reputation as an expert and elucidator of Italian Renaissance painting. The two men had become inseparable companions; they were still together at the Villa Pergola after nearly sixty years. Out of their friendship had grown the Lefcourt Collection in its present form: sixty paintings and an unspecified number of drawings which epitomized the love for Italy that both men had felt and through which—Nick didn't say this for fear of being misunderstood—their intense feeling for each other was transfigured and immortalized.

As he talked, Nick was furious with Sol for putting him in this position. As if the Lefcourt Collection, that marvelous flowing together of Max's generosity and means and Frank Sanger's taste and erudition, could be bought and sold, like a clutter of jewels in some Fifth Avenue store.

With a dozen or so exceptions, Nick related, the collection had been completed by the beginning of World War II. It had always hung in the Villa Pergola except for a brief period when it had been exhibited in Japan, and during the war itself, when it had been transferred for safekeeping to Lugano. The Villa itself had fallen unoccupied then, while Sanger and Lefcourt had spent the duration in London.

"You see," Nick said, winding up, "the Lefcourt Collection is really special. It has an Italian heartbeat, and about a hundred or so years of combined love and enthusiasm and work by Max and Frank tied up in it. Even if Max would let it go—which he never would—I don't think the Italian Government would let it out of the country."

He paused for thought. To people like Nick, governments—remote mixtures of armies, customs officials and tax collectors—were the ultimate, unreasoning impediments to human wishes. He was sure Gudge felt the same way. Maybe he could pin it on the Italian Government.

Bubber merely nodded, his pursed lips the only evidence of inner calculation. Governments held no terror for him; he'd caused more than one to be bought or sold, propped up or tumbled. What his mind was bent on was that Max and Frank were both eighty years old or better. Older than Granddaddy was when he died. They'd outlived his grandfather and father both, these two old men had, and the way it looked for him, might see him, the last Gudge, into the ground. Two old men. Living together.

After coffee, Nick and Gudge shook hands with Sol; Gudge had unmistakably been passed on to Nick—that was clear.

They strolled across to the Institute in silence. The day's early clarity was beginning to muzz over with haze. It felt to Nick as if the pressure in the air were increasing. Perhaps a thunderstorm was on the way.

Short of the Fuller, Gudge stopped. He had obviously been chewing something over. He looked at Nick.

"Queers, huh?"

"Queers?"

"Those two old boys you were talking about at lunch. They queer for each other?"

"I don't know." Nick was guarded. He found the question offensive but he minded his temper. "They like each other. They've been together a long time. They have an awful lot in common."

"Queers." Bubber's statement was final. In his mind he had rendered the ultimate, pejorative verdict. The two men took another couple of steps toward the Institute's entrance.

"Let me ask you something, Mr. Reverey. How come there's nothing but queers up here? Queers and Jews. And lawyers. We don't have all that back home. Of course, I got more lawyers than lice on a hound in Houston and Dallas and elsewhere, but where're all these queers coming from? Some boy start doodaddin' around the bunkhouse like some of the people I saw in that club last night, my Mexicans'd cut his *cojones* off."

It was a statement that required no response.

Inside the Fuller, Nick gave in to his sense of irony and forked over $15 for a Lefcourt catalogue which he handed to Gudge. As Gudge took it, Nick suppressed an urge to tell the Henry Ford anecdote that was part of every art dealer's inventory of professional lore. As the story, probably apocryphal, went, a consortium of art dealers decided that the inventor of the Model T was a likely prospect for the block purchase of a carefully assembled collection of Old Master paintings. At great expense, certainly thousands of times the $15 Nick had just spent on the Lefcourt catalogue, the dealers commissioned the preparation of two lavish volumes which illustrated and described each of the works. Ford was very much impressed with the books. But when the subject of buying the actual works came up, he demurred, pointing to the books and arguing, with some plausibility, that who needed anything more when he had pictures as beautiful as these?

As they passed through the main building, Gudge paused at the roped-off entrance to Darius Fuller's reading room. Next to J. Pierpont Morgan's study a half-mile uptown, it was the most baronial sanctum sanctorum in Manhattan, a suitable setting for the deliberations and intrigues of a reincarnated Renaissance captain-prince, as Darius Fuller had seen himself.

"Pretty fancy room," Gudge said. "Cluttered, though. Hot, too, I'll bet, in the summer, with them heavy curtains."

Nick told him a little about the history of the Fuller. And about Morgan, Fuller's rival in splendor. As he talked, he perceived that Gudge's interest was merely polite.

"Do you get to New York often, Mr. Gudge?"

"You can call me Buford. Folks do. New York? Not much. Not if I can help it. This's only my second time ever. New York scares me: too noisy, too many funny-lookin' people. I'm afraid I'm just a country boy."

They continued on into the Annex. It was the first time Nick had seen it in daylight, which was the true test of an exhibition space. Nick had to admit that the lighting seemed fine. Even on a day turning dull, the light slanted in through translucent panels which filtered out the dangerous ends of the spectrum and gave the atrium a soft glow like mellow varnish, which was dispersed on the surfaces of the pictures by the artful angling of scrims and studio lights.

They wandered at an easy pace among the larger paintings on the movable screens on the floor of the atrium. Gudge seemed to approve of the Carracci *Cooking School* and the Poussin *Death of Romulus*. Nick pointed out that while there were important works in the collection by artists who were not Italian—like Van Dyck, who was Flemish, or Poussin, who was French—every work in the collection had deep Italian associations.

"The collection's really about Italy, you see."

Gudge was thinking. He let Nick's observation pass.

"I don't like religious pictures. Not that it matters. These are the real thing, huh? The best?"

"On the whole, wonderful."

"Huh."

Bubber did not seem taken by much that he saw. He did halt for a moment in front of the Van Dyck portrait.

"That's how my half-sister'd like to look. If she was a lady."

As they moved upstairs into the hutchlike galleries which branched off the core, Nick recalled that Gudge and the ferocious Mrs. Masterman were indeed related. Again, however, Gudge's statement had foreclosed on any reply. Conversation with the man, Nick thought, was just an endless series of dead ends.

Without speaking, Nick studying the paintings and Gudge inventorying them, as it were, they made their way up through the smaller interlocking galleries. At the end of the last gallery, Nick stopped for a minute to study the small Duccio *Dormition of the Virgin*, the late-thirteenth-century Sienese panel which Frank Sanger had written "epitomizes the grace and piety of the best of Tuscan mediaeval painting; in the gleam of its golden background one senses the first dawning rays of the Renaissance." He thought of Sanger, wondered how he was getting along. He made a mental note to call Florence.

Something in the air vibrated, disturbing Nick's concentration. He shook himself back into time present and walked out onto the balcony, to find Bubber face to face across a dozen feet with Granada Masterman and Frodo Crisp, who had come from the other direction.

It was not a cozy moment. Later, over a stiff double Gibson, Frodo would liken it to those moments near the end of the war when he was a young assistant at the National Gallery and the Nazi buzz bombs would rumble overhead, then fall silent as they dropped on the city. Except that there were no shelters or helmets available on the balcony of the Fuller Annex.

Frodo had been doing his best to walk off Mrs. Masterman's obvious—indeed, vocal—outrage at having been passed by at the Board elections two days earlier. Hugo Winstead had broken the news to her manfully, gambling that her residual need for his services and entrée would overrule the stormy impulses of her disgruntlement. He had judged her correctly, although it was a much nearer-run thing than he had realized. For a minute Granada had simply looked at him, only a slight tremor around the jaw betraying the rage that was a mere locked synapse or two away from contorting her face with apelike fury. For an instant she had hovered on the brink of dismissing Winstead, firing him and his firm from all the legal business she controlled and all she could influence; such a display of emotion, however, would be a surrender to her femininity—and Granada Masterman had built her empire on stronger pilings than womanliness. She stifled her anger and disappointment and told Hugo Winstead, in that strange upper-class diction in which the vowels pursed in upon themselves, that she quite understood, that she would continue to serve the Institute in any way she could.

Winstead had raised the storm warnings for Frodo. Crisp had entertained his enraged benefactress at lunch in his office, showing her some pictures he was considering on approval—not that there was any money for them, but an experienced museum man like Frodo appreciated the efficacy, as a promotion or palliative, of taking his patrons behind the scenes, of making them "insiders." She seemed placated, so he had suggested a stroll among the Lefcourt pictures. Now it was all for nought.

Granada was first dumbstruck, then furious and finally apprehensive to find Bubber on her turf.

"Hello, Buford." It had been nearly twenty years since they had last spoken or seen each other.

" 'Lo, Gran." Four words between two people; between a brother and sister after two decades—spoken with enough poisonous intent to wipe out a regiment.

Those were the only words they spoke during the encounter.

"Well," said Frodo tensely. "Nicholas. Um. Umm." Clearing his throat,

Crisp took Mrs. Masterman firmly by the elbow and guided her away from Nick and Gudge, nodding—politely but in no way deferentially—to the opposition, and vanished with her into the next small gallery. The meeting had consumed possibly a minute, two at most, but Nick felt a dozen years older.

Gudge didn't say anything until they were halfway through the lobby of the old building. When he spoke at last, it was clear that he was choosing his words as carefully as he culled his beef cattle.

"You probably don't know this, Mr. Reverey, but that ugly old woman's the only person, man, woman or child, on God's green earth that ever stole something from the Lazy G and got away with it. I'll kick myself to the end of time for lettin' her. She got something to do with this place?"

Nick related what he knew of Granada's benefactions to the Fuller. Wanting to hand the ball back to Sol, he added a few thoughts about the Fuller board, its composition, prestige and importance, footnoting that no one understood the Institute better than Solomon Greschner. He had the feeling that Gudge would have made a bid for the Fuller on the spot, the whole Institute—buildings, pictures, even Frodo—and been prepared to pay cash.

To a degree, he was right. Fundamentally, however, Gudge was interested in buying only what was worth buying—by the standards he had been taught. He was prepared to make certain exceptions for his wife. But that was for her. Some people bought friends; Bubber didn't want friends—so he didn't buy them. Some people bought fame; Bubber didn't want fame—so he didn't bid on it. Some people bought horses, or houses, or pictures; Bubber didn't want any of those things, so he didn't buy them. Throughout his life, it had been drummed into Bubber that the only thing really worth spending good money on was more money—so that, generally, was what he'd bought.

With an invitation to the Gudges to call on him at his gallery the next day, Nick saw Bubber into his limousine. As he watched Gudge settle wearily onto the seat, it occurred to Nick that the exhilaration, there was no other word for it, of that moment of pure, focused hatred for Granada had momentarily pumped Gudge up, freed him for an instant from the marrow-deep fatigue the man wore like painful, heavy armor. As he closed the car door and stepped back, he thought he heard Gudge ask the driver to take him to Mulberry Street.

"Mr. Reverey." It was a guard at his elbow. "Mr. Crisp asks, can he see you in his office before you leave."

Upstairs, he found Frodo swiveled around facing out the window. The droop of his shoulders suggested he had spent a couple of agonizing hours on the cross. Nick let him sit, silent, staring out over Rostval Place. While he waited for Frodo to gather his thoughts, he looked around the office. It had originally been Darius Fuller's small observatory; the slice in the domed ceiling through which the telescope had peered had been glazed over.

Around three quarters of its circumference, windows had been let into the walls; they offered an arclike view of Rostval Place which swept from its northwest corner clear around to Number 17. Below the windows, bookcases to the height of a man's waist ran most of the distance around the room. There were two easels, one empty, and the other bearing a pleasant medium-sized landscape with a Roman temple and in the foreground St. Christopher carrying the Christ Child across a stream. Nick knew the picture. It was by Domenichino, a leader of the reappreciated Bolognese school of the seventeenth century, which had turned up in a Welsh convent and had been bought at an auction at Grundy's by Du Cazlet. He thought the house had paid about $300,000 for it.

"No peeking, Nicholas. That's naughty—and our Belgian friends would think the less of me for letting you see it." Frodo had rejoined mortality.

"But isn't it a beauty? Marco cleaned and it came up just as I guessed it would. Look at these passages. The picture reads as a whole now. I knew it would when I saw it. Of course, we didn't have the money, but I tipped old Du Cazlet to it—in return for letting me have first look after Marco got through with it. D'you know, he scarcely touched it? Look at these figures. I must say he is like the little girl, Domenichino—mostly horrid, but oh, when he is good he is very very good. What do you think? Look, Nicholas, look at this. And here. And here. D'you know, he can be a wonderful painter!"

Forgotten were Mrs. Masterman and the incident in the Annex. All other existence had flown out the windows. There was nothing now in all the whole wide world except the picture on the easel and the inexplicable private mystery of Frodo's relationship to it.

"Nicholas, what is going on?" The moment had passed. "Has the world gone mad? What is Sol up to? What are you doing with those Gudge people?"

Nick held up both hands.

"One at a time. Mr. Gudge is following up on his wife's newly hatched interest in great art. He can afford to do so. He is worth a hundred, perhaps two hundred of what his countrymen call 'units.' In Texas, Frodo, a 'unit' is one hundred million dollars. That will stand a man handsomely at Grundy's or Du Cazlet, or even *chez moi*, even at today's prices. Second, I suspect the world *has* gone mad, but I don't see that that helps either of us very much or that there's much we can do about it. As for what Sol is about, you will have to ask Sol. My answer to the last question has already been made. I might add, as if you didn't know it, that I make my living, such as it is, selling paintings and drawings."

"Don't be arch with me, Nicholas. You know exactly what I mean. Let me show you something."

He rose and led Nick to a large table at the back of the room. It was piled high with books and papers.

"Look at these," Frodo said, thrusting a bilious-green volume at Nick. It was a copy of something called *The Million Dollar Directory*. "Or this": a pile of back issues of *Forbes*. "All of this, Nicholas"—Frodo's hand gestured toward the table—"is my new vocation. I am becoming a connoisseur of money—especially new money. Once, as recently as a year ago, I was looking forward to completing my monograph on Piero and finishing the revision of Frank's *Quattrocento Painters*. Now I spend my nights poring over *Who's Who in American Finance* and the membership lists of private discotheques. Because we have no money to buy pictures. None. Zero. I had the good news from Hugo this morning. And now I appear to have a family vendetta loosed on my doorstep. I needn't tell you Mrs. Masterman said some very unpleasant things after we parted. She is a positive dragon; St. George would have taken one look and turned tail and England would have a different patron saint.

"The worst part of it is, the woman can't see art for beans. God knows I've tried with her. You know I was made to go to Venice with her last year. Actually, I don't know whether she can see it or not. I do know that she looks at a painting and senses, knows, that she can buy it but that she can't possess it. And if she can't possess it, she isn't interested.

"Nicholas, be serious before I have a nervous breakdown right here and now. What is going on with the Gudges?"

So Nick told him about the nature of their interest in the Lefcourt Collection. And Frodo's eyes first widened with amazement and then narrowed with calculation.

"Very interesting."

"Don't be foolish, Frodo. I hear you're thinking about going to Texas. Any truth to that?"

"I have thought about it. They have some wonderful things there. Some. On the whole, I find Texans a kindly, generous race—on their own territory. But Nicholas, how can I leave what I've built here? At my age?"

"I can certainly understand that. Remember Mr. Micawber, Frodo. Something will turn up."

"Let us pray, Nicholas; let us pray."

As Nick got up to leave, he gestured at the Domenichino on the easel. "What do the Belgians want for it?"

"Five hundred fifty thousand."

"Oh, come on, Frodo, you've got to be kidding. They paid three hundred thousand only six months ago. At Grundy's. We were both there."

"Indeed, dear boy, but they'll let us pay for it over ten years. I think we can just manage; I've got a book over here that tells all about compound interest." He headed for the table, but Nick waved him back.

It wasn't worth it, probably, now that Frodo had confirmed his worst fears about the Institute's finances, but old friends were old friends. Nick's world still made a place for harmless courtesies. He had the Rubenses marked for Bogle, but he would recognize his debt and friendship.

"Frodo, it may be academic, but I've got something coming in next week that I want you to have first crack at. It's very big; the biggest I've ever had. I'll warn you now: it'll run into seven figures."

"Seven figures. Oh, Nicholas."

"Frodo, I told you it might be academic. But come and look. I'll call you."

Outside, it was starting to drizzle, but it was that kind of day, Nick thought, looking about for a cab.

Frodo Crisp wasted no time, after Nick's departure, in telephoning across the square.

"Solomon, we've just had the most ghastly confrontation here. I'd given lunch to Granada, who is positively buzzing mad that she wasn't added to the Board on Tuesday—not that I blame them; she's really the most awful shit—and afterward I was trying to walk some of the steam out of her in the new building when, what d'you think, we crashed right into Nicholas and this great sack of bones who turned out to be the famous Mr. Gudge, Granada's half-brother, for whom she harbors, may I say, the same cordial feelings as Lady Macbeth for Banquo.

"It was the most awful minute and a half. I swear to you, Solomon, that I should have rather been back in Trafalgar Square in 1944, or anywhere else, for that matter, than rooted to the spot with these two awful people staring daggers at each other. There is no point in repeating the things she said about the Gudges, and you, once we were out of earshot; very rough talk for a would-be great lady. I'm afraid, Solomon, she rather sees your fine Venetian hand in the fact that various Gudges have appeared in this institution twice within a fortnight.

"Then, when like Perseus I've dispatched the gorgon and composed myself enough to ask Nicholas what in heaven's name is going on, he suggests to me that Mr. Gudge merely came over to price the Lefcourt Collection because Mr. Gudge proposes to buy it if he can—can you imagine Max's face? For his wife, I expect. That redheaded baggage—or cheap West Texas whore, as Granada put it, in her ladylike fashion—you were trailing about at the opening of the Annex.

"Frank Sanger was right twenty years ago when he advised me to pass up this job and stay in Florence with him and Max and write the books I should have written. Have you ever seen the young boys on the Lungarno when the first warm days of March arrive? Well, I can tell you it's a great deal better than doing battle with some Korean, or whatever that architect is that Hugo Winstead foisted on poor Calypso, or sitting next to Mrs. Masterman, knowing that she is all ambition and no taste and that that seems the wave of my future.

"Solomon, when I first came to New York, you advised me that it was crucial to memorize the social geometry. And I have done so. But my dear, what is going on now would perplex Euclid!"

Greschner heard Frodo out patiently. The world had changed from the pleasant days when Frodo had first arrived at the Fuller fresh from his position at the Caledonian, plunged from the civilized calm of Edinburgh into the noisy bustle of Manhattan. The Fuller then had been a small, cultivated universe Frodo could manage easily, drawing its governance and sustenance from sleepy trust officers and deferential, adequately wealthy widows; as long as the only music of its spheres was the clinking of teacups in Manhattan parlors; as long as a Rembrandt drawing could be bought for $25,000 and a Mozart manuscript for about half that figure.

Actually, Frodo had done very well, until OPEC had wiped out the traditional financial benchmarks and turned topsy-turvy, without sense or merit, the balance of wealth throughout the country. It was as if the last buoy marking the last remaining navigable channel had been sunk by a storm. Overnight, old hallmarks of value were rubbed out. A million dollars, once a sign of real personal wealth, no longer meant anything in some American cities. Men in Houston or New York or Denver whose literacy was limited to the stock tables calculated their personal worth and found themselves billionaires, thanks to unexpected, welcome pricing decisions taken thousands of miles away by unknown Arabs. As they prospered, old money withered away, shrunk by inflation. Old money was Frodo's natural bailiwick.

Poor Frodo, Sol thought: his world had been based on paper, if only he'd seen it. The stocks and bonds in the Fuller Foundation. The widows' mites which came the Fuller's way. Once upon a time, objects—buildings, pictures, even oil wells, Sol supposed—had been evaluated in terms of a quantity of money; now—a subtle shift but, for people in Frodo's boat, a disastrous, confusing one—money itself was measured against its worth in objects. It was an age for treasure-chasing.

Frodo and Homer Seabury were brothers under the skin, Sol reflected, listening to Frodo's voice rise in pitch as he wound up his plaint. They were like skiers fleeing an Alpine avalanche, hearing the thunder behind them, praying that somehow they could outski it or that it would subside before it engulfed and crushed them.

But, thought Sol, that was life. One had to adapt. His own career, if he was honest about it, had been one continuous, nimble adjustment, without prejudice or second thought, to the rise and fall in the fortunes of other men. It must ever be so for those of us who serve the whims and ambitions of the rich and powerful. The good courtier bowed before the throne, no matter whose buttocks it cradled. Frodo should have seen that.

"Now, Frodo, calm down." Sol spoke sternly. "I am trying to pull your financial chestnuts out of the fire." A babble of protest came through the receiver.

"To continue, if I may, without interruption, good fortune has placed in our hands—yours and mine, Frodo—two old, well, let's say aging, men nearing the end of our useful lives—the possibility of a coup that will astound our few friends and confound our enemies—most notably Granada.

"A short time ago, Mr. Gudge, the same you met earlier under what sounds like unpropitious circumstances, came to me for professional assistance. It appears his wife has social ambitions that would make Becky Sharp pale. It seems to be an epidemic in Texas these days. Mr. Gudge will do anything to see that those ambitions are consummated, which means he will spend any amount of money. There is nothing else he can contribute to get his wife into the ponds in which she wishes to swim. And, as you no doubt realize, Mr. Gudge can very nearly afford to buy the Pacific Ocean!

"It was an assignment I found on the surface unappealing, to be honest with you, no matter how remunerative it might prove. At my age, I'd prefer something more prestigious. It was partly a matter of keeping my hand in, however. My friends in industry don't seem to come around much anymore. I once worked things out so that a client was granted simultaneous landing rights in Peking and Moscow. Another time, a corporation that had poisoned a thousand children received a humanitarian commendation from the White House, thanks to me. Now I seem to be reduced to using a lifetime's connections and favors done to promote the social careers of dreary women whose husbands, through no fault of anyone's but the Arabs, are rich enough to want to make ladies of them and foolish enough to pay for it.

"Mrs. Gudge is a different matter, though. When her husband was at lunch here today, I calculated quickly—but, I believe, accurately—that his net worth exceeds the sum total of all the men who have sat down in my dining room in the forty-odd years I have owned this house. Any man who doesn't welcome the opportunity to get close to money of that size, no matter how, is a fool. I may be old, Frodo, and useless to some, but I daresay that I am no fool.

"Secondly, there is a priceless opportunity here to repay old scores. Mr. Gudge and Granada hate each other. It is an old quarrel, but apparently as lively today as it ever was. Interesting, don't you think, how quarrels over money last forever in this country? Very Dickensian, really.

"Now, Granada wants to go out in society. It seems to go with being in the cosmetics business. In any event, Granada Masterman—who, I promise you, Frodo, could have been President, for she has the brains and the unthreatening plainness, had she not wished to queen it over human garbage dumps like Monte Carlo . . . Granada is the regret of my life." He sighed.

"Anyway, we are going to pit Mrs. Gudge against Granada. It should be a terrific contest. Granada's got a long head start, but she won't do as she's told, while Mrs. Gudge is malleable clay. Mr. Gudge would buy Max Lefcourt's pictures for her if he could. If anyone could afford it, it's Mr. Buford Gudge IV. But Rome isn't going to let that collection out of Italy once it leaves the Institute, Frodo. But he might buy something else. Use your head, Frodo; make up a shopping list. I know you've craved the Tintoretto from Dunraven House. We both know that Nicholas may be getting it on consignment. Or that Velásquez at Gene Frost's. So stop wringing your hands and wailing like an old queen and think, Frodo. Think!"

He saw no need to enlarge on the sexual implications of bringing Nick and Caryn Gudge together on a regular basis; they would be of no more than academic interest to the Fuller Director, anyway. Why confide in Frodo at this point that Victor Sartorian had confirmed Sol's suspicion: whether clothed in Paris silk or Odessa cotton, Mrs. Gudge's thighs housed a merry insatiable brushfire? Nick would mind his *p*'s and *q*'s when it came to that. He had the sort of long, thin-nosed good looks those pioneer females seemed to go for and a demonstrable weakness for a handsome woman. Intrigued though he might be with Jill, Nick would go with his main chance. Sol was sure of it.

Finishing with Crisp, he dialed Nick. They spoke for a few minutes; Nick seconded Frodo's sense of the Gudge–Masterman encounter. Yes, the Gudges were due to come in tomorrow, and just as a safeguard, he'd gotten a florid Renoir nude from Johnny Sandler to show them if the Dunraven Tintoretto and a couple of other things didn't tickle them. As for Gudge's buying the Lefcourt Collection, forget it. Nick had lunched with Max before he left. Max's intent was to leave all the Florentine pictures and sculpture at La Pergola as one bequest to the Florentine state museums; the rest would be dispersed throughout Italy; the Poussin was earmarked for the Fuller, as a tribute to Frodo. But Nick *would* give it the old college try to get the Gudges hot to trot on buying great pictures, period. If he blew it, he suggested to Sol, they could always be handed on to Du Cazlet, which was said to have half of Goering's collection in its warehouse, or—failing that—to Johnny Sandler.

Sol next telephoned Homer Seabury.

"How's your calendar next week, Homer? We might have to take a little trip to the heartland. No, I can't tell you exactly, not now, but keep your datebook clear. Homer, have I ever led you down the garden path? Exactly. I'll be back to you."

Then he called a Texas number and spoke briefly to Katagira. He described Seaco Group, and Homer Seabury, in almost precisely the words that Katagira had anticipated. He had known Greschner would approach Seaco. Listening carefully, watching the rising wind whip the leaves in the cottonwoods like tiny banners, Katagira had to smile to himself. It reminded him of Gudge trying to explain football to him in their early days together, showing him diagrams which symbolized a chain of foreseeable reactions to fakes, deceptions, patterns. Football *is* life, Gudge had insisted. Perhaps he was right.

They agreed on a meeting ten days hence at the ranch. A Lazy G jet would pick up Greschner and Seabury at LaGuardia. Sol called Seabury's office and locked up the date.

Finally, Sol called Jill Newman, as he did every other afternoon. He didn't really have anything for her, although he hinted that he might have something pretty good for Robert Creighton in a week or so. They gossiped about odds and ends for ten minutes; at one point she started to ask him something about Nick, then bit her question off halfway. It was not in Sol's interest to pick up on it; his hesitation was so obvious that Jill noticed it but then let it go, and they chatted for a while longer, neither giving nor getting, like money changers swapping coins. When he hung up, Vosper was lurking in the background, with a silver tray on which rested a horn cup full of papaya juice, a Meissen saucer with four ominous-looking capsules and a stern written injunction from Victor Sartorian that Mr. Greschner was to nap every day without exception.

The Gudges arrived at Nick's shortly before twelve the next day. Caryn was full of the previous evening. They'd dined at the Tarver Meltons', and it had been very clever—and so well done. She quoted the menu to Nick with the ingratiating unctuousness of a Beverly Hills waiter describing the day's vegetarian special. Her husband looked worn out; *his* evening had been spent dodging the overtures of a former Cabinet secretary looking for a handsomely remunerated consultancy.

He settled them into comfortable chairs facing two picture stands and signaled Sarah Ruggles to let the show begin.

It started with a pair of Fragonard paintings which had once belonged to Madame Du Barry: depictions of pinching, squeezing lads and lasses disporting among topiaries cut in the shape of sexual organs. He waxed eloquent, emphasizing the royal pedigree of the paintings and their relevance to an aristocratic life danced to the tune and pleasure of the King of France.

His listeners were attentive but unenthusiastic.

The Fragonards were succeeded by a great Dutch still-life, a Kalf, the best Nick had ever seen outside of the Maritshuis in The Hague. It was a positive symphony of textures: gilded horn and ivory, a sterling knife inscribed with the artist's initials, twists and reflections of lemons and pomegranates, the dull gleam of pewter.

No reaction. Mrs. Gudge had seen better silver at Cartier.

The big Canaletto next. A view across the gondola-dotted bay of Venice toward the island of the Giudecca, with a dramatically cloudy sky pierced by the campanile of S. Giorgio Maggiore. Thinking to engage Mrs. Gudge's consumerist instincts, Nick pointed out the site now occupied by the Cipriani Hotel, where big visiting money came for a swim and a $50 pizza. It had no effect.

Nick decided to switch signals, to try something complex but characterful. Sarah brought out the Liotard *Portrait of the Comtesse de Journée*, a painting that had the striking quirkiness of a Courbet or Delacroix, but dated from nearly a century earlier. It was the sort of picture that appealed only to a genuine taste for painting.

Bland nods and dead eyes. Mrs. Gudge knew about Venice already.

Sarah dragged out the Tintoretto, a large, heavy picture still in the dark carved frame it had worn since it had left the artist's workshop to hang on the walls of the Palazzo Albrizzi. It depicted The Feast at Cana; the celebrants were all members of the patron's family, and Christ, the central figure, was believed to be a tributary portrait of Titian. In its rich coloring, the variety and energy of its poses, its identifiable relationship to the most glamorous artistic period of the most glamorous city on earth, it was—as Nick described it—the summation of every specifically marvelous characteristic of the golden age of Venetian painting.

Bubber looked at his watch. Caryn stroked her Gucci handbag. This was a losing proposition. The other works he had in mind—the Dürer sketch of *Piety*; the David *Horatius at the Bridge*; the Constable watercolor of *Stow from the Wold*—would be a waste of time. So she brought on the Renoir *Nicole sur la Plage de Saint Martin*, which Johnny Sandler had sent over.

By now, Nick didn't care about the money. Over the phone he'd agreed to go 40–60 with Sandler on any profit in the Renoir. He wanted to make the sale, and he gave it his best, intoning verities about Renoir's colorism, the documented immoralities of the model, the names of great collectors who had recently paid enormous sums for Renoirs of this period and quality.

Bubber dozed. Caryn stared blankly at the painting.

"Well, that's it," Nick said. There was no further race to run. He watched Bubber stir himself, rumbling and jerking into wakefulness. The Gudges rose to go, thanking him for showing them his nice pictures.

Twenty feet of Z-plated Cadillac was parked outside his door. They got into it; to Nick's surprise, neither of them said anything. Finally, as the driver started the car, Caryn Gudge said she'd like to come back for another look, but Nick put that down to polite, reflexive chatter. Before the limousine pulled away, Bubber leaned over to the half-opened window.

"Them's pretty pictures, Mr. Reverey. But they ain't the ones Caryn wants. What she wants are the ones I want. You get me them pictures, Mr. Reverey, and you own the world."

Nick met Jill for lunch that Friday at Maia's, which by unspoken rules was handed over every Friday to the art crowd, to honor the weekly sales at Grundy's new auction gallery a block to the east. Among the salesrooms, Grundy's was the current class act in a fickle city which changed enthusiasms as frequently as Massimo von González changed his tastemaking opinions. After letting Sotheby's and Christie's have their own way with this promising market for a time, Grundy's had stormed into town in a cloud of famous attorneys, razor-minded real estate brokers and blue-chip "advisers" of every sexual and social persuasion; when the dust cleared, a famous old foundling hospital had been condemned and razed to make way for a six-story building covering the better part of a high-class block on the Upper East Side. The operation had caused not only raised eyebrows among the older guard, but a painful revision of an opinion widely held by New York's at-heart Anglicized gentry: that the British might be many things, but pushy and commercial they never were.

Grundy's held only one major sale a week—each Friday at four in the afternoon, on the assumption that only serious bidders would forgo an early start for the country. The Friday catalogues listed no object with a guarantee price of less than $25,000. And its guarantees were ironclad, backed by a bottomless pit of Kuwaiti and Venezuelan money. Grundy's competed only for the big items, while Sotheby's and Christie's contemplated their enormous rents and, six days a week, peddled $400 trivets and $600 topazes.

The likes of Gratiane von González could command a table at Maia's four days a week; it was good business for Maia and kept the restaurant's name in front of the readers of *That Woman!* But on Friday, serious money spoke in hushed, deep tones which brooked no superficiality. Discretion was the rule of the day. Public relations types and columnists were barred unless impeccably credentialed and properly escorted, and then only under an unspoken vow of silence.

On Fridays, the big center table was reserved for The Honorable Sebastian Tubworthy, Grundy's American chairman, and his suite: favored clients, paid and unpaid publicists, beholden tax advisers; while all around, like whirling stars in a galaxy, dealers, anxious sellers, fidgety trustees and a hum of lawyers filled the lesser tables with a buzz of expectation, oiled by Maia's house wine.

Nick had known Tubworthy for a long time, from the days when the young lord, a penny-fresh apprentice at Grundy's, which was then in a far-distant third place among the London auction houses, had turned up at the Villa Pergola on summer holiday with a letter of introduction to Max and Frank, who were away at the time; it had fallen to Nick to guide the newcomer around the villa. They had spent three hours wandering through the halls and rooms and library, at the end of which Tubworthy had looked at his watch, indicated a wish to be driven to his hotel in the Piazza Ognissanti and left with Nick a bid of £15 million for the villa and its contents on behalf of a Greek shipowner. Such was Tubworthy's view of the purpose of art in the great equation of life.

Today was to be the first great test of what *Art News* had described as "the Tubworthy Theory": that the art world was so frenzied and out of touch with real values that it should be possible to sell, as a single enormous lot, a famous house and all its contents. Grundy's had guaranteed a reserve, it was understood, of $11,642,000 for the land, premises and contents of the Southampton house of Jean Traideur, a recently incarcerated wheat speculator. House, land, books on shelves, pictures on walls, cars in garage, sheets, towels, stove, pots, pans: all to be sold as a single lot.

The sale should prove interesting. These auction houses were going nuts thinking up new competitive gimmicks. Nick was curious only because Johnny Sandler thought it would confirm his view that there were times now when a whole might be worth considerably more than the sum of its parts. That an integral cycle by Rubens and the catchall possessions of a commodities crook were miles apart in every way didn't matter for purposes of argument with Johnny.

He waited for Jill outside Chez Maia. She had told him that one of her less ladylike qualities was that she was always punctual. And she was; to his astonishment, she even had her money out and ready when her taxi pulled up. They went in and were promptly seated.

"I don't think the owner knows who I am," she said, laughing, after she kissed his cheek lightly. "Barb Brown came in just after I did, and she's being made to wait on a stool in the ladies' room." Barb Brown was the syndicated columnist for the leading morning tabloid and a press agent's cooperative dream. "So it's true what they say about Maia's on Friday. Press welcome except on sale days?"

When Maia had shown them to their table, Jill looked around and remarked, "Without being too precise, I'd guess we just passed about six billion dollars of upward mobility: just at the tables I could put a name to. Does art really do that good a job of attracting money? Most of the people I have to write about are into clothes."

"Different crowd," Nick replied, finishing a palm-up, palm-down acknowledgment of the smiling, eyebrow-arching appreciation of Jill that Johnny Sandler had beamed from across the room. "Clothes for women; pictures for men. That rag of yours isn't going to write that Lipschitz or Googlefuss dazzled the crowd with a well-cut flannel suit. And they can't exactly bring their new Rolls into the restaurant; this isn't Beverly Hills, where every social columnist has an assistant who covers parking lots. The best these poor bastards can do is show up at Grundy's, acting like they're going to bid big, and once in a while buying something, so they can crawl right inside the frame and be petted by Renoir or Cézanne. And if the action heats up and emotions flow high, requiring celebrations and wakes, and what with one thing or another they miss the last train to the Hamptons, or the traffic is too great by the time they're ready to leave, so much the better. They can always go down Saturday morning. Which makes a lot of other people happy. Rumor has it there's an alliance of mistresses and restaurants which underwrites Grundy's losses on these Friday sales just to keep the men in town until Saturday. After all, chasing a Matisse or a Louis XV desk is a better excuse, to a wife, than to say you've been working late on a deal. Especially since New York's become a community-property jurisdiction."

"So I've heard. Who was that man you just waved to?"

Nick identified Sandler and, without naming names, alluded to the Rubens sketches. Although he realized that she might take his reticence as a sign of mistrust, and although he hoped she wouldn't, it simply wasn't in his province to blab about a private arrangement involving Johnny—or even so monstrously indiscreet a man as Barry Winters—to anyone else. Forget what she did for a living. That, in a way, made it even more tempting to tell all. He shifted gears and asked about her week.

For her part, Jill noted the gear change and liked it. She was frankly tired of uninvited confidences. Most men she met, and nearly all the women of the type she was likely to meet, couldn't wait to fill her ears with information either trivial or sordid. It put her on the spot. Basically, she believed that people should be the arbiters of all disclosures about themselves; by yakking about their private lives and thoughts, they laid on her a responsibility she did not want. She had her own sources: a dozen New York, London and Paris headwaiters; a handful of strategically located hotelkeepers in the choice resorts; useful, observant servitors around the world, who fed her information as guiltlessly and objectively as biologists reporting experiments. If she wished, she could have transformed their tales into oblique, anonymous items *à clef* which she could toss like kindling on the roaring fire of gossip. She preferred to do it her way and stick to clothes and parties.

Over grilled sole and a salad, they talked aimlessly, wandering from one subject to another, moving toward the kind of reassuring intimacy that only people who know themselves can develop instinctively. They didn't try to make hostages of each other by trading intimacies; it was an unsecured treaty that was building between them. Nick told her about art dealing, which could itself be called to ethical task.

"I'm doing this, really, because of all the things I thought worth trying, this seemed to be the only thing I liked that I had any kind of a gift for. I've got an eye, as they say, which is shorthand for an instinct that makes a quick sort-through of a bunch of pictures, say, and settles on the one or two that have what it takes: I don't know what you'd call it—ripeness, maybe; wholeness, electricity. There are about ten thousand words and none of them do the job except maybe 'quality.' That's what an 'eye' sees. Like the Cézanne in the sale today. Somebody with an eye takes it as it is. Sees that it can't be changed. Somebody without one asks a lot of questions. Thinks it can be explained, broken down into some kind of formula. Here."

He opened the sale catalogue.

"Look at this Cézanne. It just jumps off the page. I want to take it home and spend the next sixty years looking at it without trying to figure it out. I don't know if it hits you the way it hits me. That's Cézanne's quality. Three generations of art-history professors have gotten intellectually rich trying to explain him, but I'm not so sure that the answer, if there is one, isn't that his pictures are beautiful, pure and simple. Beautiful. When they had the big Cézanne show here a couple of years ago, I went a dozen times, after skipping the opening—which, as you doubtless reported, was a lot of bluehairs in diamonds and sables looking at each other. The first time, I went by myself—and God knows I'm in the business, I've seen Cézannes a hundred times, but never so many together—anyway, when I went that first time, I was ready for 'significance.' Cézanne as the bridge to the future —that sort of crap. And the pictures knocked me out. Including the one today, which was in the exhibition. They were so goddamn beautiful. Maybe it's the color—there's something about catching and containing the whole spectrum, like light in old wood, something Picasso saw when he was really burning in his early Cubist pictures; and the arrangement of the forms, how they work with and against each other, like this one, like the way the sitter is set off against the trees, objects balanced in a way that couldn't be shifted an inch right or an inch left. By you or me, I mean. Cézanne could have done whatever the hell he wanted and it still would have come out right. But you and I couldn't, and that's the trick of genius. Having an 'eye,' I've finally figured out, is knowing when to applaud without looking around to see what the rest of the crowd is doing. You can train an eye a little bit, tie it into memory so you can start picking out who did what and who didn't, which is a Botticelli and which is a Filippino Lippi, but in the end it's still ninety percent feeling and ten percent handwriting, no matter what the professors say."

"Quite a speech." His fish was cold. "Eat," she said, and while he did she talked lightly about her own reactions to painting and the world she wrote about, in which artists' names had become a currency as socially useful as the initials on luggage.

At quarter to two, the rush for the better seats at Grundy's emptied the restaurant. They finished their coffee. As he signed the check, Nick had a philosophical afterthought.

"You know, you don't have to be a so-called expert to have an eye. You know Harvey Bogle? Some people say he's a shlepper from the word Go, but I think he's got a natural eye."

"Harvey's no shlepper, Nick; you're right about him. He's very smart." Jill let Robert Creighton talk. "I have a feeling his time may have come. On the way up in business, Harvey ducked the bullet with his name on it. If it misses you just once, the world's your oyster. Now Harvey owns the Oyster Bar."

As he got her coat from the checkroom, a waiter went by, bearing a tray with a sandwich and a glass of milk into the ladies' room. Nick looked quizzically at Maia.

"The nerve of some people," Maia said. "Imagine that columnist thinking she can invade my clients' privacy." Maia looked at Jill, smiling. "So wonderful to see you with a nice man for a change, darling. We'll talk later, no? I have such interesting things to tell you."

CHAPTER NINE

From "The Bottom Line" by Robert Creighton, Pritchett's, May 20:

Uneasier yet lies the head, Homer Seabury's, that wears the crown at Seaco Group, the big brokerage firm. This column has learned that Seaco's largest stockholder, Granada Masterman, who controls over 20% of its common stock through her Masterman United Inc. (MUD), and is unhappy with what she is said to consider Seabury's staid management style, has reached a definitive agreement with retiring Senator Rufus Lassiter (R./Ind.-Conn). The agreement provides for Lassiter, a cofounder with Seabury of Seaco Group's predecessor firm and a glamorous, high-visibility, damn-the-torpedoes type, to stand for Seaco's board as MUD's candidate at Seaco's next annual meeting.

This will only be a first step for the Lassiter-MUD axis, however. Mrs. Masterman and Senator Lassiter are said to be personally close. Ideologically, they are practically indistinguishable; both advocate the rampant free-marketism which currently passes for economic philosophy in Washington. The Senator's recent best-seller, "Moral Money," went so far as to urge the elimination of poverty through such operations of the free market as the starvation of the poor. The book is required reading for MUD's field force of some 16,000 Masterwomen, who have built MUD's program of in-the-home "parties" featuring personal care and self-realization products and programs (cosmetics; weight loss; repigmentation; mind control; Bible study) into a $450-million-a-year direct-sales business. It is said that Mrs. Masterman sees an enormous profit possibility in the potential integration of Seaco's range of financial products and services with her empire. Especially if Seaco's reins can be handed over to the dynamic, articulate Lassiter.

Mrs. Masterman is said to have opened negotiations with corporate raider Harvey Bogle for the latter's recently acquired block of Seaco shares. If she is successful, MUD's interest in Seaco will exceed the approximately 20% interest still held by Homer Seabury by over 50%. A deal with Bogle will not come cheap. One source on the Street described the negotiations as "Lucrezia Borgia trying to make a deal with Attila the Hun." Stay tuned, fight fans. . . .

"Have you seen this?" Homer Seabury thrust the article at Hugo Winstead. They were meeting in Seaco's apartment in a midtown hotel.

Winstead looked it over and nodded. "I haven't seen it, but somebody called and told me what was in it. Where the hell does this guy Creighton get this stuff?"

Seabury shrugged. "I'm sure I don't know. In the old days, I'd point the finger at Sol Greschner—he had every columnist in America in his pocket—but not today, and surely not with something concerning Granada, especially since I'm a client of Sol's. One of the few that have stayed with him. Which is, frankly, why I wanted to see you, Hugo. You are on Granada's board. Both she and I are your legal clients. You and I are old friends. What is going on? Is this true about Rufus?"

"Homer, believe me, I don't know. Which makes me just as happy, frankly. If I knew I probably couldn't say anything. You know that. Could I have a glass of sherry?"

Homer wished he knew if Hugo was lying. Damn it, he thought, I've never been any good at catching out liars. He crossed the small living room to the liquor cabinet. Hugo had lied as long as Homer had known him. Lied like a small boy who feared that life itself was nothing but a series of reproach punishments. That fear itself was the source of Hugo's driving ambition. Hugo's falsehoods, in the past mostly little self-glorifying exaggerations, had over the years often expanded into important, risky fabrications, bubbling freely from inventive springs deep in his character. It showed up in Hugo's deceitful handling of women. And seemed to work. Women couldn't resist a scoundrel like Hugo. Not that it was much to Homer; it was just that he wondered occasionally why it was that the shits seemed to make out so well in love, life and business. He'd been raised to believe the opposite.

Seabury and Winstead were meeting, as they did once a quarter, to review the Fuller Foundation's investment portfolio. They constituted the *de facto* investment committee of the trustees.

Winstead sipped his sherry. He could see that Homer was agitated. Best to settle the dust. Seaco was money.

"Look, old friend, I don't know anything. The work we do for MUD is strictly limited to litigation, patents, SEC and Washington. As long as I'm your general counsel, and on her board, I've advised you both that there's hardly any way, ethically, for me to be involved professionally in any dealings between the two of you. Except as a friend, of course. I'll be frank with you, Homer. I may have been pretty useful when it came to working out things when Rufus sold his stock to MUD, but now, seeing what pain it's caused you, I wish I'd never been involved."

It was Homer's opinion that Hugo was no more an attorney at law, for all his talk of professional ethics, than he himself was. Like 99 percent of the big-time lawyers in the country, Hugo had become an operator, a dealmaker, an agent. Homer doubted whether Hugo still had any interest in the law: in equity, or right or wrong, or justice.

But Homer said nothing, just grunted his complaisance, knowing, shamefacedly, that he was just another basically honest man routed by a charlatan. They turned to the bound folder that listed the Foundation's holdings.

Both men were silent as they studied the list, flipping back and forth among the pages.

"Pretty lackluster performance, eh?" Winstead said. He thought, Now it's your turn to walk on a few moral eggs, you sanctimonious, boring fool. It was his responsibility, and Seabury's, to set general investment policy for the Endowment and to hire and fire, on the basis of performance, the investment advisers or managers who ran the portfolio. Both men knew that the bank trust department which managed the Fuller account was Seaco Group's largest institutional commission customer. He'd seen the numbers: Certified had powered something like $22 million in gross stock-exchange commissions through Seaco in the last fiscal year. The bank had been doing a lousy job with the Fuller's money. So what was new?—everybody knew the big banks handled too much money to be agile, and only the agile, those with maneuverable positions, had really made out in the fickle, edgy markets of the last few years. The Fuller would have been better off with a smaller investment manager, but to have gone that way could have been very painful for Seabury. The Fuller account was prestige business, the sort of name it paid off for banks to drop in chasing new accounts; for Homer to have a hand in taking it away from the bank that now mismanaged it wouldn't sit well with either Certified, Homer's institutional traders or Seaco's stockholders. In his own turn, Hugo had bitten enough feeding hands to appreciate Homer's quandary.

We are to some degree all whores, thought Hugo. It was a conclusion that reposed easily within his breast. He had long since made his peace with his own opportunism and the moral flexibility, he would have called it, that was its correlative. It seemed an easy, affordable price for what it had bought: money, social prominence, influence, access to the choicest boards and drawing rooms. And the infinitely satisfying product of all of these: the power to arbitrate the aspirations of other would-be kings of the hill.

The pursuit of personal advantage had reduced even as old a friend as Homer Seabury to little more than a chessman in Hugo's everlasting game. Hugo was like all scalp-hunters: his life was peopled with trophies. Wife, important friends, deferential supplicants, the women he slept with: pieces on a board.

Watching Seabury make his careful way down the columns in the report, Winstead felt a twitch of something between contempt and pity. Homer believed he was still back in 1944, still fighting the war; that the good guys had to win; that God was on his side. God was on nobody's side. Hugo Winstead had learned that lesson early.

He'd learned it and so had Lassiter, and so had Granada. That much had never been clearer than the week before when they'd met in Washington, in Lassiter's apartment in the Fairfax. Lassiter had already announced his intention to resign his Senate seat early next year, so that the popular

Republican governor of Connecticut could appoint himself to the balance of the term. It was clear to Winstead that Lassiter was champing to get back into capitalist harness. Too many kids in Washington, Lassiter had complained, like that blow-dried turncoat who'd been running the budget, and too many cowboys and oil barons calling the tune. Lassiter had erased the blots in his political copybook. He'd gotten elected as a liberal, but that, as he was prone to say, was long ago and in another country, and besides, that ideological wench was dead. *Moral Money* had turned the trick. It was in tune with the caveman mentality that now prevailed. Once reviled in the leather armchairs of Manhattan business clubs, Lassiter had transformed himself into an idol of the right.

It was time now to cash in. Lassiter saw the private sector awaiting his second coming with open palms proffering gold. Just look at the royalties from his books. It was the American way.

Wall Street, his old stamping ground, was the place. Money was on America's mind as never before, and so the last two years had been the best ever for making money down there; certified halfwits were pulling down numbers in the high six figures. As the author of *Moral Money*, he could count on an easy three to four million a year. When the Senator spoke of the new business he thought he could do for Seaco, and the new areas into which he could take the firm, Winstead had seen the glint of distant stars begin to shine in Granada Masterman's eyes. He'd spoken of qualifying every one of her sixteen thousand Masterwomen as a registered representative; of selling stocks, bonds, Seaco-sponsored money funds, through the same home-party system that had overwhelmed middle-class America with rouge and moisturizers and spiritual renewal. The idea was to get Seaco's wide-ranging paw into every decent-sized cookie jar in the country, to clip off a share of the national grocery money. It was a truly creative scheme. The legal work involved in setting it up was almost as mind-boggling as the fees.

"Shall we tell the bank to make any changes in the basic investment philosophy?" Homer's question startled Hugo back to the business at hand. "My bond boys tell me that the long markets might be ripe for a big turn, and God knows, the Institute can use the income. But frankly, Hugo, I'm still scared of the bond market. It'd take something major to make me change my mind that it's still headed lower. And the way the stock market's bouncing around, God knows where things'll sell six months or a year from now. One day the Dow looks like it's off and running to 2000; the next it looks headed to 750. Right now we're sixty–forty stocks and bonds; I wouldn't be against lightening up on the stock side to maybe fifty–fifty. But no more. Naturally, everything depends on Washington and how things go. If these supply-side people are right, who knows?"

"Who knows indeed, Homer? I'd go along with a fifty–fifty split. What're long Telephones going for now? Fourteen percent?"

"Around there. They're talking fourteen and a fraction on two hundred and fifty million dollars of twelve-year Pacific Telephones we're doing the day after tomorrow."

"Let's tell the bank to move the bond portion up to fifty percent. It seems to me that there's not a hell of a lot to lose. We do need the income."

As they broke up, Winstead, feeling the need for a bit more ethical insulation, said, "You know, Homer, I don't know anything about Granada's plans now. She's pretty browned off about not making the Fuller Board. At all of us, but at me particularly. She wants the Board worse than anything; she's said as much to Calypso; but you know my wife—she plays it closer to the vest than anyone. As long as Granada wants the Fuller Board, and you're on it—and you know how Calypso loves you, Homer—Granada's not going to do anything to bruise you. Calypso's ready to vote Granada on—provided we see a little more money from her."

Closing the door, Homer Seabury, thinking he was at long last seeing the light about Hugo, rejoiced that he had not been tempted to tell Winstead about his forthcoming trip to Texas. He had lunched with Greschner earlier in the day. If what Sol had intimated proved to be true, it just might be the end of all his troubles.

Sandler was furious; Nick was philosophical.

It now appeared that the pictures would not arrive until Monday. TWA had cancelled the flight without notice. Sandler started screaming immediately; rosy profanities poured over the phone at Nick, who turned them aside. No point in fighting the irreversible. It was only two days. He thanked God he didn't share Johnny's obsession with the immediate.

Wanting to quiet Johnny down, Nick called him back and invited him to lunch the next day. They met at Glenn's, a restaurant they both liked for "nonworking" meals. The excellent food was offered without affectation, and the restaurant usually offered an ogler's dream smorgasbord of fine-looking women.

Johnny took a second Bloody Mary, felt better for it and let his wrath subside.

Nick chose that moment to tell him again that he felt obligated to let Frodo have the first shot at the Rubens sketches. Johnny wasn't happy with the idea, clearly, but the second hit of Stolichnaya had worked its calming magic, so he was less forthright than usual.

"We'll piss away a week, minimum, with Crisp, I figure," Sandler said. "The Fuller's tap city. But you're the boss."

Nick could see Johnny working out the loss of a week's interest on $7 million. It smarted a little, like a mild sunburn, but it didn't really sting.

Food came, accompanied by another round of Bloodys. As always, a third jigger of Stolichnaya proved as potent a truth-telling serum as sodium pentothal.

"Sometimes I don't get you, Nick," said Sandler, destroying a chicken *paillard*. "You know how much money you could be making if you pulled out the stops?"

Nick was familiar with this sermon. He heard it out now for perhaps the dozen-dozenth time. Enough was enough for him. The fact was, he couldn't perceive the difference between, say, ten million dollars and twelve; it didn't matter to him. There were a lot of things he was afraid of in life, but money wasn't one of them. Ignorance might be courage, he sometimes told himself.

"Nick, you do great right now." Sandler's line of attack had shifted to the sincere. "But, Jesus, think of what you could be doing. You could be killing 'em, man, goddamn killing 'em. Your eye; your contacts. You got it all if you'd only really put the hammer down."

So go out and win it for Notre Dame, Nick thought, not at all meanly or resentfully. It was just a difference of style. He knew Johnny loved art as much as he did, but Johnny also loved deals. The hotter the action, the faster the chase, the happier Sandler was. Every once in a while, it seemed to Nick, the two affections got confused in Johnny's mind. It was a confusion, Nick knew, that pointed up the fundamental difference between them. Also, Johnny never looked at a picture without a powerful sense of its market value; it was as if a dollar sum, small and clear, hovered like a halo above the painting. Nick never saw that aura.

He had never discussed his philosophy with Sandler, nor would he ever. They were friends, and the essence of friendship was similarity, not opposition. Friendship needed discretion to flourish. Good friends kept each other's confidences; good friends did not wield their personal value systems against each other like sabers. His differences *from* Johnny were not differences *with* Johnny; no matter how deep they might seem in the abstract, they were fundamentally irrelevant to the friendship. So, even if the right words could have been found, which Nick doubted, these were not matters discussable between men who intended to remain the close friends they were.

"You're probably right," he said. "The hard sell's tough for me—but I'm trying."

Sandler seemed placated.

"So what else is new? How about that sale at Grundy's, anyway? Six million bid against a twelve reserve. Tubworthy's gonna put Grundy's down the toilet. How's your love life?"

Nick told him about Jill and who she was.

"No shit. Gilberte, huh? Goddamn. Deirdre'll go apeshit. I thought all those gossip columnists were about ninety years old with black moles on their tits! I'll say one thing. These women sure read that goddamn paper of hers. Deirdre won't go out of the house Monday mornings until she's read the whole thing. Son of a bitch! You want to bring her to dinner?"

"Why not?" Nick thought for a moment. "By the way, I've got a strong backup for Frodo if he folds on the sketches . . ."

"Which he will."

"Probably. Anyway, Harvey Bogle wants to see them."

Seeing that he could have stuffed a porpoise into Johnny's gaping mouth, Nick felt a good measure of satisfaction as he signaled for the check.

Over the Mississippi plain, giant rose-edged clouds seemed to sink into the earth like teeth, dwarfing the small jet that dashed westward across their face. Sol marveled at the sight. He had never been in a plane like the Lazy G Falcon; the few air trips he took had always been in large commercial airliners. Now he had some sense of the swiftness and daring of flight. It was another of those aspects of the twentieth century that he found daunting.

Across from him, Homer Seabury sipped a cup of coffee and shuffled through a pile of reports. The two men had run out of aimless conversation a bit past Pittsburgh. Homer's nervous, Sol thought. This is much more than a new-business trip. He sees this as the possible salvation I've suggested. If Homer can work his way into Gudge's confidence—and the Japanese, too—and a mutually interesting working relationship can evolve, he just may be able to persuade Gudge to rescue him from Granada's slavering jaws. It will come down to give-and-take.

"Tell me one more time about these people." Homer looked up from his reading. He hadn't been able to focus on the usually sedating branch-office reports and committee minutes.

"Homer, there really isn't much to report. You've seen those magazine pieces I asked the clipping service to send you. And that videotape of Gudge's appearance before Rufus Lassiter's Senate committee." That had been one of Rufus' better, more inhuman performances.

"These people have been out here since well before the turn of the century. They're snakebit, as they say out here, when it comes to our sort of world. The men tend to lead lonely, suspicious, bitter lives. They're reclusive people. The Gudges, of course, make the other big Texas rich, who aren't exactly sociable, look positively gregarious. Mr. Gudge's grandfather seems to have been the dominant figure, the one who set the family's course. Right up to today. He's the one that got them out of ranching and into the oil-and-gas business, starting a very long time ago. He may even have been involved in Spindletop. When I met with Gudge, he and Katagira—that's his man, as you'll see—barely mentioned the past, but there's no doubt the grandfather looms large. You've seen that piece in *Fortune* I sent you, which was probably pure guesswork, given the family's reclusiveness. Anyway, like anybody with a lot of money at the beginning of the war, they had more when it ended, and about forty times more now, thanks to OPEC. And they own it all outright; it's Gudge's: free and unencumbered, entirely at his discretion. So where you've got to be careful, Homer, is not to aggravate this nervous mania for privacy. They are suspicious of us in the East; suspicious to the point of hatred. And they have their reasons. Remember, Rufus dragged Gudge over the coals. Which gives you an edge, Homer, because Gudge hates Rufus, and Granada. That gives you something in common. Play on that. Old wounds are useful when it comes to getting new business."

"Do you think we might really be able to do some business here?"

"Of course I do." Sol sounded impatient. "If I didn't, do you think I'd have the two of us sitting here in this airplane? You know how I hate flying."

"Still, it seems strange, Sol. This family that has done about as well as could be, without ever touching the Street, and suddenly they do a complete about-face and want to talk to us. I find it very curious."

"Yours not to reason why, Homer—nor to inspect the teeth of gift horses too closely. First, we don't really know exactly what they have in mind. This might be a case of this Buford Gudge taking wing on his own, rebelling against the party line."

Sol looked at Homer as if to say: and you, Homer, should understand if anyone does how long can be the shadow from beyond the grave.

"Anyway," Sol continued, "we're first of all here to listen. Then, if it's appropriate, you can make a pitch about Seaco's sterling qualities. Our conversation at Number Seventeen was pretty general, although they left no doubt that they're thinking of doing something in the bond market. Which is one of your particular strengths now, isn't it? With those aggressive young men you pirated away? They obviously have something specific in mind. I think you're a natural for them. Katagira apparently was on the Street in the Sixties—with Kahn, I think. I gather he has little use for the so-called new breed—another point of personal empathy with you. So just get the drift before jumping one way or another."

Despite the fact that he spoke as if addressing a neophyte, he could see that Homer was reassured.

"You know, Sol," said Seabury, warming to the possibilities, "it really does make sense to look at long bonds. We won't see prices like this again in our lifetimes. Treasuries with a dozen years to maturity selling at a yield of 12.60 percent! It makes a man's mouth water. If I didn't have this Masterman problem, with Harvey coming along to make it worse, I'd be tempted to take a flyer for the firm; as it is, I have to keep my powder dry."

"Well, Homer, let's just see." Sol was satisfied to have stimulated Homer to the conventional investment pieties.

Seabury returned to his papers, and Sol once again stared out the window. The cloud towers had been left behind. The landscape below had turned into a patchwork of large fields, pale and dark, yellow and brown. Here and there a small town interrupted the remorseless flat stretches which extended in every direction.

It had been a long day already. Sol let his head drop back and drifted off. He was awakened later by the copilot's voice on the intercom; they were turning onto approach vector.

The Falcon slid down over a countryside now uniformly yellowish-brown. The earth was streaming past under the wings; just before it turned into the oil-stained cement of the runway, Sol caught a glimpse of a large house bordered by a crescent drive, with a stand of tall trees a small distance beyond it. Then the wheels shrieked, bounced, and they were firmly on solid ground, rolling past the small control tower, in front of which a big car was parked, with two men standing beside it. One was a short man, almost dwarfish. The other, leaning on the hood as if to keep himself erect, was Bubber Gudge, there to greet the first overnight guests to come to the Lazy G Ranch in nearly fifty years.

When Nick rang her doorbell, Jill had just finished brushing her hair. Shaking it into shape, with a bathrobe wrapped loosely about her, she went to the door and opened it to find Nick grinning like a foolish, slightly embarrassed teen-ager, proffering a single rose. She took it with a slight curtsy, bobbing her head with a little snap that Nick remembered from Jenny.

"Why, thank you, sir. I'm running a little behind, as you can see. Can you get yourself a drink?"

"I can and will. Take your time; I'll yak with Jenny while you finish."

"Jenny's not here. She's gone for the weekend to friends in Easthampton. I'm supposed to go out tomorrow. I've had a hell of a day. And you? Jenny'll be disappointed to have missed you. She's become quite a fan of yours."

"And vice versa. Damn—I brought this for her." From under his arm Nick took a book: *The Story of Great Paintings*. "I think she'll like it. I checked it out carefully. No baby talk about Krazy Vincent Van Gogh. I thought it might prepare her for our much-meditated trip together to the Fuller and the Met."

He was delighted when Jenny accepted his invitation. Aside from believing that it had to make a favorable difference with Jill, he liked the little girl. She was a spunky, forthright child, very much her mother's advocate and protector. He was sorry not to see Jenny this evening. He'd taken to calling Jill every other day or so, just to chat, to make sure he remained a live presence in her life. As often as not, Jenny answered; Nick believed he and the little girl had become phone pals.

Jill left him in the living room with a vodka-on-the-rocks and the following Monday's copy of *That Woman!* She made herself a drink and went back to her room. Days like this happened every once in a while. The telex hadn't stopped chattering. There had been a lot of stuff for Gilberte from the resort hotels that tipped her off about the more interesting merriments taking place under their roofs—balls and galas and soirees and, gratuitously, what she called "the bedroom Parcheesi" of their newsworthy guests. These last items she'd as usual discarded, shredding them, although she had smiled in amusement at some of the reported goings-on; from the London telexes, one would gather that all of Belgravia was in rut, although that was nothing new. There were wires from the Paris couture houses detailing the monumental extravagances of women of a dozen nationalities. She wondered why her sources kept transmitting the more vicious gossip. With so many more rich people in the world, the luxury hotels were all overbooked and the famous dressmakers oversold; they couldn't still need her help. She guessed it was sheer habit that accounted for the flow. And a kind of perverse vengeance on the part of the hotelkeepers, who, now that they were rich themselves and no longer needed a mention by Gilberte to fill empty rooms, were simply getting even with the sort of people who had patronized them, in every sense, for years.

Then there'd been a tip about Bogle and TransNational which had obliged her to rewrite the lead item of the next week's Creighton piece, but first she'd spent a couple of fruitless hours trying to run it down. As expected, Marvin Terrace' office hadn't returned her call, even after, posing as Creighton's stringer, she'd advised one of Terrace' three secretaries that Mr. Creighton was going to run a piece saying that Terrace and associates in management were working on a deal to take TransNational private in order to protect TEC's stockholders from being "exploited," which was a corporate euphemism for management's fear of being found out and fired. Marvin must be running really scared. He'd milked TransNational very handsomely: living like a prince on the company cuff, in the accepted fashion of the day.

Then, after a boring lunch with two effeminate Irishmen who'd insisted on bringing their wolfhound into the crowded bar at Dove Sono, she'd had to get Jenny packed and picked up by her Easthampton friends; and after writing and correcting her story and sending it in to *Pritchett's* and, with energy that now seemed to have vanished, blocking out the next week's columns for *That Woman!*, she'd finally locked up the harmless telexes from Antibes and Baden-Baden in the filing cabinet, and shut down the office. Only then had she seen that it was close to seven-thirty and realized Nick was due to pick her up in half an hour. What a day indeed. But of course there was the $65,000 a year from *Pritchett's* and the $50,000 from *That Woman!*, so life had its compensations. And there'd been some more noises about syndicating Gilberte; and agents had been calling, as they did every week, about getting her to do a life-style book; and then there had been the five pages of the new novel she invariably began out of envy and resentment after wading through the first dismal paragraphs of the manuscript of Esmé Bogle's latest verbal swamp.

She finished dressing. She blessed her mirror for telling her she didn't look as tired as she felt. As she made up her eyes, she speculated on the evening ahead. She hoped it would be simple. She wasn't cynical, but she was past being impressed by show and expense. She wanted a vodka martini, a good meal, the better part of a bottle of red wine, a cigarette and a laugh. Am I thinking like a man, she wondered—is this what men think about before a date? Should I be thinking about getting laid? She shook her head at the mirror, abandoned her preconceptions and went to join Nick.

Nick stood up as she entered the living room.

"You look very beautiful. I'm very glad to see you." He was holding *That Woman!* "Can you really do this crap with a straight face?"

He was pointing to a double-page spread titled "The Sweet Life—with Responsibility." It was a celebration of Granada Masterman's Palm Beach and Southampton houses.

"In most countries this brings on Communism," he continued. "Look at this." He indicated a photograph of Granada, beaming like a bug-eyed buffalo, beside Gratiane von González, hyenalike in her own self-satisfaction; the two women had been photographed in the middle of the recently redecorated Masterman living room. " 'Decorating must be entirely contemporary, and totally suited to the location. You can't do a resort house the way you do a principal residence. Resort life calls for a different kind of statement.' " Nick read the caption with obvious sarcasm. " 'So says In decorator Gratiane von González, shown here with her client, tycoon and cultural benefactress Granada Masterman, in the latter's Palm Beach residence, Villa Dinero. The furniture and floor have been entirely re-covered in custom-made fabrics and tiles, all American-made, designed to reflect the nation's commitment to economic self-reliance. Dollar-green and Saudi-umber velvet has been used for the seats of the gilded wicker chaises and sofas, which are set on a pavement of Attica-kilned tiles which display variations of the Stars and Stripes, from Betsy Ross to the present. 'It's a question of what is appropriate and what is not,' says Madame von González. 'In a resort house we want a lighter theme, but something truly contemporary, of course; something which speaks to the national consciousness. That's why Mrs. Masterman and I decided on 'America' as the theme for the principal rooms. Especially here in Palm Beach, where people tend to eat lightly and therefore forget our national ideals."

"Christ almighty," Nick said. "Why don't they use 'hunger' as a theme and cover the armchairs in food stamps?"

"Now, don't get excited," Jill said, adding a generous splash of vodka to each of their drinks. "You want to know why we print this? Look." She flipped through the paper, pointing out at least a dozen full pages advertising various Masterman products.

"Understand?"

"I suppose." His voice was grudging.

"You're a little too holy, you know. I've done a little homework."

She went over to an armchair near the window and picked up an armful of magazines.

"You don't have to say it." She took a sip of her drink. "You're thinking how can I write for something that prints this? Well, how about you?"

She started to open each of the magazines, which had been marked with slips of paper. Nick knew them. *Art News*. *Art and Society*. *Art and Investment*. Each page she opened had a half-page ad: "Reverey and Company/ Old Masters."

"Every one of these has you in it," she said, "and look what else they have." She had other markers: on articles headed "Buy Cheap, Sell Rich: Art as Investment"; "Beat the Dow with German Expressionism"; "How I Retired on Rembrandt Etchings."

She looked at him with a wounding sympathy.

"Don't you see? It's the same everywhere. Money, money, money. That's what people want to read about. What rich is—and how to get there. Even your discreet advertisements pay for this, Nick. We're all in this together."

He looked chagrined.

"Don't pout," she said. "I'm just making up for your interrogation at our first lunch. What's for dinner?"

"I made a reservation at a little French place over on Sixtieth Street. It's quiet and simple. I doubt we'll run into Woody Allen and his Rolls. I couldn't face one of those restaurants that give you two slices of quince and a piece of quail liver on an eighteen-inch plate and call it a meal; but if you've got a better idea, speak now or forever et cetera."

"That's just fine. More vodka?"

"Why not? Been busy?"

"Yes." Feeling that he was off his high horse, she told him about next week's column in *That Woman!* which would be devoted to a carat-by-carat comparison of the estimated wealth and annual personal expenditures of three very competitive Texas matrons who had dominated recent social scripture.

"And then, at the bottom, we're going to run a little one-column on Caryn Gudge, as a new but definitely formidable challenger, just to keep the ladies on their toes. Did I tell you Gratiane von González got the decorating job on the Gudge apartment in the Esmé Castle?"

"She's sweeping the field, huh?"

"Like Secretariat. She's leaving next week for a tour of industrial society: places like Pittsburgh, Cleveland, Canton. It seems she can't make her mind up on just the right industrial theme for Caryn Gudge. Smokestack America's very In this year. Look, this is depressing. Can we go eat?"

"You bet."

Jill looked so appealing to Nick's vodka-fueled eyes that he wanted to kiss her. Not now, you idiot, not now, he said to himself.

They shared oysters and a bottle of Chablis, followed by roast chicken and a salad and a bottle of Bordeaux.

"What a nice dinner," she said over coffee. "Would it be awful if I had a brandy?" She felt relaxed and easy. Her other lives seemed far away. Life was acquiring a smoothness.

When they left the restaurant, they'd both drunk and confided enough to feel that the evening shouldn't end.

"There's a hell of a piano player a few blocks from here," Nick said outside. "Are you into singing a few of the old ones?"

"Try me."

Jill took his arm as they walked down Third Avenue in the warm night; the night itself seemed good enough cause for Nick to break out in a deeply felt, if flat, tenor rendition of "I'll Get By."

"I'll be Irene Dunne," Jill said, and joined in: "Poverty may come to me . . ."

The piano player was as good as advertised. He knew everything. They interrupted each other, "Imagine" cutting in on Nick's passionate rendition of "Celeste Aida," until it seemed there was nothing for it but to go dancing.

Outside, the air was streaked with summer. Off they went to a club. In the taxi, he kissed her, and then, embarrassed by his boldness, launched into a half-sung, half-hummed version of "Mack the Knife" in something that sounded just like German to him.

The club was hopping. It was the last big weekend before the serious summer weekends claimed the fun people. They had a stinger at the bar. Danced. God, they both danced well with each other. Her hand rested securely on his neck; he kissed her.

A shout of recognition broke into their absorption. The Sandlers were sitting at a floorside table with a couple of Italian dealers. Chairs were pulled up. There was champagne in a bucket. Extra glasses were brought. The Italians were charming; everybody was charming; everybody was laughing. Everybody loved Jill. "*Te voglio bene*, Jill," he sang, seeing her dimly across the table, listening abstractedly to Johnny Sandler. More champagne; more dancing; the room was alive with delight. Two more stingers, waiter, please.

"Get out of here!"

The order came from a voice three parts gravel, two parts husk, somewhere off to Nick's left. He prised his eyes open, blinked and saw the familiar features of his bedroom.

"Now, wait a minute," he tried to say. Reason came slowly. All that emerged was a croak. Had he been changed into a frog prince? He tried again: "Now, wait a minute." That was more like it. "This is my room. I don't have to get out." There was a low moan, mournful and pained, then silence. Breathing. Nick let his eyes slap shut, let the room swim away again. There was something terribly wrong with his head. He let himself slide off into sleep.

Later: someone poked him. There was less of a fog in his mind now.

"What am I doing here?" A snake was hissing at him hoarsely. He turned his head and looked into an angry, accusing eye.

"I'm damned if I know, madam." His skull was a balloon filled with cement.

"I can't move. I'm paralyzed," the voice said. "What did you do to me? What time is it?" So many questions bouncing like sharply thrown pebbles off a brain as sore as an open wound.

"I don't know. Wait." He struggled to glance at the clock. "It's seven-oh-eight. Or six-oh-eight; who cares? Nothing's wrong with you." He was trying to find some tiny measure of recollection somewhere in his mind. "No. Nothing happened. Look. Let's try to sleep."

"No. Got to go." A moan. The figure next to him straightened up; then there was a groan and the sound of a head, a body plopping back down, heavily. Another moan. Sleep.

Later: light invaded the edges of his awareness. How had he gotten here? he wondered, blissful. He was cupped like a warm spoon around her. He reached under the sheets, aroused, touching the back of her neck tentatively, letting a less tentative hand stray along a tempting, warm angle of flesh. He pressed himself close to her. Kissed her neck. So warm. He was unable to move away from this penumbra of warmth. Another moan, but this time not painful or resentful.

"Ummmm." A hand reached back, took him fondly. "What's this?"

"No one you know." A silly answer turneth away wrath. "Oh, God, don't stop doing that."

"Ummmm." Purring now. Shifting, adjusting to him. He slid into her as if she had been waiting for him forever. He had never felt more warm or enclosed. He felt as if someone else were conducting the music to which they were moving. Moments later, with a deep murmur, she shifted again, signaling with her hand on his hip that she wanted him above her. It all seemed effortless, out of time. Somewhere he heard small sounds from the back of her throat, but by then he was hopelessly involved in what was happening to him and what he was trying to give to her.

Afterward, they slept. Drifting down into the deep, disembodied dreaming that follows lovemaking. Sometime later he awoke again; it was like swimming up from the blackest depths of the sea. He looked up and saw her leaning on an elbow, saw her looking smiling at him; the casual affection of her expression, the indifference to her own nakedness, to her breasts loosely touching his arm and chest, offered him something comforting and tempting to which he was too kitten-weak to respond. He drifted off again.

Later, waking for good, he found the other side of the bed empty. The smell of coffee filled his scraped senses. He put on his bathrobe, groaningly trying to reconstruct a jigsaw of half-dreams. Downstairs, he heard noises.

Jill was in the kitchen, wearing his raincoat, drinking a cup of steaming coffee. The *Times* was spread out on the kitchen table.

"There you are," she said, pouring a second cup.

She looked at him with a smile both mischievous and affectionate.

"I have to tell you," she said, "that I expected that if this happened between us, it would involve murmured, civilized endearments, intimate rustlings of silk and taffeta against skin, the discreet click of snaps and buttons. Something very artful and literary. Instead you got me drunk and took me to your place and bedded me like a shopgirl. What would my readers think? Isn't there any romance in this cruel, cruel world?"

Before he could make any kind of a smart reply, she came around the table, took the cup from his hand and kissed him. Her breath was fresh.

She drew her face away and looked at him.

"Your toothbrush. I hope you're not too fastidious to be romantic."

He wanted to be suave, but he was tongue-tied.

She kissed him again.

"That's more like it," she said, handing him his coffee. "You carry this. Let's go back to bed. You can skip the silks and taffetas; it's strictly Burberry now. But I would like something in the way of endearments. To salve my own sense of value, you understand. And remind me to pick up Jenny tomorrow."

Nick was only too pleased to oblige. From the heart.

As the Falcon arrowed up from the Lazy G airstrip, Homer Seabury's grin was as wide and sweeping as a searchlight.

"Goddamn, Sol, this could be the biggest thing to hit the Street since Hughes Tool went public. Assuming they go all the way. Even if they don't, what a feather!"

Homer rubbed his hands.

Sol couldn't disagree. The day and a half at the ranch had gone better than he might have hoped. Even though the ranch itself had been something of a surprise. It was hot when they arrived. After they had been shown to their rooms, on which a flurry of painting, washing and polishing had obviously been expended to conceal years of neglect, Homer and Sol joined Gudge for lunch on the west porch, which looked up the sweeping rise behind the house. Afterward, they were to be given a helicopter tour of the ranch. Dinner would be time enough to get down to business, Gudge had said.

Before going down to lunch, Sol lowered himself achingly onto the edge of the bed. The mattress was hard and lumpy, promising a night of anguish for old flesh and weary bones. The bed was covered with an inexpensive chenille spread. The rest of the furniture, a wooden dresser and two ladder-back chairs, was plain factory stuff; at least forty years old, Sol guessed. He washed his face and hands and dried them on a thin towel. He brushed his whiskers in the mirror over the bureau; he lived, these days, with the fear he might die an unseemingly inelegant death. Opening the closet, he smiled wanly at the five wire hangers scattered along the rod. He made a mental note to secure an invitation for Caryn Gudge to a first-class English country weekend, to learn about hangers and valets and gain instruction in the care and treatment of discriminating guests.

His overnight case, an old leather friend, sat on one of the two chairs where the houseman had placed it. Sol eyed it nervously. It had been at least ten years since he had packed or unpacked a bag himself. As he opened it, he wasn't sure he'd ever get his things back in.

Consoling himself that it was all in a good, profitable cause, and feeling restless, despite Sartorian's stern order to nap, he found his way downstairs. There was nobody about and the rooms were dark and curtained, so he wandered freely. He found himself first in the entryway to the darkened dining room, its shutters closed against the late-afternoon heat and glare. His arm brushed a switch and the glass cases on either side of him flashed alight. They were full of maps and documents, bits of barbed wire, branding irons, bottles of dark fluid which he took to be oil, cylinders of rock; he realized he was looking at the Lazy G's private museum. Square in the middle of the lowest shelf of one case was an old revolver, resting on the velvet bed of a box made from what looked like rosewood, with an ornate label in the upper case which read "COLT'S PATENT FIREARMS." Peering closely, he saw that a small plate had been set into the pistol's ivory grip; it was engraved with the recumbent G that was the ranch's brand and a date. Sol's eyesight wasn't what it had been, but by bending close to the glass, he could make out that the brass plaque read September 14, 1938. He looked closely at the weapon. It gleamed against its deep maroon cushion; all its parts—barrel and cylinder, grip, trigger guard, hammer—had been freshly polished and lightly washed in oil. It looked ready to be picked up and fired.

"Real interesting, huh?" said Gudge's voice behind him. Sol was too old a hand at prowling around in other people's lives to act startled. He straightened up slowly. Gudge was smiling with pride.

"Very interesting," Sol said. "What's the revolver? Your great-grandfather's? The gun that tamed this great land?"

"My granddaddy's. Your room all right?"

"Very nice, thank you." Gudge seemed at ease. "What's the date on the gun mean?"

"Don't rightly know." Gudge seemed hesitant. Greschner didn't press.

"How about a little barbecue? Show you the rest of the house later."

They strolled out through the living room, past a small den which seemed to contain little besides a desk and a large television screen, to find Katagira and Homer Seabury chatting on the porch.

"Ah, Mr. Greschner. I apologize for not accompanying Mr. Gudge to the airstrip to greet you, but we've been having a rather complicated time in Qatar and the telex won't stop chattering." He bowed. Sol was amused to see that Katagira was in traditional Japanese costume, except that a pair of lizard cowboy boots peeped out from the bottom of his robe. He caught Sol's curious glance and smiled.

"The boots? A necessity of frontier life, I fear, Mr. Greschner. While I find Japanese dress more comfortable for working, occasionally a rattlesnake—a 'narrow stranger,' as our great poet Miss Dickinson would say—will stray into the compound. The boots are just a little added protection against one of the few remaining terrors of the plains, now that the rustlers and wolves are gone or fenced in or working in Dallas." Katagira chuckled apologetically at his little joke.

The four men lunched on barbecue and beans. The only liquor offered was beer; Seabury was the only taker. Their conversation was limited to small talk, the tentative, exploratory chatter ritually preparatory to any really serious business pitch. Gudge said very little; it seemed to Seabury that he was also a meat-and-potatoes man. The realization made him comfortable.

Afterward, a helicopter clattered noisily in to land on the wedge of lawn bordering the crescent gravel driveway in front of the house.

"Y'all don't mind if Stumpy here shows you around. Mr. K and I got some more business downstairs. We'll see y'all about five. Get down to the serious vistin' then." It was interesting, Sol noted, how Gudge's Texas accent appeared to come and go.

For forty-five minutes, the chopper ranged above the ranch, with Gudge's foreman at the controls, shouting over the racket of the rotor blades to point out various Lazy G landmarks: the original landholding, now the much-truncated North Section; the arroyo where Gudge's grandfather had killed the biggest buck mule deer ever shot in Hutchinson County; the coppice where the Texas Rangers, under the fabled Captain Frank Hamer, had caught and gunned down three men who had robbed an oil-company paymaster in Borger. Sol thought the violent history of the ranch seemed to fit with the careless vastness of the landscape.

He was glad, finally, when the helicopter cleared a rise and the Main House reappeared, with the stand of cottonwoods off to one side, shading Katagira's house and casting pool; across the road were clustered the bunkhouse and the ranch hands' houses; beyond them were the tanks that stored gasoline and jet fuel and the rest of the working infrastructure. A mile or so southwest, across a grid of fenced-in fields punctuated with infrequent dots the color of bright mahogany—feeding cattle—he could make out the landing tower. The sense of isolation, of being a traveler in a private, secluded kingdom was overwhelming.

Helicopters were poor conveyances for old bodies, Sol agonized; he felt as if some gargantuan hand had shaken him like a rattle. He saw by his watch that it was 3:20. Time for a good nap and bath and a regrouping of the whole man before the business of the evening. Sol wasn't used to performing on other men's territory. He missed Number 17; it was like a limb to him; as he aged, he feared to leave it, feared that he might die in a strange bed, under strange ceilings, with none of his treasures to see him off.

Upstairs, he took a book from his suitcase, trying to disturb as little as possible the military neatness with which Vosper had arrayed its contents. It was one of his treasures: the copy of *Vanity Fair* which Thackeray had presented to Charles Dickens. He settled as best he could on the lumpy mattress and tried to read; he knew the book as well as his own character, yet it never lost its freshness, its relevance. "This, dear friends and companions, is my amiable object," he read, picking up his place; "to walk with you through the Fair; to examine the shops and shows there; and that we shall all come home after the flare, and the noise, and the gaiety, and be perfectly miserable in private."

Let that be my epitaph, he thought, feeling the weight of age on his eyelids.

At five-thirty the four men reassembled in the living room. They were offered well-iced margaritas and settled down on two sofas flanking a large, square table inset with a mosaic map of early Texas. There was a long instant's silence; later Sol would liken it, to himself, to the moment before the first shot was fired on Fort Sumter.

The few seconds' pause impelled Sol to begin:

"I think it might be best, Mr. Gudge—or Mr. Katagira—if you explained to Mr. Seabury, as you did to me when we met in New York, what your aims and interests are. Then perhaps he can tell you something about his firm, Seaco Group, and how their capabilities might serve your own objectives—to see if I am right to surmise that there is in fact a genuine mutuality of interest here." It was nothing more than a downbeat to set the quadrille in motion.

"Well, sir"—it was Gudge, surprisingly. He had taken a nap and felt much better. Bubber's intervals of strength were becoming increasingly irregular. Katagira had encouraged him to use whatever energy he had to speak his piece.

He turned to Seabury. "I don't know how much Mr. Greschner has told you, and, of course, neither of you has seen our figures, so as to get some picture of the metes and bounds of what we've got here, but we got a mess of numbers for you to take back to New York, Mr. Seabury. Anyway, I'm going to let Mr. K here talk about the details, when we get to them, assuming there's a way we can do business.

"Mr. Seabury, I inherited these assets when my granddaddy died. This ranch has been here since my great-granddaddy traded for it in 1885. Most of that time whatever we had here, other folks, mostly in Washington, a lot of Indian-lovers and nigger-lovers and poor-people-lovers been trying to take what's ours and pay nothin' for it. First they gave away the land, and lately they been trying to tax the oil and gas. The way we see it, the state of Texas has just been a big free lunch for a bunch of city folks back East."

Katagira entered the dialogue on cue.

"Please don't be alarmed, Mr. Seabury, if Mr. Gudge reflects the feelings of this part of the country. The politics of our nation do little to bind its regions together in any feeling of interdependence. I know you, as a New Yorker, with your problems, understand that."

He nodded back to Gudge.

"Once we owned close to three million acres out there, Mr. Seabury, but my granddaddy saw that there was no use tryin' to fight Washington and the droughts, so he started gettin' the Lazy G into the oil business and other things besides. He was real smart, Granddaddy, and he built the Lazy G his way. With his own brains. There isn't much I own today, except a couple of banks, and the radio-TVs, and the service companies and maybe some other little things, that wasn't thought of by Granddaddy; and those things was paid for with what Granddaddy was smart enough to get our money in.

"Granddaddy figgered it was best to keep our money in the bank or the ground. Over time, Granddaddy used to say, cash and land always counted. Whenever we'd get a few million extra, we'd buy us something for hard money: a radio-TV in Bakersfield or a shopping center in Del Rio, or some li'l pissant country bank to fit with what we already got.

"But we never bought paper, Mr. Seabury. The only stocks I got is of businesses I own one hundred percent. Pieces of paper in the vault downstairs. There's about maybe sixty, maybe ninety of those—huh, Mr. Katagira? One certificate apiece. That's it. We got no bonds, no stocks. No government paper. We never could trust the government anyway. Not with people like that Lassiter whispering in the President's ear."

Gudge paused to let it sink in. Katagira had advised him to emphasize a strong antipathy to Senator Lassiter. Then Gudge continued.

"But now, I'm not so sure. Things have changed. I mean LBJ was a traitor to the folks that made him; and the next fellow, the one that didn't shave, he just wasn't anybody's kind of folks; and the next one, walking around in them high-water pants, and couldn't spell his name; and I wouldn't let that Carter cut the balls off a dead calf. But now it's different.

"Now we got folks up there, we can get on with our business. Get the closet Commies and queers and nigger deadbeats out of the pants pockets of our government. Nowadays, a man can charge what's fair for his oil, and the gas'll be next. We've got twenty trillion cubic feet behind pipe that's shut in waiting for a fair price. And we're gonna get that price, Mr. Seabury. I mean, nowadays, a couple fellows figure they'd like to throw in together, do a merger, cut up a market, ain't no two-bit Democrat Jew lawyer from the Justice Department gonna show up first thing waving papers at them and ruin their deal. Gonna let the folks with the money have a fair chance at pulling the country out of the dirt. Money's the glue, Mr. Seabury."

"Amen," said Homer Seabury: pious, sincere, expedient.

"Times've changed, and we're gonna change too here on the Lazy G. Give you one last example. We used to spend, maybe twenty-five thousand dollars with Schlumberger on a nice well; now it's close to two hundred and fifty thousand. To do what we want to is going to take a whole lot of money, and planning, and being, praise the Lord, as lucky as we have been. But it's a whole lot easier to be lucky if you got the money to start with. You know what I mean, Mr. Seabury."

Seabury did.

Gudge looked at Katagira, sitting beside him.

"Why don't you take over here, Mr. K?" As he handed the discussion over to Katagira, it struck Sol forcefully how limited Gudge's energy and concentration seemed to be.

"Mr. K's kind of my general manager around here, Mr. Seabury. I expect Mr. Greschner's told you about him. He's our planner. Plus being a lawyer and financial man. He's on top of all the figures and stuff like that. He'll tell you what we're thinking about. See if maybe you folks can help us."

Seabury looked like a motherless kitten who had just been led into a field of catnip. Well, Sol thought, here's your chance, Homer; just listen. Play your cards right and your troubles may be over.

"Basically, Mr. Seabury," began Katagira, "our concerns, our areas of interest, are three. Financial planning. Investment diversification. Access to the capital markets, should the need arise.

"We have a complex group of companies operating in many countries; the group's complexity arises from the pleasant fact that Mr. Gudge is its sole owner—in some cases in his own name, in others through trusts or similar intermediaries designed to take advantage of differing tax jurisdictions. He is thus relieved of the many inconveniences which attend public ownership and the demands of outside stockholders. Outright proprietorship has many advantages, Mr. Seabury, as you well know, having once been in that position yourself; and the greatest of these is the freedom to do exactly as you please. However, Mr. Gudge's privacy and outright ownership, as I indicated to Mr. Greschner when we called upon him in New York, is today less of an advantage than before. He wishes to continue to expand the Lazy G and its satellites. As he said, it would seem an era of great opportunity is at hand.

"Opportunity, however, which may require commitments of a magnitude or type which Mr. Gudge and his forebears have heretofore been reticent to make. To do this, as we in our forthright, unsophisticated way understand it, necessitates experienced, irreproachable assistance. In several areas, Mr. Seabury. We need to have a market appraisal of the Gudge holdings. And an overview from a sophisticated, experienced house like yourselves as to the best means of deploying the assets at Mr. Gudge's disposal to produce the most beneficial financial effect. Such an overview might encompass a recommendation that some part of the Lazy G system—say, the oil-field services units, to suggest one possibility—be reconstituted so as to make up an attractive vehicle to raise capital through a public offering of common stock. Not that I could say that Mr. Gudge would necessarily respond favorably to such a recommendation. But he is aware of the success Mr. Hughes, who was an acquaintance of his grandfather's, although a much younger, if equally difficult, man, had with the sale to the public of Hughes Tool."

Katagira was moving on. "Then there is the investment question. One must always seek the most advantageous allocation of one's resources. At any given time there are invariably several alluring claimants for attention. The last ten years have seen what I might call a canonization of hard assets. Land; minerals; precious metals and many other sorts of treasure. Mr. Gudge wonders whether the pendulum hasn't perhaps swung too far, perhaps even off the very face of the clock of investment sense. Can money itself, he has asked himself, be really worth as little as it now seems to be, especially with courageous, intelligent and determined men sitting in Washington? The finest credit instrument in the world, the promises-to-pay of this splendid nation, now that a new spirit of enterprise is abroad in the land, seem very cheaply priced indeed."

Homer's head nodded in time to Katagira's concepts.

"This leads Mr. Gudge to question whether his family's historic aversion to securities of any kind may represent a prejudicial attitude which could prove very costly in terms of financial opportunity. Do you follow me, Mr. Seabury?"

Seabury did. His own rhetoric was ready to come out of the chute; he was obviously impatient to have *his* say. This could be bigger than the Hunts' silver play. And ever so much more prudent, handled by a conservative firm like his own. Yet even as he panted to respond, he remembered Sol's adjurations on the flight west. Moreover, like a lonely drunk in the wee hours, he was reluctant, for the sake of his own intoxication, to interrupt the delicious, comradely stream of possibilities at which Katagira was hinting.

"The Lazy G as it stands today, Mr. Seabury, is an amalgam of hard assets. All good, solid businesses, Mr. Seabury; ably managed in the field and extremely productive. Without indulging in confidences of a sort which would be premature, I can say that Mr. Gudge controls several hundreds of millions of dollars of annual cash flow in excess of the sustaining requirements of the assets now in place. It is getting very expensive to purchase 'things' in a world which seems to want only 'things.' Perhaps, Mr. Gudge has asked himself, and me, it is time to consider the orphans of the storm?

"Prudently, mind you. Mr. Gudge is no speculator; not by inclination or temperament, let alone his devotion to the philosophical underpinnings of the fortune which is his to command. This is a conservative house, Mr. Seabury. Mr. Gudge is a wealthy man, by any standard. And an observant one. As am I, here at his elbow. He does not intend to risk his heritage. His only wish is to make money."

Katagira let this sink home, pausing for a moment. Sol looked at Homer. Seabury's eyes were whirring like slot machines.

Then, with much the same feeling and technique with which he had often sent his line looping easily, softly over his trout pond, he added, "Of course, to work together on the basis I am speaking of, Mr. Seabury, would require closeness and single-mindedness. And the assurance that each of us would be able, without interference, to proceed as we had started; that the partners in this joint voyage of discovery and opportunity would be in a position to carry out their respective roles without disruption or distraction.

"I speak bluntly, Mr. Seabury. Mr. Greschner—and my own inquiries, I might add—have made us aware of certain pressures on Seaco Group which could compromise your firm's undoubted ability to guide us. Mr. Gudge has weighed these against your unquestioned reputation for competence and discretion. Yours is a firm which, by and large, has eschewed speculation without surrendering its competitive energy. At least, that is the way we see you, here on the Lazy G. Without saying a great deal more, may I simply indicate, on Mr. Gudge's behalf, that he believes, given the resources in his control, and of course assuming that we can find an acceptable basis for working with you, that it seems likely that a way can be found to mitigate any pressures which might disturb our joint effort."

Gudge nodded on cue. Katagira watched his statement float across the room and settle in front of Homer Seabury's self-interest as gently as a fly on the water. And then, as expected, he saw that concern come rolling to the surface like a giant trout and snatch the bait.

Sol saw it too. Skillful middleman that he was, he knew that it was time for their side to take on some of the burden of persuasion. He hoped Homer would be equal to the moment. He feared that Homer's dogged, anachronistic belief that hard, intelligent work and prudent, ethical behavior deserved the keys to the kingdom might not have prepared him to respond artistically when this kind of great good fortune came flying out of the wings like a stagecraft god to rescue him.

Homer didn't disappoint him. He possessed sufficient intelligence, and more than enough desperation, to recognize the potential. Gudge could be a white knight clad in the invincible armor of more money than his foes could ever array. Homer described Seaco Group's capabilities almost poetically. His words took on theological coloration; it was as if, at Seaco, investment banking and brokerage were divine missions, robed with moral responsibility.

As Homer launched into his pitch, as convinced of the virtue and efficacy of his calling as any evangelist, his bulk and heft seemed to underscore the devious earnestness of his words. When Homer extolled his firm, he preached the right, the true religion.

He spoke of Seaco's Financial Engineering Section: ten experienced executives overseeing the efforts of sixty MBAs from Harvard, Stanford and Chicago, each of them a wizard with calculator, computer and the entire arsenal of received opinions that contemporary business sought and treasured. He expounded on the combination of prudence and dash that characterized his newly acquired Fixed Income Section. He rhapsodized on his Mergers and Acquisitions Section, which concluded great consolidations with a panache a musketeer would have envied. He summarized the statistical profile of his firm: its capital, number of branches, number of registered representatives, the great deals it had been responsible for doing and undoing. Investment-policy triumphs were described, as were those moments of market hysteria when Seaco, to believe Homer, had stood as a pillar of judicious, analytical calm while heads and fortunes were lost on all sides by other, less steadfast men. Homer became in human form the brochure he had once hired Sol to write: telling a convincing tale of fortunes spun and dissolved like cotton candy; he produced an annual report assembled by the best design firm in New York; it was illustrated with quiet-hued photographs of responsible-looking men talking into telephones or posed in front of the factories their cleverness and foresight had caused to be financed.

Katagira had heard this sort of thing many times before. It was hot in the room, and his eyes wanted to drowse, but his hereditary inscrutability served him well. Bubber's large, pained frame rebelled at all this sitting and jawing, but he stayed with it; sat stolidly, chin on chest. Sol was a veteran listener; there was no foolishness or pomposity under the sun that he had not heard or had a hand in propagating. It went well.

That evening, over the best steak Seabury had ever eaten, the talk turned to generalities. Homer responded expansively to queries about the economy, the outlook for the markets, the policies of the Federal Reserve Bank. Katagira talked about Japan. Gudge, briefly, discussed the oil business. Too much fools' money chasing deals, he opined. It was time to send money into places the fools had abandoned.

Afterward, Bubber pleaded weariness and went off to bed. An ulcer, Katagira explained, taking his two guests on a tour of the house. The other rooms were as nondescript as the guest rooms. In the living room, Sol looked curiously at the photographs on the sideboard. A man with the angry look of an eagle in clothes that dated from the '30s. The grandfather, Sol guessed. A photograph of Gudge, apparently about eighteen, standing next to a man with a weak, lost smile. Father and son? A large, hideous color photograph of Caryn Gudge. On a shelf, nosing around while Katagira and Seabury talked at the window, he found an odd thing: a tattered copy of an old Dr. Seuss book, *To Think That I Saw It on Mulberry Street*. Sol felt a twinge. It was a book he knew; once he'd read it to his own son.

Back downstairs, the three men paused before the lighted cases next to the dining room. Katagira pointed out various deeds and maps, called their attention to the changing braidings of barbed wire, spoke of the great oil finds commemorated in the small, sticky bottles lined up like soldiers.

"What's the pistol?" asked Seabury.

"Just a memento," said Katagira. "Mr. Gudge's grandfather was a true frontiersman. I think it marks his recognition that the old days were at an end."

They finished the evening with a drink in Gudge's study. On the big screen, Clint Longley was letting it fly for sixty yards and six and a big Dallas win.

The next morning, over breakfast, it was agreed that Seabury would get back to Katagira with a firm proposal as to how Seaco might interface with the Gudge interests. Homer looked a little blurred. Sol assumed he'd done some private celebrating with the flask in his briefcase.

An hour later, the Falcon was a diminishing speck in the bright, hot sky. Watching it wheel into its high, eastbound course, Bubber turned to Katagira.

"What'd you think?"

"Perfect," said Katagira. "Perfect. He's our man. And Greschner, too. He's a resentful man; we'll use him. It couldn't have gone better."

He looked at Gudge. "You can get some rest now. I know it was tiring, but that's the price."

"Perfect," he muttered to himself again, following Gudge to the Rolls. The sky seemed surreally blue, full of mystery and possibilities.

CHAPTER TEN

As it happened, Winters, his mistress and the pictures arrived Saturday afternoon. Sandler was away for the weekend, and since the partners had agreed that all should be present for the unveiling, thc four crates spent the weekend in Nick's basement vault.

Monday afternoon, Nick stood with Johnny Sandler and Barry Winters in his upstairs gallery watching Sandler's man Raul unscrew the lid of the last case. The first nine pictures had been taken from their cushioned plastic wrappings and were leaning against the wall, reunited with the Hydra. Raul unwrapped the Apples of the Hesperides and placed it with its fellows, so that the sketches—Nick reminded himself to start calling them *modelli*—were at last arranged in narrative sequence, from the Nemean Lion to Cerberus, around three sides of the room.

Winters popped the cork on a magnum of champagne he'd brought over from the Tennyson.

"Wonderful, eh, Nick?"

"No other word for them, Barry. My congratulations." The three men clinked glasses.

"Now, Nick, what's the form?" asked Winters.

He was a large, florid man about Nick's age, who seemed to grow heavier and more flushed with each passing day; Nick sometimes thought that Barry's high rate of living would cause him to beach like a whale on the sands of his fifth decade. He was dressed, as always, in a manner that would have made him conspicuous at a racetrack. Perspiring—it was one of those June days which hovered between the warm zephyrs of spring and the vaporous heat of summer—he mopped vigorously at his brow with a large mauve handkerchief; sweat ran down his great, mottled cheeks, darkening the quarter-inch green stripes of his shirt, turning the orange of his necktie to dark amber.

Nick brought his partners up to date on Sarah's research, and gave them typescript copies of the test of the brochure.

"I've got Marco Carraccino coming tomorrow to look them over. I'm assuming they won't have to go over to his place. Torberg's finishing a job at the Met; he says he'll photograph them by the end of the week."

As he spoke, he strolled around the room, giving each painting a brief, searching look.

"You know, guys," he said, turning back to Sandler and Winters, "these are so fantastic, I think we ought to go first class. Let's have them framed."

"Jesus, Nick," Sandler moaned. "Who by? Hartmann, probably? You're looking at another month. A month; a point and a half at today's prices. Come on, give us a break."

"I think we ought to do it, Johnny; I really do. It would really dress them up. What's your thought, Barry?"

"I must say, Nicholas, I rather agree with you. C'mon, Johnny, let's dress 'em up. With what you're worth, old sod, what's a few thousand going to mean?"

Sandler sulked. "Well, I didn't get there pissing it away, that's for sure." He was outvoted, however, and their money was in there next to his, so his fiscal anguish was bearable.

"Another thing—and I suppose Johnny told you this, Barry—I'm going to let the Fuller have first whack. I owe it to Frodo." Nick was firm.

"Johnny did say something. I gather they haven't any money, though."

"Frodo's pretty resourceful. I doubt he can step up on these, but even if he can't, I want him in our corner. I've got a prospect in mind with whom Frodo might prove to be very helpful." He told Winters about Bogle.

"You understand, Barry," said Sandler, "that Nick's simply planning to sell eight million dollars of pictures to a guy who's never bought a painting in his life. This is some deal. We're springing for frames; we got Nick's honor to defend; we got a virgin collector. I'm gonna lose dough on this."

"Bogle's not completely cherry, Johnny," Nick said. He couldn't resist the needle. "He's got a hell of a pretty little Fantin-Latour. Purple and burgundy anemones in a brass bowl. You may know the picture."

"Bogle owns that picture? How the hell'd he get it?"

"Bought it out of your Christmas show, he told me."

Sandler grimaced.

"Bought it out of my Christmas show? Harvey Bogle? Billionaire Bogle? Harvey Bogle walked into Sandler and Sandler and bought a picture and nobody told me? I am going to fire every one of those tightasses I've got in the gallery. My Christmas show? Shit!"

He left with a great show of fury.

Winters lingered behind.

"You think you can do something with this man Bogle, Nick?"

"It's a feeling, Barry; just instinct. And Bogle, you see, has very warm feelings for the Fuller. He likes it. And he's got more money than God."

"Or Johnny Sandler."

"Amen to that."

As he was leaving, Winters said, "I feel terribly badly for poor old Crisp. D'you know, I had the loveliest little Brueghel landscape drawing last week; just Frodo's sort of thing. I called him and he started to cry over the telephone. They really don't have any money, Nick."

"I know that, Barry. But Frodo's a pal. Right?"

"Right."

They agreed to meet the next morning, when Carraccino came.

"Thanks for the hospitality. It's tiring, this international dealing, you know. And now I've got to go back to the Tennyson, where my darling Delphina awaits the hard and tasty fruits of her demon lover's lust."

"Give her my best. How's your wife?"

"Prospering. It's Del's turn for a nice trip, so Daphne has to content herself with a trinket from Bulgari. In the fall, it'll be the other way round. Tiring and expensive, but keeps a lad rosy-cheeked."

Left to himself, Nick walked around the room, looking at each of the pictures in turn, more carefully this time. It was hard to choose a favorite, although he thought the way Rubens had laid out The Girdle of Hippolyta, showing the Amazon Queen kneeling before Hercules on a field littered with her slain sisters, imploring with outstretched arms for the return of her broad jeweled belt, the source of her strength, had a nice sexist turn to it. Lovingly, he put each of the sketches into the steel-doored closet.

He looked at his watch. Time to run. He was off to Jill's for an early evening with her and Jenny. Jill had hinted that they could make love after Jenny went to bed, although his staying overnight was out of the question. It didn't matter. He liked seeing Jenny, and as for Jill, even if she hadn't shown, the morning after their first tricky night together, that she knew her way around eggs and coffee as well as anyone, Nick would have been no less desperately taken with her, no less anxious to spend every moment possible near her, drinking her in, and no less rapturously happy that she seemed to want him around as much as he wanted to be with her.

Divide and conquer was Homer Seabury's administrative rule of thumb. Putting the lions in the same cage with the tigers was for circuses, which Seaco sometimes resembled. In preparing a response to the requirements established at the meeting with Gudge and Katagira, Seabury needed to consult with both his corporate-finance types and his bond-trading people. Two entirely different species.

He started with corporate finance, summoning the heads of Seaco Financial Engineering and Seaco Mergers and Acquisitions to come to his office after the close of trading. Homer would have found it difficult to control these aggressively intelligent, action-oriented young men, except that they were so prodigiously self-important that he was able to guide them with the reins of their own conceit. His emphasis on delaying meetings with them "until after the close" was designed to make them infer that he recognized the necessity of their remaining close to telephone and tape, to be on top of possible fast-breaking developments requiring the crisp, blab-first-and-think-second response imprinted by their first-class business school educations.

They arrived within minutes of each other, each accompanied by younger MBAs carrying the artifacts of their vocation: yellow legal pads and hand calculators. Financial Engineering was the older of the two, just under forty. He had graduate degrees in Business Administration and Law, and had taught both those subjects at the postgraduate level before ever having seen the inside of a legal or business office, let alone a courtroom or a factory. He was a whiz with figures; to him the world was totally reducible to numbers: every atom and value and thing.

His counterpart in Mergers and Acquisitions was a tougher, more worldly article. He had been the gem of his college ROTC unit, had gone straight into the Marines with a commission, but a low-grade infection contracted at Quantico had fortuitously spared him the nastiness of 'Nam. He had served out his time in the Corps Commandant's Washington headquarters. On discharge, he had gone off to the Harvard Business School; kept his eyes and ears open, giving his mind some much-needed rest, and struggled to construct a public persona mixing frontier terseness with a part-obscene, part-snappy banter that he fancied as "street-smart," although there weren't any streets of that kind in the Chicago suburb where he'd been raised. Seabury couldn't stand him, but the clients seemed to like him. Part of Homer's antipathy was confusion; he couldn't understand why Mergers and Acquisitions persisted in speaking part of the time like a colored person and part of the time like a Dead End Kid.

Mergers and Acquisitions was good at his game; whether defending against a hostile takeover bid or quarterbacking an offer, he followed a merger philosophy right out of the Pentagon. He believed in financial firepower: to keep blowing those dollars at 'em until the other guy quit. It earned Seaco $12 million a year on fees, and the fun was just starting.

Seabury began, "I have met recently with a prospective client. This could be an enormous piece of business, gentlemen and, uh, miss." Homer hadn't gotten used to the prevalence of women on the Street. It was the sort of thing Lassiter could have handled more gracefully. "Anyway, uh, this client, whose name I'll keep under wraps for the minute, is a very large private corporation—a very, very large corporation—closely held in its entirety, which is considering forming an investment-banking relationship. At the outset, the relationship will be principally advisory, concentrating on long-range capital planning, which is your area"—turning to Financial Engineering—"and a structural reorganization of certain of its larger components, which falls in your bailiwick"—a brief smile for Mergers and Acquisitions.

"Down the road, there is the possibility of handling an initial public offering which in my judgment could rival Hughes Tool and Apple Computer as a hot deal."

Big and hot, like what I've got for you, Mergers and Acquisitions said to himself, thinking tough and sexy as he smiled at the girl who was one of Engineering's assistants. He was the house ass-man. Just like up in Bedford, where he stashed the family, he was the ass-man at the country club, the yacht club and the bar at the local steak pub. A fighting man needed a little 'tang after a tough day in the trenches.

"What I think we're going to need," Seabury was saying, "is a study which outlines for the client what his alternatives are vis-à-vis financing strategy, based on his assumptions and our own as to markets and the economic outlook, and which groups his operations in the most effective fashion and is most palatable marketwise. And of course, we'll be talking valuation, too, which means you two will have to interface, put your heads together. This is a full-service proposition. It'll call for us taking our best shot.

"What I need now is a rundown on our expertise. The usual bushwa. And a price. What'd we charge Amalgamated on that study we did for them?"

"Four hundred fifty K," Financial Engineering answered promptly.

Chickenshit, thought Mergers and Acquisitions. Chickenshit pay for chickenshit work. I don't take my dick out to pee for less than five hundred grand. He slung zeroes as casually as a kid skipping stones.

"Well, this client can pay easily as much as Amalgamated. What I think we ought to do is quote him a fee that's not insulting: not too big, not too small. This client has a very full sense of a dollar, but he's not cheap. I can safely say we're talking about two, three billion of value here, plus a major potential financing business—maybe as much as five to six hundred million of future financing, near term. And we ought to give him some idea—at today's prices, of course—of what it'll cost him to do this, do that.

"Give me your ideas in a memo. Something that I can use with the client, whom I'll deal with personally. If we get the business, then the next step will be to get down to specifics, and that will mean a little trip for us all. Can I get that memo shortly?"

They would get back to him, they said, and left, grumbling about old farts like Homer who didn't really understand their dynamite new banking techniques and yet still insisted on dealing with the clients.

Twenty minutes later, the head of Seaco's Fixed Income Securities Group came in. He was a chubby, short man in his late twenties, with shifty eyes and a mouth as quick at producing justifications and excuses as his mind was at making calculations. He was a cold-blooded, ambitious cherub with a thirst for empire.

He and Homer were getting used to each other, but it was taking some doing. Fixed Income was a very raw gem indeed. He had risen through the ranks at three other firms; Homer had hired him away from the last of them. He liked big scores and lived an unconcealedly flashy life replete with thousand-dollar cocaine and five-hundred-dollar hookers, with limousines, and rinkside boxes at the Ranger games, third-row seats at the big musicals and choice tables at the Third Avenue jock restaurants where the Knicks and Yankees hung out. Homer had snatched him after he'd gone head to head with the senior partners of his previous firm and lost; his taste for taking billion-dollar T-bill positions with a head still popping with last night's juice had scared them witless. He'd stormed back to the trading room and put it on the wire that he and his entire unit could be had for a price, and Seaco had popped. Now he was making Homer nervous, although the trading and underwriting profits flowing upstairs from the spanking-new trading room were, on balance, consoling. He was a very tough article, aggressive and abrasive beyond his years.

Sol, who had a better sense of gutter brains than Homer, understood. "It is what Thackeray called 'the dismal precocity of poverty,' " he'd told Seabury, somewhat pompously, when Homer complained about his new superstar's lack of couth.

Homer told Fixed Income little about the possibility, as he put it, that a highly conservative new customer might want to "invest"—that was Homer's phrase—several hundred million dollars in the long-term bond market.

"Leveraged?" asked Fixed Income enthusiastically. He loved leverage.

"I don't know. These are very conservative people."

"Size?"

"I can't imagine they'd want to do much less than a hundred million."

Now, that was more like it, thought Fixed Income. With $100 million as equity in a bond portfolio, another $1 billion could be borrowed. That kind of figure was worth a man's time.

"There's a lot of money around now. If they'll leverage, we can make a bundle on the carry." He saw that Homer looked puzzled; Seabury, he knew, was a cash customer. "On the difference between what I borrow for in the market and what we charge the client for carrying his position. The commission tickets'll be okay, but the real dough's in the spread."

"Well, we'll see about that," said Homer, finally; but he sounded very dubious.

Shit, thought Fixed Income. No point in arguing the point with Seabury. Get in the customer's pants first; then teach him about leverage. Dangle profits at him. The way to make money for yourself was to use a bundle of someone else's. He did some fast arithmetic. Take the 8¾-percent Treasuries due in seven years. They were trading at around $75, or $750 for a $1,000 bond. At that price, they yielded about 13.9 percent to their due date. Since they were selling at a big discount from face value, an investor could finance about 95 percent of his cost, which meant he'd have to put up only about $40 of the $750 purchase price.

He started to run some numbers in his head, figuring money costs, interest offsets. Any first-rate bond trader was born with a calculator in his head; he had nothing but contempt for those MBA jerks upstairs who needed a Hewlett-Packard to add two three-digit numbers. Which was one digit more than their average I.Q. He was aware of the speed with which his mind could massage figures; it was a source of pride to him. In a few seconds, he calculated that a fully leveraged investor who started with $100 million of his own could make a 200-percent money profit if the long-term bond market rallied up 14–15 percent from its present levels. Put in $100 million; take out close to $300 million. It was the leverage that did the trick. Leverage was magic. Leverage was better than God.

He turned his mind to the risks. Bond markets could turn to shit; look at this one. It was tough to figure it getting worse, but who could say?

Just as quickly, he calculated the downside. A 10-percent decline would be the point where trouble started, when the lenders would want the loss covered; but if that happened, the prime rate would probably be at 25 percent and the markets would have shut down, so that worry looked purely theoretical.

He left Homer with the reassurance that they could handle a big customer better than any of the other big houses. Unlike some of his opposite numbers in other firms, Fixed Income didn't bet the firm's own capital on his feeling about the direction of interest rates. His was a service business. He took positions in the billions, however, to facilitate his institutional customers, to make a market, and used all the capital he could lay his hands on to carry them. He liked the sound of "billions." The word had a truly triumphant ring. When he left, Seabury was mentally rubbing his hands over the prospect of the hundreds of thousands, even millions, even more, in commissions and trading profits and financing spreads that an account the size of Gudge's could generate for Seaco. Naturally, there was no way of telling how vigorously he might have kept rubbing had he known that a thousand miles away, Katagira was also reflecting on the bond market, and leverage, and the way Wall Street worked. He did so with the same refined calculation that enabled him to send a quarter-gram Brown Coachman, riding the tip of a translucent weightless leader, twenty feet across a pond to land within six inches of its intended target. Where it would float, tempting and succulent, until it was taken by a trout succumbing to the sheer force of appetite.

"They're beautiful. Extraordinary." Marco Carraccino took the gold-framed monocle from his eye and put down the ultraviolet lamp. Lovingly, with as obviously careful a responsibility as if he had been handed someone's infant, he took the last *modello* from the easel on which, one by one, he had inspected the entire series.

"There's nothing wrong with any of them. Oh, there's a bit of discoloration in the varnish; two or three need a little surface cleaning, perhaps; but nothing urgent. They're as fresh as if Rubens had painted them yesterday. Such a fantastic artist. *Guarda, che bello.*" Carraccino's second vocation was to be Italian.

He pointed to the Augean Stables, making vigorous small circles with his index finger to indicate and enclose a passage showing Hercules carrying an old river god, symbolizing the Alpheus, the river that was diverted through the royal stables to carry off in one day the accumulated filth of years. "Nobody, not even Michelangelo, could interweave figures like this man. *Fantastico.*

"You are very lucky," he said, a round, elegant figure turning to smile on Nick, Johnny and Winters, who had been hanging back, like anxious relatives in a sickroom awaiting the doctor's verdict on a beloved relative. "Very lucky. I have seen nothing like this. Oh, many fine sketches, *sicuro.* But a whole series? In perfect condition."

"Have you shown these to Frodo Crisp?" he asked Nick. "He will die from pleasure."

"Not yet, Marco. We wanted you to bless them first. I'm glad you feel about them the way I did when Johnny showed me the Hydra. What do you think about the date?"

"Oh, late, of course. But late for Rubens doesn't mean the work of an old man. He was not yet sixty-three when he died. Still in the prime of life. These must be for Spain. The subject, the style. Perhaps for the Torre de la Parada. What does the *Corpus* say?"

"That there has always been speculation that a Labors might have been included in the program, but nothing concrete. A lot of Hercules pictures were mentioned in eighteenth- and nineteenth-century inventories."

"Nicholas, when you decide to do something don't let anyone touch these except me. And then I'll only kiss the dust away. One must be careful with Rubens. You know what those *banditti* did to the big group portrait. *È stronzo!*"

Nicholas knew. The thought of the crimes committed in the name of "scientific" restoration made him shake his head. Nick knew that it had taken all of Carraccino's indubitable artistry to re-create the original values of a hundred paintings defaced by earnest but insensitive restorers.

"Don't worry, Marco, but thanks anyway for the reminder. How about a glass of something?"

Downstairs, while Torberg moved into the small upstairs gallery to set up his lights and camera, they chatted further over sherry about the condition of the world in which all four of them were involved. It was terrible how many important museum jobs were going begging, for lack of qualified people. No one had an "eye" anymore, and the "eye" was still the key, the core, the kernel of the vocation.

"It's a disgrace," said Carraccino. "The art historians know only documents and photographs; the restorers are all chemists first and painters last. *Poveri quadri*; poor pictures. *A l'occhio*—to the 'eye.' " He raised his glass in a mournful toast, drained it and departed.

The three dealers lunched at the Tennyson and walked back afterward to await Frodo.

The Director of the Fuller was invariably late. He was a great student of the opera and understood the value of an entrance. And punctuality was, after all, the buyer's prerogative. At Winters' request, a bottle of champagne was sent for and opened. Nick winced inwardly at the $60 tab he could expect from his wine store; the English inhaled champagne like oxygen.

Forty-five minutes later, Frodo appeared, hands fluttering like light-becalmed moths to excuse his tardiness. Frodo might be out of the market, but his famous manners had not evaporated along with his purchase fund. He behaved with the grace of a princess royal opening a pig show.

Nick opened the door to the working gallery. Torberg was casing his cameras. There was only one picture on the easel, The Cretan Bull.

Crisp looked closely at the sketch for a minute or two.

"Very nice, Nicholas. Rather like the two little pictures at Princes Gate. Except much more finished. It's really very good. Wonderful, in fact. Good condition, too, I might add." Frodo's manner said: What's the fuss? It's lovely, to be sure, but surely there's more?

Nick smiled at Sandler and Winters. "Can you give me a hand?" He went to the closet and unlocked it. The three men started to range the other eleven sketches along the baseboard.

As Sandler placed The Hydra on the floor, Frodo's quick dark gaze darted to it, probing back and forth, a radiant finger sweeping the room, making connections. As they kept bringing the sketches out, until Winters had finally leaned The Horses of Diomedes firmly against the wall, Frodo surrendered himself to the luxury of seeing. He emitted small, orgasmic exclamations as he circled the room like a cormorant searching out food: bent, angular, awkward; pausing before each picture in turn, obviously overwhelmed by the rarity and beauty presented to him.

He made three circuits. Finally, he turned to stare at Nick and the others, huddled like the Graces awaiting Paris' final judgment.

"I owe some apologies here." He looked first at Johnny Sandler, then at Barry Winters. "I have perhaps been ungracious on the subject of certain art dealers." His eyes turned friendly behind his pince-nez; the line of his nose, usually pointed up, as if to delineate by extension a boundary between the permissible and everything else, lowered perceptibly. Frodo was opening the gates of his private kingdom.

Rounding on Nick, he announced: "There is captured in this room everything that Rubens is or can be. The only thing comparable to this is the Decius Mus pictures in Lichtenstein. They are wonderful—but they are huge, in some ways terrifying pictures which belong in a collection as impregnable as dear Max's. This is a gold mine, Nicholas. I would weep at the sight of them, except that my emotions are suddenly constipated by envy and frustration. It's cruel to show them to me. They are as great as the Maria de' Medici series in the Louvre, and they can be savored without a million schoolchildren and German tourists interposing themselves."

While Frodo continued his review of the sketches, now bending six inches close to one for the breath of a detail, or stepping a yard back from another to catch the impact and excitement of its whole, Nick surreptitiously gestured Barry and Johnny out of the room. They went unquestioningly, recognizing that Frodo and Nick must now speak privately. There was nothing they could contribute.

After his eyes had clearly absorbed all they could, Frodo turned away and looked at Nick.

"There's nothing in the literature, of course?"

"No."

"I thought not. These are absolutely beautiful. I suppose they cost about as much as a rocket ship?"

Nick told him.

"I see. Well, you must let me reserve them for the Institute."

"Of course, Frodo. But I must tell you the rumor is that you're short of money." Nick owed that to Sandler and Winters.

"Of course we are, Nicholas. But I must have a try. Surely you'll grant me that boon?"

"Of course."

Nick could hear invisible wheels start to turn inside Crisp. The messianic aesthetic fervor with which Frodo overwhelmed the frugality of donors, the consoling confidence with which he subdued the furious need to belong of the Granada Mastermans of the world would be quickly mobilized. Frodo would marshal his formidable inner armies to try to finance the purchase of the dozen little pictures, whose combined surface totaled perhaps sixty square feet—less than the size of Granada Masterman's new sauna. This was the real thrill of the chase, the ultimate point of the museum life. People like Frodo worked for little money and suffered the often dreary company and condescension of rich, ambitious, ignorant men and women in order to pay for the only victories they felt were worthwhile: the acquisition of great works of art. The discovery and capture of masterpieces. Before other, equally driven curators or collectors in London or Malibu, Stuttgart or Yokohama could steal the prize, his prize, Frodo would have made his move.

Granada Masterman's apartment took up several floors high up in a tower on Central Park South. The back half of the top floor, which faced south, across a water tower and a patchwork of spindly-hedged asphalt rooftop gardens, had been assigned to her stepson, a loop-jawed young man whose broad, stupid face perfectly mirrored the mind that revolved slowly behind it. He was content to lurk in there, generally unseen, venturing out only to a half-dozen discotheques where his stepmother's credit was unquestioned. Among his records and his gossip magazines, he awaited his turn to be called to greatness, to join the elect: to take his place among the otherwise useless young men for whom ultimate salvation from the travails of responsibility would be the purchase of a seat in the United States Senate.

The other half of the floor was given over to a communications office, not unlike the information center at the Lazy G, over which a rotating cadre of thin-faced secretaries presided, busying themselves with a chattering telex network and a battery of word-processing machines plugged into a private telephone system which spread Mrs. Masterman's nocturnal inspirations to her sixteen thousand Masterwomen.

On the next-lower floor, a small chapel had been built. The altar was a pale marble facsimile of the Subtreasury Building topped with a shelf on which rested various appurtenances of Masterwomanhood: flash-frozen eucharistic Brie, a promotional Hermès scarf showing the Seven Stations of Personal Development, a copy of *Moral Money* bound in violet calfskin. Above hung color photographs illustrating the history of Masterman United, Inc., from the first clotted, creaky mud truck beside a pipe rack in East Texas to the smiling face of The Lady Founder Herself on the floor of the New York Stock Exchange, holding the fragment of ticker tape that marked the first public trade of MUD.

The rest of the floor was devoted to closets holding shoes, gowns and fifty-two fur coats, each carefully marked in terms of the Masterwoman devotional calendar. Tucked into a corner were a small bedroom and bath for her husband, Waldo, in the unlikely event he might leave his beloved golf courses and dahlia beds and venture into Manhattan.

The seventeenth, or lowest, floor was the showplace. The front of the apartment, overlooking the park, was a large ell. Granada's bedroom ran longwise away from the northern exposure. Floor-to-ceiling windows on its northern and western sides filled the room with bright sunlight for most of the day, slowly rotting and fading the cowboy watercolors on the east wall, which backed onto the living room.

This room, through which one passed to reach the dining room, the kitchen and pantry, and the three maids' bedrooms, was entered by a broad elevator foyer, customarily occupied by an armed security guard. It was a wide, fair chamber, welcoming in the full blaze of afternoon, subtle and disarming after dark. Above the fireplace hung an abstract sculpture, silver and gold, fashioned from the molten remnants of her husband's golfing trophies—his sole contribution to the aesthetics of the place. The furniture was French and English, as good as could be expected from ten years of underbidding at important auctions. Except for the silver-framed prison photos of recent government officials, whose sullen expressions above the numbers on their chests were mitigated by the light flowing south over the park, there were no pictures in the room. The walls were paneled; no nails for good wood.

Left alone in this room to finish his drink, after his interview with his Granada, Hugo Winstead once again wondered if he had taken the right turning in life.

Not that he was unused to unpleasant tasks. His willingness to perform them, even when they verged on outright betrayal, had underwritten his career. Ethical or moral or sentimental second thoughts were not reactions native to him. They would have hindered his mad dash to freedom from his shamefully inelegant background. He was not a man to underestimate the effects of luck. After all, nothing but luck had put him on the same aircraft carrier with Homer Seabury, whose father was the most consequential lawyer in New York; nothing but luck had caused him to break his ankle tripping over a cable on the flight deck, so that he had to be ferried back to Ulithi on a PBY the day before the Japs came steaming out of San Bernadino Strait and sank the carrier; nothing but luck had plucked Seabury and Rufus Lassiter out of the ocean while a thousand others went to the bottom, and then reunited them with Winstead in Honolulu; nothing but luck had kept them together so that they could go drinking at Solomon Greschner's house in 1945, Homer with both burned arms in slings, Rufus on a cane and himself appearing just as valiant as they because of his ankle cast; Greschner then had suggested that old Morgan Seabury offer Hugo a job.

Luck, in those years, had often as not worn the shape of Solomon Greschner. Sol had fixed up the job; Sol had put Calypso in his path, and the Fuller Foundation, and the introduction to Granada and much else. Sol had hammered into deep sand most of the pilings of Homer's life. They said Rufus was lucky. Compared to me, Hugo thought, Rufus has been downright deprived in the luck department. Hugo regarded luck as his innate gift, a talent like shrewdness, or charm, or a smooth golf swing, all of which he had also come to possess; luck was a dependable personal attribute of Hugo's makeup; therefore, as he rationalized it, whatever fortune might be seen to have brought him was, by his lights, of his own doing.

Loyalty was another matter. Did this Navy thing have to last forever, the way Homer seemed to think it should? Well, now he had his marching orders from Granada, and Homer would be in harm's way. He'd lined up with Granada. She'd forced any betrayal of Homer on him. He took a pull on his vodka. Hell, he thought finally, there would be ways of making it up to Homer. Between him and Rufus, somehow, some way they would manage. And, if worse came to worst, he could always start reminiscing about the war.

Comforted, having found, as he always did, some acceptable excuse for another mortgage taken out against his equity in the past, Hugo drained his glass and went to the telephone. He asked Homer if they could meet uptown late the next day; perhaps at the club, on Seabury's way home. What he had to say would take an hour, Winstead figured, no longer. Right now he needed something to pick him up. A restorative, one might say. For Hugo there was only one sort.

He took up the phone again. When he explained his problem about a pending case, the girl who worked for his litigation partner said she'd be happy to meet him at the Coach House in an hour. Such a pretty voice, Hugo thought. And nice legs, too.

At about the same time, Nick put down his own phone and let himself laugh. First, Bogle had called, in a mood of great annoyance.

"You know someone named Winters? An Englishman; real snot-ass accent. Says he's one of the most important art dealers in London. Talked down to me, like I was some Sheenie kid pricing a Mickey Mouse watch. And he was the one who called, not me. Using your name. That was for openers. Now he's called up here about six times since. Sounds drunk most of the time, at least to me, although maybe it's the accent. Says he heard I was interested in collecting pictures. I asked him where and he wouldn't say, but he kept mentioning you. Says he has a Brueghel drawing to show me. He wants to come up here, for a drink, which I wouldn't say he needs; he wants to take me to dinner. I told him to get back to me. What's the story, Nick? I'm not buying anything. Yet."

Nick advised Bogle that he had never heard of a dealer named Winters. Poor Barry—he never learned, did he?

"This happens a lot, Harvey. I'm sorry that you were bothered, but sometimes being in this business is like being on a mailing list. I've had a lot of problems with people using my name. If this Waters, or whatever his name is, calls again, tell him to call me. I'll set him straight. We dealers have a professional organization to deal with this sort of thing."

Before he hung up, he told Bogle that, by coincidence, he had been on the point of telephoning to see if Bogle could come by early the following week to look at some pictures. They made a date for that Thursday after lunch. That, Nick decided, would be Frodo's deadline.

Then he called Johnny Sandler. First he reported that he and Bogle had an appointment. Then he told him about Bogle's call.

"This means Barry stays out of sight, as far as I'm concerned. He now becomes a true silent partner, until my sixty days are up, Johnny. Bogle is tricky new money. You know how it is, Johnny. He's got to be rocked and lullabied. Bogle won't go for that Bratt's Club crap of Barry's. He's got a real eye for bullshit. I'll handle Bogle, but it's up to you to keep Barry away from the deal—okay? Send him back to his wife in London. It'll be good for him. He's got to be about screwed out and shopped out by now, wouldn't you think? Isn't it about time for Ascot?"

Finally, he called Frodo Crisp and invited him to dinner night after next to talk further about the *modelli*. He knew that the Fuller's director generally reserved Thursday evenings for a tour of the leather bars, but he guessed that the pull of art would prevail over the longings of the flesh in this case, and it did. He and Jill and Frodo could have a good time together, and if they made a reasonably early evening of it, Frodo could still make it down to the piers in good time. Saturday night they were dining with the Sandlers.

Socially, it looked pretty heavy, but Jenny was again going away for a long weekend with a chum—now that summer vacation had started, the child's schedule rivaled that of the busiest professional houseguest—and Nick and Jill were determined to seize the days and the nights, to start bringing their separated lives into some sort of phase, and make their too divergent orbits coalesce.

The memorandum from Financial Engineering and Mergers and Acquisitions was on Homer Seabury's desk when he arrived at seven-thirty that Friday morning. It was a concise rehash of hundreds of presentations that Homer had seen over the years. Investment bankers preferred to huckster by example, showcasing an impressive client list as proof of capability. A firm's competence was ratified by the company it kept. New clients were attracted by the prospect of joining an exclusive club, of keeping perhaps better corporate company than they knew themselves to be, of mingling with the quality. Respectability by association.

Homer Seabury knew that none of this would count with Buford Gudge or Katagira. The lists of important-sounding transactions and famous corporations which made up the main body of the memo were filler and would be seen by them as such. The Lazy G people, especially with Sol at their ear, would have known, well before they had ever laid eyes on Homer, that Seaco was professionally as capable—well, more or less—as Goldman, Sachs or Lehman or Kidder, Peabody to carry out the functional tasks which Katagira had outlined. What appealed to Homer was the innate conservatism of the Lazy G people. These weren't wild men trying to corner a market segment or bull a commodity. They weren't promoters looking for a top-notch Wall Street name to crutch a shaky offering of speculative securities over the barricades of investment dubiety. They were, he thought —thankfully—his kind of financial people; for all the inevitable cultural differences between the frontier, the domain of the open collar and the red neck, and his cosmopolitan, silk-hosed, establishmentarian world, Homer Seabury believed that he and Bubber Gudge were moral and philosophical brothers under the skin. The thought warmed and comforted him.

For brothers stuck together, he thought. In the way that hope unreflectively transforms possibility into likelihood, Homer had already forged, in his mind, an alliance with Gudge: a pact of mutual advantage, defense and satisfaction against Granada Masterman and her minions. His mind had already polished up the trophies of victory and set them on the mantel in the Seaco Partners' Room. In Seabury's case, hope had been fused with imagined justice. With Gudge on his side, taking what Homer by now was sure could be the decisive hand in the game, Seaco could continue on the path he had set for it: fiscally impregnable, doing fewer things than the flashier competition, but doing them stylishly and well, a model of old-school banking transported safely and profitably into the chaotic riskiness of the modern world. It had taken him long enough to expunge the presence of Rufus Lassiter, with his taste for gimmickry and the fast dollar; he was damned if he would go along with his return to an active role at Seaco, let alone with Granada calling the signals from the shadows. There was no telling what she had up her sleeve, but he would bet that it had something to do with tying Seaco into her purple army of saleswomen. Gimmicks. Advertising. Publicity. To Homer Seabury, these were the characteristics of contemporary Wall Street that resonated the unsoundness of the new thinking. Imagine, at some firms, people could write checks on their brokerage accounts! Well, never at Seaco. There would always be a niche—a damn good one, too—for the firm that was a little out of date, that incarnated the old values—the killer, Homer thought slyly, in laced-up shoes and a dark tie.

The memorandum concluded with a recommendation that Seaco seek to obtain a three-year advisory contract, at an annual retainer of $500,000, to provide "ongoing financial consultation, econometrics, diagnostics, capital-structure engineering and maintainance, and evaluative overview and support in the area of acquisition and consolidation: including strategic and tactical planning; mobilization, infiltration and negotiation; capitulation design." Reading it over, Homer wished Mergers and Acquisitions didn't always have to sound like one of the Joint Chiefs of Staff.

He called Sol and read the memorandum to him.

"Homer, you can leave out the references and history. You saw those people. By now, they probably know more about Seaco's history than you do. Just tell them that the resources and expertise of your firm are a matter of record—Gudge isn't going to be impressed by the fact you handled fifty million dollars of financing for X, Y or Z last year; he dribbles fifty million out of the side of his mouth—and that you will put them at their disposal. And put in something about the character of the firm. Your philosophy. Your solidity and conservatism. Homer, that's what'll sell Gudge on you and Seaco. You've got to seem his kind of folks, as he might say himself.

"The fee's too high. Gudge knows what money's worth. Cut it by a hundred and fifty thousand a year. Go back to the way things used to be on Wall Street; make your money on the deals. People like Gudge want closers; they usually hate experts. Make the retainer count for credit against whatever fees you earn for transactions, such as mergers. Homer, these people didn't get to be worth several billions by being dopes. They still tie money to value; which means they don't mind spending it but they do mind wasting it. They aren't going to like putting up a half-million a year for what you and I know you mean by 'ongoing financial consultation,' et cetera. Translated into English, that means that every six weeks or so, some twenty-five-year-old just out of business school is going to call up Katagira with a half-assed, self-serving idea which will, one, display an appalling ignorance of the operational realities of this or that Gudge business, and two, will show, just as transparently, that it was conceived as much to make money for Seaco and a name for this junior-grade wizard as to do something of real benefit, or advantage, for the Gudge interests."

Thanking Greschner, Homer had mixed feelings. It made no difference to him if he asked for $500,000 or $50,000. He had never gotten used to these retainers. He certainly would never have paid them if he'd been running a corporation. In what he thought of as "his" day, you collected from an investment-banking client only when you did a deal for him, just as Sol had said; you got paid only when a client thought enough of an idea you offered him for nothing to pay you to turn it into a reality, a transaction completed and closed. But retainers were all the rage on the Street now, and a firm needed them to be able to pay its new MBAs $40,000 a year in order to attract enough MBAs to supply to the clients in order to justify the retainers. An ironic circle, Homer thought, but corporate America seemed determined to keep the Street happy and fat, and whose money was used to pay for all this foolishness, anyway? Nowadays, the Street's most lucrative game was to help corporate America spend its money buying other companies' used assets.

Homer sometimes wondered at this. Wasn't industrial America pretty run-down? Wouldn't the billions spent by corporations buying other corporations buy a hell of a lot of new machine tools and industrial robots and continuous-casting units? Well, the Street didn't make the kind of fees off machine tools it stood to make off corporate takeovers, so it had persuaded the corporate clients that takeovers were what they wanted. And the rule had always been: the client knew best; the client was always right.

He asked his secretary to get Mr. Katagira at an unlisted number in Texas. Their conversation lasted fifteen minutes, during which Seabury outlined the ideas in the memorandum, as modified by Greschner. Neither Homer nor Katagira was much given to verbal embellishment. Katagira would get back to him as soon as he could, Seabury was told at the end of their conversation, once he had had an opportunity to confer with Mr. Gudge, who was out of town and might not return for several days. Katagira asked for Seabury's home telephone number, in case it might not be possible to ring until sometime over the weekend.

Homer had tried to discern some hint of approval or disapproval in Katagira's voice, but it was impossible. Ah, well, he thought, rising to head downstairs for the regular Friday meeting of the Transactions Committee, nothing now but to wait for the telephone to ring.

Neither Jill nor Nick was used to sleeping through the night with another soul inches away, so it wasn't surprising that they had awakened within minutes of each other. It had seemed completely normal to be lying there in the dark, with the small noises of the city outside, chattering as idly and cheerfully as if they were in a restaurant. Jill told him more about herself. There had been a lot of wounding there, Nick saw. He made a vow—an unseen, unheard promise to himself, a knight errant's private compact—that as far as Jill was concerned, he would always be numbered among the not guilty. He reached for her then, feeling the irrepressible, miraculously repeatable physical charge that seemed always to pulse at the heart of every new, true romance. Other important, everlasting things were said, as they burrowed deep in their cocoon of sensation and white night, until at last they fell apart and off the edge of wakefulness.

Once, later, Nick awoke. Listening to her on the next pillow, feeling the line of her pressed warm along his length, sensing some vibration, some inwardest quiver, that went beyond mere pulse or breathing, he began to be aware of the consternation he was capable of causing in someone else's breast. It was not an altogether comforting awareness; it implied so much responsibility.

Saturday had been a morning for separate errands; a reunion at lunch for some good, cheap Greek food; on to the Met to see what was happening. Hand in hand, they wandered through a show of a private collection of Middle European Romantic Painting. It was a lot of crap, Nick felt—as he had known he would. He could see Jill was puzzled at finding these dreary, uninteresting pictures given an important display by a major museum.

Finally she looked at him. "Forgive me, but isn't this junk, really?"

"Indeed, my dearest love," he replied. "But hot junk. Steaming, in fact. A new school to be celebrated. Pap for the writers, fad-discoverers and folks like me who suddenly have museums and heavyweight collectors calling up wanting unknown Czech and Rumanian painters."

They walked on toward the American wing. "The art market gets restyled every few years. Like cars. The immortals—Rubens, Cézanne—stay above the hurly-burly."

They turned into the galleries that housed American works and finally stopped in front of a large painting depicting a storm-clouded black sky over a beach running off into cliffs, with three ships at various distances making for the lee shore while fishermen on the beach furled their nets and made fast.

"I like that," she said. "It feels like life."

"And it's large enough to fight these big gallery spaces. The Met likes things big. There's not much intimacy around here. Drama; that's the game here. It's why I like the Fuller. Sometimes I think the Met's gone crazy trying to draw people. Like that photography show they had here a few years ago. You must have covered it; every society and literary clown within fifty miles was there, staring at these pictures this jumped-up fashion photographer had taken of not-very-attractive people, with their warts and tics. They were blown up to life size or bigger, so you found yourself looking at an eight-inch nose or a size sixty-eight bosom, and everyone figured because it was big and black-and-white, it must be art. Big *does* better, by and large, in crowds. The Met likes crowds. But that doesn't mean it *is* better."

The night before had been one of those miserable evenings during which everything was said too loudly, too much was eaten and drunk and nothing was tasted or heard. Jill and Nick hung apart from the uproar. At last, while the rest of the group headed off on a disco foray, they made their escape.

Central Park West was a welcome refuge; they were worn out by the effortfulness of the dinner. They made love vigorously and affectionately, and then slept soundly, touching each other frequently in the night. Now they were sitting, a happy intimate Sunday couple, with the sun painting the dining room, a Haydn flute quartet whistling softly in the background and the New York, Boston and Washington papers splashed about the table.

"This is nice. I'm glad you came home with me. You're very good value, Nick." She touched his cheek. "Lots of good ways. Bed and breakfast; morning, noon and night. But can you be trusted? I think you can."

"I can. This thing's gone fast for us, but it's gone far, too. I don't think I can stand loving you by appointment only. I mean, I don't think we have to live together, but what about Jenny? You've been pretty strict on the overnights, but isn't there a point at which—"

"Of course there is. I told you when we started you have to be trusted in little pieces, one by one. Children are serious about a man in their mother's bed. There are two of us here to hurt. Don't you forget that." She was serious; she was terrified of betrayal.

"Listen, don't I know it." He was full of the overconfidence that his euphoria brought. He wasn't really hearing her. "I heard a story once. This guy—married, I think—got loaded; I mean really knee-walking; one night while his wife or live-in or whatever was away, at a country-club party in some dump like Greenwich where he was a houseguest, and the next thing he knew he wakes up next to this pretty good-looking new divorcée in what he guesses is her bedroom. He's about to pile on, they're both as randy as goats, but he has to pee first. Of course, she forgets to tell him that she and her children have a kind of Sunday code, that the sound of the john flushing on weekends is a signal that Mummy's awake. So he comes back, and is just climbing on, you can imagine, out to here with evidence of his ardor, when the door opens, and in come three kids, all under seven, with flowers and orange juice and the *Times*, and here's this man they've never seen before mounting their mother. My God, how awful can life be? For all concerned."

"Awful enough." A special chilliness in her voice made him look up and examine her closely. The sun outside was shining as brightly as before, but her face had darkened.

"I'm sorry. Did I say something? I just thought it was kind of an object lesson. A drastic one, perhaps. It's a stupid story. I'm sorry."

He reached out his hand and let it rest, tentatively, on her forearm. She didn't draw back. She looked sad, as if a disappointing, distasteful memory had passed through her mind like a quick cloud across the sun. Something private, not yet able to be shared.

"Don't worry. It's nothing. It's just that something very like that happened to me." She saw Nick turn grave. "No, I wasn't in the bed, darling. You men are always so jealous of the past and so careless of the present. It was just a man I knew and liked once upon a time. It's a silly story. Not worth getting excited about; I'm sorry."

Further comment would be unwelcome, for Nick now recollected that Sol had told him the story, and that it had been about Sol's son, Mickey, and that Mickey Greschner had once been Jill's lover. He buried his attention in the papers until Jill suggested that they shower and walk back across the park for lunch. By then, Nick had resolved one thing: to be careful of the present. He was not going to be lumped with the likes of Mickey Greschner—on any grounds.

Gudge and Katagira decided that it would be good tactics not to call Seabury back until Sunday. Keep him eager.

Gudge had only one question when Katagira related his conversation with Seabury. "What do we get for our three hundred and fifty thousand dollars?"

"If my experience on Wall Street is any guide," said Katagira, "nothing. But then, we don't want anything. Oh, they'll send us countless memos about this and that, and I'll pretend to study them carefully—you certainly don't have to bother with them, unless, as seems unlikely, they come up with something really creative or useful. We pay them to bring them into the orbit of our plans, to make them think they are the active, the initiating party in the relationship. It's merely step one."

Sunday afternoon, a call from Katagira summoned Homer Seabury from the lunch table at which his wife was entertaining the other officers of the Morris County Beagle Club. The talk was of dogs exclusively, and it was boring in the extreme. Homer was happy to make his escape.

"Mr. Seabury?" Katagira's voice was cheerful. "Mr. Gudge and I have reviewed the thoughts you gave me the other day, and without wasting time and words, since I'm sure I've taken you from the lunch table, we feel the basis you propose for commencing a relationship is perfectly acceptable."

Seabury was overjoyed. And proud of himself for pulling it off.

"In the next few days," Katagira continued, "I'll be sending you a package of material which your people can review. It will be, of course, descriptive and financial. What we'd specifically like Seaco Group's opinion on would be, first, how we should deploy our service and production interests, respectively, in a manner that would maximize their value in the event we should wish to make one or more public offerings. Secondly, we would like you to design a large-scale program for the purchase of, say, half a billion dollars in long-term and medium-term Treasury securities. For cash, of course. Mr. Gudge has decided that the present Administration's actions clearly indicate a fundamental turn, not yet fully appreciated, in the economic affairs of this country which must be reflected in the bond market.

"When you have completed your review and analysis, hopefully within the next few weeks, I'd suggest that we have an all-hands meeting here at the ranch—we'll send a plane, of course—to decide on a course of action and begin implementing your recommendations. Is that agreeable? Good. I might say, before letting you return to your meal, Mr. Seabury, that Mr. Gudge has been very favorably impressed with the punctuality of Seaco Group's response to our inquiries."

Bidding Seabury goodbye, Katagira went to tell his employer that he had patted Seabury, whom Gudge had once compared to an anxious dog that was making noises like a polar bear and walking around on its hind legs.

"Good deal," said Gudge. He was slumped on his couch, watching Roger Staubach paralyze the Redskins. Bubber was preoccupied; it had occurred to him that Caryn hadn't been back to the ranch in nearly three weeks. Maybe she was mad at him for not getting those pictures she wanted so bad. He asked Katagira to get that art fellow up in New York on the phone for him. He'd get some action; that was the point of being a Gudge.

Fifteen hundred miles to the northeast, Sol Greschner had listened to Homer Seabury blurt out his triumph. He congratulated his friend and smiled with the satisfaction of a successful marriage broker—after all, he would receive 20 percent of Seaco's fee from Gudge and a privileged allocation if there was a public offering and it looked hot. Then he called and left a message on Jill's answering machine.

Jill and Nick had tried a Sunday-afternoon movie, but it wasn't very good and they couldn't keep their hands off each other, so she'd taken him back to her apartment.

Later, after Nick was gone and Jenny had been fed and was settled in front of the television set, Jill retired to her office. On the telex was a message from the proprietor of a desperately expensive remote Caribbean beach hotel informing her that a famous movie star had checked in under an assumed name with a woman who was certainly not his wife. She pondered that for a moment, shook her head and turned on the telephone-answering machine. Sol's voice came on. She listened to his message several times, carefully, making notes.

Then she sat down at the computer; while waiting for the screen to light up, she composed the opening lines of Robert Creighton's next column: "Just when smart Streetwatchers were starting to write off Homer Seabury's tenure as chief executive of Seaco Group, it appears as if he may have pulled off a career-saving coup. It's too early to talk specifics, and no one at Seaco is saying anything, but the firm may just have landed one of the biggest, most highly sought-after investment-banking accounts in the world. . . ." This'll keep them talking, she thought, as her fingers started to fly across the keyboard.

CHAPTER ELEVEN

The summer after he came down from Cambridge, Maximilian Lefcourt went to stay for a weekend with his friend Ivo Crouchback at the latter's family *castello* in the Italian coastal town of Santa Dulcina delle Rocce. He was returning to the South of France after his annual visit to his parents at La Pergola, the villa on the Fiesole road, outside Florence, which his father had built as a wedding gift to Max's mother. In those days, Florence held few attractions for the young Englishman who had not made up his mind about much of anything: vocation, politics, the precise character of his sexuality. Little engaged Max in Florence; he took polite walks with his parents in hills buzzing with the heat of early summer; in the evenings, after dinner, the family was driven into town for coffee and ices in the Piazza Repubblica, where a brass band played; he passed his mornings reading the London newspapers in the hedged garden, beneath which the city was spread out like a visual buffet. The expatriate summer colony of which his parents were a part circulated among themselves at a series of dinner parties, teas and elaborate picnics with parasols and Fortnum and Mason hampers. In the course of his visit, they went over the hill to lunch with Berenson at I Tatti, his villa in Settignano. Max was not much impressed; he found himself unawed by the self-centered little man who dropped names and ideas in six languages to the swooning admiration of the rest of the table.

Max had no real feeling for Florence then. His daily rounds were not much different from what they would have been in London: tobacconist, bank, news agent, shoemaker, club. When his family's calendar permitted, he lunched alone with the latest Michael Arlen novel in one of a half-dozen favored cafés; though he might walk in the shadow of the Duomo, under the arcades of the Uffizi, in the gardens of the Pitti Palace, his daydreams were of casinos and champagne cocktails in his beloved "Monte"; he saw nothing of the artistic glory at his elbow. When his family duty dance ended, after a fortnight of utter neglect of the archstone of European art, he took the train to Genoa, where he was met by the Crouchbacks' chauffeur and driven to Santa Dulcina delle Rocce. Just twenty-four at the time, he was already the utter prisoner of a self-imposed routine of dinners and dances and watering spots which he expected would keep him content for a lifetime.

His meeting with Francis Sanger changed all that. It transformed Max's life and his personality.

Sanger, then just thirty, was a guest at another villa to which the Crouchback ménage had been bidden to lunch. Francis Sanger was already, like Berenson, "an attraction." Sanger had made his mark with the publication of a history of fresco painting which had caused the art world to change the way it looked at the great cycles in Assisi and Florence. In the course of preparing the book, he had argued that a fresco cycle in an obscure church tucked away in the Umbrian foothills was an early, uncharacteristic work by Piero della Francesca. It was a major coup of connoisseurship; shortly afterward, Sanger's instinctive judgment was confirmed by the discovery in the church's sacristy of a document that completely set forth the commission and payment for the cycle.

At the time of his meeting with Max, Sanger was riding a cresting wave of celebrity occasioned by the publication of his autobiography at thirty, *Trent'anni: An Aesthetic Life.* Yet nothing he did paid well; he scraped out a living scouting for dealers, selling attributions and sleeping at least two-thirds of his nights in the guest bedrooms of covetous hosts who accepted his mind and presence in lieu of rent.

After lunch, Max and Francis Sanger, who preferred to be called Frank, wandered off together for a stroll. Both were weary of the brittle, meaningless conversation of the luncheon party. No evident electricity had passed between them at lunch. Nor had they overdrunk the straw-gold wine of the region. What they may have said or done as they wandered the paths that twisted among the cypress-alleyed hills was between them. When at last their walk took them back into Santa Dulcina, after the heat of the day had passed and the picnic party had packed up its hampers, they knew their destiny was to be together.

Frank persuaded Max to return with him to Florence. Florence epitomized everything that was civilized, he argued; Max must learn Florence; it was as essential to a truly cultivated man as speaking French or knowing Shakespeare. Max consented. He would have gone to the moon for Frank. One of the Lefcourt automobiles was summoned from Florence; the two young men sent the driver back by train and set off together along a road which they would still be traveling together nearly sixty years later.

It took them two winding weeks to reach Florence. As they grew closer, finding an eloquent solace and joy in each other's company, Frank Sanger inoculated Max with the virus of Italy. It had a benign virulence, he knew, more powerful than that of almost any other culture. He watched happily as Max became enslaved, as the germ took hold in provincial picture galleries, in small cheap cafés, in churches so dark that a flashlight was needed to make out grim apocalypses painted at the time of the Black Death. By the time they turned the dusty car into the carriage yard of La Pergola, Max Lefcourt had found his vocation. A year later, his parents died and he became sole master of a large fortune and of La Pergola.

Max had no taste for the public sort of spectacle that Berenson had created at I Tatti. La Pergola was organized for the comfort and pleasure and working requirements of its two inhabitants. Thus began the torrential production of the next five decades: a flow of books and monographs on Italian painters and painting; volumes of autobiography and aesthetics; a commonplace book; essays polite and contentious; reviews; occasional pieces and tributes; delicate, unmemorable verse. To the villa, over those fifty or so years came the gifted and agreeable young men, Nick and Frodo Crisp among them, to study with Sanger; to live and breathe the great collection he and Max Lefcourt had built together on the foundation of Max's inheritance.

The collection was not "historical." Its guiding principle was an absolute dedication to quality. The collecting was selective, value-conscious, severely judged, effortful, creative.

Most of the greatest works were acquired during an intense dozen years before World War II. Treasures seemed to come from every corner of the world. The Lotto *Allegory of Penitence* was discovered in an antiques shop in Sussex. An Easter trip to Sicily yielded the smaller Raphael Madonna. The *Gugliemedonna Triptych* by Lorenzo Monaco was bought from the Russians. The greatest paintings and drawings were purchased during the years of Mussolini's ascendancy: the Bronzino portrait of the famous publisher Lorenzo Amicabile; the Modestini *tondo* by Fra Filippo Lippi; the great Titian *Judas*; the attributed Giorgione portrait of Paolina Nera; the Antonello *Saint Luke with the Donor Giacometto Cane*; works by foreign artists working in Italy: Claude, Poussin, Ingres, Turner.

By 1939, when the collection went into hiding for the duration, the collection had attained essentially its final shape and character. A small number of great paintings and drawings were added after the war. Finally, there was no space left on the walls of La Pergola, but by then Max and Frank's taste for the hunt had been spoiled by the commercial extravaganza the art market had become.

There would never be another collection like it, thought Nick, steering his rented Fiat off the Autostrada Firenze–Mare onto the road that led into Florence. He was glad Frank could see him, as suddenly as he'd called. He needed Frank's opinion.

Bogle had been called away to Hong Kong and Singapore, which meant a ten-day delay before he could be brought together with the Rubens cycle. Nick had needed to escape what had become a daily torture: calls from Sol and Bubber and Caryn Gudge about buying the Lefcourt Collection. Gudge had even offered him a $50,000 annual retainer as an "art adviser," and a 10-percent commission if Nick could make a deal with Max Lefcourt. Nick had politely refused. The trouble was, he couldn't send Gudge to another dealer; there wasn't another one who had the entrée to Max. He would just have to weather the storm.

Whenever he had time on his hands, Nick tended to go to London, where there was always business to be done. Harried by the Gudges and Sol, and with Jill having taken Jenny out West for an interminable two weeks, he left for England. He still got a kick from London, even though the old city had all but capitulated to the general high-priced cheapness that oozed in with the new money.

Nick stayed two days. He looked in on Barry Winters, who took him to lunch at a "club" which seemed to be dominated by Arabs and Greeks, the unpleasant sort of people who formed the backbone of Winters' client list. Over a piece of chicken that cost £20 and a bottle of Spanish plonk that cost £40, Winters talked disparagingly of "wogs," but he never stopped waving and smiling unctuously toward most of the other tables. Afterward, declining an invitation to dinner, Nick walked across Berkeley Square and up Bond Street to a gallery with which he was 50–50 on a Hogarth conversation piece.

Richard Creel, one of the partners, was expecting him. The picture had only that morning come back from the restorers. It showed a family of four posed carefully on the terrace of a classical house on the bank of the Thames. The picture had come up beautifully; its original coolness and restraint had been returned to it, so that the pleasing awkwardness of the figures was admirably matched and balanced by the repose and serenity of its atmosphere.

"Looks wonderful," said Nick.

"It does, doesn't it? We had to do a little patchwork here. And here." Creel pointed to small vaguely neutral areas in the sky and in the face of one of the figures. "And we had to put it on a new canvas. But basically it was really a matter of taking off that yellow Victorian varnish and letting the picture speak for itself."

"Well, it's a knockout. Is Yale going to take it?"

"I should think they would do," said Creel. "They haven't got anything quite this fine. Not *quite*. They've reserved it. Incidentally, Nicholas, I don't know what your plans are while you're here, but I should look in at Grundy's if I were you. Get them to show you Code Name 'Padua.' " Creel flashed a mysterious, mischievous smile which interested Nick.

After lunch at the Garrick Club, Nick telephoned Grundy's and made a date for the next morning, giving him plenty of time for the afternoon flight to Pisa. He visited Agnew's, had his eyes knocked out by a stunning show of Turner watercolors, found that Mr. Julian was in Düsseldorf until the end of the week and spent the rest of the afternoon at the Wallace Collection. On his way back, he walked through the Burlington Arcade, looking for something to take back to his ladies; everything cost at least 20 percent more than at Bloomingdale's. Unskilled shopper, he dawdled and hemmed, finally settling uncertainly on a pair of Fair Isle sweaters that he guessed would fit.

That night, for the first time ever that he could recall, he dined alone in London, in his hotel room. He had no urge to howl. He tried to read the book Jill had raved about. It was all about wonderfully talented, amusingly vocationed, enviably sublimated men and women who led the sort of life he hoped he was drifting into with Jill, an existence from which the last tooth of pain had been drawn. It didn't seem very real. The night before he left, he'd taken Jill and Jenny out for an early hamburger around the corner from her place. Afterward, in her living room, she'd hugged him and kissed his cheek with her daughter looking on. To be so demonstrative, to admit him thus into the deep privacy of her relationship with Jenny was a kind of confession, he knew. He intended to prove worthy of the confidence.

He was almost through the commercial outskirts of Florence. Keeping north of the old, historic center of the city, he passed under the railroad tracks, drove down the Viale Filippo Strozzi and swung through the Piazza di Libertà and the Piazza delle Cure and finally onto the Via San Domenico, the main Fiesole road. Just before the little village of San Domenico, he turned east on a rougher road, bumped along for just over two kilometers and, at last, found himself on the cypress-lined avenue that led up a fold in the hill to La Pergola. As the weathered stone of its enclosing walls came into view, Nick felt the same tingle in his spirit that he had experienced when, twenty years earlier, he had first come to La Pergola, in search of the secret of Italian painting. It was a shrine, a holy place.

As he turned the car in the carriage yard, the main door of La Pergola opened, disclosing Max, leaning on his stick, with a cheery hand waved in greeting. He and Nick embraced, while Giovanna, the cook, boss of the household and indispensable governess of her two old charges, cooed over her young friend.

"Come in, come in, come in," Max exclaimed. "Frank can't wait to see you. He's in the sitting room; we took a bit of a long walk this morning, three times around the garden and almost to the bottom of the arbor, and I'm afraid he's rather overdone it."

As they walked down the hall, Nick looked curiously about him. The Collection was still in New York; the exhibition at the Fuller was due to close in a week. He was interested to see how the villa looked stripped of its noblest ornaments. There were no blank spaces; everything had been replaced. Above the pilastered, waist-high wooden bookcases that ran the length of the hallway, in place of the three small Sassettas that usually hung there, were three panels depicting what Nick took to be episodes from the life of Saint Benedict.

"Where did those come from, Max?"

"The three Neroccios? The people down at the Uffizi got them for us.

From things they had in storage. I expect they realized how lonely Frank and I would be without the pictures. Really very nice of them, don't you think? You should see the so-called Veronese they dug up to put in the dining room where the Titian was. It's very grand, even if it is probably a later copy. Ah, here we are. Frank, here's Nicholas."

The room was warm with pale afternoon sunlight. Frank Sanger was sitting in an armchair near the French doors leading to the terrace and the gardens beyond; they had been left ajar to catch the last fresh breath of the day. He had a cashmere blanket over his knees and a book and a notebook open on his lap, but he seemed to be staring out across the gardens and the hills, like a sailor on watch.

"Oh, Nicholas, I am glad to see you. You won't mind if I don't get up, but it's quite a process and I know I'll manage to drop everything."

They shook hands. Nick thought that age had turned Frank transparent; his skin had the texture and translucency of vellum. But his voice was clear and forthright, and his eyes seemed as alert and assimilative as ever.

"Now sit down, Nicholas. Have you eaten? Max, see that Nicholas is fed. What's new? How's Frodo? What's the gossip? Is it true the Le Nain that was in Lausanne is going to Texas? Who arranged that? Did Max behave himself in New York? Have you read this? It's called *Pedigree*, and it's very stupid. I'm reviewing it for the *Burlington*. Why must people write about art who don't know anything about it? How are you, now? Max, did you ring for food for Nicholas?"

Nothing wrong with Frank's spirit, Nick thought. He had frequently reflected that if the Lefcourt-Sanger ménage had been a marriage, Frank would have been the shrewish, demanding, irresistibly frivolous wife and Max the complacent, confident, unbothered breadwinner.

He tried to answer Frank's questions between bites of the salami and fresh bread and bitter Italian beer which Aldo brought. Yes, the Le Nain, a very rare, very fine seventeenth-century French painting, was indeed going to a Texas museum. And dirt-cheap, too. There had been a scholarly ruckus about the picture's authenticity, which had been challenged by a famous connoisseur for reasons of jealousy and pique. This whiffy little academic tempest had ruffled enough feathers to oblige the owner of the picture to drop his asking price by $2 million, which was when the director of the Texas museum, who believed in his own eye, had pounced. The storm soon blew itself out. Technical analysis and newly researched documentation had vindicated the picture's genuineness.

"Why didn't Frodo buy it?" Sanger demanded. "I know the picture. It's marvelous. I saw it at Du Cazlet before the war, when everyone except Sterling thought Le Nain was a figment of the imagination. Frodo should have gotten it; there's nothing like it in the Fuller."

Nick was surprised that Max hadn't reported on the Fuller's financial calamity. He risked making Frank choleric and told the facts as he knew them.

"There really ought to be a law, you know," Max added mildly. "About these social-climbing, nonprofessional trustees, especially when they're spending money that was never theirs. I tell you, Nicholas, I don't like that fellow Winstead. You remember the Winsteads, Frank. Two years ago. They came with a letter from Frodo. She's a very pretty, scared-looking creature, too pale to sit in the sun even at dawn, I should think. He's very crisp and self-assured. A slick, nasty bit of work. I personally can't abide any man who's publicly rude to his wife. And he's the most awful lecher; I had to dine at their flat before my opening, and my word, he had his hand on every fanny in the room."

"Let me tell you why I had to see you, Frank," Nick said. "It just came up yesterday, in London. Hang on to your hats. Old Herr Frühlingstein has decided to sell his altarpiece. Grundy's is going to handle it. It will go under the hammer in November."

"I don't believe it!" exclaimed Sanger. "That altarpiece has been in that family for three hundred years, since before the Thirty Years' War. It was carried over the Alps into Switzerland to keep it away from Wallenstein's armies. You surely must be joking, Nicholas."

"I'm not, Frank; I promise you. I saw it—in London, at Grundy's, yesterday afternoon."

Code Name "Padua." The languid young aristocrat who was number two in the Old Masters department of Grundy's had been happy to take him downstairs in the gallery.

"Top secret, naturally, Nicholas, y'know," he'd been warned. In the shorthand of the trade, that meant that only a couple of dozen of the more important—meaning well-heeled—dealers, collectors and museum officials around the world had been or would shortly be advised, in deepest sworn secrecy, that at Grundy's annual Major Old Masters Fixture, usually in early November, the world would be given the opportunity to bid on the legendary Calabrian Retable, showing the Blessed Virgin with donors, and four scenes from her life in the *predella*, still in the original frame carved with the arms of the kings of Naples and Calabria, thought to have been painted around 1330 by Giotto di Bondone, the father of all modern European painting.

It was a mystery how the altarpiece had come into the possession of the Frühlingstein family, which had fled from its Saxon homeland to Switzerland early in the seventeenth century, to a forbidding stone chalet overlooking Lake Constance. Archivists could trace the picture back in family inventories to 1587. Then the past closed over the painting's history.

It was the first time Nick had seen it. He was struck with how well it looked. The gold ground was dulled by age, but on the whole unscarred. It showed the Virgin and Child enthroned, flanked by a cortege of adoring angels, with Robert of Anjou, King of Naples, and his son Carlo, King of Calabria, kneeling in devotion in the foreground. Below was a row of five small panels showing the Birth of the Virgin; the Annunciation; the Nativity; the Crucifixion; the Death of the Virgin. Each was a masterpiece. The work perfectly expressed the naturalism, the sense of real volume, the realization of space as tactile which had been Giotto's triumph; by which Giotto had directed European painting away from the flat, hieratic frontality of the Byzantine tradition. To unschooled eyes, the drawing of the bodies and faces and the handling of folds and surfaces would appear primitive, even ugly, Nick knew; yet place it next to one of its Gothic or Byzantine predecessors, and not even the rankest amateur, with not a page of art history in his head, could fail to see the advance that Giotto represented—something truly different.

"Photographs of Code Name 'Padua' won't be available for some weeks, I'm afraid, Nicholas," his guide had informed him. "We're going all out on the catalogue. Sebastian's going to ask Felix Rothschild to write it up. I'd personally have plumped for old Sanger, but Sebastian thinks he's over the hill. Sebastian had rather hoped to get Sanger over to bless it, though; give us a juicy paragraph or two for the catalogue; but I gather the old boy's too frail to fly. Pity. He was a great one."

Taking a last look at the Giotto, Nick thought there was no need to pump up the catalogue on this work. Giotto had been celebrated by writers from Dante to Proust. He was an authentic, transcendent, transforming genius on a level with Michelangelo and Beethoven and Shakespeare; one of those who reshaped a tradition so deeply and completely that it could never return to the safe, accepted path along which it had come. This picture was fuller, more advanced, richer and more assured than the Ognissanti Madonna in the Uffizi, painted a decade or so earlier.

"What are you going to put on it?"

"Oh, we'll do it justice."

Leaving Grundy's, Nick knew that he had been looking at a minimum of $5 million on Grundy's velvet wall. This could be the most expensive picture ever sold at auction. The question was, what was he going to do about it? He would sure as hell check with Felix Rothschild, as soon as he got back to New York. Damn, he thought, why not hop a plane and get Frank's view of the thing? And so he had come to Florence.

Sanger still refused to believe Frühlingstein was selling.

"It might be gossip, Frank, but the official word in London is that the old boy's got a young, born-again wife and she wants a lot of money to endow a center for religious medicine. He's got religion too, they're saying, so he's a determined seller."

Sanger shook his head.

"I simply don't understand. Money seems to have turned the world quite upside down. One wonders about loyalties. Selling that picture would be like Max selling me. I know the picture well. It's among the greatest Italian paintings I've ever seen, and it's absolutely by Giotto, of course. I should think there'll be a merry chase for it."

"It won't be cheap."

Sanger had answered the question on Nick's mind. He still believed the attribution to Giotto. His opinion would make or break the price of a picture on which there was no signature, no documentation; the "authenticity" of which was no more than a gathering of expert opinions and conjectures.

Max cut in. "You must go for your nap now, Frank. Especially if we're going to be suitably amusing for Nicholas at dinner."

At twilight, Nick walked alone through the gardens, pausing now and then to look at the statues that punctuated the walkways Max and Frank had laid out among the flower beds. At the bottom of the garden, the high surrounding hedges had been notched to give a view which carefully excluded the industrial wasteland east and west of the old city. It was like a porthole to the past, Nick thought, a telescoped view across five centuries to epochs made eternal by admiring history. It was wonderful to be able to feast on the panorama spread before him on the Arno plain. The upright strut of the Campanile glowed pearl and rusty-pink in the sunset, majestically mated with the squat brick dominance of Brunelleschi's dome. The watchtower of the Palazzo Vecchio guarded the eastern edge of Nick's vision; to the west he could just make out the tower of San Lorenzo and beyond it the tip of the belfry of Santa Maria Novella. He felt like a particle suspended in a falling sunbeam. Then, sipping his Campari, he thought of the two old men in their villa, and of the awful presumption of someone like Bubber Gudge, to think men like Frank Sanger and Max Lefcourt might take a sum of money for the treasure of their lifetimes.

For two days, Katagira had been locked up downstairs in the computer room, immured among his humming and clattering machines, creating the corporate fictions he would be showing to the people at Seaco. He was pleased with the way things were shaping up; the system was working just as he had planned; the machines themselves—the small minicomputer at which he worked out the programming; the mainframe; the word processors and printers, teleprinters, signature machines, collators and copiers—were functioning just as he had hoped. The system spoke well for the consultants who had chosen and installed the hardware, and formulated the software to perform the jobs he described. He had worked intensively with them for the better part of eight months. He was fortunate to have had a good working knowledge of computers to begin with. Now he was complete master of the system.

Emerging only to eat meals with Gudge, whom he could sometimes hear restlessly tramping around upstairs during the rare quiet intervals when the machines were idle, he went methodically through the steps he had plotted. First, he printed out a complete list of the sixty-seven accounting units into which the Lazy G domain was statistically broken down. From these, he isolated the nineteen energy and energy-related lines that seemed to suit his purpose. From the memory banks, he summoned up, line by line, five years of historical operating figures and balance sheets, as well as the most recent results. He arranged these in two groups which made what seemed to him a tasty-looking investment mix. Then the hard work began. For the next two days, apart from meals and sleep and three sorties to his casting pond, Katagira and his machines manipulated and massaged the figures, combining, changing, rearranging, recasting, reorganizing. The computers produced two new companies, each with a plausible legal and financial picture: its history, figures, description of properties and a précis of the relevant documentation of its existence and entitlements: instruments of incorporation, by-laws, legal forms. All the paper impedimenta that testified to the very being of a business organization.

Finally, he had assembled two quite thick packets of material, each different, copies of which he locked away in the safe along with a third. He then prepared covering letters for the remaining packets, in his capacity as attorney in fact for the Lazy G. The first was to Homer Seabury; the second would go to a lawyer in Wilmington, a harmless hack barely capable of making the most perfunctory, commonplace filings with the Delaware corporate office. He had been carefully chosen for his ordinariness.

He summoned Stumpy and ordered the helicopter to fly the packets to Amarillo and put them in the hands of Federal Express. Then he went upstairs, where his employer was watching Dandy Don put away the 49ers on the videotape.

"All done," he reported. "Seabury will have the information tomorrow. The legal business is a matter of form and has been relayed to Wilmington. I believe we may expect to hear from the Seaco people by the middle of next week. I should think they'll be quite excited."

He was pleased. The deployment looked attractive. As they appeared on paper, both Gudge Undersurface Technology and Gudge Oil Development, two newly constituted entities roughly modeled on existing Lazy G units, would whet the appetite and tickle the fancy of even the most conservative, wary investment banker.

Yes, on paper they looked very good indeed. Which was probably appropriate, he thought, since it was on paper, and on paper alone, that these fictions, so enticingly titled, existed.

The two new companies would now be eagerly scrutinized by the corporate-finance minions at Seaco for financial-planning opportunities; ultimately, as Katagira planned, they would be alluringly described in prospectuses and their shares sold to the investing public by a Seaco-managed underwriting syndicate which would presumably include most of Wall Street. Yet what the syndicate would commit its name and reputation and capital to underwrite; and what the public would pay hundreds of millions of dollars to purchase, would have no existence beyond the pieces of paper across which the figures concocted by Katagira and his machines mesmerizingly danced. Figures presumably symbolizing real operations and actual assets, flows of cash and profit ringing in real cash registers. Katagira and his machines had created an imaginary empire, using actual parts of the

Lazy G as raw material. Gudge Oil Development might appear a vast production and exploration complex; legal title to the Lazy G's reserves was vested, however, in units that had nothing to do with Gudge Oil Development. Gudge Undersurface Technology was an imaginative composite; there were, to be sure, trucks and pumps, wire-line crews and seismic units, out in the field, generating profits for Gudge accounts around the world, but those trucks, pumps, crews and units, those bank accounts, were as legally walled off from the entity described in the package on its way to Seaco as if they had been on another planet. He telexed a transfer of $275 million cash to the newly opened account at Seaco and instructions to start buying long Government bonds selling at a deep discount. For cash, of course. The Gudges were, after all, conservative people.

Jill did not really want to have lunch with Caryn Gudge.

This was the time of year when she hated being Gilberte. Being Creighton was easy and nonseasonal. There was always something to write about. It was tricky sometimes; Granada would let slip something about Seaco; Calypso would mention something that could have come only from Harvey Bogle. That kind of material required careful handling. Sol would have his information. But mostly, between what she read in the financial press and what she knew about human nature, it played itself.

"Gilberte" was another matter, especially at this particular time. By June, the big Manhattan charity parties, with their gilded lists, were over. The beach resorts weren't really cranked up. Her office at *That Woman!* was flooded with press releases looking to autumn: about charity committees and events to come. But those evenings and unrealized snobberies were some months off. She needed something now. That was when she envied her sisters who worked the celebrity lane; they could get by on P.R. handouts from studio flacks, or book chat served up by people like Milty Mosker, the famous literary accountant.

She really had no choice, therefore, than to accept Caryn Gudge's invitation to lunch. Mrs. Gudge was very much in the eye of Gilberte's public. The woman hadn't gone to the bathroom without its being duly noted, with special attention to the labels in her clothes, in the papers. Sol had gone overboard. He kept so much pressure on Jill that she felt like a seal with a ball on its nose. She tried to ration mentions of Caryn Gudge; Granada had complained that Caryn was getting too much ink, so Jill had given Granada a healthy play, with an item—and photograph—about Granada's appearance as Wyatt Earp at the Cattle Barons' Ball, and prayed for peace. If this went to its logical conclusion, "The Party Line" would soon be entirely about Mrs. Gudge and Mrs. Masterman.

She met Caryn at Dove Sono—at the table occupied on Tuesdays by Granada. Luigi hovered over them helpfully; his accountant had filled him in on Mr. Gudge's net worth, and Luigi was, in any case, a devoted reader of *That Woman!*

After they ordered lunch, with Caryn struggling manfully through the wine list, the talk started.

"Jill, I've got the feeling you either don't like me or are mad at me. I mean, I go everywhere, but you just write me up maybe once a week, like I was dust on the rug, and never a photograph. There's a whole lot of people gettin' paragraphs, and pictures too, from you who aren't worth the money I could spend in an hour." Caryn didn't fool around.

Jill tried to be tactful.

"I'm not mad at you, Caryn. But there's a great deal going on every week and they only give me so much space."

Caryn pouted. She really was pretty, Jill thought; damn her.

"I s'pose so. It just gets me down, sometimes. Folks up here are so hard to get to know, to really know. Why is it Europeans are so much nicer to me?"

I could tell you, honey; oh, I could tell you, thought Jill. But the answer wouldn't do much for your self-esteem.

Caryn brightened.

"Anyway, that's not the real reason I wanted you to come have luncheon with me. I've got a real exclusive. Just for you. Here it is. Buford and me are just about to make the biggest art purchase you or anyone ever heard of. I can't name names; not just yet. But it'll be humongous. Hundreds of millions of dollars! There, now; how's that for news? We've even got Nicholas Reverey working on it. He's the famous dealer. And the cutest boy!"

Either Caryn was lying or she was fooling herself, Jill thought. Jill guessed she was alluding to this ridiculous business of trying to buy the Lefcourt Collection. Nick had told her about it. He'd said he hadn't even mentioned it to Max Lefcourt when he'd gone to Florence to talk to Sanger. They'd have laughed him out of La Pergola. Of course, thought Jill, people like the Gudges always believed that money could work any miracle. What she particularly didn't like was the salacious way Caryn talked about Nick—or was she imagining things?

Be a lady, she told herself.

"Well, that is news, Caryn. When can I use it? It's bad luck to talk about something like that before it actually happens, so why don't you let me know when it happens? That way I can get a special photographer up to you and really do a feature spread."

She observed a truly happy smile appear on Caryn's face. Jill Newman, she said to herself, you are a fine person. You have made another human being genuinely happy.

The three-column advertisement appeared on page 44 in the second section of the New York edition of *The Wall Street Journal*. It was approximately seven inches across by six inches down, printed with the self-satisfied understatement of an Episcopal vestryman. It also appeared in the regional editions of the *Journal*; *The New York Times*; papers in Dallas, Houston,

New Orleans, Tulsa, Amarillo and Midland-Odessa; the *Financial Times* in London and the *International Herald Tribune*, and was scheduled to appear in the next issues of *Pritchett's*, *Barron's*, *Business Week*, *Forbes*, *The Economist* and *Oil and Gas Journal*.

"We are pleased/to announce that we have been retained/as Financial Advisers," the advertisement read, in the discreet fourteen-point Garamond typeface favored by the financial community for gloating in print, "to/ Gudge Oil Development/and/Gudge Undersurface Technology." Then came several spaces before the Seaco logotype and the legend "Seaco Group/investment bankers and brokers."

It was on its face a simple, straightforward announcement, but it caused considerable reverberations wherever it was knowledgeably read. There was no question, thought Katagira, that Greschner had been right to recommend that they go along with Homer Seabury's earnest request to make public the now-formal relationship between his firm and the Gudge interests. Gudge had at first been downright opposed when Katagira had broached Seabury's entreaty. Katagira had himself been very cool to the idea; it was almost too dramatic, too abrupt a break with tradition; a switch in character that could arouse suspicion. Nevertheless, it had been agreed that in matters involving the public face of this business, Greschner's advice would rule. And it would add to Homer Seabury's quantum of exploitable gratitude.

"I can't see much harm in it," Sol had told Katagira over the telephone. "Of course, the principal beneficiary will be Seabury. An announcement that he's become the investment banker to Mr. Gudge will make Homer a big man on the Street. His friends will be pleased, his competitors envious and his enemies—most particularly Mrs. Masterman, I expect—outraged. It's going to strengthen his hand in a lot of ways, and for that, of course, he's going to be most grateful—which could prove beneficial to you in case you should ever want Homer to really push on something for you. He'll owe you one for this."

Listening to Greschner, Katagira again wondered if it mightn't be judicious to fill him in completely. One of the critical casualties would be Homer Seabury; in casual conversation with Greschner, Katagira had gotten the impression that Seabury represented one of the few lasting loyalties in Greschner's life. Better, Katagira thought, to keep Greschner unconflicted, at least for the time being.

Greschner was an older man—presumably healthy, but at his age surely fragile. It might be too much to tell him now that they were planning to cause a panic on Wall Street by collapsing Seaco in a seemingly plausible multibillion-dollar adventure in the long-term-bond market, and by inducing the financial community to underwrite the public offering of hundreds of millions in common stock of two fraudulent companies. The game, after all, was just barely afoot.

So he accepted Greschner's advice, and the advertisement celebrating the professional bonding of Seaco and the Gudge empire appeared on the Thursday morning before the long July 4 weekend, causing varied but distinct emotions wherever it was noted by readers with something at stake.

To Homer Seabury, it was joy, triumph, glory, infinite relief, vindication, champagne and laurel wreaths. Grins and backslaps in the hallways from his colleagues. Praiseful phone calls from his friendly competitors, contemporaries, veterans like him who had remembered what it was like in the trenches. "Nothing like it since Blyth got the Ford business," said one. There could be no higher compliment. Later, there were more congratulations at the Hiatus Club, and in the club car that evening. A day for public appearances, Homer had thought, eschewing his private dining room and letting his driver go home early; a day for a man to show himself. Several times that day he found himself stroking the opened newspaper page on which the advertisement appeared. He'd made certain that Publicity had ordered several dozen miniature replicas embalmed in Lucite cubes; now, be sure to remember to send one to Sol, he instructed his secretary with the benign severity of one who has discovered his utter worthwhileness. Then there had been a congratulatory phone call from Morgan, Stanley, no less, an accolade which produced such rapturous confusion that he forgot to telephone Sol to thank him for bringing the Gudge business to Seaco. Rapture, that was the word. He had an extra bourbon with the fellows on the train; so buoyant was his frame of mind when he stepped onto the platform at Morristown that the prospect of three days in the company of his wife seemed bearable.

There was opportunistic delight, although perhaps not quite so immoderate, to be found elsewhere in the Seaco offices. Financial Engineering was the envy of his fellows. A man who resembled, even at his most self-effacing, a large, arrogant mouse, he was now positively insufferable. He had requisitioned a huge floor safe for his office in which he ceremoniously and visibly locked up Katagira's confected figures each evening. A man was as hot as the business he worked on, he knew, and this was of the hottest. He pushed all his other work aside, alienating at least one long-time corporate client, and with his team of eager young MBA pencil-pushers, devoted long hours to formulating and reformulating capital structures; blocking out recommendations; puzzling out the right number of shares, whether preferred stock made sense, possibly a trust for the producing properties. Weighty questions.

Chickenshit in a sandbox, thought Mergers and Acquisitions. Kids playing with themselves. He had put together a shopping list of companies for Gudge to buy through Seaco in big public and highly publicized tender offers. He could use some of the press those guys at First Boston were getting. The list included a steel company, two food packagers, several airlines and an aluminum extruder. That none of these businesses had any overt fit with the Gudge interests didn't bother Mergers and Acquisitions. The numbers played themselves, and they were dynamite. The companies on his list were all vulnerable or on the block, so deals could get done. He'd also made sure that Xeroxes of the Gudge figures had been discreetly circulated to key clients and prospects who might want to do a deal themselves. Nobody'd said anything about permission; didn't he know what he was doing?

Fixed Income was happy without even seeing the ad. Just before the close he'd worked out a swap with a bank in Chicago, cleaning them out of a big, unhappy position in the Treasury 7⅞s of 1993, the 8¾s of 1994 and the 7¼s of 1992, using the remainder of the $275 million he'd started with in the Gudge account and some tag ends in his own trading inventory, plus some markdowns on a triple-A utility turkey that one of the majors had stuck the Street with the week before. He liked the mix he'd put together for the account. At cost, it was priced to yield an average of 13.78 percent to maturity, with an average dollar cost of around $82. If this bond market would just get some juice, there could be big money for all hands in trading this account. Nothing like what it could be if they put a little leverage in there. He had a string of country banks just wetting their pants to repo a big Treasury position if he could put it together.

Harvey Bogle picked up a copy of the *Journal* in the San Francisco airport where he was changing planes for the last leg of the flight home from Sydney. He didn't come across the Seaco-Gudge tombstone until he was settled in his seat and the plane was mounting the sky over the Sierra Nevada foothills, but when he did he smiled, whistled softly and unthinkingly touched his forehead in a fleeting salute to Homer Seabury. Then, tired as he was, he felt suddenly more energetic, as refreshed as if a window had been opened on a morning ocean, his mind homing in on what this surprising turn of events might mean for him. The equation was a little more complicated; the wheels were spinning just a little bit faster. Wait and see would be the order of the next few days. What was clear to Bogle was that Homer had gotten in bed with a guy with an awful lot of bullets in his gun—if he chose to start firing. He gave himself to a minute's deeply satisfying reflection: one thing for certain, Granada Masterman's bloomers would have started to fill up at this news. As he let his eyes slide closed, Bogle thought with relish that Tuesday afternoon, at last, after two weeks of being promoted by a bunch of Diggers and Slopeheads, he was going to see whatever it was that Reverey had been hinting so tantalizingly about. His competitive juices were in a state of ferment.

Rufus Lassiter was in his Senate office when he saw the tombstone. He had been practicing his sincere, confident look in the mirror, trying to play down the boyish hustle that had suited his liberal days. Returning to the Street wanted something more clubmanlike and solid. The country wanted grown-ups, he thought, stretching his lips into a smile that displayed his teeth like a trophy case, the grin of a man wise and witty, with money in the bank. An aide had come in with the morning papers, *The Wall Street*

Journal open and marked; the aide had instructions to keep a sharp eye out for anything about Seaco. The marking and clipping had been going on for about two years, ever since Lassiter and his old shipmate Hugo Winstead had put their heads together to try to figure a way to unseat their third old shipmate, Homer Seabury. It had been shortly after the publication of *Moral Money*. Their paths had crossed at the Beverly Hills Hotel while Lassiter was on a publicity tour, doing talk shows, and Winstead was on the Coast buttoning up the deal between Marvin Terrace of TransNational and Granada Masterman.

"Granada's become a great fan of yours, Rufus. Have you seen her recently?" Winstead had said after the small talk. "She's read *Moral Money* five or six times already. You're bigger than Ayn Rand in her head."

That kind of praise was always music to Lassiter's ears. He and Hugo were confederates in vanity, a quality that set them apart from Seabury.

"Granada's trying to work out a financial self-realization program to fit with her Masterwoman concept," Winstead continued. "We've been looking for a fit: the Street; insurance; banking; money funds. You get the picture."

"What about Homer?" Lassiter had asked. He knew Winstead was also Seaco's general counsel.

But both men knew that Homer might be disposable, and disposed of. For a few seconds their thought paths had diverged, as each calculated the possible returns to himself; then they had gotten back on the track. Lassiter was sick of Washington. The liberalism he had adopted to get elected was a thing of the past. There was a new breeze ruffling the forest. Niggers and old people were out of fashion, or about to be. If he had to bet, rich was going to be okay all over again. Mink coats and a crease in the blue jeans. He liked the look of Reagan; he could be told what to do. Lassiter calculated that he could hang around, take a shot at Treasury or Commerce in a Republican Administration—something you could trampoline off to a big job in the private sector; if he got it, fine—he could always quit if it got boring. But if he didn't, where the hell was his safety net? The royalties from the book were okay, and he had another one in mind, the one about Constitutional guarantees of deprivation, and the project one New York publisher had proposed: rewriting the Book of Psalms and the Gospels in terms of the "supply-side" economics that nutcake from California was talking about. But that wasn't what he wanted. Bigger fish were required for Rufus Lassiter's frying pan. Like getting Seaco back.

He and Hugo had fixed up a date in Washington. Then he had met Granada and she fell for him. Not sexually; there was no energy left for sex in Granada's metabolism and no blank spaces on the pages of her appointment book. She liked what she heard; he knew what to say. He made her feel good about being rich, about the conspicuousness with which she consumed the world's goods, including the lives and time of others. Their intimacy became bound up in their little conspiracy, with Hugo included.

They had kept it secret, pretty much, at least until Hugo had been able to inveigle Homer Seabury into curing his capital deficiency by selling additional stock to MUD. Now everything was in place for Rufus' triumphant return to Wall Street: capitalist guru, champion of the rich. The business would pour in.

Maybe. But what the hell did this Gudge deal mean? He telephoned Granada in New York. She hadn't seen the advertisement; obviously Hugo had been too chicken to call her. Lassiter read it to her.

"I think we'd better have a meeting, Rufus. Can we do it down there? I'll get Hugo. Tomorrow, say."

Her voice was calm, controlled. An admirable, decisive lady, thought Lassiter.

In her tower office, Granada sat trembling after replacing the receiver. This was what she had feared worst. Just when she had thought herself safe. She should have guessed something when Caryn Gudge had suddenly materialized in New York, bearing the surname she thought of as rightfully hers. They were coming after her.

For fifteen years, Granada had believed in her deepest fibers that the Gudges were lurking out there, biding their vengeful hour, waiting patiently like wolves stalking a bison to bring her down and punish her for having taken from them. Greschner was in with them now too. He also had a grudge against her. She knew what was at stake; the fiscal stability of MUD was largely committed to her investment in Seaco. Bogle too. Enemies, enemies, enemies. And she just a weak woman. She began to sob—great cowlike shudders that racked her enormous frame.

"Well, well, well," said Jill.

Nick looked up, squinting in the sun. They were sitting on the beach at Wainscott, facing the ocean, fully equipped with lotions, towels, cameras and a copy of *War and Peace* that had known many beaches. A friend had lent Nick the guesthouse on his place and fixed it so they could use the Beach Club, which was a treat for Jenny, brimming as she was with the natural sociability of most young ladies of ten. She had already scampered off in the middle of a giggling covey of friends old and new, leaving her mother and "NickHe'sMummy'sBoyfriend," now unselfconsciously pronounced as one word, by themselves to enjoy the first morning of a four-day weekend.

"What 'Well, well, well'?" asked Nick.

"The Seaco battle's been joined. You probably aren't interested in this sort of thing, but there's an ad in *The Wall Street Journal* announcing the fact that Seaco Group—that's Homer Seabury—have become the investment bankers to what sounds like Mr. Buford Gudge IV, the famous 'Bubber,' billionaire husband of the vile Mrs. Buford Gudge IV, Caryn to her few friends, who as much as told me she wants to go to bed with you."

Nick let that slip, remembering his one dance with Caryn Gudge.

"Just give the news, please. So what about Seabury?"

"So—Mr. Gudge is the half-brother of the equally famous Mrs. Granada Masterman, to whose house we are bidden this evening. After dinner—with the 'B Group.' It's my fault, actually. I told Granada I wasn't working this weekend, so we were demoted. No pad; no pencils; no photographers mine to command. You'll probably hate me for it; if I'd been working, you'd have had to go downtown and get some of those acid-green pants and a belt with pigs or whales on it and spend the evening under Granada's tent talking to some woman covered in pink appliqué frogs and bunny rabbits. If you want me to, I can still call."

"I think not. I'm going to buy a very large steak and I brought down a good bottle of wine and you and I and Jenny are going to cook out. Now, what about Homer Seabury and Granada Masterman and the curious Gudge family?"

"Well, Granada has been moving in on poor Homer, who, as I understand it, runs a safe, conservative brokerage house, and rumor has it that she's planning to vote her shares—she owns twenty-odd percent of Seaco—to bring back Rufus Lassiter to run the firm in a more go-go way. Rufus was Homer's original partner. He's a swinger in financial matters."

"He's a complete, raving asshole."

"Nick, darling, nobody argues that. He loudmouthed his way out of a Cabinet job he thought he had a lock on, so he wants to get back in the private sector and out of the Senate, where he doesn't think he's a big enough deal, and Granada's his meal ticket. But now Homer's obviously made some kind of arrangement with the Gudges. Nick, this is a big step for them. Like a bear coming out of his cave. I don't really understand, but mine not to reason why. I'll bet it's the talk of Wall Street. Gudge can't be thinking of doing any financing, let alone going public. He's dripping money. He may be thinking of selling off something and needs a professional evaluation. Everybody knows the Gudges hate paper; they keep their extra money in cash or in gold, so they can't be looking for a stockbroker to love them. Whatever it is, it gives Homer a really strong potential ally. MUD's a nice company and Granada's made a lot of money, but I can't see her going toe to toe with Gudge. He's just got too much money!

"And your friend Harvey Bogle's involved too, Nick. He's right in the middle of it with a big block of Seaco stock. The swing man; Harvey's favorite position. He'll go with the flow or to the highest bidder and take a few million out of it. I admire him. Harvey likes nothing better than to see a couple of jerks flailing away at each other in a takeover fight or a proxy contest with other people's money. He gets right in the middle, stirs the pot, and the flies stick to Harvey's flypaper. Whatever happens, it's going to be exciting."

"How do you know all of this? I thought gossip and parties were your thing. Flounces and ruffles. The things that count. You sound like Harvey Bogle yourself."

"Just a hobby left over from the old accounting days. You read gossip for kicks; I read the business pages. Keeps a girl's head from being turned. Ah, there you are."

Jenny had returned. A small, doughty figure, hands on hips.

"Can I eat lunch with my friends and go over to Julie's house?"

"Of course you can." It was Nick who answered.

Jill rose. "How about a walk?"

Her legs looked ten feet long. She had all the glamour parts, Nick thought: legs, enough bosom, dark shoulder-length hair shaken free. But it was the sharp intelligence of her features that held and mesmerized him. In his entranced condition, questions he might have asked went by the board as he took her hand and they set off down the beach, just filling up with the first real crowds of the summer, the sky clear and the still-chilly, barely swimmable water sparkling like shadowy glass under a high sun.

There was not a moment of the weekend that Nick would have exchanged. That evening, after they had eaten and drunk half of a second bottle of Rioja and tucked Jenny in, watched over by Gudget, busy with his nocturnal spinnings, they had walked a few hundred yards down the road to Granada's house. The party was even more ridiculous than they had expected. All those unstylish, awkward people looking gloomily unhatched in their brilliant plumage; puffy, overmoneyed younger people gulping smoke and booze and buzzing back and forth into the encroaching gardens to feed their olfactories with the sweet white powder. After twenty minutes, and half a glass of champagne, and a wave and a fixed smile to their hostess, enthroned at a center table on the right of the Duc de Besoin, they were home again.

It was an important weekend, for all that it was carefree. They were together in the same room with Jenny next door; it was another big step for Jill. The shapes of each other's life and way of thinking became more clearly defined in their minds. He asked her about Sol and the job at *That Woman!*. Why had he been so helpful? What was in it for him?

"I think he felt sorry for me. Mickey Greschner treated me pretty badly. Messed up my life, and Jenny was just a baby. Mickey was a real shit, Nick. It was a good thing for everybody when he died, even his father."

Nick hadn't suspected the depth of Jill's involvement with young Greschner; maybe he didn't want to know, to admit that there were deeper linkages between Jill and Sol than either let on. He slept on it. In the morning Jenny came in to see them, smiling, anxious to get going to the beach. It was eight o'clock, brilliant, and Nick let his misgivings slip away.

Monday night, as the traffic edged sweatily along the expressway, Jenny slept in the back seat of the rented car, her hamster's cage in her lap. Jill dozed beside Nick. In the difficult light, her perfect, sleeping profile seemed exquisitely mysterious. Love was wonderful, he thought; life was wonderful. Ennobled by loving, he felt himself to be a positive storehouse of virtue and manliness. Looking down the bright avenue of the future, all he could see was bands playing and flags flying.

CHAPTER TWELVE

"The trouble is, based on these numbers, they really don't need any outside financing." Financial Engineering's voice was gloomy. He was describing an investment banker's nightmare. No financing need meant no deals. No deals meant no money to be creamed off the Gudge relationship, apart from the annual retainer. The atmosphere in the conference room was sepulchral.

There were a dozen people seated around the table. Homer was at its head. Ranged on either side of him were Financial Engineering and Mergers and Acquisitions and their lieutenants. Syndicate and Equity Sales were also represented.

"Based on the figures they sent us," Financial Engineering continued, "their oil and gas production is throwing off around six hundred million a year of free-cash flow, and that's with half their gas production shut in until we get decontrol. Their reserve estimates put a discounted present value on the proven oil and gas properties of close to nine billion, and that's using current gas prices."

"Who does their reservoir engineering? D&M?" Homer asked, liking how to-the-point and professional he sounded.

"They do most of their own now. Gudge has got his own firm. He bought out McFarlane and Wogg, the big Tulsa firm, about five years ago. They had a pretty good reputation."

"Well," said Seabury, "if we come close to a deal we'll certainly want an independent report—or at least a reliable consultative overview, don't you think?"

"Absolutely."

"One more thing before we move on." Seabury was right on top of things and showing it. "Who's their accountant?"

"I don't know. The preliminaries that we've been working off haven't been signed off on. Again, they probably do their own. These look like inside stuff. Anyway, numbers this big are real confidence-builders."

"Well, we'll have to have a clean accounting certificate." Seabury liked the way he sounded. He was easily as crisp and decisive as the young men. "Anyway, I apologize for interrupting. Continue with your wrap-up. You were saying the Gudge interests don't appear to need any money. What about their bond investment program? You're aware, aren't you, that as of today they're long four hundred fifty million and change in Treasury bonds?"

"Homer, I wasn't thinking in speculative terms." Financial Engineering looked smug. He cast a resigned, dubious glance across the table at Mergers and Acquisitions. How demeaning, his look said, to sully the lofty arithmetic of corporate finance with mention of the vulgar dollars and cents of the trading room.

"They have a big inventory," he continued, "of undeveloped acreage. The majors are just watering at the mouth to get into bed with Gudge because a lot of their leases look like real elephants." Take that, Homer, thought Financial Engineering; you're not the only one who can talk Oil-speak.

Homer looked puzzled. "Elephants?"

"Yessir. Million-barrel prospects."

The oil companies were Wall Street's best customers these days. Investment bankers were playing a critical role in the national energy crisis; assisting oil-company clients to stand foursquare and deploy their windfalling profits buying cable-TV companies, or department stores, or insurance companies.

"The Undersurface businesses will do about thirty-five million in after-tax profits in the fiscal year just ended. For some reason, these Gudge companies are on a May 31 fiscal year, which means their next regular audit wouldn't be completed until sometime in the fall next year, well over a year from now.

"Anyway, the bottom line is, it's hard to see where they'll need much outside capital."

"What, then, do we propose?" Seabury launched a fusillade of indignation. "Nothing? Do I get hold of Mr. Katagira and advise him that we have contracted to take three hundred and fifty thousand dollars of Mr. Gudge's money each year for five years to assist him in formulating financial strategy, and that our best idea for financing strategy is that he do nothing? Doesn't anyone have an idea?"

"No, sir. That's not what I recommend." Financial Engineering raised a placating hand. He wanted to keep control of the meeting. Across the table he could see Mergers and Acquisitions' dorsal fin breaking water. "What I meant was, there's nothing obvious. So what is necessary is to propose a possible need. Put the need in place first, and have on the shelf a creative long-range financing strategy to meet it. Sell the cart and then get the client to buy an expensive horse to pull it, the way we did with Enscon. Accordingly, we've been doing some work with our colleagues in M&A. We've got some pretty good ideas. You want to take it from here?" He beamed over at Mergers and Acquisitions. There, he thought: that puts it on a collaborative basis with me at the head of the team.

The other man took over smoothly. In the past dozen years he had inspired the spending of billions of dollars belonging to thousands of stockholders of whose existence he was morally unaware. He was a prophet of the business-school theology that management had *droit de seigneur* with a corporation's assets; it was a lucrative mission he preached. He had developed a dozen platform manners, as many routines and shticks as a Grossinger's *tummler*, in order to persuade a hesitant chief executive to ride into a takeover fray, armed and armored with cash and credit, snorting with the exhilaration, the intoxication of battle.

"Our analysis of the Gudge situation says that if ever there was an over-concentrated situation, egg-basket-wise, this's it. These people are betting their house, car and boat on the oil and gas business. Not that it hasn't been good for them. The numbers say that plain enough. But I'd have to say if I was the man in charge, looking at the going-in, getting-out costs of oil and gas exploration, I'd be thinking diversification. And major diversification; something on the order of a twenty-five-to-thirty-percent reorientation of their earnings mix, which means adding maybe as much as one hundred million in after-tax profits from new sources."

It sounded good, he thought. Forget the fact that these people had been making a lot of money year in, year out for close to eighty years, when oil had sold for $2 a barrel and when it sold for $40. Where were the investment-banking possibilities in people that stuck with businesses they knew and understood?

"Now, with the Dow selling at around six times estimated earnings, and Standard and Poor's about the same, we'd have to figure a minimum fifty-percent freeze-out premium in any merger or takeover, which comes to, say, a ten-times multiple, which means it takes one billion to buy a hundred million of earnings. Now we're getting up to some numbers that make their free cash flow start to look a little skinny if we're thinking a billion-dollar price tag on acquisition X."

This sounded more like it, thought Homer.

"So it becomes imperative to fill up the old quiver," said Mergers and Acquisitions.

"Quiver?"

"Yeah, the thing you keep your arrows in. You want a lot of arrows. Different kinds of weapons. You want to be able to use cash, if the numbers are good and the deal will fly; or to be able to trade stock if it has to be tax-free or if the goodwill looks like it'll eat you alive. I try to get our clients to visualize their capitalizations as holsters, Homer, filled with every sort of defensive and offensive weapon. Cash. Paper. Whatever the situation calls for. That way we can bang the bad guys with both hands when it gets down to infighting.

"Now, the way Gudge is set up today, their arsenal is pretty shabby. Too damn few arrows. They could hock their oil and gas, maybe set up a line of a few billion against the reserves, but, shit, anybody can do that, and it would eat up an awful lot of cash flow for the next ten years or so. From the way you've talked, Homer, I don't see these people hocking their cash flow.

"But if they set themselves up with some good-looking paper, which I believe they can based on the numbers they've shown us, they can cut it both ways. The market still likes the oil service companies: Schlumberger, Hughes, Gearhart, Baker, Halliburton—the prime names—are selling at around twelve, thirteen times current earnings against six on the Dow. Throw a name like Gudge out there, and our guess is you could do an initial public offering at maybe fifteen times, which on thirty-five million makes the Gudge service companies worth something over half a billion in the market. And that would be pretty powerful currency. Do you fellows disagree on the values?" He looked around the room at Syndicate, at Equity Sales and, finally and longest, at Financial Engineering. All three nodded agreement with varying degrees of enthusiasm. Syndicate was near to wetting his pants at the prospect of doing a Gudge deal; the aristocrats of the Street—Morgan, Lehman Kuhn Loeb, Goldman, Dillon Read—would bust their butts to get in on a Gudge offering. He could make them dance to his tune, for once; maybe even trade into a special-bracket position in a choice deal of theirs. Equity Sales was also pretty moist at the possibility. The institutional interest would be out of sight and it was axiomatic that the firm running the books stole the cream off the top of the institutional book. But it would be the public that would really go apeshit on something like this. A chance for the common man to be in partnership with the legendary Bubber Gudge. In his head he was thinking a $25 offering price; respectable, but low enough to catch the moms and pops. Figure a gross discount to the underwriting group of a buck and a quarter, which meant, using the usual rule of thumb, a five-eighths selling commission. Christ, he thought joyfully, I'll have to get a goddamn whip and a chair to keep the salesmen at bay.

Financial Engineering's mind was turning too fast to be either elated or downcast. He nodded merely to keep on the team while he tried to find a way to break out of the pack. He kept a Rolodex of possibilities in his head; now it was spinning like a rat driving a treadmill. Then it hit him and he raised a hand, still formulating what he was going to say as the eyes around the table shifted to settle on him.

"You know, I have a thought. Suppose we propose two pieces of paper. Do a straight common-stock deal on the service business, but—and I've got to check this out further—how about selling a trust-type deal on the production? Real widows-and-orphans stuff. Put, say, a billion, a billion five worth of producing properties into an income-bearing trust, with some prospective acreage thrown in for sex appeal, price it to yield seven percent and stand back and watch the action. Like the Mesa deal. It's cheap money to Gudge. He'd have to pay fifteen percent, minimum, three or four under prime, to discount his acreage, and since he doesn't pay any cash taxes, what with depletion and redrilling, that's a real fifteen percent. Against seven percent on the trust. And he's got two pieces of paper to play with."

There was general approval at the table. Now they were looking at two public offerings. A total of $400 million to $1 billion, assuming that between 20 and 50 percent of their horseback estimate of the market value of the two Gudge entities would be initially offered. The managing underwriter, the firm that put the deal together and allocated the underwriting participations along the Street and around the country, normally took a fifth of the underwriting commission off the top, which meant that Seaco was looking at somewhere between $4 million and $10 million before it started to ring the cash register actually selling stock to its customers.

Heady wine indeed.

"Well, gentlemen and, umm, ladies," said Seabury. "I think this gives us the parameters of a presentation to the Lazy G people." He turned back to Mergers and Acquisitions. "Now what areas might we suggest Mr. Gudge be thinking about? As a stimulus to putting together this war chest you prescribe?"

There wasn't a man at the table who wasn't eager to answer that question, including Seabury himself. They were all realists. They read the papers; they read Creighton in *Pritchett's*, and while they did, they absently, unconsciously fingered the backs of their necks, tracing an imaginary line where the guillotine might fall.

"Well, sir," said Mergers and Acquisitions. "The hot area right now is financial services. It fits new technologies, new demographics, new attitudes. The biggest growth industry in the world in the last ten years has been the creation of rich people. They need services. Cash management. Credit. Investment products. Insurance. That's the sector where the real prospects are. I'd be advising Gudge to look at insurance. Thrift institutions. He's got a little savings-and-loan on the Coast. To add to his banking interests. And of course, there's the brokerage business. Companies like ours."

Ours. The word gladdened Seabury's heart. Just what he'd been thinking. He adjourned the meeting, pleased and proud to have assembled such an outstanding team.

Two hours later, his secretary buzzed the offices of Financial Engineering and Mergers and Acquisitions. A meeting and presentation had been scheduled in ten days' time in Texas. Mr. Seabury assumed they'd have their material in order by then. Once in a while a little hump-busting didn't hurt. They would be picked up at Butler. Wheels up at 8 A.M.

Then she called Fixed Income. Mr. Seabury would be grateful if he could get himself to Amarillo the day after the Corporate Finance people. Mr.

Seabury felt it would be useful to bring the Lazy G client up to date on the bond investment program.

Caryn Gudge had shrugged off the shoulder straps of her $1,500 sundress, which had bunched about her waist, exposing her marvelous breasts, which Victor Sartorian was stroking more or less in time to the bobbing of her head between his parted legs. He was wearing a quilted blue silk dressing gown, sashed at its middle, with a black velvet shawl collar, and a black silk ascot at his throat. With his sleek, slicked hair and his small, untrustworthy mustache, he looked exactly like a parlor snake in a period play.

This was the way Caryn liked him to look. It conformed to her notions of romance, the movie-magazine ideals she had carried in her heart since girlhood. Feeling him thicken between her lips, hearing the rustle of his silk robe, smelling the incense in the room and tasting, at the back of her throat, the vague sourness of the champagne they'd drunk, she squeezed her eyes shut, imagining it was a good-looking, younger man, someone like that Reverey that Jill Newman had, to whom she might be giving herself.

They had long since abandoned any pretense at psychotherapy, she and Victor. He'd rearranged his schedule so that she was his final appointment on the two afternoons a week she came to him. Before then, she'd put in enough time on his couch for him to know her fantasies, which he now dressed to suit. The incense and champagne had been his inspiration and contribution.

She was happy with the arrangement. A good part of her life back in Odessa had been sex. She'd always liked fooling around. That was the problem with Buford. She sure did like all the things he did for her and the way he loved her so much. But he wasn't much good in bed, and up here . . . well, the problem with New York, the only problem, was that all the men were so faggy, at least in the circles where Mr. Greschner had her moving. Victor wasn't the greatest in the looks department, and he was kind of old. But he sure had energy, and he was real big down there, and he knew how to get a girl juiced up better than anyone she'd ever known back in Texas. Still, it would have been nice to get a young man for her arm at all those openings, and afterwards, and not some fancy, stuck-up foreigner, either.

She felt Sartorian push gently on her shoulders. She let him slide away and stood up, unzipping her dress as she did and letting it fall to the floor. Tuesday and Thursday afternoons, when she came for her hour, she never wore anything underneath. She stretched out on the couch and felt, rather than saw, Victor bending over her.

"Now something to make you feel all crazy, darling." His fingers brushed between her legs, leaving a residue which started a tremendous tickling, making her as sensitive as if the wound were raw. She heard him sniff, twice, loudly. He lowered himself beside her, stroking, titillating, making her moan and squeak with excitement. No one could have told her then that she was riding on the underside of the moon.

Then she was on top, taking him in long rising postings, with her right hand reaching back under her, wrapping him gently. Making him do some moaning. Her hand felt the first tremulous expansion that always signaled the onset of his ejaculation. She bent forward, thankful that the exercise class Mr. Greschner had recommended had made her limber enough to stretch forward to receive the snapped ampoule of amyl nitrate which Sartorian pressed up against her nostrils.

Later, when she had left, and Sartorian's heartbeat was somewhere near normal again, he reported in to Greschner. What he learned of the business affairs of his patients' husbands seldom bore on their therapy, so there seemed little wrong with confiding in Sol, who seemed interested in that sort of thing and had done Sartorian enough favors for a dozen lifetimes.

"No, I'm afraid there's nothing new to be known of Gudge, Solomon. He just gives her enormous amounts of money and endless charge accounts and apparently never discusses his business. She did say he hasn't been feeling well recently, but I must say she didn't seem worried."

Sartorian hung up. He was the greatest admirer there was of his old friend Solomon. How clever of the man to have seen that Mrs. Gudge was the sort of woman who needed a touch of thrill-seeking to make her New York experience complete. Of course, Granada mustn't find out. He was still getting $100,000 a year as chief psychiatric consultant to the Masterwoman Realization Program, and that bought a goodly amount of the sweet white powder.

Nick felt nervous, but wasn't sure whether it was apprehension or elation that had him in its grip. Bogle was coming in, finally, to see the Rubens sketches. The extra fortnight's delay had given Carraccino time to replace the old yellowed varnish with a clear dressing that brought out the brilliance of the ripest, liveliest passages and pulled together the compositions, enriching the tonalities that intervened between highlights, deepening a pink touch here, an azure or viridian streak there, sharpening hazy blurs and meanderings into meadows and mountains. They'd decided not to have them framed, after all; the delay would have been intolerable.

He and Sarah had reviewed the brochures and double-checked the Kodachrome transparencies and the color prints for tonal accuracy. Now, like a schoolboy rehearsing his graduation speech, Nick found himself running through his presentation. With an experienced hand, a museum director like Frodo, little or nothing need be said; it was simply a matter of letting the works of art speak for themselves and, at the end of the communion, quietly handing over the documentation. With checkbook collectors, usually a pitch of some sort was necessary. Checkbook collectors were like people who lived on the telephone, seeming to need a crackling voice to reassure them they were still alive. Checkbook collectors tended to see price as the imprimatur of quality. The few great amateur collectors—a German baron, a California dried-fruit mogul, a department-store owner in Lyon, the widow of a Canadian oil billionaire—had their own methods. This one consulted a battery of experts; that one made up her mind in ten minutes and paid in ten months; another would take weeks, vanishing incommunicado to travel to perhaps a half-dozen cities to look at comparable works, before deciding.

The brochures Sarah had prepared, ten copies—which was all Nick thought he would possibly need—were dark green loose-leaf binders with "NICHOLAS REVEREY/OLD MASTER PAINTINGS AND DRAWINGS" stamped on the front cover; they were about the size and heft of a desk atlas. The bulk of the contents was photographs: color prints and matted transparencies showing each sketch in its entirety. Since color photographs, no matter how carefully made, were notoriously unreliable, each was followed by a black-and-white photo of the whole sketch, accompanied by blowups of especially telling or seductive details: the audaciously painted head and mane of the Nemean Lion; the seascape from the Geryon; the torso of the river god from The Augean Stables. They had been chosen to illustrate various facets of Rubens' genius. The photographer had done his job brilliantly.

The textual portion of the brochure was headed:

Sir Peter Paul Rubens
born 1577 Siegen (Germany)—died 1640 Antwerp (Belgium)
THE LABORS OF HERCULES
Sketches in oil on uncradled panel executed ca. 1635–1640.

There followed a list of the individual pictures by subject, with the size of each. Next came the section headed "Provenance" which traced the history of the pictures' ownership. Here Sarah had done a little embroidering. Although all that was known was that the series had turned up three months earlier in the vault of a cantonal bank in a well-known Swiss resort, Sarah's entry read:

Collection of Philip IV, Madrid (?)
Collection of Dukes of Infantado, Madrid (?)
Private Collection, Switzerland.

The question marks hedged Nick against allegations of misrepresenting the paintings' genealogy; it let him mention kings and dukes; royal associations still added a tangible measure of allure when it came to clinching a sale.

The bulk of the textual introduction was devoted to Sarah's laying out her thesis that the sketches represented work performed by Rubens in connection with the Spanish king's two major building and decoration programs of the late 1630s. It was buttressed by extensive quotations from Brown and Elliot's work on the Buen Retiro, from Held's great catalogue of

Rubens' oil sketches—to which these would now surely be added in future editions—and from a mass of supplementary material that Sarah had dredged up from the Rubens bibliography.

In working with Sarah to get her text in good, final form, Nick had been impressed with the work she had done in pulling in the symbolic importance of Hercules to give the sketches an added dimension of intellectual interest. She had taken as her point of departure a quotation from Brown and Elliot:

> To the seventeenth-century mind, Hercules was a polyvalent symbol, a fact that the planners of the [palace] exploited to the hilt. First and foremost, Hercules was a popular symbol of Virtue and Strength, meanings which he had represented since antiquity. In the course of the sixteenth century, the virtuous and heroic Hercules was appropriated as a symbol of the prince. . . . numerous claims [were made] to Hercules as an ancestor. . . . The events of ancient and modern history conspired to make Hercules a logical symbol of the Habsburg kings of Spain.

It pleased Nick that she had incorporated the paintings' symbolic aspect into her discussion. Although most collectors shied away from the verbal, extravisual ideas, symbols, associations and meanings that were integral to European painting before 1850, preferring the intellectual simplicity of Impressionism, Nick still felt that the traditional—well, literary—interpretations helped the eye to see. A work of art was not one thing; it was everything. It was not this or that; it was all. There was no single, certain path to its meaning and significance or the pleasure it gave. It was of its maker's time, and of its beholder's time; it held woven into itself what Botticelli heard in the piazza on the way to his workshop; what Rembrandt thought walking beside the Prinsengracht on a misty afternoon; it could incorporate the morning light on the facade of Santa Croce, or a letter from Rubens about the English court, or Cézanne's view of the corner of a house through the woods, or a program for the decoration of a palace ceiling handed to Tiepolo by a prince's astrologer. There was no legislation governing or limiting the meanings that might be found in a work of art.

Sarah's little essay moved on from her summary of the Hercules symbolism and her speculation as to the possibility that Rubens might have concocted these to show up the pictorial weaknesses and programmatic stiffness of the Zurbarán cycle to a brief review—largely pinched from the catalogue, Nick saw—of the views that knowledgeable critics had taken of Rubens' sketches through the centuries. She ended by quoting directly from the catalogue:

> Collectors evidently quickly saw that Rubens' sketches, no matter what their original function, were highly desirable as works of art in themselves. . . . As to their monetary value, we know that twelve sketches for the cycle of Constantine

> . . . were appraised . . . at more than twice the amount allowed for the large cartoons from which the tapestries were originally woven.

An excellent job, Nick thought. Sarah had postulated a compelling historical context for the pictures, made a good case for royalty in the family tree and dropped a useful suggestion as to their value. These were unusually powerful associations to claim for works of art that had appeared from nowhere.

The balance of the brochure consisted of a note on condition graciously contributed by Marco Carraccino, and twelve single-page summaries which related the stories of the Labors and filled in the comparative information on each subject. Although Carraccino had not examined the pictures by infrared reflectography, his close visual examination had indicated minor early restorations in the background of the Stymphalian Birds, doubtless to correct an exposure to dampness in the far-distant past, and the insignificant abradings, skinnings and irruptions that three and a half centuries might normally be expected to produce. All things considered, Carraccino's verdict on the condition of the sketches was "superb."

In her comments on each *modello*, Sarah had used judicious selections from Bulfinch and Robert Graves to tie the painting to its mythological origin, as well as apposite pictorial references and associations. It was an impressive job. He wondered whether it would impress Bogle.

Bogle was punctual to the minute.

"Nice place," he remarked, looking around the downstairs sitting room. He paused to look at a newly acquired pair of Longhi paintings of a Venetian masked ball. "Don't let my wife see those, or she'll want to give a goddamn costume dance around them." Nick led him upstairs.

The sketches had been reframed and hung in four vertical groupings of three on the longest wall of the comfortable upstairs room in which Nick showed important paintings. Its walls were covered in dark brown linen; it was furnished with good but not exceptional English country furniture. Two chairs had been placed close to the sketches. Beside them, a George I walnut side table, which had been a moving-in present to Nick from Sol Greschner, held copies of Sarah's brochure, the two volumes of Held's catalogue and a small book, Burckhardt's *Recollections of Rubens.* It was inscribed: "*To Nicholas Reverey/from his friend Francis Sanger/with affection and the reminder that not all artistic genius is Italian,/a statement with which the subject of this book might have disagreed/La Pergola/April, 1965.*"

Nick showed Bogle to one of the two chairs. There was nothing in the room to distract from the pictures before them. Against the opposite wall was an unlighted case holding a collection of eighteenth-century French terra-cottas that Nick was assembling for a Wall Street broker who was "into small things."

Nick liked the way the pictures looked. He had fussed with them several different ways, trying out variant groupings this way and that, lugging in several picture stands and trying the sketches one at a time. There was no doubt that in unity there was strength. Together, they seemed to feed on, to nourish each other. A fleck of vermilion in the Horses of Diomedes found an echo in an orange tunic in the Girdle of Hippolyta. The suggestion of a grove in the background of the Apples of the Hesperides resonated, green, cool and tempting, in the foreground of the Erymanthian Boar. Through all twelve of them, fugal and insistent, coursed the thrusting, physical energy which it had been their creator's special genius to be able to convey.

Nick had no intention of starting with a hard sell. Nor was he about to overdo the diffident routine. The relationship between art dealer and client was at best difficult. Some qualitative initiative, like the notes establishing the key of a musical composition, had to be taken.

"Rubens," he said simply. Bogle might be inexperienced, but he was no illiterate. There was a good Rubens head of Catullus in the Lefcourt Collection—Bogle would surely have looked at it in the catalogue—and there were the great paintings in the Met. Bogle might have seen them.

"The Twelve Labors of Hercules. *Modelli*—highly finished oil sketches for large paintings. Oil on panel. Probably painted for King Philip IV of Spain around 1635–1640. The greatest things I've ever had in my hands."

That was enough. He moved to the back of the room, discreetly leaving Bogle head to head with the pictures.

For a time, Bogle neither spoke nor moved. Nick could sense his eyes moving up and down, across, then up and down and at random, taking in the cumulative effect of the entire group, then narrowing their focus to concentrate first on one, then on another. At length he got to his feet and moved close to the pictures, bending to study the lower ones, moving along the rows like an inspecting general.

He turned to Nick. "What's the subject of this one? I kind of like it the best."

Nick moved over to him, mildly surprised. Although he hadn't expected Harvey Bogle to keel over in a transport of appreciative ecstasy, he'd anticipated a strong general reaction first. Bogle was clearly a man for specifics.

"That's Hercules stealing the oxen from the shepherd Geryon." He instructed Bogle from his recently replenished store of mythology. How Hercules had been instructed by the Delphic oracle to indenture himself to King Eurystheus for twelve years. The Labors which Eurystheus set him were the price of immortality. Not knowing the exact turn of Bogle's mind, or of his sense of humor, he left out the alternative version of the legend, which Sarah had told him about while they went over the first draft of her brochure, which was that Hercules and Eurystheus were male lovers and that Hercules had carried out the labors as a token of his affection.

"Interesting that you like this one," Nick continued. "It's very beautiful. These two mountains in the distance are the Pillars of Hercules—the Straits of Gibraltar. King Geryon was believed to be the mythical ancestor of the kings of Spain." He told Bogle a little more about the symbolic character of the cycle, cutting himself off short when he saw that the other man was back immersed in the paintings, no longer hearing Nick's prattle.

For the next forty minutes Bogle studied the pictures, asked Nick about them, returned to studying them. He disdained Nick's offer of a brochure, saying he'd leave that for later. He asked for a glass of water.

Finally he sat down again, took one more searching look, like a man finishing a drink, and turned to Nick.

"These're great. I'd like to read that stuff you've got together on them. I like the size; and they've got a lot of zip. You know, funny, when I was a kid, I thought Rubens always meant fat women."

"So do most people," Nick said. "Let me read you something." He picked up Burckhardt's little book on Rubens, which not by chance was lying close to hand.

" 'It is an exhilarating task,' " he read, " 'to evoke the life and personality of Rubens; good fortune and kindliness abound in him as in hardly any other great master. . . . In the consciousness of his own noble nature and great powers he must have been one of the most privileged of mortals. . . . He saw at one and the same time a restful symmetrical arrangement of the masses in space and vehement spiritual and physical motion . . . his triumphant color harmonies, his near and far distances and scheme of light and shade rose before him . . . till all was matured to the harmony and power we have spoken of. . . . When he paints a subject from Homer, then meet the Ionian and the Fleming, the two greatest story-tellers our earth has ever borne—Homer and Rubens.' "

He could see Bogle was getting the message.

Bogle turned back to the sketches with an intentness that suggested he was trying to verify Burckhardt's words in the pictures hanging before him on Nick's wall.

"Great," he finally said. It was an admission as much as an expression of enthusiasm. "Terrific. I figure you're selling them as one lot, right?"

"That's right. It would be a crime to break them up."

"How much?"

"We're asking eight million."

"*We're?*"

"I have partners in this. They didn't come cheap. We have to spread the risk. And the interest."

"Eight million is a lot of bread. Eight million buys a lot of stock. Buys the equity in a condo development, an industrial park. I could buy another five hundred thousand shares of Seaco for eight million dollars."

"So you could. And that would only leave, what, another ten, fifteen, twenty million shares of Seaco you don't own. And there'll be another condominium or another shopping center just like yours half a block away. But there are only these twelve little pictures. There aren't any duplicates of these. That's the point."

"Look," said Bogle evenly, "I get you. Everything's relative. Things have to be laid on the line. I mean, you'll admit, this is real art—which costs real money. This is no piece of shit by Leroy Neiman. If I start now, up here in the major leagues, what's next? I don't intend to be a one-shot player. I know too many guys had one good book, one hit play, one good round of golf, and that's supposed to last them the rest of their life. That's not my ball game."

Nick thought about the Giotto he'd seen in London. He remembered, also, Johnny Sandler's First Rule of Selling: "Stick with what's on the wall."

"I wouldn't worry about that. Look at the Kimbell Museum in Fort Worth. A great museum, a great collection, all done in barely ten years! Norton Simon's done the same thing. It takes brains; taste; guts; good advice. Money. When something like this turns up, bang! They pull the trigger."

It never hurt, old Zauber had told Nick, to establish the inference of a competitor in the client's mind.

"Maybe so. You're doing the telling and you've got the pictures for sale. So. That's the name of the game. Tell you what. I'm interested. Put a hold on these. If you want some earnest money—two, three hundred thousand—say the word. Let me look this stuff over." Bogle nodded at the binder in his hand. "Tell me, has Crisp seen these?"

"He has. As a matter of fact, he's got them on reserve for the Fuller, so I can't ethically hold these for you until he's gone one way or the other."

Bogle looked at him carefully.

"You're probably carrying these with borrowed money. The Fuller hasn't got eight million. Crisp wants to keep someone else from buying them, that's all. He shouldn't worry about me. Another thing, Nick . . ."

It was the first time Bogle had called him by name.

"Yes?"

"If you're into the banks to carry these, don't forget: money that costs twenty percent has its own ethics, since we're talking ethics. Do you mind if I call Crisp? Maybe have him come up and look at them with me? I'll protect you with the Fuller; don't worry."

"I'm not worried. Would you like me to call Frodo? Or anyone else you name. Money's expensive these days, but we've factored that in. That's the chance we take for being in this business."

Bogle took out an appointment book.

"Ten o'clock tomorrow morning okay with you? If Crisp can make it, I can."

Nick saw him out downstairs. Then he called Frodo and set up the meeting. He left word at the Tennyson for Bogle that they were on. Then he called Sandler.

"Johnny, we just might have ignition. He liked them a lot. He didn't fall over dead when I talked price; I started at eight; after all, Bogle didn't get rich hitting the bid, as you'd say. I put the pictures on ice for him. He's coming back tomorrow morning. He wants Frodo to look at them. He's interested, all right; my guess is, though, he's going to want a lot of expertise before he puts up or shuts up. He's the kind of guy who doesn't flinch at the price, but doesn't want to make a mistake."

"Christ. Not another ———!" Sandler abusively described a famous West Coast collector who was notorious for keeping dealers hanging while he consulted around the world. "We gonna have to put together a goddamn art-historical congress before the sonofabitch can make up his mind?"

"I pray not. I can't guarantee it. Bogle really wants to collect; which means, as he puts it, Johnny, that he wants to form a collection. This is only Step One. But what a step. What do we do for an encore?"

"C'mon, Nick, c'mon. A deal like this gets around, stuff comes out of the woodwork. Half the goddamn Old Masters the British Government thinks are still hanging in stately homes waiting to get taxed are copies; the originals are in bank vaults in Zurich waiting to get sold. How about that Giotto that Grundy's is going to be selling this fall? They're pushing the shit out of that sonofabitch. Tubworthy even called *me*! Anyhow, what'm I bitching about? You handle Bogle; you found him, and he's got the bucks. Just to be safe, though, Nick, line up a couple of experts. Who's the big honcho on Rubens? The guy from Oberlin? Get ahold of him."

"I'm sure he's still in Japan. I know he was in Tokyo when the pictures came in, and I think his office said he wouldn't be back till the end of the fall term." He heard Sandler snort with annoyance. "I'll call Oberlin and check. Will you clue Barry in?"

The History of Art Department at Oberlin confirmed that the scholar was on teaching leave at Tokyo University until the following January. Was there something they could mail him?

Nick was sure that by now Bogle would be devouring the brochure. He believed that Bogle had the heart of a student, that he wasn't all action and improvisation.

He took Jill and Jenny to an early movie and a plate of fettuccine at a little Italian place around the corner from Lincoln Center. It was still light as they walked back toward Central Park West through crowds making for the Mostly Mozart concert. Jill had been very much interested in Nick's account of his session with Bogle.

"Don't worry about the price," she advised Nick. "Harvey can stand it. Everyone knows he's made a ton of money, Nick. That foundation of his showed about ninety-five million dollars in assets in its last report. And God knows what he's worth himself. Harvey's very decisive, but careful. Just stay with him. Hold his hand. I think you could have a winner here."

He sat up with her watching an old Bob Hope picture after Jenny had been put to bed. The evening was hot, but there was a breeze flowing across the top of the park, so she left the windows open. The Philharmonic was in the Sheep Meadow that evening; fragments of music—Berlioz, Sibelius,

Rossini—drifted in intermittently. Jill had the lights down. Across the park, the lights of Fifth Avenue apartment buildings sparkled. Curious, Nick thought, how it's possible to feel so romantic, here, in the middle of this sweaty, noisy, dangerous city, in the flickering light of a television set. He held Jill's hand and kissed her and told her he loved her. When his eyes returned to the screen, his mind returned to Bogle.

It was close to midnight when he got home. Five minutes after he got in and finished checking the lights and the alarm system, the phone rang. It was his answering service with an urgent message: Please call Mr. Bogle whenever you come in.

Bogle came right onto the phone.

"Sorry to call this late," said Nick. "I hope I didn't wake up your wife."

"You crazy? She's doing Tom Snyder live on NBC. Then she's got a limo taking her to the Island to catch a few *z*'s in a hot-sheet motel in Roslyn so she can get up early and pass out doughnuts and coffee in some paperback warehouse. They're shipping out the fortieth printing of *Salon* tomorrow.

"Anyway, I've been reading this stuff you gave me. I'd like to read those books you refer to. Can I get them?"

Nick said he'd send them over in the morning.

"No. I mean, if I'm going to think about owning these pictures, I figure I better own the books first. There's a fancy art bookstore down the street. Think they'll have them?"

Nick said he'd see that the books—the sketch catalogue, Brown and Elliot on the Buen Retiro, Burckhardt on Rubens, Alpers on the Torre de la Parada, Karpinski—got to Bogle in the morning. Bogle pushed the date two hours later, to give him time to do his homework. He'd be there at noon. Nick was sure he could get Frodo to readjust his schedule. He was a little off balance. He wasn't used to the rapid, shifting clock of the high-speed entrepreneur.

"Now let's talk about experts. Who's this guy from Oberlin? Is he around? I'd like to hear what he has to say. You're quoting him up one side and down the other. Can he look at them?"

Nick explained that the man was in Japan and that it was probably impossible to get him back.

"How about sending him this brochure you gave me? You say he's at Tokyo University? Look, I do a lot of business with one of these Jap trading companies. They send a pouch to Tokyo every morning on JAL. How's about I get this out to JFK right now, and you can send me another? You call the guy tomorrow in Tokyo, and explain. He can call us up. Collect. Now who the hell else is a big deal on Rubens?"

The only other, Nick explained, was Ludwig Karpinski, the head of the Rubens Institute in Antwerp.

"Tell him to get his ass over here. First class. Shit, I'll put him in a suite in the Castle. Tell him to get his ass over here and take a look. Now who's this Guinea who's doing all the talking about the kind of shape the pictures are in? Can he be there tomorrow? I don't want to be a pain in the ass, but eight bills is eight bills, and a country boy like me needs all the help he can get."

After hanging up, Nick reviewed the tasks at hand. The world of connoisseurship and scholarship moved at the slow pace of teacups handed across silver trays in stifling drawing rooms. Bogle's pace would be tough to put over. But the game was sure as hell worth the candle. He turned out the light. He dreamed first of Hercules, and that dream merged delightfully into a picture of him and Jill and Jenny, Jill with a reporter's pad in her hand and a wire trailing behind her, bouncing through broad fields watched over by a big house, which was and wasn't La Pergola, with two old men waving affectionately from a balcony.

Katagira took it as a good omen that two of the oldest, most suspicious trout in his pond had recently risen to his flies. When Seabury had telephoned to ask for an appointment the following week, he'd agreed immediately, sure that Gudge would be available. His employer was in bad spirits. It had now been six weeks since Mrs. Gudge had gone East. Gudge himself seemed stronger than he had been at any time in the last year; Katagira guessed that he was in remission. The wife had pleaded the necessity of carrying out necessary planning assignments in connection with a number of social functions scheduled for the fall season. Functions that Mr. Greschner had ordained as important, essential.

"You think she's all right?" Gudge had asked at dinner the night before.

"I'm sure she is, sir. I spoke to Greschner yesterday and he reports she's become very involved in a number of worthy causes."

He'd gotten that from Sol, with whom he had become quite confiding over the last month. Mrs. Gudge's social and sexual antics were marginal to their discussions of Seabury and Seaco. If Mrs. Gudge was preoccupied with her New York life, that suited Katagira. It was important for him to concentrate on diffusing Gudge's worries; his employer had too much time alone.

That mustn't be allowed to happen, he said to himself, straining to send the soft curve of his line to reach a darkened spot on the far reach of the pool. They must do something about getting those paintings on which she seemed fixated.

It took three weeks for Harvey Bogle to make up his mind about the Rubens sketches. During that time, the stock and bond markets gyrated wildly to news from Washington, Tel Aviv and London. Meetings that would touch the nerve strings of nations were held. Summer boiled to a steamy end.

Nick was raveled, but in the end it was worth it. First, there had been the meeting with Bogle, Frodo Crisp and Carraccino. Frodo had praised the sketches; Carraccino had endorsed their condition; Nick had prayed.

The deliberations had been punctuated by assertive hints to get going from Johnny Sandler, ensconced with his glamorous houseguests in Easthampton, and nervous inquiries from Barry Winters in Cap d'Ail.

Karpinski had been flown in from Antwerp. He was a hulking shambles of a man, bald and clever, from whose lips a dying Sobranie eternally drooped. Quarts of Glenlivet whisky magically vanished in his presence. In Nick's upstairs gallery, even Bogle had hung back, struck dumb in an aura of knowledgeability which left no room for the man of action. Karpinski had lumbered close to the pictures, his black cigarette a bare centimeter from their surface, seeming to enter their space, to depart the room and enter the sunny distances of Rubens' imagination. His intensity seemed to thicken the air in the small room. At length he emerged from the caverns of his concentration to praise the sketches as authentic, perfect, of major importance. He would like to drink to that.

A telegram had arrived from Tokyo:

> NO DOUBT PHOTOS ARE OF MAJOR AUTHENTIC RUBENS DISCOVERY. CONSIDERING EARLY TERMINATION MY APPOINTMENT HERE TO SEE WORKS OF THIS QUALITY. MY CONGRATULATIONS CONVINCING HYPOTHESIS AS TO ORIGIN. WILL CERTAINLY INCLUDE FUTURE EDITIONS CATALOGUE. MAY I PUBLISH EARLIEST POSSIBLE BURLINGTON MAGAZINE?

Of course he could, Nick replied by return wire, after conferring with Sandler.

Finally, Bogle had requested one more session with Frodo. They met for an hour. When he left, Frodo was smiling.

Bogle was a man on whom endless quantities of salesmanship had been heaped. He was a rich man, known to be adventurous with his money. But this was something else again. He told Nick he'd like to walk around the block. There wasn't any point in jerking anyone around any longer. Time to cut bait.

While Nick and Frodo waited, wanting but not daring to knock back a brandy to hammer down their agitation, Harvey Bogle walked six blocks south along Park Avenue and six blocks back north. He walked debating with himself. Buildings he understood; stocks, bonds, the anxiety of nervous men. Toughness. The calculable love of women. The money wasn't the issue.

When he had made up his mind, he returned to Nick's.

"What can I say?" Nick thought he looked sweated out. "I want to buy them. You want to make a deal at seven eight, you got it. The two hundred thousand saves my pride as a negotiator. The deal is subject to certain conditions regarding Crisp."

At $7.8 million it was a sale, if there was no problem with Frodo. Bogle seemed certain there wouldn't be.

The deal was done. The air in the room broke apart; Frodo and Bogle made their goodbyes quickly and were gone. None of them wanted the bubbly atmosphere to evaporate down to second thoughts.

Nick called Johnny Sandler in Easthampton and got Deirdre. Sandler had shot a 79 at Maidstone, was drunk in the bar at the club and might be home sometime in the twenty-first century. He left word at Barry Winters' Riviera villa. He called Jill and offered her and Jenny a major dinner at Benihana. Then he poured himself the largest Scotch in history.

CHAPTER THIRTEEN

Hugo looked out the window of Rufus Lassiter's Nantucket house. It stood on a bluff overlooking Surfside Beach. He guessed it was about forty minutes past first light. He had awakened, shaking, from a bad dream; something about the war. From his window, he could just see the first gleam of daylight on the southern tip of Miacomet Pond. Below, on the sand, he made out Rufus Lassiter's elegant figure, laboring at the edge of the surf with a long casting rod.

He thought he might as well wander down to the beach and talk to Rufus. If they got their business resolved, he might be able to catch the first plane out after lunch, before that cursed fog set in.

Below, Rufus Lassiter thought how much he hated Washington in general and in the summer in particular. When Congress recessed, he had headed immediately to the big Surfside house which his wife had brought with her as her dowry. By day, he worked on his third book; it was tentatively titled *God and Greed,* and he thought it Gibbonian in scope; in the evening he and his wife would drive to town, sit on the yacht-club veranda and accept adulation.

In Nantucket, no force of man was permitted to disturb the Senator's blissful contemplation of himself and his future. It was as if he were hooded behind a camera, oblivious to everything except his own image in the ground glass, an image he worked tirelessly to pose and compose just so. He fished in the surf, not to catch bass and blues, but as a test of might; to see how far he could throw the lure; whether he could reach the line of combers a hundred yards out that marked the sandbar pushed up by the winter's storms. For Rufus Lassiter, length of carry was all. The long cast; the big hit. When Hugo Winstead made his way down the wooden stairs that descended the face of the dune cliff, Lassiter had gotten into a rhythm. When Granada put him back in, he was going to rename the firm "Seaco Lassiter Group." Just like old times. It sounded right. "Seaaaaaco." Back with the rod. Pivot. Set. Then—whoosh—"Lassiter." A staccato movement sending the line bellying off the spool, propelling the flip-flopping lure out almost to the combers. Again. "Seaaaaaco." Pause. "Lassiter!"

"Good morning, Rufus."

Lassiter lowered the rod.

"Well, Hugo, you're up and about with the gulls. Trouble sleeping?"

"Oh, a bit. We old folks don't need as much, however. It seemed a nice morning, and then I saw you from my window, so I thought we might talk. Before everyone's up and about."

"Why not?" Old friend though he was, Lassiter would just as soon be rid of Hugo. Hugo was a reminder; Lassiter never saw Hugo these days without being seized with a vague unease, as if he saw something of himself mirrored in Hugo's joyless opportunism. He planted the butt of his rod into the sand, took Winstead's elbow, and they set off along the beach, backs to the sun.

"How was your session with Granada, Hugo? I'm sorry I couldn't make it, but those arm-twisters in the White House won't let go on this tax thing. And since the principal beneficiaries are folks like thee and me, who am I to absent myself? I gather she's upset about this Gudge tie-up with Seaco. It does look like a real feather in Homer's cap."

"She's on an absolute tear about it, Rufus. She wants us to do something. You know how she is. She made all sorts of nasty threats and said some very unkind things about my legal ability. She's gotten very full of herself, Granada has. In a way I rather wished we'd kept Greschner around, instead of getting him out. But that's spilt milk."

"Of course it is, Hugo, and all three of us know it. What matters is to keep her eye on the main chance. This arrangement with Gudge doesn't mean a damn thing. It's just an investment-banking relationship, not a safety net. It won't mean a speck of difference to Granada's objectives with Seaco. That's what she's got to be made to see."

"If Granada can hook Seaco into MUD, Hugo, the possibilities are limitless. All those dried-out suburban women at those hideous Masterwoman parties, nursing the money in the sugar bowl. Just waiting for MUD/Seaco to help them. I'll bet there are billions out there."

"Certainly you and Granada think so, Rufus, and conceptually it makes sense. There's no arguing that; so there's no point discussing it at any length. What we must make certain is that nothing goes off the track. When we spoke after my last unfortunate meeting with Granada, you were going to sniff around Washington on the Gudges. Any luck?"

"None, I'm sick to say. I got the bloodhounds out at the SEC, the IRS and even the CIA. Mr. Buford Gudge is, regrettably, clean. Except for that business in Africa four years ago—you remember that, Hugo, my last fling as a liberal. I sometimes wish I hadn't boiled Gudge so red. He's very rich."

"Granada wouldn't have stood it otherwise, Rufus. Besides, Gudge may be rich, but he's not generous. And we both know Granada has been."

"Oh, of course I know that, Hugo. Why in the world do you think I subpoenaed him in the first place? Granada insisted. Her people dug up the evidence."

"So there's little to pull on Gudge?"

"Nothing. Clean bill with the tax people. His companies don't file a consolidated return, but it looks as if Gudge has been paying taxes world-wide at around a twenty-percent rate, cash to cash, the last few years. Since that beats the major oil companies and I'd guess three-quarters of the Fortune '500' by a fair piece, it wouldn't even pay to set up a media stink, get the bleeding hearts out crying for blood. If we tried that, Greschner'd P.R. us to death. The people at Treasury are starting to think Gudge is a hero. He's bought about a billion in long governments already, and it's starting to get around. The bond market's been stronger, and he's getting the credit. So Washington's a bust, Hugo. What about your end?"

"Zero. He never leaves that ranch of his. Been to New York once. To see Sol. Greschner's handling the wife's case; which is another—quite separate, but equally impossible—problem with Granada."

"So I'd heard. What about the wife, anyway?"

"Needs asbestos drawers, I hear. Another little number from the sticks with a rich husband and hot pants. Very social. Waves all that money around and has attracted a few of the sharks. Mrs. von González, in particular, is currently treading a very thin and dangerous line, trying to be all things to all women. And Victor Sartorian. He's taken Mrs. Gudge on as a patient. If I know Victor . . ." Winstead's arching eyebrows finished the sentence without words.

They walked a way farther, each with his thoughts, and then turned back into the sun, now well up in the sky. The surf pounded over the squeals of feeding gulls.

"So," said Lassiter, "as I see it, here's where we stand. Homer has landed Gudge as a client—which we are certainly powerless to prevent. Gudge could buy and sell Seaco a hundred times over, or Granada, or thee and me, if he wished. But why would he wish? He's done nothing but buy a lot of discounted bonds—and so would I, if I had his money. My God, they're giving that paper away. But it's bonds, Hugo. Bonds. This isn't the Hunts; this isn't silver and a corner and futures and all that crap."

"Quite right, Rufus. I must defer to you on matters of the Street. I do think we ought to get Granada to buy a little more Seaco. MUD's got a lot of cash right now. Just to be on the safe side."

"I don't disagree. One other thing, Hugo. Where does Bogle fit into all of this?"

"Who ever knows what Harvey Bogle's up to, Rufus? He's got a good-sized piece of Marvin Terrace, too; Marvin's on my Fuller Board. Harvey's a troublemaker—and no gentleman."

"Are any of us?"

Winstead chuckled. "I suppose not, Rufus. Not with these kinds of stakes. Anyway, I really can't speak for Bogle."

"You know, Hugo"—Lassiter had been doing some thinking—"why don't you, why don't we, get Granada to tender for enough additional Seaco to bring her up to twenty percent? Another million shares'd only cost her, say, another sixteen, seventeen million. Then she'd have a blocking position. Maybe Harvey Bogle'd make a deal on his stock. He'd sell his mother if the price was right. Hell, maybe Granada could trade him her TransNational? That's what Bogle really wants, I hear."

"It's an idea." Winstead wasn't enthusiastic. He knew Bogle didn't like him; if he got control of TransNational, Seabury, Winstead could kiss that very lucrative account goodbye. Fortunately, Granada liked the idea of becoming an entertainment *impresaria.* Visions of those sound-stage parties the Terraces were always throwing danced in her head. Hollywood was, after all, respectable these days.

They had arrived back at Lassiter's rod. Their brisk walk had left both men breathing harder; it reminded each of them that they were no longer young and carefree. They might have their own ways of hiding from the fact: Rufus with his solipsism; Hugo with his seductions. But time was running out; there was less room for delay. Neither considered the fact that, although their conversation had largely revolved around Seaco, they had mentioned their old shipmate-benefactor Homer Seabury only marginally, and thought of him even less.

Hugo returned to the house and telephoned to reserve a seat on the midafternoon plane to LaGuardia. That out of the way, he sat in the warm shade of the porch, politely acknowledging Louise Seabury Lassiter's freckled bustlings, and read through a stack of papers. Lassiter stayed at the threshold of the surf. His casts grew longer and more accurate, but no fish took his plug. Shortly before lunch, Winstead was summoned to the telephone. It was his wife, instructing him to call a board meeting of the Fuller Foundation in the next two weeks, preferably right after Labor Day. When she explained why, Winstead's composure buckled for an instant. Harvey Bogle's capacity for mischief had always seemed limitless, but at least he'd kept away from the Fuller. Until now.

The meeting with the Seaco people had begun early that afternoon and was still going on. Bubber had never heard such bullshit in his life. Goddamn, there were nine of them from Seaco plus another one to come out the next morning. Which was about eight more than was necessary. Katagira had explained to him that investment bankers worked that way these days; they came in "teams"; the objective was to overwhelm the prospect's reticence with personnel, to show by sheer weight of numbers of people that the matter at hand was complex enough to justify the fees being charged, and to crowd out, with the clouds of pro forma figures in the impressive, logotyped folders bound in maroon Lexan, whatever reservations the client might have about what he was being "advised" to do. The stack in front of Bubber's place at the table—the dining room was doing makeshift conference duty—now numbered five. On the bottom was "LAZY G ENTERPRISES/FINANCING STRATEGIES/ANALYSIS AND IMPLEMENTATION." Next came "GUDGE UNDERSURFACE TECHNOLOGY/GUDGE OIL DEVELOPMENT/ FINANCING ALTERNATIVES"; then, "GUDGE ENERGY EXPLORATION TRUST/A PROPOSAL"; then "GUT AND GEET/INITIAL PUBLIC OFFERINGS/A PROPOSAL." Uppermost in the stack was "STRATEGIC DIVERSIFICATION OPTIONS: A STUDY PREPARED FOR THE GUDGE INTERESTS/BY SEACO MERGERS AND ACQUISITIONS DIVISION."

Bubber thumbed the top folder idly. The first page contained a neatly typed list of diversification possibilities for the Service Company that Katagira had made up. His listless attention turned to puzzlement. Why would these people suggest that a company they had been told did testing and fracturing and seismic work and cementing—all related to the drilling and placing in production of oil wells—spend $500 million of its own and borrowed money to buy an airline? Or a bunch of five-and-dimes? Katagira had been right: these Wall Street people sure thought in funny ways.

Bubber felt no differently about this sort of foolishness than he had the first time he'd heard it from Seabury himself; of course, now he had these fancy books with all these numbers they'd made up from Katagira's original made-up numbers, so he figured they'd bit. He couldn't get his mind properly set on all this business anyhow. He was worried about his wife. She sure sounded pissed off at him about not getting those pictures. And she obviously had a real bad cold in her nose, the way she kept sniffling. If she hadn't been up there in New York and all those other fancy places that Greschner kept finding for her to go to, she'd get real well real quick in the dry air of the High Plains. But when he'd suggested that she come down to the ranch for a stretch, her voice had turned all snotty. Goddamn, she was some woman, he knew, but he wished he had a little more control over her. He shoulda made her sign the prenuptial agreement like Katagira had urged; but hell, he had to go to Venezuela that afternoon to negotiate that Maracaibo concession, and anyway, she sure did love him, the things she did to show it, so what was there to worry about? He just kinda wished he'd put a little salt on her tail. The way those old boys in Houston did.

About two they'd broken for a stretch and a breath of air, after the skinny kid with the snotty voice had finished going on about how they were going to do something called "an initial public offering," talking about syndicates, and group account, and institutional distribution, after-market positioning, comparative PEs. Bubber was sure that he could have understood it all in about five seconds if he'd had a mind to concentrate on it. From his cursory riffling of the books before him, it didn't seem to amount to any more than kindergarten arithmetic all dressed up for church. It was funny. The fancier they sounded, the more people seemed to get sorta drunk on their own words. Like the kid doing the talking. Keep talking, and maybe you'll get to believe it, son, he said to himself; all this talk was making him sleepy. He looked over at Katagira. The Japanese sat there, as still and expressionless as a cat watching a bird. And old Homer, he'd kept nodding vigorously, like he was beating time with his head, looking first at Gudge, then at Katagira. Gudge could see Seabury was trying to get a feeling for how his folks were doing. He guessed his own blank expression couldn't have given old Homer much satisfaction.

"You and I know we're going to buy practically anything they propose," Katagira had said as they'd awaited the brand-new Gulfstream bringing their guests. "Unless what they propose is absolute foolishness—which, they being from Wall Street, is always a possibility. But let's let them think they're selling two very tough customers. The more they think that, the more they'll congratulate themselves; the happier they are with their success in handling us, the less wary they'll be."

When they broke at teatime, Bubber went in to call Greschner. He was troubled.

"Mr. Greschner, this is Buford Gudge again. Just wonderin' if you'd heard anything from Miz Gudge since we last visited."

Sol knew Gudge was ill at ease with the amount of time Caryn Gudge was spending in New York. He knew from Sartorian that Caryn Gudge was being petulant and difficult with her husband for not getting her the Lefcourt pictures. Greschner himself was a little put out with Nick for refusing to be helpful. Those paintings meant a lot to Mrs. Gudge. She had fixed on them as the key to being welcomed in the bastions she wished to storm: the Fuller Institute and, beyond that, a White House dinner. Anybody could buy their way into the latter, Caryn knew. She wanted to go legitimately—and would, as a patroness, a sovereign of the arts, once she got those pictures. Unlike Granada, who was possessed of a rational intelligence which envy alone seemed to unbalance, and therefore believed that hard work was part of the equation of gratification, Caryn believed that wish alone made right and that her husband's money was the just instrument of that rectitude.

"No, Mr. Gudge, I haven't," Sol replied. "I believe she's in Newport this weekend; staying with the Tarver Meltons. Oh, yes, a charming couple. Older. Very well connected. I'll call if you like. I expect, though, that the houseparty's out on the Cushing yacht. The houseparty? No, no, don't worry. Just the Meltons; Dr. Sartorian—you've met Dr. Sartorian? Ah, well, he's very well known here; some people from Maine and Germany, I think. I know there are balls—dances—tonight and tomorrow. I'll tell you what, Buford: let me call Newport. I know you're in a meeting. No, of course. Homer told me he was on his way down with some of his people. How's it going? Good, good. Anyway, I'll call Newport and have Mrs. Gudge call you."

Greschner hung up and looked at his watch. Five-thirty. The yachting party should be home by now. He rang for Vosper and asked to be connected with Dr. Sartorian at the Meltons' rented cottage.

"Tell him to call me within twenty minutes from a public telephone," Sol instructed. Lucienne Melton was famous for eavesdropping on her houseguests' telephone calls.

Fifteen minutes later, Sartorian was on the line. The toast calling the butter knife.

"Victor, this thing with Mrs. Gudge is getting out of hand. She's got to go back to Texas; she's got to see her husband, if briefly; and she's got to forget about Max Lefcourt's pictures. And you can use the rest. You've been looking awful. Act your age. Granada must know what you're up to by now; but if she doesn't, and Mrs. Gudge isn't bound for the ranch by Tuesday morning, I can personally guarantee that it will be very chilly for you at Dove Sono at lunch, assuming you're invited—ever again. What is Masterman United paying you this year, Victor? I hear it's going up to close to two hundred thousand dollars. Even by your standards that will buy a great deal of cocaine. Stop sniffling, Victor. There's too much in this for everyone to throw it away for the pleasures of the moment."

In movies, men like Victor Sartorian, confronted with the law Sol was laying down, would have chattered and gibbered their indignation. Sol knew better about Victor. Sartorian was practical. There was a brief silence while Sartorian digested Sol's remarks.

"I think I can get her to go back to Texas at least for the long weekend, Solomon. And you're right, I could use the rest. She's an active, demanding lady; very attractive, very exciting, but also very young." Sartorian's chuckle was blessed with a hint of salaciousness, like bitters in a drink.

"With respect to the Lefcourt Collection, I can only tell you—as a psychoanalyst, of course—that it has become a fixation which is beyond the sort of therapeutic postponement that is my specialty. And Nicholas Reverey hasn't helped either, I might add. She was very taken with him at your house; she finds him cultivated, which is catnip to these Texas women. And now she's heard about him and Jill, and women like Caryn Gudge are always going to be jealous of women like Jill. Before you start blaming me entirely, you might lean on young Mr. Reverey—who, I believe, is not completely unindebted to you, Sol."

"I know, Victor, I know. I don't disagree. I'm trying, but Nicholas can be very difficult. Anyway, his is a sin of omission. Now do have Mrs. Gudge call her husband. He's wasting away in her absence."

"I should think."

"And I'll try to get Nicholas to be more useful, or at least more pleasant."

Sol thought for an instant that he should telephone the Lazy G and inform Gudge that his wife had been located and would be calling him. Of that he was certain. Victor Sartorian was a good manipulator of people when necessary; it was just that they preferred to paint on canvases of different sizes and textures. No need to call Gudge, he thought. As for Nicholas, what could he do? How silly he'd been not to fuss and fool over Lefcourt and Sanger years ago; but then they never came to America and Frank Sanger didn't work for dealers. He had seen nothing useful in such a relationship, and had let it go by. Now what to do? Sic Frodo on Lefcourt? Frodo would never do it. No, he would have to prevail on Nick, just to give it a try at least. It couldn't have come at a worse time. Nick was in love with Jill Newman, which meant his already impossibly high standards were probably worsened by the virtuous posings of courtship.

Dunno why this boy feels he has to growl like a bear, Bubber reflected. Mergers and Acquisitions was winding up his part of the presentation. It was as convincing a demonstration of his specialty as he had ever made, he believed. He'd combined what he thought to be a pithy, incisive overview of the future of capitalism with a gallus-snapping, man-to-man, down-to-the-details, what-are-you-and-I-going-to-do-about-it look at a few hard prospects.

Mercifully, José came quietly up behind him just as the kid was starting in on a list of inflation-discounted asset plays that, combined, had earned less last year than three of Gudge's Yates Field wells.

"Mrs. Gudge is on the phone, sir."

He hurt too much to jump out of his chair; these days, he felt as if the center had been sucked out of his bones. But all his tired agony dropped from him when he heard her voice.

"Buford darling, how are you? Honey, I'da called, but we were on this yacht, and honey, the ship-to-shore didn't work for stink."

"I sure miss you, Caryn. Been beautiful here." Gudge wished he could've borrowed some of the eloquence from the other room to say how happy he was to hear her voice. "We got a real good new well down in the Chalk. Lots of folks here now; all of them Seabury people. I think you met him—Homer Seabury, that is; at least, he said he did."

"Oh, honey, I sure miss the hell out of you too. Can you send the plane to fetch me? Sunday maybe. There's a couple of parties up here that Mr. Greschner thinks I shouldn't miss. It'd look bad if I left now. I mean, sweetheart, well, there's some important people coming up . . ." She named four viciously competitive Munich automobile scions whose jets were at that moment vying for landing slots at Providence to rendezvous with hornet-angry helicopters racing over from Newport.

"No problem, sweetheart. Plane'll be there Sunday nine o'clock. Got a little surprise for you." Goddamn, he thought, wait'll she sees the new plane. He'd bought the new Gulfstream as a surprise for Caryn.

"Oh, Buford"—her voice had a yielding tenderness even his imagination had never been able to hear before—"you sweet thing; don't tell me. A surprise. You got those pictures. Oh, you sweetheart man." She purred over the telephone. He felt like he had that first time back in that motel room in Odessa. Oh, damnation, he thought, there had to be a way. He saw that the usual sheet of paper had been placed on the table. Picking it up, he looked quickly at the bottom line: "$13,024,728,000."

"Oh, honey, I got lots of surprises for you." He could count on that to get her attention. Through the receiver, her farewell kiss seemed to reach wet and tempting right into his groin. Aching to get her back, he added, "And sweetheart, you take care of that cold, hear?"

The Gulfstream had gotten off a little after eight o'clock. Seabury had remained behind, standing beside the runway with Katagira and Stumpy, waving farewell. Gudge had said his goodbyes at the Main House.

When the plane had settled into level flight and the radio operator had come back to show them the liquor cabinet and make sure they were comfortable, the Seaco team celebrated.

"I think we killed 'em," said Financial Engineering's aide-de-camp.

"You better believe it," answered Mergers and Acquisition's number two. Drinks were poured all around, emptied and repoured.

For the rest of the three-hour flight to Butler, they flew higher on the wings of their exuberance than any aircraft could have taken them. In the strange way of their calling, they discussed the meeting as if they had conquered an adversary, instead of having wooed and won an ally to whose service they were pledged. It was a time for impassioned self-congratulation. Labor Day was coming up; a long weekend for basking under many suns.

"Why do you think Mr. Seabury stayed behind?" said the good-looking young woman from Financial Engineering's squad. Her question was addressed, student to supreme master, to Mergers and Acquisitions, who was leaning easily against the bulkhead, as if he owned the plane, working on his fourth Jack Daniel's.

"Not to worry. Old Homer's a pro. He stays for the kill. Just in case there're any second thoughts. Any more questions. Although, frankly, sweetheart, I'd rather be there to answer them myself. If I wasn't here talking to you." He set his face in a crisp, knowledgeable mask, half-profile, his best angle, jaw jutting into the night.

After talking to Caryn, Gudge called Sol again. It prompted Sol to track Nick down and try to get him back on the Lefcourt case. As he had expected, he found Nick at Jill's.

"Nicholas, I'm sorry to bother you."

Nick was sleepy. He and Jill had taken to going to bed early, often before eleven, now that Jenny was at camp through Labor Day. Nick himself was on hold; the sale of the Rubens cycle to Bogle was conditional on the affirming action of the Fuller Board, and although Frodo had assured him that Calypso would back Bogle's extraordinary terms, and that therefore the Board would go along, it would still be two weeks before a quorum could be assembled and money would change hands. He talked to Bogle every day, or nearly. Harvey was holding firm. Nick had ventured to mention the Giotto to him—just that and no more. Bogle had grunted; it was clear to Nick that the Rubens acquisition was a done deal. Bogle gave no indication whether he intended to pause; whether, for the moment, that was it as far as Bogle's collecting was concerned. They'd run into the Bogles at a party in Easthampton early in August and had briefly shared a table at a party. Afterward, he had sent Bogle Grundy's circular on the Giotto, and left it at that.

"No problem, Sol. What can I do for you?"

Jill's sleepy head kept tumbling to her breastbone under the reading light. It was amazing, Nick thought, how quickly habituated to each other he and Jill had become. It worried him sometimes.

"Nicholas, I've had two calls from Buford Gudge today. It seems he must have those pictures of Max Lefcourt's. And, I regret to say—and it's probably my fault—he seems absolutely glued to the notion that you're the only one who can get them."

"Sol, I will not go to Max on this matter. It would be insulting."

Beside him, Jill had drifted off, her book sliding onto the coverlet. The air conditioner hummed quakily. They'd been to Mostly Mozart that evening: there had been a lovely performance of the E-flat Sinfonia Concertante. The mood had been peaceful, right. Now here was Sol. He tried not to sound impatient.

"Sol, there's nothing I can do. Or will. It's foolish. Max has got plenty of money. He's seventy-eight years old; Frank's over eighty. The collection is their life; the things are their children. Sol, there just isn't any way!"

He could hear Sol breathing reflectively on the other end. Poor old Sol, he thought: the great figurer, the great fixer; coming up empty.

"Oh, I know." Sol sounded worn out. Nick's watch on the night table said midnight.

"I know," Sol repeated sadly. Then, more brightly: "Maybe there is one way you could deal with Gudge. Make him see the problem."

"What?" Nick was skeptical.

"Look, why don't you just jot down what you think it's worth. Picture by picture; you've got the catalogue. Then Gudge can review it. Then we'll see. My guess is, he'll find the sum appalling."

"Sol, will you promise me one thing? If I do it, strictly for you, can that be the end of it? On your word?"

"On my word."

"I'll be back to you."

Nick hung up. He looked down at Jill, sleeping, barely stirring the covers with the rise and fall of her breathing. How forceful emotions are, he thought. It took rockets months, even years to reach the planets; in seconds a man could traverse the entire universe of feeling.

Nick was correct in his feeling that Harvey Bogle's mind was elsewhere. Bogle was preoccupied with TransNational, the communications demesne over which Marvin Terrace uneasily presided. He had decided to give Terrace a final chance to negotiate an agreeable settlement. If Terrace remained obdurate, Bogle was quite prepared to launch one of the weekend blitzkriegs for which he had acquired an unenviable reputation among the corporate fat cats who were his favorite targets. He liked to strike over holiday weekends, when the principal executives of the target company, their advisers and the judges and regulators to whom they turned in times of stress were well on their way to cocktail parties in the Hamptons, salmon camps in Nova Scotia, goat shoots in Mexico and the host of other executive entertainments for which it was the privilege of the stockholders of America to pay.

By the time they could regroup, Bogle generally owned the stock necessary to force the conclusion he desired. Sometimes he insisted on an active voice in management; more often than not, he was perfectly willing to be bribed to go away by a management willing to spend whatever of its stockholders' capital it took to ensure the continuance of its perquisites and prominence. Bogle had done deals on Good Friday, on every Jewish holiday, once even on Christmas Day. Thoughtful money, he contended, worked outside conventional clocks and calendars.

Thus it was that Marvin Terrace, Chairman of the Board and Chief Executive Officer of TransNational Entertainment and Communications, sat fretting in the lobby of the Beverly Sunset Hotel on the Friday evening of the Labor Day weekend, waiting for his investment banker and dreading the upcoming session with Bogle.

He examined the clocks in his socks to make sure they were running dead parallel up his shins, and reached behind him to twitch the double vents in his Huntsman suit into precise alignment. He looked around the lobby. No one was about. It was Labor Day—not a real Beverly Hills weekend. How should he deal with Bogle? he wondered.

Perhaps he should strike a conciliatory note. He was in pretty good shape, what with his options and his stock-award units, and his profit-sharing deal on *Draculite, the Killer Shark of Mars* was just about vested. When Bogle appeared on the scene, he'd gotten TEC's lawyers to write up a safety net of a $500,000 severance bonus and another $200,000 a year in pensions and consultancies for the next decade, plus a "humiliation award" of $150,000 annually for five years if he got fired for incompetence. It could be a living.

If Bogle got control, he'd be out. He and Mellie wouldn't be able to hold their heads up in Hancock Park; that was the thing. At least, though, they'd have enough money to stay there, which hadn't been true before he'd arrived at TransNational.

The only thing about the old life: it had been peaceful, and something he could understand. Sometimes he missed his clipboard and his pencil scabbard. When all he had to do was go around and ask what people were doing and then make marks on his piece of paper and look serious. Then they'd asked him to look after the TransNational loan, which was going bad, and before he knew what was happening, everybody who had anything to do with TransNational was gone, and he was installed as its new chief executive. It didn't matter because, the next Monday, the banks were going to throw the company into bankruptcy. But on his very first Saturday night as interim CEO, New York had called to say *Draculite* was doing $20,000 a day in Manhattan, and then it had done $200 million worldwide, and he and Mellie were getting their pictures in *That Woman!* and going everywhere.

It was tough running a so-called creative business. He knew everybody at the studio thought he was a cretin. So what?—because he was lucky. *Son of Draculite Goes to Saturn* did another $250 million at the box office; *Ouch, Darling*, a TV series about gay dentists, took off and was in its fifth season and was worth probably $60 million in syndication plus cable; Lake Windfall, a table-tennis resort in New Mexico which had been on TransNational's books for a few thousand dollars, was sold for $115 million after spirited bidding between two diversifying oil companies.

"Marvin, sorry to be late." It was S. Marcus Hochheim, his investment banker.

Terrace jumped up. "Marc. Good to see you." He took the other man's hand warmly. "Thanks for coming."

The two were old allies. They had met when Hochheim, a trainee at a minor investment-banking firm controlled by his mother's first cousin, had appeared at Terrace's bank to count bonds. Marvin had been in the basement of the bank, new on the job himself, with his clipboard ready to hand and a plastic pocket scabbard stuffed with pencils. The two had become instant fast allies in the eternal struggle of the stupid against the smart, a struggle which even after thirty centuries was still too close to call.

Since that first meeting, the genetic splicing of Wall Street firms had propelled Marc Hochheim into a partnership at a large and prestigious house, which had justified Terrace's bringing him onto the board he had carefully shaped from a motley of degunned generals and unshipped admirals. In a captive board, he knew, might lie salvation. In addition, Hochheim's firm, Kuhn, Kahn, Cohn and Co., was paid $200,000 a year to advise TransNational.

Terrace looked at his watch. "We're due in his bungalow now."

He led Hochheim into the hotel gardens, luxuriantly flowering alleyways lined with topiaries sculpted in the image of the film colony's immortals.

Between hedges shaped like Leo Carillo and Ern Westmore, Terrace stopped.

"Marc, do you think Bogle knows we're working on buying the company in? There may be an item in *Pritchett's* coming up. We had a tip. Is there a leak in your shop?"

"Of course not," said Hochheim. "Who do you think we are? Morgan Stanley?"

Bogle answered the door. "Evening, Marvin. Who's this?"

"Evening Harvey. This is my investment banker, Marc Hochheim."

"How are you, Mort?"

"It's, uh, Marc."

"Oh, sorry. You kinda look like a Mort I once knew."

They followed Bogle into the bungalow. A bar had been set up, and a side table with dishes of crab legs, chicken salad and cold beef.

"You come from New York, Marc? Have some of this. You must be hungry. You want pastrami? Sunset salad? You name it. Marvin?"

Bogle liked to start fast. It made for a distinct negotiating advantage. Eighty-five seconds into the meeting, he had Hochheim pissed off, and piss in the mind made for stupid. He pressed on. Now for Terrace.

"Glad you could make it, Marvin. I don't think you're missing anything in that party in France. Your wife's over there? So is everybody in the world. Must be a pretty fancy party. Esmé left three days ago with a crew from ABC."

"Uh, yes, Harvey, Melissa's there now. I was supposed to join her, but, you know, the interests of TransNational, heh heh . . ." Under stress, Terrace regurgitated an irritating, twitchy geniality. These guys all squirm the same way, Bogle thought; he'd noticed the same thing in Homer Seabury when he'd put a hot brick under his ass.

Hochheim broke in: "Mr. Bogle, I've had a long trip; there's a holiday weekend coming up; I think we ought to—"

"Call me Harv, Marc," Bogle interrupted back. "What's on your mind?"

"It's your mind that's got something on it, Mr. Bogle; you called the meeting."

"Indeed I did, Marc, indeed I did. So let's get down to cases. A little bird tells me your deal to take TransNational private is a lot further along than has been indicated to us poor jerks who only know what you let us read in the papers. Forty bucks a share, all cash—the money to come from a bunch of banks headed up by the Coastal National and the Certified Guaranty with a big slice of long-term financing from the Fiduciary Farm Life. I hear you're damn near set to close."

He looked them over. Terrace seemed flushed. Hochheim, whom Bogle had already figured for a natural-born gifted liar, said nothing. He continued pleasantly.

"Now, you know I own sixteen percent of TransNational. A couple hundred thousand shares more than Masterman United. Your bank group is going to insist on your getting eighty percent of the stock to close your buy-in. Mrs. Masterman's agreed to go along with you. I don't know what kind of a special deal you cut with her, but knowing you guys, there's got to be one, probably something social for your wife. This whole thing's full of special deals, right, Marc? But I'll get to that in a minute.

"I could go into the market Tuesday and buy another five percent, but that's gonna cost me another fifteen million, and then where am I? So I want to make a deal. I just don't want to be dumb about it. You guys are saying the company's worth forty dollars a share; presumably you've got an opinion to that effect from Marc's firm. I just want to see the real numbers."

"The real numbers?" asked Terrace.

"Yeah, the ones you're using with the banks and Fiduciary Farm Life. See, I figure if the banks'll lend you on the basis of forty dollars a share, they must have seen something that says the company's worth closer to eighty dollars. They like their cushion."

Terrace drew himself up.

"What you're suggesting, Harvey, is outrageous. Right, Marc? This is a private transaction involving ourselves, who are management, and a group of investors. These are inside company figures to which you refer. Confidential figures which, so long as I am Chief Executive Officer of this company, go no farther than the boardroom and our existing lending group. To permit their wider dissemination might cause harmful speculation and disorder in the trading market. We have had preliminary, exploratory discussions with certain financial institutions—that I can confirm—but only on the basis of information that has been publicly disclosed."

Bullshit, thought Bogle. He had the figures in his briefcase in the bedroom. A small bank in the group had approached him to see if he might consider making a competing bid. As the young Midwestern banker had put it: "Our tit's in a wringer, Mr. Bogle; we have no choice but to string along with big boys like Certified and Coastal. They throw us too much business. But Christ, if that idiot Terrace really gets in the driver's seat, with no one looking over his shoulder, this sonofabitch is likely to go right down the tubes, and with it our buy-out loan." The analysis he'd turned over to Bogle indicated TransNational was worth $83 a share.

"Cut the shit, Marvin," Bogle said. "I have some exciting news for you. You're trying to steal this company. Which I can sympathize with; except that you're not going to steal it from me. So, to make your deal, I want in. I want thirty percent of what you boys have carved out for yourselves at your price. And I'll go for your price."

Terrace affected an expression of deep indignation.

"Harvey, I resent your implications. This is a fine deal for TransNational and its constituencies. It rewards our stockholders. It lifts from over the heads of our employees any shadow of uncertainty as to the company's future direction and management. And, I might say, it fittingly recognizes the contributions that this management team has made."

Terrace felt confident. This Bogle man wasn't going to throw $15 million into an uncertain game. Harvey was too smart for that.

His sonorous, assured tone pleased Bogle. He'd guessed right about Terrace. Marvin's success and the money he'd made—which was peanuts compared with the size of the pot now on the table, but beyond dreaming about for a guy who'd once quick-marched a clipboard around a bank basement—had caused him to believe in his intelligence. When you started thinking that way, Bogle knew, you started getting trustful. And that's when you got your nuts cut off.

Hochheim, on the other hand, did know how dumb he was, Bogle guessed, which was why he spent most of his time protecting his own flanks, even if it meant selling out an old client.

"Look, Marvin," he said in a voice as calming as a scoutmaster's, "no need to push to a quick answer. Think it over. You know, I said a minute ago, your deal is loaded with special gimmicks. I wouldn't go bananas betting on the loyalty of your institutional friends. The banks are whores; just ask the guys at Conoco and Marathon about their loyal institutional stockholders and their friendly banks. In the stock market, Marvin, friendship has a price. You've got a lot to think about; like, for example, your own future. Right, Marc?"

Hochheim scowled. Bogle smiled at him.

"Which was why I was surprised, Marvin"—Bogle's voice was mild and conciliatory—"to hear that Marc here had made a deal with Coastal Bank to bring over that whiz kid from Metro." He named a driving young studio executive who was currently the hottest name in Hollywood. "Do that, Marvin, and you'd really be letting the camel's nose under the tent."

As he'd expected, Terrace reacted as if he'd been shocked by a cattle prod. Bogle sat back.

"What's he talking about, Marc?" Terrace had turned angrily to Hochheim.

Hochheim was red.

"Well, he's got it all wrong. I was going to mention it to you later, Marvin. A couple of the banks did suggest that it would be a good idea to add a little depth to the management picture here, and since they seemed pretty set on it, and since obviously we wanted to move things along, I did indicate that I was sure you'd give it serious consideration. But that's as far as it went. I give you my word, no commitment was made."

Paranoia was flashing a scenario onto the screen of Terrace's mind. He could see himself forced out of his own company. No more private screening room or dinners with the stars. No big compensation settlements. How could Marc have done this to him? He needed to regroup. He was damned if he was going to get into a catfight in front of Bogle.

"Harvey"—there was a discernible quaver to his words—"I think it's pretty underhanded of you to try to confuse the facts with innuendo. I happen to have absolute confidence in Marc's loyalty and ability."

Terrace knew that he could get to the bottom of that with a phone call or two. In his heart, he already knew the answer. Smart guys like Bogle didn't tell lies. Liars got tripped up, found out. Dummies like Marc tried to get cute; they were the ones who fell flat on their faces.

"Now, as to your other proposal, I'm certain what the answer will be, but as a matter of courtesy I will consider it and get back to you. Certainly, as our largest stockholder, you deserve every consideration. I would ask, in the same spirit, that you not do anything precipitate until you hear from me one way or the other."

Bogle saw them out. It had all played right to the script he had worked out beforehand. The kid from the Midwestern bank had been right; Hochheim was so hot to get this deal done, and get the agent's fee, he had been ready to sell Terrace down the toilet. Now Marvin was in a real bind. If he let the banks bring in the Metro guy, or if Harvey became a 30-percent partner, Terrace had to figure his ass'd be kicked so high he'd think he was riding the space shuttle. Terrace had been a poor boy once; the meganumbers of a $440-million buy-out of TransNational would be vaguely unreal, while the birds twittering in the hand, the perks and the million-dollar salary, the house in Hancock Park with two Mercedeses in the driveway, the membership in the Los Angeles Country Club were all real. For someone with Marvin Terrace's background, things like that had a reassuring taste and feel to them. If he'd been a betting man, thought Bogle, he'd have to say that the buy-out was dead.

He went into the bathroom to shave. He had a dinner date with an astrophysicist from UCLA; she was one of a series of occasional paramours around the country whom he'd lined up by answering "personals" in the *Manhattan Journal of Literature.* They were all smart. The only dummies Harvey Bogle tolerated in his life were the ones he had financial dealings with. Poor Marvin, he thought briefly, looking at his face in the mirror. He could have been worth $25 million if he'd hung tough. And Hochheim—to have pissed away that kind of relationship.

"Do you really think they're that stupid?" he asked his reflection out loud.

They're that stupid, it seemed to answer back.

After a summer in the sun, the trustees of the Fuller Foundation looked uniformly, expansively fit and, with the exception of Calypso, expensively tanned. The inner glow displayed by Calypso Winstead and Homer Seabury was positively triumphant. Not even a miserable rainy Labor Day weekend in the Southampton mausoleum that was the Masterman "cottage" had dampened Calypso's elation at the prospect of Harvey Bogle's gift of the Rubens sketches to the Institute. The trustees had been informed of his unusual conditions. Her husband, she knew, was, for one, prepared to declare them insupportable; Calypso was entirely in favor of accepting the gift as offered. Of course, Harvey had talked it over with her, seeking her advice, and wanting to couch his gift in a manner that might help ease the pressures from the Board—especially where Granada Masterman might try to apply some countervailing pressure.

The Institute was really the only part of her birthright that Hugo hadn't somehow been able to commandeer, thanks to the Agreement of Settlement. Her rationale for marrying him now seemed obscure, difficult to fathom; all she could remember was a great deal of persuasive, generalized approval from the trusted older men: Greschner, Morgan Seabury, Smithers Ward from the bank, who collectively meant "father" to her. They were all removed from her life now. Death had taken care of the lawyer; Ward was retired in South Carolina. Uncle Sol had been effectively exiled by

Hugo, who had squeezed out of her life every influence he thought competitive. He had taken over her trusts, administered her money, presided over the Foundation and its resources. He had filled the Board with his clients, using her birthright as a stepping-stone to solidify his business relationships and to "cure" himself socially, in the way that fine tobacco was cured in bonded warehouses.

She had let Hugo mesmerize her too long, she had decided over the summer. The cumulative traumas of her father's death, marriage to Hugo and two miscarriages, and the sudden, reproachful departure of Solomon Greschner from the Board and from her life had been permitted to linger too long, and too influentially, in her spirit. Anesthetized, she had watched as the Institute was backed into a financial corner, which compromised its artistic function. She knew what Hugo had in mind for solutions. Turn the Institute into an arena for big traveling loan shows; make it another stop on the artistic vaudeville circuit. This week the Fuller; next week Fort Wayne. Open the Board up to his clients. If another way could be found, she would prefer it. She did rather enjoy being cosseted by Granada Masterman, who had real, tangible hooks into the other three members of the Board. At least, it was a switch. Calypso didn't think Granada was "Fuller quality." In theory, it was a snobbish thing to say, but Granada didn't even like art. Of course, neither did the majority of the Board; all they knew about was money—but that was the funny part, because if they did, why was the Institute virtually out of money? What good, then, were they? Their predecessors had been men of some cultivation: Uncle Sol had his first editions and his bronzes and his drawings of musicians; Uncle Morgan had his Cycladic figurines and his Rivière bindings; Mr. Ward was prouder of his Japanese swords and *netsuke* than of being president of American Surety Trust.

For perhaps the first time in her adult life, Calypso thought, she was seeing things realistically. She now heard other voices clearly; the sounds of the world were no longer muddied by Hugo's persistent obbligato. It was a pleasant feeling, but tiring, in the way that entirely new enjoyments could be. She still needed the investment of Harvey's bottomless stamina and energy to fund her self-confidence. It would have been nice to have an ally on the Board. Homer Seabury would have been the logical one; he came from her world; but he was such a pallid imitation of her recollection of his father. Anyway, she had made up her mind. She waited for Hugo, who had just come in—a few minutes late, as usual—to call the meeting to order.

Two seats down the table, Homer Seabury was himself feeling as ebulliently liberated as Calypso. If everything went according to plan, he would sign a deal next week that would put his troubles behind him and let him get on with the business of building Seaco without having to worry about protecting his flanks. Watching Hugo Winstead shuffle his papers and say his postholiday hellos, Seabury was strangely glad that Katagira had taken on the task of preparing the necessary papers. To put Homer's mind at ease, it had been agreed that there would be a thirty-day cooling-off period following the signing and announcement of the transaction. That would give the Winstead firm time to vet the papers. It seemed eminently sensible to Homer and he'd readily agreed.

So much for the joy at the table.

Seabury turned to Marvin Terrace.

"I saw you called off your going-private deal, Marvin. Too bad. Your people must have put a lot of work into it. And the banks."

And Marc Hochheim too, he thought, feeling a tremor of polite glee that a competitor had failed to bring off a big one. The people at Kahn, Kuhn, Cohn must be really browned off at Terrace, he guessed; that must have been the reason for Marc Hochheim's sudden resignation from the TransNational board of directors.

"Anyway, you may be able to resurrect it. Why don't we lunch on it one of these days, Marvin? I've got a lot of very bright people in my corporate-finance shop; we might be able to be of service. We've signed on as advisers to Buford Gudge and his interests, you know."

"I wouldn't mind the lunch, Homer, but the deal is dead. Win some; lose some. So we'll just go ahead as we have. Our prospects are excellent; our Christmas release schedule has got our people all fired up. I think our stockholders will be happy."

Not likely, both men knew. When Robert Creighton's column had first hinted at a management buy-out, which had forced an announcement by Terrace that a preliminary study was in fact in the works, TNE had run up from $28 to $37. When Terrace had announced that the deal was off, the stock had fallen back to $27; experienced stock-watchers thought it looked as if it would stay there for a long time, even if TransNational brought in six *Star Wars* and ten *Godfathers* and found oil on its studio property. The Street didn't like companies that announced deals and then let them fall through. The arbitrageurs—the smart boys who inventoried the sell side in a merger against a fat profit on the buy-out—had gotten killed; some people were talking a $70-million bath. The consolation for the traders was that the bond market was showing some real tone, and that, Homer knew, was largely due to the wave of confidence the Gudge investment program had just started. The Gudge purchases were being widely talked about. Just wait until next week's announcement, he thought, feeling wonderfully pleased with himself. That'll give it a real shot in the arm.

At the head of the table, Hugo Winstead was vexed. The Puerto Rican woman who cleaned the Village apartment hadn't come in, it seemed, since June; there were old dishes in the sink, and the little kitchen appeared to be swarming with roaches. The videotape was on the fritz. Which was just as well; he wouldn't have wanted a record of his performance. After two months in dry dock, he'd barely gotten it out of his pants and started to slip it in when he'd shot off. It had been very embarrassing. Thank God it was one of his regulars and not that new associate from Yale he was making great plans for.

He cleared his throat. "Well, shall we start? It's a pleasure to see everyone looking so well. Calypso and I hope you all had a pleasant, interesting summer.

"Now, we've had to call for this special meeting—and Calypso and I are very gratified that you could be here on such short notice—well in advance of our customary October date. For any of you whom this may have inconvenienced, you may console yourself with the knowledge that Frodo has cut short his Florentine stay to be with us." There was a murmur; Crisp's July-to-October sojourns at La Pergola were sacrosanct.

"No agenda has been mailed to you. This was not only in the interest of time, but of confidentiality. I think you all know what we have on the table before us. Of course, whatever we decide here today must be kept confidential until a suitable public announcement, should one be necessary, can be framed and made, and that can only be done in the event an understanding is reached.

"Before asking Frodo to join us, after which I expect we'll want to go into executive session, it would perhaps be useful if I summarize what has transpired.

"Harvey Bogle, whom you all know, has offered the Institute a group of paintings, twelve in all, which Mr. Bogle is considering purchasing. These are, I understand, oil sketches by the seventeenth-century Flemish painter Peter Paul Rubens. *Sir* Peter Paul Rubens—thank you, Calypso. Depicting the Labors of Hercules, a mythological subject. I have not seen them. I am told by Frodo that despite their small size, and the fact that they are sketches, they are of the utmost rarity and value. He can tell you about that. I must add that Mr. Bogle has also agreed to provide whatever sum is necessary to establish a special gallery for the pictures so that they may be shown to their best advantage under ideal conditions of temperature and humidity.

"In proposing this gift, Mr. Bogle has attached certain conditions to which I, personally, am opposed. First, he requests that we invite his wife, Mrs. Esmé Bogle, who is a well-known writer of popular fiction, to give the Fuller Reading this year." There was a gasp, over which Winstead quickly rode. "I urge that we table any discussion of this until we are in executive session again. I do think you should be aware that Mr. Bogle has somehow been made privy to the fact that the poet who was to be this year's Fuller Reader will be incapacitated for at least another eight months. Thus this October's reading *is* at present available."

Words could be tabled, but thoughts could not. To be offered a Fuller Reading was one of the loftiest honors that could be paid to a living writer. The first Reading had been given in 1940 by Robert Frost. Thereafter, except for two of the war years, the third Thursday evening in October had found Eliot and Faulkner, Liebling, Malraux and Perelman, Graham

Greene and St. John Perse reading in the mahogany-paneled Reading Room on the mezzanine of the Mansion; the only exception had been in 1947, when the Reading for that year had been held in January to accommodate the traveling plans of Evelyn Waugh.

Of the people at the table, only Calypso had read *Salon*. Men were not normally interested in the carryings-on of a hairdressing establishment. But the thought of Esmé Bogle declaiming on Parnassus was at the very least unusual. It disturbed Hugo, but not Calypso. She had heard Frodo on the subject of the Rubens paintings. How awful could one evening possibly ever be, against the chance to have these glorious things in the Institute forever?

"There is one other condition that Mr. Bogle has made clear. He has asked for the right to designate a member of this Board. That in effect requires Calypso to create a proxy for her powers as sole voting trustee under the Agreement of Settlement. I find this intolerable. Mr. Bogle did state, in a letter to Calypso received approximately a month ago, that neither he nor any of his immediate family would be so designated.

"There it is, in brief. Now, before any of us are tempted to premature discussion, let's have Frodo in."

Whenever a potentially controversial acquisition was before the Board, Frodo contrived to don a halo of mystical, frail aestheticism. When he entered the room, it was apparent that he had somehow managed to organize himself physically so that his angular, birdlike figure seemed, if anything, more spinily delicate and his features more pointed and refined. Under his arm were two large volumes—props, the trustees each knew; Frodo didn't like to confound his own viewpoint with the opinions of other experts; the divine laws he carried down from the mountain of connoisseurship were usually writ by his own hand.

He plunked the books down heavily and purposefully at his place at the table, between Hugo and Calypso, next to a stack of copies of Reverey's brochure. He sighed once, deeply, as if communing with inner truths of unimaginable depth and portent, and then looked around the table, greeting each of the trustees in turn, examining them as a stork might examine a particularly delectable grub, until he came to Calypso, whom he fixed with a smile of undeniable fondness.

"I have been the Director of this Institute for twenty years," he began, "during which the foresight and generosity of this Board and other friends have enabled us to acquire many wonderful things. In all that time, however, I cannot think of any work of art—works of art, I should say—which have become available to us, under any circumstances, as exciting as these—which are offered at no financial cost to the Institute."

He nodded his head prayerfully at the end wall opposite Winstead. The trustees saw that the velvet curtains had been drawn. They could be sure that Harvey Bogle's Rubens sketches had been arranged on the grid of display brackets and runners which Crisp had caused to be installed on the wall some years earlier.

"Before we look at these extraordinary paintings, it might perhaps be useful for you to examine an excellent brochure which the dealer Nicholas Reverey, who is handling the sale of the paintings, has made up. Unlike most similar productions by dealers, which usually bear as much relationship to real scholarship as detergent advertising to the poetry of Keats, these are of a very high standard indeed." He slid them across the table.

While other people at the table thumbed through the brochures, Crisp summarized their findings and hypotheses. "I must say," he concluded, "that I can find small room for disagreement with the dealer's conclusions as to the origin and *raison d'être* of these extraordinary little pictures, which are absolutely from Rubens' own hand. Surely they date from the late 1630s, at which point Rubens was essentially preoccupied with the enormous commission for the King of Spain's hunting lodge. That no program for a Labors of Hercules has turned up until now has been an abiding mystery, for if ever a subject and an artistic temperament were suited, one might say destined, for each other, it would be Hercules and Sir Peter Paul Rubens. I think you will see that for yourselves when we come to look at the pictures.

"Now, I think one last thing should be said. Rubens, on the whole, hasn't done as well in this country as he should, considering his inestimable greatness as an artist. Until quite recently, really, he wasn't the sort who appealed to frontier tastes, and I need not say that his amply, abundantly endowed female nudes hardly appealed to the sort of Victorian prudishness that was to be found here until really quite recently. Thus the best large Rubens paintings in America, the Wrightsman portrait uptown at the Metropolitan, the *Holy Family* in Raleigh, the *Saint Catherine* in Toledo and the early *Diana* in Cleveland, each in its way remarkable, don't really show him at his most mature and heroic, in that visually complex, epic manner which I believe displays him most characteristically and wonderfully. There are some very fine oil sketches here and there, such as one of the Duke of Buckingham in the Kimbell Museum and the model for the Whitehall Ceiling at New Haven. But in no single place elsewhere in this country, if these pictures come here, will one be able to see an entire cycle. Nowhere."

He rose and made his way to the far wall, where he drew back the velvet curtains. The dozen sketches had been arranged in two rows of six.

The trustees followed Crisp. As always, their eyes had been prefocused by the Director. In each mind was posed the question: what am I supposed to see that is so wonderful? Each came up with a slightly different answer. Marvin Terrace thought they looked sort of Impressionist, which he knew was at least fashionable. Homer Seabury was taken by their quality of being finely made, by the gloss of the surfaces and the jewel-like brilliance of certain passages. For Hugo Winstead, artistic judgment was a matter of small consequence—one look sufficed to tell him that the things couldn't be kept out on artistic grounds; he would have to find other reasons. Only Calypso, who had spent long hours over two decades learning about art from Frodo and from the experts to whom he sent her with glowing letters of introduction, thought she could see what it was that had electrified Frodo Crisp and Harvey Bogle. As far as she was concerned, the pictures must come to the Institute. When she had gone with Frodo to see them at Reverey's, her last reservations had been allayed. Rubens had always meant something vaguely immoral, but these pictures would have passed even the puritanical scrutiny of her grandfather.

The trustees spent perhaps half an hour before the sketches, asking questions, making the appropriate exclamations of wonder and delight, the three men hoping to drown out the subaural grinding of axes taking place in their minds. Then Frodo was dismissed and Hugo called the meeting into executive session.

"I think the issue is clear. We have to take Frodo's word—and the word of these other experts in this booklet—that what we've got on the wall there is the real McCoy. Ordinarily, we'd jump at the chance of getting them. But are we willing to submit to blackmail to do so? I personally like to think I have a higher opinion of the Institute than that."

"I must say, my first instinct is to second Hugo," said Marvin Terrace. "I mean, aren't there other things to think about? And these are just sketches, didn't Frodo say; and they're awfully small." In his laborious way, Terrace had figured that Bogle must want something pretty important from the Fuller to be willing to make an offer like this. Those pictures must have cost a fair piece; Terrace knew that pictures were expensive these days. Hell, it'd cost the company close to $400,000 for those whatever-they-were flower pictures that decorator friend of Mellie's had got for his office. "Any idea what Harvey paid for them?"

"The price was more than seven million dollars, according to Frodo," Calypso answered. "And you know he's apparently willing to redo the Limewood Room to hang them in? I don't see how we can refuse—in conscience."

"Well, now, Calypso," Terrace said, "maybe there's something we don't know here. And what about turning the Fuller Reading over to his wife? Do you know the sort of stuff she writes? Sex books, that's what!"

"Marvin has a point, dear," Hugo said. His voice was like a lubricating unguent. "We have fifty years of great distinction invested in the Readings. There are larger considerations."

"I don't think so": Homer Seabury, unexpectedly. He knew what Terrace and Winstead were up to. Fronting for Granada Masterman, that was what. If he were in their shoes, he'd probably be thinking that way himself. But he wasn't; not any longer, he hoped. In any case, he'd never had that poor-boy mentality which goaded Hugo and Marvin. He didn't have any impoverished, lower-caste history to worry about sinking back into. Even if he hadn't worked things out so that he was going to be able to be quit of worrying about Granada, and Bogle too, when he signed that deal with Gudge next week, he'd probably have voted for what he thought was the true best thing for the Institute. So he said firmly, "This is a museum. A place for the greatest things we can acquire and display. These appear to fit our purposes, and at a very reasonable price, especially for an institution that has no money left to buy art. Esmé Bogle can come here and read and it will be forgotten. It won't be the first time. We had Upton Sinclair here in 1941. My father was apoplectic; three days later it was forgotten."

"Well, that's all very well," challenged Winstead, "but what about this commitment not to elect a new trustee for a year? What about that?"

"Yes, indeed, what about that?" demanded Terrace. "It seems to me, Homer, that we'd be abdicating our rights."

Terrace was now absolutely certain that Bogle would barter his right to elect a trustee for Granada Masterman's stock in TransNational; Granada could attain the Board and Terrace would be in Bogle's clutches; if that happened, Marvin knew, given the spirit of his meeting with Bogle in Beverly Hills, it would be time to dust off the clipboard. Of course, only Calypso could do the actual voting; but she always went along with Hugo.

The talk went back and forth for another hour. The half-baked, unpromising schemes invariably trotted out in discussions of this sort were all paraded and found wanting. No, there were no other Rubens experts who should be consulted. No, there was no possibility of Bogle's equivocating his terms.

When Winstead finally called for a vote, he knew he was beaten. It was clear that Seabury was taking a firm stand; with Homer sticking to his guns and voting with Calypso—who, Hugo knew, was committed to accept Bogle's offer—that would make it 2–2 and under the Settlement Calypso would break the tie. There was one consolation, he figured. He could lay the blame off on Homer when it became necessary to tell Granada what had happened. Homer had broken ranks, unexpectedly. That would do it. He found the thought so comforting that he troubled himself no further about the source of Homer's newfound fortitude.

Crisp was delighted when Hugo advised him of the Board's decision. His calculations had suggested a near-run thing. Calypso was one he could count; Winstead absolutely not. Crisp had known enough mongrels—it went with the museum vocation—to understand that birthright had no meaning for them. Terrace was another *parvenu*; scared of his own shadow, Crisp knew, but perhaps anxious enough to curry favor with Bogle to vote yea. Maybe a vote there; he didn't know, of course, of the Beverly Hills meeting. It would come down to Homer Seabury, thought Frodo. Homer was our sort; if he voted what was in his blood, Homer would come through. Although these days, self-interest could make a cur out of the finest-bred greyhound.

Nick was delighted with Crisp's call. He and Bogle had been in his upstairs sitting room, looking at a few drawings which Nick had chosen to illustrate certain ideas he had about what made a drawing good. Neither man was particularly attentive to the lesson; both jumped when the phone rang.

Walking back to the Tennyson, Bogle was pleased. He knew how deeply happy this had made Calypso. It was she who had suggested putting a lock on the trusteeship; to keep Hugo off her back, she said. With no money in the Institute's treasury, it was best to keep the seat vacant until one should appear who would be truly helpful. Granada was not that person, she knew. And Esmé was ecstatic; he'd caught up with her in the greenroom of *PM Winston-Salem*. She knew exactly what she'd be reading, she told him; she'd get her public relations people to coordinate with the Fuller on her allotted invitations. All in all, a coup, thought Bogle. And he was happiest of all. He was a convert; there was no other word for it. It was as if he had been waiting all his life to be called to the enjoyment of art. Nothing he had ever done had so totally and pleasurably engaged his instincts and his intellect. Unlike buildings and stocks and bonds and the expensive fripperies demanded by wives and girlfriends, here was a really sensible way to spend the money you didn't need. So satisfied did he feel that he hugged the big folio volume under his arm, Felix Rothschild's monograph on Giotto, now long out of print, thoughtfully marked by Nick to the page displaying the altarpiece that would be auctioned off in London in a month and a half.

CHAPTER FOURTEEN

There were two stories, and a brief notice, in *The New York Times* for the last Wednesday in September which were read with similar avidity but varying degrees of pleasure by the several trustees of the Fuller Institute, as well as by other individuals who for one reason or another were interested in the Institute and its Board members.

The most prominent story appeared on the first page, in the lower left-hand corner, under the by-line of the paper's senior art critic. It was headed "FULLER INSTITUTE OBTAINS/MAJOR GIFT OF ART" and underneath, in smaller type, "N.Y. FINANCIER DONATES/RUBENS CYCLE VALUED/IN EXCESS OF $5 MILLION." The report began:

> The Fuller Institute announced yesterday that it has been given an extremely rare series of oil sketches by Sir Peter Paul Rubens (1577–1640). The small paintings, which average approximately 30″ by 15″ in size, and depict the twelve Labors of Hercules, have been donated to the Fuller by Harvey C. Bogle, the well-known financier and industrial investor. According to Sir Frodo Crisp, the director of the Fuller Institute and a noted expert on Western European painting, the sketches were purchased by Bogle from a European private collection through a consortium of art dealers represented by Nicholas Reverey, the New York dealer. Although information as to the price paid for the cycle is not available, knowledgeable sources believe it may have exceeded $5 million. In 1980, a large painting from Rubens' early period, the "Samson and Delilah," dated by experts around 1610, was bought at auction by the National Gallery, London, for $5,474,000 (£2,300,000).

Turning to follow the story to the inside pages, Nick chuckled. The *Times* was attuned to the character of the public interest in art; the $5-million hypothesized price occurred three times in the heading and first paragraph. Nick would have liked to be more open with the *Times* critic, who'd telephoned nosing after the price, following the press conference at which Winstead and Crisp had announced the gift; that information was Bogle's alone to dispense, however, and Bogle had made himself scarce; he'd called Nick to say he was heading out of town, but that he'd be in touch soon about the Giotto. Before hanging up, Bogle had indicated a wish to get together with Felix Rothschild to talk about the altarpiece.

The remainder of the *Times* story was a predictable rehash of reactions from Rubens authorities and envious but gracious museum directors. Livermore Green, the director of the National Gallery in Washington, had said how wonderful it was for the nation to have the pictures; the Mayor had rushed uptown to be photographed between Crisp and Winstead, holding the Hydra over his head like a tennis trophy. The report concluded by repeating the theories concerning the paintings' origin, a review of Rubens' career, a touch of art-historical showing-off with some interpretive flights of fancy and a speculation on New York collecting:

> Whether the purchase of these paintings by Mr. Bogle marks the emergence of the sort of major individual collector of Old Master pictures that this city has been short of in the last decade remains to be seen. Since the death of Robert Lehman in 1969, only one truly distinguished collection has carried the standard borne so nobly in this city by private collectors since the turn of the century; Mr. Bogle's entry on the scene is therefore to be welcomed, with a prayer that he may be inclined to continue in both his acquisitiveness and his generosity.
>
> It is fitting that these pictures, apparently painted for a royal residence, should find a home at the Fuller Institute. Together with the Frick Collection and the Pierpont Morgan Library, the Institute is one of this city's three great "ducal" collections, reflecting an independence of means and spirit which sets it apart from other institutions increasingly deferential to arrogant government functionaries, celebrity-seeking corporate executives or egocentrically self-commemorative individuals willing to barter their own or someone else's dollars for status. One would have expected the announcement of the Bogle gift to have been accompanied by a statement of Mr. Bogle's having been elected to the Fuller's Board of Trustees. A source close to the Fuller Institute and to Mr. Bogle has assured this newspaper that this is not to be, nor is it Mr. Bogle's wish or intention.

Nicely handled, Sol, thought Nick. Sol had been "a source close to" a number of New York institutions for fifty years. The men who covered the city's cultural and financial beats for the *Times* looked to Sol for the right dope on any story like this. When Crisp had telephoned to say that the trustees had accepted Bogle's conditions, he and Nick had bustled down to Number 17 to confer with Greschner. Bogle still trusted Sol to be able to handle something like this so that it got just the right press, that its best face was displayed at its best angle in the best light. It was important to get that last part in, about Bogle's lack of personal interest, in order to set up the right reaction to the second meaningful item which appeared in the news that day, that Esmé Bogle had been invited to give this year's Fuller

Reading. It was just a sliver of news buried in a column of miscellany in the section the paper devoted each Wednesday to double boilers, mineral waters and recipes for Afghan goat stews. Sol had arranged for Jill to slot an item about Esmé in the coming Friday's *That Woman!*, to the effect that the invitation to Esmé had been tendered by the Fuller Board acting on its own, an inspired act of gratitude for Harvey Bogle's unprecedented generosity.

"Calypso must be delighted," Sol said. "This will get Granada off her back for a while."

Sol and, he knew, Jill had alerted Calypso early on that Granada, for all her talk, was a very unlikely benefactress.

"Granada's quite a story," Jill had told her. "Smart, tough. As successful as any big corporate entrepreneur in this country. But like them, she's all business. She wishes the world spoke numbers, so she wouldn't have to bother reading anything. Not that she reads much, anyway. Esmé's last novel, maybe. *The Wall Street Journal*. The rag I write for. Anything about expensive, fancy people—the sort of garbage she wants so badly to mix with. Hotel dwellers. She thinks nobody believes that once upon a time she was a child who was close to all that Gudge money. Except something happened. She's got this ambition to prove that point which makes her quite blind to the fact that it all is too long ago and far away, that she can't get back there from where she is; that that whole world is gone anyway; there aren't any more dukes and milords sipping tea in the lobby of the Carlton—just a bunch of Arabs and Texans with a lot of traveler's checks.

"Granada's a successful modern woman. The most complex creature there is, the American self-made woman. Her success didn't just happen, Calypso. She made it happen—and in the course of it, all the salon, hostessy qualities that make a lady, as usually defined, got washed away. And she can't relearn them. That's what's so sad about Granada's kind of woman. They can have all the money in the world, but all they do is end up at the expensive tables in the spotlight. Looking somewhat ridiculous—big females in five-thousand-dollar evening dresses with paid-for friends."

Sol had also told her about Granada. There had been something sad in his voice when he talked about her, though; something that Calypso felt went beyond his disappointment at Granada's desertion. Hugo had deserted Sol too—and had insulted him by maneuvering him off the Board of the Institute with that age thing—but Sol, when he mentioned Hugo, spoke in terms of a mistake, a forgivable error of judgment, an incontinence worth a scolding but no more. Granada he had spoken of more seriously. There was something . . . well, tragic, about his voice.

"Granada won't do you any good, Cal," he'd said, rising and crossing the room to a bookcase. "She's like Julia in *David Copperfield*: peevish and fine, and nothing blooms near her. The air around her is poisoned by her corrosive envy. She wants and values nothing you or I would want or value: which is sad, because she has great ability, and it's going to waste. She has an instinctive urge for power which so few people and practically no women have. Granada won't do anything for you, Cal. She has no time for cultivation."

While Calypso pridefully reread the *Times* story, Jill found even more interesting a two-paragraph article on the second page of the Business Section, which was headed "SEACO GROUP, GUDGE INTERESTS/FORM $80 MILLION/JOINT TRADING VENTURE."

Jill, who had been expecting the story's appearance, had allowed herself to be scooped, in a limited way, on this one. Sol had promised some good deep background for Creighton, which he had said would reveal the entire iceberg. She told her secretary at *That Woman!* to hold her calls, and to get her that morning's *Wall Street Journal*, and settled down with the *Times* report. By the time she finished, the *Journal* was on her desk; its story, as she had anticipated, was considerably fuller than the one in the *Times* and somewhat more to the point. Jill had very little respect for American financial journalism; it displayed contemptibly shallow analytical powers, and showed little grasp of what was going on behind the numbers and corporate maneuverings and press releases it dutifully regurgitated as rendered. Once or twice a year she would happen on a story that seemed to penetrate close to what she perceived to be the heart of most business stories: the purely human motivations—not the statistical or conceptual pap fed to the press and the public—inherent in a particular deal or corporate policy. That was the angle—confluences of greed, apprehension, thirst—from which she had fashioned Creighton's reportage. In an odd way, she attributed her point of view to her experience as a society reporter. The more she saw of rich people, many of them retired entrepreneurs or executives, the less she accepted the simple ability to write a check, no matter how large or on whose account, as an earnest of intelligence or shrewdness.

Sol had kept her briefed on Seaco's courtship of Bubber Gudge. In his selective way, he had omitted Katagira from his accounts of the developing relationship. Tucked away in Jill's memory, however, was something Caryn Gudge had said about "Buford's Jap" one Sunday night at the Von Gonzálezes', where Mrs. Gudge now dined regularly every third week. She intended to pursue the subject further, but the opportunity to slide easily into an inferential conversation about the Gudge setup hadn't arrived.

According to the newspaper accounts, Homer Seabury had announced the organization of a partnership between Seaco and certain entities controlled by Buford Gudge IV, "to whom Seaco Group acts as financial adviser," with the objective of "investment trading and dealing" in Treasury and other high grade long-term bonds. Seaco Group was to manage the resources of the partnership and act as the general partner. Which meant that Seaco would have the unlimited liability, Jill reflected fleetingly. The partnership's initial capital would be $80 million, contributed in equal $40-million shares by Seaco and the Gudge interests. Jill's eyebrows had risen slightly when she first read this; she wouldn't have thought Seaco had

$40 million kicking around to sink into something like this. But then, reading on, she had learned that Seaco's participation was to be funded with the proceeds of a direct sale to the Gudge interests of $40 million of a special voting convertible preferred stock, of which the terms were yet to be determined. Wow! Homer had 20 percent, and with Gudge now taking a substantial interest, presumably as Homer's ally, that ought to scotch Granada's snake. Good for Homer, she thought. Somehow, he'd gotten Gudge to put up all the cash—which made sense, since the Gudge Treasury-bond positions were getting to be the talk of the Street. There had been a rally worth a hundred basis points in the long-Treasury market since Gudge had moved in, even in the face of pretty dismal economic and monetary news.

The two stories concluded with speculations as to the current size of the Gudge bond positions, now thought to approach five billion dollars, and some generalizing historical information on Gudge and Seaco.

Well, well, well, she thought. Everybody had come to play in the Seaco sandbox. Since Homer's bond trader was known to be a real gunslinger, Jill did some quick figuring. They could probably leverage the partnership 95 percent which meant that nearly $1.5 billion could be borrowed on an equity of $80 million. If they were really bullish on the bond market, and believed that rates would continue to fall sharply and bond prices continue to rise, they'd push as far out into the maturity range as the creditors would let them. Long bonds would react most sharply to market moves; the profits —and risks—against highly leveraged positions would be more dramatic on a portfolio with an average maturity of ten years than on one with less than a year. The creditors would fall all over themselves on this. Banks that had lent money to Poland would jump at lending to a Seaco-Gudge axis. And there were billions out there in funny-money land: repurchase agreements, rollovers, not to mention what that kind of cash could do in the futures market. If the market went their way, Jill calculated, the new partnership could probably swing for close to $10 billion. Not that Homer Seabury would ever let it get that far.

Nevertheless, she thought, Granada's hot breath has scared Homer onto a very fast track indeed. She made a note to check with Sol as to what he knew about some of the details of the arrangement. Now, she sighed, back to the featherheads, temporarily banishing Creighton to a niche in the back of her mind. Rolling a sheet of fresh paper into her typewriter, she began to write:

> THE PARTY LINE/by Gilberte: Lovely Lady turns Literary Lioness . . . *Tout* literary and every other kind of Manhattan is expected to turn out next month when ESME BOGLE, our (and everyone else's) favorite lady writer—her fabulous, everyone's-talking-about "Salon" just went into its sixth million in paperback—gives the annual Fuller Reading at the to-die-over Fuller Mansion. She'll be reading from her new novel in progress which has her publishers

> blowing kisses all the way to the bank and her agent, MILTY MOSKER, singing movie, movie, movie. The choice of Esme to join such other literary immortals who've read at the Fuller Institute as RICHARD FROST, S. G. PERELMAN and THEODORE S. ELLIOT was engineered by urbane, silver-haired HUGO WINSTEAD, the Fuller's chairman and suave attorney husband of CALYPSO FULLER, descendant of the Mansion's founders . . .

Jill leaned back in her swivel chair. She couldn't get used to the need for getting the names of cultural immortals deliberately wrong while getting every last umlaut right in a German title, but all the other columnists did it, and it wouldn't do for Gilberte to seem dangerously literary. The things we do for our children she thought, and went on typing.

> A famous couple (she's on everyone's lips, including those of a leading Broadway star; don't guess the gender) have agreed to ring down the curtain . . .

It was a cheap shot, but once in a while she indulged herself out of sheer exasperation; she hoped Nick wouldn't see it.

That evening, at home, she switched on the *Pritchett's* word processor; sat staring for a while at the greenish screen as if it were a seer's globe, gathering her thoughts, then tapped out:

> THE BOTTOM LINE/by Robert Creighton/ . . . The Big News on Wall Street is that the biggest bucks in America appear to have lined up foursquare behind the decrepit dollar. The announcement of a joint-venture bond investment partnership between Seaco Group and the massive Gudge interests appears to confirm what has been an open secret for weeks: Buford Gudge IV is betting on the Administration's anti-inflation policy. The word has been that Seaco has not-too-quietly been accumulating close to $2 billion in long Treasuries for various Gudge accounts. Essentially for cash! This despite the fact that the prime rate continues to hover around 20% and the Friday money figures don't look comforting to anyone except Mr. Gudge—and, one guesses, Seaco now—but after all, rich people have their own crystal balls. Spell that c-o-n-n-e-c-t-i-o-n-s. Nobody's talking, but a lot of smart money is betting that there'll be a big downside breakthrough in M1-B in the next few weeks; which accounts for the fact that the bond market has had a nice bounce in the last few weeks. The Seaco-Gudge announcement puts to flight a cloud of fear that Gudge has simply been using big money to make it bigger; that he used a little loose cash and a minimal amount of credit to give the market a push, and planned to take a quick profit, lay his positions off on the big trading houses and hustle back to his legendary Texas ranch a few hundred million richer. . . . Gudge looks to be in for a big play. And the bond crowd is jumping for joy. As this goes to press, Treasuries eight years out or better saw a dramatic pop at the close of Friday's trading: bringing their upside move since the beginning of the week to 50 basic points on average, with more expected next week when the bellwether houses get their sheep in line. . . . And the bond boys aren't the only winners. In a neat bit of financial legerdemain, Homer Seabury, Seaco's taciturn chairman,

appears to have gotten out from under the gun of Granada Masterman's MUD, by financing his interest in the new partnership through the sale to Gudge of a 15% special voting interest in Seaco. Strange bedfellows? Maybe . . . but apparently more to Seabury's liking than Mrs. Masterman and her crony, waiting-in-the-wings Senator Rufus Lassiter, whom smart tongues had tabbed to wake up Seaco . . . Congratulations, Homer. . . . Now, for us poor guys who haven't got billions to turn the money markets around, there are still a few undervalued equities on the Big Board worth looking over, among them . . .

Before transmitting the column, Jill wondered for an instant whether she should enlarge the Seaco item to say something about Harvey Bogle. That made it too complicated. Wait and see. Harvey could be counted on for a story on his own. And MUD hadn't reacted yet; surely Granada would show her hand, if only in the Hell-hath-no-fury department. Close to midnight; Nick had spared her from having to dine with two Colombians who had flown in hastily from Bogotá to see if there were any more Rubens pictures around. She might just have time for a bath before he arrived. He'd probably be slightly, sweetly drunk, she anticipated. As she turned off the lights, she dwelt for an instant on the frustration of being an anonymous name at the head of a column. This could be a hell of a story to report; what a cast! Then she remembered that Nick was going abroad next week. Why the hell did love have to make every moment together so indispensably precious—so that tomorrow ceased to exist for fear of its not coming and every moment together lost was a lifetime?

The pressroom supervisor at *Pritchett's* who was in Greschner's pocket had been his usual reliable self, so Sol saw that the advance of Jill's story was on Katagira's facsimile printer the next morning. Katagira read it through several times; it was very satisfactory. He must show it to Gudge, who had not come out of his room for a week. He had been assured by José and Stumpy both that the boss wasn't in pain, or physically unfit—just depressed. Mrs. Gudge had been away for nearly two months this time; she was in France—last week it had been London—with Madame von González, buying furniture on her way to taking the waters at Montecatini. There was nothing Katagira could have said to Gudge by way of consolation or counsel about his wife.

It was the second time that Fixed Income and Katagira had met. In the interim, Fixed Income had done what he would be first to admit was a terrific job for them in the market. He'd set the Gudge accounts up so that it was difficult for anyone else at Seaco to know exactly what he had done. Not that it mattered. This was cash business, topped off with a little credit buying, maybe $200 million, that he covered easily with his overnight lines at the banks and took a nice quarter-point on. When he drove through the gates of the Lazy G, a little fuzzed from a lot of booze drunk the night before while trying to make a lady carpet salesman in the hotel bar in

Amarillo, and a Yellowjacket swallowed this morning to get even with the hangover, the Gudge accounts owned something over $978 million in long Governments, most of it in six- to twelve-year maturities. That wasn't enough to spark the kind of self-fulfilling rally he had in mind down the road, but he knew his traders and salesmen drank long and boastfully at the bars around Hanover Square, and by managing the innuendo and gossip which buzzed in his division between trades, he had ensured that the Street was thinking that Gudge had $2 billion minimum in the bond market. No one ever knew how much money anyone else had, but that didn't stop traders from betting on their guesses. Shit, the goddamn government didn't know how much money it had in circulation, but it kept publishing figures, so that every Friday afternoon the money market went apeshit. The effect of the $2-billion rumor was enough to mark up the Gudge portfolio about 33 basis points on average, which meant it was up about $20 million in real dollars plus net interest, which gossip would translate to around $100 million in effective psychological value on the Street. And $100 million, real or imagined, was incentive enough to talk rally at Harry's Bar.

Fixed Income was pleased enough, and hangover-indiscreet enough, to boast about this when he and Seabury and Katagira sat down over *huevos rancheros* and chuckwagon coffee. And articulate enough so that Seabury took it all in approvingly and would have rubbed his hands with pride if he hadn't been such a gentleman. Katagira observed these two fat trout swimming pridefully in the pond of their self-esteem; listening, watching, waiting; letting the sun and the calm, lucid water of companionability dull their wariness.

"Hearing you, sir, one would have to conclude," he said at length, seeing Fixed Income's fifth cup of coffee send a jangling belt of confidence into the young man's bloodstream, "that great opportunities do indeed exist. Perhaps we have been too modest, too circumspect, in our objectives. The problem is, from our point of view, that while we believe in our investment philosophy, and its ultimate truth, it seems difficult for us to take full advantage of the possibilities of leverage without exposing ourselves to the scrutiny of the regulatory authorities. Public and private, I mean. On one hand there is the Federal Reserve; on the other, the elected governors of the market. Always the suspicion of the potential power of a man as rich as Mr. Gudge is known to be. The possibility of rules' being changed to our disadvantage. I feel certain Mr. Gudge would have no financial problem in committing several hundred millions more to this program. Psychologically, however, he finds it difficult, despite his confidence in the workings of the Administration's fiscal policies. You see, sir, Wall Street has not been kind to its Texas friends, such as the Hunts and Mr. Perot. Millions of dollars have been lost on what seems to us to have been bad faith. People down here remember such things."

He smiled with an expression of wistful apology. Ah, his regretful expression seemed to say, would but that such men of good intention as they could find a way to do really substantial business.

Then, seemingly as an afterthought: "Frankly, Mr. Seabury, it's the reason, despite the very excellent impression and the very ingenious suggestions made by your group, that Mr. Gudge feels that public ownership of certain of his interests would open him to a kind of scrutiny which he would be obliged to face alone. Without tangibly interested, influential allies."

Katagira let his voice trail off and drift in the room, much as a cast would settle quietly, unsuspiciously on his pond. Again he smiled wanly at the other two men.

Later he would tell Gudge that Homer Seabury's expression became that of a fish seeing the fattest midge in the history of Creation hover tantalizingly above the surface, bare sufficient millimeters out of reach.

Seabury and his associate looked quickly at each other. Again Katagira inserted himself into their silent, mutually prayerful dialogue.

"I suppose what I'm saying, Mr. Seabury"—it was time to treat with the opposing chief—"is that however tempting the investment possibilities, and we believe them to be extraordinary, we would be outsiders. And outsiders take momentous risks on Wall Street. Not from the market, sir, but from the insiders. That, I believe, is a matter of history."

Seabury started to harrumph in reply, but was interrupted by his younger colleague.

"Mr. Katagira, would you excuse Mr. Seabury and me for a couple of minutes?" Another swallow of coffee was gulped. "I think we might have an answer."

"Of course."

They were back in ten minutes; from the way they walked into the room, Katagira could see that the young man was now leading for Seaco.

"Mr. Katagira," Fixed Interest said, "we've been thinking, and it seems to us that maybe there's a way to do business so that you'll be comfortable. Where we'll assume an equivalent risk. We happen to agree with your view of the money markets; matter of fact, we're even more bullish." He sounded very positive, even though all three men at the table knew that Seaco's most recent econometric model of the nation's outlook argued for lifeboats instead of yachts.

"Would you consider forming a separate general partnership with us for the purpose of trading? We'd run it on the regular commission basis, which would compensate us for our supervision. Otherwise, we'd be equal general partners, and divide everything fifty-fifty. We could start by each contributing five million dollars. Using leverage, that'd give us one hundred million in investible funds. How's that?"

Katagira answered immediately. "I don't think so, really—although the idea in the abstract has merit. But it's too small, a fraction of what we should be committing, given the scale of the opportunity."

He sounded regretful; ah, if only there were a way . . . The trout that was Seabury looked as if in his water-distorted vision he were watching a live grenade descending slowly toward his feeding place.

Then Katagira reached up and snatched the falling bomb out of the air before it burst. "May I propose an alternative for consideration? There's money to be made. We're agreed on that. And, Mr. Seabury—I shall be frank—different problems to be solved. From our side, volume: Mr. Gudge can afford only investments which justify his attention. From your side, politics, shall we say? Mr. Seabury, you have a large stockholder whose rumored purpose is to unseat you. Let us blend the two: fire and air. Here is what I propose . . ."

When he finished, Seabury and his young man had scrambled over each other to agree, suggest minor modifications which Katagira accepted without a murmur and then, with more coffee and José's margaritas, to justify, enthuse over and celebrate the creative perception of mutual interest that had led to the forging of this bond.

An intelligent plan, all agreed. Gudge would contribute all the cash, $80 million, but half of his commitment would be invested in Seaco, for a voting interest sufficient to give Seabury the insulation he thought he needed. Seaco would reinvest this $40 million back in the bond-trading partnership, in which it would be the general, and the Lazy G the limited, partner.

On behalf of his employer, Katagira had contributed a celebratory element more giddy than champagne: the Lazy G's second-best jet stood ready for the triumphant, now-secure head of Seaco and his genius boy, who would laurel themselves a dozen times over with whisky and wine on the journey home, until they fully believed themselves to have conjured up the plan Katagira had propounded. It seemed to them, as they descended through the night to the glittering city, that it rose to greet them, tall and proud and respectful, saluting its warriors returning victorious from distant, dangerous lands with the fruits of unconditional triumph.

"There is nothing I can do about it, Granada. It's closed and done. Homer's put it over. It's legal. No one knew about it until last night when he got the board together. I voted against it. We've got thirty days to look it over, legally, and the Exchange insists on a stockholders' meeting; but Granada, he showed us enough proxies—including one on Harvey's shares somehow, damn it—to push it through."

Granada Masterman stared at Hugo and said nothing. Her expression was as dully dangerous as a shark's. He fell silent, wishing he could sneak away.

"I must say, Hugo, this smacks terribly of carelessness on someone's part." Rufus Lassiter was settled like a jackal next to Granada on the puce plush sofa in her library. He was also in a rage. He'd been with Granada the evening before; after a party at the Ethiopian Embassy; they'd been having a quiet vegetarian nightcap in her apartment when the *Pritchett's* story had been phoned to her. Having a nightcap and making plans. Plans which included $500,000 a year plus bonuses for Lassiter when Seaco became part of MUD. She'd heard it, taken in its meaning, and lapsed herself into a menacing silence.

"Homer's a fool," she said at length to the two men. "A fool." Then she lapsed into silence. Neither man spoke.

After a time, she said "Don't blame Hugo, Rufus. This is no time for fighting among ourselves." More silence.

Behind the unspeaking, primeval mask of her unhappiness, behind the blank-eyed disappointment, Granada's intelligence was functioning. Tears and emotions were for private life. She shut down her womanly reactions; problems produced a surge of logical thinking that was like adrenaline. She hadn't slept since the *Pritchett's* report had come in. First, she'd rinsed her mind of the anger that rose like steam from her hatred of Bubber. She believed Bubber would have no stomach for a public fight, not over any reasonable haul. This war would have several battles; only the last would count. It was essential that she get Seaco. The entire Masterwoman program for the next year was keyed on an investment scheme centered on control of Seaco.

"I'm all right now, you two," she said. "You can go. I'll call you."

To them, because they had mentally prejudged her as a woman, she looked mournful, broken-down, helpless and weak. Hugo and Lassiter were glad to be able to go, to flee this display of feminine frailty. She turned her drained cheeks to their solemn kisses, pressed their damp hands gratefully, sighed and heaved and bade them goodbye.

After the men had gone, Granada rose and punched up her night secretary.

"Find me Mr. Harvey Bogle, please."

It took a while. But finally, at three in the morning, she found him in Spokane, and shortly after four, made a deal to trade her block of Trans-National for his shares in Seaco. They would close as soon as it was mutually practicable.

Bogle had anticipated hearing from Granada once he learned that Gudge had bought into Seaco. He was mildly surprised that Seabury'd brought it off. These Old School types could surprise from time to time. With Gudge in there now, head to head with Granada, he wanted no part of Seaco. This could go to the death—which was longer than he wanted to play for. He had what he wanted, anyway. He could now turn his attention to Marvin Terrace; poor old Marvin—his nuts'd be right up next to his tonsils when the news of his trade with Granada got out. He'd agreed to let her handle the publicity any way she wanted; Harvey didn't fool around with appearances if he could help it.

The town of Sta. Marta, which Nick's train from Zurich was approaching, was appropriately named. Its patron saint, who had welcomed Christ into her house and fed Him, could also be considered the patron of the town's historical vocation: hotelkeeping.

Sta. Marta lay at the head of a valley, some three hours by train or car from Zurich, or a fifty-minute helicopter jaunt from the industrial cities of the Lombard plain on the other side of the Alps. The town occupied the heights above the largest of a necklace of lakes that was strung in the shadow of the mountains. For a good part of the year it could be reached by car through a number of twisting passes which connected the valley to the points of the compass. In the dead of winter, the passes were generally closed by snowdrifts or fog, slippery and unnavigable, so that the railway or, in good weather, the airport was the only means of safe entry.

In the summer season, the attractions were the air, the sun, the medicinal baths fed by a sulfur-charged spring and the high flower-flecked meadows which turned russet and ocher as August became September and the breath of night turned chilly. In summer, the lake became a pool of forest poetry, reflecting the green palette, deep, dark viridian to pale olive, of the parks and trees that bordered it. It was a season for long, invigorating walks, sometimes picked out among the boulders and clefts of high, gravel-strewn glaciers barely covered with grass; other times in the lower meadows, dappled with gentians and forget-me-nots; or among the pines, when the sun was at its height, along shadowed paths which broke upon unexpected ponds or waterfalls. It was a season for older people, for the secure of heart and spirit, for contemplation, rustication and renewal. In winter, youth dominated; the crowd was noisy, flashy and boisterous.

Two hotels dominated Sta. Marta physically and socially. The higher, some thousand feet above the lakefront, was the Bellavista Muntana, owned by Signora Ermapista; the other, on the fringes of the center of the town, looming over the lake, which reflected it gloriously on sunny days, was the Gastpalast Kratsch, the pride of its proprietor, Herr Kratsch. Although both hotels, and their owners, radiated great dignity, and were, in the six languages in common usage in the town, outspoken about their exclusivity and quality, they had been branded as "Armpit" and "Crotch" by the famous American novelist who had drunk himself to death in the *Stuebli* of the Kratsch, and it was by these sobriquets that they were familiarly known in the town and, indeed, around the world.

The two hotels reversed their relative ascendancy with the change of the seasons. In summer and early autumn, the Bellavista Muntana was the undoubted queen of Sta. Marta. It stood higher up on the mountain, where the air was fresher; it encompassed a carefully articulated series of pathways through forest and meadowland suitable to the exertions of its elderly clientele; it had its own spring and spa and a private chairlift to the lower glacier, as well as a team of excellent therapists and masseurs from Hamburg. It attracted a guest list of solid citizens, mainly of a certain age, as deep-pocketed and creditworthy as any innkeeper could wish.

Once the snow began to fly, the older, more centrally located Kratsch seized the advantage. Winter brought a flashy, racy crowd, rich and obvious, who filled every hotel in the village at prices that stopped the breath of normal people. But if the cost of a season in a decent single room at the Bellavista would have outfitted an invasion, the rates at Herr Kratsch's establishment would have underwritten a space flight. When Signora Ermapista grumbled that this was possibly due to Herr Kratsch's well-known propensity for adding the date into his guests' bills, equally knowing souls would point to her own practice of treating the standard daily 25-percent service charge as compounded interest. Both hotels were equally luxurious; both hotelkeepers were equally mean. The two establishments glared balefully at each other, summer and winter. They were keenly competitive. His Greeks came from marginally better islands than hers; her Arabs were fractionally less disgusting than his; her Americans could still afford a full season, which his apparently could not; but his English fortune-hunters seemed, on balance, to buy more champagne than hers did.

Their rivalry was immensely profitable to the town: to its plumbers, plasterers, hairdressers, disco teachers, ski-waxers, lifeguards. Laugh though they might at Crotch and Armpit, it was done out of earshot, for no Sta. Martan could deny the skill with which Herr Kratsch and Signora Ermapista skinned their guests and publicized their lodging houses. Although it had been years since they had spoken, the owner of the Bellavista and the proprietor of the Gastpalast shared the conviction that the preponderance of those who clawed and intrigued for rooms, especially in winter, could afford to do so only because of money dishonestly gotten; thanks to fortunes earned not by hard work and saving, but by the speculative luck and inflation of assets brought on by the machinations of oil sheikhs. It was their obligation, as good Swiss, to appropriate these ill-gotten gains, which they did with a zestful vengeance.

As might be expected, Solomon Greschner stayed at the Bellavista. He had begun coming there twenty-five years earlier, shortly after his wife had been institutionalized for chronic depression and his son had become estranged from him. The stately atmosphere of Signora Ermapista's hotel and the excellence of her Parma chef suited him. Nevertheless, he had—in the ineffable, mysterious Greschner fashion—contrived to strike up excellent relations with Herr Kratsch as well. The relationship had been helped along by Dr. Frucht, to whom Sol had carried a letter of introduction from Victor Sartorian, many of whose patients stayed in the winter season at the Gastpalast Kratsch, where Frucht functioned as the notional house physician. Greschner had become fast friends with the Swiss doctor, whom he recognized as the genuine article. Frucht was much more than a doctor, Sol thought; just in the way that Victor Sartorian was much less. He was a polymath: an accomplished pianist and watercolorist; an admirer of Goethe and Turgenev; a man of integrity and philosophy who fearlessly prescribed aspirin and broth to Park Avenue heiresses berserkly screaming for amphetamines. During the two weeks of Sol's annual sojourn, he and Frucht dined together almost nightly, on odd nights with Herr Kratsch in his private dining room. The hotel proprietor had been quick to perceive that there was more than enough of the Greschner effect for both himself and his rival up the hill. So long as Herr Greschner's recommendations filled suites at the Gastpalast and the newspaper connection which Herr Greschner had established kept the name of the hotel on the most fashion-conscious, extravagant tongues in America, what did Kratsch care if Herr Greschner slept under Signora Ermapista's luscious eiderdowns?

On the evening that Nick arrived in Sta. Marta for his annual three-day communing with Sol, after a flight from London and a pleasant train ride through the mountains, Greschner had scheduled them to dine with Dr. Frucht at the very good restaurant in the neighboring village. As usual, Sol met Nick with a horse cart at the railway station; there was plenty of time before they were due to meet Frucht in the bar of the Bellavista.

"So, Nicholas, what's the news from London?" They were settled in the cart for the peaceful twenty-minute clip-clop from the station to Sol's hotel. Nick told him about the Giotto.

Along Bond Street, the word was that Grundy's had put a £4-million reserve on the picture and was going to stick to it. The seller was a rich man, after all, and not English; he was not some penniless county noble obliged to sell to pay death duties. To get the picture into its rooms, Grundy's must have promised a very handsome minimum figure. That worked out to close to $8 million—which would make it the most expensive picture ever sold at auction, if it got to that price. As to potential bidders, who could say? The German museums who had dominated the Hirsch sales in 1978 were out of gas; the end of the *Wirtschaftswunder* had seen to that. It seemed unlikely that the California museums which had teamed up to buy the Chatsworth Poussin could be back for more so soon. So who was there? The German prince? the Greek? the mysterious Argentinian? the old Chicago tycoon whose wallet seemed as limitless as his vanity? He had to be running out of money by now. Possibly someone out of left field—maybe a Texan. There wasn't an Arab in creation who'd buy a painting of the Virgin and Child. It could be a small field. Too small to justify the kind of reserve that was being talked about over the fried plaice at Wilton's.

Nick thought Bogle should go after it. It might take as much as $9 million. He wasn't just idly playing about with his client's money. Bogle had told him that he wanted to go after only the best and rarest of what was left. If it happened that Giotto came on the heels of Rubens, so what? That was the turn of the cards. He could handle $9 million, Bogle had told Nick; at much over that, it would start to look expensive. But he wanted to be sure that Nick thought he should. Which meant going to London with Carraccino for consultation; when he got back, he would head up to Boston for a soul-search with Felix Rothschild. Then he'd get back to Bogle and tell him what he thought. Bogle's objective wasn't complicated: he just wanted the best and was willing to pay market for it. The only caveat was that Bogle had to have some empathy with what he was buying. As it happened, he would be coming to London in nine days, and Nick had arranged with Grundy's that Bogle have a private view of the picture. That was certainly no problem. Since the announcement of the gift of the Hercules cycle to the Fuller Institute, Harvey Bogle's name had acquired magical powers in the upmost circles of the art world.

"Well, here we are." The carriage had drawn up under the looming porte-cochère of the Bellavista. Sol bustled Nick into the lobby and up to his room. "I'll see you in an hour in the bar. Frucht's coming to join us; there's a marvelous little restaurant in Saas."

They dined with Dr. Frucht. Over *Bündnerfleisch* and an excellent local white wine, they talked of many things. Frucht was a man for whom no subject was without interest, nor on which he was ever without some information or insight. Later, veal with morels and gnocchi and a bottle of old Dôle lent a weightier, more philosophical tone to their conversation. Nick watched Sol open up; in Sta. Marta, Nick knew, the inner Greschner had a way of coming to the surface, leaving the other people's lives in which, like a hermit crab, it lived so much of the time.

Over brandy, Frucht and Sol, in the fashion of elderly men mourning better times, spoke of the worsened state of life and society.

"It's right out of *Vanity Fair*," said Frucht. He quoted Thackeray: " '. . . A title and a coach and four are toys more precious than happiness in Vanity Fair.' A sad situation, my friends; a sad situation." He drank deeply of his brandy. Nick looked across the table at Sol. He could not escape the feeling that something malign was rising in Sol, moving slowly toward the surface like a sulfurous bubble in a prehistoric swamp.

CHAPTER FIFTEEN

"Well," said Jill, as she and Nick went up the steps and entered the old Fuller Mansion, "this marks the beginning of the silly season. It'll end in late March, probably in Palm Beach, and I will be a very busy lady. Except this year, my consort, when and if I can, I will draw considerable comfort from your presence at my side."

It was not a prospect that thrilled Nick with expectation. He saw himself being stitched, like a helpless thread, into an awful tapestry of foolishness that would cover winter like a tent.

Not that he hadn't been warned.

Jill had said, "You've got this thing about rich people, Nick, yet I'm not sure you really know what you're muttering to yourself about. So I'm going to head you through my landscape."

Tonight was step one.

They climbed the stairs to the Reading Room. To Nick's dismay, the square hall at the top was filled with people he thought looked very peculiar.

Jill anticipated his reaction.

"Esmé's got them all out tonight, I see."

"Who's 'them all'?"

"The 'Bucks 'n' Books' crowd. Her peers in best-sellerdom. I'm surprised to see them all here, and then again, I'm not; these people watch each other like hawks."

To Nick, who confined his novel-reading to thrillers, Dickens, and P. G. Wodehouse, with occasional happy venturings into the social comics like Lardner and Powell, it was all quite mysterious.

They found Frodo Crisp near the door to the Reading Room, which, they could see, was filling up rapidly.

"Good evening, Frodo."

"Nicholas; Jill. I am utterly exhausted by this. My system is too frail to endure anything like this ever again."

It seemed, as Frodo explained, that the Fuller Reader was normally allotted forty seats for her claque. The balance of the three hundred were issued to the Fellows and Associates of the Institute and to the Manhattan literary and academic establishment; roughly twenty seats were available to the Director, whose guest Nick was, and the trustees. There had never been a problem before—not when Faulkner, Robert Lowell or Arthur Miller had read at the Institute. The announcement of Esmé as the Reader had, as Frodo put it, "unleashed the dogs of war." First, it had turned out that Esmé numbered an extraordinary number of clandestine fans among the black-tied, blue-haired, lisp-voiced Fellows and Associates. Esmé herself had required no fewer than seventy seats. Fortunately, her Reading was boycotted by the Critics Council and PEN, so that enough seats were found. But the mess had brought Frodo's administrative staff to the brink of resignation.

As Jill and Nick went into the Reading Room, Frodo said, without a smile, "I believe this may be the most extraordinary evening in the history of this Institute."

They found seats halfway down the room, which was buzzing with anticipation.

"Have you ever read Esmé's novels, Nick?"

"No."

"You've missed something. They're quite remarkable. The sex in them is not only multidimensional but multidirectional. You can open them at any page and read in either direction and it all makes about the same degree of sense."

Finally, the hall was filled, the lights along the walls dimmed and it was painfully apparent to Nick that the hour was at hand. He winked at Sol, a late arrival, who had found a seat at the end of the row in front of them. Sol replied by lifting his eyebrows almost to the ceiling.

A hush fell on the room. Frodo advanced to the lectern and addressed the audience in what Nick knew to be his most elegant, civilized manner.

"Ladies and gentlemen; Trustees, Fellows, Associates and other friends of the Fuller Institute; honored guests: For close to forty years, it has been the custom of this Institute to present distinguished practitioners of the literary traditions of Europe and the United States. Among these, the popular, vernacular novel has perhaps not been sufficiently recognized in our programs—an oversight which I believe tonight's reading will do much to correct. From Richardson and Fielding through Dickens and Trollope, Galsworthy and Henry James, to the Marquands, O'Haras and Anthony Powells of our day, the broad novel of social context has been at the forefront of popular letters. As much as any single group, the fair sex has carried its honorable share of this tradition. One need only mention Jane Austen, Emily Eden, the Brontës, Mrs. Wharton. Artists who spoke in their own special way, in a vocabulary rich in the detail of lives of privilege and cultivation, for their times, their milieu and their gender. In tonight's Fuller Reader, those concerns are once again conflated. May I give you Mrs. Esmé Bogle."

Stepping down, Nick saw on Frodo's face an expression which suggested that the Fuller Director knew, to the shame of his sense of harmony between subject and technique, that he had used a cannon to salute the launching of a rowboat.

Esmé mounted the small platform on which the lectern was set. The triumphant, radiant smile that she had presented all day was infinitesimally troubled by a microscopic frown. She wasn't sure about Crisp's introduction; "conflated" sounded suspiciously as if it had something to do with "fart." But the sight of the audience whisked any doubts away, and as she took her place at the podium her little eyes sparkled with delight, and she flashed the smile familiar to a nation of talk-show viewers.

"My God," murmured Jill. "She looks like a gift candle."

"Hush," said Nick. But it was true. Esmé's couturier of the week had responded to her request for something "*très* Emily Dickinson" with a chaste white gown tied under the bosom with a broad crimson sash which was knotted at her ribs with an enormous bow; it did nothing to elongate Esmé's admittedly compact figure. Her hair was swept up in a single stiffened pigtail, which did in fact give the effect of a wick; it was the fashion of the week, "Manhattan coolie," which Massimo von González had decreed in belated recognition of normalized relations with China.

"I am going to read tonight," Esmé began, "from my best-seller in progress, *Countess*, a novel of wealth, passion and power.

"Unfortunately, as film and first-serial rights are in the process of negotiation, it won't be possible to disclose the plot, except to say that it concerns the life of an alluring American doctor named Perdida, a beautiful, troubled woman with a secret in her past as dark as the flashing eyes that win the love of cruel, sadistic Sir Reservoir Eagle, heir to the Earldom of Clermont —a countess, you see, is the wife of an earl—and thus leads her into a tempestuous world of society and internal medicine."

Esmé gave a pretty little flounce, donned a large pair of gem-ornamented harlequin glasses, opened the folder before her and began to read.

> "Perdida Ashcroft had the largest nipples and most thickly fleeced pubis in her class at Miss Simsbury's, the exclusive girls' boarding school located in an exclusive suburb of Willimantic, Connecticut, some hundred miles north of New York City which cost $8,325 per year tuition plus uniforms that had to be ordered from the couture department of Saks Fifth Avenue, the exclusive department store on the corner of Fiftieth Street, just across from Saint Patrick's Cathedral, which was built in 1879–1888, proud bastion, and specialized in exclusive *haute couture* clothes such as those of Oscar de la Renta, on Fifth Avenue . . ."

A silence fell on the Reading Room. Her slight voice carried clearly to her transfixed audience. As she read on, the audience, divided equally between stunned trauma and rapt, adoring attention, seemed in a trance that would have done Tristan credit. Nick, stupefied, squeezed his hands and tried not to look at Jill.

Esmé read for the next forty-five minutes. As far as Nick could follow, her female characters, when they weren't at boarding school, spent most of their time either at Gucci, or at Pucci, or at various well-known restaurants. The male characters were constantly at "exclusive" clubs in New York and London, none of which Nick, who got around in both cities, had ever heard of. The characters of both genders spent much time becoming "engorged," which seemed to prefigure "coming to Orgasm," the last presumably a state of extreme physical excitement, although from Esmé's dislocated prose and peculiar pronunciation of certain words, it might also have been a resort in France. As best Nick could judge, Esmé's novel featured more Russian princes than *War and Peace* and a vocabulary equally as specific as but sadly less erotic than Dr. Van de Velde's *Ideal Marriage*, a work that his eighth-grade class had considered the summit of libidinous wickedness.

At last, she seemed to be winding down.

> ". . . Mamie had helped Perdida into the once-in-a-lifetime gown which Ramón Finisterra had confected for her. 'Yo' sho' am de bes' belle ob dis ball, Perdy,' said the grinning Negress, a descendant of slaves whose ancestor was reputed to have slept with President Millard Fillmore. Perdida looked in the mirror and saw the gentle dumpling of her chin melding with the two little rosebuds of her mouth. With the comb and brush that her grandmother had given her mother at the latter's debut in 1939 at the exclusive Piping Rock Club where her family had been members for six generations, with its luxurious white clubhouse and facilities for all sports including golf and horsemanship, Perdida finished the tripedal geometry of her toilette and rose, so that the skirts of her gown spread about her like rose-petaled water. She felt someone behind her and turned, so that the light on the brilliants in her auburn tresses made splinterlike glints which reflected off her father's stern face. She saw that he was engorged. 'Oh, Daddy,' she murmured, because she loved her generous father, reaching for his fly, which still had buttons because the Savile Row tailors, Snood and Grewbury, which he had been going to on the advice of many of his partners insisted on buttons, while he encircled her swollen nipples with his tongue and her vulva grew incredulous. 'Oh, Daddy,' Perdida sighed, hoping her father wouldn't break too many sequins, but she was burning now with icy ripples which ran from her follicles to her rosy toes while downstairs her guests waited, including many photographers from leading magazines."

Esmé closed the folder and stepped back, head bowed, in the modest attitude of Callas at her farewell. The Reading Room erupted in applause; there were tears in many of the women's eyes. Graciously, Frodo let Esmé wallow in the clapping for another minute before he rose to lead her from the platform and out the side door that led through his office to the Book Room, in which, appropriately, the reception was to be held.

It was enough to be carried along by the crowd pushing out the main doors of the Reading Room, so that Nick and Jill said nothing until they were inside the double-storied Book Room, champagne in hand.

"I'm speechless."

"My darling, five million women can't be wrong. It's fantasy, which a lot of women need. Just ask Granada. There's no point in being snooty. Esmé's audience doesn't care about style."

They were joined by Sol and by Frodo, who had left the star of the evening surrounded by admirers. "Wasn't it marvelous?" said Crisp. "There's something positively awesome about an absolute lack of talent and taste."

Sol nodded and looked around the room. "All the leading lights seem to be here, I must say. The Pantheon of best-sellerdom."

Downstairs, Jill excused herself to work the room; Nick remained with Sol, surveying the scene.

It was quite something, he thought, seeing all the movers and makers of commercial fiction compacted like garbage into this one room. He recognized a number of faces from the personality press: a man gotten up in a camouflage suit whose innuendo-filled thrillers catered to the conspiracy paranoia of the day; a gloating Englishman famed for generational page-turners containing no adverbs, adjectives or any sign of interest in language; at the vortex of one eddy of favor-seekers stood a spiky-haired, assertive man: Milty Mosker, the legendary accountant/agent who had broken the bank at a dozen publishing houses. They made quite a sight, these frantic purveyors of literature to an illiterate age.

His gaze fixed on a scowling, blue-jeaned fireplug of a man leaning against a far wall, besieged by adoring blue-haired ladies.

"Isn't that Henry Grappler over there, Sol? The dwarf that looks like he's got gas pains."

"Not gas pains, Nicholas. He is merely looking writerly. That is his *métier.*"

Grappler was currently in vogue. His scowl, hinting of profundities and enigmas beyond ordinary ken, grimaced from the pages and covers of dozens of periodicals. His first successful novel, *Plop*, had become the intellectual banner of adolescents of every age. His latest, *Condo Poopoo*, had been hailed by a leading newsweekly for its "exuberant fecal pyrotechnics."

"Actually," Sol continued, "Grappler should be gloating. Milty's just done him a fabulous licensing deal, with that other little man who designs fashion versions of lumberjack clothes and cowboy suits; they're going to do a line of writer's gear. Prefrayed work shorts and baggy sweaters; tweed jackets impregnated with pipe tobacco; patched flannels. Milty's thrilled. They're going to call the line 'Clothes According to Plop.' "

They were joined by Frodo.

"Well, my friends," said Crisp, "and what do you think of our little collision with literature? Wild and wondrous, no? I've just been talking to the most extraordinary man who seemed to have parachuted in for the evening; at least, he was dressed that way. He kept going on about how all my nice old ladies in the Junior League are actually Russian agents. Is this country mad, or am I? Anyway, come with me, Nicholas; Jill; Solomon. I want you to see something."

He took them down the hall, around a corner and down a short flight of stairs, to a large door beside which Bogle was waiting. Frodo unlocked it and flicked on the lights.

The room was about fifteen feet square, Nick guessed; the walls had been covered in dark green velvet. Frodo flicked a switch, and pinlights set in the picture molding picked out the twelve sketches, which had been hung on three walls. The sketches had been framed in Flemish and Italian period frames, Nick saw, of dark wood; no two were quite alike, but they worked well as an ensemble. The sketches were arrayed in the order of the Labors, beginning with The Nemean Lion and ending with Cerberus. A rail running around the room about a foot off the floor kept viewers at a safe distance from the sketches and supported a large, legible label for each painting. These complemented two large, poster-sized labels on either side of the door which expounded the paintings' hypothetical history and summarized Rubens' artistic career.

"Terrific framing, Frodo. I'm glad you didn't settle for copies. They look just right."

"Thank you, Nicholas, although I must admit that Harvey helped me make up my mind. We found six of these right here in the city, and scrounged another five in Paris, Rome and Brussels; and the Metropolitan, I must say, was extremely decent about letting me have one off that perfectly odious Brouwer that Sir John *will* insist on hanging."

Nick looked overhead. There was a skylight crisscrossed with alarm tapes. He guessed the room enjoyed good natural light in the daytime.

"Have you got them sonically protected?"

"Absolutely. The very latest and best system—and at a good price, too, since it turns out Harvey owns the company that makes it. Put a hand within an inch of the surface or the edge of the frame and off go the trumpets of Hell."

The small group spent twenty minutes admiring the room and the sketches. As he locked up, Frodo sighed, "Of course, the pity is that we'll not be able to show them this way for some time. We'll have to put them over the way in the Annex to accommodate the crowds. The public clamor to see anything expensive is considerable, but in a few months I expect it will have died down, as it always has. Just like the Lehman Wing at the Metropolitan. They pack in like sardines for six months and then silence. Six-day wonders, that's what this country likes."

On the way back, Nick asked, "Do you mind if we cut and run? Are you through, love?"

"I guess so. No, I don't mind. Let's say good night. I know what's on your mind; this crowd of phonies is tough to take after just twenty minutes with the real thing."

While Jill bade Esmé good night, Nick wandered over to a glass case that had been set up in the vestibule. It contained first editions of Dickens. One was Sol's copy of *Little Dorrit*; Dickens had presented it to George Eliot. The author's inscription, in Dickens' forceful, unruly hand, was scrawled across the bottom of the last page, under the book's closing lines, which Nick read aloud, feeling Jill take his arm:

" 'And so they went down . . . while the noisy and the eager, and the arrogant and the forward and the vain, fretted and chafed and made their usual uproar.' " He looked back into the Book Room, hearing the chatter and babble; then he and Jill made their way out.

CHAPTER SIXTEEN

"So—the bottom line is, they've decided to go public with GOD and GUT, and to hold off on the energy/exploration trust for the time being. Right, Homer?"

Seabury nodded at Financial Engineering and then around the table. He had convoked a meeting of Seaco's Executive Committee to give final approval to the firm's commitment to act as managing underwriter for the initial public offerings of Gudge Oil Development and Gudge Energy Technology. The formal invitation to Seaco had come two days earlier in a call, surprisingly, from Gudge himself. Seabury had expected to hear from Katagira; he had Financial Engineering waiting in his office in case there were additional technical matters to be discussed. Instead, over the speakerphone came the shy voice of the proprietor himself.

"Mr. Seabury, Buford Gudge here. I wanted to make this a personal call to tell you that I've decided to see if you good folks would be interested in helping us get a public market for two of our units. I want to say we've been right impressed by the work that's been done by you and your people. You seem to be our kind of people."

Listening at Gudge's side, Katagira was pleased to hear the words emerge just as rehearsed.

The two men on the Seaco end could barely contain themselves; Seabury made hushing signs with his hands, then replied, in a voice Financial Engineering found rather pompous, "Well, that is certainly good news, Mr. Gudge. How exactly do you wish to proceed?"

"Well, we'd like to get some real distribution for these securities. I mean, there doesn't seem to be much point in *goin'* public if you don't *get* public, don't you see. I was thinkin' maybe to sell two hundred and fifty million dollars of common stock for th'oil company, Gudge Oil Development—sell ten million shares at twenty-five dollars, like you recommended—and raise 'bout the same for the service business, Gudge Undersurface Technology

—say, maybe eight million shares at thirty dollars, again like you suggested. That sound doable to you?"

Seabury looked over at Financial Engineering questioningly. The younger man identified himself into the speakerphone. "Mr. Gudge, that's nicely within the parameters we had discussed. What about our idea for the royalty trust on your U.S. production?"

"Well, sir, I b'lieve we'll wait on that one a bit. We got to put some pretty decent producing acreage in the oil company along with the wildcat leases, kind of to dress it up a bit, and I'd like to leave myself some options. Then you got to get a trustee and all that stuff; and frankly, Mr. Seabury, now I've decided to go, I'd sure like to get going."

"I understand." Seabury hoped the connection would have blurred the obvious disappointment in his colleague's voice. These young men surrendered their inspirations grudgingly.

"So, those are the metes and bounds," Gudge continued. "What's the next move? Y'all want us to gin up some more figures?"

"Quite possibly." Seabury wanted to enjoy a few more minutes bringing this fish he'd hooked to the gaff. "The ball's in our court now. We'll have to run this by our Executive Committee; I explained to Mr. Katagira that their final approval is necessary for any transaction involving a possible capital commitment by Seaco Group."

He had not explained that approval by his executive Committee on *his* deals was a foregone conclusion. He liked to be gentlemanly, to hear out the objections, suggestions and apprehensions of the other members of the committee and treat them with decent intellectual respect. But he had a way of making it unspokenly clear that heel-digging dissenters could expect to begin the next week selling insurance.

"I understand that. Now there's just a couple other things. One, I got to put a couple of boards of directors together for these two companies. I'm gonna need you to help me with that. We don't know a whole lot of folks of the kind that sit on boards. 'Course, I b'lieve you'd agree with me that we don't want a bunch of independent directors who're too darn independent and make it hard for us to do business. D'you get my meaning?"

Gudge's second problem was more complicated, he said, and he thought it would be better if Mr. Katagira huddled long-distance with Seabury's young man, who'd be honchoing the deal anyway. It was left that Financial Engineering and Gudge's side would confer later in the day to pick up on any unresolved matters, prior to rubber-stamping the deal at an Executive Committee meeting.

"We'll be back to you, then, Mr. Gudge, in a couple of days, with some ideas on timing and spread, and to figure who does what to whom."

As he hung up the phone, Bubber couldn't help noticing that Katagira, who had been on an extension, was smiling.

"Well?"

"It couldn't have gone better. You did extremely well. Every Wall Street firm has some kind of committee to approve its underwritings and capital exposure. It spreads the blame within the firm if anything should go wrong. After what I have to tell Mr. Seabury's financial engineer this afternoon, there might be some commotion on Mr. Seabury's Executive Committee, but I expect, in view of the sums involved, he will prevail and carry their votes. I predict the following: when Seabury—or that overcogent young man of his—gets back to us, they'll want us to bring in some independent experts to look at our accounts and oil and gas reserves: accounts which are made up out of thin air; oil and gas reserves which exist only on paper. We'll bully them out of the first, as we've discussed, and I think we can rely on Buckets Maxwell to help us out on the second. When they find out how easy, and generous, we are to deal with on the question of underwriting compensation, their breasts will be at peace."

"Well, you're the expert. I got to say that if I was going to lay out a commitment of five hundred million dollars, I'd want a real good look at the figures and the engineering."

"Certainly. But that would be your money you'd be laying out, not the investing public's. And no one would be waving, say, twenty-five million in underwriting fees to tempt you to think twice about sticking to your guns, and possibly losing a very lucrative piece of business. Mr. Gudge, twenty years ago, Wall Street houses of Seaco's caliber didn't touch commodities or hostile takeover bids or unaudited figures—from anyone! But there are a great many people down there who need to live well, and the business was there, and it proposed to pay exceptionally well, and the older generation was dying out, so the ancient standards—scruples, if you will—died with surprising ease. All it took was one, you see; the first mold-breaker did his bit and the race was on.

"I think," concluded Katagira, "we may reasonably rely on the old siren song to drown out any reservations. 'If we don't do it,' Seabury will say to his people, 'someone else will.' "

Seabury turned to Financial Engineering. "Why don't you run down the gray areas? And maybe Hugo can fill us in on the legalities." He smiled at Winstead, whom he had asked to join the meeting in his capacity as Seaco's outside counsel.

"Well, none of us have any problems with the numbers. The oil company's got strong assets; no debt; a great-looking acreage position, domestic and overseas, and a good cash flow. Hell, if you wanted to design a big, independent exploration-production company from scratch, you couldn't do better than this. Same thing with the service business, which is essentially a recombination of a bunch of existing Gudge/Lazy G businesses renamed and put under one flag. Which the exploration company is too, for that matter. But on the basic businesses, there's no problem. The numbers tell the tale.

"The only problem arises from the fact that this is a private empire we're dealing with. It belonged to one man. Of course, it's worth several billion dollars. Which is some comfort, because you can't keep track of anything as big and diversified as this on the back of an envelope. But they use captive accountants of their own: they bought out McQueen & Kimmel, the Dallas firm that ranked about fifteenth in the country, a few years ago. It's maintained as a separate unit, and it only handles Gudge's regulated businesses, the banks and TV stations, plus a number of outside engagements. It has a good reputation, but it's still a Gudge unit, which, for us, means not much cold comfort on the numbers. We're talking about two prospectuses relating to offerings totaling around five hundred million dollars, which are going to have this firm's name on them. And we're not going to get even a fresh internal audit—which is, frankly, what we ought to have —because they're on a May fiscal, so the internally audited figures will be six months old, which is pretty out of date. To get Price Waterhouse or another Big Eight firm in to scrub the books would take six to eight weeks and cost somebody about a million bucks, and I can tell you there's no way Gudge'd stand for either the delay or the cost."

"Are you saying that there's no chance of a special audit?" asked one of the older officers.

"That's the way it looks."

The senior man looked at Homer. "Good God, Homer, are you even considering putting our name on a prospectus without fresh figures? I've been here thirty years and we've never done that!"

Homer eyed him serenely.

"We've never had a shot at a piece of business like this. Use some perspective, man. Don't you realize who this is? This is Buford Gudge IV. This is the richest man in the country!"

He signaled Financial Engineering to continue.

"On the reserves, there's something of the same problem. They use in-house engineers for their reserve reports; Gudge started the unit with a couple of defectors from DeGolyer and McNaughton. The scuttlebutt in Houston and Denver is that the work's state-of-the-art, but it's not the same as having D&M or Keplinger massage the computer runs and look over the engineering. But there we may be able to work something out."

After much discussion and several glares and sniffs from Homer, a consensus was reached. The Gudge business was, after all, potentially the hottest new offering ever to come to Wall Street. These weren't chickenshit operators; this was Buford Gudge IV, as Homer had emphasized; the Lazy G—names that caused heads to dip deferentially wherever men got together to talk oil or money. To risk losing the business on technicalities would be dumb. So they decided that they'd settle for whatever the McQueen firm could give them, and as reassuring a letter as they could get on the interim quarterly figures, provided they got an indemnity from Gudge himself. On the reservoir engineering, they would have to persuade Gudge to let an outside firm vet the reserve reports; the list included three or four outfits the experienced energy hands around the table knew to be likely to report what was required. After all, reserve engineering—unlike accounting —was not an exact science.

"How's this all sound to you, Hugo?" Seabury asked.

Winstead's firm wasn't paid its half-million-dollar retainer to cause problems or exacerbate internal disputes. He adopted a serious mien.

"Well, Homer, these are all really business judgments. If it was anyone other than someone of Gudge's scale and known probity, I'd say think twice before forgoing a special audit on a new issue and settling for an indemnity. I think we all recognize the risks implicit in making a significant exception in our normal practice for any client of this firm, especially if that client is also its largest stockholder. But on balance, considering who that client-stockholder is, and what he's known to be worth, I think your exposure's tolerable."

Very statesmanlike, Hugo, thought his listeners. Just the words we want to hear. You walk a dozen tightropes a day professionally and personally and not a wavy, splendid hair is ruffled. I admire you, you ice-water sonofabitch.

Financial Engineering was deputed to work out the details of preparing the offering. As usual, the prospectus would be drafted by Gudge's counsel and the underwriting and other papers by Winstead's firm, which would act as counsel for the underwriting group.

"Who'll Gudge use for counsel?" asked someone. "Hagerty and Duvall? Didn't they represent him in Washington once?"

"I understand he's got his own people in-house who'll handle the registration statement. These people don't like to go outside." Financial Engineering was very firm; with the deal having safely passed the Executive Committee, he was now sitting squarely on the side of his new client, and reveling in the details.

"What about marketing?" asked the head of the Syndicate Department; he would be responsible for putting together the underwriting group—which would probably include two hundred firms of all sizes—and allocating the shares of GOD and GUT within the group. From him, and through the head of the Sales Department, would come the sense of the market's reception of the two offerings, which in turn would determine the price at which GOD and GUT would be sold to the public.

"What are your ideas?" asked Seabury.

"I'd like to dog-and-pony it."

Seabury exploded. "Are you insane? Drag Mr. Gudge around the country like a vaudeville act for every regional broker that wants a look? This isn't going to be a circus!"

"Well, will he come up for the Due Diligence meeting? Christ, Homer, he's got to face the underwriters and let them ask him questions, so they can say they've at least done some looking into this deal on their own and aren't just taking it on our say-so."

"Mr. Gudge will, I'm sure, attend the information meeting."

"What about spread?" asked someone.

The issue of what to charge a client for a service, whether it was arranging a loan or taking a stock issue public, was always a critical matter. Corporations had a fairly complete understanding of what other companies paid for equivalent services. Except for the merger business, in which absolute, irresponsible madness seemed to be the rule, investment-banking fees were carefully scrutinized in the interest of comparative equity. Within any firm, it could be expected that each officer would fight like a tiger to see that the firm's other officers' corporate clients paid more than his.

Financial Engineering's reply sedated them.

"We've had preliminary conversations on the subject; Gudge is prepared to spring for the high end of the scale. That's one of the trade-offs on the audit matter."

Savage hearts pumped reposefully in savage breasts.

"So, then . . ." Seabury wrapped it up. "We accept his indemnity on the accounting, and get a decent engineering firm to bless the reserve report. We expect to be able to make the offerings in early December. Price and spread will be determined by market conditions at the time."

The rest of the table nodded consensus, although one or two of the older men seemed to fall short of genuine ebullience.

As the meeting disbanded, Financial Engineering threw a jovial, familiar arm across Seabury's shoulders. "You know, Homer, that's the thing about these Texas people. Their word is everything."

The next morning, the older partner, showing the signs of a sleepless night, showed up in Seabury's office.

"Homer, I'm handing in my cards. Quitting."

Seabury looked at him without much care or attempted understanding. There was too much going on to deal with each man's neurosis.

"Mind telling me why?" he asked; his voice showed little interest in what the answer would be.

"Well, I suppose the catalyst is this Gudge thing, but maybe it's just that the world's changed. That's probably it. We seem to have kicked all the old standards out the window. I doubt, for example, that your father would have given the same advice that Hugo Winstead gave us yesterday."

"What's my father got to do with it? He's been dead for years."

The older man looked at Homer.

"Not for all of us, Homer. If you don't mind my saying: not for you either, until recently."

Seabury had work to do. A business to run. Hands-on. He had time only for those who were along for the whole great adventure that Seaco had suddenly become. His impatience was obvious.

"One last thing, Homer. Those are very glib, bright men you've brought in. Very quick. And very glib, if you don't mind me repeating myself. But they are different from us, Homer; from you and me—don't you see? They make me uncomfortable. They are so action-oriented." He shook his head sadly. "This firm was my life, Homer; it must be almost more than that to you. It bears your name."

"The times have changed, I'm afraid." Homer extended his hand. "We must change with them. Even if it's difficult."

Alone again, he reflected for a minute, no longer, on what his departing associate had said. Like it or not, he really had no choice but to grasp the hand of salvation as firmly as he could. How could a savior be other than benevolent, anyway? For the first time in many months, he felt in command.

Katagira's conversation with Financial Engineering was a model of satisfaction on both sides. He took down Seaco's thoughts as to reliable reservoir engineers; they knew Maxwell and Good pretty well, he said. He'd get the material to them. He was certain Mr. Gudge would indemnify the underwriters, and Seaco in particular, against any misrepresentations or accounting problems. Even though their accountants were part of the Lazy G family, it remained a fine, independent firm. He'd get the inside lawyers cracking on making a facsimile transmission of the relevant documents to Winstead's offices so that the attorneys for the underwriters could satisfy themselves on matters of title and other boilerplate. And his people would get started forthwith on putting the registration together. All the SEC matrices were stored in his information system; to get a draft was mainly a matter of turning the machines loose to winnow the Lazy G's data base for what was needed and fit it into the matrix. Then that too could be facsimile-transmitted to the Winstead firm for comment, reedited back in Texas and facsimile-transmitted to the financial printers in Manhattan to be finalized for filing with the Securities and Exchange Commission. There might be no need at all for an all-hands, face-to-face meeting, thanks to the telecommunications interface.

When he had finished with Seaco, Katagira thought for a minute. His computer battery was programmed for SEC filings. It would be roughly an hour's work for the machines to dredge up the raw information on his imaginary companies and print a draft for his review. The work normally performed by a half-dozen young attorneys boilerplating and scissoring and pasting a registration statement. With the information room at his disposal, he could act alone as house counsel and staff. He was also *de facto* senior partner of McQueen & Kimmel and therefore able to sign off on any figures or representations that went out on that firm's letterhead. Corporations, investment bankers, buyers and sellers routinely received and relied on the signatures of "Price Waterhouse," "Touche Ross" or any of the Big Eight public-accounting firms. What they saw were handwritten, generic signatures that gave no clue who personally had done the signing. The ultimate in self-protective institutional anonymity. With the right tools to hand, life could be so easily organized, he thought. All that remained on the day's agenda was for Gudge to telephone Buckets Maxwell in Houston and visit a bit on the subject of old times and old favors. Buckets was a grateful man.

The world became truly a manageable place, he reflected, if one owned it.

Bogle had returned to New York on the four-o'clock shuttle, after spending most of the morning at Felix Rothschild's office at the small, all-girl liberal-arts college near the Gardner Museum, followed by a long lunch at the Ritz. Felix was the ornament of his faculty. He had spurned repeated offers to move across the river to Harvard, or to convey his reputation and following to New Haven or New York. His mother had come from a rich Jewish banking family, so Felix had no need of money. Twice widowed, he lived in a large frame house in a leafy cul-de-sac in Cambridge, tended by a series of jovial Irish women.

Nick had accepted Felix' invitation to stay for dinner and the night. They had seen Bogle into a taxi after lunch. The meeting had been productive. Felix had reassured Bogle on the merits of the Giotto; he had shown him a group of large, detailed photographs, including an infrared series, which he planned to include in the new edition of *Giotto and His Century*. He was entirely convincing—as Nick had known he would be. Felix wore the fourteenth century like a rich, tapestried cape that had been specially woven for him. It seemed that like a sorcerer, he could spread his arms and envelop his listeners in his magical cloak. Nick thought him the noblest of men: wise, attentive, honestly cultivated, possessed of a rich, compelling measure of theatricality. His deep, mellifluous voice resonated the echoing halls of Tuscan palaces and the sleepy noontime streets of otherwise bustling hill towns. He was still handsome; his dark sleekness couldn't totally obscure how gorgeous a young man he must have been. Even now, as he approached seventy, it remained a matter of scandalous buzzing among the weaving spiders of the Harvard Faculty Club that not a few of the comely Radcliffe girls who hastened across the Charles to audit Felix' twice-weekly lectures sooner or later awoke to hear the birds in the dawn-lit branches overhanging the gracious house in Ellery Place. It was in fact this delightful benefit that kept Felix anchored in the still backwaters of the Fenway.

"You realize, Nicholas, that I could never teach at Harvard. I am too utterly dedicated to Radcliffe women, which could prove complicating. Their combination of mind and sheer sensual enthusiasm produces the most extraordinary priapic effects in me."

When Felix had declared this, it had struck Nick that his former mentor had the only truly tumescent voice he had ever heard.

The Ritz doorman hustled after Felix' Mercedes. Professor Rothschild had the sort of presence that sent busboys and porters jumping while billionaires cooled their heels. It was the sort of afternoon that showed Boston at its best; a crisp wind gusting off the Common, riffling the surface of the ponds and tearing the leaves from the trees. There hadn't been much in the way of autumn this year—more a series of postscriptive, unpleasant little summers separated by odd streaks of cool weather. To Nick's relief, it looked as though the seasons had finally broken.

"I shall see you later at Ellery Place, Nicholas. Don't be too early. I have given Mrs. Denehy the afternoon off and I have a conference with a student. About five, shall we say?"

That suited Nick. He wanted to stop by the Museum of Fine Arts and show some photographs to an old school friend who was the chief curator of paintings. Boston had some money these days, he'd heard—and the museum needed to beef up its sixteenth-century Italian holdings. There was a wonderful, big Jacopo Bassano rumored to be coming on the market, an *Adoration* from an Italian private collection that was almost as good as the great *Flight into Egypt* at Pasadena. And he had a line on a Constable *Midsummer Landscape* in the collection of a church school that was running out of money; there wasn't a museum in America that wasn't chasing after what Nick thought were hopelessly overrated German Romantic paintings. The Boston Museum could well be interested in both of these. He wanted to stop by the Fogg and talk to Pfeffenselz, the drawings expert, about three so-called Signorellis that a Swiss dealer was after him to go shares on. He had the photographs in his briefcase. They were nice drawings, all right, and probably from the right time and place, but they lacked the forcefulness that was Signorelli's dominant characteristic. Nevertheless, getting Pfeffenselz's imprimatur would be worth the $250 it would cost.

It was just after four o'clock when he left the Fogg, having finished a good afternoon's work. Pfeffenselz, who preferred error to indecision, had unhesitatingly pronounced Nick's drawings contemporary copies of drawings by a Signorelli follower; burrowing into his files, he had substantiated his hip-shot opinion to Nick's satisfaction with photographs of similar drawings in Vienna and Paris.

Nick had declined Pfeffenselz' offer of a schnapps at the Faculty Club. As he looked across Quincy Street into the Yard, the familiar bulk of the Library reminded him of a question that had been tickling the back of his mind for some months. He had plenty of time; it would take only a half-hour at most to walk to Rothschild's house in Ellery Place.

He found his way to the section devoted to class books and alumni lists. He started with the class following his, looking for "Manship, Robert." He finally located Bobby Manship two classes after his own; a blond, confident face smiling out from the page, well off and well fed. The sort of boy Greenwich mothers liked their daughters to marry. Safe and employable. He turned to the alumni records, where he found what he was afraid he was looking for. Bobby Manship had died well over twelve years ago. Yet Jenny, Jill's daughter by Bobby, was only just about to be eleven, and Nick knew from his own nephews and nieces and the sons and daughters of friends that if there was one thing children knew to the day, if there was one thing that was never kept from them, it was exactly how old they were. A child might not know his father, or his address, or the name of his doctor, but with almost his first utterance, a child knew his birth date and his age. Which meant that Jenny was not, as Jill had told him, Jill's daughter by Bobby Manship—but must be her daughter by someone else, out of wedlock. And that someone else, Nick was suddenly certain, could only be Mickey Greschner, Sol's son, himself dead for ten years or more. Which explained a great deal, Nick thought. Especially the relationship between Jill and Sol. Sol knew. He knew, and—though he kept his distance—he helped.

Walking in the early twilight, through the clatter and hubbub of Harvard Square onto the shaded pavement of Brattle Street, Nick pondered his great discovery and found, to his relief, that to him it made no real difference. Jenny was no bastard hidden in the attic. That she had something of Sol in her veins drew her closer to Nick, who had caught himself looking over his second floor not two days earlier to see if one of the rooms could be converted into a suitable bedroom for a small, positive girl. Jill was ashamed of her liaison with Mickey Greschner because of the cad Mickey had been; but Sol, of course, would never admit publicly to an illegitimate granddaughter out of quite different motives. Some might be social, questions of face in the world to which Sol pretended. Yet if Nick knew him at all, Sol would fear to brand the child with his Jewishness. It was the darker side of Sol's personality: this belief that he had been denied the full measure of his deserved esteem because he was a Jewish tailor's son. Nick had never discussed it with Sol. But Sol moved among men to whom nasty little ethnic slurs were second, unthinking nature, and Nick knew he must be marked with a thousand painful cuts. And how would Jill think about that? Well, that was a question for the asking.

He took an extra, reflective turn around the block and arrived on Felix' stoop, as requested, comfortably after five. His host looked ruffled and ruddy after his afternoon's exertions.

Over drinks, Felix remarked to him, "Your Mr. Bogle is a curious one, isn't he? You've made him an important collector with one coup, Nicholas; that's rather hasty, you know. But he looks the genuine article to me. He's not like one man who consults me endlessly and has developed a rating system: 'Is this picture class one, class two, or class three?' he'll ask, and I know he's asked or will ask Frank Sanger, and Grizzi and every other expert, the same question, and plugs our answers into some sort of computer to make his mind up. And pays us nothing. But Mr. Bogle is merely being prudent, I think. He likes the Giotto; he told me so himself while you were away from the table, and I can assure you I stinted nothing in my praise of the piece. But he doesn't wish to seem an improvident fool. He doesn't want to give you *carte blanche* at Grundy's next week to buy the Giotto and have another, just as good but at half the price, turn up the next day. Which I assured him would not be the case.

"Now, I think we should go out to dinner immediately. The mother of one of my more enchanting pupils has taken to dropping in for a glass of sherry at around this hour, and as charming a woman as she is, although perhaps a touch mature, I'm afraid this evening I'm simply not up to it. So you shall be my beard, Nicholas, my sword and buckler—and, as seems fitting, you shall also pay for dinner."

The night before he was to leave for London to bid for Bogle, Nick took Jill to dinner at Maïa's. He had been thinking about how he might approach what he had guessed about Jill and Mickey Greschner and Jenny. It seemed important that he let Jill know that he knew. He was not quite sure why, except that it seemed to him that a covenant of mutual, all-encompassing honor had been struck between them, and that it just wasn't in the cards to keep important secrets from her.

When they had settled at their table, and ordered drinks, and Jill had graciously acknowledged the deference of a number of mention-seekers around the room, Nick decided he could no longer play it cute.

"There's something I ought to tell you."

She was too happy to be with him to be really listening, and she cut him off with her own thoughts.

"I'm going to miss you horribly, you know. It's no fun without you, and I find myself getting frightfully jealous about what you're going to get up to in London. Sol tells me half of that city's in love with you. Or something like that. Maybe it was that you'd been to bed with half of London. Were you really that busy?"

"Actually, it was Sol I wanted to talk to you about—in a way. Now, just sit still until I finish." He told her about his trip to Boston and Cambridge and his nosing around in the alumni files. "I wasn't checking up on you, believe me. I'm just curious when it comes to dates; they make a difference in my business, and the first time I took you out, the first time I met Jenny, something rang wrong. I knew Bobby Manship was too close to my class to have died when he did and leave a daughter Jenny's age. So, now, I know —or think I do—why Sol takes such an interest in you."

She looked at him for a spell with a clear, candid expression. She had never seemed so wise and beautiful.

"I see. Does it make a difference?"

"Not in the least. Not for ten seconds. I just wanted you to know that I knew. I don't even know why."

"Can we order? Truth makes me hungry. Will you buy me a good bottle of wine, really good, and I'll tell all."

As they ate, she told him about discovering that she was pregnant just three weeks after she'd sent Mickey Greschner packing. She'd gone back to Wyoming when Jenny began to show, taking a leave of absence on account, as she'd claimed, of her father's failing health. Her family had been staunch as bricks. After her daughter was born, though, she knew she couldn't stick it on the frontier and she'd come back to New York, to her old job at the accounting firm. Someone in New York had to know in case anything happened to her, and so one day she'd gone to see Sol. He'd been very understanding; he'd even come to see Jenny, once, but so long ago that the child didn't remember.

"Sol got me onto *That Woman!*, Nick. He was really wonderful. But he didn't want to identify himself with a granddaughter. I've always wondered about that. He said it had something to do with not crucifying her with his Jewishness. I never knew whether to believe it or not. I think there's some suffering there, on that account; but you know Sol, Nick—he'd never tell. What I really think it was, was that Sol simply couldn't have any normal, human, family, loving—whatever the hell words we want, Nick—relationship in his life. Do you know what he said to me once? It was so awful and cynical and sad it made me feel like weeping, and you know I am not a sentimental woman. Sol said, 'We always love the wrong people, although once in a million years it's redeemed because they give us the right children.' I think that's what happened with Jenny, Nick. Her father—I can't really bear to say his name—was a real shit. A vulture about women. His own father called him 'a panhandler in the streets of the heart,' and that's what he was. Self-pitying, boastful, jokey-smart; every cheap woman-tricking gimmick in the book.

"Do you know that Czech writer, Kundera? He has a phrase that describes the philosophy of the Mickeys of the world. 'Sorrow,' he says, 'is the fastest way to a woman's genitals.' That was Mickey's game.

"But I got Jenny out of it, and now I have you. I think I do; don't I, Nick?"

"Of course you do."

"Thank God for that. So, while all the deck is being dealt, I think there's one more thing you might know. But it's a deep, deep secret, Nick. You'll see why."

And she told him about her second identity: about Robert Creighton.

"That was all Sol's idea. It was about two years after I'd gotten started at *That Woman!* I was still doing a little accounting work on the side, some of it for Sol, and he got interested in this thing I have for numbers. And 'Robert Creighton' was invented. In those days, Nick, there wasn't a corner of the financial world Sol didn't reach. He had every financial journalist in New York in his pocket. And half the security analysts on Wall Street. He can still pull some strings, but not the way he could then. My God, he could make a stock move! Get it mentioned on TV, even; puff pieces in the papers; analysts to write it up and recommend it. It was like watching an invasion being mounted. That's what he did with Granada Masterman; before he even got around to building her up personally, he'd made MUD the hot stock of the decade.

"But he was always a bundle of contradictions. There's a lot of vengeance in Sol. You probably see that as clearly as I do. He used to complain that there wasn't any good investigative, Washington-type financial reporting in America; imagine how this sounded coming from the man who was paid millions a year to undermine the objectivity of the financial press! So he helped me to cook up Robert Creighton, and here I am."

"And I am about to faint." A thousand questions presented themselves in his mind, so many that they pressed so hard and insistently in such a small space of time that suddenly there were none. Stupefied by her disclosure, he found there was nothing he could say. Not now. This would take private hours—which, tonight, they didn't have.

"Look," he said, "we'll have to straighten all this out when I get back." Not that there was anything to straighten out, he realized, feeling a great sense of relief. All that her Creighton persona added was another intriguing dimension. That world didn't touch him; what didn't touch him couldn't threaten him. His first reaction to her revelation had been that he was somehow threatened. He saw, without reflection, that it wasn't so.

She must have seen the expression of relief succeed the confusion on his face.

"You don't mind that I've got a present as shady as my past?"

"How could I? That's the trouble with love. I'll have to get used to your being so formidable, that's all. Twittery Gilberte and the Terror of Wall Street are one and the same! I can't take it."

"Don't make light of it, Nick. Creighton's what makes Gilberte bearable." She was very serious, he saw. He liked her serious. Following on that, he realized that this cleansed him of misgivings about her work; thus he started to forget that she was, and would be until she quit, Gilberte no less than Creighton.

He took Jill home, relieved the neighbor who was staying with Jenny and talked for a while with his two favorite women. He helped Jill get Jenny to bed; then it was time to go. He was leaving early the next morning; their involvement no longer needed the rubber stamp of hurried lovemaking.

As she took him to the door, she reached into his pocket and took out his address book and pencil.

"Here," she said, writing something in the book—"here's Creighton's telex number. You're so clever, you can send me a love telex." Then she kissed him with a deep affection that he felt to his toes, and sent him home and off to England.

There was a lot to think about, Nick realized as he watched the lights of Windsor crawl under the wings of the descending Concorde. How much had changed since he'd first come to England years before! From the sky it was still substantially the same: baguettes of light strung along the banks of the Thames; the now-darkened patchwork of fields and forests; a country that once had promised such a good, foursquare time and was now of a piece with a truculent, clawing world. He was lucky with Jill that way, he knew. She was always in his mind, clearing the skies even on mornings so slimy and odoriferous that Manhattan felt like the interior of a cistern, perfuming garbage-cluttered streets.

He planned to spend the weekend at Creel's house in the country, catching his breath and readying himself for the auction Tuesday. New Du Cazlet revelations occupied the front burner of scandal, to the relish of the world art-dealing community, now congregated in London for a week of important sales. The Giotto was the prize, no question; there seemed little reliable gossip in St. James's and along Bond Street, however, as to who might be doing some important bidding. The real talk was about the curator at the Louvre who had come forward and confessed to having taken kickbacks from Du Cazlet for disqualifying a number of important masterpieces from the French national patrimony. For twenty years, Du Cazlet's ability to secure export licenses had been a matter of obscene speculation among the old man's competitors. Now it was all coming out. And Nick enjoyed it.

Felix Rothschild had warned him. "*Schadenfreude*, Nicholas—a wonderful word: pleasure at the misfortune of others. A wonderful word, indeed, but an unhealthy emotion. I myself have taken an occasional stipend from Dumas du Cazlet. He is just cleverer than the rest, not more dishonest. Believe that, Nicholas." Well, clever or not, the old man's scrawny nuts were in the vise, and Nick found himself getting an enormous kick out of it.

His enjoyment was, if anything, increased when he was walking up Brook Street, on his way to rendezvous with his ride to Creel's house near Oxford, and encountered Caryn Gudge coming out of Claridge's. Nick was in a hurry; he didn't have much time to talk—and she left him little room.

"Why, Mr. Reverey, what a pleasure to see you. Are you staying in London long? Are you stopping here, at the Claridge? Mrs. von González and I are just doing some shopping. I'm in Room 612; whyn't you stop by for supper Sunday night?"

She looked very disappointed when he explained he wouldn't be coming back up to London until Monday morning. It was apparent to him, but worth no more than passing, amused notice, that if he should choose to stop by, he could have everything and anything on the menu.

When he arrived at Creel's house, his host informed him, "Nicholas, when Daphne heard you were in England, she insisted on having us to lunch tomorrow. Poor thing, Freddy's having another one of his customer shoots. You won't believe the people. It's a good lesson as to what's become of this country. Is everything in the world for sale?"

The next noon, they drove thirty miles into Gloucestershire to a fine house set in a splendid park. As Creel maneuvered up the private road, they could hear the bangings of the morning's last drive.

Their hostess was on the steps. She was a blond, handsome rose of England who hated the country; hated shooting and people who shot, most particularly her husband; but managed to sustain a commendable enthusiasm for the latter's large, self-made fortune.

She rushed to the side of Creel's car. "Hullo, John; hullo, Bernard; hullo, Nicholas; my God, how wonderful to see you; all of you, actually. You won't believe how ghastly this all is. Freddy's got his ship-chartering and stock-brokering crowd here. And they've taken Bunny Chesterfield's shooting next weekend, so we have to start all over again. My God, I needed reinforcements. Oh, Jesus, here they come."

A small file of Range Rovers pulled stertorously into the drive and disgorged a crew of sullen, sallow men dressed uneasily in plus-fours and tweed caps. Introductions were made. Most of the group seemed to be Greeks, along with an American and an unsmiling Swede. Lunch was painful. The shooters discussed tanker rates and how much they'd paid for their Purdey shotguns and where to buy the best shooting suits. They sounded like a Macedonian theater company trying to play Lonsdale. The way of the world, Nick thought: the wrong walls for the right pictures; the wrong people for the right pleasures. England had sold out and become a world in which money alone had come to mean anything.

His sobered frame of mind was redeemed, however, by his hostess. After lunch, the shooting party had been loaded back into the Range Rovers, which bore them away, under lowering skies, to their grim and gloomy recreation. Walking them back to their car, his hostess had slipped her arm through Nick's, halted him so as to get a good look at him and remarked, "Nicholas, you look wonderful. As though you're in love. Are you? God knows I wish I was."

He was pleased and proud to admit that, in fact, he was.

CHAPTER SEVENTEEN

With everyone's attention focused on the Giotto altarpiece, the bargain hunters had themselves a fine time during the first hour of Grundy's Old Masters sale. Nick himself bought a fine Koninck landscape with a splendid, spacious sky for less than $400,000. He was in his usual seat, four in from the end of the sixth row, where Sebastian Tubworthy, who was conducting this big sale himself, could keep an eye on him. He'd made certain of not sitting close to another important dealer; he didn't wish to chance a repetition of the embarrassing episode in New York last season, when each of two dealers, sitting one behind the other, believed himself to be the successful bidder on an important Cézanne.

Looking around, Nick thought that Grundy's had made a good thing of seeming slightly anachronistic and vaguely shabby. Its saleroom featured none of the electronic marvels of its larger competitors: revolving stages and quote boards that showed the bidding in six currencies. In these same high, pastel-colored rooms, nearly two centuries before, the first Henry Grundy, a long-distant ancestor of The Honorable Sebastian Tubworthy, had set himself up in competition with Mr. Christie. From their appearance, Nick guessed the rooms had been painted perhaps twice since the time of the original Mr. Grundy.

Nick had been advised by a mole he maintained within Grundy's, for the price of a yearly fortnight's holiday in Cornwall, that there was considerable unease in the higher echelons of Grundy's about the prospects of the Giotto's making the stratospheric reserve that Grundy's had quoted the seller in order to lure the painting into its rooms. Only Tubworthy himself knew what it was. Nick's original guess of £4 million, or roughly $8 million, still seemed likely. But the interest necessary to support such a high price simply hadn't developed. Some of the problem was political: large sections of Leeds and Hull were aflame with riots, and it was unlikely that Her Majesty's tottering Government would come forth to buy the painting for the National Gallery. Germany's long-enchanted economy had lost its magic. The world remained in the vise of inflation and stagnation; in France and Italy, it was not a propitious time for a lavish expenditure of public money on a cultural artifact, no matter how precious.

The American scene looked equally unpromising. Culture in the White House was largely defined by hairdressers and appliance salesmen. Most American museums were broke: the Met was still paying off on that Japanese collection, Washington on its building; the Getty's vast fortune was still tied up in litigation, and its trustees were said to be reluctant to borrow against its future. The National Gallery, like the Fuller, was letting its collections pay the price of its architectural extravagances. And Grundy's had experienced some flat bad luck: the two wealthy South Americans on whom Tubworthy had been counting to stage a bidding war were in the hands of terrorists.

Still, with an object as extraordinary as the Giotto, there was always the likelihood of someone's wanting the dubious honor of paying more for a single work of art than had ever been paid. Texans tended to think that way, Nick knew; he wondered if Du Cazlet had tried to hook Caryn Gudge on the picture. His own experience told him the Gudges were quantity buyers. And fixed on the Lefcourt pictures.

He had formulated his bidding strategy accordingly. He would wait and see what happened. Stay out until the bidding started to gasp, and then step in with a determined but not manic tread. Do not get trapped, he repeated to himself. He had arranged with Tubworthy that as long as his arms stayed folded across his chest he was bidding.

The auctioneer finished knocking down a dreary little Steen of peasants quarreling in a tavern.

"Lot Ninety-three," Tubworthy intoned. Stylish, thought Nick, not to describe the picture; it spoke for itself. A thrill of expectation went around the room; several hundred people inched perceptibly forward on their seats, murmuring as two gallery assistants hoisted the altarpiece onto a stand to the auctioneer's left. The languid young men and women stationed below the auctioneer's stand to pick up bids became tense and wary.

"Do I have a million pounds?" Nick let his hands rest, interlocked, in his lap. He was embarrassed to feel his palms sticking moistly to the glossy paper of the sales catalogue.

"A million . . . a million three fifty . . . a million seven fifty": the bidding was moving up in increments of £150,000.

"Two million . . . against you, sir . . . two million one hundred": slowing up now as the price got fancier; ". . . two million three hundred." Nick unclasped his hands, and saw Tubworthy's eye catch the movement: ". . . two million four hundred . . . two million five hundred . . . against you, sir"; Tubworthy looked past Nick's ear, but he was talking to Nick. One more time, Nick said to himself. "Two million six hundred . . ." There was a gasp in the room: a new London record. Nick folded his arms against his chest and looked at the ceiling; as far as he could figure, from the movement of Tubworthy's eyes and the actions of the bid-watchers, there were at least two other bidders in the room and possibly one for whom Grundy's itself was acting.

"Two million eight hundred"; Tubworthy looked in Nick's general direction; ". . . against you in the back of the room, sir . . . three million . . . against you, sir . . . three million one hundred thousand . . . against you, sir . . ." Again he looked just past Nick.

There was something wrong here, Nick suddenly thought. Something wrong with the rhythm of the bidding. At these levels, there should be breath-catching, pocketbook-checking pauses, but this was altogether too slick, too quick and facile and automatic. "Against you, sir, three million one hundred thousand . . . once!" Tubworthy's hand, holding the ivory spool he used as a hammer, was poised over his walnut lectern. He was looking at Nick directly now; the third bidder must have dropped out.

". . . Do I hear more . . . three million one hundred thousand against you, sir . . . second." Tubworthy was giving Nick every chance. Nick's mind was racing. He had to bet his instincts. He was certain Grundy's was jerking him around, running him against the reserve; there hadn't been another real bidder for at least four raises; the only bidder was Tubworthy, faking an auction, just the way the other people had jerked the old guy around on the manuscript a couple of years ago. The hell with them. Nick shook his head barely perceptibly, unfolded his arms and pretended to study his program. He hoped to Christ he was right. By any standard of relative value, the altarpiece was worth £4 million. But it was Bogle's money.

". . . All done, sir, then? . . . at three million one hundred thousand pounds it is, then, to a buyer not in the room." Tubworthy rapped his desk sharply. As if hastening to get on with the business, to extricate himself from the tension of the previous lot, he moved quickly to the next item in the catalogue. Fifteen minutes later, the sale was over.

The audience milled around briefly; Nick accepted the commiserations of several other dealers. The room was speculating, as it gathered up its catalogues and umbrellas and made its way toward Wilton's and Mark's for champagne and postmortems, that Tubworthy had a third South American on the telephone—or possibly the reclusive Los Angeles collector who, rumor said, had been seen in London not a week before. Nick tarried, chatting amiably with some of Grundy's staff; he thought he might stick around for a bit; his instincts said that the day wasn't finished yet, so he declined a lunch invitation at the Agnews'.

He was right. A uniformed commissionaire presented himself at Nick's elbow while Nick was half-attentively examining a galleryful of Italian drawings to be offered for sale that afternoon.

"Excuse me, sir, but Mr. Sebastian would like a word with you."

Nick followed the man through a door into the foxes' lair of backstage offices and storerooms. He was led past a small sitting room occupied by a small, white-haired man with a furious expression, and into Tubworthy's office.

"Glad we caught you, Nicholas. We've had something happen that's rather rum. Bit of a misunderstanding, actually. It seems . . ." He launched into a lengthy tale involving duplicity on the part of the Berlin Museum and the Preussische Kulturbesitz, faulty communications, expected them to bid, and so forth and so on. As he listened, Nick became very pleased with himself; he'd guessed right after all. Tubworthy was in the soup. He had promised the seller a sale and he didn't have one.

"It seems," Tubworthy concluded, "that we have misunderstood Dr. Frühlingstein—he's the angry little chap in the next room; we believed him to have indicated that he would sell only at the reserve price we suggested for the picture. It didn't make that figure, so we, um, bought it in, without, um, exactly saying just that. No point in embarrassing anyone, what? Except now he tells us that he wanted a sale at whatever price the picture would bring."

Nick had to admire Tubworthy; the man actually sounded indignant.

"What did you have on the picture, Sebastian?"

"I don't really think that matters now, does it, Nicholas?"

"I suppose not."

Nick was sure Tubworthy had promised the old man at least £4 million. That would handily break the old record of $6.7 million which Sotheby's had gotten for the Turner *Juliet and Her Nurse*.

"Anyway, it seems Dr. Frühlingstein does want a sale. Something about nuns and health machines; it completely escapes me. Anyway, Nicholas, what about it? You were the last, highest bidder. Why don't we work out something? You know the picture's worth it."

Nick didn't disagree with Tubworthy's estimate of the altarpiece' value. But like most dealers, he felt the auction houses had been playing fast-and-loose for too long. A lesson couldn't hurt.

"Hell, Sebastian, you know I'm interested in the picture. But you own it now, so why don't you tell me what you've got in mind."

"Suppose you take over the winning bid, three million one, and we'll just forget the buyer's premium? How does that sound?"

"Terrible."

Nick had been doing some more fast thinking. At any price under £3 million, Bogle would be light-years ahead of the game; for rarity, historical importance, condition and sheer artistic quality, the Giotto was infinitely more desirable than the Turner, or the Rubens *Samson*, or the Codex Leicester/Hammer, the Chatsworth Poussin, the Velásquez in the Met or any of the works that had stunned the art world with the prices they had made at auction. It was surely as fine and valuable a work as the Rubens cycle for which Bogle had paid $7.8. Nick would admit that readily. The fact was, Bogle was gutsy and lucky. If the painting had come up just three years ago, when the Germans had gone berserk at Sotheby's, paying millions for medieval armbands and medallions at the Hirsch sales, the Giotto would have brought £7 million or £8 million. But in these miserable, confused, unconfident times, Bogle had a bargain. Nevertheless, some rubbing-in needed to be done, even if Bogle didn't need the hundred thousand or so pounds it would save him.

"Sit down, Sebastian, and I'll tell you where I think we can make a deal. The man in the next room heard a bid for three million one, which means two million eight to him after he pays you full commission, which I doubt is his deal with you. But that's your problem. The public's thinking two million eight net to the seller, which is where I'll start."

"Uh, Nicholas, I think we'd better think of three million; in order to get the finest things under one's roof, one, uh, makes concessions, don't y'know?"

"Indeed I do. So three million net, or better, is what we must find for Dr. Frühlingstein. Now, I think—think, mind you, Sebastian, because you did a first-class acting job out there—that I started bidding alone against your reserve at around two million six, two million seven, maybe two million eight. Don't look so pained, Sebastian. I won't make you confess anything. Just hear me out.

"I'll put up two million seven; you put up the rest, whatever it takes to get you out of this mess. Otherwise, my goodness. If the papers got hold of this on top of the Du Cazlet business. Not to mention the Art Dealers Association. This way, my lips are sealed—as will be the good Dr. Frühlingstein's, I'm sure, and yours, of course. Just a deal among gentlemen."

Nick extended his hand. He had assumed that Grundy's was charging Frühlingstein full commission only if the picture made its reserve. The commission schedules printed in the front of the catalogues were only for the little people: the old ladies who brought in Aunt Maud's Tabriz carpet or Uncle Sylvester's Daumier etchings. That is the way the world works, he thought, lounging against Tubworthy's desk, idly examining a photograph of a weedy young man in boating costume whom he recalled seeing with Tubworthy in New York in the spring. The managing director of Grundy's had gone off to tell Dr. Frühlingstein the good news that he could start construction on his homeopathic abbey.

After he let Tubworthy buy him a $200 pasta lunch at Cecconi's, Nick walked back to his hotel. He found Bogle in Midland, Texas, where he was looking at some office property, and told him the story, raising a good laugh from Bogle with his tale of the auction house's shenanigans and his own shrewd handling of the situation. Nick was pleased with himself. This sort of fun-and-games was, presumably, routine to Bogle.

"You did good, Nick. I really wanted to get that picture, you know. I couldn't get to sleep last night thinking about it, so I called that friend of yours, the professor, in Boston and talked to him about it. Listen, Nick, I want to be the one who tells Frodo Crisp, okay? I'm going to send it to the Fuller, except this time I think I'll do it on a long loan. I want some leverage on some of those people."

Then he called Jill, finally tracking her down at her exercise class, and alerted her that he'd be back in the morning. Before he could tell her the rest, she broke in.

"I can't wait to say it. Oh, Nick, I'm so proud of you. Calypso's here in class, and Frodo called her after Harvey Bogle called him. Just seconds ago. They're all so excited; and so am I—but at seeing you. Hurry home, my love."

Then, just before hanging up, she added, "I've got a terrible surprise for you, and I mean terrible. No, I do love you. But block out the first two days the week after Thanksgiving. At the end of the month. We're going to Disney World. In Florida. No, I'm not going to tell you any more. Surprises are good for growing boys."

The astonishing revelation that the Seaco-Gudge partnership had contracted a possible obligation with a group of thirty-nine banks and insurance companies for future delivery of $1.4 billion of long- and medium-term corporate bonds hit the firm like a thunderclap. For some, it was a pride-enriching affirmation of Seaco's new drive and power; for others, it was an ominously dramatic statement of conviction in a financial environment that was at best uncertain, at worst fraught with danger. All realized that it was potentially the biggest, most bullish bet ever placed by anyone on the direction of interest rates.

In *Pritchett's*, Robert Creighton, usually an advocate of prudence and common sense, surprisingly took the Seaco-Gudge side, although some of his thoughts seemed double-edged:

> One has to be impressed by the sheer magnitude of Buford Gudge IV's commitment to his belief that Administration fiscal policies will reverse recent trends in the money market and damp the fires of inflation. Although there has been scant hard evidence to date which substantiates this conviction, one should remember that the Gudge fortune, built on an instinctive appreciation of the future of oil and gas which dates from the early years of this century, has not grown thanks to nearsightedness; nor, in fact, can the family's historic aversion to paper money and paper securities, now reversed with a bang, be seen to have been anything other than foresighted and farsighted. Coupled with Seaco's undoubted skill in trading and financing, this is a formidable combination, sailing along in the van of what veteran bond-market observers are starting to call the "Gudge Bull Market."

Reading on, Fixed Income saw with pleasure that Creighton had indeed mentioned his name. Which was the sole reason he was reading the article. It was his custom to read nothing except the flashing boards in the trading room which marked the momentary movements of the several thousand debt issues, public and private, for which Seaco stood ready to make a bid or generate a swap. The quote boards and the hourly, computer-generated position sheets, which showed the firm's inventory of notes, bonds, marketable certificates of deposit and other debt securities, as well as the bank and other borrowings that carried this inventory, were normally the extent of Fixed Income's literary life. Putting down *Pritchett's*, in the glow of knowing that the three-piece suits upstairs never got their names in the papers, let alone a mention by Robert Creighton, which was better than Abelson in *Barron's*, or Rukeyser on the tube.

He checked his position sheets. As of noon, Seaco was carrying slightly over $5 billion of money-market securities and bonds, of which $1.6 billion, marked to market, were deep-discount medium-term bonds in the Gudge account. His overall position was peanuts compared with that of Salomon Brothers or Merrill Lynch, but it was still the biggest in the firm's history, and it was climbing nicely. Most of it was carried with loans from a group of twenty-six banks and commercial finance houses. He was doing some borrowing in the repo market on the short stuff, but it hadn't made the kind of move he was looking for; the effect the Gudge action had caused in the long-term-bond market hadn't spilled over onto the short side, but he was certain it would, sooner or later.

The Gudges were nicely ahead on their trades, he saw. The portfolio was up almost 15 percent on average cost, and just about 30 percent on their average equity. The leverage was starting to talk ever so sweetly. He thought he could pump in another $200 million and take a couple of his lending banks' trust departments out of some troublesome positions. Cash to cash they were having no trouble with the interest spread. The real market action was now in long bonds. What with Merrill Lynch spieling bonds, and the papers full of bullish bond talk, the streets were full of little guys looking to lock in fancy rates; Gudge owned close to a billion of bonds with a maturity of ten years or more and they'd tucked away another $200 million in the partnership, and those bonds—old, low-coupon stuff, 7½s, 8⅜s, 8¼s —had been bought in the high 60s and low 70s, to yield around 13½ percent. Most of them were up close to 80 now, or better. The man in the street was following Gudge as if he were the Pied Piper of Hamelin, and it was grist for Fixed Income's money mill.

This deal with the institutions was his biggest coup. The banks and insurance companies were still sweating their bond positions, he knew; even with the recent rally, they still showed losses in their bond values that made their portfolio records look like shit; in the bank trust departments around the country were rimless-spectacled, underpaid guys in unshined black shoes, second-class citizens whose job was to tend the bond positions. A bunch of jerks who read papers on economics and went to symposiums and had no feel for the market. He could sense this market really starting to build under him, like the first swell of a great oncoming wave under a surfboard; it was in his toes, in the adrenal flashing of the quote boards, the pulsing murmur of his traders on their phones, the shouts, the papers, the messengers moving like ball boys among the trading stations.

So he'd gotten his traders together one night in the basement room at Margo's in Hanover Square and put it on an "us against them" basis. Us down here against the boys upstairs. Us of great faith against the guys in the banks.

Circularize the institutional accounts, he'd commanded his troops. On a "what if" basis, see who'd be interested in writing a put-call option to the Seaco-Gudge partnership on a position in long Treasuries, agencies and AA or better corporates and utilities, a contract that would give the institutions the right to put their bonds to the partnership, and the partnership the right to buy from the institutions, at current prices, for a one-year period.

As he had expected, an offer this dramatic scared most of the customers back into their holes. People for whom decisiveness on someone else's part was occasion for alarm or sudden prudence. A few, who wanted to play because they thought the bond market full of air and the government economic program full of something else, backed off because they didn't see enough visible financial strength in the partnership, the Gudge name notwithstanding, in case it came time to shove the bonds to it. But for most, the mention of the Gudge name sufficed to dismiss any concerns, especially when Katagira agreed to have the Gudge interests co-guarantee the partnership's possible obligations under the option.

While some of his senior associates fumed, Fixed Income barged ahead. He soft-soaped their misgivings by lining up backstop financing with a group of banks for $1 billion of repo financing, if and when needed; it was written as "subject to market conditions" and with the other usual caveats, which was just so much boilerplate welded by lawyers against contingencies that could never occur. He was already carrying about $500 million in the off-Fed market, overnight loans which made everybody a little money, and was nicely outside the Fed's regulatory orbit; regulation meant reserves, and reserves meant lower profits, so that the banks were hungry for this kind of business.

To a cantankerous senior associate's objection that a 10-point drop in long Governments could result in the technical impairment of Seaco's capital, he talked blurringly fast and implored Homer's intervention. The Gudge flag was the one to sail under at Seaco, no matter how rough the seas ran. He talked about "Gudge profits" and waved the Gudge flag as hard as he could until the smoke cleared. The two Gudge offerings were being processed by a Securities and Exchange Commission heartily into the spirit of laissez-faire deregulation which suffused Washington, and brought roses to the cheeks of corporate leaders everywhere. They were the hottest deals on the Street. Seabury was receiving suppliant calls from men who'd scarcely spoken to him for a dozen years. A fistfight broke out in the Stock Exchange Luncheon Club between specialists competing for the GUT and GOD books. That was, in the end, what carried the day. The climate itself was as persuasive as any argument Fixed Income could muster. The signals were clear everywhere one looked; the day of the rich man, the man with assets to bloat and income to shelter, had arrived. The scent of money hung in the air like incense. The rich, it had been decreed by Washington and sanctified by the resident wizards of the new economics, should get richer.

What Seaco executive, looking at the rise in the firm's profits and standing since Gudge had entered the picture, could take issue with that?

From his distant pinnacle in Texas, Katagira watched it unfold. He had succeeded in his initial aim, he thought, which was to balance a giant inverted pyramid atop the point of a pin. As he had guessed, the trick itself was so artful and engrossing that those in the audience lost sight of how wobbling and uncertain the accomplishment was. Now they were venturing right into the shadow of a trembling weight that might be dislodged and crush them. No matter: it was surely glorious to see. Soon all that would remain would be to kick the pin.

He was troubled about his employer, however. Gudge was pining his heart away over that whore wife of his, spending his priceless remaining strength wishing her back. It would not do for him to give up the ghost until Katagira had completed the exercise. In rare generous moments, Katagira wanted Gudge truly to savor the process of victory, and the larger change in the order of things that it should cause. To be robbed of this perhaps final pleasure by Caryn Gudge struck Katagira as next to tragic; yet the conditions of tragedy were in Gudge's own heart, and the malaise seemed as incurable as his cancer. In an unenslaved state of mind and heart, Gudge would have relished the way things were working out. The news from Greschner that Mrs. Masterman was buying deeply into Seaco was an unexpected but fulfilling bit of news. Gudge wanted the carnage to be particularized; wanted to see labels—Granada, Lassiter—on the bloody fragments his explosion would scatter across the face of the East.

Nick was on a high. His business was fantastic. Harvey Bogle was catching his breath after having burst onto the art world like a tornado; the Giotto was now also on display in the Fuller Annex; along with the Rubens sketches, it was playing to heartwarmingly long weekend lines. But there were other clients. The Koninck landscape he'd picked up in London, a lovely low view of the *polders* near Utrecht under a fresh summer sky, went quickly to a Texas museum for $100,000 profit. The Cranach came down off the wall and returned to Leipzig as the chattel of the largest Burger King franchisee in West Germany. Nick had never seen so much private money chasing art. It seemed that word had gotten round that Harvey Bogle had stolen the Giotto; now every painting for sale was the last picture on earth. Johnny Sandler reported the same thing. In the middle of November, ten days before the gala opening of Sandler Contemporary Art, Deirdre Sandler's brainchild and baby, he'd had to scuttle off to Paris to buy stock for Christmas.

"I spent damn near a million and a half bucks," he complained to Nick at the Tennyson, "and for that I got a late Léger, a Pissarro the size of a stamp, two Ernst drawings and the ugliest Picasso I ever saw. If I get two and a half million for 'em I'll be luckier than a pig in shit." For the first time ever, Nick felt he had outgunned Johnny Sandler.

The joint Due Diligence meeting for Gudge Undersurface Technology and Gudge Oil Development was as well attended as any in Wall Street memory, and the only such meeting ever to have had live television coverage. Seaco's syndicate manager had twice been obliged to move the meeting to larger quarters. It was apparent that the meeting was shaping up as an "event" instead of a forum for the dissemination of information. Homer Seabury was greatly, if privately, thankful for this. He was well aware of Gudge's breakdown on national television before the Lassiter Committee. The audience had accordingly been seeded with prerehearsed questions—a common practice. Homer intended to gavel the meeting to an abrupt conclusion if Gudge began to get nervous or confused. The offerings were in fine shape; in the parlance of the Street, they were "riots"; it looked as if GUT were oversubscribed by 50 percent and GOD by just a bit less. Both would go to a fat premium in the aftermarket.

As the offering date drew near, the excitement subdued even the most nervous of Homer's associates. The Gudge offerings claimed the spotlight of attention within the firm. The Syndicate and Sales departments had become the emotional and functional nerve centers of Seaco. No senior executive of the firm failed to find his way to their floor in the course of a working day. And why not? These were the sorts of deals that made a firm. The appearance of the preliminary prospectus, with its ignored disclaimers printed in bold red letters along its edge, had made the investment community aware of the specific virtues of GUT and GOD. The GUT "red herring" showed that the company had grown almost as rapidly as Baker International and Gearhart-Owen, was as basically positioned in its operating sectors as Halliburton and had nearly the profit margins, as well as a breath of the technological sex appeal, of Schlumberger. The "red herring" for GOD showed an ever-increasing cash flow derived from an acreage spread that included the large prospective, undrilled holdings in exploratory zones particularly dear to investment fashion-setters. Institutions, which had always kept Seaco down on their list of preferred brokers, suddenly opened their hearts and commission purses to their newfound friend—in return for generous allocations of GUT and GOD. Surly accounts long dissatisfied with Seaco's ideas and service overnight turned childlike and gentle, and begged their brokers for a few hundred shares of each. A rumor swept the Street that a dozen top hands at Halliburton had besieged Seaco's Dallas office for shares of GUT; the same was related of an Arco group in Los Angeles—or were they from Superior Oil in Houston?

It didn't matter. The deals were on fire, and getting in on them soon was less an investment objective than a question of status. On Broad Street, Montgomery Street, West Sixth, LaSalle Street; in the rue de la Corraterie in Geneva, and along the Paradeplatz in Zurich and on Cheapside in the City of London, the opening gambit among jowly men at bars and lunch tables was "How much GUT and GOD were you able to get?"

It was axiomatic on the Street that the manager of a public offering could steal the institutional orders blind, since most of those orders, notionally for the account of the entire group, or designated to certain firms within the group, passed through the manager's hands. It had never happened that Seaco had enjoyed this privilege, because it had never managed a deal that was both big and hot. But its Sales and Syndicate directors had learned their trade well elsewhere; by creaming off a little bit here and a little bit there, they managed to double the firm's year-to-date volume in institutional equities.

Homer Seabury took personal charge of certain of the cosmetics; with Katagira's concurrence, he assumed responsibility for the recruitment of outside directors for the two companies, and assembled a select list of superannuated executives, retired military officers and pastured lawyers to whom the figures in the prospectuses, not to mention annual retainers of $20,000 (plus fees of $2,500 plus expenses for attendance at quarterly board and committee meetings) were sufficient grounds for accepting the call to high public service.

Those were glorious weeks for Seaco; a time to create due bills, and to exact retribution from the Street for years of gentlemanly disparagement. Old detractors choked back their Mickey Mouse jokes; the firm was now perceived with eyes wiped clean of old preconceptions. Like lovers frolicking in some tropical surf, Seaco and the Street embraced amid a froth of high excitement.

The group at the head table that faced the packed auditorium in the Hilton Vista was a strange one. Homer Seabury sat in the middle, with Bubber Gudge on his immediate right. The complaisant Wilmington lawyer was on one end, as the counsel for GUT and GOD. Buckets Maxwell was there, to opine on the reserves, if anyone asked. Stumpy, dressed in a new suit, was introduced as representing the accountants for GUT/GOD. Everyone knew accounting firms were full of strange people, and they were never asked anything anyway, especially when the books were as straightforward as these. Representing Seaco, and the underwriting syndicate, were Hugo Winstead, counsel for the underwriters; Financial Engineering and the head of Syndicate.

At eleven o'clock exactly, Seabury rose.

"Good morning, ladies and gentlemen. This is the information meeting in connection with the public offering of ten million shares of new common stock of Gudge Undersurface Technology and eight million shares—two million for the account of certain stockholders—of the common stock of Gudge Oil Development. I am Homer Seabury, Executive Managing Director of Seaco Group, Inc., which has the pleasure of serving as manager of the underwriting accounts which have been formed for these offerings. To my right is Mr. Buford Gudge IV, Chairman of both GUT and GOD . . ." Seabury went on to introduce the rest of the table from left to right.

After some remarks on the expected timing of the offerings, he turned the meeting over to Gudge.

To his own surprise, Katagira's long-distance delight and Seabury's eternal gratitude, Bubber acquitted himself well. He read from a ten-minute prepared statement, devoting five minutes apiece to the current business picture and the outlook for GUT and GOD. He had actually helped Katagira construct these interim figures; it was the only fun he'd had in a couple of months. He didn't stumble once. Perhaps because he saw for once a roomful of faces over whom he held the unquestioned sway of knowing something crucial that they didn't. It gave him confidence.

The question-and-answer period went smoothly. Katagira and Financial Engineering had choreographed a series of planted questions that were typical of every Due Diligence meeting ever held. There were a technical jeté: what new developments in wire-line services was GUT working on? A competitive divertissement: who were GOD's principal competitors in terms of Overthrust acreage position? An antigovernment gavotte: how did GUT presently stand with respect to the Foreign Corrupt Practices Act? An us-against-the-knee-jerk-liberals bourrée: what were GOD's environmental difficulties? And finally, a pas-de-deux celebrating the laissez-faire muse: how did Mr. Gudge view the new political/economic climate as affecting the two companies' earnings prospects? The last word on this was scarcely out of Gudge's mouth when Seabury, not wishing to risk overplaying a pat hand, adjourned the meeting. Even then he did not in fact relax until the limousine had taken Gudge, who had been delayed in the auditorium by autograph seekers wanting his scrawl on their prospectuses, to Newark Airport, where the Lazy G jet was waiting.

"God help us," Nick mumbled, fumbling in the dark of the unfamiliar room for the telephone buzzing close to his head.

"Four-thirty call, Mr. Reverey," said the cheery voice of the hotel operator. He replaced the receiver and rolled over to poke Jill awake.

"Four-thirty, my angel; time to rise and robe and make our way to the Mount of Olives."

An agonized "Uugghh" came from the sleepy heap sharing the bed.

Thirty minutes later they had struggled into their clothes; Jill had made up and checked to make sure that Jenny still slept soundly in the adjoining sitting room and they had found their way along torchlit paths to the lobby of the Polynesian Hotel of Walt Disney World; hostesses in long purple gowns were offering coffee in plastic coconuts to the invited guests at Masterman United's Tenth Annual Sunrise Service and Awards Breakfast.

Nick leaned against an ersatz palm tree, sipped the acrid, thin coffee and hissed, "I just want you to know that I am seriously reconsidering this relationship."

"Be quiet. It only lasts two hours. And then we can get out of here. Besides, Jenny had a lovely time yesterday. You were sweet with her."

"Well, I'm crazy about her, even if I don't quite get her enthusiasm for the place. I have a very low tolerance for plastic. I need living things."

A few minutes later, they were herded politely onto the monorail that would carry them to the Magic Kingdom. Young men and women in imitation hard hats showed them to their seats with a bright affability that Nick found peculiar so early in the day.

"Don't be such a sourpuss," Jill rebuked him. "This is the shape of Middle America in the twentieth century. That's why Granada holds it here. This is the mecca for people who otherwise haven't got much to dream about. You fancy yourself a keen, skeptical social observer, so just shut up and watch; you'll learn something."

As the train bore them soundlessly toward the gates of the amusement park, Jill explained what was to come.

"This is a combination of a 4-H breakfast, Party Day at Nuremberg, and the Sermon on the Mount. Granada uses it to announce next year's Mastertheme. Last year it was Christian Clarity in Prayer and Pore.

"Practically all sixteen thousand Masterwomen are here with their families. Only the halt and dying dare not show; there must be a dozen funerals and births and hysterectomies being postponed around the country until this is over. By noon today, Granada will have a printout on the absentees."

"There weren't any sixteen thousand people, let alone families, that I could see."

"They're mostly in hotels scattered around the countryside; the quality of their accommodations is computer-determined according to last year's achievement. The fifty top Masterwomen, the ones who'll receive their laurel wreaths—no, I mean it, *laurel wreaths*—at the Awards Ceremony, are all staying within Disney World itself. The radius begins here and extends out, so that the young girl who just started last year and only sold a few thousand dollars' worth of Masterproducts is probably at a Quality Court Motel in downtown Kissimmee. The Masterlady, the one that'll get the gold wreath which is the top award, which means sales and overrides of close to two million dollars from a Masterterritory in a rich suburb, is fixed up with a suite at the Polynesian."

"Don't these women hate being put down that way? I thought Masterwomanhood was all about self-expression. How about equal rights?"

"Masterwomanhood is about money, Nick. And it's a second family to these women. Something dependable in their lives. It's a fabulous, effective concept. Granada's a genius; take it from Creighton. You'll see. Well, we're here."

They walked up Main Street. The ink-dark sky showed only a faint undertracing of daybreak. The street was floodlit, as was the castle that bestrode the park's central mall. The circular drive in front of it had been filled with grandstands. For the first time, Nick became conscious of the people around them: smiling, expectant Masterwomen, strangely impressive in their gowns, followed by obviously befuddled husbands and companions in their Sunday best. There was no getting away from the religious feeling in the air.

They found their seats in the second row of a small, obviously exclusive section of cushioned bleachers. Taking the scene in, Nick saw that a high, purple-draped platform, its lectern looking altarlike in the eerie floodlighting, had been placed to one side and in front of the castle's grilled gateway. The seats around them began to fill with familiar faces. Calypso and Hugo Winstead, with Victor Sartorian tagging behind. A large woman Nick couldn't at first place, then recognized as Louise Seabury Lassiter.

"No Von Gonzálezes?" he asked.

"Temporarily in exile. She's being punished for decorating Caryn Gudge's apartment."

As he watched the spectacle, he thought of Sol; there was something Greschnerian in all of this.

"How long has this been going on?"

"I think Granada told me it was the tenth."

Which meant it had begun when Sol and Granada had still been a team.

The little temporary stadium was almost full. Nick looked at his watch. Five-twenty. A final group was making its way toward five seats that had been held in the front row of the section where he was sitting.

"Oh, my goodness"—even Jill gasped in surprise.

They were five middle-aged women, minked against the mild predawn chill, who somehow, despite obvious differences in stature, figure and feature, looked exactly alike. Nick knew who they were; those frosted, puff-cut, desperately youthful heads were familiar to him from his society columns. The White House Auxiliary. He turned to say something to Jill, but as he did, the lights went down and so reverent a hush fell on the crowd that it would have been sacrilege even to whisper.

Only the chairs on the mall were illuminated now, along with a lone spotlight trained on the uppermost battlement of the enchanted castle. There was a vague murmur. Slowly then, with the self-consciously deliberate dignity of bridesmaids, a procession made its way between the bleachers along the central axis of the mall. These were the Masterwomen laureate, Nick guessed, watching them make their solemn way, gowns trailing in the dew-swept grass, to their chairs. It struck him as strangely Druidic, but as perverse a version of ancient midsummer rituals as the plastic fantasies around him were of the rich inner imaginings of childhood. He was seated close enough to see that they made up a composite of middle-class American womanhood. Tough, middle-aged small-town women, their lined, knowing faces at odds with the demureness of their gowns, were followed by peach-cheeked young things whose still-innocent expectations were evident in their wide, wondering eyes. An unlikely, unappealing group, he thought, as the last Masterwoman took her seat. But no worse than the kinds of dreams that were left to them, to the world.

Now all the lights were out. There was a motion at the base of the castle, and the song of a small, all-female choir rose in the night; the upper towers and turrets of the castle were dimly visible in the beginning light of day. Nick couldn't make out what the choir was singing; it was some kind of hymn. The women's voices floating through the dark, barely audible, had a mesmerizing effect; the audience seemed to be breathing in unison.

Suddenly, a sharp beam focused on the tower, perhaps seventy feet above them. A figure was standing on the battlements: Granada, her purple gown sashed in magenta and edged in gold, with a golden ornament at her bosom, her arms extended to complete the arc of the bleachers. It was as if she had taken the entire crowd into her embrace.

"Welcome, Masterwomen." Her voice was higher, less momentous, than Nick had expected from her appearance. On her lofty fiber-glass perch she looked mysterious and monumental, an imposing amalgam of Brünnhilde and Juno, but her voice was coarse and plain; she was like a silent-movie star who could not speak. "Welcome, honored guests. Welcome, Masterfamilies. Welcome, my Masterwomen." She intoned her greetings like a high priestess.

The spotlight on her slowly withdrew, casting her back into darkness, the mere suggestion of a figure against a rose-black sky, while another spotlight flared on, to pick out a gowned figure on one of the lower, flanking turrets. Nick recognized a well-known country-and-western singer, a TV spokeswoman for Masterproducts; she proceeded to sing a musical setting of the Twenty-third Psalm; as she reached the final verses, the choir added a swelling undertone; the skillfulness of the arrangement disguised the banal, nasal rendition. The spotlight died as the sound trailed off, and for an instant all was dark.

Nick, for all his instinct to resist, felt himself start to slip into a kind of suspension out of time and place. Damn, he said to himself, in his drowsiness, it's so artful that it works.

Then, on the other turret, a second light revealed a tall, male figure, gowned like a lay preacher. Over loudspeakers placed among the bleachers came Granada's voice: "The invocation will be offered by Senator Rufus Lassiter."

"Dear Lord. Hear our prayer and keep us in the paths of Thy wealth, and suffer us not to be among the meek and poor, for they shall not vaunt the fruits of Thy handiwork nor the treasures of the earth that Thou has laid up for the strong and the entrepreneurial that their works may magnify Thy glory. Let us celebrate Thee with all that Thou hast supplied us. Be ever on our side; let us shine and prosper in the knowledge that among Thy chosen are those who govern us, and who will make Thy way clear against those who would challenge Thy divine law and take from others that the sinner might be lifted from his disgrace or the beggar from his gutter. Make Thy face shine upon us; grant us wealth and happiness so that our tongues may be as golden trumpets in the service of Thy glory."

The spotlight stayed on Lassiter for an instant before being extinguished, but he seemed to Nick to burn with such an inner radiance of piety that no other light was needed.

Dawn was now starting to patch through in earnest. Streaks of crimson edged in pale yellow were splashed on the horizon. The lights were no longer necessary to make out Granada's stern figure on the tower.

She was again the focus of attention.

"Masterwomen, this is your occasion. Ours. Last year, bless each and all of you, our revenues passed five hundred million dollars. Net income after taxes and earnings per share achieved record levels, as did the value of each and every share of your company. At such a time, it seems wholly appropriate that our theme for our next fiscal year, around which we have created a wonderful new family of Masterproducts and Masterservices, is 'Mastermoney: The Woman Made Whole Through Wealth and Opulence.' You will see sample kits at the breakfast after the ceremonies. Let me just say that this is the most exciting Masterconcept ever, so much in tune with the times. It promises so much. Release and liberation through such essentials as tax planning and interior decoration, just to name two. Let the hand that ties the apron from this day forward tie the purse. For the next twelve months, the Masterwoman's credo will be 'Self-realization Through Self-gratification.' Our new line incorporates those qualities which have come to be recognized as central to the American ideal and which have, thankfully, found expression at the very pinnacle of American life.

"Which brings me to the moment for which we have all been waiting. The presentation of this year's awards to the fifty Masterwomen, a number of them past Mastermistresses and Masterladies, but also several who are to be honored for the first time. This level of achievement deserves special recognition. That, and the theme of our next year's campaign, make it so specially wonderful to have with us today a woman—no, a goddess: the goddess who represents all that is rich and opulent and exciting in this great democracy of ours."

Granada then sank to her knees; only her large head appeared above the crenellated edge of the turret.

Even in his ambiguous condition, the gesture surprised Nick enough to cause him to sharpen his senses.

A second figure had materialized on the tower. She was dressed, he could see, in a Masterwoman gown, worn under a calf-length mink coat. Just as he felt a thrill run through the crowd, and the first patterings of applause begin to spread, he recognized who it was: the bouffant hair framed a head with bony, handsome features which seemed almost too large and dramatic for her facial planes, a smile like a fun-house grimace.

Granada was on her feet again, clasping her guest's hands.

"Masterwomen, Guests, Masterfamilies: the First Lady of the United States of America; the First Lady of the Fashion World." Again she lowered herself in a deep curtsy.

With applause first scattered and polite, then thunderous and concentrated, the crowd responded to the magic of the royal smile being beamed from the plastic-and-wallboard castle, now revealed in all its ersatz splendor by the breaking light of day.

Jill and Nick could only stare at each other, silent with astonishment.

Granada and the honored guest had made their way down through the castle's polyvinyl chloride intestines to the speaker's platform. One by one, the laureates came forward, to be crowned and embraced by the Supreme Masterlady, and given a rose, a smile and a crisp handshake by the First Lady. In the background, the choir hummed waves of intense, formless harmony. At last, the gold wreath, celebrating $4.5 million in Mastersales, was placed on the stiff beehive of a tight-lipped woman from Enid, Oklahoma, who specialized in servicing oil-field trailer camps.

From the platform, Granada signaled for silence. The laureates had formed two lines on either side of the paved path which ran to the main gate of the castle. The choir launched into "America the Beautiful," which was picked up by sixteen thousand voices. At the front edge of the platform, Granada and the First Lady, joined now by Rufus Lassiter and the country-and-western singer, lustily led the throng in the anthem. One by one, and then in pockets and whole sections, the crowd rose to its feet, seemingly pulled erect by its own sense of community.

The sun was on the horizon now, a fiery red slice spilling premonitions of the warm hours to come. The anthem died; the voices of the choir faded ghostlike into stillness. The two lines of laureates stood frozen beneath the rostrum. A quivering, silent tension took possession of the crowd, as the widening light of the sun slowly spread to warm it. To Nick, it was as if he and the rest had sucked all the breath out of the air. Then, just as it seemed the collective lungs of the crowd would burst, the gates of the castle rose creakily, and with a bright burst of color, out pranced Mickey Mouse and Minnie, Goofy and Pluto, Donald Duck and all the rest.

Nick shook himself thankfully. Watching the new arrivals caper merrily in orlon fur and vinyl snouts, he welcomed the passing of the night's enchantments. It was good to be back in the real world.

CHAPTER EIGHTEEN

Although Bubber wanted desperately to flee New York, he and Katagira remained long enough to watch the launching of their arks on the floodwaters of the efficient market. Katagira was in an excellent frame of mind.

He was pleased to have avoided Greschner's dinner on the eve of the public offerings of GUT and GOD. Talking later with Greschner had confirmed his expectation that the mood of the guests was celebratory, and of those who stood to earn very large near-term profits, exultant. Katagira found that gloating tended to impede his digestion.

He had gone to a Japanese restaurant he liked on West Forty-fifth Street and had a really good meal. Returning to the Hotel Akira on lower Park Avenue, he had exchanged a few words and $50 with an accommodating bell captain with the right connections, who saw to it that Mr. Katagira's moderate fleshly requirements were promptly and skillfully taken care of. He preferred the Akira for that reason, among others, to the guest room of Gudge's apartment at the Esmé Castle.

Gudge had further disturbing news over breakfast in the hotel coffee shop.

"Darn it, K, she threw a real screamin' fit on me. Can't figure it out, but she says she ain't coming back to the Lazy G until I get her those pictures."

This was just exactly what was not needed now, Katagira knew. He looked across the table and saw the pale, gray, exhausted, emotionally confused man Gudge was. A man possibly in great pain, although Gudge never complained. From what José and the house people at the ranch had gossiped through the back door, Katagira believed that there was nothing Mrs. Gudge offered her husband that could not be substantially duplicated by ladies as near to the Lazy G as Amarillo. Sex was nothing if not undiscriminating. But while one wet tongue or voracious mouth was much the same as another to an analytical sensualist like Katagira, it was not that way to his employer.

Seabury ushered them into an office overlooking the trading room.

"I thought you'd enjoy watching the early action. We filed our price amendment last night, printed and distributed the final prospectuses." He handed each of his two guests two thin, stapled booklets, one for GOD and one for GUT. "We expect the Commission to declare the registration statements effective within the next half-hour, and frankly, we expect the offering to go extremely well, even in an iffy market like this one."

That was an understatement. The stock market was a mess. There had been no basic improvement in short-term interest rates; the prime stood at 19 percent against a high of 21 percent. There were signs that the Administration's fiscal policy was taking hold, but this was no longer universally applauded as bullish. Business investment was firming, as reported by corporate purchasing agents, but seemed to be heavily concentrated in industrial robots and other laborsaving devices; the unemployment statistics therefore looked ominous, especially in the older industrial sectors. The Texas Railway Commission had followed the lead of the Saudis and cut back production allowables so that prices were holding at just over $30. The long-term bond market was the one bright spot. The herd was following the bell cow. Gudge and Katagira had left the cheese out for almost six months; no one appeared to have died from eating it, so the rats were now gorging themselves.

The Gudge mystique had created good demand for GUT and GOD. Moreover, at the pricing meeting the afternoon before the offering, always a nervous time for investment bankers, the dark hour when final reconciliation must be made between the celestial price that has been hinted and intimated to an issuer, and the giveaway figure dangled before prospective buyers, Buford Gudge IV had blessedly proved to be a perfect pussycat.

"Whatever y'all suggest is okay with me" was all he'd said when Financial Engineering had spread out computer printouts comparing GOD and GUT statistically with similar companies. The sheets proved irrevocably, as Financial Engineering glibly interpreted them, that GUT should be offered at $24.50 a share, which represented a price/earnings multiple at a slight discount to what the market was paying for what he called "seasoned" firms. The same reasoning, with an emphasis on asset values, plus what Financial Engineering termed "a couple of bucks for sex appeal," indicated an offering price of $29.375 for each share of GOD. The way Gudge figured it, since all this fancy calculating was based on figures concocted by the collective imagination of Katagira and his computers, it didn't much matter what price you sold the shares at. Whatever could be gotten for them was fine; he wasn't doing this for the money.

"That's fine with me," he'd also said when they pulled out equally impressive spread sheets to demonstrate that the commission for the underwriters should be $1.50 a share on GOD and $1.25 on GUT. He readily bought their logic. If a fellow needed to charge 5 percent, or 6 percent, or 4 percent, to be able to sell nearly $500 million worth of fairy stories, well, he was worth his price.

Gudge's ready acceptance of the recommended price and spread made Seaco's syndicate manager's joy complete. This was a dream deal. From day number one, he had known it would be hot, which meant he wouldn't have to twist arms, kiss asses or promise the undeliverable in order to put out stock. Now he had a guaranteed riot, a stampede.

There wouldn't be any loose stock, so he went to work cleaning up the syndicate, flushing out the liars—the houses that took down their allocation to pocket the full commission and would leak unsold stock back into the aftermarket. The clan of syndicate managers knew who the liars were; they ranged from small firms in third-rank cities which had some family tie-in to Seaco to a couple of very big outfits not a quarter-mile away. Big or small, these firms couldn't have sold their full allotment of tickets to the Crucifixion. Next, the syndicate manager took care of his friends. Old Street favors he repaid by allotting a few thousand of the shares here and there. Personal considerations were respected. There was a girl on the syndicate desk of the big firm in the next building he'd been trying to lay for the last three months. She got 500 GUT and 300 GOD.

Now, awaiting confirmation that the SEC had given the green light for the offering to proceed, he had a good tight book on a fairly priced deal, strong demand and a generous spread. He couldn't have been happier. And around the Street, he had become a man of respect.

A few minutes later, the SEC came in and all systems were go. The syndicate wire flashed the word to its partners that they were now effective: GUT and GOD were launched on friendly waters. He turned, grinned at Homer Seabury in the glassed-in office overlooking the syndicate/trading area and gave him a hearty thumbs-up. He saw Seabury grin back and pump the hands of Gudge and the Jap.

Two hours later, Bubber watched the ugly industrial flats of New Jersey flow away beneath the wing tip. This had to be it, he hoped. Too many trips to New York in one year.

"How 'bout that?" he said to Katagira, across from him. "It's like everything else in the world these days. All you ever see about what's goin' on is a lot of numbers on screens and sheets of computer paper, and guys shoutin' on the telephone."

Katagira smiled.

"Mr. Gudge, how long has it been since you've actually seen a barrel of *your* oil?"

Gudge shook his head, and went back to his contemplation of the landscape, while Katagira returned to his consideration of the problem of the Lefcourt Collection.

At about that time, Homer strutted into the trading room, went up behind the syndicate desk and laid a hefty, paternal hand on his syndicate manager's shoulder.

"How're we doing?"

"Pretty good. GUT's 26½–27; GOD's 31–32. I've bought a little stock for the syndicate from Morgan. An institution they'd circled for a hundred thousand shares took it on the Jesse Owens late yesterday."

"Well, keep on top of that short," Homer said. He thought he sounded pretty professional. As he left the syndicate area, it occurred to him that, by God, there were worse things in the world than being Homer Seabury.

The Christmas season surged upon New York. As in most recent years, it was a time of tempered ebullience for those with a conscience. Fifth Avenue was as gaily decorated as ever; the crowds were as dense and noisome. Fingering catalogues advertising $5,000 doghouses or watching Italians in pointed shoes dicker over jeweled watches in Van Cleef diverted the attention from starvation in Somalia or misery north of Ninety-sixth Street. The man in the street, preoccupied with his own tribulations, rushed about his business, ever more inward, less communal.

The affairs of the nation seemed strangely at odds with the relaxed, confident mood emanating from Washington. To charges that the Administration's failure to commit to a humane social policy must sooner or later leave the nation's social fabric in tatters, the President expressed his profound disappointment with the minimally waged, the hungry and the jobless; they had failed to use their tax incentives to lift themselves entrepreneurially from their miserable lot; the foodless holidays they faced were nobody's fault but their own. His sentiments were to be echoed by Rufus Lassiter in his Christmas Eve sermon at St. Willoughby's.

Although seasonal unemployment and crime rates were soaring, and the economy breathed but fitfully, and the banking system made its usual pious noises about the consequences of illiquidity and an uncomfortably high prime rate, along Wall Street and on Pennsylvania Avenue the business of prosperity proceeded as usual. Dust and cobwebs filled what had been the Justice Department's antitrust division. A series of deals announced during Christmas week indicated that the nation's seven major oil companies would soon become three. If the transactions closed, a heavenly nourishing drizzle of close to $1 billion in commissions and fees would shower on Wall Street. The bond market, which had been the Street's sore point for two years, had real momentum now. On the Monday following the GUT/GOD offering, Robert Creighton had the inside information that the Gudge interests, for their own account and in partnership with Seaco, having put several billion dollars into short and medium Treasuries and high-grade agencies and corporates, were beginning to buy aggressively into lower-rated corporates on a longer spread of maturities. For the moment, what Creighton did not report was that these positions were being financed with billions of worldwide borrowings channeled through Seaco.

In setting up the arrangement, at an enriched interest rate to the lenders, Fixed Income had induced the banks to finance a qualitatively broader and longer-maturing range of instruments than they normally liked. His persuasiveness was enhanced by the very size of the business he offered.

Now, with the happiest Christmas of his young life but three days off, he stood alone in his darkened trading room, lit only by the lights blinking the key indicators of the Hong Kong and Tokyo markets, the only sound apart from his breathing the clack of the telexes which monitored the twenty-four-hour business Seaco had become. Master of his realm. He had changed the direction of an entire market, perhaps of a financial generation. He was on the way to the top; only the night before, at the enormous office party at the Waldorf that Homer had unbent to give, his captain's hand had smitten his shoulder in affectionate salutation. Soon he would sit at Homer Seabury's right hand; from there, it would require but a small effort to take over the throne itself. Homer would never know what had hit him. A nice guy, Homer, but not smart enough, or tough enough, for this business. Not a real pro.

Outside, the lights of the surrounding glass towers were flickering off, crystal points, now here, now gone, in the frosty night. To Fixed Income, it was strangely, truly romantic being there alone, surveying his domain of empty desks and silent telephones and quote boards. If he had had any sense of history or metaphor, he might have seen himself as a young Alexander; but neither history nor metaphor was integral to his philosophy, nor that of the world he proposed to conquer.

"You wouldn't believe it, Nick."

Jill was telephoning from Washington. To celebrate the alacrity and geniality with which the President had sent Special Forces units into the ghettos of Akron and Detroit to suppress food-stamp riots, a number of his most withered, wrinkled cronies had thrown together a bash at the F Street Club. Jill was covering it for *That Woman!*

"Nice group, huh?" Nick thought of himself as a fairly docile political animal, but the antics in and around the White House were starting to gnaw, especially during this cold, difficult time. Winter had rushed in early and bitter. The streets of the city smelled of trouble, even under the misleading blanket of early snow.

"Just awful. Everyone's about five hundred years old. If they're not a hairdresser."

What do you expect? Nick thought; this is your beat, after all, my darling.

"It's total plastic, Nick. Even I'm surprised; of course, I haven't worked the White House set. I don't think these people have hearts or insides, even. Just tube things that go beep. The President's face looks as though it'd been left in the sun too long and needs to go into the shop."

"Lots of blacks and Jews, I'll bet?"

"Don't be stupid. Jenny all right? I'll be home for supper; see you then."

"Hurry, hurry." She's got to be running out of gas on this kind of work, he thought, pleased at the possibility.

Five minutes later, the phone rang again.

It was Gudge.

"Mr. Reverey, you got to get me those pictures. I suppose there's no way to get 'em by Christmas, but right after New Year's maybe?" He sounded plaintive, urgent—almost desperate. There was something so beseeching about his voice that Nick carefully masked his impatience.

"Mr. Gudge, I just don't think I can. I've told Sol Greschner so a dozen times. I can appreciate your interest, but I just don't think there's a ray of hope of getting them."

"Mr. Reverey, Mr. Greschner says you valued them pictures at three hundred and fifty million. That right?"

"Mr. Gudge, that's what you might call a horseback estimate. It means nothing."

"Mr. Reverey, will you do me a favor? Please, sir." Gudge was imploring; his voice quavered, as if something in his larynx were loose and uncontrollable, like a broken rudder.

"Yes, sir? What is it?"

"Mr. Reverey, will you offer them old boys four hundred million dollars? Just put it on the table; you don't have to do anymore'n that."

Nick couldn't help gasping. Gudge must have heard him.

"Mr. Reverey, you do that, and there's a million-dollar commission in it for you—just to put the offer on the table. You don't have to do more'n that. If they take it, there's five percent in it."

There was one thing Nick was not going to do: sell out. But he did feel sorry for the man.

"Mr. Gudge, I'll do this for you. I'm going to Europe in February. I'll lay your offer before Max, but no more. But there'll be no fee. I'll be your messenger boy." Out of pity, he added silently.

No fee, by God; but if Max, so help me God, should take four hundred million dollars, then I'll take some too.

"Sure 'preciate that, Mr. Reverey. I sure do. Well—Merry Christmas and Happy New Year."

"And to you, sir."

This was all foolishness—these amounts, this task, the whole conversation. But what harm could it do? He was taking Jill skiing in Austria in late January anyway; they could slip down to Florence for a couple of days. He'd like her to meet Max and Frank, and Florence was a wonderful, curious place in the winter.

On New Year's Eve, a benevolent deity had mantled both coasts and all between with a clear night, so that the contented could go to bed in the promise of a pleasant New Year's Day and the fretful could at least see the stars during their midnight pacings and try to find hopeful auguries in them.

Homer Seabury slept secure, untroubled by the bassetlike snufflings of his wife in the next bed. It had been a glorious finish to a year that had begun questionably. As late as April, he had been under siege, his leadership in question, his job at risk. When the year ended, he was firmly ensconced, his adversaries routed, firmly and dependably partnered by the richest man in America. His struggling days as "Pluck" seemed as distant as the sack of Troy. He had metamorphosed into Homer Seabury, dynamic leader of the most vigorous, adventurous firm on the Street; mentioned, one heard, as a possible president of the Bond Club. The only shadow, and it had been as brief and insignificant as a gnat passing across the sun, had been at the closing of GOD and GUT before Christmas. He would have liked to be photographed handing the two checks, for $222,987,625.38 and $231,754,813.76, representing the net proceeds of the two offerings, to Gudge himself. Gudge had apparently been incapacitated, so Homer had to make do with posing with a man whom the *Financial Gazette* identified in the captions to the photographs as Eula Parsons, corporate secretary of GUT and GOD, whom Homer knew only as "Stumpy." Anyway, the little man had gone back to Texas laden with typical souvenirs of such occasions: miniature prospectuses embedded in lucite like flies in amber; framed reductions of the tombstone ad. The two issues would be listed on the New York Stock Exchange in mid-January; perhaps he could get his picture taken with Gudge then. On the Floor.

And people were listening to him. Even Hugo Winstead, who'd high-hatted him pretty much since their Navy days, in spite of all he'd done for Hugo, had gone right along when he suggested they put the Fuller Endowment 60 percent into bonds. That had been eight weeks ago, before the market really took off, and the Endowment had a nice profit. Next week they'd kick out a little more IBM and buy some long Telephones. And only the day before, Hugo'd suggested, on the phone from Hobe Sound, that they switch the Endowment's fairly large holding in Merrill Lynch into common stock of Seaco. What a vote of confidence! Well, Hugo had declared, if they were going to be in interest-sensitive securities, they ought to go with the best.

Homer Seabury was a decent, honorable, reasonably intelligent man. They were qualities of which he had often despaired; they seemed to bring him so little by way of reward and left him vulnerable to so much difficulty in a world ruled by the expedient. Now, as he slept, his subconscious seemed to tell him that at last right had made might, and the thought brought a smile to his sleeping lips.

The light of the moon outside the window of the Lassiters' Hobe Sound house streamed bright yellow across the guest room in which Calypso Winstead slept while Hugo lay staring at the ceiling.

He was, as usual, pondering how to protect himself against feedback from his own duplicity. The secretly prepared documents for Masterman United's forthcoming surprise tender offer for an additional 20 percent of Seaco were ready. Winstead's firm had not handled them directly; following his advice, proffered strictly in the interest of discretion, of course, MUD had given the work to a Texas firm that handled a portion of its legal business. The specialist at Seabury, Winstead had reviewed the Texas firm's work and pronounced it satisfactory. That was the extent of his involvement, however. His open involvement. He was sure that Homer wouldn't hold it against him that his firm, not he, had looked over some documents for MUD, which after all was nearly as old a client as Seaco. It wasn't as if he were taking sides between friends. The record, if interrogated, would show that he had asked to be excused from the MUD board meeting when the Seaco matter was brought up. Of course, Rufus, who had been there *ex officio*, had briefed him—off the record. He hoped Granada was correct in her assumption that her half-brother would have no inclination for a public brawl. Having seen Gudge at Sol Greschner's at that party before Christmas, he was inclined to agree. The man looked as if he were losing air. That was what Rufus said too, and God knew Rufus had faced Gudge down and beaten him in a fair fight at those committee hearings. Anyway, even if Granada got in, and then somehow lost a proxy fight, the millions she'd have invested in Seaco could always be liquidated. Homer'd surely give her a free registration statement just to get her out.

He went over it again, checking for chinks. Satisfied that the many flanks his self-destructiveness persisted in exposing were all covered, he turned his mind to private matters.

Caryn Gudge. He got hard just thinking about her. They'd had lunch once and drinks once, and seen each other at a couple of parties after Greschner's dinner, but she'd made it clear that she was just beyond his grasp. Barely. Well, he was taking her to lunch next week at the Coach House, which was just two blocks' walk from his Village apartment. Calypso was complaining that she not only looked pale, she felt pale, so she would remain in Florida for a few days longer. That made dinner with Caryn a possibility. Like all avid adulterers, Hugo hoarded free evenings like nuggets. He was pleased to have thought of dangling a seat on the Fuller Board before Mrs. Gudge.

In his mind's eye he was already delineating the scene in his apartment if he could get Caryn up there. He shifted on the bed. To discuss a Board seat with her might provoke mighty expensive retribution, if bruited to Granada's ears. Two socially ambitious women could grind a man like maize if he got caught between them. Anyhow, thanks to Bogle, the vacant seat had been frozen for a year by the terms of the Rubens gift. Good old Harvey. Hell, a year was a long time from now, and next week at the Coach House was, after all, just next week.

The thought bestirred him. He couldn't get the fantasy of Caryn out of his mind—shedding her clothes, walking toward him. Those breasts. His state of excitement made him uncomfortable. In younger days, he would have sneaked across to the bathroom and dealt with his condition himself, but at sixty, he valued each ejaculation as a pearl in a diminishing string. He lay back and stared at the moon, waiting for himself to subside.

Down the hall, Rufus Lassiter lay swaddled in self-satisfaction. He was a truly contemporary man, ideologically nimble and concentered all in self, as the poet said. He had a bloodhound's nose for the spoor of change, and it had served him well. Once a darling of the liberals and the disadvantaged, now the smiling but severe evangelist of the political economy of the managers and proprietors, he had gone to bed anticipating rejoining his sort of people in the New Year, showing the Street what a real athlete could do on the fast track. The heartaches and disappointments that might befall others, that he might create for others, including Seabury, his ancient comrade, old friend, former partner, went undisclosed to Lassiter's unemotional soul. So confident was Rufus of his future and himself that he didn't bother to dream.

Entwined like some dissolute Laocoön, Caryn Gudge and Victor Sartorian lay on a sweaty bed in Caryn's rented villa twenty-five miles to the south. The ammoniac aftersmell of poppers hung in the air; empty, overturned wineglasses, straws and razor blades, fine white dustings littered the side tables. Caryn's hand brushed lightly against Sartorian's gray-furred chest; he breathed in little short grunts. It was a thoroughly modern scene: expensive, loveless, dreamless. Peace at a price.

The smell of poppers and much else also filled the sweaty basement room in Manhattan; the bumping thrust of the guitars and the wailing of the dyke singer sent the dancers flailing in a jutty, sweat-soaked *caramagnole*. Right in the middle of the floor, Frodo gyrated, his stork's frame making pallid angles under the unlikely black leather vest. His gold-rimmed glasses had steamed in the thick heat of the cellar, but he could still make out Ralph pumping across from him. It was a triumphant finish to a triumphant year. Out of the ashes, Frodo Crisp, out of the ashes. He reached for the popper Ralph was offering and inhaled so hard that the reeling fumes seemed to course right down to the soles of his feet.

It was quieter some blocks to the north and east where Harvey Bogle sat alone in the drawing room of his town house, a glass of Scotch at his side, reading the thoughtfully inscribed photocopy of the manuscript of *Giotto and His Century* that Felix Rothschild had sent him. Like Nick, Bogle was impressed with the richness of Rothschild's erudition, which seemed to mirror an equivalent richness of soul. He thought back on the year and decided that he had missed his vocation. The art historians were the lucky ones. They spent their lives in the right company. Well, so would he. Once he got through with Marvin Terrace.

He looked at his watch and took a sip of the whisky. Happy New Year. Esmé wouldn't be home for hours. She was at Avery Fisher Hall, at a midnight performance of the *Salon* Suite for Voice and Orchestra that one of her retinue had written for her, and then was on her way to do a phone-in in Hackensack. He yawned and went to bed.

The object of a portion of Harvey Bogle's attention, Marvin Terrace, was nervously hosting a party at his Palm Springs house. Granada Masterman was present. She had driven over from El Dorado with her husband,

Waldo, who was at that moment boring a small group with an account of his afternoon's golf game. He had come out to get ready for the Bob Hope Pro-Am. Her mind was in idle, as it always tended to be when her husband was around. She was looking forward to the New Year, still two hours off, and to dispatching Homer Seabury with her takeover *Blitzkrieg* so that she could get her Mastermoney program started. Her financial people had estimated that plugging her sixteen thousand Masterwomen into a captive brokerage organization would empty the nation's cookie jars by as much as $50 million in year one, with 65 percent of that flowing right to the bottom line, the way she planned to run things. Rufus could take over the business; that smile of his would become the front for an entire range of financial self-realization products and literature.

This crowd was a real waste of time, she said to herself, sweetly smiling at the deferential traffic which eddied around her. She watched Mellie Terrace hustling around the room. Poor thing, she thought, she must be petrified inside. To have worked so hard to get here, and now Harvey Bogle's going to tie a can to Marvin's tail. They'd have money enough, but without TransNational, well, how could they know who their friends were? In Granada's cosmogony, character and charm, paving stones to friendship for most of the rest of the civilized world, were decidedly ranked among the lesser forces. She would have said that in any case it was all the same for Marvin Terrace, who lacked charm and character, and much else, except that one enormous piece of luck, and the will to hang on to it.

In the background somebody tooted a horn, which put her mind on the New Year. She thought of the people in her life; when she thought of people, Granada thought mainly of enemies. She started running down the list, laying envious, spiteful ill wishes on Homer Seabury, Harvey Bogle and above all Bubber and that trash wife of his, and Solomon Greschner. And Solomon Greschner. And Solomon Greschner.

Jill and Nick had called Sol to wish him a Happy New Year, called her parents and his, and gone to bed to watch a Jack Benny movie.

In the middle of it, Jill asked Nick, "Did I ever tell you people think I look like Carole Lombard? What do you think?" She pointed at the screen.

"I think you do. I always have. I love all four of you. Carole, Jill, Gilberte and good old Bob C."

"And Jenny makes five?"

"And Jenny makes five."

Man and master saw the Old Year out together at Number 17 and at the Lazy G. Sol was not much for sentimental occasions; sentiment was for families, and he had no family. He had never really taken the little girl to his heart, although she was provided for in his will. He wondered how it would turn out for Jill and Nick. The world was so full of trouble; so many unpredictable, unpleasant surprises.

Vosper appeared at a quarter to midnight, and they took a glass each from a bottle of champagne. When the Regency clock on the sideboard struck the hour, they raised their glasses wordlessly, first to each other and then to Dr. Johnson glowering from his frame over the mantel. As he had done each New Year's since Vosper had entered his service, Sol took a twenty-dollar gold piece from the pocket of his evening vest and gave it to Vosper. They wished each other a Happy New Year with extreme courtesy and parted. After three hours of watching ghostly shadows parade across his ceiling, Sol's eyes finally closed and he drifted down into uneasy slumber.

Far to the southwest, Katagira and Gudge dined, as they generally did, in silence. It had been a dismal holiday fortnight at the ranch. Mrs. Gudge had not appeared and had called only twice. Gudge was piteously despondent. Even Katagira, whose humanity was locked up by his mechanistic view of life, felt a twinge of heartache for his master. A tree had been set up in the bunkhouse for the vaqueros and their families; Stumpy had hung it with colored lights and cotton tendrils so that it made a brave show against the austere furnishings of the bunkhouse parlor. On Christmas Eve, Gudge had gone to the bunkhouse and presented each of the vaqueros with a $500 bill; there were silver dollars for the children, and presents, toys and sweaters and new jeans, that José and his wife had brought from the Penney's in Amarillo. The skies were dreary; it looked as though there might be snow; the ranch seemed to be curling in on itself like a dying leaf.

Over their cheerless dinner, enlivened only by a red candle José had found for the table, Katagira discovered there was nothing he could say. Despair made an already inarticulate man like Gudge draw in further, until all that could be glimpsed of his feelings and troubles was small hints that a man was in there somewhere—hints like the barely visible glitter of a turtle's eyes from within its shell. There was no advice he could give. No confidences he could draw out. Nothing to say. Nothing to ask. Nothing. Just the job to do.

At length, he put down his chopsticks. Across from him sat a man for whom the tolling of midnight meant the start of a year whose end he might not see. Gudge chewed carefully, industriously.

He looked at Katagira. "Well, guess you'll be going to bed now. G'night."

"Good night."

Happy New Year.

CHAPTER NINETEEN

For historians of the American financial markets, the arrival of the New Year marked the start of the bond market's furious, final push to the peak of what would come to be known as the "Gudge Bull Market." The statistical evidence would be recorded in the market technicians' charts. The causes that underlay the surge were varied, as they must be in any proceeding where large numbers of normally careful men are suddenly turned into lemmings. Certainly present was the irrepressible, market-animating fear of missing out on a good thing. Certainly the "sponsorship" of so demonstrably vast, and therefore fiscally virtuous, a participant as the Gudge interests had its effect. Certainly Washington helped; the seers and prophets of the Administration looked up from the statistical entrails from which they had been trying to divine some kind of proof that things were getting better, saw better numbers rushing by on the bond quote boards and publicly applauded all those responsible, among whom they numbered themselves, for making at last come to pass the harbingers of the long-predicted, seldom-evident great day of glory. That short-term rates remained high, as money flowed out of certificates of deposit and project notes into signicantly discounted obligations of Uncle Sam and his *Doppelgänger* in the private sector, was but a speck in a flea's eye, worth scarcely more notice than the escalating number of small-business failures and a stubbornly standfast unemployment rate. There were other places to direct hosannas. By the end of January, the Treasury 9s of 1944, which had stood at 71 barely six months earlier, were 10 points higher. The IBM 9⅜s of 2004 had moved from 73 to 84; the Illinois Bell 7⅝s of '06 from 57 to 63; the Con Ed 4⅝s of '91 from 50 to 57.

These remarkable trading profits and portfolio markups were much talked about. They cast a seductive, rosy glow which tinged the financial news, all the financial news, with a fine positivism as opalescently rosy as the first beams of sunrise. What had until recently been perceived as no better than an interim pause in the inflation rate, due mainly to an oil glut, the general business recession and the collapse of the residential-housing market, was now hailed as the dawn of a major economic trend that would carry the nation back to the glory days of cheap prosperity. Wishful thinking, and its academic stepchild, optimistic forecasting, showed their faces to the warm sun every day now; for the first time in a dozen years, the world began to look like a pretty good place in which to be living.

On the crest of this floodtide of joy and profit rode Seaco Group. It was clearly the "hot" house on the Street. Common rumor and skillful public relations saw to that. Solomon Greschner was back working with the exuberance of his youth; the financial world was his line of country, known and charted, so that within a month he had placed Homer Seabury on the cover of *Forbes*, arranged for Seabury to be honored as Man of the Year at the Financial Club's annual beano and seduced two of the Street's most respected stock-pickers into including Seaco Group among their "Picks for Profit" as reported in the *Pritchett's* annual survey. A profile of the firm and its leader was being prepared by *Institutional Investor*.

Seaco positively foamed with activity. Fixed Income had just about doubled his sales and trading force since the first of the year, added six new traders in financial futures, recruited a busy arbitrage section, and was expanding his intraoffice empire into commodities, so that now the 8ths and 16ths muttered by his minions into their headsets or shouted the breadth of the barnlike trading room denominated not only the value of pieces of paper but quantities of Ghanaian coffee or Iowa pork bellies.

There were comforting signs that the economic program put forward by the Administration and mooed, neighed, clucked and quacked into law by Congress was doing exactly what was intended. Levels of executive compensation continued to rise. An informal census conducted by the Internal Revenue Service showed that the population of certifiable millionaires was expected to rise by more than 20 percent. Measured as a percentage of annual cash revenues after allowable deductions, the rate of cash taxes paid by the nation's fifty largest corporations approximated that paid by a Puerto Rican family of twelve in the South Bronx. Nor had industry turned a deaf ear to the "unspoken social compact" with the private sector which the nation's newspapers had assumed to be implicit in the new economics: a plea by the First Lady for funds to buy decent Chippendale for Blair House had produced a rush of over $6 million in corporate contributions, and it seemed that the reduction in federal welfare payments had combined with the new affluence in the upper brackets to produce what the Budget Director described as "a stimulative level of ethnic reentry into domestic employment," confirming his earlier prediction that the economy of the '80s would emphasize the service component, especially in those categories—such as doing floors and shining shoes—which were traditionally "Afro-American."

No grass was allowed to sprout under Homer's sturdy brogans when it came to living up to his new image. Within the firm, only its more adventurous voices had his ear now. He had clearly come out from under the shadow of his background, his upbringing, his father, his early defeats—whatever causes there may be that freeze the scared child within the adult's body and voice. Homer had broken with all of that; he had become a man of the times. No longer did he speak of the American Stock Exchange as "the Curb" or recall over martinis the halcyon time when young men with enough money to buy an exchange seat and just enough brains to find it did something called "odd lots." Gone for Homer was the antique notion of his vocation as a matter of hushed discretion, as a respectful, podgy existence, a diligent intermediary well paid for fueling the financial needs of industry and the nation. He shed his fogeyness like a snakeskin and joined the crowd. The object, he had at long last come to understand, was to be the big man on the block, own the biggest car, have the biggest share of whatever his grasping hands could touch or his salivating appetite could imagine. Now, at night, when Homer Seabury slept, the dream he dreamed was truly American: as revised and vulgar as the re-Englished Bible he once had been so incensed to find in his pew at St. Willoughby's.

Toward the middle of the month, the Seaco Discount Bond Fund was launched. The offering was underwritten by a consortium of large firms whose principal officers, all young, tough men with calculator minds, had sniggered at people like Homer for most of their careers. The SDBF was announced at $150 million and finally sold close to double that figure, so hysterical was the public's demand to get right in there with Seaco; the inrush of subscriptions necessitated an initial sale of $285 million. It was followed by six similar funds. Bond-buying was replacing *Pac-Man* as a national pastime.

SDBF was Fixed Income's inspiration, although it was Homer who was its Chairman and national Chief Executive, who got his picture in the three-color prospectus. Fixed Income had no quarrel with this. Homer had a broad, placid face, one to be trusted, while his own features were a little too quick and darting under the baby fat, his eyes a touch too boldly ambitious. Besides, he was preoccupied with his expansion into retail bond sales. Taking a leaf from one of the Street's best-known names, he had hired a cadre of smooth-voiced unemployed actors to man a bank of telephones; working from a spiel written by a TV writer with six Emmys to his credit, they sonorously recited investment pieties to selected prospects. In the first week of Operation Neil Simon—who Fixed Income was pretty sure was a famous playwright, and "Isn't this kind of a play, and all? With actors, I mean"—Seaco signed up 327 new retail bond accounts.

But Fixed Income was merely the busiest of a humming crowd of activists within Seaco. Financial Engineering had added thirty people to his department and had received a hunting license for up to fifteen new MBAs in the annual talent safari to the business schools. Mergers and Acquisitions had a lot of deals in the works but nothing right on the fire. The commercial banks were using up, in financing the bond orgy, the powder that he'd expected to be available for another round of the great takeover binge. It didn't matter, though, because he was on his way to media glory. The agency that was preparing Seaco's network TV campaign—"Seaco Group: An Outfit for Real Men"—had tested the firm's top executives for screen presence, and Mergers and Acquisitions had walked away with the honors. He wasn't bothered by the fact that his role merely called for him to stare manfully into the camera, say "Seaco, a Man's Firm" and wink as if he'd just handed over a prime telephone number. Last night he'd balled the ass off that little chick that did casting at the agency, and she was talking maybe a weekend at this really great little country inn she knew.

The metamorphosis of the firm and its Executive Managing Director was altogether too rapid and complete for some of its few surviving original partners, who grumbled openly around the lunch table between courses ferried downtown by Dove Sono. Nor were they as complacent as the younger people seemed to be about the status of the various Gudge accounts. They had been around long enough, through enough changes of market weather, to have become convinced that nothing lasted forever, for good or ill. The growing weight of the Gudge accounts struck them as astronomical, the partnership and Seaco increasing their borrowings in awesome increments as climbing prices expanded the leverageable value of the portfolios. One of the older partners, a relic from a day when a liberal-arts education was deemed a nonvocational asset in itself, would look around the table at the smart, confident young men and murmur about "hubris"; another, who had contented himself for twenty years with a professional life that paid for a slightly musty East Side apartment and a modest cottage on the Jersey shore, once made so bold as to ask Fixed Income about the firm's exposure and was immediately enfiladed with such a rat-a-tat-tat of fast talk that he withdrew into himself like a hermit crab. Who should, or could, complain? Who could be so foolish? Weren't profits at record levels, and capital, and new accounts? Wasn't the firm on everyone's lips? Was anyone else worried? Were the banks hesitant to lend more money as needed? No, they were not. In fact, the Fed was said to be giving them secret encouragement. Homer had even been on a White House dinner list; what greater confirmation could there be? This wasn't throwing a lot of good money at niggers. This was the bond market. This was where the country lived. Bingo bango bingo.

In the end, the older partners kept silent, sullenly accepting that the men of the moment and the hour have as their privilege immunity from the hauntings of history.

Although he was not yet truly alarmed, Katagira was beginning to feel a vague concern that Mrs. Gudge's behavior might precipitate a crisis of some sort which might complicate matters. It was all very amorphous in his mind, yet he felt instinctively that his employer's passion for his wife, whether justified or not, was an untrustworthy emotion. Caryn Gudge's protracted absence—there seemed to be no way of inducing her to return to the ranch, even for a short visit—seemed increasingly to weigh on Gudge. Katagira worried that his loneliness might impel Gudge to join his wife in the spotlight, much as he loathed it. Infatuation was potentially treacherous to a design as rational as Katagira's.

There was no "solution" to the potential problem of Mrs. Gudge. She was decidedly in the *picture*, although whether she might actually prove to be in the *way* couldn't now be known. Katagira judged that it was better to leave things as they were, at least until the woman's influence, demands or absence created intolerable pressure on Buford Gudge. Only then would he have to make a decision about the lady. The pieces were otherwise in place. Seaco was locked in on an automatic pilot vectored to disaster. The publicity and praise being devoted to the firm amused him. Homer Seabury lumbered innocently toward the jaws of the trap, too large and sleek and proud to suspect the possibility of trouble: a bear luxuriating in the warmth of the sun, innocent of the peril at the edge of the woods. There were men in Washington whose heads had been turned by the music, too. On Gudge's desk was a letter from the Secretary of the Treasury praising him as a "farsighted fiscal patriot." Consideration was being given to putting it downstairs in the memorabilia case, with the gun and the deeds and maps.

Greschner had proved as useful as Katagira could ever have expected, within the limits to which he had been involved. Now the question was if —and when—Greschner should be included in the affair as a full-fledged accomplice. Katagira was sure that he would involve himself with enthusiasm; the wellsprings of disillusionment and resentment that he had sensed at the first meeting with Greschner must still be flowing, feeding the blacker parts of the man's soul. As, too, must flow a growing sense of his own importance; no less than Seabury, Greschner was a beneficiary of the association with Gudge's fortune. He had taken the King's shilling; was he the King's man? Katagira guessed yes, given Greschner's age and pretensions. If fully informed, Greschner could make fuller use of his advantages; certain men seemed to be inspired by malevolence to levels of ingenuity that jollier, contented types could never attain. As far as Katagira was concerned, it was only a matter of letting Wall Street wind itself up to the high whine of hysteria before it would be appropriate to sit down with Greschner and orchestrate the final stages of the financial bloodbath.

In the meantime, there were details to be busy with. The bleakness of a Panhandle winter kept him indoors; he missed the use of his casting pond. Gudge had offered to cover it with an air bubble, but that offended Katagira's sense of the natural order of things and he had politely declined. He had his information room, and he was quite content to work in it four to five hours a day, recasting the programs that deployed and recorded the Lazy G's assets and operations. There were other matters: the question of survivors, those who would go on living and spending after Wall Street was turned into a sty of crumpled paper. He sent Stumpy to Oklahoma City to deal with an errand.

Feeling stiff, he rose and went upstairs and out onto the porch. The leafless trees and frost-stubbled ground under the bare, gray sky struck him as unspeakably desolate. The blood in his veins felt as frozen as his pond. From out by the bunkhouse, he heard the sharp crack of a pistol being fired; it seemed to splinter the air. That would be Gudge shooting with Stumpy, he knew. Strange, he thought. In all their time together, Gudge had never so much as picked up a gun, until recently. While it was in the nature of Texans to blast to pieces anything that moved or flew, feather or flesh, Gudge had virtually disclaimed his heritage. Now, with the growing enthusiasm of a peacetime soldier at target practice, he spent an hour or two daily at the pistol range Stumpy had set up. Perhaps, Katagira guessed, he expected he might have to defend his home when the time came and the East in its turn came howling for revenge. Perhaps.

Katagira thought he might read a bit before lunch. He was halfway through *Moby Dick* and deeply absorbed. It was the fourth or fifth time he had read it; it was very much a book for these elemental, winterswept times, he felt.

The snow seemed to blow parallel to the ground, so fierce was the wind, and Hugo Winstead felt fortunate to have been able to get into LaGuardia. Although the cab was making heavy going, barely twenty miles an hour, the usual traffic seemed to have been driven to cover, and it seemed likely that Winstead could be at the apartment in Greenwich Village in time for his date with Caryn Gudge. He was glad he'd been able to break away from Washington on the early side. And it wasn't just thankfulness at having enough time to get to the Village; he hated these weekly meetings that Granada now insisted on having in the capital just to suit Rufus Lassiter.

At least, he could now see an end in sight.

As usual, he, Granada and Lassiter had met in Lassiter's suite in the Jefferson.

"Well," she'd declared, "I believe we're finally ready to go. I'm happy to say the Royal Industrial Bank of Montreal has syndicated a credit of eighty-five million dollars to finance MUD's offer for an additional three point two million shares of Seaco."

"That's what, twenty-seven fifty a share?" asked Winstead. He knew that the stock had closed at $23 and a small fraction the night before. It seemed a generation earlier, although it had been less than a year, the night of the opening of the Annex, when Seaco had stood at $14. He was watching SECX carefully these days. He and Seabury had bought 235,000 shares for the Fuller Endowment at an average price of $21; through a bank in the Bahamas which asked decently few questions, and lent money happily to persons of unquestioned standing, he'd picked up 75,000 for his own account, fully borrowed, at a little less than that. Then there were 102,000 shares he'd put into Calypso's various trusts. And another 27,000 in the law firm's pension account.

"That's right, Hugo. Rufus and I think that ought to do it. Of course," she giggled toughly, "we couldn't consult our investment bankers for their advice."

"It doesn't make any difference, really," said Rufus Lassiter with a wide, confident grin. "I keep pretty close to the Street these days. I'd say there's a better grasp of what's going on right here in this room than on all sixteen floors of Seaco."

"I'm not questioning the price, Rufus, just asking. I just want to do a little figuring in my head." Winstead reached into his attaché case and took out a copy of the most recent report of MUD. Turning to the financial statements, he examined the balance sheet for a moment, put on a gravely reflective expression and said, "You realize, of course, Granada, that this will bring your consolidated borrowings up to over one hundred thirty-eight million dollars short and long. Moreover, it will bring your aggregate investment in Seaco, counting everything from the day you bought Rufus' stock through the purchase from Bogle and now this, to something around one hundred twenty million, which makes a very heavy debt–equity ratio, especially for a service business."

His comment was purely academic, a boilerplate fiscal piety. Hugo was a client's lawyer; he never went further with a declaration of principle than the first trace of a client's frown. He would traipse without qualm from this session to a meeting of the Seaco board. To Lassiter's undeceived eyes, Winstead was like a small dog carrying tidbits between master and mistress.

"I think Granada can read the figures as well as any of us, Hugo."

"Of course, Rufus. I was just making an observation."

"Well, Hugo, I appreciate that," said Granada, "as does Rufus. I know it does seem like a lot of money, but the banks didn't make a squeak. They're awfully helpful, those Canadian banks. Marvin Terrace told me about them. D'you know, he's lining up a lot of money to fight off Harvey Bogle? Poor Esmé. I hope this ruckus doesn't interfere with her new movie."

This was the fourth of these meetings, and Granada was anxious to defuse what she felt was a growing tension between Lassiter and Winstead. She needed them both in a cooperative mood. The difference was, she guessed, that neither of them any longer felt he needed the other. It was as if they were jealous of each other's potential futures, and that jealousy had obscured all that had gone before between them. Which made it all the more difficult for her to manipulate them so as to get the most out of each, to get what she wanted. Rufus was an ideal figurehead. He had a national reputation. She wanted powerful-appearing men for her figureheads. Rufus suited. He wore his ego like antlers.

Hugo was a different piece of goods—a slick operative in shadows and crevices. Where Rufus talked so noisily as to drown out his own hearing, Hugo listened and judged the situation before declaring himself. Hugo always looked twice, and that, added to his luck, was why he had gotten on top and remained there in spite of himself. Granada valued him for where he was, not what he was.

She owned these two, she reflected. She had bought them like dogs from a kennel, paid good money and promises for them, and now she had one, sleek and vain, and another, mangier, sniffy, humping every passing leg and post. She intended to work them in harness.

"How do you see the timetable, Hugo? I believe you spoke with our friends in Texas yesterday?" Granada's tone was placatingly deferential.

"Well, they tell me"—Hugo chose his words to emphasize his moral distance from the plot—"that we—that they—that MUD, that is—can formally make the offer within twenty-four hours of your giving the word. I presume you'd want Executive Committee approval on this?" Granada nodded. That was *pro forma*. She was her own Executive Committee.

"I'd say go. Blow 'em out of the water," Lassiter broke in. "No point in letting the stock run further."

"You're confident, aren't you, Granada, that the Gudge interests will sit still?"

"Aren't you, Hugo?" The question made him uneasy. Did she know of his attentions to Caryn? Then she put his mind at rest. "The record's clear, and Bubber'd never get in a public scrap with anybody, least of all me. His grandfather'd come back from the other side of the grave and kill him."

Hugo thought she spoke awfully confidently for someone who'd spoken to her half-brother only twice in twenty years. Might she not be overrelying on the newspaper Gudge, the silent publicityphobe? On the other hand, nothing Caryn Gudge had told him, in the moments when they lay together, waiting for him to rise to another bout, suggested otherwise.

The taxi was now plowing down the East River Drive, slowing to turn off at Houston Street.

Well, we'll soon know, he thought. The plan was to announce the tender offer in two weeks, after Seaco's board had dispersed to sunny February climates. He was thankful that he'd be out of town; he had an urgent meeting himself on the Coast with Marvin Terrace. Poor Marvin. He didn't see how he could hang on against Bogle.

The taxi turned north on Sixth Avenue, then skirted Washington Square, and deposited Winstead in front of the distinguished brick-faced town house in which he kept his *garçonnière*. He looked up and down the street, but there was no one out in this weather except a sharp-faced woman towing a reluctant corgi through the drifts. He let himself into the building and went upstairs to the apartment.

He didn't have long to wait. At exactly four-thirty the doorbell sounded, and he admitted Caryn Gudge.

"Well, hello, love," she said.

She kissed him. "I've missed you." She took his hand and guided it up her thigh, carrying her skirt before it; she was wearing stockings and garters and no panties—*That Woman!* was pushing "The New Wickedness in lingerie." "Umm, what's this?" Her hand was at his fly. "Did you save this for me?"

Her very cheapness and forwardness had found something kindred in Winstead's psychological makeup; they were both small-town kids; she'd captivated his drugstore cowboy's sense of sexual derring-do. Hugo believed there was something dashing and hypermasculine about sex flaunted just below the threshold of the rest of the world's awareness. When, at their first dinner date alone together, she'd reached under the table at Jack's and brought him to climax just as the sommelier was pouring the wine, she had won him in a way that all the other women with the mere offering of their bodies or, at times, their affections could never do.

"The machine on?" she murmured as they settled on the bed, fumbling with buttons and zippers.

"Mm-hm." The breath caught in his throat as she covered him with her mouth; the spread of her hair blinded him with its auburn brightness as he fell back, scrabbling with his hands to lift her, to turn her so that he could enter her before it was too late.

Later, they drank white wine and watched a retrospective of their assignations. Caryn lay languorously across him, one hand idly busy in his crotch, the other in hers, watching herself appreciatively on the television screen. He wasn't too bad for an old boy, she thought; he sure wanted what she had—no doubt of that. And he had what she wanted.

"Darling," she said to Winstead, who appeared to have ceased quivering, "you mind running that one of you and that girl in your office?" While he dutifully got up to change the tape, she rubbed a little cocaine on her sex. "Honey"—the tape was running, and Winstead was pouring himself a glass of champagne—"you don't care if I fool with myself a little?"

Ever deferential to the wishes of his ladies, Hugo didn't care at all. Of course, in deference to his sense of detail, he bade her wait while he loaded a fresh videocassette.

In New York, the announcement of MUD's offer for the 20 percent of Seaco that would give it working control burst like a thunderclap on the sanguine dreams and plans of the top officers of the securities firm. Homer Seabury had been planning his remarks as incoming vice-president of the Bond Club and newly elected chairman of the Financial Round Table. These notes were hastily put aside as he first summoned a meeting of his Executive Committee and then telephoned Katagira.

"I don't know whether you've heard, but Mrs. Masterman has made an offer for 3.2 million shares. At $27.50, which comes to some $85 million. Assuming she gets the stock, she would own 51 percent of the votes, as against 31 percent for ourselves. Needless to say, if she should be successful, given the hard feelings between herself and Mr. Gudge, this could terminate what has been a most profitable and, hmmm, amicable, may I say, working arrangement. It was my hope, given the resources at your disposal, that you might see fit to, ummm, enter the fray yourself to protect this arrangement."

The suggestion did not please Katagira. This business of competitive bidding for public companies, like squealing pigs squabbling over apple cores, was best left to the presidents and captive boards of directors of other public companies, who were psychologically impervious to the delay and expense of suits and countersuits. Their malefactions might be extreme vanity and profligacy; heedless stewardship; stupidity, even; but these were explicable, and sentenceable only by pension, and generally disregarded by a puppy-dog financial press. Katagira, however, was proceeding on a bold scheme of make-believe. And an implacable schedule. The risks implicit in a public dogfight, involving batteries of lawyers and squadrons of experts, was too great. Katagira had studied enough of these corporate melees to recognize that as in all battles, the little picture was what counted. Winning the war became the business not of the grand strategists but of the nitpickers. He didn't want any legal termites burrowing through his records; he couldn't permit the precious, smoothly humming machine he had set in motion to be damaged or diverted by a hailstorm of subpoenas.

On the other hand, it was clearly inadmissible for Seaco to be taken over by this particular adversary this late in the game. The thought of all or a great part of Mrs. Masterman's borrowed $85 million having been somehow lured onto a ship which he had squarely in the cross hairs of his periscope was enticing. It increased the likelihood of sinking her, which was what Gudge wanted. Moreover, Gudge was in a fresh, combative frame of mind. Mrs. Gudge's surprise visit had been as rehabilitative as a hormone injection. The bedroom kept its secrets; but whatever mysteries were practiced in the sober upstairs room in the Big House undeniably worked. She was a sexual sorceress, Mrs. Gudge. At least to her husband.

"Mr. Seabury," he said after a moment's pause, "obviously we are inclined to be helpful to a good friend and partner. If we can be, within the limits of prudent self-interest. And I am sure we can. Provided we can come up with an appropriate formula. Which is possible. Although it will not be easy."

Goddamn mystical Japanese, Seabury was thinking on the other end. Yet there was a chance.

"Well, Mr. Katagira, you put your heads to it and we'll do the same up here. I've got an Executive Committee meeting set up after I hang up with you. We'll be talking to counsel. I'll get back to you this afternoon."

Before Seabury got down to substantive matters in the meeting, the routine details to be dealt with by the target management in any unfriendly takeover bid were gotten out of the way. Full pension benefits were retroactively vested in all the firm's senior officers, whether or not earned. Ten-year consulting contracts ranging downward from $200,000 a year were executed with Homer Seabury and the other directors and principal department heads of the firm. These contracts were to be activated in the event of a change in the composition of Seaco's board of directors, as was a five-year extension of Homer Seabury's employment contract at $537,500 a year plus a 15-percent annual cost-of-living escalation, payable in a lump sum in the event he should resign as Seaco's chief executive.

As he executed the papers passed across the table by Hugo Winstead, who had prepared just such a set for Marvin Terrace the week before, Homer kicked himself for having been old-fashioned. Seaco had no option plan, no phantom stock benefits, stock-appreciation units—none of the enriching paper party hats managers in other companies had fashioned for themselves. Morgan Seabury had preached to his son that cash was the only suitable measure of a job well done, and the lesson had stuck with Homer. All too well.

"Well, now," he said, returning the papers to Winstead and looking around the table, "what are we going to do about this little problem?" He wanted to sound affably confident, to give no hint that his bowels had turned to marmalade. He stared at Mergers and Acquisitions and asked, "What's your plan?"

This was the moment for which the younger man had been born. To slap leather with the bad guys in a shoot-out in dusty, cattle-trodden streets.

"Well, first, we ought to try to nuke them legalwise. Check their passports. Run 'em ragged on 10-b-5 and 16-b, for manipulation and insider trading. I've asked Irving here to guide us in this area."

He nodded to an unprepossessing bald man on his left. Irving Voler, the legendary mergers-and-acquisitions lawyer. Senior partner in the law firm of Inganno, Voler and Lugen, which numbered 457 of the Fortune "500" among its clients, which fancied itself to be Solomon when it came to dividing up corporations. Which charged annual retainers of $375,000 with no guarantee that if two of its clients went to war, it might not act for both. Nonpareil among experts in the refined legal arts of the takeover bid: harassment, prevarication and delay.

Voler leaned forward, elbows on the table, and spoke with a strangely wizened voice. Wise men, he had long before decided, should be wrinkled in every way.

"It won't be easy." He let this sink in. "Their tender documents seem to be in order. Isn't that correct, Hugo?"

Winstead nodded, equally ponderously.

"The financing's Canadian. We're working on that angle with some friends at State. Of course, the other side's got some stroke there; Senator Lassiter will be putting his oar in, and Mrs. Masterman's got some friends close to the President. Very close. At this stage, I can't say the Canadian angle will be entirely fruitful."

Which didn't surprise Homer. He had never believed the anti-Canadian argument made any sense. When the oil-company bidding wars had opened up, it had been made to sound as if the Canadians were going to send a million tank trucks down to pump up all the oil and carry it back to Winnipeg and Ottawa.

"There're a couple of other Washington angles worth looking into," Voler continued. "Food and Drug. We've put a team of scientists at Sloan-Kettering on a round-the-clock retainer to see whether any MUD products cause cancer. And of course, there's Affirmative Action. Apparently, there aren't too many black or Hispanic Masterwomen. I assume you're clean on that here at Seaco. How many Spics and jigaboos you got working here, anyway?"

Voler finished outlining his strategy, which struck Homer as pretty farfetched. He turned to Mergers and Acquisitions and inquired: "Suppose none of this flies; what then?"

"Then we outgun 'em."

The young man looked very resolute. Like Errol Flynn on the bridge of a cardboard LST approaching the darkened beaches of a soundstage atoll.

"Blow 'em out of the water with a preemptive bid. I've put a pencil to it and it figures they—she—can't go much better than $31–$32 without her banks' saying 'Time out.' I think $40'll do it for our side."

"That's nearly $130 million!" exclaimed Homer. "We can't do that, even if the banks would give it to us; to buy in that much stock would wreck our capital ratios. What about our customers and the employees? We can't run that kind of exposure. Not on top of our bond position."

Mergers and Acquisitions' face registered a mixture of pity and contempt. This was no game for chickenshits, he thought, and yet that was what he was stuck with. Why wasn't he lucky like those other M-and-A guys along the Street? Shit, they had the kind of clients whose egos you could light a real fire under; get 'em so steamed up they'd bet their kids rather than lose a target company to someone else.

"What about your friends in Texas?" Voler asked Homer.

"I've spoken with them. They've promised to give it serious consideration. But I seriously doubt that they would want to be involved in the sort of highly visible bidding contest you appear to be proposing."

"Well, then, there's no choice but to white-knight it," said Mergers and Acquisitions. "Which should be possible. Everybody right now's got a hard-on for financial services. You want me to start calling the insurance companies? People like that will give a fast go or no-go on the concept. They're all apeshit on concepts. I mean, some guy actually paid real money for Bache. You can talk field sales force, new financial products, marketing synergy: that kind of crap. Others—Europeans, Japs—want to look at numbers and assets, and that takes too much time."

Field sales force, new financial products, etcetera, etcetera, thought Homer bitterly. That was what Granada herself was after. Of course, an insurance company wouldn't be bringing Rufus along to sit in his chair. But maybe there would be someone else.

"Meanwhile," said Mergers and Acquisitions, "we play for time. Crank up the P.R. Get Greschner off his ass. Sign up a couple of friendly analysts and columnists. Run ads in the *Journal* and *Pritchett's* about underlying values, management's record; sing the old song 'Don't give your stock away.' Get on the banks who've got stock in their trust departments; let 'em know if they tender, we'll kick their asses off the depositary and call-loan list. Let the bond boys handle that. Check the other institutions. Who has our group insurance? Do they own any stock? What's here in street name? Who owns it beneficially? Any other friends on the Street we can count on? Isn't there stock in the Fuller Endowment?"

Barking out these directions and questions, he felt clear-eyed and in command, no matter how violently the deck timbers shifted under his feet or the raging tides beat against the hull.

When the younger man mentioned the Fuller Endowment, Homer turned to look at Hugo. Both of them recognized their clear fiduciary duty. If Granada was successful in her quest for 3.2 million shares, only a small number would remain in the public float; a number too small to ensure any kind of liquid market. Just the way it had been in Western Electric before AT&T bought in the remaining scraps. A market for stamp collectors. It would be incumbent on any responsible trustee or adviser, given the facts, to tender any stock under his control. Homer felt as if his own hands were tied to the dagger being plunged into his bosom.

He spent a rueful, aimless afternoon and a worse evening. If staring and wishing could make a telephone ring, his would have sounded like a carillon. By ten-thirty the following morning, Katagira still had not called back and Homer's mood was suicidal. At ten forty-five, Mergers and Acquisitions rushed into his office, streaming expletives and a ripped fragment of the broad tape.

"We are in the shit," he announced. "Here!" He shoved the piece of paper at Homer.

Homer read it carefully twice, the second time with a lifeless, desensitized stare, as if he had been lobotomized by the words on the page. Dow-Jones reported MUD's announcement of a signed agreement with four investment institutions, including the trust department of Seaco's principal clearing bank, providing for the irrevocable purchase of 1.2 million shares of Seaco at $27.50 net. The money had changed hands. The institutions had agreed to be pro-rated back if MUD's offer was overtendered, and were guaranteed any raise MUD might make in its bid, but otherwise the deal was set in concrete.

Homer's first instinct was to call Hugo. Then a dull signal somewhere reminded him that Hugo was on his way to the Coast. Why, thought Homer, was everyone always en route to the Coast when you desperately needed them? He waved a hand to dismiss Mergers and Acquisitions. The magicians might as well pack up their rings and scarves and bottomless hats and go home. Granada had won. Rufus had won. They had stolen his life for nothing more than money. So depressed was he that he didn't hear his secretary's buzz; she had to come into his office to tell him Mr. Katagira was on the telephone from Texas.

By midafternoon, after driving under skies still stained with the pale washes of winter sunlight, they had turned off the main road at Vetta le Croce and were twisting through the hills toward Max's villa.

"I can't wait," Jill said. Being brought to La Pergola was, she felt, the ultimate admittance into Nick's life. This trip had been an odyssey to his cherished places. They had skied for ten days in the Austrian Alps, in the little resort where he had been taken as a child by his father. Now La Pergola; beyond this, what secret places could there be?

Nick sensed her excitement. In Austria, she had astonished him, swooping down the snow-filled chutes in long, fluent serpentines. He knew she would do no less well at La Pergola.

In another ten minutes, they were there. Max met them on the steps, embracing Jill as if she were a child come home. Frank was napping.

While Aldo bustled their things upstairs, followed by Jill, Nick asked if he could have a moment with Max. He wanted to get the Gudge business over with first and quickly.

Max Lefcourt didn't blink at the mention of $400 million for his collection.

"Mind, Nicholas, I'm not blasé, don't you see. It's just that such a sum of ready money is unknown to any time and place with which I'm even vaguely acquainted." The old man sat elegantly straight in a velvet armchair. Nick felt embarrassed to have vulgarized this room, this friendship with Gudge's offer. Too badly embarrassed even to apologize, other than to say, "Max, I promise that's the last you'll hear of this from me."

"Don't give it a thought, dear boy. Now—what's the news? How's Frodo? He must be ecstatic to have old Frühlingstein's Giotto. What an extraordinary chap your Mr. Bogle must be! An instinctive collector, I gather. They're the rarest, but the best. Frank had a long letter from Felix Rothschild which did nothing but talk about him. I gather you did yourself proud in London. What tricky swine these auction-house people can be! They used to come sniffing around here all the time until we shooed them off. Practically had to use a stick. And now, what about this divine young woman you've brought us? Is there a chance Frank and I can keep her? I'm sure we could make peace with Giuseppina."

"You won't part with your collection, Max. I won't part with Jill."

"Not even for ready money?"

"Not even for ready money."

Later in the afternoon, through the windows, Nick watched Jill walking at the bottom of the garden with Frank Sanger, her arm through one of his, while the old man supported himself on his stick with the other. She was smothered against the cold in an old Viennese coat of Max's, a great leather production with frog closings and wide fur collar that all but covered her face.

Max followed Nick's gaze.

"Frank is very taken with her—as I am. So few young people who come here seem to want to enjoy anything; they're all so professional. They think Frank's got some mechanical trick for recognizing a Botticelli. It's all games and gimmicks. They don't even go outside to look at the city, let alone our pictures. All they want is gossip."

Max swept his arm toward the view. The late-afternoon sky was a deepening gray, pocked with a bluish scud of clouds that swept across the plain of the Arno, bound for the Adriatic. Nick had forgotten how fierce and infernal Florence could look in winter, stripped of its customary sunlight. The warmth of the drawing room, a fire alight and crackling, made cozy, protective contrast to the darkening garden where Jill and Francis Sanger were making one last turn among the bare alleys of yew and box. Shadows were deepening in the old Roman wisteria arbor from which the villa took its name.

"You should see this place in the summer," Nick had said, when they had gone out into the garden the afternoon they arrived, after Lefcourt and Sanger had retired for a nap.

"Oh, but I love it now. Just as it is today. And I love *them*, Nick. And they love you."

Nick knew it, but it still made him redden. "See that arbor over there? That's La Pergola; they say Boccaccio's dames and gallants fled here during the plague, under that same wisteria. Maybe that's where the tales in *Decameron* were first told."

The next morning they went down into the city. It had been a mild but dismally sunless winter; the Arno flowed sluggish and crusted under its bridges. The narrow alleys were clotted with frozen muddy traces of snow. They could see their breath in the arcades of the Uffizi. The statues before the Signoria seemed to shiver. In the galleries where the pictures hung, it was stifling and close. After the bleak days they were thankful to return to the villa, to savor the conversation and company of their hosts.

The day before they were to depart, Nick was summoned to the telephone. When he came back, he reported, "That was none other than Mr. Harvey Bogle. He seems to be in Sta. Marta and has urgent need of me. Duty calls, I fear, which means that you must undertake the dangerous flight from Milan to New York alone, my angel; or—better yet—accompany me to Sta. Marta for two days. Will you? Please."

"Oh, Nick, I can't. I promised everyone"—she sent him a meaningful look—"that I'd be back at the typewriter Monday, and Mother will be deranged by now. I just can't do it. Do you really have to go? Sta. Marta will be full of every phony in the world."

"I'm afraid I have to. I remember something from my school days. Housman, maybe. Something about trumpets holloing and I must go. And so I must."

Dinner was a sprightly affair. All agreed that Jill must be brought back to see spring's bright mantle spread across Tuscany and the city. Plans were made for picnics and excursions.

"We have real springtime here," Frank told Jill. "It's got the breath of summer in it. None of that bittersweet, blossomy business they go for in Paris. The stones of this city need sunlight and a fresh heart."

Nick enjoyed watching them play shamelessly up to Jill.

They left before first light the next morning while Lefcourt and Sanger still slept. "I can't wait to come back in April," Jill said, as they drove toward the *autostrada* leading to Milan. "Wouldn't it be wonderful to bring Jenny?"

She dozed most of the way. Outside Milan, she awoke with an observation on her lips: "Isn't it truly marvelous to see what real love is like? Aren't we like that, Nick? Will we be?"

"Of course we will." His answer sounded offhanded; she sensed that his mind was already across the Alps.

In the airport, she watched him hurry away toward the Zurich flight. When he had vanished, she reached into her carryall and took out a book bound in light brown cloth. Francis Sanger had given it to her the night before.

"I can see you love Florence, my dear. And I can see you love Nicholas. It's very good for him. He's needed somebody for a long time—almost as long, really, as Max and I have known him, when Felix Rothschild sent him to us as a young man. How gifted he was, you know. And he loved the landscapes in the paintings, and the strong faces of the saints, much, much more than he ever enjoyed being able to guess right off who painted what or when.

"That's what I found so interesting—and exciting—in Nicholas, my dear. And so, I expect, do you. He's an idealist, you see. An idealist in the right way: full of feeling and decent conviction without being intellectually purblind.

"Anyway, that's neither here nor there. What is, is this book. It's called *Indian Summer*. By William Dean Howells. Look here—it was published in 1886. Fourteen years before I was born, if you can believe such a thing. It's a wise and wonderful book. Nobody reads Howells anymore, of course. But he had something to say. It's fine on Florence in the winter, when so few know the city, and quite as good on men and women and matters of the heart. And it moves right along. Here—I want very much for you to have it."

Taking a fountain pen from his pocket, he had written on the flyleaf: "*For Gilberte—dear Jill—with the homage and affection of her admirer Francis Sanger/Florence/La Pergola.*" He dated the inscription and blew upon the wet ink. When she took it from him, she saw that his handwriting was strong and confident, nothing like the infirm spider tracks she would have expected from a man this old.

Now, waiting for her plane to be called, she opened the book and began to read, thinking that La Pergola was just as Nick had described it: Parnassus; Paradise; Perfection. Now that she had seen perfection through his eyes, she thought she finally understood him, and knew why she loved him.

Nick's train arrived at Sta. Marta after dark. Harvey Bogle was waiting on the platform.

"Thanks for coming, Nick. I hate to bug a man on his vacation, but I wanted you to look at something. Anyway, have you ever seen this place before? At this time of year? It's a zoo. Esmé dragged me here while she picks up some local color. Wait till you see these people!"

The hotel car brought them to the porte-cochère of the Gastpalast Kratsch. It was blazing with lights. Uniformed minions took Nick's bags and led them into the hotel. A Babel of noise greeted them. It was clear that the cocktail hour was at its height. Nick guessed there were three hundred people in the main hall, and every one of them was dressed to the teeth—the men in black tie and studs, the women in gowns and jewels. A string quartet sawed manfully away from a corner platform, barely breaking even with the multilingual clink and clamor.

"I don't guess you brought a tuxedo," said Bogle, "and here they won't let you take a pee after eight o'clock unless you're wearing one, so we had one fixed up—me and my new asshole buddy Herr Kratsch, who runs this place. It'll be in your room."

Nick had been given an adequate small room on the *entresol*, the mezzanine rooms where Herr Kratsch traditionally stashed his wickedest single men, last-minute arrivals and old, favored guests whom economic fortune had treated comparatively unkindly. Room arrangements were a matter of critical strategic importance at the Gastpalast Kratsch, which at its peak season resembled a sexual board game. Back-hall sneakings and scutterings went on twenty-four hours a day. Puffing Bavarian chemical magnates lumbered off to the slopes in the morning while their youthful wives awaited the gentle rap of the young Italian with the dashing eyes who'd danced so divinely the night before. Slim-hipped Spaniards set out to take their elderly companions' poodles and Yorkies for constitutionals and ended up in the arms of Hollywood stars or Greek shipping tycoons, depending on their mood and the relative desperation of their finances. Romance flowered—causing impassioned pleas to Herr Kratsch for relocation—and died—sending the suppliants back to the front desk with angry requests for something more suitable.

When Nick came downstairs, pleasantly surprised that the borrowed dinner jacket was an acceptable fit, Herr Kratsch was at his command post, dealing with another crisis. The hotel beauty salon had run out of the industrial-grade hair spray that cemented in place the elaborate coiffures of the hotel's ladies, ensuring that not a hair was disturbed by the windy rotors of the helicopters which flew them up the mountain to the Skihawk Club. That was the crux of Herr Kratsch's current problem. In one way or another, the Skihawk was the center of daytime life for a goodly number of Sta. Marta's more obvious seasonal residents. Some could spend the late mornings sipping $30 Bloody Marys or $20 bouillon in the low, timbered clubhouse at the top of the Gozmatsch run, followed by baked potatoes stuffed with caviar; others were obliged to lurk in the village, talking loudly at lunch on the terrace of the Gastpalast Kratsch and pretending that only an inconvenient doctor's appointment or the need to send an urgent telex, not social or personal shortcomings, kept them from enjoying the voluptuous rusticity of the Skihawk. As with all clubs based purely on snobbism, the pleasure the Skihawk offered its initiates was easily as much derived from watching the misery, discomfort and striving of those who tested its threshold and fell short as from any delight they might take in the company of their fellow members. But no one, member, striver or fortunate guest, would dare appear at the club in less than the absolute peak of ordained current fashion. Hence Herr Kratsch's hair-spray crisis. The style-setters of Paris, New York and Milan had decreed a "lacquered outdoorsiness" for the season, replacing the preceding year's "contained rambunctiousness." Herr Kratsch prided himself on being able, year in and year out, to supply his female guests with whatever necessities were decreed by that season's fashion oxymoron. Now, through an unforgivable failure of his computerized inventory-control system, there was no suitable hair spray in the hotel, nor, indeed, anywhere in Sta. Marta except possibly up on the hill at the Bellavista, to which he would certainly not apply. And the very next day was the gala "Déjeuner Americain" at the Skihawk, for which argonauts from Spetsai and Hong Kong, auto magnates from Torino and Rio, beer barons from Manila and Monterrey and real estate speculators and slumlords from a dozen capitals, and their lady wives and mistresses, would be paying 500 Swiss francs to lunch on hot dogs and Cheez-Wiz. Wars had been started over lesser crises.

As agreed, Nick met Bogle in the small bar.

"I'll say one thing for this place, Nick. Money talks. It's like Kratsch runs a Dun and Bradstreet on every new guest. He's quite a character, Kratsch is. Nosy. Oh, boy, Esmé's going bats here. There aren't any important talk shows in Switzerland, so nobody knows who she is. There's this club up on the mountain where all the fancy folk hang out that she's dying to get into, but even Milty Mosker struck out on arranging that. Anyway, I'm glad you came. I need your advice on something. Well, not really your advice: I guess your approval."

Nick knew immediately that Harvey was telling him he'd gone out and bought something on his own.

The next morning Nick presented himself at Bogle's suite at ten o'clock. Bogle opened the door; he detained Nick for an instant in the foyer.

"You're probably going to think I'm sort of a shit, but I stopped in Zurich on my way here. Felix Rothschild suggested I look at something he knew about. I guess I didn't tell you, and maybe he didn't either, but I put Rothschild on retainer—just to help me out. I guess he does all right, but there isn't a professor in the world who can't use an extra twenty grand.

"Anyway, Nick, I saw this thing and it knocked me over. Maybe it was the plane trip; tired, bleary; you know—the smarts come slower after sitting up all night. So I reserved it for the Foundation. For the Fuller, if they want it. Or the Met. They've started to suck around. But then I figured you got me into this, and you're my right arm, the one I'll have left after paying for this picture—if I buy it—so I hustled to the phone and your office told me you were in Florence. Anyway, come take a look."

The sitting room was flooded with clear winter sunshine. An easel had been set up to catch the light streaming across the lake. The painting on it was faced toward the window, away from Nick.

As he followed Bogle into the room, an elderly, gray-haired man got up from an armchair where he had been drinking a cup of tea and came painfully over to Nick extending an arthritic claw.

"Nicholas."

"Heinz." A light went on in Nick's mind. He grinned. "Don't tell me. I don't believe it. You're going to sell it?"

The old man spread his arms, palms up, and nodded with an expression of calm resignation.

"I think the time has come, Nicholas. It's better to see it to a good home now, while I can, than go to my grave worrying about my nephew. He's a nice boy, but ambitious. He wants to be the next Johnny Sandler, and that's impossible. So, that's it."

Nick looked at Bogle. "I don't have to look at it if it's what I think it is." He turned back to the other man. "The Watteau, right, Heinz? The *Commedia*?" The old man nodded.

"Harvey, if you buy this picture, you are going to break the hearts of every other collector, museum, you name it, in the world. Except for the Louvre and the Berlin Museum, and maybe the Wallace Collection. They've each got a great Watteau."

He walked around the easel and looked at the picture. It was every bit as beautiful as he remembered it from the first and only time he'd seen it, almost twenty years ago.

The picture was perhaps a yard and a half wide by a yard high. It depicted *The Italian Comedians in the Garden of Love.* A low landscape, framed by willow and cypress, with a lake in the middle ground and beyond, hidden in a rose-gold haze, the suggestion of mountains. The eye was led back to a melding of earth with sky which suggested that the canvas opened onto interminable spaces that only the imagination could take the measure of. In the foreground, the familiar characters of the Commedia dell'Arte were ranged in easy attitudes on the grass, bowered in banks of flowers, shaded by the drooping trees. In the rear, Harlequin had taken Columbine by the hand and was gesturing toward the mists in the distance, making her ready to go with him out beyond the picture plane, beyond the farthest edge of vision, into, it seemed, eternity. It made the heart ache with bittersweet longing.

Nick thought it perfectly encapsulated the eighteenth century the way he wanted to think of that age: sumptuous, artificial, yet with an edge of sadness, as if the machine age hulked just beyond the horizon like a dim, threatening presence. Watteau captured that.

"Don't think for a minute, Harvey. Pack it up and be done with it. It's a miracle." He turned around. "Heinz used to have about a dozen drawings Watteau made after Rubens. Do you still own them?"

"No longer, alas, Nicholas."

"Too bad. It would have been interesting for Harvey to see them."

"Nicholas, Nicholas. What can I say? He has. He's just bought them, you see."

The early train for Zurich left at seven in the morning, so Nick dined early. The Bogles had been invited to a dinner party before the evening's full-dress gala in the basement discotheque, leaving him to his own devices, which made him perfectly happy.

Reviewing his day over dinner in the hotel *Stuebli*, with a bottle of Dôle to keep him company, he judged it a success. He was pleased that Bogle had bought the Watteaus. Frodo would be ecstatic. For himself, he was satisfied that he had kept the inside track with Bogle. Too many dealers were jealous and selfish about their clients. Nick had guessed Bogle wouldn't put up with that kind of girls'-school behavior.

He took a deep sip of the Dôle. For an instant he felt a sliver of sadness for his friend Heinz. It was always wrenching to part with a treasure, to bid goodbye to the companion of a lifetime. Yet, why not? This was Heinz's business. He pretended to be a scholar and an amateur, but Nick estimated that Borgner's volume and profits were easily as much as his own. And the Borgner vaults under the old city of Zurich held what small part of the French eighteenth century hadn't been appropriated by Frederick the Great, the Louvre and Du Cazlet.

Through Dr. Frucht, he'd arranged lunch for the Bogles at the Skihawk Club. Esmé's eyes had bugged at the clothes and jewels: ruby-studded ski mittens and jump suits of cloth-of-gold seemed routine. She wouldn't get it right, of course, Nick knew; writers like Esmé never seemed to get inside the fancy world they served up to their slavering audience of middle-class fantasists. All they ever got right was the labels. There'd even be a touch of drama during lunch when an angry little millionaire from California had practically come to blows with a storm-faced ex-Uhlan over the last package of Hostess Twinkies.

It was close to eleven when Nick made his way to his room. He was a little drunk. It had seemed a good idea to follow his dinner with a couple of *Pflumlis* and then a sedating Scotch or two in the little bar upstairs. He threw off his clothes and settled down on the bed, trying to read the story in the Paris *Herald Tribune* that Harvey had told him about. It seemed that Homer Seabury had outsmarted Granada Masterman. Something like that. The print blurred. He thought he could ask Jill about it tomorrow in New York. Drowsiness overtook him.

He was roused by a rapping at his door. His watch said 11:45. He would have sworn he'd been asleep for more than a half-hour. He threw on a bathrobe and shuffled to the door.

Caryn Gudge was standing there.

"Well, hi," she said conversationally. She was wearing a long silk bathrobe. Her hair was loose.

"I saw you come in this afternoon. Can you believe it, it took this long to get my room switched down the hall. Thank God money still talks somewhere."

Nick could say nothing. He was randy with liquor and unspent dreams. As casually as she might have flicked back an errant hair, she reached for his hand and guided it inside her robe to her breast. She let the gown fall open; he saw the long sweep of legs and belly, the auburn moss at her crotch. He felt paralyzed; unable to heed the alarm bells in his head which grew fainter with each second. Her other hand reached up and slid inside his bathrobe, taking him gently. He felt himself grow hard in her grasp; something irresistible spread through him from his groin, drowning out the last small warning tinkle.

"Let's have us some fun," she said. She smiled up at him, but her eyes weren't laughing. Holding him as if he were as inert and manageable as a skillet, she guided him back into his room, pushing the door shut behind her.

Two hours later she let herself out of Nick's room, leaving him foolishly asleep in the wreckage of his bedclothes. She made her way quietly down the hall to her room. Live and learn, she thought, as she closed her door behind her; he wasn't half as good as he'd looked. Funny, being that young and all, he didn't have a patch on Hugo.

In his pantry, the floor waiter watched her. He had a mirror that commanded a view of the corridor. He was a young boy from the town; this was his first employment, and he was anxious to make a good job of it. Which meant obeying orders—and the first order around the Gastpalast was that Herr Kratsch was to be notified about any unusual commerce of any kind between guests in his hotel, especially guests not married to each other or traveling together. The waiter put down his month-old soccer paper and made a note of the particulars and room numbers on a sheet of paper. It was a matter of an instant to carry it down to the front desk, marked to the attention of Herr Kratsch, and return to his station. Slightly out of breath, he was pleased to see that the lights in his call box were dark. All was calm, all was well.

Nick arose late the next morning, bathed and dressed and went downstairs. The hazy memory of a few hours earlier filled him with a trepidation that soon became guilt. Hell, he tried to convince himself, he wasn't married to Jill. Like most men in the situation he had created for himself, he needed to drive in some tent pegs of reassurance, to hurry back symbolically to the order of things he'd briefly, carelessly thrown aside; anxiety had to be shoved back into the farthest, most nearly invisible reaches of his mind, where the line between recollection and fantasy disappeared. His effort was a sorry one.

At the front desk, he asked for a telex form and sent an affectionate message to Jill at the number she'd given him. Another small gesture, this time of reaffirmation, by which he hoped to fool himself about the reality of what had taken place.

Kratsch saw him into the car that would take him to the Zurich train. Then he returned to his desk. Keeping a hotel like the Gastpalast was a twenty-four-hour job. Around Sta. Marta it was joked that Herr Kratsch, like a marmot, slept only out of season.

It was his practice to inspect all incoming and outgoing telexes. Through this habit, Herr Kratsch had, over the years, learned valuable details about tanker movements, future titanium prices, stock-market activity and such other matters of interest as bore directly on the value of his varied holdings at the Banco d' Oltremare. He scanned Nick's telex quickly, admiring the young man's romantic facility, until the name and number to which it was being sent caught his eye.

Herr Kratsch frowned. He hoped there would be no difficulty. By nature a man who let live, he did not wish that the telex he himself had sent off just hours before to the same telex number, recounting the day's activities at the Gastpalast, including certain goings-on in the *entresol*, would cause any inconvenience for anyone. He was not, after all, a troublemaker; simply maintaining his end of a relationship that kept the name of the Gastpalast Kratsch before the eyes of the fashionable, moneyed world. It was, after all, not his business what people did with their lives. His life was the Gastpalast. He turned away and busied himself with the more difficult matter of that evening's gold-and-silver *Kegel* party.

CHAPTER TWENTY

The morning papers contained much economic news of the sort that prudent men found ominous and which caused even the stompingest market bulls hot flashes of uncertainty. Not Homer Seabury, however; his antennae had been dulled by triumph. He and Katagira had mousetrapped Granada Masterman. There was no doubt of that. Two days before the expiration of MUD's hostile tender offer, Seaco had stepped in with a preemptive bid for 3 million of its own shares at $35, which it had financed by selling $105 of capital notes and preferred stock to Gudge Cormier Holdings, Ltd., the Lazy G's Bermuda-based insurance company, which operated with a swaggering lack of restraint and regulation that suited its *pukka* colonial antecedents.

Seabury was finally impregnable. Counting the stock owned by Gudge with his own, he had an absolute majority in his pocket. Eight million votes out of a total of 15 million plus. What a vote of confidence by Gudge!

Katagira was not displeased. The money was to be lost in any case, so that it came down to a simple question of where, not whether, it was placed. Mrs. Masterman was nicely on board, too. Their preemptive bid had caused her to withdraw, but MUD for some reason was hanging on to the 1.2 million shares it had bought from the institutions, on which, technically, it had a paper profit of close to $9 million; by Katagira's reckoning, MUD now had a total of $88 million invested in Seaco—and nowhere, for the foreseeable future at least, to turn, since, through MUD, Mrs. Masterman owned enough Seaco stock to be, legally, an "insider." It would be a long time before MUD could legally sell its Seaco shares; time enough for Katagira to see the whole business blown to smoke. To lose $88 million wouldn't kill MUD, but, as Gudge had said, "It'd damn for sure smart." That Granada had lost face on the Street was unarguable. Her defeat was fodder for the chauvinists at the Stock Exchange Lunch Club; "It just goes to show," gloated the specialist in Seaco, "if you have to squat to piss, don't get in a pissing match."

Katagira was also pleased to have euchred the institutions. His brief time around Wall Street had convinced him of their basic intellectual dishonesty; the Seaco business had proved him right. The three institutional blocks of Seaco stock that had been prematurely, irrevocably committed to MUD just happened to come from the investment arms of two banks and an insurance company that just happened to do a great deal of other, profitable business, none of it connected with investments, with Masterman United. This had been pointed out by Robert Creighton in *Pritchett's*; substantial lawsuits on behalf of fiduciary and advisory accounts were being mounted against the offending institutions.

It was all very satisfactory, he reported to Gudge. Give the fish a little more line, a slightly longer run to weaken it, and it would be time to start reeling. When he recounted how that would be, Gudge, for all that his disease was tightening its grip and squeezing out his already diminished vitality, was able, weakly, to stomp a couple of times for what passed in his life for joy.

In the last month or two, Jill had more than once speculated on the possibility of being freed of Gilberte. That things would work out with Nick so that she could resign that odious commission. It was a dangerous kind of daydream, she knew; it smacked more than vaguely of dependence. Or at least of the possibility of dependence. Whenever she felt it come on, she scolded herself for not being more thoroughly modern. Most of her contemporaries would more willingly suffer killing emotional deprivation than admit to the possibility of letting some part of their independence go. She couldn't go that far.

So she thought.

She had flicked on the light in her workroom, gone over to the telex and seen at a glance that a series of items had been received from Herr Kratsch.

Kratsch was real scum, she thought as she tore the paper from the machine and carried it back to her desk to read. This was the part of the job she hated worst—relying on this kind of backstairs peeking and snooping for "items." But "items" were what dictated her value to *That Woman!*; they were what Gilberte bartered for, exchanging mentions of hotels and restaurants and limousine services and masseurs—even doctors; Victor Sartorian was a prime source—for tidbits of fashion information. The trouble was, she thought, her purveyors persisted in dishing dirt to her, even though they must have realized by now that she, for one, didn't print them. Kratsch was among the most comprehensive, and worst, she thought. If his clientele knew what he passed on, the Gastpalast would be empty and its proprietor, if he was lucky, washing dishes at the Bellavista. She supposed Kratsch sent this same stuff to other columnists; once or twice, she'd elsewhere spotted an item that had also been on her telex.

As she settled to read Kratsch's telex, she blessed herself for having worked it out so that she neither suffered nor made others suffer from the slimy world of which Gilberte was, technically, part and practitioner. Somehow, thanks to Creighton, and her own character, she thought, reading disinterestedly, I've transcended it.

Then Kratsch's seventh item, reporting Caryn Gudge's midnight sortie in the Gastpalast *entresol,* hit her with the force, the more shattering for being so entirely unexpected, of a sniper's bullet striking a random victim.

Not quite making sense of it, she read it twice more.

She would later recall that something strange had happened then. A fierce energy rose within her, quite blocking out all the implications of what she had read, and she pounded at her typewriter until she had finished her column, getting business out of the way, purging herself of her vocation; barely making it to the end before the onrush of tears and sorrow overtook her.

She threw the column aside and, like an animal on whose leg a hidden trap has sunk its sudden teeth, she gave a cry—part moan, part sob, part howl—so shocking and uncontrollable that she stuffed her fist against her mouth for fear of frightening Jenny awake.

She felt as if she were outside herself, looking into a burgled room, seeing the place where her precious private things were kept now trashed and savaged by a stranger. The thought made her sick, and she rushed to the bathroom.

Then—for a while—she wept softly with disappointment and hurt. The futility of tears came to her; she was behaving like a baby, she thought, or a poor, dumb animal trying uncomprehendingly to lick itself well. Well, she thought, she was neither baby nor animal. This was the twentieth century; be tough, she instructed herself. She began to appreciate the enormity of the insult she had been paid. Men, she said to herself ferociously; men! Always slaves to that thing between their legs; that twisp of flesh with its funny nicknames; that boy's toy, that gun that armed itself and demanded to be shot and wouldn't abate until it was. She became angry with herself. What was wrong with her? she demanded. Would she always stick herself with weak ones, like Bobby Manship, who went out windows, or Mickey Greschner, with his whore's mentality, or now Nick, Nicholas—yes, Nicholas now—who couldn't keep it in their pants?

The final admission was the most wounding of all. It was this dirty business she was in that had brought this to her. All across the city, women slept in peaceful ignorance of their men's fallings from grace and fidelity. Other women rose and went to offices, or shops; sat in banks or wrote advertising copy; or edited novels; or built empires. Other women didn't spend Sunday nights reading the parings and scraps of the dirty-minded and vicious-hearted of the world. She knew then how foolish she had been to expect that the filth wouldn't someday rise high enough to stain her.

What she needed was time to think. To take a walk in the freezing air and let it clear her head and senses. She half-rose, thinking to get her coat and stalk out into the night where she could walk miles and blocks and continents, whatever it took to get herself together, to figure it out. Then she thought of Jenny, sleeping down the hall, and knew that the ominous Manhattan night was no place for a single, now suddenly solitary parent to venture. The hopelessness of it brought up a phrase from that Howells novel Francis Sanger had given her: "A *man would have plunged from the house and walked the night away; a woman must wear it out in her bed.*" She found herself gasping, as if her hopelessness were pushing the air from the room. She jerked the window up and let herself suck in great clarifying drafts.

Nick must go. There could be no mending. The insult was too great. Totally unforgivable. Angrily, she had drawn her chair to the typewriter and started the letter on which she was now working. A crowd of crumpled paper gobbets grew around her chair, burying the ball of paper that had been the strip of telex containing Kratsch's informings and causing to perish, forever unread, Nick's message to her.

The morning's financial pages carried a number of articles that commanded Katagira's interest and attention. In an interview on the front page of *The Wall Street Journal*, a member of the enforcement division of the Securities and Exchange Commission had come out for a reduced burden of disclosure on the nation's great corporations: "The function of the Commission is to expedite the sale and propagation of corporate securities, not to hinder the process," the august functionary was quoted as having decreed; later in the interview, he had pointed with pride to the ease with which the Commission had cleared the way for GOD and GUT to come to market. Katagira wondered, offhand, what that worthy gentleman, formerly a well-known securities lawyer, might have wished to add to his statement had he known that the assets and profits reported by GUT and GOD, both of which had been among the most actively traded stocks on the Big Board since their issuance, were entirely fictitious. The two issues had brought nearly $500 million at the initial offering; now, three months later, still haloed by the golden glow of the name of Gudge in a very edgy market, they were worth some $100 million more than at issuance.

Katagira was ensconced in his warm, small office next to the information room. Outside, a late-winter storm was howling itself to death; it was a good time to be inside. Crossing to the Big House that morning, he had felt the wind tear at him and prayed, only for an instant, that spring might soon arrive and the whole business could wind itself up, just as the gale and sleet outside were wearing themselves out across the landscape.

Ah, he smiled to himself, seeing that Homer Seabury had been named a special adviser to the Treasury Department. "Mr. Seabury, chief executive of Seaco Group, the firm closely identified with the resurgence of the long-term-bond market, will advise the Secretary on capital-market decisions affecting the sale of long-term obligations," reported the *Times*. Which reminded Katagira of something. From a neat pile of papers at the corner of his worktable, he picked out the latest computer run from Seaco. The Seaco-Gudge partnership now held $11.6 market value of government, industrial and utility bonds with a face value of approximately $14.5 billion. The partnership's equity consisted of $470 million of GUT, GOD and Seaco stock provided by various Gudge interests, plus $160 million in cash contributed equally by Seaco and Gudge, the balance of the financing, nearly $10.5 billion, consisted of loans from an international syndicate of banks and commercial finance companies; in addition to the bond portfolio itself, the loans were collateralized by $4.3 billion of Seaco Group's free customer balances and just over $1 billion in securities dedicated to Seaco's stock-loan program.

At the moment, the paper profit in the partnership's bond position stood at nearly $1.7 billion, which meant they had a paper triple on their equity. The earliest maturity in the portfolio was seven years out, which meant that it had not been possible to hedge in the conventional financial-futures market. Ever ravenous for new paper to create new action, the futures markets were planning to commence trading in "Gudge Futures," as they were inevitably nicknamed, by which speculators in long-term bonds, an army growing daily in size and frenzy, might hedge their positions or speculate on the direction of the market. Always pleased to see anything that would enlarge the ripples when it came time for him to drop his boulder into the already teeming pond, Katagira wished them and their ingenuity well.

There was more Seaco news, he found. In Creighton's *Pritchett's* column, it was reported that Seaco Group had been engaged by Harvey Bogle as part of the team with which he proposed to do battle for TransNational Entertainment Communications. "The hired guns," wrote Creighton, listing their retainers and minimum commissions as a football program might list the players' numbers,

> constitute a very Cooperstown of the sharks that can be expected to gather over such a succulent piece of takeover blubber as TEC. Harvey Bogle, the contender, has in his corner: Seaco Group, investment bankers, $2 million minimum; Quayle, Sopwith and Phelin, lawyers, $1 million against $600 an hour; Polans Associates, financial public relations and solicitation, estimated $500,000. Wiping the brow and patching the cuts of Marvin Terrace, the leg-weary incumbent, will be Kuhn, Kahn, Cohn and Co., investment bankers, $3 million; Inganno, Voler and Lugen, attorneys, $2 million against $600 an hour; Black and Chestnutt, Federal Communications Commission specialist attorneys, $500,000 estimated; Behrens, Kapp and Staff, corporate P.R., $500,000 estimated.

"In addition," the item concluded, "it is understood that Bogle has engaged Solomon Greschner, the legendary dean of big-league public relations, as a special adviser."

How unlike Greschner, he thought, to permit mention of his name in such a matter. Reflecting further, he recalled how he had heard, years ago, that a principal source of Greschner's influence and success, especially on Wall Street, was his unparalleled connections with financial journalists and stock analysts. Very likely Greschner himself had planted mention of himself in Creighton's column, Katagira guessed. That would be a most valuable capability when the time, which now approached with a rush, was finally at hand.

Which brought Katagira back to present matters. Having been left alone at the ranch while Gudge accompanied his wife to Palm Beach for two weeks, he had seized the solitary time to put the next, final stages of the plan in order. He had just about completed the redivision and repackaging of the assets of the Lazy G for the ultimate distribution he planned for them. His processors and data files had proved up the necessary titles, drawn up the requisite instruments of conveyance and certain related deeds and documents, all now awaiting only Buford Gudge's signature. There were roughly one hundred pieces of paper to be signed, along with approximately forty covering letters.

So that part was virtually complete; on the shelf, to be executed by Gudge on his return from Florida.

Now, he thought, we must address ourselves to the execution. The audience has been shown the hat, and the rabbit, and seen the rabbit put into the hat. Now, as in any good conjurer's performance, must begin the business of gradually revealing that the hat is empty. He had bored into the structure and weakened it; in a matter of weeks, it would be time to give it that first, gentle, precisely placed little shove which would set it imperceptibly trembling. At first there would be just a faint surface disruption, a clod set jiggling by the volcano climbing surfaceward from the boiling core of the earth; a minuscule spill of sand from the sea wearing through the earthen dike; a rumble of thunder so faint and distant as to seem a figment of the imagination. In their case, there would, first, be vague rumors, hints of trouble or irregularity; then a mounting crescendo of small facts and large innuendos, the rumors gathering centripetal force, fusing like blown glass with a core of actuality so that the facts themselves seemed to grow in size and terror. Next would appear the large cracks, fingers of the abyss to come, and then, panic: the terminal state of markets.

He had known from the beginning that he would probably need help with this; from the beginning he had believed that Greschner would provide it. Like himself, Greschner was an outsider to this world and would always be. Unlike himself, Greschner could not accept the fact of his ultimate exclusion. He might be a servant smarter and more perceptive than those he served, but he was a servant still—now and always. A valued presence—yet somehow always to be vaguely apologized for. Greschner had been assigned a role in the lives of others that practically ensured his cancerous dissatisfaction and resentment.

And Greschner liked real power; liked his actions to have acknowledged consequences; wanted to be "The Man Who . . ." All that had been plain to Katagira practically from the beginning. Greschner would find it irresistible not to join with them, Katagira thought. The very idea of power of this degree and effect would simply be too transcendent not to surrender to.

It was time to invite Greschner in. He went to the telephone and dialed Greschner's number in New York. Outside, the wind whirled and cut through the leafless trees, skidding gustily along the bare, frozen ground under skies as gray and lightless as dead skin. Waiting for Greschner to come onto the line, Katagira thought that the gale somehow prefigured the storms to come.

Nick's plane finally lumbered onto the runway at JFK seven hours late. The storm had completely disrupted traffic in the air, so his Swissair flight had spent three hours on the ground in Newfoundland before refueling and heading on to New York.

Nick was desperate to see Jill. In truth, he was desperate with guilt by now, practically gasping, like a man drowning, for the deep, unconstricting sigh of relief men need to assure them they have gotten away with something they wish they had never done. Only Jill could give him that reassurance. He needed to be able to reach out and touch her and thus know that she was real and so was he and that it was just a nightmare that had swept over them.

By the time he had made it through Immigration and to a pay phone, he was throat-caught with anxiety.

There was no answer at Jill's. Strange, he thought; it's almost ten at night. Sunday night. Jill never went out on a Sunday night. It occurred to him then that she might be outside, in the terminal, waiting for him. Cheered by the thought, he endured the wait at Customs, got a skycap to take his bags and practically burst into the crowded, confused arrival hall.

She wasn't there.

On the cab ride back to Manhattan, his chest felt crushed. He tried to force back the "How did she find out?" which had pushed its way past "She doesn't know; she can't know" in the near-hysterical inner conversation taking place in his mind.

He heard the letter before he saw it. It had fallen through the letter slot onto the floor, and he kicked it as he let himself into the maisonette. Snapping on the light, he stood holding it as if it contained some malevolent genie he feared to release, but only for a second. Ripping it open, he read:

Dear Nick:

I must get to the point and tell you that I know what happened between you and Caryn Gudge in Sta. Marta. I know because of this filthy business I am in.

Nick, I don't want to see you. I won't say "ever," but don't get your hopes up.

There are many things that could be said. I won't torment you and I won't torment me with them. Let's just say thanks for what we've had and please, you must know, I just can't continue to be with someone who is that way. The way I didn't think you were. But you turned out to be just like Mickey Greschner and all the rest.

I'm sorry for that. It's a cheap shot, but then, I think I owe you at least one of those.

There's everything else to say and there's nothing. We're both old enough to know them without saying them, and I'm not writing for publication now.

Please don't call. I've got the phone turned off, and Monday my number will be changed. Now it's over between us, I guess, and I must take care of Jenny. I know she'll want to know where you went, and I don't know quite how I'll explain. Maybe I'll say you died.

He kicked his bag aside and ran out and got a cab on Park Avenue and asked it to take him to Jill's. The transverses through Central Park were blocked by snow, and it was a long, dismal trip around by Central Park South, even on a Sunday night. The cab didn't go fast enough to suit Nick's pounding nerves, nor did the elevator up to Jill's floor, and when he got there he remembered that his keys to her apartment were back at his place.

So he knocked politely and called her name in a hushed voice, and then louder. "Please!" he implored. "Please, damn it; please, please! Just listen. Just let me talk for five minutes, one minute, that's all, and I promise I'll go. Promise." She must have been listening on the other side of the door, he later figured, perhaps wavering, because suddenly he heard the "klock" of the deadbolt sliding shut. Although the noise was on the other side of the door, Nick felt that it was he who was being locked up, in a cell that was the rest of his life.

CHAPTER TWENTY-ONE

Robert Creighton in *Pritchett's*, April 9:

> Easter seems an especially suitable time for thinking about eggs in baskets, and Marvin Terrace, chief executive of TransNational Entertainment Corporation (TEC-NYSE), must be worrying about his, which corporate raider Harvey Bogle seems bent on turning into an omelette.
>
> In the next few weeks, the financial community will see an intensifying of the proxy battle for control of TEC that Bogle initiated last month. Unlike the oil-company bidding contests of the last year, the TEC fight doesn't appear to be another case of corporate Ping-Pong, with the ball being the stockholders' and employees' relative interests and the paddles the egos of the contending chief executives. Most insiders on the Street believe that there is real merit in Bogle's position. He believes that TEC, notionally a creative company, should be managed creatively. As one major institutional trader commented: "The only place Marvin Terrace is creative is in protecting his own skin."
>
> Certainly TEC in recent years seems to have been run principally for the entertainment and social ambitions of its management and the remuneration of the horde of advisers Marvin Terrace has surrounded himself with since he was forced on TEC by the company's lenders a few years ago. If Bogle prevails —and he is said to be adding continuously to his nearly 30% voting interest in TEC—it will probably mark the end of those $100-a-head catered sound-stage buffets which the Terraces have been throwing for the White House crowd. The prospect of a Bogle victory in the proxy fight is said to have cast gloom over every caterer, florist, bartending service and wine merchant from Santa Monica to the San Fernando Valley.

Bogle put down the paper and smiled at Nick, who had come to the Tennyson for a drink.

"I'm going to eat this guy Terrace's ass with a spoon. I know you don't get much of a bang out of business, Nick—business-type business, that is —but this is some deal. It's a course in itself in what's wrong with this country.

"Terrace, you see, makes about a million a year, maybe more, at TransNational. He owns about a million bucks' worth of stock, mostly paid for with an interest-free loan from the company. So he's making a million on a million-dollar investment, or 100 percent return, and the stockholders are getting about 3 percent a year."

Bogle smiled. He'd enjoyed his interview with Terrace, a frightened accountant cowering behind the Duke of Wellington's campaign desk amid a decorator's mishmash of crossed Zulu spears, Boule cabinets, mediocre Victorian watercolors, narwhal horns and dhurrie rugs.

"But Harvey," Terrace had pleaded, "I'm management, senior management; this company is my life; that's what management gets paid for. Those sums you're throwing at me—well, these days that's what management gets paid."

"I got news for you, Marvin. 'Paid' and 'worth' aren't synonyms. I'm sick of you guys in management. Guys in Detroit making a million a year and the Japs own the car market. What're they getting paid for? Coming to work? It's worse than the government. You're all paying yourselves about five times what you were five, ten years ago and your companies are doing worse. That's inflationary, Marvin; that's unpatriotic. You give speeches and go to parties and every six or eight months you get a hard-on to piss away the stockholders' money in some big tender offer. Which makes all you guys feel like real big deals, I guess."

Then Terrace had tried to buy him out, using bank lines which had been arranged for the purpose, but Bogle had insisted on the same offer's being made to all stockholders; at which Terrace had turned ashen.

"I'm gonna make an example of you, Marvin. And maybe other guys who own stock in other companies will take it to heart and kick some butt in their own backyards. Personally, I'd like to kick ass in a couple of oil companies, but they're beyond me; you I can afford, which is your bad luck."

"Harvey, I must say I simply don't follow you. Why this vengeful tone?" Terrace was trying to sound patrician. "This is very disruptive to this company."

"And is going to be to your social life, Marvin. Let's just say I'm sick and tired of your type of guy, Marvin. Sick and tired; and rich enough, and secure enough, to do something about it. I'm not part of the club, you see, and I don't want to be. I don't want to go to the Bohemian Grove or the Greenbrier, or get elected to big-time boards. You can't put me down by talking to me like some kid that's puked in the bar of the Links Club. I'm gonna talk with my money, Marvin."

It had been a successful meeting by Bogle's standards. In the relish of relating it, however, Bogle failed to grasp the moroseness underlying Nick's apparent attentiveness. Later, after Nick had left, he did; and resolved to lend his own distractful effort to cheering his friend up.

"It was real embarrassing, K, I tell you." Gudge laid down his fork and looked at Katagira, to whom he had just finished relating the story of

Greschner's exclusion from a dance at Palm Beach's Seagrape club. Caryn had invited Greschner to stay with them for the last long winter weekend; she had even cajoled her husband into coming to Palm Beach. The Gudges had been taken to the Seagrape dance by the Tarver Meltons.

"Oh, I don't know, Buford," Caryn broke in before Katagira could comment. "I mean, I don't see how he possibly could have expected to be asked. It's not just the Jewish thing, sweetheart, although that's bad enough. But he is a public relations man, and that's just not the kind of person we want at Seagrape."

Masklike as always, Katagira's expression betrayed no unusual interest at Mrs. Gudge's conversational appropriation of a membership in a Palm Beach club to which it was unlikely she would ever belong. How predictable were her metamorphoses, he thought; at first, she had been grateful and grasping, conscious of superficial labels, a copyist. Then, during the time she had stayed away from the ranch longest, there had clearly been a decadent phase, the discovery of new thrills; Katagira had recognized the signs. Now, after a winter amid the manicured lawns and minds of Palm Beach, she had become rather grand. She was starting to talk like an insider.

"You know, darling," she continued, "I'm just not sure we need Sol so much anymore. I mean, I do know a whole lot of people now, you know, and—well—it's just that Sol's so kind of, of . . . professional. I mean, you can't take him just anywhere. I mean, well, after all, he was . . ." She paused, chasing the right word like a dog snapping at a moth. ". . . well, hired." And if hired, could be fired, went the unspoken logical conclusion.

Gudge looked at Katagira. Handle it, his weary glance said; handle it, please. Gudge truly feared personal dealings of all kinds, but especially unpleasant ones.

"Perhaps," said Katagira measuredly, "it might help if I went to New York to speak with Mr. Greschner; to discuss some modification of the existing arrangements respecting Mrs. Gudge."

"Oh, would you?" Caryn said, adding, "But I'm going to need the Gulfstream, so could you take the Falcon or the Lear?"

"Of course." One answer to both questions.

Inadvertently, Mrs. Gudge—Katagira almost blessed her—had supplied him with what he needed. The man was right: the moment surely approached; and now Mrs. Gudge had given him the motive. Between the Palm Beach incident, and now her disavowal of her manufacturer, Caryn Gudge would tip the balance in Greschner's mind. After all, without her husband's money and name, who was Caryn Gudge? To Katagira, nothing. No more than she had been before Gudge; no more than she would be after what was to come.

He told the Gudges he would leave for New York as soon as he could make a date with Greschner.

They dined together at Number 17 three days later. Greschner had been surprised to hear from Katagira; he had assumed their dealings would have effectively concluded with the forging of the Gudge-Seaco connection, perhaps the most celebrated, mutually profitable alliance in Wall Street history. He was greatly pleased, therefore, by Katagira's call, which told him inferentially that perhaps he had not been as completely forgotten in the whole business as he had thought. Typically, Sol did not for a moment consider that Katagira's proposed visit might involve termination of his engagement as Caryn Gudge's public relations counsel. In a perverse way, he had tried to underplay her disloyal behavior in Palm Beach by telling himself that the Seagrape should be taken as a symbol of how effective he had been in her behalf. He had made her what she wanted to be.

"You're looking extremely well, Mr. Greschner. Nice color—for this time of year. I gather you spent the weekend with Mr. and Mrs. Gudge in Florida."

Katagira had decided to circle the principal matter on his mind like a courting mantis, to feel Greschner out and take one last determining sounding of the man.

"Indeed so. And very pleasant it was, although I must confess I found it a trifle rambunctious for a man of my years. And you? Has it been an arduous winter at the Lazy G?"

"Tolerable. By no means as wearing as some we've had in my tenure there."

Over dinner they exchanged small talk centering on Seaco. Katagira was effusive in his praise of the firm, Homer Seabury, his associates and the businesslike efficiency and singular creativity with which the bond investment program had been transacted. He let fall the impression that all that had been accomplished was in greatest measure due to Solomon Greschner's judiciousness and wisdom in guiding the Gudge interests to Seaco.

"Do you know, Mr. Greschner, that we're now approaching fifteen billion dollars of total commitments, for our own account and in our partnership with Mr. Seabury? Total borrowing—in all forms—against our existing bond positions is very close to thirteen billion dollars. And of course, we've infused another three hundred million dollars cash which Mr. Gudge borrowed from his banking group against certain of his producing properties. It's really remarkable, isn't it, if you think that as recently as a year ago the total indebtedness of the Gudge interests was less than three million dollars?"

Katagira was extremely pleased with the way things had worked out. The indebtedness drawn down from the banks, some $400 million of which was from Gudge-controlled banks and stretched their legal lending limits to the utmost, was secured by the same properties which the investing public believed to be cornerstones of the asset base of GOD. He regarded this transaction as a nice fillip which might intensify the velocity and extent of the damage that would ensue when he gave the final puff and collapsed the financial house of cards his computers' legerdemain had erected.

For the time, he stayed away from the business of Mrs. Gudge. Although he liked having the weapon at hand, he preferred, if he could, not to throw Caryn Gudge's disloyalty like dog meat at Greschner's feet to bait his ire. Katagira regarded anger, no matter how fairly provoked or how well justified, as a most unsatisfactory, unsuitable motivator. Especially in circumstances that required calm, efficient play of the hand. So he intended instead to draw Greschner in by appealing to his most piercingly felt inadequacy, to what Katagira perceived as the great raw hole at the seat of his being. He proposed to hold out to Greschner something which he believed Greschner was acutely, miserably aware of never having grasped. He would offer Greschner the chance to share in the exercise of real power.

Back upstairs in the firelit study, with the flames reflected richly in the dark paneling, settled in the fat stuffed armchairs flanking the fireplace, Katagira got down to cases.

"Mr. Greschner, I have from our very first meeting been of the opinion that you are a philosophical man. A man, may I say, much more attuned to our Oriental view of things than to the hurly-burly pragmatism of the mercantile civilization in which we both find ourselves."

Greschner smiled.

"You have been an integral part of the New York culture—may I call it that?—for half a century," Katagira continued. "I expect you have observed and analyzed many changes. Might I beg the indulgence of being privy to your thinking? How would you characterize these changes? We are both, after all, of a certain age, and, I must tell you, I myself feel increasingly ill at ease in this world. I suspect you may feel the same. But I would be greatly interested in hearing you express it in your own terms."

Greschner neither fulminated nor poured out a torrent of vindictive self-pity. He spoke instead in a tone that Katagira might have taken for his own in the same moral circumstances. His words resonated with the disappointment, the resignation of a man of long experience finally convinced of the irreversible tawdriness of everyday human behavior.

"It is a paper world we live in, Mr. Katagira," Greschner finished. "Because it is that, grown men are permitted to act out fantasies with the money of others: corporate shoot-outs with dollars instead of bullets. Once upon a time, when I was most active, the great men on Wall Street and from industry got their pictures in the papers only when they died or were convicted. Then, just about twenty years ago, as I recall, stardom came to the Street. They acquired press agents; craved publicity; wanted to see themselves in the public eye. I regret to say in hindsight that I made rather a good thing, financially and professionally, of this thirst. I might add, also in hindsight, that I am not entirely comfortable living with it."

Greschner sounded like a mildly repentant false prophet. Katagira felt this was all palaver; that Greschner was a morally guilty, philosophically embittered man. Certainly few individuals below the level of great captains of state and their immediate lieutenants could have contributed as much to the decline of private responsibility as a man like Solomon Greschner. A man who could manipulate a world that believed what it read in its papers, or saw on its television screens, into accepting as genuine Solomon Greschner's fabrications of character and accomplishment.

That was Greschner's misfortune, Katagira believed, although he could now see that Greschner himself might have described it as "tragedy." But there was nothing truly tragic even in puppets: even if made so well and manipulated so adroitly. There was nothing innately tragic about social climbers' being guided adroitly upward toward worthless summits; about pinched and anxious inheritors' being advertised as industrial statesmen; about dollars' being traded for the appearance of virtue or cultivation.

He believed, however, that Greschner truly saw himself as a tragic figure. From Katagira's point of view, it was a very serviceable belief.

He nodded solemnly as Greschner finished. Before responding, he paused, letting his silence further impregnate the room with a sense of momentousness. He wanted Greschner at his most Olympian.

Finally: "Mr. Greschner, I have come to discuss with you a matter of the greatest urgency and significance. Of mortal significance, I might say."

For the next half-hour he described in detail everything behind Bubber Gudge's sudden, stunning involvement with Wall Street, everything that underlay the miracle of "the Gudge bull market" in bonds. He spared nothing. He disclosed that GUT and GOD were paper creatures, holding legal title to none of the assets that Seaco's offering documents and the investment world at large assumed them to own. Figments of the "imagination" of his information room. He described Gudge's motivation: basically to avenge himself on his half-sister, Mrs. Masterman, and on his taunter and torturer, Senator Lassiter, and, in a larger sense, on the alien world and culture represented by New York, a city toward which Gudge seemed to have wellspring antipathies beyond even Katagira's understanding. How he, Katagira, had seen this as an opportunity to strike a purgative blow for his own values.

"Now, Mr. Greschner, we are at last ready to rush to judgment," Katagira said firmly. His finality didn't escape Sol. "To cut, one by one, the strings which make the marionette dance. To dismantle our cardboard temple to Mammon. You are the acknowledged master of the reverse of these arts—a notable builder of illusions. We are inviting you—that is, Mr. Gudge is inviting you—to join in unbuilding what is the greatest illusion ever visited on Wall Street. Largely by itself, I might add."

Greschner felt strangely calm, considering what the Japanese had just told him. Reflexively, he saw immediately that Katagira had run no risk in telling him all. Although his guest hadn't said as much, it was clear that everything was in place for the denouement. Greschner might go to the papers and reveal what Gudge was up to. With what consequences? None—things would just happen earlier and faster. And less artistically.

What about Homer Seabury? he thought. Poor Homer. His association with the Seaburys went back a long way. Yet, he realized, although Homer had paid him well, Morgan Seabury would never dine at his table.

Wanting to buy a little time, to think further behind a thin screen of words, he said, "This is quite a piece of news, Mr. Katagira. I think you've figured out something about me. Mine has not been a grateful profession, as I suggested. But there are loyalties . . ."

"Of course, of course. And debts to be repaid also, I think."

Indeed there were, Sol thought. He'd once told an interviewer: "I get paid an average of three thousand dollars a week an assignment and at least twice that in contumely." At least ten times that from the likes of Granada Masterman, he calculated. Homer Seabury was a small price to pay for the carting off of the incidents of insolence and disrespect heaped like ash and offal in Sol's memory.

Suddenly Sol recognized that there was nothing to be gained from further reflection. He had been duped, which was the ultimate in disgrace for the shrewd, world-wise, insightful man he took himself to be; now here, in Katagira's outstretched hand, was recovery, absolution. In his mind, his world reshaped itself; the puzzle came together; the pieces joined, and he realized that this was the answer: the maker of pedestals would now hammer them to pieces. It was right and meet to do so. A fine, even a noble conclusion to a career less than fine and less than noble.

"A very intriguing idea, Mr. Katagira. I'm flattered to be considered. And at my age, and with my memories, I really don't see how I could do other than accept. When would you like to discuss specifics? And I'd have to have some idea of your notions on timing."

Watching Sol immerse himself mentally in detail, as if this were just another assignment—much grander, of course—to put something or someone over, Katagira wondered if his new collaborator perceived what he, Katagira, thought he saw. That Solomon Greschner had just accepted an invitation to participate in the ultimate revenge. On himself.

He let matters rest for a minute; then, as he had promised, he again brought up with Greschner the possibility of acquiring the Lefcourt Collection.

Nick settled into himself with a fierce singleness of purpose, stayed at home most nights except for completely inescapable business engagements and spent long hours talking to himself.

His principal distraction was his work. The art-buying frenzy of the 1970s was finished; mediocre works by great names no longer made premium prices. The faddish boomlets too were mercifully over. Picasso masterpieces sold flourishingly and for very high prices; Picasso junk languished in the inventories of dealers whom the art papers characterized as "overoptimistic" and whom Nick and Johnny Sandler described as "blind." Dutch and Flemish flower pictures returned to price levels suitable for the botanical curiosities they were. Price and artistic merit once again seemed linked.

Nick had work to do. Johnny Sandler had managed to wheedle a great Van Gogh out of a movie magnate's widow, and Nick shared his conviction that it was a picture that Harvey Bogle must acquire, the vehicle by which they might bring Bogle down toward the present. Bogle had made it clear that Old Masters were his thing, but the Van Gogh, a late view of a hot summer field near Arles, was purely and simply a great work of painting. It was priced at $4.6 million—"to sell," Sandler said. It had a quality of blazing positive ferocity to which Nick was sure Bogle would succumb; its mood matched Nick's sense of Bogle's temperament. The Van Gogh turned Nick on, made the hair at the back of his neck tingle, just as the Rubenses had; just as Callas' singing had, or Prospero's farewell. As Jill did.

He planned to take it to the West Coast, where Bogle was dug in and exchanging canister and grape with the Terrace forces at TransNational. Nick found himself intrigued by the whole business. Since his parting from Jill, and having heard Bogle talk so often about his own dealings, he had begun to read the business news. *Pritchett's* was, of course, a sort of way of keeping in touch with her. But the business section of the *Times* no longer was dumped, barely glanced at, on the floor on Sunday mornings, and now *The Wall Street Journal* arrived each weekday morning; Nick still had no interest in calling a broker about Mismer Hermeneutics or speculating his art-dealing profits on October corn; still, he began once again to know what was going on.

If Nick's world and life held few comforts, and those gray and threadbare, with the taste of ashes, Jill, while she remained unyielding in her commitment not to readmit Nick to her life, was not doing much better. Though hers was a morally unyielding position, high-minded beyond cavil, it gave her little satisfaction and less fun.

Yet she was pretty certain—*pretty* certain—that she was doing the right thing, the only thing, she could do to preserve an iota of self-respect. Her moral absolutism shone, she felt, like a sure, small light in a dark world, in which everything might be murkily tarnished by prior sale or compromise. It was, to be sure, a brave little light, she thought ruefully, yet it seared as painfully as acetylene.

More than ever, she found her public existence loathsome. It came home to her how important Nick had been to her ability to continue Gilberte's life; alone, it seemed barely possible for her to make, in any way, the round of those awful, garish parties peopled by awful, garish sacks of money masquerading as human beings. As Creighton, she was philosophically more respectable, but frustrated by the secrecy imposed on her. It was like a crusade conducted by a spy. All merit and no glory. Damaging as the realization was to her ego, she came to see how vital Nick's adoration had been to her entire existence; how it mitigated what she felt about herself; how it permitted her to disguise from herself the feeling that—how had Nick told her Harvey Bogle had put it about Marvin Terrace: that he was "in life for the money"?—she, as Gilberte, had sold out to the Granadas and Gratianes of the world and that any talk to the contrary was just so much self-deception.

The worst part was the sympathy of her friends. As she'd expected, her women friends of a certain age, especially those in whom happiness or fulfillment had not atrophied the prized kernel of self-pity, took up their accustomed roles: wailing beside the dusty, jeering road as she dragged the cross of man's awfulness to Calvary. That bored her. Nick had done no more, she began to feel, than what men might always do; compared with this lousy, lonely state, what was the big deal?

She thanked God for Jenny. With Jenny around, the need for a man, or any other companionship, seemed remote. She and her daughter plunged into New York as into a massage bath. Movies on weekends; and zoos and walking tours and the park and restaurants. No museums, though. No art. Nick was art. Jenny was a good companion. Like most children, she was strong on the facts of existence but uncomprehending when it came to motivation. She took the mysterious ways of adults as a given. If it seemed to Jill that Jenny sometimes verged on asking about Nick, pausing as if on the edge of a cliff, so that Jill's heart momentarily sank at the prospect of being evasive or uncandid or emotionally cowardly to her own daughter, the child invariably did her mother the immense favor of retreating, of choosing to prattle on about pandas or Burt Reynolds or a skirt she'd liked at Bendel's.

At night, too exhausted to indulge in the city dweller's little fiction of calling loneliness solitude, Jill confronted the ultimate depletion of her broken affair. Nick's love, his outright adoration, had given a quality of importance to her and her life. That he was out there, somewhere in the night, with this telepathic heartful of love wasn't the same thing as having him around to say it. Love needed saying. Life needed significance. She stuck to her guns, but she was fair game when Sol called to say that within weeks he would bestow on her the greatest story of any financial journalist's lifetime. She thought of Anne Sexton's poetry: "*At night, alone, I marry the bed.*" She could do worse than to have that line, that destiny carved into the headboard.

To the clipping from the *Times* was attached, simply, a slip bearing the logo of Greschner Associates and the rubric: OF INTEREST. The story, in its entirety, read:

ITALIAN COUNT
TO SELL COLLECTION

Rome (AP): The famed collection of Roman and Etruscan antiquities of Duke Federico Corto, whose family traces its Ligurian ancestry back at least five centuries, is to be sold at auction in Rome this fall under the auspices of Grundy's, the well-known London auctioneers. The collection, which includes important Roman copies of sculptures by Phidias and Praxiteles, the most significant holdings of Etruscan art outside the National Museum in the Villa Giulia and other important Roman works, including the triumphal relief of "Marc Antony in Egypt," is considered to be the single greatest concentration, outside of the Italian State Museums, of works of art representing Italy's ancient past.

In response to inquiries concerning his decision to sell a collection formed by his family over the last three centuries, Duke Federico, 75, stated, "Terrorism is now out of control in this country. It will not be long before they stop murdering our present and start murdering our past. It is no longer sensible to maintain this collection in our palazzo."

Duke Federico's nephew Count Giuliano Corto, 42, lost a leg in last year's terrorist bombing of the Arsenale Ferrorurgica, outside Breschia, of which he is Executive Director General.

Katagira read the clipping with interest, pursing his lips, as if pursuing a second line of inquiry in the back of his mind, while the front concentrated on the article. Gudge was very ill; their grand plan would soon start unfolding. He went into the information center and punched up ITALY. The first time, they had gone through channels, but there were always alternatives, especially for someone with the Lazy G's financial power.

Nick arrived in Beverly Hills to find Bogle under siege by Maxwell Pflug, a New York dealer with a sound eye for names and no sense of art. Pflug knew his lists and dates cold; time after time he had walked into provincial auction rooms across Europe and spotted—somewhere in the third or fourth row of pictures indiscriminately crowded onto a wall—a second-grade painting, but possibly by an important master, lurking under a hundred or so years of dirty, yellowed varnish. It was one of these discoveries that Pflug was hawking, a very early still-life almost certainly by Velásquez.

Nick knew from Bogle's first remarks that Pflug, as usual, was making heavy water for himself.

"Nick, this is an okay picture, but no better. But who is this guy Pflug? All he wants to talk about is dukes and money. He comes in here, plunks the picture down without talking about it, tells me about all the important people he's stayed with here, there and everywhere and how much money he made yesterday closing out his TransNational options. The last hour's the only time I've had to look at the picture. I had to send him down to the hotel—probably to get laid, since he spent a lot of time talking about that too. How are you, Nick?"

"Fair. Poor Pflug. Don't get upset with him, Harvey. He just wants to be everything that he isn't. He wants to be Casanova and J. P. Morgan and Mr. French Riviera and Escoffier. Anything but Maxwell Pflug, art dealer. But he has got an eye for certain kinds of pictures, and that picture there is okay, as you put it. What's he asking?"

"Nine hundred thou. What do you guess he bought it for?"

There were no secrets in the art trade, so Nick knew that Pflug had paid something like $1,900 in sterling for the picture, plus maybe $10,000 to Marco Carraccino to clean off the old varnish, lay a paint blister and transfer it to a new canvas. A big profit, but the more power to Pflug. It was Nick's practice, and an unbreakable rule of the game, never to discuss his competitors' margins of profit.

"I don't know. I heard he found it somewhere in England, and these days the English don't give anything away."

"What do you think?"

"I think it's a nice picture. What else can I say, since I've got a very expensive painting of my own sitting in your front hall hoping to get sold? You know the Met paid over four million for a Velásquez portrait—in pre-OPEC dollars. It comes down to what you think, Harvey. I hope you don't think that sounds chicken."

What Nick didn't say was that the Velásquez was like most of Pflug's pictures. It was "right" in the parlance of the trade: 99⁴⁴⁄₁₀₀ certainly by Velásquez. But it wasn't top-drawer. A stroke here, a patch there hinted at the artist's future greatness, just enough to confirm the important attribution, but that was as far as it went. Pflug's eye was strictly for big names at bargain prices; a Velásquez was a Velásquez was a Velásquez to Pflug. He was a quantitative type, pure and simple.

"I'll buy that," said Bogle. "I'll offer him four hundred thou."

He looked at Nick. "You look like shit. No wonder. Still moaning over the fact you couldn't keep your dick in your pants and got canned by Jill?"

How sweetly Harvey put it, Nick thought.

"It's been kind of a rough time. How's it going with you? I've been reading about this TEC thing. You going to win?"

"So the experts tell me. Meeting's next week. I think Marvin Terrace's going to find his lunch has been eaten. You want a drink?"

While Bogle poured a Scotch, Nick unscrewed the lid of the Van Gogh's packing case and lifted the picture from the polystyrene pads that held it in place. He leaned it against the back of a sofa.

Bogle whistled.

"Strong, isn't it?"

"Harvey, I think it's the greatest Van Gogh to come on the market in years. Better than the Ford picture; better even than the Niarchos picture. It grabs you; it says everything Van Gogh seemed to be wanting to say at his maddest and most inspired. You get the feeling that the heat in his mind was just as strong as the heat on those fields—and they are hot in late summer. I know; I've been to Arles."

"You're doing this with Sandler, aren't you? What is it: four million six you said on the phone—right?"

"That's right. We had to pay up ourselves for this, and with money at 18½ percent, like all small businessmen, we have to cover ourselves for shelf time. I hate to guess what you'd be paying if Sandler hadn't blocked out Grundy's."

"Well, let me live with it for a week." He looked at Nick sternly. "All business, aren't you? This fight with Jill rob you of your boyish charm?"

"Let's just say learning how dumb I can be has been a deeply sobering affair."

Bogle was obviously thinking of something else. He grinned at Nick and asked, "You doing anything for the next few days? You need some distracting. What's your plan?"

"Nothing in particular. I thought I'd hang around. Go visit the Getty and the L.A. County and the Norton Simon." He didn't say that New York was full of ghosts.

"How'd you like to join me on a fast flying tour of the so-called 'Bogle empire'? See the U.S.A.? I'm getting itchy here, and Esmé's due in tomorrow on her book tour, which means I'll have P.R. types and hairdressers all over the place. Jesus, I haven't seen her alone in four months except a couple of times sitting on the can. How about it? Get you out of the sulks."

Nick agreed. Why not? he thought. Why not, indeed? His entire life these days seemed to be about live and learn.

Afterward, when he was sufficiently recovered, Nick thought he might someday assemble *The Wit and Wisdom of Harvey Bogle* out of his gleanings. They were on the road five days, conveyed by a JetStar belonging to Bogle's hotel corporation. The Bogle "empire" turned out to be situated entirely in the "new" America—the shiny, thrusting glass cities which had come to the fore as the old regime of the Northeast slid into sooty decline. Portland, Seattle, Denver, Dallas, Houston, Atlanta all boasted Bogle hotels, or commercial properties, or industrial-parts distributors, or convenience-store chains controlled by the man who spent the hours in the air curled up with a variety of reading that, to Nick's astonishment, encompassed everything from Gibbon to the lastest issue of *Celebrity Beaver,* but seemed never to include business reports.

"Harvey, I have to ask you something," Nick said as the jet circled to turn back in over Puget Sound, aflame in the early twilight. "I thought you tycoons never read anything but reports and *The Wall Street Journal.*"

"Nuts. Who needs all that crap? Everywhere we stop I get one sheet of paper. It tells me how we're doing, there and now, cashwise. I'm a private guy. No stockholders to butter up—to shut up, you might say—with a lot of fancy earnings made up by a bunch of accountants. I want to know how much is in the bank; how much we owe and are committed to spend; how much we're owed and how current that is; how fast we're turning our inventory, whether that's hotel rooms or cases of Seven-Up or grosses of widgets. That's all. Cash-on-hand counts. I don't get a hard-on reading about return on investment or discounted future cash flow or the rest of that business-school bullshit."

Nor did Nick encounter squadrons of the glib, bright young men he had believed to be the backbone of American business. After driving around Dallas looking at a bunch of low-lying warehousing complexes and touring a facility that turned out helicopter components, Nick remarked that all the people he met seemed, well, weathered.

"We don't hire MBAs. I'm a value-conscious buyer, so I won't pay forty grand a year for nothing, no matter how smartass it comes packaged. I want guys with time in the outfit; who know the business and know they've got a job with us until we go flat-ass broke, so they're loyal. I don't want a lot of kids sitting around with their thumb up their ass looking at the pictures in *Fortune*. I'll tell you something, Nick. I was in England years ago and I got worried because every guy I met running anything had been to one of about three schools. Mostly Eton. You got a class system over there that wrecked England just the way you wreck dogs if you inbreed them. We've got a class system in this country now, and don't fool yourself that we don't. I got guys working for me started as mail-room guys or messengers or janitors and who're now managers and making good money. That's not true most places. It used to be true everyplace, but now you got to have a goddamn MBA to get your foot on the ladder. So what happens to the smart kid who can't go to Harvard or Stanford and has to get a real job? He ends up where he started. On a factory floor, looking out the window, watching the snot-noses park their Mercedes-Benzes. That's a class system, Nick, and that's a ball-buster.

"I'll tell you something else. I couldn't've done this today. Just to get into business you gotta have about fifty million bucks just to pay the goddamn lawyers and paper-pushers, and it's all bullshit. But it doesn't leave anything for the business itself, so you get into the banks, and with rates up where they are, they eat you alive. But don't get me started on banks."

But Nick did anyway, at a very fancy French restaurant in Houston. They'd had a long day. Schedules had gotten confused, so they'd begun in the smog of the Loop and finished up out by the Ship Channel looking at a little factory turning out complex electronic seismology equipment for the oil industry. The manager of Bogle's oil-field-parts distribution company wanted to buy the plant and add its products to his lines.

Over dinner, Harvey had taken an extra martini.

"Take that guy this afternoon, Nick. He's getting killed. He has to spend on research, to keep ahead, or some big-time outfit'll Chinese-copy his equipment and take his market away by underpricing him. Except that he has to pay his friendly bank probably two over prime, so there goes the R.-and-D. money. He had to borrow because he spent his equity on lawyers and accountants and consultants—and the bank's lawyers: don't forget that bill—to get the loan in the first place.

"A very big reason we're in the shit in this country is because somebody told that guy at Citibank about earnings per share and all of a sudden bank stocks, which you used to buy for yield, because you maybe had an aversion to gambling, are coming on like electronics companies. Fifty new, untested ideas a day. Which is why today the banks are out bidding for money in the open market so they can make their loans grow and their earnings grow, and suddenly we are up to our ass in Eurodollars and Asiadollars and loans to Zaïre and the banks are selling negotiable CDs and here come the money-market funds to educate you, me and every Joe on the street that why should we give our deposits for nothing to our friendly banker if he has to pay Exxon or Bubber Gudge or some other rich guy the going rate? That's a big change, Nick. It's changed the country. All these assholes in Washington and Wall Street are running around mouthing off about 'inflation premiums,' but what's happened is that the day is over when the banks can count on getting the use of billions, trillions, of other people's money for nothing. That, Nick, is what our friends the economists call a structural change. You know how much I personally keep in the bank day to day? About three grand. Just enough for tips and hookers. And I'm not going to go back to the way it was, giving the banks my cash for nothing, and neither is Joe Blow now that he's tasted blood."

On to Denver then, for a helicopter ride over a new industrial park, Nick marveling in sorrow at the foul, sulfurous pall smearing the distant white splendor of the Rockies, and lunch with a nearly apoplectic oil man with whom Bogle was drilling for gas in Wyoming.

"Harvey, this fuckin' world is crazy. You see this?" He produced a column of print torn from the morning's paper. Nick had noticed it. A third major company, armed with a $4-billion credit line from its banks, had entered the bidding fray for South Louisiana Gas and Oil, the largest remaining publicly held independent.

"Harvey, this here is shitass dumb. Here we're dying for oil—new oil—and instead these goddamn banks gonna take four fucking billion dollars which they could be lending to big operators like me or Gudge—except he's in bonds now—to finance drilling, to get some new production, and they've taken this money right out of the oil business so that one of these dumb New York sumbitch lawyers and accountants that run most of the majors can get his rocks off by gettin' bigger. Goddamn, Harvey, what this country needs is to find *new* oil—which ain't the same thing as Mobil buyin' Conoco. So here's four billion fucking dollars which could have, should have, gone into new wells, pissed away to a bunch of bank trust departments and pension funds, and the U.S. of A. ain't got one fucking new barrel of oil or one fucking cubic foot of new gas or one goddamn new B.T.U. of coal or steam or shale to show for it. Shit!"

He took a resolute pull on his Rob Roy. Bogle nodded his resigned agreement. It sounded commonsensical to Nick.

He and Harvey parted company in Atlanta, and Nick flew back to LaGuardia; Bogle returned to Los Angeles, to see to the completion of his trial by proxy with Marvin Terrace and, Nick hoped, to consummate a lasting affair with the Van Gogh, which had languished during their absence in a bonded warehouse.

It had been an edifying journey. Nick felt as if he had been to the other side of the world. The barren sameness of the American commercial landscape had depressed him. The sheer optimistic energy that ran through the streets of Houston, Denver and Dallas like unleashed lightning was truly impressive, and, he could see, almost violently exhilarating to its possessors. Yet it was, still and all, alien corn to him.

He slowly got back into New York gear, and loneliness soon enfolded him once again in its clammy wings. He took to sitting alone in the park, watching the embraces of springtime lovers and thinking suitably mournful thoughts. He listened to Wagner. Often he would leave his house on no mission, just to walk: something might turn up.

One day, he found himself crossing Central Park, on his way to look at some drawings owned by one of those old women holed up with their treasures in once-great Broadway apartment houses. In front of him, he noted the progress of a man, not old, who walked with such a painful, surrendered hesitancy that Nick got the impression the man hoped he would wear out his life before he reached the other side of the park. Nick felt a shudder of sympathy; on the western skyline he could make out Jill's building, which drew his eyes as if he were hypnotized.

Another time, returning from one of these meaningless perambulations, he passed his old school just as a tumult of small boys in blue caps poured out the door. He saw himself as a boy instantly reproduced a dozen times there on the sidewalk, and the thought of time's irreversibility was almost physically painful. He bought the evening paper; among its shrillnesses he noted, almost absently, a wire-service dispatch that Harvey Bogle had won the right to elect a majority of the board of directors of TransNational Entertainment Corporation.

For distraction, he went to an early movie.

It was barely six o'clock when he let himself into the maisonette. The phone rang soon after, and he was startled to hear Frodo's shrill voice on the other end.

"For God's sake, Nicholas, where have you been?" Crisp sounded hysterical, almost to the point of tears. "Now, listen. You must get packed and I'll pick you up outside your door in half an hour. No longer. We're on the overnight flight to Rome. Felix will meet us at the airport."

Nick blurted out the obvious question.

"Of course, of course, dear boy, you can't know." There was something he had never before heard in Frodo's voice. "Max telephoned this morning. Frank's been killed, Nick. Killed."

CHAPTER TWENTY-TWO

The carabiniere who stood at the crossroads outside Pratovale, shivering in the early chill, was an inexperienced boy from southern Italy. He was still sleepy and mentally a little confused by having been rousted out of the barracks and stationed in this lonely place—told only that his duty was to keep watch for the gray Fiat that had been used by the old American's abductors.

He had been seized the previous afternoon, during his customary constitutional on the road outside the gates of La Pergola. Because Max Lefcourt didn't feel up to it, Sanger had been accompanied by Giuseppina's husband, Aldo. Two old men, having a peaceful, wordless stroll on a clear April afternoon. It had been only a matter of an instant for the car to overtake them; for Aldo to be pushed roughly aside and Sanger as roughly bundled into the back seat of the Fiat; for a note wrapped around a stone to be tossed at the feet of the howling Aldo as the car sped up the hillside toward the Fiesole road, from which any number of possible escape routes tentacled out.

That night, while Sanger slept fitfully in a barn outside Donini, and his captors grumbled the night away—since it was strictly a money job, without any ideological overtones—the police authorities had worked to lay a thorough net over a hundred-mile radius of Florence. While they did, Max Lefcourt, his feelings obviously drawn out fine as wire, so that his very skin seemed to quiver with the effort of self-control, prayed in the villa chapel; the note the kidnappers had left said that he would be contacted about a ransom. The police were confused: there was no understandable motive for kidnapping an eighty-year-old American who had done only service to Italy and to Italian art. A disgraceful business, they murmured.

The young soldier at the crossroads was a very small filament in the wide net laid down by the police. Small and unsure. When he saw the gray Fiat come barreling around the narrow curve below his watch post, he lost what little presence of mind he'd ever had; forgetting his orders to report anything—anything—over his walkie-talkie and act then only according to instructions, he clambered to his feet under the tree that hid him from the driver's view and unslung his Beretta submachine gun.

The driver could not have seen him. The automobile's lights did a poor job of cutting through the interlaced wisps of ground fog that still hung in the air, and the road wriggled treacherously through the hills. His vision and concentration were totally directed to the business of negotiating the curves and dips. When the soldier suddenly stepped out from behind a large pine on the road's shoulder and started shooting, he was too surprised to react.

It would not have mattered anyway. At that range, the emptied magazine turned the car's interior into a hornets' nest of bullets. The Fiat skewed across the road and smashed into a rocky escarpment. Cautiously the young soldier made his way over to the car; the hiss of its broken radiator made a strange counterpoint to the noise of morning church bells drifting up the valley.

It was very bad, he saw, starting to shake. They were all dead. At least, he thought, the old man, pitched awkwardly against his unwanted companion, must have gone immediately. Part of his head had been blown away by the first slugs to enter the car. It was very bad. He must make a report, he remembered, now at last reaching for his radio.

For months now, Katagira had been systematically unbundling—the papers would later say "gutting"—the composite of assets, properties, rights and values which the public knew as GUT and GOD. His computers had broken down and retransferred legal title to drilling and production rights on nearly a million acres of domestic proved and producing lease and fee land. Thus, the Gudge position in the Anadarko Basin had been re-created as the original patchwork of small, unrelated leases it had originally been, before Gudge's grandfather had bought them up and fused them into a unit.

To complete his plan, Katagira proposed to rearrange the Gudge interests so that when the collapse came, they would be carrion for lawyers. His plan envisaged arranging matters so that every piece and particle of the vast dominion would, in the end, be subject to several competing valid claims, liens and interests in equity. In a way, he thought, this would synopsize the evolution of the country: a realm staked out by the determination of a pioneer, expanded by vision and enterprise, to finish as a tired nub ground down and worn away in litigation. Over the last three months, therefore, he had been systematically tendering his Anadarko interests to seven different swap funds. These were paper empires, organized by brokerage firms, which stood ready to exchange their shares for the tens of thousands of vestigial nonliquid partnership interests that had been acquired over the years by tax-shelter investors. Thus the Anadarko block, redistributed by Katagira's computers into eighteen hundred–odd individual names taken from a 1957 Des Moines telephone directory, and still believed by GOD stockholders to be the holding shown on the map in the prospectus, was also believed to be the property, in its fractionated form, of five different swap funds.

The largest, most amusing and inventive element of his scheme would be implemented only when the smoke and fire were at their blazingest. It too was now in final form. The paperwork was complete; the envelopes stamped and addressed, ready to go.

Now for the rumors, he thought. Step One. Rumors which he and Greschner had formulated and would now send on their way, like buzz bombs. The natural course of events was also working for them; the steam was fizzling out of The Gudge Bull Market. As the Hunts had learned, no single fortune was, in the end, substantial enough to throw back great market tides, which moved implacably, as if pulled by the moon.

Robert Creighton in *Pritchett's*, April 20:

> . . . Dr. Jasper Purchase, Wall Street's so-called "Merchant of Misery," predicted last week at a Bond Club meeting that there were sufficient signs on the horizon to indicate that some major correction—for which read "collapse"—is called for in the recently ebullient bond market. This could affect certain major bond dealers and investment houses which have been on the cutting edge of the rally on bond values and have put their own and their customers' money where their mouth is. Using recent Federal Reserve data, Dr. Purchase suggested that the monetary aggregates and economic data suggest that bond prices might decline at least 20% from the levels to which this frenzied market has driven them.

When Granada Masterman read this, she felt close to panic and immediately telephoned Rufus Lassiter in Washington and had her secretary summon Hugo Winstead to her office.

Lassiter tried, in his suave, credible fashion, to push her concerns aside.

"Granada, there isn't any doubt that Homer's got Seaco practically underwater if you assume that bond prices are going to go back anywhere near what they were a year ago. But that doesn't bother me because, personally, I don't think that's going to happen. The President's program is working, by God. There're a lot of people down on Wall Street that are, well, frankly, jealous of how our team's new economics has worked out just the way we said it would. The people I think're going to get hurt are the sort who are going to keep betting on high interest rates. Nossir, Granada, what you're hearing is just a lot of technical foolishness from a lot of panicky professors who never met a payroll. Who're trying to make us look wrong. Well, they'll see."

Listening to this, Granada found herself wishing, in spite of her admiration for Rufus, that he didn't always have to feel the need to answer even the simplest question with a major political statement.

"But Rufus, you do realize we've invested close to ninety million dollars in Seaco shares. If the bond market collapses, you can imagine what it will mean for Seaco—and for us."

Granada had been worried for some weeks now. Some of the more conservative members of the MUD board had privately expressed to her their concern about the size of the Seaco investment. Her bankers and her top financial man had suggested taking the nearly $100-million paper profit on the total position and adding it to MUD's equity.

Lassiter was aware of her misgivings, but it didn't suit his purpose. Seaco was going to be his baby, his forum, his triumphal arch. And Homer, bless him, had put in place the kind of team that he could really manage. Plus cutting loose all those Masterwomen to cut the country's purse strings. He would show he could run an empire like MUD/Seaco and once he did that, why, hell, they'd want him to run the country, which he surely could do a damn sight better than all those used-car salesmen over at the White House. Sensing the extent of her concern, he switched courses.

"Well, Granada, of course, it's really up to you; after all, it is your show, although we've put a lot of loving time into it and the whole Masterdollar concept. It's just that—well, dammit—I hate to see you give in to Buford. I can just hear that wife of his gloating."

He could hear her stiffen on the other end. He applied the killer stroke.

"Incidentally, there's going to be a major, but very private, very select dinner in Georgetown in three weeks at ———'s." He gave the name of a famous savant. "Yes, of course the First Couple will be there. And anyone else who counts to this Administration. I think I can arrange a couple of places at the table. It's going to be quite a crowd—all the top people." He rattled off a list of couturiers, warehousing magnates and charity-ball chairwomen which made Granada's heart thrill. When he hung up, finally, Senator Rufus Lassiter counted it a job well done—which meant, as always, that his own interests had been served, first, last and foremost.

Nevertheless, after hanging up, Mrs. Masterman advised Hugo Winstead that, "just for the sake of prudence," she wished to explore the possibility of selling the Seaco block, or a significant piece of it, as soon as possible. Her woman's instinct told her that all these men on Wall Street seemed to get wound up like tops and spin their heads off. She wished she'd stayed after TransNational; Marvin Terrace would have given her anything she could have asked if only she'd been able to save his job for him. But there was only so far she could go. And Harvey Bogle was known always to be available for negotiation. Unlike Buford. Of course, Buford was a billionaire and known to make gold from anything he touched. Which was some small source of confidence.

There was a part of herself that Granada wouldn't often admit to, except at odd occasional moments like the present. She knew she had behaved just exactly like a woman—well, it was more that she had behaved the way men said a woman would behave—in trying to outstay Buford in the Seaco business. She had had no business doing that. Except she could tell herself, she had had every business doing it. There was the whole thing of the Gudges' wanting to throw her into the street, as if with the billions they had there hadn't been miles and miles of room to spare for the scraps she'd been given with which to make a life. And then Buford had turned up in Seaco, for which she had had such plans, she and Rufus. And all the while there was that awful tramp wife of Buford's getting all the attention. Woman or not, you had to fight for yourself. Anyway, she would at least pay lip service to her advisers. It never hurt to be ready.

Homer Seabury had enough on his mind without the call from Hugo Winstead to set up a meeting to discuss freeing up MUD's Seaco stock for public sale.

For one thing, Homer didn't want to call Katagira. Not that there was a real problem so far as he knew. But earlier that morning he'd had a brief conversation with Fixed Income that had raised a tingle in his mind.

"You know, the put's coming due in three weeks," the younger man had reported, reminding Homer that Seaco-Gudge had entered into a put/call arrangement some months earlier with respect to $1.4 billion of long-term bonds owned by a syndicate of banks and insurance companies. In those palmy times, it had seemed like a splendid, statesmanlike maneuver which had unlocked a rush of funds into bonds; now it looked like an awful lot of money to have to come up with.

"They don't have to give notice until fifteen days prior, which is next Wednesday, but a little bird tells me they're going to put the paper to us. The option's only underwater about thirty million, but all these assholes are listening to this shithead preaching this doom-and-gloom crap. And now the bond market's on about a five-minute temporary hold, after six months of going straight up, so that's got 'em crapping in their Levi's. The bottom line is, Homer, seven hundred million apiece for Gudge and us if they exercise their put."

The young man's insouciance before so large a number struck Homer as downright disrespectful.

"Eight hundred million?" The amount loomed over Homer like a tyrannosaurus.

"Yeah, except we've got extra collateral in the partnership which'll cover almost half, which means only a couple hundred mil apiece. That's peanuts to Gudge. I can bank another one hundred million; there're still a few hayseed banks that'll repo us; and pick up some loose change around the Street. This market's gonna stay this way about another two, three days, I figure, until the ribbon clerks are out and the Merchant of Misery's got egg on his kisser. I loaded up on ninety-day T-bill futures this morning for the dealer account. Just a bil—nothing big; but when this market gets cranked up again, it'll make us a nice little profit."

Homer heard a total lack of reflectiveness in the young man's words that first astonished and then scared him.

"Aren't you getting us a bit far out on a limb?" he asked. He knew he wasn't ever forceful enough with these aggressive young people.

"Nah," said Fixed Income, "no way"; but instead of reasoned, market-annealed confidence, Homer now heard the dangerous, often fatal resonances of gut thinking. He had no way of knowing that the younger man was now living on the thin edge of what a more objective soul would have recognized as fear. Fixed Income had seen that the juice was out of the bond market; most days he felt as if he were pushing against an invisible, resistant wall, and so he popped a couple of Tranzines to dull his apprehensions and took aboard enough snorts of prize Colombian coke to maintain a self-deceptive state of confident elation. He'd turned his head into a drugstore.

"Don't you think," Homer remonstrated, "that given the size of our positions, both for our own long account and our dealer inventories, we should stay at these levels, maybe even work off some? I certainly don't want to get into jeopardy."

"Is that an order?"

"Well, I suppose you might instead call it a strong suggestion."

"Okay—if that's what you want." Fixed Income's quick sullenness betrayed his youth. He preferred to get out of tight corners by talking faster and faster, by letting the machine-gun glibness for which he was famous carve an escape route among his adversaries.

"Anyway, get hold of our buddies in Texas and grease 'em up," said the younger man, leaving to return to the trading room; he was happier amid the noise and flurry of the trenches, where the action frequently got so fast and busy in itself that the participants would have been hard put to explain what it was that the action itself was about. It helped a man forget his own troubles. In Fixed Income's case, his sense of trouble was the aftermath of an unpleasant conversation with the V.P. who handled the drawdowns and overnight loans with which Fixed Income was financing his departmental inventories as well as funding Seaco's investment positions as a principal.

"I don't want to sound threatening," the banker had said in the way that bankers do just before they pull the plug, "but our people"—implying that someone else had forced this onerous task on him—" would like to see a little housecleaning, qualitywise, on the collateral package." He made it clear to Fixed Income that no whistle would be sounded in Homer Seabury's own ear—at least, not for the present; but that the bank would very much prefer it if, well, some of the lower-grade bonds backing their loan were replaced with AAA stuff.

Now the insurance companies and pension funds with whom he'd negotiated the billion-dollar buy/sell back when it looked as if the bond market were blue sky all the way were sounding as if they were going to exercise their contractual put and sock the bonds to Seaco-Gudge, and those noises were making faint tremors in a market that was starting to act a little fragile. So far, it was just thin, worrisome keening, barely audible in the bustling roar and cacophony of daily dealings. As Fixed Income made his way back to the trading room, he thanked Christ he was in bed with a certifiable billionaire.

Homer turned back to the business of the MUD holding. Much as he wanted Granada out of Seaco, which would utterly remove the threat of Lassiter's taking over the castle, common sense told him that a big offering of Seaco shares just now would be taken by the Street as evidence of a loss of confidence, as a vote for trepidation. The Street might be sliding into one of its bad patches. Events had not measured up to expectations; real life had failed to confirm the bubbling euphoria of a few months earlier. Momentum was petering out—and Homer Seabury had been sucked into betting the store on momentum.

He guessed he could count on Winstead to help divert Granada. Indirectly, Hugo was up to his ears in this, since it was with his full blessing that the Fuller Endowment was now 60 percent in long-term bonds, as well as the owner of 250,000 shares of Seaco. And Hugo had strongly recommended, and the Fuller board had unhesitatingly approved, the deployment of Fuller's stock portfolio to Seaco's institutional stock-loan program. Close to $23 million in common stocks owned by the Endowment was now "at" Seaco on loan, helping to collateralize Seaco's operational borrowings. The interest paid by Seaco on the borrowed stock was income which the Institute could well use; Seaco profited on the spread between what it paid the Fuller for the use of its stock and what it earned, net, by lending the stock on the Street. The Fuller kept title to the shares it deposited with Seaco. It was a good deal for everyone.

No, Homer thought, no worry about Hugo's assistance. Hugo was in deep enough with Seaco to ensure that.

Harvey Bogle also sensed the Street's itchiness and started to act on it. He was sure there was money to be made in Seaco. On the short side. It seemed to him that the firm was badly overextended. The fat profits of its early bond purchases had been hocked to buy more bonds, on which the subsequent profits, these too hocked, had been thinner and thinner. As far as he could judge, the so-called bull market in bonds was out of gas; it was running on the vapor. When that became obvious, the hot-money guys would start banging away with both hands until the public hit the panic button.

So he methodically began to sell Seaco short. The stock was at $33 when he began, having stolidly, remarkably, held its ground in a nervous market; he opened by having his foundation go short 5,000 shares and planned to sell a few thousand a day until he got obvious enough for the sheep to hear the tinkling of his bell and join the rush for the exits.

The rest of his life was ordered with the same confidence and conviction.

Life at home was tranquil. *Countess* was to be published officially in a month, and Esmé was in full flight. The book was already in the stores and being reordered at the rate of twenty-five thousand copies a week.

The new team he had installed at TransNational, with instructions to make haste slowly, looked to be doing its job well, and with remarkably little friction, even allowing for that unpleasant business about sending the marshals over to the Terraces' Brentwood mansion to repossess the studio's antiques.

Bogle was now, by his own calculation, 99 percent immersed in his art collection. He had tried to keep funneling business to Nick, but he found Nick changed, and nothing he could do seemed to relight the old schoolboy spark he had found so intriguing. That trip around the country should've been like a cold shower, he figured; should've woken Reverey up to the fact that there was a whole ridiculous world out there clanking and clinking away and worth having a laugh at because of its bullshit. For his purposes, he wanted Nick to stay untamed and fresh, just a kid in love with art and no more, all eye and enthusiasm totally dedicated to the Bogle Collection. But no, Nick now seemed to have turned kind of tough and abrupt. Not that he wasn't working hard, Bogle admitted—turning up objects, helping the collection shape and grow. Just now, thanks to Nick, Bogle was taking a hard look at a Delacroix *Lion Hunt* that had been scared up in France which Reverey and Agnew's were joint on. But he was aware that Nick now had other things on his mind. Which wasn't the plan—not as Harvey saw it.

On an easel in his apartment was the fine Baldung of *Eve and Death;* it caught his eye as he put down the phone from giving his West Coast broker the first shortside order in Seaco. Strange, he thought, how in the Italian pictures of the same period, early sixteenth century, Old Man Death never stuck his face in—but in Germany, whether it was Dürer or Baldung or Cranach, the guy with the sickle and the skin flayed down to the bare bones underneath was always there, a constant remonstrative presence. He looked closely at the obscenely smooth figure of Eve, apple in her hand, snake curled at her ankle like a metallic scourge. Woman, women, he thought. Women and death. Banging down on his friend Nick's head and heart like mortar shells. Christ, Bogle reflected, first Jill Newman and now this business with old Sanger; he hoped it wouldn't make Nick any stonier inside. He didn't want Nick to be tough; tough, thought Harvey Bogle, is for guys like me.

Jill had seen the front-page note in the *Times* about Francis Sanger's killing and had immediately gone to her back-bedroom office and wept wrenchingly and silently at the awful waste of it all. Integral to her grief was the recollection of her days in Florence with Nick, of the candlelit evening when Frank had given her the copy of *Indian Summer* and of the walks she and Nick had taken through the cold-caked winter city. Walked in the eternal way of lovers in cities, as if their feelings had somehow bestowed on them the proprietorship of the town, the privilege of seeing secret mysteries placed there especially and exclusively for them.

With a twinge, her mind went to Nick. She hoped this wouldn't break him. It would break her, she thought. Would have, rather. Would have in the old days. The days B.N. Before Nick.

Something in her had hardened, Jill believed; this hardening, she also believed, had gotten her past Nick. "Over" him. Defensively objective about her grief, she told herself that what twinges she felt for Nick were no more, no less than what any educated, reasonably sensitive person would have felt for another human being who'd lost a friend: a good, good friend.

The new hard Jill Newman. Also the new hard Gilberte. For five years, Gilberte had ignored the real juice and dirt that came her way; now, suddenly, the column dished up the scum she was fed by the scum-dealers and whisperers; instead of converting the stream of scandal and talebearing into a weekly series of allusive little florets of social and fashion chatter about as incisive and provoking as a tea cozy, "The Party Line" had started to play rough.

In just a month she had transformed "The Party Line" into a repository of real dirt. Jill had been inspired to add a dimension to the column that made it indispensable reading for the world of gossip; in each column, she managed to drop nonlibelous hints which made clear exactly who her sources had been for this or that item. Thus old feuds were rekindled and new animosities fired up, and more sources were created; friendships that had lasted for decades were breached, and new thirstings for retribution were born; personal and institutional confidences that had long been taken for granted were revealed, and new hatred distilled. All of which produced more material.

The publisher of *That Woman!* was delighted with the new tune Gilberte was singing. The newly vicious column had in six short weeks brought about two divorces, a failed suicide and the dismissal of a highly placed insurance executive and uprooted a catamitic love triangle said to involve at least one person, well, close to the very center of government. Gilberte was at it sword and buckler now; no quarter, no discretion, no decency. And as the column's transformation became recognized, Jill's phone scarcely stopped ringing, as the slimy beasts of the city emerged from their rocks and algae to whisper in her ear.

Well, if that's what they want, give it to them, she'd thought just that morning, savoring a tear-stained letter on a thick, crested paper that bore the fashionable new name and fashionable new address of an adventuress recently married to the wealthy proprietor of New York's most prestigious insurance brokerage. The letter complained of a mention in Jill's last column of ". . . a certain free-spending matron known to wicked, witty insiders as Madame Bon-Ami, because she seems determined to give her husband's wallet a scouring . . ." The subject of the item was not amused;

this sort of pandering to the maliciousness of her readers, however, had gotten Jill a $10,000 raise.

She had toughened up Creighton, too. Greschner had kept her apprised as to who the real ax-grinders on Wall Street were; the jealous ones; the closet cynics; the enemies within. She started making calls: "I'm calling for Robert Creighton, and Mr. Creighton would value your off-the-record opinion on . . ." These people, as she'd always suspected, were also real dirtmongers; men and women in brokerage houses, banks, money-management firms, corporate financial offices, whom envy, slights, real or imagined, or an evolved hatred of the system had brought to the edge of what Wall Street viewed as real rebellion: telling things as they were.

And back of it all, she was sitting on the Gudge-Seaco story, which had become something far greater and more significant than a financial scoop. Emotionally, Jill had refocused the story in her mind and given it a larger personal dimension than pure journalism would perhaps have dictated. Caryn Gudge was wrapped up in there somewhere, and Hugo Winstead, and the sycophantic universe of Granada Masterman; she added her own collection of ogres and lesser monsters to the swarming crowds of the financial district that would eventually populate the tale.

Letter to Nick, she thought. Letter to Nick about Sanger.

She took an hour over it, but all she could come up with was

Dear Nick:

I know how close you were to Frank Sanger and what a wonderful man he was and I wanted you to know that I am thinking about you.

Love,
Jill

She took a dozen stabs at it, and found herself unable to say more than that, and each time, because she simply would not let herself say what she wanted to say, for all her being "over" Nick, she found herself dissolved and weeping.

The notice of Sanger's death produced considerable surprise and disappointment in Katagira. It had not been anticipated to come to this, surely. Whether it would change Lefcourt's mind about selling, who could say? Only time would tell.

He turned to the financial papers. Ah, the excellent Creighton had a story about impending failures among certain of the more speculatively managed California savings-and-loans. Mentioned among them was Gudge's own Golden Grove Savings and Loan, although its controlling stockholder was not mentioned, nor was he in fact known to be such. Golden Grove was a Gudge fiefdom; but its link to the Lazy G could have been traced only through a circuitous maze of holding companies. For six months, Golden Grove's aggressive managers had been encouraged by Katagira, in Gudge's name and over Gudge's signature, to play aggressively in the financial futures market. Mounting losses had been met by loans from one of the Gudge-controlled banks and by a $10-million equity infusion from GOD. According to Katagira's schedule, Golden Grove would be allowed to collapse in two weeks. The money involved was not great; Katagira had calculated that less than $100 million would be lost by depositors and creditors. It was the principle of the thing that would count. As he and Greschner had agreed, Creighton would report that Gudge had walked away from Golden Grove and let it sink. With the Seaco-Gudge bond option coming up, the knowledge that Buford Gudge IV, the legendary Bubber, had disavowed the semimoral commitment the world expects rich people to have to their commercial chattels would surely send tremors along Wall Street. Gudge's assumed financial *noblesse* would have failed to *oblige*.

He was pleased. There was now enough disquiet at the very heart of the system so that any spasm would be magnified, and just as he intended, events and reactions would start to run out of control.

So, out beyond the edge of vision, just the sort of wave which, among those who might have known enough to see it building, Harvey Bogle alone had anticipated and prepared for began to rise. It was still too faint to drive the feeding birds to shore; in the late sunlight, one could have said, the sea remained calm and inviting, even though it could also have been said that the water was chillier than one would ideally have liked, but that could be put down to the fact it was late in the season. So the winds that ruffled and cooled the ocean's face were assumed by would-be swimmers to be purely transitory; surface breezes that would be gone by the bright, warm dawn of the next day.

Those who knew—Katagira, Jill and Greschner, and Gudge; those who, like Bogle, were merely suspicious but trusted their suspicions; those who were apprehensive but uncertain—Hugo, Granada—and those who had so great a stake in being reassured, like Homer Seabury and his ungovernable minions, all toiled on the shore in varying degrees of preparedness. The forming wave was only a flake of excitement, a hint of a shadow across their lives. Its time would come. And so the market steamed on, but with a sharply diminished sense of direction.

CHAPTER TWENTY-THREE

Even in grief, Max Lefcourt's unfailing courtesy remained intact. A car and driver were waiting for Nick, Frodo and Felix Rothschild when they arrived in Milan. Three hours later, the car entered the driveway of La Pergola; Giuseppina and Aldo were waiting on the front steps of the villa. As the three men stepped out of the car, they were each tearfully embraced.

"Il Signor Lefcourt is taking a nap," Giuseppina advised. "Il Signor Francesco is to be found in the library."

There Frank reposed, in a closed coffin, amid the ceiling-high shelves of the reference library he and Max had assembled over fifty years. It struck Nick that he and Felix and Frodo came as mourners to a temple of scholarship; there was something oddly sacred about the moment, as if Frank's presence, if that was the word, sanctified the rows of books. Awkwardly, uncertain of quite the right thing to do but feeling that it was essential to do something, he made a small, unsure bow to the dark mahogany box and turned away quickly.

Max appeared about seven. To Nick he seemed infinitely weary, as if the marrow had been drawn meltingly from his bones over the last few days.

"Nicholas. Dear Frodo. Felix." He greeted each in turn, searching their faces as if wanting to find some vestige of Sanger.

"Such a miserable business—and so absolutely unlike the way Frank would have wished to take his leave of us." He looked around the drawing room, letting his eye rest quickly in turn on the objects around which he and Sanger had formed their lives: the *Kiss of Judas* above the credenza which had once decorated a Medici villa; *Saint Lucy* on the opposite wall, the last addition to the Lefcourt collection; the Laurana bust of a Florentine noblewoman, cold, elegant, perfectly featured; the small Raphael *Madonna and Child with Saint Joseph.* Dim, comforting presences on the walls with which Max seemed to be making a reaffirming communion, finding something of Frank Sanger alive in each of them, some crystallized memory.

"I shall want you to say something short and praiseful, Felix. Frank always thought you the most gracious user of the language who ever came to us. We shall be having a service in the Carmine tomorrow at ten; the Sovrintendenza has very graciously allowed us to use the Brancacci Chapel. I know it would have pleased Frank to be able to bid farewell to the Masaccios. It was his first book, you know. He . . ." The old man's self-control cut off the sob, but he was nonetheless forced into a momentary silence.

Then he gathered himself again. "You shan't mind if I don't join you at dinner? This has all been very exhausting. Very." He embraced each of them and made his way out of the room. There was nothing to say; the low lights, the dim paintings on the walls seeming to lurk like spectral creatures in the shadows, the sense of smothering darkness made for an eerie half-world punctuated by the sound of Lefcourt's cane tapping its way along the hall.

The next morning Nick was up early, before the others. He wanted a walk, so he telephoned for a taxi and had it drop him outside Sta. Croce. At that hour, the church was hollowly empty except for a few praying women. Genuflecting as a matter of reflex, he walked quietly down the side aisle, not wishing to disturb the old women's devotions; he entered the Bardi Chapel and stared up at the great Giotto frescoes, remembering Sanger's praise of the great master, his salutation of "the temporal made timeless by a monumentality and humanity which no European painter before Giotto could have conceived, let alone executed."

Thanks, Frank, he thought as he left the church. Thanks for teaching me to see. He walked through the streets of the gradually activating city: through the Piazza della Repubblica; past the cloister of Sta. Maria Novella, under the odd parapets of the Signoria and the grotesque heroism of the statues in the Loggia de' Lanzi. It was a gray, sourish day, its dull light muting the ochers and reds of postcard Florence into something somberer, something deprived. A good day for a sad occasion, he thought, crossing the Ponte alla Carraia on his way at last to the Carmine. He halted briefly on the bridge and watched the muddy Arno rush underneath.

The Piazza del Carmine was filled with cars. It seemed as if the entire Italian art world had assembled to honor a fallen chieftain. But in contrast to many such ceremonious funerals which Nick had attended, no one seemed inclined to chatter on the steps. There was an undertone of apology present in the gathering congregation, a palpable feeling of common shame —as human beings, as Italians—to be of the same race that could so miserably, unnecessarily steal an old man's last few unbegrudgeable years.

It was a simple ceremony. The young priest who had given Communion for the last ten years in La Pergola's private chapel read from St. Francis. Felix spoke movingly and well of Francis Sanger's love of life and art and his devotion to his teaching and his students. "A priestly man," he concluded, "rich in friendship, rich in endowments, rich in the company he kept and the company he was, who takes some part of each of us with him now. *Addio, caro maestro, caro amico, Caro Francesco. Addio.*" Felix' voice came close to breaking; Nick felt tears start.

The chapel seemed alive with ghosts and memories; Nick felt that if he strained he could hear their voices. Old conversations, old visions pushing back across the years. There was a stir at the rear of the chapel then, as two men made their way up the aisle between the rows of folding chairs. The older had a corona of brilliant white hair which danced flamelike as he made his halting way, nearly blind, dependent for guidance on the hand with which he gripped his companion's shoulder. Nick knew him at once. He had been the greatest pianist in the world until his eyesight had failed and he had abandoned the concert stage for a hermit's existence at Fontainebleau. It had been years since he had played in public, Nick knew, but of course he would have come for Frank. His companion had been the violin prodigy of his age; he too was all but retired, but he too would have come however many miles in whatever condition life had left him to make farewell music for his friend Frank Sanger.

The old man settled at the piano, back straight as a guardsman's. Through the chapel windows a beam of light fixed and played on the rich wood of the violinist's instrument; it seemed to make a halo of the old pianist's hair. Some imperceptible sign passed between them and they began to play the slow movement from Beethoven's "Spring" Sonata. The music was heartbreaking, rending. It hung above the heads of the mourning crowd, sealing the chapel from the rest of the careworn, fractious world, spinning its attenuated sorrowful song like a rope around the heart of each listener. Above, the great figures in Masaccio's cycle of St. Peter seemed to have come to life. It was as if, Nick thought, they were standing surrogate for the entire history of Italian painting, official mourners deputed from the netherworld to be present at their friend's last moments.

The music died, and the violinist sat down while the old pianist began to play. Nick knew the piece at once: one of Liszt's "Petrarch" sonnets. The No. 47. It had been a favorite of Frank's. "*Benedetto sia il giorno,*" the poet had written: "Blessed be the day and the hour and the moment when I met my love"; and Liszt had set it to music, catching the inexorable sadness of Petrarch's nostalgic recollection of the transcendent moment when he had seen his beloved Laura.

As the music continued, he turned to look at Max, sitting across the aisle. His friend was ramrod-straight, staring ahead, a slight smile on his lips. Nick knew instinctively that Max was no longer with them, that his spirit had passed through the walls of the chapel, out into the wide plain and beyond, to the long, late-afternoon landscape of memory, where the failing sun slanted down on the avenue of cypress at the bottom of the garden; where Francis Sanger, restored by recollection to his youthful fairness and vigor, stood waiting to greet his friend. Nick's own tears now came freely, as it rushed upon him how much had been taken from Max, and in the same instant of recognition, how much he wished, he needed, Jill to be there.

That afternoon Frank Sanger was buried in the garden of La Pergola, under the notch in the privet, which seemed to be filled with the bulk of the dome of the cathedral, orange and red in the sun. The captains and kings gradually dispersed. The last muted conversations in the *salone* died away. Felix had left to spend the night at I Tatti and then was to rush back to Boston for a lecture. Frodo had departed for London to see his mother. Max had asked Nick to remain at La Pergola—"for company," he said—and so Nick, having nothing pressing to do, had stayed behind.

For nearly a week he was left to his own devices. Max stayed in his room upstairs; Giuseppina carried his meals up to him on a tray, shaking her head solemnly. The villa seemed unable to shake its residual sadness, which hung damply in the air like mildew, although the weather had turned brilliant and fresh. Nick filled his time by reading in the garden and taking long solitary drives into the countryside. For some reason, he felt no urge to go down to Florence. It was enough to know that it was there; that its arsenal of distractions was his to command if need be. Vaguely, Nick sensed that his presence at La Pergola had a specific point which was locked up in Max Lefcourt's mind. So he waited to be summoned. New York was a haunted house of might-have-beens, and he felt no rushing need to return.

One evening he finally did go into the city. In the *caffè*, a mournful flutist and a string trio played a hokey arrangement of airs from Verdi. It was the cheapest sort of music, and like the cheapest music, it produced infinite, sad longings. He fled back to La Pergola.

Finally, one evening before dinner, Max came into the *salone*.

"You must think me terribly rude, Nicholas; I hope it hasn't been a trial for you, being alone." The old man was emaciated by grief, wrung out, so that no further tears were possible.

"Not at all, Max. I just wish there were something I could say or do to make it easier for you."

"There is." Lefcourt managed a smile. "Shall we go into the garden? It looks a lovely evening."

They strolled down to a bench at the bottom of the garden. The evening air was soft and lemon-scented. The lights of Florence sparkled in the distance.

Lefcourt gestured Nick to the place beside him. He nodded at the modest stone that marked Francis Sanger's grave; it was inset with a Pisanello medal of John Paleologus: the first personal gift that Max had made to Sanger, years before.

"I suppose someone will come along and rip it out someday. That's the way the world is. Poor Frank—he may be better off than any of us." Lefcourt paused. "Frank saved me, you know, Nicholas. When I came down from Cambridge full of bad ideas, I might easily have gone rotten, like Tony Blunt or Bill Haydon or the others. But Frank gave me Italy, you see. And himself. And now he's gone—and so, I fear, is this once-wonderful country which I have loved so dearly.

"That's why I want you to help me, Nicholas. I've spent the time since poor Frank's funeral—it was a nice service, wasn't it?—thinking. There's nothing left for me here now. Nicholas, I've decided to sell your Texan the pictures in this house."

"Oh, no, Max. For God's sake, no." Nick's resentment sent him to his feet. "No, no, no!"

Lefcourt patted the place Nick had vacated.

"Sit down, Nicholas, and listen to me. Carefully, please." His voice sounded surprisingly firm and commanding. Nick obeyed.

"Nicholas, I have formed a terrible suspicion, from which I cannot escape. I believe that Frank was kidnapped for a purpose. Had the ransom demand ever come, I believe it would have been for a sum of money so large that I would have been obliged to sell the collection—or perhaps they would have demanded the collection itself. That really doesn't matter, does it? What does matter is my feeling that Frank was taken for a purpose; the last throw of a desperate man, may we say; and that man, I think, might well be your Mr. Gudge."

"Oh, Max, come on!"

"Nicholas, I told you. I cannot escape the feeling."

"So—I'll grant you your suspicions. Let's just say you're right. Why in the world sell him the pictures? Frank's gone; it makes no sense."

Max seemed to shiver.

"I believe I'm getting a slight chill."

He rose and, gesturing for Nick's arm, started back up toward the villa.

When they were seated in the *salone*, near the fire, Max said, almost absently, "Nicholas, go over and take a *close* look at the little Piero portrait behind the piano."

Nick did. The light was dim, so he raised a lamp from the credenza, thinking, as he did so, that it had been years since he'd given the collection a real study.

The picture was dead. Everything superficial was right: form, style and surface. Superbly worked out. But it had no soul, no electricity, no emanation. It was a stroke-perfect copy.

The astonishment in his face as he turned to Max, who smiled mischievously, said everything.

"Clever, aren't they, those Japanese? Come over here, Nicholas; I have a little story to tell you.

"You will remember before the war—of course, you'd not have been born then—that Frank and I sent the collection to Japan. In honor of dear Yashiro. He stayed here, you see, when he was doing the revision of his book on Botticelli. The collection had a great success in Japan. And when it left, the Japanese, in that funny, mysterious, secretive way of theirs, made me the most extraordinary gift. They'd had the collection copied. The entire collection. Exactly to scale. Copied by a group of artists in, of all places, Hiroshima. They are the most extraordinary people. And they can copy anything. Not just alarm clocks and automobiles. You can see; they've got everything right except the soul; they don't really understand it, and they can't take it apart to see how it works, so the spirit is beyond them.

"Anyway, with the exception of things that Frank and I bought since the war, of which the Velásquez and the Caravaggio are the most important, everything here"—Lefcourt's arms spread wide—"is a copy made in Hiroshima in 1938."

"That's not possible!" exclaimed Nick.

"It is indeed, my young friend. And has been for the last five years, since Frank and I decided that things were turning for the worse. Only Frank and I and Aldo knew about the copies; they'd been crated as furniture and stored in Florence. So we had them brought up and we reframed them ourselves. It wasn't very difficult, you see. The only really large painting I have is the Titian, and that did give us a bit of a time."

"I don't believe it."

"Well, you must, Nicholas, because it's the truth. I must say that it did give Frank and me a bit of a good laugh—because, you see, nobody came here to see the pictures: they came to see us. So they seldom gave the pictures a second look. They wanted to see us two old decrepit monuments. You and Frodo never really looked at the pictures any longer; you know you didn't, Nicholas. You simply cast a careless eye to reassure yourself that all was as you expected—these were old friends, after all—and got down to the gossip and Giuseppina's *bollito*. And they are good copies, you know. And we kept the lights dim after we made the change. You know how Frodo has complained about the light. Now, Nicholas, don't look so sour. You just took things for granted. Most of us do. No harm in that."

Nick was stunned, and abashed. Max was right, though: it had been years since he'd really looked closely at the pictures themselves. The mere glimpse of them, of the something in the frames, set off a rush of memories and associations which he, and Felix and Frodo, probably, substituted for the act of seeing.

"Max, I'm speechless."

"Hardly, I should think. A bit wounded, perhaps. But you know—not to be remonstrative, Nicholas—that was what was so wonderful about Frank. He never stopped looking, so he never stopped seeing. He believed that works of art demanded that kind of attention; they oughtn't to be reduced to mere clues to our preconceptions and recollections. Frank took nothing in life for granted, except man's innate genius and humanity. How sadly wrong he was about that."

Nick felt dubious.

"Max, you're not going to try to tell me the pictures at the Fuller weren't genuine?"

"Of course they were. It took some arranging, but your Mr. Gudge isn't the only one who can arrange things. I also have friends who are men of parts. Along the way, identical crates were exchanged. When the exhibition in New York ended, the copies returned to La Pergola; the originals went back to a home in the mountains I'd found for them—where they're safe and well tended. It wasn't really very complicated. Not when the collection's owner is in on the game.

"Now, Nicholas, what's important: I want you to handle the sale of these pictures here to your Mr. Gudge. That will make you my accomplice, but I gather from Felix you've no love for those people anyway. Come, let's go up to dinner. I know Giuseppina's done a *Scrigno di Venere* just for you. Put some flesh on those slender bones of yours. Let me tell you what I have in mind."

Over dinner, Nick said, "Max, I don't know. It's a terrible risk for me. For you, for Frank's memory; even if you're right about Gudge. How can I knowingly become involved in selling something I know to be spurious?"

"There are motives in life, Nicholas, which sometimes must outweigh our normal inclinations. I understand from Frodo that you lost that nice girl you brought here to us. Because of the Gudges. And you, after all, first mentioned the name of Gudge in this house. I understand you took Mr. Gudge to see my pictures in New York. Oh, Nicholas, I know what you think; but you see, I do think you owe me something by way of compensation. I can see in your face that you also think you do."

Nick thought it over.

"I suppose I do, Max. I suppose I do. But there must be conditions. I won't take any money, nor will I pass on authenticity. I'll be a go-between. Anyway, what makes you think you can put it over?"

"Mr. Gudge. He's offered this vast sum of money twice, sight unseen. He lives in a world of assumptions, perhaps to a greater extent than the rest of us. He's a billionaire—so says the world; but who's counted his money? This is the Lefcourt Collection. Do I look like a forger? Is it any less improbable, given the nature of the world, that my pictures are fakes than that Gudge isn't a billionaire?"

"I suppose not. Does anyone else know?"

"Frodo does. I told him before he left; we may need him. But he'll be silent. I'll see he gets the Caravaggio for the Fuller. And he hates these people."

"And the money, Max. What will you do with the money?"

"The point is not the money, Nicholas. I don't know; perhaps I'll give it to the Queen. There's always a use for money. You see, it's getting it away from Gudge, defrauding him, taking his money and giving him less value back, that will injure him. It will come out, someday. These very rich people are that way, you know. Their souls are the color of their money; it's a terrible stain, that."

"And the genuine pictures?"

"Safe in the bosom of the mountains, Nicholas. In a safe place and in safe hands. Frank would approve. And there they'll sleep, like Brünnhilde in her circle of fire, awaiting the right time to reappear. It'll be my little gift to what remains of mankind, if anything does in fact remain fifty years from now. After the darkness falls. If it ever lifts again, those pictures will be needed. Think of the way the light of humanism was kept alive in the monasteries in the Dark Ages. Now, Nicholas, perhaps a little more? I seem to have regained my appetite. How healthful it is to get even, as you Americans say."

CHAPTER TWENTY-FOUR

"The art event of the century," went the front-page story in *The New York Times*,

> was consummated yesterday with the announcement that the bulk of the Lefcourt Collection, an assemblage of approximately two hundred paintings, drawings and sculptures, principally by Italian masters from the 13th to the 18th centuries, has been acquired by Texas oilman/investor Buford Gudge IV, 49. Although the price paid for the collection was not revealed, knowledgeable opinion suggests that close to one-half billion dollars has changed hands.
>
> The Lefcourt Collection was gathered over the past 50 years by Maximilian d'Auberville Foxe Lefcourt, 73, third Baron Lefcourt, and his close friend and companion, the American art historian Francis Sanger, whose recent death in a tragic terrorist incident is thought to have been a factor in Baron Lefcourt's decision to part with the collection. It is also rumored that Baron Lefcourt proposes to transfer his fabled villa La Pergola, acquired by his family late in the last century and rumored to have been a site known to Petrarch and Boccaccio, to Cambridge University as a center for humanistic studies.
>
> An interesting aspect of the sale of the Lefcourt Collection was the participation, as a beneficiary, of the Italian Government, whose official permission was required for the export of the collection. Under the terms of the contract of sale, it is understood, the "Portrait of a Man," thought to be the Baroque artist Lorenzo Bernini (1598–1680), by the Spanish painter Diego Velásquez (1599–1660) will go to the Doria-Pamphili Gallery in Rome, to join Velásquez's "Portrait of Pope Innocent X," the other masterpiece dating from Velásquez's Roman sojourn in the early 1650s. Similarly, a large drawing of monkeys and lions by the Venetian artist Gentile Bellini (1429–1507) and a panel depicting the "Coronation of the Virgin," attributed to Pietro Lorenzetti (c. 1280–c. 1348), an important follower of Giotto, will go to the Uffizi Gallery in Florence, as will a "Portrait of a Young Woman," popularly known as "The Italian Girl," by Hans Holbein the younger (1497–1543). In addition, it is also understood that certain commercial interests, notably oil and gas properties in the Adriatic Sea, have been ceded to the Italian energy monopoly ENI. It is

> also understood that Lord Lefcourt has agreed to donate a substantial portion of the proceeds from the sale, perhaps as much as $200 million, to the Italian state arts fund.
>
> These four works, as well as roughly a dozen paintings and as many drawings to be retained by Lord Lefcourt, who is rumored to be leaving his Italian home of 50 years for Switzerland, are all among the most recent additions to the Lefcourt Collection, to which a relatively small number of objects have been added in the years since World War II. Another relatively recent acquisition, a painting of "St. Lucy" by Michelangelo Merisi da Caravaggio (1573–1610), will be given by Lord Lefcourt to the Fuller Institute in New York City, with which his Lordship has enjoyed cordial relations for many years.
>
> The separation of these works from the collection does not lessen its impact as a whole, which rivals in quality, art-historical scope and highlights the Italian holdings of the National Gallery in Washington, the Metropolitan Museum and the Johnson Collection in the Philadelphia Museum of Art. Among its notable treasures are Titian's "Kiss of Judas," perhaps the noblest of the great Venetian painter's darkly dramatic last works; two Raphael Madonnas representing his youth and full maturity; a small Nativity by Botticelli (possibly a pendant to the Annunciation in the Robert Lehman Collection at the Metropolitan Museum); a "Portrait of a Youth," thought to be Pigello Portinari, a son of the Medici agent in Flanders, by the Flemish master Hugo Van der Goes; the "Madonna of the Grackle" by Giovanni Bellini; three panels of scenes from the Life of St. Andrew by Filippo Lippi and his son Filippino Lippi; two large sketches for the gran salone of the Palazzo Bragadin, Venice, by Giambattista Tiepolo . . .

The list continued for two paragraphs.

> . . . Although Lord Lefcourt has remained silent as to the reason for his decision to sell his collection, sources close to him, as well as Florentine social and artistic circles, believe that the death under tragic circumstances of his long-time companion Francis Sanger, 82, the noted American art historian, has disenchanted him with Italy . . .

Nick put down the paper and let his head slump against the back of the sofa.

He was exhausted.

It had taken nearly three weeks of constant going back and forth to complete the sale. Not that there had been any dispute about price. Or any investigation by Gudge of the pictures for which he was laying out $397 million. Which worked out, on the paintings alone, to an average price of nearly $3 million—ranging from nearly $10 million apiece for the Titian and the large Raphael to several hundred thousand for the Bellotto *View of Munich* and the Tiepolo sketches. Nick's main task had been to set the prices. The contract had been drawn up by Max's London solicitors and the Japanese who represented Gudge. It was the Japanese who had worked out whatever oil deal it had been necessary to make with the Energy Ministry in Rome to buy a passport out of Italy for the pictures. Max himself had taken care of the Ministry of Fine Arts, arranging for the gifts to the Doria and the Uffizi and for the cash benefaction.

The Japanese had been an odd one, Nick thought. He'd arrived within two days of Nick's call to Gudge and checked into the Excelsior Hotel on the Piazza Ognissanti. Except for the working sessions in the library of La Pergola, he'd returned alone to his hotel—keeping entirely to himself. When it had seemed the government was going to get sticky about an export permit, he'd vanished for two days, presumably to Rome. When he'd returned to Florence, the producing properties of Idrocarburi Gudge S.A. had been deeded to ENI, along with some valuable lease interests.

Max had been impressed. "That Mr. Katagira is most assuredly a man of parts," he said to Nick during one of their predinner garden pilgrimages to Sanger's graveside. "He knows how to get things done here."

It made Nick sorry to see how effectively money greased the skids these days. Sure, he admitted, nickel-and-dime stuff had always been the name of the game in Italy. A small touch here had opened this door; a few million lire there had sent the odd good painting on its transatlantic way—remember the Signorelli *tondo* you and Creel managed to get out, he admonished himself, feeling himself becoming hypocritically sanctimonious—but never part of Italy's national patrimony, which was what the Lefcourt Collection was. The Arabs, he thought, have made whores of us all, as Frodo had said to him once when they were wandering through the antiques show at Grosvenor House.

He hoped Mr. Gudge was happy.

"He is extremely pleased," the Japanese had said. Period. End of report. Nothing about the fate or future of the collection. At least the handful of genuine works: the Guercino *Samson in Chains* and that lovely little Mantegna of *The Harrowing of Hell*, and the best things Max had bought since the war—the Velásquez, the Caravaggio, the Turner, the Ingres double portrait of the Saumarez girls, the Fra Angelico fragment, the Fra Bartolommeo landscape drawings—would be spared the possibility of a Texas exile.

Nick was certain that the Lefcourt Collection would be renamed the Gudge Collection. The Gudge Collection! Well, they could call it that, but it would never be anything except the Lefcourt Collection.

He thought he would have a hot bath and give Frodo a call. Perhaps they could have a good laugh together. Perhaps. He needed a laugh.

The news of Gudge's acquisition of the Lefcourt Collection, which Frodo had tipped him on two days before it came out in the papers, filled Greschner's mind with possibilities.

Frodo had finished his report with a plea.

"Solomon, I'm quite prepared to retract the rather unkind things I said about your Mrs. Gudge a few months ago. Provided you give us a bit of help, which I believe you're in a position to do." He outlined what he wanted.

Later, Katagira called. What he wanted done Sol knew exactly how to handle. Then, with Frodo's request in mind and because in any case he liked to let on that he was conversant with whatever was going on, a form of tacit indiscretion which Katagira knew gave Greschner a feeling of power, he asked about the Lefcourt purchase.

"There most assuredly is no keeping of secrets from you, Mr. Greschner. Actually, I was about to tell you about it. There certainly will be a critical role for you to play in this as well, but that I think you should discuss with Mrs. Gudge directly. She's in charge of cultural affairs around here," Katagira chuckled.

Mrs. Gudge would be in New York in two days, the Japanese said.

"And Mr. Gudge? He must be very happy about this. I know it's been on his mind a great deal over the last year—really since Mrs. Gudge first saw the Collection. He must be triumphant."

"So-so, I'm afraid. He's not well at all, Mr. Greschner. Terribly weak. Some days I think the end must be not far off. The pain seems to be worse; but he's a remarkable man with remarkable willpower. He seems determined to live this out, all of it—to see the end. And I believe he will. Now, just to recapitulate, if you don't mind: you understand the implications of the Golden Grove failure as they are to be presented to the public?"

"Indeed I do. Have no fear of that. You're not fearful that this might trigger things prematurely?"

"I think, frankly, Mr. Greschner, it's an unavoidable risk. Given Mr. Gudge's condition, and the condition of the financial markets. Further deterioration might set events on their own course, and it's very much Mr. Gudge's desire that he be identified, and recognized, as the author of circumstances, not their creature. You are aware, Mr. Greschner, from our talk six weeks ago, that this is a crusade for Mr. Gudge; a holy war; a *jihad*."

"Of course. You can rely on me. As for Mrs. Gudge, I expect I can reach her at the Esmé Castle?"

"I'll make sure she's in touch."

Greschner hung up. He understood Katagira's apprehensions about the bond market. His sources on the Street, including a few thoughts Jill had passed on during their now almost daily conversations, told of an overbought market teetering on the edge of a major collapse. A fad had outlived its useful life, had lost its majority, and was being sustained, if that was the word, by sheer nervous energy and, one might say, the prayers of those, like Seaco and its banks, who were in too deep to get out. The only thing that would probably turn it around was a big bullish change in the money-supply statistics to be released in three weeks; it was a mercy that the Fed was now publishing its money counts monthly, so that the market was at least spared the yo-yo Friday-night cycles of earlier years. It could go either way, the experts felt. There was a lot of optimistic talk coming out of

Washington, including some encouraging cost-of-living figures. But the money funds kept growing, which wasn't exactly a sign of investor confidence in the long-term markets. Back and forth, back and forth, Sol reflected.

Jill had reported that the Street was saying a big short position in Seaco was being built up, according to her sources. No names yet, but it was presumably an important player, a likely bellwether. She was following up on the rumor.

He turned his mind to Caryn Gudge and Frodo's request. He was sure he could work it out, but since he had only two days, no time like the present to get started. He picked up the telephone and dialed Calypso Winstead.

The collapse of the Golden Grove Savings Association, an innocuous little savings-and-loan headquartered south of Los Angeles, would not in itself have been important enough to cause trouble for Wall Street. The total of the Golden Grove haircut was less than $200 million in capital and reserves, uninsured deposits and the cash market value of the small float in the stock; the loss was shared by the association's depositors, the federal insurers, speculators who had written options against the association's mortgage and bond portfolio and its stockholders, in themselves an insignificant number by the Street's current measures of calamity. These days, with a sense of uncertainty as heavy in the air as exhaust fumes, the Street didn't bat an eye at any blowoff less than a quarter-billion.

Creighton reported it differently. This ought to make some real waves, Jill thought, reading over her column for the next Monday's *Pritchett's*. She had been working at it for most of the day, writing and rewriting the item, trying out several different locations within the body of the column. Shock without panic. That was what Sol had suggested she aim for. It was good advice, she guessed. Working through the day—while Jenny was at school—she found herself adrenally charged up by the disclosures Sol had made, as he led her stage by stage into the Gudge story. She was thinking ahead; she thought now she knew what was coming. Surely Gudge was up to something. She scented a first, faint whiff of rottenness from the shores of Denmark. If her guess was correct, wasn't she a co-conspirator, she wondered, seeing that her information came from Sol, whose obvious self-satisfaction on the telephone told her he was in on something?

Jill recognized that in any market ploy, a lot of innocent people could get hurt. Yet her sympathy for other innocents was used up, along with her tolerance for the selfish antics of the rich. Gudge had uncharacteristically walked away from the Golden Grove collapse. What if Seaco and the bond-trading partnership got into trouble; would he do the same?

She finished the column. The Gudge item was a mere five lines to the effect that did Wall Street know that the freshly defunct Golden Grove Savings Association, which had gambled itself into insolvency in the financial-futures market, was an orphan abandoned by its largest stockholder, none other than Buford Gudge IV? Of course, she knew, her readership would make the Seaco-Gudge connection quickly. She couldn't help that. She wouldn't want to be in Homer Seabury's shoes Sunday night when the advance copies of *Pritchett's* went out; but then, she'd thought all along that what Homer Seabury was doing with his firm was suicidal.

When she had finished transmitting the column to Union City, she got up and made a pot of tea, needing a break to reconstitute herself mentally for her other journalistic task. It was a nice bright day outside the kitchen window: a good day for walking and talking; for being arm in arm, she thought ruefully; for being in love. She needed to get out. No new men, though. The hell with that routine. Maybe she and Jenny could catch a movie, even though it was a school night. Who cared? Who indeed, she said sadly to herself, carrying her tea back to her workroom.

The lead-in to her Gilberte column was in the typewriter.

> GILBERTE hears that the fabulous CARYN GUDGE, whose husband, BUFORD (Don't call me BUBBER) GUDGE IV, has just bought the fabled LEFCOURT Collection, with its RAPHAELS and REMBRANDTS and other treasures, may become the leading benefactress not only of the Texas Panhandle, but of CALYPSO and HUGO WINSTEAD's fabulous FULLER Institute. While Mrs. GUDGE is in New York huddling with top Vietnamese architect NGUYEN TRANH—he did the fabulous FULLER Annex, you know—about a new museum to be built on her ranch in Texas, she's also talking with SIR FRODO CRISP, the FULLER's director and everyone's favorite extra man, about a major gift of some of the LEFCOURT treasures to the FULLER. If that happens, the empty seat on the FULLER Board won't be empty any longer, or so a little bird perched at the end of the table tells us . . .

She threw the last in to cause Hugo Winstead a little disquiet.

Wait until Granada sees that! Jill smiled. In a way she felt sorry for Granada: she'd done so much, spent so much, tried so hard. But after all was said and done, Granada hadn't been able to grow beyond her money.

She closed out the column with a puff on a forthcoming $400-a-ticket olive-oil tasting.

Just as its author had anticipated, Creighton's column caused a stir. The Golden Grove item produced a broad range of reactions, ranging from mild quizzical vibrations to deep anxious rumblings.

By nine-fifteen Monday morning, the chief financial officer of the bank that had led the syndication of the buy/sell arrangement with the Seaco-Gudge partnership had his chief bond trader on the carpet.

"You see this?" He waved *Pritchett's* at the other man, who nodded cheerlessly and said nothing.

What the hell am I supposed to say? he thought. When we stitched this deal together, the guy behind the desk and the bigger cats upstairs were the ones that crowded to get their pictures in the papers. Nobody from *Forbes* or *The Institutional Investor* had come rapping on the trading-room door to quote him on the future of interest rates. Nobody had wanted his opinion of the supply side, or the Laffer curve, or the gold standard. He wasn't surprised to be here, though. The way the bank worked, there would be a menu of shit being prepared upstairs in the president's office for the chief financial officer and in the chairman's office for the president. The buck would work its way upstairs until finally, smokelike, it would dissolve in the ionosphere of the boardroom, lost in a haze of excuses acceptable to a board of directors drawn from the bank's largest debtors. After all, it was someone else's money that had been lent; that it might be lost was therefore someone else's fault.

"Well?" Again—pompously, querulously—from behind the desk.

"I saw it. Look, I talked to Seaco last night. Not to worry, they told me. When the option expires next week, they'll be there. Gudge is with them one hundred and ten percent. We come up with the bonds, they'll be good for the billion four on their end. I'm not sweating it."

The financial officer didn't look appeased. His ass was on the line, he knew. They had been counting on using their profit on the option to offset the hosing they'd taken on that currency shot in cruzeiros. If Seaco-Gudge defaulted and the bank was stuck with $300 million of bonds on which it'd mentally booked a $30-million profit, his nuts were going to be served for breakfast.

The bond trader could see that his superior was really worried.

"Look," he said, "Gudge isn't gonna drop the ball on Seaco. This isn't some chickenshit S.-and-L. in the Imperial Valley. The sonofabitch has got eighty big ones tied up in Seaco, plus maybe three, four units' equity in the bond partnership. Plus, I worked it out, the guy's holding close to a billion six in the market value of those two companies went public last year. So he's good for the dough. And Seaco looks clean. Sure, they've taken a bath on some of their positions; who hasn't? But if push comes to shove, they'll show up at the closing. That I think we can count on."

Both men knew what he meant. So great was the value of being able to book profits from the bond sale on the profit-and-loss statement, which would make top management look good, that the bank and its sisters in the syndicate would surely lend Seaco-Gudge enough money—suitably collateralized, of course—to buy the bonds, and pay the syndicate with its own money.

The realization made the chief financial officer feel suddenly better, as if an ulcer had been emulsified into submission.

"Well, keep an eye on it." He tried, half-successfully, to put the right note of bonhomie in his voice.

No worry there, thought his trader. He was keeping a very close eye, and ear, on the Seaco trading room, and he didn't like what he was seeing and hearing. The night before, just as soon as he'd seen the Creighton note on the Golden Grove collapse, he'd called Fixed Income at his home in Roslyn; although it was difficult to hear precisely over the noise of a television set and the babble of young children in the background, the Seaco man had sounded wired-out, his nerves working overtime on the near edge of hysteria. Drugs, he'd guessed. The young guys on the big positioning desks were all on them. Uppers, mostly, he knew, designed to promote that whiz-bang sense of self which seemed integral these days to the trading game. And cocaine, which lent its own sweet unreality to the delicate process of tiptoeing over ice growing progressively thinner. Tiptoeing, my ass, he thought: floating.

The bank's trader was a gray veteran of twenty-five years on the Street. The bond market had really scared him for the last six months, and he'd been down on it for close to two years. When the present Administration had come in, he'd listened briefly to the rhetoric; looked closely at what he felt to be the salient fact in the economy, which was that the use of credit by all hands was running wild and uncontrolled—the ultimate stage of that free market about which all the fat cats babbled while they waited for their tax cut like a diner waiting for his steak. So he started taking the bank out of its position in long bonds. To his regret, he'd been only about halfway successful. The chairman was kissing ass in Washington, so to run counter to the prevailing euphoria was thought to be bad manners in terms of social politics; then this goddamn Gudge thing had come along, and really screwed his strategy up. Not that he wasn't somewhat to blame: the way the kid from Seaco had presented it, it looked like enough of a lock to be worth the study. But then a lot of buzzwords—"creative financing," "Gudge," "market stratagems," "two-way street"—had gotten thrown in, like an alchemist's incantations, capable of turning lead into gold, and the deal had gotten signed up. Naturally, no one knew at the time that Seaco was going to go apeshit leveraging itself in the bond business.

Thankfully, the bank's trader reflected that Seaco's financial strength or weakness outside of this deal wasn't his business. The boys over in the Wall Street Division covered the broker loans; it was up to them to decide how much rope to let out before it started to make up into a noose. It wouldn't give them a hell of a lot of comfort to know, if they did, that they were several hundred million bucks exposed—and they weren't alone—to a trading position being run by a kid whose nerves were starting to go on him, who sounded like he was being propped up by dope and delusion, two very frail supports if the going got rough.

Homer Seabury was starting to feel as if he were going fifteen rounds with Sugar Ray Leonard. Only a fortnight earlier, Katagira had assured him of Gudge's dependability in a crunch. Now, like a roundhouse to the chin, came this fellow Creighton implying that Gudge had done just the opposite in another situation. Even though it seemed like peanuts; a little S&L out in cloud-cuckooland; not the same sort of thing at all.

Mercifully, Creighton hadn't even mentioned the Gudge-Seaco relationship—which meant, thank heaven, that the firm's customers weren't any more nervous than might ordinarily be expected in a very nervous market. The bond market was frozen tremblingly in place, like a deer in a jungle full of tigers; the stock market, which had first bubbled, then boiled, was back to simmering and looked as if it were cooling fast. A long way from margin-call problems, but looking gillish and pale. The prime rate seemed stuck at 19 percent. The President had made six televised appearances: cajoling, exhorting, excoriating an unmoved class of upper-bracket tax beneficiaries who were busy hoarding the abundant fruits of what now looked to be the temporary, passing harvest of ill-advised political foolishness, putting them into Switzerland against the severer winter whose chill breath could be felt even on a bright April day.

It was not a consoling picture for Homer Seabury as he sat staring out his window, looking through the passage between two challenging high-rise buildings up the East River, watching airliners rise from LaGuardia, stately darts against a sky unusually blue, unusually clear. Things should be going measurably better than they were. For a while there, even as recently as a month earlier, Homer had thought himself finally liberated from life's tireless unfairnesses. Now, in the window, he saw his jowly, listless reflection: a lion in trouble; no longer the fiscal statesman, innovator and leader whom more powerful men had once crossed dining rooms to congratulate.

His secretary's buzz announced a call from the chairman of the firm's principal bank. The buck had percolated to the top. It was barely eleven o'clock.

"Homer, would it be too much to ask you to come over after the close? Just a few routine things; a matter of getting our signals straight. Haven't seen much of you recently, anyway. Not since that dinner for Kissinger at the Gorse." The voice was rich with detectably fake affability. The chairman hadn't made a routine call, other than to his barber and his wife, in a dozen years.

Seabury said he'd be there. Then, as he had all his life, as his father had instructed him, when trouble loomed, he telephoned Solomon Greschner.

He summarized the situation.

"Sol, we really must do something about the banks. The Street's pretty nervous right now, and frankly, we're just a bit more exposed than I'd ideally like to be. Technically, that is. You know—or maybe you don't—that we—that is, the bond-investment partnership we organized with Mr. Gudge—entered into an agreement six months ago with a group of banks, including our friends over on Cedar Street, and insurance companies to buy a substantial amount of bonds from them?"

Greschner thought it judicious not to comment on the fact that, as Seabury described it, the contract, which Katagira had described in detail to Greschner, had been altered in Seabury's telling from a contractual right on the part of the banks to stick the bonds to Seaco-Gudge to what sounded like a gentlemanly handshake committing the banks to let Seaco buy away their cherished bonds. As usual, it's all in the semantics, thought Sol.

"What's the amount, Homer?"

"Well, um, it seems to work out to one billion four hundred million dollars."

"Seven hundred million apiece?"

"That's correct."

"How's it look?"

"Well, frankly, it's a little underwater right now—maybe fifty or sixty basis points. This little technical correction we're having, you know. Not that we don't think we won't do wonderfully well on it, you know, when all's said and done." Seabury's confidence-inducing chuckle sounded effortful.

"And you're afraid that Mr. Gudge might not honor his side of the arrangement—is that it? I think Mr. Gudge would be very disappointed if he thought you were harboring such thoughts, Homer." Greschner recognized that he sounded unduly severe, especially considering Seabury's doglike loyalty through the years. He softened his tone. "I expect this has been brought about by that snip in Creighton's column? About that California mishap?"

"So it seems, Solomon. Not that I—we—anyone at Seaco has anything less than absolute confidence in Mr. Gudge's integrity—and his ability to make good on his commitments." Again the nervous chuckle. "But, well, you know, not everyone reads the newspapers the same way. And not everyone knows Mr. Gudge as well as we do."

"I understand, Homer. Perfectly. Now how can I help you?"

"Well, as it happens . . ." Seabury went on to explain about his conversation with Katagira.

"So you really don't wish to appear unconfident, shall we say, by telephoning again? Perfectly understandable, Homer, perfectly understandable. I shall be happy to call. After all, it is a media problem, more in the area of public relations than anything else, and that is my bailiwick." Greschner felt positive admiration for Katagira welling in him. It was all happening exactly as the Japanese had indicated it would.

Seabury expelled words of gratitude with a violent rush that suggested his nerves had pounded him on the back. Then he recaptured his sense of the moment.

"Um, one other thing, Solomon. I believe you've got a pretty good connection to this fellow Creighton?"

"Good enough."

"Well, um, do you think you could manage to keep anything about this option business out of *Pritchett's*? At least until all the loose ends are buttoned up."

"Homer, I'll try. Muzzling the press isn't easy, but I'll see what I can do. After all, the market runs on confidence, and it hardly is to anyone's interest to have unfounded rumors loose on the Street." At the other end he heard a heavy sigh of relief.

"And Homer, one thing. I'm speaking to you now in your capacity as a member of the board of the Fuller Institute. And very much off the record." His tone left no doubt that any breach of confidence would result in an immediate call to Texas, with possible grave consequences to Gudge's feelings about his bond-trading partners. "You may not be aware"—which Homer wasn't—"that Mr. and Mrs. Gudge are contemplating a major gift to the Institute. Of art. Certain things that are presently part of the Gudge Collection which Frodo desperately wants. It may be that the board will find it appropriate to recognize this contribution by giving Mrs. Gudge a seat. There are two vacant now, what with Marvin Terrace's resignation. One must remain vacant, as per the agreement with Harvey Bogle in connection with his long-term loan of the Rubens sketches. But the other, well . . ."

He need say no more, he knew. A grunt from Seabury indicated that his implication was clear. He ended their conversation with a few pleasantries.

Stretching, he rose from the armchair and strolled across the room, which seemed to glow rich and vibrant in the late-morning sun pouring through the large windows that faced Rostval Place. Green and shiny, the trees were at their best. Mothers with very young children idled on the benches. The flow of traffic was slight at most. Around the perimeter of the park, the facades of the town houses were a bright motley of orange and gray brick and basalt. This is the way it once was, Greschner thought, and the way it should have remained.

Then he went back across the room to telephone Katagira.

Hugo Winstead was suddenly beset by small discomforts which attacked him like horseflies. He desperately needed to talk to his old friend and shipmate Homer Seabury.

His wife and his patroness were both after him about this Gudge-Seaco business. There were rumors in the Street. He needed to know how bad the trouble was, assuming there was trouble; and if there in fact was, he and Homer had to get their stories aligned.

He'd expected to hear from Granada Masterman, once he saw that piece in *Pritchett's* about Gudge's savings-and-loan. He hadn't counted on Rufus Lassiter's making a complete about-face and supporting Granada's decision to bail out of Seaco while and if she could. And she had deputed Hugo to inform Seabury of that decision and to set in motion the registration process that would permit her to sell her stock as soon as possible. Interesting switch by Rufus, Winstead said to himself; the Senator had a sense of self-preservation even more finely tuned than his own, itself a miracle to the generation of rivals, competitors, clients, lovers and even a few admirers that had watched with astonishment as Hugo had risen until he was a figure to be reckoned with in the highest circles of commerce, culture and society. If Lassiter had changed his mind, Winstead guessed, things at Seaco must be pretty bad. Bad enough so that the mere thought was convulsive enough to make him cancel an assignation with a pretty young accountant from the IRS he'd met the week before in Washington. Now he was twiddling his thumbs waiting for Homer Seabury to return his call.

He was in the soup.

Although his lawyering days were behind him—like most senior partners, he spoon-fed clients, ran political errands and negotiated deals—he knew that his position as MUD's counsel, and a director, made him an insider, as far as Seaco stock was concerned. Which meant that the Endowment, where he was a fiduciary, and Calypso's trusts, where he was not a trustee but had exercised investment supervision, were locked into all the Seaco that he and Homer had so optimistically put them into months before. Not to mention the bonds. They were already at a slight loss; fortunately, the Endowment was accountable only once a year, and the next audit wouldn't come until the following February, which gave them ten months to get back to no worse than square one.

Fortunately, it hadn't all been a mess. Homer had seen to it that the Endowment and the trusts, and Hugo for his own small account, had been generously allocated GUT and GOD, which were still selling at close to their postoffering highs. So there were some consolations.

But if Seaco fell out of bed, or the bond market cracked; or, what was unthinkable, both happened—and they were surely linked—the Endowment would lose 50 percent of its value overnight. Which would put the Institute in trouble on its mortgage. Hugo's institutional pillars, which he had opportunistically converted into watching posts, would be knocked out from under him like stilts in a hurricane. The Winstead game could well be over.

Goddamn Homer, he thought angrily, drumming his fingers on his desk. Goddamn goddamn goddamn. If it was going to take this long, I could have kept the date in the Village. He pecked at his sandwich. The remembrance that he'd put the firm's retirement plan heavily into Seaco didn't improve his appetite.

It was after two when Seabury called.

Winstead wasted no time.

"Homer, Granada's decided to sell the Seaco stock. Right away. We want to get a registration statement cranked up A.S.A.P. At our expense. We'll indemnify the purchasers."

To his surprise, Seabury betrayed no indignation. He sounded downright jolly—unsuitably so, to Winstead's ears.

"Well, Hugo, you can tell her I think she's making a big mistake. Not that I regret her decision, you understand, even though my position's absolutely secure here. But if that's what she wants, we'll certainly do our best to cooperate. Have you got an underwriter?"

Winstead named a rival firm that would take a canoe out in a hurricane if the underwriting spread was fat enough. Lassiter, who knew them from his old Wall Street days, had contacted them on behalf of Granada, dangling all sorts of other potential MUD business—pension accounts; commercial paper; Europaper—before their greedy eyes. Hugo was sure that Rufus had made a deal assuring himself of a nice post-Senate fee or consultancy for acting as the finder. That was perfectly in the cards; what wasn't was Seabury's flabbergasting calmness.

"I must say, Homer, you're taking this surprisingly casually. A month ago, as I recall, you jumped out of your shoes at the suggestion. And surely things have not improved since then? In the general markets?"

"Quite so, Hugo. No argument there. But frankly, I must say we think we've seen the bottom here. And we're in good shape. Of course, to get everything into a prospectus and be ready to go is probably going to require three or four weeks, assuming we start now. And assuming your firm will act for us, Hugo. What about that?"

"I think we can." The money was made from representing the issuer, anyway.

"Anything else?" Seabury spoke in the bustling manner of a man with important affairs to conclude, dealings to incite. Oddly, Winstead found his confidence perplexingly infectious. Homer was a worrier, he knew. He must know something. So he forbore further discussion of the Fuller investments in Seaco and the bond market—a discussion he was not able to forbear later that evening, over martinis before dinner, with his wife.

"Hugo," Calypso asked, in her mild way, fingers working resolutely at her needlepoint, "doesn't the Endowment own a great many shares in Homer Seabury's company?"

"Why do you ask?" Winstead looked up sharply from his perusal of *That Woman!*; a conversation he'd had with Granada just before leaving the office had alerted him to trouble brewing in Gilberte's column. And there it was. What was all this crap about Caryn Gudge and the Institute?

"Oh, it's just that I heard somewhere it's not doing very well. I wouldn't want the Endowment to be hurt, especially not after the problems with the Annex. And I believe we do have a great deal of Seaco. I thought they were very close to that Mr. Gudge. Hasn't he helped Homer in the past? With money? He's so enormously rich. Can't he help out again?"

"Calypso, there's no problem at Seaco. I spoke with Homer just this afternoon. Everything's fine—as a matter of fact, the outlook's better than it has been in some time."

"Oh, that's comforting." Her head remained bent, face averted, watching the wool draw into and out of the canvas. "I hope I wasn't premature to sell my shares; I just had a few thousand in the trusts."

"You sold your shares?" The question squeaked out with such surprising shrillness that Calypso lifted her head and looked at him curiously.

"Yes. I just called the bank who's co-trustee with me and Uncle Sol and told them to sell. They called Sol and he said it was up to me. Shouldn't I have?"

"No." But that was all he could say. No point in trying to bring Calypso up to date on forty years of securities law. He returned to his paper, agitated inside, praying fiercely that nothing should happen to Seaco. Because if something did, even the most lenient SEC enforcement officer would hardly look kindly on the day's trading in Seaco by Mrs. Hugo Winstead, wife of a director of Masterman United, and therefore an insider. Who was also general counsel to Seaco Group, Inc., whom he had that very day advised that MUD wished to sell approximately five million shares of common stock in a public offering, the announcement of which could only depress an anxious market. Caesar's wife had sullied Caesar.

Hugo's rotten afternoon and worse cocktail hour had their sources in a series of conversations to which he was not privy.

He had not been present at the lunch, for example, at which Harvey Bogle told Calypso Winstead that something smelled funny about this whole Seaco business.

"My nose tells me there's something going on. And the market says that Homer's made a terrible mistake with this bond thing. I'm a seller, and you should be too, sweetie. And push Hugo to get the Endowment out."

Nor had he been present at the interview at Number 17 Rostval Place at which Granada Masterman, for the first time in a half-dozen years, on purpose, at her request, confronted Solomon Greschner and asked him to come back onto the payroll.

"I'll pay you twice what the Gudges do." She was obviously very much upset at the item in *That Woman!* intimating Caryn Gudge's possible election to the Fuller board. "I underestimated you, Sol. If you can put that tramp over—and it seems you might just do it if you keep at it—you can handle me." She had looked at him as beseechingly as she could. He stared back at her over his huge nose as if it were a high lectern, an altar, so that it seemed that he looked imperially down on her as from a great height. How ridiculous she seemed, this large, plain woman with no particular affection for art, or anything cultural, totally fixated on this Fuller thing.

"I'm sorry, Granada. No, actually I'm not sorry," In this situation meanness came easily. "There's too much bad blood already spilled. My task—for which I'm handsomely and fairly paid—is to promote Mrs. Gudge, just as once I was paid to promote you. If she gets something you want, I fear that's just one of life's little injustices."

For an instant he thought she was going to reach into her large alligator bag, take out a gun and shoot him. But the anger lasted in her large cow eyes only for an instant before it was replaced by anguish and tears and heaving wet sobs, which Greschner recognized as coming more from frustration than from sorrow. He rose and left her there.

As always, Vosper was on the landing.

"When she stops that awful noise, Vosper, dry her off and put her in her car."

Nor was Winstead privy to three conversations that Homer Seabury had been involved in during the course of the day.

The first, just before lunch, was with the same banker who had peremptorily summoned him to an afternoon meeting to discuss "routine matters."

"Homer, good news: You'll not be needed over here this afternoon. We've been in touch with the Gudge people—that is, they've been in touch with us—and we've worked things out to everyone's satisfaction. Our Wall Street people will be talking to their opposite numbers in your shop, to iron out the details. The closing will be Tuesday, when the agreement expires. We'll be making good delivery, don't worry. I'd hate to have you fail on a billion four of bonds." He chuckled. Homer, who had been racking his administration people's minds for ideas as to how to put the banks off, even for a few days, perhaps by finding something technically amiss in the transfer powers, was not amused.

Now the whole problem seemed to have vanished. Stunned, he barely gulped out goodbyes. He felt like kissing the very earth which only minutes earlier had seemed ready to open and swallow him.

Then he called Greschner and poured out his gratitude. Greschner assured him there was no need to call Katagira, who would be calling him in the next day or so. There was, however, one call to make. Which Homer gladly did, although it took him until late afternoon to reach Calypso Winstead and assure her that whatever she thought best for the Institute, in terms of filling the empty seat on the Board, why, he was with her all the way.

Only three people had any general idea of each of the strands that had made up that afternoon's filigree of conversations. Nick did, because he had talked to Frodo, who had been separately in touch with Calypso and Sol about the negotiations with the Gudges. Frodo was anxious to secure for the Fuller the genuine pictures that had been bought along with the Hiroshima copies. These were a little Corot view of Orvieto; the fragmentary fresco *Head of a Magus* by Piero della Francesca; a Masaccio *Saint James*, a pendant to the painting in the Getty; a Crucifixion on panel by an unknown recent Riminese painter and a sheet of drawings by Poussin after Michelangelo's statue of Julius II.

It was merely a matter of trading off a seat on the Fuller Board for the pictures. These the Gudges seemed to regard as secondary, in any case, because they hadn't been mentioned in the *Times* article. Again, Nick found himself thinking how differently Bogle would have handled things. Carraccino would have been summoned, for one thing, and the forgeries instantly detected. Felix Rothschild would have been brought in—and other experts from New York, Paris, Florence and Toledo. And on top of it, Nick was sure, Bogle's own antennae would have sensed false emanations.

Frodo could bring it off. In passing Sol had mentioned something about Seabury and his firm, and the Gudges, and so had Bogle, with whom Nick was having a new go-round, on a great landscape by Constable, a painting so instinct with a feeling for England that it was tempting to step through the frame and find oneself on Salisbury Plain, under a high, cloud-dotted sky. The problem was that the London dealer with whom Nick owned the picture insisted on asking a price that Bogle, who liked and wanted the painting, found almost offensive.

"Doesn't that asshole know there's a financial crisis coming up?" he'd asked Nick, which had been followed by a disquisition on the impending failure of Seaco Group. All Nick could do was give the oral equivalent of a shrug; his hands were tied and his attention elsewhere.

Katagira and Greschner alone knew all the facts. After Greschner reported back, Katagira was pleased. It couldn't be going better. The banks had bitten on his idea that they lend the total $1.4 billion to the Seaco-Gudge partnership to buy the bonds; the loan would be secured by the bonds themselves, as well as by Gudge's shares of GUT and GOD. As the partnership liquidated the bond inventory, at the favorable prices which (he and the bank president warmly concurred) would ensue in what would surely be an upturn in the bond market (again more warm concurrence), the loan would be paid down. To give the deal the appearance of permanence, although he was within a month of pulling the trigger, Katagira proposed that the entire GUT-GOD collateral position be held by the banks until the loan was reduced to $400 million.

"Well, that might take a while. Are you sure Mr. Gudge would want to be locked in that long?"

Katagira assured the bank president that it would not disturb Mr. Gudge in the least. Mr. Gudge was substantial, after all. This was not one of those situations where people were stretched so far they had to hock their wristwatches. This was Mr. Buford Gudge IV.

Before going over to the Big House for dinner, Katagira reviewed the situation. Seaco was now entirely supported by Gudge—or rather, with bank loans backed by his GUT and GOD stock, which in turn was worthless paper, in turn backed by entirely fictitious earnings and assets. Ironically, GOD's financial statements, prepared by Katagira's computers and drafted and refined into glossy quarterly reports written and distributed by a network of advertising, printing and financial communications consultants chosen by Greschner, who was acting as Katagira's media agent, included a number of properties already pledged to some of the same banks in the earlier rescue operation. Which meant that when the crunch came, different departments of the same bank might find themselves pulling internally on the same piece of collateral, admittedly under different names. The rest of Katagira's work had been done. It was only a matter of pulling the trigger, now.

How easy—ridiculously easy—it was to fool the system, provided one steered clear of the insider exposure that had brought down Equity Funding. He allowed himself a smile, thinking of the first quarterly board meetings of GUT and GOD which had been held the previous week in Dallas. A wing of chartered jets had been dispatched to resorts in Florida and California, and a half-dozen university towns elsewhere, to gether the superannuated generals, retired lawyers, bankers and businessmen and pro bono publicans with whom the combined wisdom of Solomon Greschner and Homer Seabury had formed the boards of the two public Gudge companies. They were cozied into suites at the Fairmont Hotel; golf games and vivacious companionship were variously arranged to suit; a boozy early dinner was held in the private room at La Mansion.

The next day, half-anesthetized with foie gras and Château Lafite, they were herded into two meeting rooms at the Fairmont, handed elaborately bound and voluminous folders of figures, charts, plans—all cooked up by Katagira's information room—and shepherded by Gudge himself through an hour each of useless resolutions, including a vote on whether to hold the—as Katagira knew—never-to-be-held next meeting in Monte Carlo, London or Pebble Beach. At each man's place was a check for $7,500, plus another for $1,000, representing service on *de facto*, invisible committees. By three that afternoon, the jets were wheels-up out of Love Field, bearing their woozy human cargo out of a dream of luxury back to their palm-shaded wives, truculent faculties, indolent students or violent hospital workers.

"It went smoothly, didn't it?" Katagira had said to Gudge in the plane on their way back to the Lazy G.

"Real smooth. This going to be over with soon? I'm sure beat up bad now, K."

Katagira could see that. The gossamer gray mantle of impending death had settled on Gudge.

"We can let it go anytime now, sir. But I think it will be best to let Mrs. Gudge enjoy her party. After that, things will be very different for her."

Mrs. Gudge's big party, to celebrate the arrival and rechristening of the Lefcourt-now-Gudge Collection, which would be stored in a special warehouse under rushed construction until a proper personal museum could be built, was to be held at the ranch in two weeks. They didn't have to spoil her party, he'd promised Gudge—extracting in return the promise that he wouldn't have to attend.

A blessing, surely, he thought, moving through the dusk toward the lights of the ranch house.

He would always want to remember Florence this way, thought Max Lefcourt, standing at the end of his garden, at the notch in the hedge, a few steps from Sanger's grave. It was the last daylight hour; the light had taken on a mellowness which seemed to give added weight and depth to the profile of the city, blurring sharpnesses into an abstraction of browns and deep reds. The customary smog had been pushed off toward the west, toward Pisa, by a fresh breeze from the hills. The air was clean; the city seemed centuries distant, restored by light and breeze to times forever fresh in memory, when Dante might have been encountered in the Via dei Cerchi, or Donatello glimpsed supervising the hoisting of his Saint George into its niche on the facade of the guildhall church of Orsanmichele, or the young Leonardo trailing after his teacher Verocchio through the Piazza Signoria. The Florence of the great centuries had been planted in Max's heart and memory by Frank Sanger; it remained an image as alive and enduring as the tall pines of San Miniato.

He stood there alone until the light finally faded and the city became a twinkle of sparkles seen through a hazy blue curtain. Around him the cypresses gradually became one with the starless night; when he felt the first chill in the air, he took a long look around and went inside.

After an early, lonely dinner, he went upstairs and finished his letters. Periodically, he glanced up at the photo of Sanger on his writing table. It had been taken in 1949, in Venice, when he and Frank had gone up to see the Bellini exhibition at the Palazzo Ducale. Frank, posed on the terrace of the Hotel Gritti, so that behind him the Grand Canal spread into the Bacino, with the Salute dominating the right background, looked the way Max wanted to remember him. Young for his age, with the partisan toughness acquired during the war years in Val d'Orcia starting to wear off, eyes clear and merry.

Max finished his letters. He rose and went into the bathroom and started the bathwater running. Returning to his writing table, he examined the list he had made earlier in the week. Everything in order. He laid the letters out neatly. His solicitor from London and the *avvocato* from Florence had taken care of the legal details.

He got up again and went to the window, opening it a sliver to admit a trace of the cold night air. No longer softened by the twilight, the lights of Florence glittered fiercely.

He undressed and put on a robe. From a drawer in the table next to his bed he took out a knife. It had been Frank's OSS issue. Frank had always kept it razor-sharp, even when it was used for nothing more than to slit open envelopes.

He carried it into the bathroom. The Roman way, he thought, slipping out of the robe and climbing delicately into the large tub. He placed the knife on a stool that stood by the bath, next to a small, opened book which he had put there earlier. Meticulousness in all things. That had been one of Frank's earliest lessons.

> I have often thought that the painting and sculpture produced in Florence during the first three-quarters of the fifteenth century represents not only the finest, most manly flowering of Italian art, but of Western culture in general . . .

he read. It was from *Quattrocento Rambles,* the elegant little volume of artistic reminiscences culled from his occasional pieces that had been presented to Sanger by his students on his seventieth birthday. Scarcely a dozen years ago, thought Max; the water felt like a warm shroud around him.

He read for a while longer. Then it seemed to him the moment had arrived. He picked up the knife and was pleased to see how easily the job went. It was true, images did flood in. Places and faces. Max hated goodbyes, and now was no different. There was time, it seemed, for just one farewell tear before a mist as red as the bathwater had become swam up before his eyes and blotted out his vision forever.

CHAPTER TWENTY-FIVE

Nick heard of Max's suicide from Felix Rothschild. He was stunned. What kind of world was he living in? Four months ago he had been happy, successful, in love and loved, the world at his feet. Two old men, companions and lovers and his friends, who had done no one harm, had bestowed infinite gifts of civility on the world, and love on each other, had been alive and happy on a quiet Tuscan hillside. He now stood in the middle of an ugly junkyard of rotted values and wrecked lives, surrounded by twisted, bent and burnt scraps which closed in on him like iron jaws. Were the Gudges, he wondered, some sort of giant vise sent to crush him, to squeeze his happiness to pulp? Some pestilence? Some plague?

Max's last letter arrived two days later. It was written in his own careful hand.

> *Dear Nicholas:*
>
> *I am saying goodbye with this. I'll be gone when it gets to you. Don't weep for me. I have had a long, rich life and you have made it greatly richer. Dear Frank and I found so much of our own young selves re-created in you. There will be no funeral for me; when I buried Frank, you see, I buried the greater part of myself. And I doubt Florence could stand another such funeral, not just now. Giuseppina and Aldo will look after me, as they have for so long.*
>
> *I know you are concerned about your part in our little deception of Mr. Gudge. He was, after all, deceptive himself; he never indicated what he was prepared to see paid for my pictures. Please realize, dearest Nicholas, that, as I told you, in a wicked world one must sometimes be wicked oneself, if only in a small way and if only to preserve some sense that the honest and forthright and decent will prevail; they have such insubstantial weapons.*
>
> *Now, goodbye: I trust we will meet again. I have sent you a memento, something to remember us by. Don't be a bad boy and sell it.*
>
> *Yours,*
> *Max*

A week later, a thin crate was delivered at Nick's office. It contained a framed sheet of furious random pencil sketches, which made Nick gasp: it was Max's Michelangelo. The little drawings represented probably no more than an hour's worth of the artist's time, but what an hour! The subject was the crucified Christ. What the sheet held was Michelangelo's efforts to get the torsions and volumes right, to achieve a satisfactory arrangement to suggest the superhuman weight of the figure, as if it were lead, instead of flesh, straining against nails and wood. It had never, until now, left La Pergola since Max had bought it in 1936 at the Oppenheimer sale. It had simply been withheld from the Gudge lists. Now it belonged to Nick.

At the time the drawing arrived, Nick's fierce grief was, in the normal way of things, starting to be subdued by the press of life. Max's will, as reported in the papers, caused a commotion. Apart from routine bequests to his servants—who by his instruction had scattered his ashes next to Sanger's grave—the entirety of his estate was disposed altruistically, with considerable good humor. Nick, Frodo and Felix Rothschild had each been given a work of art: Frodo was bequested the marble angel by Desiderio da Settignano he had discovered twenty years before outside San Gimignano, which—too poor to buy it himself—he'd brought to Max's attention; Felix was left the portrait of Luigi Corno, the famous wool speculator, which he had been the first to recognize as by the hand of Andrea del Sarto; Nick got the Michelangelo drawing. Then came the surprises: Max's Swiss banker was instructed to cross the street in Geneva and deliver to the Vatican-controlled bank on the opposite corner a check for $100 million, to form a fund to be administered by the Holy See to aid disaster victims in Italy. To Cambridge went La Pergola, its remaining contents and a fund of $20 million to endow it as a center of humanistic studies; now Harvard, with I Tatti, and Cambridge, with La Pergola, could each offer the Tuscan twilights to scholars. Bequests of $5 million apiece went to the Fuller Institute, the Metropolitan Museum, the National Gallery in London, the Louvre and the Fogg Museum, and $10 million each to the Uffizi and the Accademia in Venice, which were also to divide Max's remaining pictures. The balance of the estate went to the city of Florence.

Jill called.

She sounded shaken. "Oh, Nick, I didn't want to, but I just had to call. What is going on? The two of them? Within a month? Is the world crazy? I'm sick for you on account of Max. Sick."

Then, calmer; before he could say anything: "Are you all right? You've taken some beating."

"No, I'm okay, I suppose. And you?"

"Fair."

Was this the old game? he wondered; some kind of emotional chess, your move, my move, until there were no uncontested squares on the board and the game was suddenly over?

"Job all right? Jobs?"

"Well, I guess so. I've brought an exciting new bitterness to Gilberte which the readers seem to like."

"So I've noticed. A regular Louella." Could there be anything worse than talking on the telephone when something desperately important wanted to be said?

"I was going to write you about the Gudge purchase. But then I thought you mightn't be very proud of it. Although I suppose you earned your commission." A little gratuitous acid.

"Don't be petty, Jill. How's Jenny?"

"She thought you'd never ask. Maybe . . ." She broke the sentence off.

"Maybe?"

"Just woolgathering. I expect you'll be going to Mrs. Gudge's hoo-ha in Texas next week?"

"As a matter of fact, no. The Gudges have had enough out of me this year."

"Very nicely put."

"Hush. No. I'm not going."

"Well, I have to. This is the year for Texas. Massimo decided that a couple of weeks ago; no surprise—Gratiane's cleaning up on the Gudges."

"That's your alter ego talking. How's friend Bob doing?"

"Mr. C is about to blow off the top of the barrel—according to his good friend Mr. G. who says he is going to feed Mr. C. some crucial information."

"So what's new? Sol going to Texas too?"

"He says so. Nick, they're going to throw me out of the Equal Rights Movement for this, but I would like to see you again. Friends, you understand; just friends."

"How about when you get back from Texas? If you get back. Those're savages down there. Sure, when you get back. Maybe we'll do Family Night. And in case you're wondering, I miss the hell out of you, as they say."

They hung up. The world looked a tad rosier, Nick thought.

There was a message to call Bogle; Harvey was hooked on the Constable but was still unhappy with the price. Nick picked up the phone. Max would have wanted life to go on—as long as there was love in it. Love of fair men and women, food and art. Art. He thought he might go to the Lazy G after all; Sol could fix it up so he'd surprise Jill. Surprise surprise. And to his own, he found that he was whistling as he dialed Bogle's number.

The party to welcome the Gudge Collection was held at the ranch on a Saturday night barely three weeks after Caryn, with a little conceptual stimulation from Greschner and a hearty, lip-smacking push from her lifestyle adviser, Gratiane von González, had decided to give it. Once the date had been astrologically endorsed by Victor Sartorian, whom Caryn still saw, but now only as a matter of form and pharmaceuticals, on her visits to New

York, the button was pushed—with Gratiane acting as grand marshal on the battlefield itself and Caryn in the empress' tent behind the lines: consulting, pondering, weighing the breathless reports rushed hourly from such critical operational sectors as Catering and Floristry.

The rush of events of the last two months, beginning with the purchase of the Lefcourt Collection, had transformed Caryn's life. For the first time, she truly understood just how much her husband's money could buy; with this realization, she ceased to be governed by the belief that she needed to please her way into the social stratosphere, that it was essential to curry favor in any way she could with the people she had imagined counted. She had got her husband to part with $400 million to purchase something which neither of them understood, but which the world generally agreed was about the best thing there was. It was Victor Sartorian's loss, therefore, and Winstead's, and here an English marquess or there an Italian count's, that Caryn no longer considered the russet garden between her legs to be her ultimate weapon in a world that might at any moment send her back to Odessa. Now she could redesign the world she coveted. Out of gratitude, she made herself available to Gudge whenever he wanted her, but thankfully, that wasn't very often. Busy as she was with her plans and her career, Caryn scarcely noticed that her husband seemed wan and weak.

Anyway, she felt they had truly, finally, come together in the embrace of his immense wealth, and that was a mercy to them both. Buying the Lefcourt Collection had been the key. Now it was the Gudge Collection, His and hers. The Caryn and Buford Gudge IV Collection; to be installed in the Caryn and Buford Gudge IV Gallery to be built down the road from the Ranch House from a design by Nguyen Tranh.

"I mean, if you own it," Caryn had said to Gratiane one morning, "it does seem fair to put your name on it."

"Of course, darling." They were pondering sketches for the tent village that Gratiane proposed to erect on the bluff overlooking the Main House.

Gratiane had decided to build the party around the ideological theme of the frontier and free enterprise, with special little touches to emphasize the role of oil and gas. The tent city had been her first inspiration. The Lazy G wasn't the King Ranch, after all; it was remote and simple, despite the score of carpenters, plasterers and painters who were sawing away and splashing paint in an effort to outdo the Shah's party at Persepolis. As Gratiane had programmed it, the Big House would serve as the communications center and, if needed, a field hospital for the weekend. Two downstairs rooms had been set aside as a dispensary to be supervised by Sartorian, who would be a working guest; these would be stocked with the prescriptives which a gathering of this type might require: Librium and Valium in 5s and 10s; Quaaludes; Dexamyls and Benzedrines; Nembutals and amyl nitrate; Black Beauties; gallon bottles of Victor's Vaccine. A safe downstairs would contain the secondary prescriptives: two pounds of Colombian cocaine; Rainbow acid; hash and grass, and, for the old-fashioned, three tubes of LePage's airplane glue.

It was finally arranged that "core groups" of guests would assemble at a number of mustering points—Mexico City, Nice, London, Zurich, New York, Chicago, Los Angeles—to be picked up by a fleet of chartered jets ranging from a DC-10 and two DC-9s to long-range Gulfstreams and Jet-Stars. Scheduling was coordinated so as to disgorge the glittering hordes at Dallas' Love Field (for the East Coast contingent, Canadians and Europeans) or Houston's Hobby (South Americans and West Coast) in the middle of Friday morning. There they would be herded onto buses, given $3,000 gift certificates and driven to Cutter Bill's, the leading fashionable Western emporium, to be outfitted with suitable high-style cowboy gear. Then to Tony's (Houston) or Calluaud's (Dallas) for a lunch and fashion show and afterward back to the airports for a series of departures closely timed to ensure that the limited, if up-to-the-moment, facilities of the Lazy G strip wouldn't be overtaxed.

On arrival, they would be taken to the tent city, to be chopped, clipped, hemmed, tucked and pruned by the waiting legion of grooms and coiffeurs. Trimmed, gussied and abluted, they would reconvene about seven around the chuckwagon—actually a landau purchased for the occasion from the Queen of England, but weathered by New York's leading wood-distresser so that it might well have made the trip from the Lazy G to Dodge City. There Gratiane had planned "a little cocktail—just nonvintage champagne, to stress the simplicity of the occasion" and some home-style cooking: Tex-Mex reorchestrated by New York's leading caterers to symbolize the reunion of the Old World with the New. Feuilleté of Tacos; Gratin de Queues de Coyote; Enchiladas in Borscht; Cactus Smörgåsbord; Three Alarm Cassoulet. Eighty waiters had spent the afternoon decanting as many cases of Lafite-Rothschild '67—"the only wine, darling, if you want people to see what living expensively is really like"—into gross after gross of rinsed-out Lone Star long-necked beer bottles.

Afterward, around a series of campfires, the partygoers would gather, to drink espresso and eighty-year-old cognac from tin mugs, and listen to Waylon and Willie, in person, sing songs of the West: about bars in Austin and truck drivers in cowboy hats. Then down the bluff to the disco tent, a black canvas affair erected a few hundred yards back and away from Katagira's house and pond, which had been closed off by a six-foot-high temporary fence. For the duration of the weekend, Katagira would dwell on a cot in the cellar of the Main House, in a cleaned-up storeroom near his small office and the information center. Getting him out of the way had been Gratiane's sole thought about Katagira, for which both he and Gudge were grateful.

Full of heart, with Caryn's *carte blanche* Gratiane bent to her task.

Frodo's plan to travel to Texas a day early suited Nick, who had changed his mind about going to the Gudges'. He desperately wanted to see Jill. He could fly up from Forth Worth directly, after meeting the Lazy G plane; Frodo was being taken to Fort Worth for the day to do some business. Frodo had been at the Lazy G for the last three days, getting the pictures from La Pergola onto the racks in the special warehouse that had been built to hold them during the year and a half it would take to build the new Gudge Gallery.

Nick got to D/FW early, as planned, rented a car and, as instructed, drove over to Oak Grove Airport, south of Fort Worth, to wait for Frodo to arrive from the Panhandle. He had to wait about a half-hour, during which he visited with the airport manager, a handsome, twinkly man who seemed to know a great deal about toy soldiers. Finally, as they were getting immersed in the intricacies of various W. Britain editions of the Welsh Guards, a trim Citation zipped down out of the pale blue sky, ran out the runway and taxied back to the terminal building.

"Where'd you get *him*?" asked Nick's new friend, nodding as Frodo's cranelike figure unfolded itself out of the Cessna's narrow door and made an uncertain descent of the aircraft's steps. Although it was well over 90 degrees, the Englishman was buttoned up in a heavy black flannel suit which could have stopped a bullet.

"English, you know."

"Sure is funny-looking. Well, y'all take care."

"Nicholas."

"Frodo. How's life on the untamed frontier?"

"I'll tell you in the car."

They headed onto Route 30.

Frodo turned and fixed Nick with a humorous eye over his severe, rimless glasses.

"Can you imagine, Nicholas; the Gudges have managed to put up a building in less than three weeks that is completely air-conditioned, dehumidified and perfectly secure. Painting racks and all. I hate to think what it cost. The work was done by one of Gudge's companies that makes refineries or something like that.

"It is the most extraordinary little world up there, Nicholas. That aircraft I just arrived in, which is perfectly suitable for dwarfs, as you will discover when we return this evening, is what they call their 'fooling-around' airplane. By the time we get back, all those dreadful people to whom Sol's introduced Mrs. Gudge will doubtless be there. Anyway, it's a perfect zoo. Gratiane von González in perfect bull form, as you might well imagine, ordering everyone around. Absolute swarms of workers doing the most unbelievable things. Such as pouring Lafite, of decent-enough lunch quality, into empty beer bottles. In the interest of authenticity, Gratiane said; the woman's poisonous, you know. The laird of the manor changes from shades of gray to shades of green when he pokes his head out of his hidey-hole. Doesn't say much, that one. Is he sick? I should think so."

Frodo was babbling like a man released from a long confinement.

"Anyway, halloo, hallay, she's given us the pictures we wanted, you'll be pleased to hear. Since only you and I—and Felix, too, I do think, although neither Max nor he ever said as much—know Max's little secret. It's all fixed up with Calypso—and, can you beat it, with Homer Seabury, who seems to have jumped Hugo Winstead's ship, which, from what I hear, is looking more and more like a rowboat."

"You got your shopping list?"

"Just so. And we're going to give Mrs. Gudge a seat on the Fuller board. Poor Granada. If only she hadn't tried to sneak by on the cheap. She's quite a sad case, you know. Just like all those rich people who were once poor. Not like Mrs. Gudge—she's just now learning how rich she is. And she knows how she got there. Or what with, rather; very juicy, so Victor tells me . . . oops!—and you'd know too, so I hear, Nicholas."

"Don't be naughty, Frodo. It doesn't become you. Not at your age. Besides, I've had the courtesy not to mention Ralph, if one is to dwell on momentary indiscretions. Do you and Victor spend a great deal of time together?"

"By the bye; by the bye. I shall look forward to seeing Sol tonight to congratulate him. It's just like the old days."

Nick guided the car down the exit ramp. "Sol won't be there, Frodo. No invitation."

"I don't believe it."

"That's the way it is. He's still getting paid, I gather, but he's been relegated from upstairs to downstairs."

"I see." Frodo's euphoric babble had been corked at the insult to Sol. "I'm surprised he hasn't made a commotion with Calypso. She'll still do whatever 'Uncle Sol' wants, you know."

"I know. And I'm surprised too, Frodo. Normally Sol would have raised hell with both the Gudges." He pulled into the museum parking lot.

"Well, we're all getting old, Nicholas. Even you. And age, as you're discovering, does make for patience. Ah, here we are."

While Frodo met with the museum director, to discuss a forthcoming show of Georges de la Tour, Nick took a leisurely turn around the galleries. The building had been designed by a famous American architect; it was a light, airy success, completely opposite to the clotted complex of grottos that had been tacked onto the Fuller. As a dealer, he had to marvel at what had been accomplished at the Southwestern. In a very short time, a first-class collection of paintings had been assembled; it was an example of what could flow from the combination of a generous principal donor, a director with an adventurous eye for quality and the courage to believe in it, and an enthusiastic, dedicated board prepared and able to supplement the institution's normal funds. Along with the Pasadena Gallery, he believed it to be the great museum success story so far in his lifetime. And it would continue, he believed, even though the initial director had been cruelly snatched away by an embolism and there were other, newer collectors in the field, museums and others, who could put billions on the table in the competition for increasingly scarce objects. The Southwestern represented a mixture of discrimination and opportunism—a nose for news which let it stay paces ahead of its competitors, who puffed under the weight of their money bags.

While Frodo transacted his business, Nick wandered through the museum, pausing to gloat, as dealers do, over a wonderful Devis conversation piece, *Sir Moncrief Richard and Mr. Miller with Their Wives* and *The Stallion Honeybear* which had come from him.

In time Frodo came out, Nick shook hands with the museum director and they left. An hour later they were at the Lazy G.

To his immense disappointment, Jill did not arrive until just before dinner. There had been strong headwinds, which had obliged the Gudge flotilla to make an unscheduled stop at Nashville for fuel; on landing, the JetStar carrying Jill, the Tarver Meltons, the Seaburys and Calypso Winstead had blown a tire. They thus arrived in Dallas almost two hours late, too late for lunch, with barely enough time to be outfitted at Cutter Bill.

During the flight, Jill wondered what had become of Hugo Winstead. She hadn't laid eyes on him since the Palm Beach incident; she didn't want to ask, although she was sure the telepathy that existed among women had carried the story to Calypso's ears and that she had been adjudged blameless. Hugo was what he was, after all, and recognized as such. And Calypso had been very warm to her when they'd assembled at LaGuardia for the flight.

Far and away the most bumptiously agreeable member of the party had been Homer Seabury. Jill tried to focus on him through Creighton's eyes. She saw pretty much what she had always seen: a large, affable, narrowly intelligent man born thirty years too late. He radiated an uneasy confidence; Homer handled his success—and his challenges—like a man who's had a windfall and gone out and bought himself too much car, she thought. Looking at him closely, she thought she detected a shadow hovering at his shoulder; it was only a trick of mind and eye, the imagination creating hallucinations, but she was sure that it had something to do with the story Sol had promised her as soon as he tied together some loose ends.

Poor Sol. Another lady client screwing him out of the social recognition he craved. Watching him operate over ten years, she'd come to the conclusion that what Sol really wanted was to be able to share the prominence he'd created for his clients. To bask in the same light. What galled him, she judged, was the knowledge that although he might be smarter, more devious, more acutely perceptive than most of his clients, his clients somehow escaped the taint of pushiness, of distastefulness, that attached to Sol's vocation. It was the way of the world: the dirt stuck to the man who dug it and not to him who paid for the digging. Poor Solomon Greschner; he needed a Sol Greschner of his own.

The forced put-down at Nashville ended Jill's musing. During the hour it took to change the blown-out tire, Homer went off to call his office. He was on the phone for quite a while. When he returned, it was clear to Jill that some of his cheery bloom had been rubbed away.

When they were again airborne, Jill moved over next to Seabury, who was staring purse-lipped out the window at the clouds. In the background, the Tarver Meltons prattled on about which weekend invitations they planned to accept during the coming summer. Calypso was reading Esmé Bogle's new book, with a look of slight shock which deepened as she moved from one vaginal armageddon to the next. Seabury's wife, making her first foray out of the New Jersey hunt country in five years, was engrossed in a newsletter about beagles.

"How are you, Homer? You don't look as bright and shiny as you did. The market off today?"

He turned with an expression of mild startlement that Jill had come to recognize as the reflexive reaction of males of a certain age and upbringing when a woman asked a man's question.

"Why do you ask?"

"Oh, I'm like a lot of women. I have my little nest egg in the market. It's fun to keep up. You'd be surprised how many letters we get at *That Woman!* asking for investment help."

That seemed to placate him.

"Umm," he garrumphed in the authoritative tone used by men of his type when addressing inferiors. "Was up over ten during the day, but sold down badly at the close. I think the Dow was off three and change. Bond market was terrible. We were expecting the monthly money-supply figures this afternoon, but they've been delayed until Monday. Computer trouble at the Fed. So the nervous Nellies who don't like to be long over weekends went bombs away in the last hour. It's too bad, too, because my bond people tell me the figures are going to be surprising. About time, too, if you ask me. Show all those doubting Thomases that this market's really got some foundation."

The troubles of the financial markets were invisible to the merrymakers at the Lazy G. Nearly two-thirds of the guest list were party-attenders by avocation. Nick thought it was a desecration to clutter these splendid plains with these dreadful people, capped fangs gleaming from schooled winter tans, all duded up in glitzy cowboy costumes, grinding mercilessly away to screaming disco music when they weren't lumping doggedly at the Varsoviana and Cotton-eyed Joe.

His peevish mood was worsened by his frustration in getting close to Jill. He was, after all, a man on a mission, and the mission didn't seem to be able to get started. They'd ended up far apart at dinner, as well as the coffee-and-brandy powwow, and once the dancing began she'd been borne off by Caryn and Gratiane to the other side of the tent. Nick knew enough of the stagecraft of romance to perceive that any approach to Jill had to be made under just the right circumstances. Better to wait, he told himself.

While the revels proceeded in the Panhandle, Granada Masterman, Rufus Lassiter and Hugo Winstead shared a mournful, expensive supper at L'Arena. None of them was adept at communicating on a personal level; nor was any of them willing—or indeed, this late in life, able—to expose his or her worries in an effort to win consolation from someone else. They were soloists. So although the three of them talked sporadically, in bursts, the picked-at meal was essentially passed in silence, as they meditated on their private concerns—while behind them the room buzzed with the chinking, clinking noise typical of a fancy New York restaurant.

Of the three, Winstead was in the sourest frame of mind. His handsome features were marred by a combination of disgruntlement and apprehension. He was disappointed—and scared. Granada had categorically forbidden him to attend the Gudge revels under pain of losing MUD's legal business. Off with his head, he knew, would be the sentence carried out if he committed the treason of paying homage in the rival queen's court.

"What about this business about the money-supply figures' coming in late, Rufus? The market's a shambles."

"I've been in touch with a few people I've got on the inside over on Constitution Avenue, and they assure me that the story about the computer mixup's true." Lassiter spoke in the ponderous, orotund manner he employed whenever describing the view from Olympus. "A glitch in the system, pure and simple. The data bases in St. Louis and Minneapolis went down, and to top it off the Fed's had a problem of its own. Admittedly, it couldn't have happened at a less opportune time, given the nervousness on the Street. But you'd have to say the Administration acted pretty forthrightly to come right out and announce the problem before the close. It's just a little mechanical thing, Hugo. Not to worry." He greased his dinner companions with a confident smile as oleaginous as margarine.

"Well, it certainly came at a hell of a time, that's all I can say." Winstead sounded doubtful. Before coming to dinner, he'd made a rough reckoning of his personal exposure. The T-bill market had fallen twenty basis points in the two hours preceding the Fed's announcement, and that had rumbled through the system like a runaway truck. The financial-futures markets were collapsed; AAA-rated utilities and telephones with more than five years to maturity had fallen between 5 and 8 points during the day; for many issues, there were no bids. The effect on the equity market had been pretty drastic, too. The Dow had closed off 16, and they were saying Monday would be worse.

The financial planets which Hugo orbited were wobbling. Sixty percent of the Endowment's portfolio had been invested, by Homer Seabury and himself, in long-term bonds, which now showed a paper loss of around 15 percent on cost; they had been bought about midway through the Gudge rally. Of the equity portion, three-quarters was in institutional blue-chips —IBM, Exxon, Dow Chemical, Kodak—but the balance was evenly divided between Seaco common, which was off about 20 percent from the high it had touched six weeks earlier, and about 10 percent from the Endowment's cost, and GUT and GOD, which had stood rock-firm throughout the nervous weeks past, although the general shellacking of the last two days had extorted its toll on them as well.

"What about Seaco?" put in Granada. Hugo thought she looked even larger and more slablike than usual.

"You can be sure we're keeping a close eye on the situation. I can understand your concern, Granada, and I think there is some question as to whether Homer's been entirely prudent getting himself and his firm this far exposed in this bond operation he's got with your half-brother. But I don't think there's anything to worry about there. I had my people check it out. The amount of Gudge stock that's backing up the bond position, even if we discount it substantially from its current market value, leaves a cushion of several hundred million dollars. So that the area of greatest risk is hedged handsomely, even if this market drops another fifteen or so percent."

And goddamn the fact, too—he added silently. Seaco's footings showed heavy borrowings to support loans to customers who had speculated in the bond market alongside their broker. Customers' free credit balances over and above the legal reserves had presumably been put to work for Seaco financing its own activities. Although he was primarily a big-picture man, as accustomed to speaking with his hands as with his mouth, Lassiter's position as "the Senator from Wall Street" kept him enough in touch to know that without the Gudge prop, Seaco would be over the edge. With Gudge behind him, though, Homer would probably stagger through. The rumors from 1600 Pennsylvania Avenue were that a program based on selective credit allocation was being forced by his saner advisers on a President who up to now had refused to budge from the free-market orthodoxy of the pre-Hoover brontosauruses who had financed his rise to power, an orthodoxy in which wholesale speculation, using money as a commodity, was as legitimate an objective of fiscal policy as the stimulation of productive competition.

Yes, Homer would make it, Lassiter thought ruefully. How tough it was to recognize that no one held a monopoly on the world's opportunities. Here Homer had been about to lose control of his firm, and he to seize it, when Gudge had come along. Six months ago, he'd been in the catbird seat. Out of the Senate into Seaco in one flowing movement, just the way he'd taken the pass and run it in for a touchdown against Yale the month before Pearl Harbor. But this ball had been batted away.

He had one chance that he'd been kicking around for a week or so. Coming up on the shuttle, he'd decided to try it out on Granada. He sounded good, and to his mind, what sounded good was good.

"You know, Granada, I think there might be a real opportunity here. Your half-brother's got a paper loss of about fifteen million on his Seaco stock. He didn't get into this thing to own a piece of a brokerage firm. He just might be a seller—provided he got his money back. Eighty million, wasn't it? Why not take a pass at it? If you bought his stock, you'd have 67 percent of Seaco. You'd own it virtually outright and you could merge it with MUD. Insulate yourself from taking a write-down."

Granada chewed heavily, forking a ruminative cud of turnip greens vinaigrette from her salad plate, ingesting her Insalata dell'Anima Nera along with Lassiter's suggestion.

Winstead liked the idea. Another offer by Granada would help Seaco stock—which would be good for the Endowment and take him off the hook for not having tendered it earlier. And of course, he still had 10,000 fully margined shares in his private account at Merrill Lynch; he'd been getting great service in recent weeks from the charming account executive who'd made the cold call. Great service; just the thought of it made him twitch with arousal.

Granada finished chewing.

"I don't think so, Rufus. A poor weak woman like me has no business trying to compete in Wall Street. I'm going to sell the Seaco and take the loss, whatever it is. When can we start, Hugo?" She stared right through his disappointment and Lassiter's chagrin. Her mind was made up, and, it was clear to her tablemates, had been made up well before they sat down to dine.

"Another week at the earliest. More likely two."

"But then we'll be free to sell?"

"I should think."

"Well, if that's how long it's going to take, so be it." She filled her mouth again.

Granada felt better, having made her mind up. The knowledge of how much she had put at risk in trying to buy Seaco—in being promoted by Rufus into buying Seaco was more accurate, she saw now—had chilled her into objectivity. She was at home with the creative exploitation of the lonely, dismal lives of the sort of women who made up her market, and she knew what she wanted, which was the security of wealth and acceptability, thick walls and hedges in Southampton and Palm Beach and the right people eating finger sandwiches. Not that her opinion of Rufus was less; she admired his easy, grinning confidence and the glib splendor of his conceptions. And she needed Hugo; he jangled the keys to the right locks.

It had been a chance remark by Esmé Bogle over tea one day—about how Harvey thought Homer Seabury was "over a barrel"—that had made her reconsider the Seaco business. She didn't much care for Harvey, but he was very smart. She didn't hold with placing all her conceptual eggs in one basket, so she'd called in a second set of consultants and accountants, told them of her concern and asked for a solution. Fast. She made no mistake about herself. She knew that all she came down to, candidly, was what her money could buy, and that hanging on to the money she'd made —a notion which had been somewhat supplanted, over the last year, by

Rufus's sweetly talked dreams of empire—must be her first priority now. The advice of her consultants was simple: sell Seaco.

Now she was within a fortnight of escaping, if Hugo was correct.

She turned again to Winstead.

"Hugo, are you going to be able to keep Buford's wife off the Fuller Board? I'm not at all sure I would even be able to sit in the same room with her; and I trust you haven't forgotten your promise to me when you went along with that stupid thing of Harvey Bogle's about keeping the seat empty. But now there are two empty seats. And I could be very helpful to the Institute, you know, Hugo. One hears that the First Lady's very anxious to have someone from the Fuller on her consultative committee on the arts."

"I've heard the same rumors. You're our next choice; you understand, I can't control Calypso."

"Well, I must say I was upset and not a little hurt to discover that Calypso had gone to Texas for the weekend. I can understand the Bogles' going. Esmé's a writer, after all, and *he'd* do anything for money. And all those treacherous old fogies looking for handouts. Like the Meltons. But Calypso?"

"You do know, Granada, that Frodo's been trying to arrange a long-term loan of some of the things. He told Calypso it would help if she came. I assure you she went very reluctantly."

No point in making things worse by admitting that Frodo was trying to set the seal on a major gift from Caryn Gudge. With strings attached; strings that Calypso, as usual thinking of the Institute first, seemed prepared to accept. Fortunately, he could count on Seabury; no matter what Gudge had done for him, Winstead thought with pleasure, that was one thing about Homer: he was Old School; you could lend him money, but you couldn't buy him.

"I know. Frodo told me."

"Well, that's as far as it's gone. And is going to go, believe you me. We're not the Metropolitan, you know—taking just anyone on because they've made a little money so as to be able to pay all those janitors. No, ma'am. Now how about a little dessert? Ah. A rutabaga sorbet. How about that?" Winstead looked around the room. "Isn't it nice to be here, after all? Think of those people in Texas, picking manure out of their hair. The whole thing is so ostentatious and vulgar. Really."

His chuckle, meant to reassure, sounded hollow against the dissatisfaction that lingered gloomily at the table like another diner.

CHAPTER TWENTY-SIX

Saturday began with a hunt breakfast prepared by a catering team from London. It was served at a series of trestle tables set up back of the bunkhouse, from which the ranch's vaqueros peered at the rows of underchinned men, and women mostly too bony to be of any use, scarfing down such oddities as kippers, eggs scrambled to the fineness of foam and crumpets. Afterward, a fleet of vans and limousines waited to carry golfers and tennis players to a country club outside Amarillo; helicopters waited to carry sight-seers on a tour of the principal natural attractions of the High Plains, from Palo Duro Canyon to lesser notabilities like the Adobe Walls battle monument and the Alibates Flint Quarries—sights to resuscitate eyes grown jaded on Alpine vistas or the glories of the Acropolis. The ranch's three jets had been put on a regular schedule to transport indefatigable shoppers to the consumer paradises of North Dallas, just an hour away by Lear. At the ranch itself, there were swimming, strolling and for riders seeking a taste of the real West, a remuda which Stumpy had cajoled out of the neighboring ranches—no mean feat in an age when it might be argued that there were more Ferraris in the Panhandle than cow ponys.

Dr. Sartorian did a brisk business. Being a member of international society was at its best a strainful occupation, so that there was among the younger guests good demand for most varieties of mood restoratives. The old folks stuck to their traditional, proved palliatives: gin, tobacco and criticism of the hand from which they guzzled. Which was not heard by their hostess, who spent the day inside the Main House, cloistered like a royal bride, reconstituting herself for the evening's Bal d'Élégance. Her husband stayed in his study, watching the Tech–Alumni scrimmage on the cable, happy not to be missed and wondering vaguely at the commotion. He was happy in his wife's triumphant pleasure, which was riotous, but he was in terrible pain.

He tried to limit his use of the painkillers he'd been given by the Minnesota doctors when he'd left the clinic for what they all grudgingly realized was the last time. The drugs made the world fuzzy and dreamlike. But this thing in his gut was like a squirming porcupine with fire-tipped quills; it was hollowing him out from within, as if his body were merely a casing.

Katagira feared that Gudge was failing faster than ideal timing would have decreed. So he was thoroughly pleased by the news that the Federal Reserve had been obliged to postpone releasing the money figures. There must be real trouble, he thought, pleased. The computer explanation must be a pretext. Reality was reasserting itself.

He welcomed the distraction that Mrs. Gudge's party represented. It kept him and Gudge out of sight; it occupied her so that she paid no attention to, perhaps did not even see, the extent of her husband's deterioration. The household staff did, and Stumpy, but their loyalties were rooted in the land under their feet. The land held its own secrets and expected that they keep them too.

The donation letters were all finished. Gudge had signed them that morning, when his daily energy was at its high point. Now they were locked in Katagira's safe, ready to go. All was in position.

He had conferred with Gudge about the next steps. Gudge had agreed with his schedule and his specific suggestions. He could relax now. He would have liked to work out a minor tension around his shoulders with a visit to his casting pond, but there were too many gabbling fools walking around outside. So he settled on the cot and picked up his copy of De Tocqueville.

Upstairs, Caryn saw that it was getting dark. Time to make her appearance. Bathed and coiffed, dressed in her underwear under a negligée, she thought she'd better look in on her husband. In his study down the hall she found him staring blankly at the oversized television screen. His eyes became less dull when she came in.

"Hey, honey." She sat next to him. "You going to miss Mamma tonight?" She took his hand and pulled it under her robe, there, where he liked to touch her; her other hand started to slide his zipper open. She had a little time, and she owed him something for this real nice party.

"Uh, I'm kinda under the weather," he said with an immense weariness. "Don't feel real good." She took her hand away. His own felt cold and limp against her. His breathing sounded rough, desperate. "Anything I can do for you, then? I ought to be getting ready to go downstairs. Oh, honey, it's so beautiful, the tent and all."

She saw then that he'd been reading a book, a little kid's book by its appearance, which had fallen beside him. She reached over him and picked it up. ". . . *To think that I saw it on Mulberry Street*," she read. Was he getting crazy? she wondered, but as she was about to ask him about the book, she saw that he'd fallen asleep. Just as well, she said to herself. Flicking off the television, she went back to her room to anoint herself to receive the laurel and palm that Society, gathering under the pink-and-white-striped tents on the lawn in front of the Main House, waited to bestow.

Nick finally found Jill late in the evening.

"Hello," he said as he slid onto the seat next to hers. The man on her other side was talking to a gaunt woman. "Dance?"

"No, thanks."

"I've been looking for you. Actually, I've had my eye on you, but you've been kept pretty surrounded."

"I thought you might have been. I saw you too. Yes, I have been stuck. Some party. What did you think about Architempo?" He thought she sounded awfully unaffectionate. Don't expect too much, he reminded himself; don't push too hard; you're the animal in the doghouse.

"That was the goddamndest thing I ever saw. Or heard, to be strictly accurate." As the tables had been cleared following dessert, the tent had darkened; then a spotlight had picked out the massive, unlikely figure of the world's most renowned tenor, dressed in a cowboy suit. He looked like a tank impersonating Roy Rogers. He had been flown in from Buenos Aires, where he was singing Radamès, to deliver a program of Western songs, ending up with "Yellow Rose of Texas" and "The Eyes of Texas," sung in a heavy Italian accent that had created highly unusual phonetic and musical values.

So much for culture, Nick had thought, as the tenor took his bows amid wild applause and he'd gotten up to seek out Jill. Across the table, Tarver Melton, in a tall white Stetson of the Johnny Mack Brown school, was beating his palms enthusiastically, hoping his hostess would notice how much he was enjoying her party.

"You look tired, Nick." Jill was scrutinizing him closely. "Long day here on the ranch sap you?" Her voice was a mixture of mischief and nastiness, respectively intentional and unavoidable. "What did you do?"

"Read, walked, took a turn through the hangar with Frodo and Harvey. Ate barbecue. The things one normally does on a ranch in the Panhandle. Eat brisket and look at Titian and Raphael."

Earlier, Bogle had insisted on going to look at the Lefcourt pictures.

After their tour, during which Bogle had said nothing, he and Nick took a turn around the corral fence, watching with amusement as horse after horse jiggled the luncheon caviar and champagne out of one overstuffed guest after another.

"Jesus, these people work hard having a good time."

"Harvey, this is a tough line of work, this partygoing. Glue the smile on your face."

"Nick, don't tell *me*. Esmé's a big partygoer. 'It's *material*,' she tells me. Material, my ass. Nick, let me ask you something."

"Sure."

"I may be out of my gourd, but those pictures in there—at least, the ones

I remember from the show in New York a year ago—Nick, are those the same pictures?"

"What do you mean, Harvey?"

"Well, take the big Titian. I mean, that painting knocked me on my ass a year ago and this time it didn't. Nothing I can put my finger on; I can only say that it looks right but it feels wrong. The signals are different. Different vibes. Not good; not bad. But different."

Nick kept his quizzical expression unchanged.

"Harvey, it's the light and that dump they're hanging in, and seeing them up here in cow country. Put them back in Florence or at the Fuller, you'll see: they'll sing the old tunes."

"Maybe so." Bogle didn't sound convinced.

Nick had been secretly pleased. Bogle had the gift, the nose. The qualities that made more difference than a headful of names and dates and the opinions of experts. Bogle had an eye. And a closed mouth.

"It's weird, seeing Max's pictures here, Nick." Jill's voice brought him back. "Weird and very sad, if you ask me. God, I loved those two old men." Something crackingly tender caught in her voice, making her pause for a second; then her sly composure was recovered. "I was going to write you congratulations on making the deal with Gudge but I couldn't. I don't know, it just seemed to me that it was something you probably weren't very proud of. Down deep. Where I know you. Or thought I did."

That hurt. "You know me, Jill. You know you do."

"Maybe so."

"Look, nobody can talk in this zoo. Maybe tomorrow. You going back early or late?"

"Early. I'm working this party, Nick. I've got three photographers here. Massimo's going to do an entire section on Panhandle chic. Those women in Houston are going to wet their drawers when they see it. No matter what I think of your Mrs. Gudge, she's done a hell of a job getting where she has."

"And not too bad a performance by Sol."

"Not bad. I suppose you know Caryn Gudge has dumped him."

"Frodo said as much."

"Poor Sol. But he's been around. This is a stinking business, and nobody knows it better than he does. Even a little virgin like me, never hurt a fly or betrayed a confidence, gets her nose rubbed in the gutter every now and then—as you know."

"No comment on that last bit. How about it? Lunch maybe, when and if we get back to civilization?"

"Maybe. No promises. My heart needs mending."

He got up.

"I'll call you, Jill. The worst that happens, we can be friends."

"Maybe. Nick?"

"Yes?"

"Come here." She drew his face down and kissed his cheek, fleetingly, with the same scalding butterfly's wings he'd felt after their lunch a year ago. "That was from Jenny. She asked—no, she insisted—that I deliver it. Personally."

"Give her one for me."

Sunday was a scorcher. Overnight the earth had turned the color of fire and hot ash. Swollen, aching heads beaded with champagne-tinted perspiration blinked in the ravenous sunlight and fled. In pockets and patches, the Lazy G's guests bade goodbye to their hostess, who was smiling at a bar set up in the shade of the control tower, and climbed gratefully into the jets that would speed them homeward.

Nick sat with Frodo watching them leave. The two men were sitting in camp chairs in an arbor of umbrellas that had sprouted in the fenced pasture to the west of the Main House; white-jacketed servants handed around mimosas mixed with Dom Perignon and the juice of blood oranges flown in from Spain. As had been the case all weekend, the waiters carefully articulated the ingredients of each drink or dish by brand name, if applicable, and country of national origin.

"I'm surprised they don't give the price too," said Frodo. "It would be useful if one were budgeting a dinner of one's own."

"Or the type of aircraft in which said comestible got here. Anyway, let's not be bitchy. It's nice to see money on parade." In his canvas chair, shaded from the beating sun, Nick felt like a character in an English colonial movie: solar topees and palm fans under the tropical sun and a last gin-and-squash before going out to give the wog another good thwack for Queen and Country.

"What did you think of the party?"

"I thought"—Frodo mulled his words carefully—"that it was an extremely good bad party. By which I mean that the food was good; the decor excellent; the wine delicious; the music on the whole tolerable, except for poor Architempo squalling those awful songs, and the guest list absolutely unspeakable. Preferable, on the whole, to a bad good party, where, generally for reasons of poverty, a first-class guest list is made to eat tuna casserole and drink plonk. Very rich people practically never give a good good party, because they can only understand what they can buy, and that is never the right people. To give a good party, Nicholas, is ninety percent anticipation, a quality almost impossible to achieve if people like the Meltons, or those dreary old men with new young wives who keep turning up everywhere these days, are going to be the heart of the guest list. I always try to ascertain who will be at any party I'm considering attending—unless I'm there in pursuit, for the Institute: in which case my standards fly right out the door. And it's also nice to know what wine to expect. A good wine—like that Lafite, now—can compensate for swine to one's left and right.

"I must also tell you that I felt something vaguely ominous about all this.

Something people must have felt at the Duchess of Richmond's ball before Waterloo, or at Nebuchadnezzar's feast; I can't quite put my finger on it, except that it had an edge of hazard; it simply was never jolly. Not once. Anyway," Frodo concluded, with a deeply satisfied sigh, "the party served its purpose."

"Which was, to your way of thinking, what?"

"This weekend, Nicholas, represents Mrs. Gudge's penultimate payment on her installment purchase of what seems to pass for the right society in this tiresome age. She now owns every dreary last one of those horrors we've been looking at for two days."

"And the final payment?"

"My pictures, Nicholas, my pictures and drawings. The real ones. The ones on my little list. They're being given to the Fuller. It's all drawn up. That Japanese they've got lurking in the basement appears to be an attorney —can you believe it? That's why you're staying with me. To accompany them home to New York. My word, won't that Guercino look wonderful in the Oval Gallery? And those Fra Bartolommeos. The whole business is fixed up—can you beat it? Mrs. Gudge will be elected to the Board at the fall meeting.

"The rest of the things will stay here, in a private museum, as The Gudge Collection. I've urged Mrs. Gudge to keep it very private. That leaves one empty seat, which Calypso and I think we'll auction off. It's all rather good fun, watching the chase, twitching the carrot. Calypso's been absolutely wonderful; thank heaven that god-awful Hugo stayed away. For very good reasons, I suspect."

So Nick and Frodo waited through the day, as the horde dispersed, until the cased and crated pictures could be loaded on the last JetStar. It was well after midnight when they finally left, flying with their precious cargo into the flaming dawn of a day that would crack the Gudge Bull Market like an eggshell.

CHAPTER TWENTY-SEVEN

Although the more scurrilous papers would refer to the episode as "Fedgate," it was never conclusively established that the Federal Reserve Board, presumably under pressure from the White House, had stonewalled the money-supply figures to prevent a panic from building up over the weekend. As it turned out, in the month since the last release of the figures, the average of all series, from M1 to the new M7, which incorporated official estimates of overseas deposits in hidden corporate slush funds, Mafia accounts and other multibillion unchartable coigns and crannies, showed the money supply increasing at an annual rate of close to 9 percent—about twice the target rate preached by the strict monetarists, and well above the expectations of the Street. On Monday, finally, a reluctant Federal Reserve Board, with the grudging acquiescence of the White House, released data which proved irrevocably how precipitately, especially in the last month, it had been pumping money into the system.

The long-term bond market stopped in its tracks, shuddered, and plummeted.

By one-fifteen, the leading bond traders had dropped their quotations an average of 15 percent. Bids up and down the Street were all "subject." The ATT 8.80s of 2005, which had stood at $61 seven months earlier when Seaco had made its first purchases of non-Treasury securities for the Gudge account, and had risen to $76 in April, had been selling at around $72, or a point below what Seaco-Gudge had paid for the $55 million of the issue included in the $1.4-billion institutional put. Two hours later, they were $63 bid, and every trader's orders from upstairs were to limit his size to $5 million of any given issue, with a buy-back.

The money-supply news was the biggest, most shocking, most brutal, but only the first blow to the financial markets over the next three days. Monday night, after the close, while the traders picked through the smoking rubble in search of some smoldering but useful scrap with which to begin to rebuild, the *New York Post* and ABC disseminated a Washington leak to the effect that the Consumer Price Index would show a hefty rise in the rate of inflationary increase. Tuesday, business inventories were calculated to have risen at a seasonally adjusted rate of over 9 percent. Wednesday, the president of the Bond Fund Institute, the organization representing the $100 billion of long-term-bond funds which Wall Street and the big financial institutions had hurried to create, in order to bleed lucrative distribution and management fees from a reigning investment fashion, reported that at the rate redemptions and withdrawals were running, the bond funds would be out of liquidity by week's end.

On Thursday, a blue-ribbon deputation from the Street, including Homer Seabury, as well as the president of the Bond Fund Institute, members of leading trading firms, creditor banks and investment institutions, made a trip to Washington to ask the government to close the bond market.

The Undersecretary of the Treasury for Capital Markets heard them out politely and denied the request.

"A couple of years ago, I heard the same thing when the silver market got in trouble. You guys never seem to be able to pass up the commissions and God knows what else you get out of this, so you push it too far and too hard, and then when the cardboard gets wet and the bottom falls out of the take-home containers, you come crying to Uncle."

He sounded very tough and entrepreneurial, beating these stooges about the head with the rubber club of free-market enterprise. He was also speaking policy. The Administration was probusiness, but the business types it understood had made their money gobbling up forests and national parks; they dug their wealth from the ground, or from sending words and pictures over the air or through cables; they were not like these Eastern paper merchants. Wall Street was where the action once had been, but no longer. The Administration had already enjoyed some success beating up on the sophisticated philosophical scapegraces of the East, the spoilsports at the new-economics kiddie party who refused to believe that if you put on your funny hat and honked your tooter and gave a big, confident smile, and grabbed every favor in sight, you could make something out of nothing and life would be just chicken à la king from there on.

It was policy, then, that the man from Treasury spoke. Tough shit, said Washington, and went back to its own problems. Let the blame roost in Manhattan's concrete canyons for a while, it was saying. Nobody loved New York anyway.

The deputation returned sullenly to New York, hardly knowing that the worst was yet to come. Not anticipating the blow from the Merchant of Misery which would fall on Friday morning. Not knowing that one among them, Homer Seabury, would be, in his decent, hopeless way, the instrument of final judgment.

The Street's mind pictured the Merchant of Misery as a squat homunculus who dwelt in a moldy cellar amid lizards and snakes and retorts bubbling with noxious evil potions; he was in fact a short, intelligent, middle-aged man, with a pleasant, mild face and a disagreeable tendency to stick with the provable facts when all about him were spouting concepts. "There is nothing wrong *per se* with being optimistic," he was fond of saying, "but it is also not a moral necessity."

With a look of vague apology, he told his audience at the Friday Economics Forum that his analysis, based on his own model of the dollar-based financial system, suggested that the rate of growth of the inflationary segments of the money supply, most notably nonproductive bank credit, was back over 10 percent; that although the government's spending policy might now aptly be termed "slingshots and margarine," federal deficits for the next two fiscal years could exceed $100 to $125 billion and that he forecast the prime rate to rise to 22 percent in the foreseeable future.

It was not an upbeat speech. The financial editorialist for the *News* wrote: "*Counted on to be present at any economic apocalypse, the Merchant of Misery once again thundered onto the scene, like the deadly horseman of legend, his forecasts and data forged into a pestilential scythe.*" His verbal elegance drew slim appreciation from a financial community doomed to pass a rainy, muggy weekend licking its wounds and pondering its desperate future.

None more desperately so than Homer Seabury.

Friday evening, he sat sequestered in the upstairs study of the heavy Tudor house, listening to the wet, uncomforting drizzle outside.

He had studied the sheet before him a hundred times. It had been prepared by his comptroller Friday just before the close. To Homer it seemed less a financial statement than a damage-control report.

It could be worse, he supposed. At least there was a way out, thanks to Gudge. Seaco itself was looking at paper trading losses on its inventory positions of around $65 million, or roughly one-third of its capital. The firm had sent out margin calls to the tune of $7 million to its retail bond customers. Another 10-percent drop in the market would really open the floodgates, his comptroller had warned. But if things just stayed relatively not much worse, Homer estimated, Seaco could limp along. Just.

He wasn't sorry to have lost his young bond trader. At least there was some good out of all this mess. Fixed Income had come flying into Homer's office on Friday morning, before the opening, and spouted in a single, unbroken sentence that he was tired of working in a chickenshit outfit and was leaving with his girlfriend to start a mulch farm in Oregon and they could all go fuck themselves but he wasn't going to be fucked around with and that was it. Period. Goodbye. The young man had seemed even more highly strung than usual—he had the look of a man who'd lain wire-stiff and sleepless through the last five nights—and Homer had been glad to get him out of the office. And the firm.

His thoughts returned to his immediate difficulties. The partnership he'd been talked into. Thanks to that big purchase from the institutions—close to the top, Homer thought miserably—the Seaco-Gudge venture was now almost $275 million underwater. They were back to square one on their original purchases. And everything else showed a loss, ranging from merciful pennies in many cases to outright disaster in others. To be sure, Gudge's stock was up as collateral, still over $800 million worth, although the Dow had been off more than 70 points on the week. Seaco shares were nearly 45 percent below their high of just weeks earlier. The fact was, without Gudge's stock holding off the wolves from the partnership, Seaco was insolvent.

The SEC was making noises. Winstead's firm had advised him to get a release or guaranty from Gudge that would relieve Seaco of any contingent or conditional liability on the partnership. He hated to ask for it. In any case, Gudge was locked in by his guaranty agreement with the banks, but the Winstead people didn't think that would do it with the Commission and the Stock Exchange. Reluctantly, he agreed to call Katagira and see what he could work out. Monday, he told himself; Monday would be time enough.

His study was stuffy. He opened a window to look out. A ground fog had begun to rise from the warm, wet earth as the temperature sank. He stared out, looking at nothing in particular. For an instant he thought he imagined that the mist shaped itself into a face: his father's. For shame, the apparition said; for shame, Homer; see what you've done. Before Homer could respond, his imagination settled, the figure became nothing more substantial than wisps and tailings of grayish fog, flecked with orange by the fading sunlight, and Homer turned back to his worries.

A summary of the Merchant of Misery's speech appeared in the morning *Times*; Greschner immediately called Katagira and read it to him.

"I think now's the time," he offered when he had finished. "The Street's on the near edge of panic. We can push it over. But we've got to know in the next hour or so—so I can tell Creighton. Otherwise it's wait until next week and who knows what'll happen?"

"I don't disagree," said Katagira. "Everything is ready at my end. Are you taken care of?"

"Oh, indeed," Greschner replied. And indeed he was. All his securities had been liquidated and the cash remitted to his banks. Out of the market for the first time since I had five bucks to put into it, Sol had thought, when the last broker confirmed the last sale to him. Out, for the first time in sixty years.

"That's excellent. I'll call you back shortly."

Katagira hung up. He thought for a minute, then got up, moving in the fragile way of a man much older than his years, and went out to cross the lawn to the Main House. It was eleven-thirty: lunchtime at the Lazy G. Gudge came down at a few minutes to twelve. His breathing was now largely a sequence of wheezes. He carried himself as if everything inside his skin were loose and jolting about painfully.

They ate for a while, the usual, silent meal, until Katagira finally spoke.

"Mr. Gudge, the time has come."

Gudge looked up at him slowly as if he had sat down to eat and found destiny opposite him at the table.

"You think so, huh?"

"I do, sir. How are you feeling?"

"Just awful. Never felt worse. Ever." Gudge paused. "Be good to get it done with, won't it?"

"I suppose so, sir." But I really don't know, Katagira thought. Yet there is no more time. "Yes, it's been a strain."

"Well, what's left to do?"

Katagira explained. "I think," he concluded, "it would be desirable to get Mrs. Gudge back to the ranch to wait out the next week or two. She would be better off here, and since she knows nothing, there will be nothing she can say, if in fact anyone can get to her."

"No problem. She's coming back tomorrow night. Bringing that Vietnam fellow, the architect for the gallery. Getting those pictures has sure made her happy, K. You did real good work there."

"Thank you sir. I'm pleased. And you're ready, sir?"

"Ready when you are."

"Then, if you don't mind, I'll leave you now. To call Mr. Greschner. Have a good afternoon, sir. I'll see you this evening."

When Jill finished typing the story Saturday night, she was shaking.

Being Robert Creighton had heretofore worked out easily. It had consisted of tips from Sol—that perverse, unadmitted grandpatrimony which allowed her to make enough money to live decently and send Jenny to the best school; it had been guarded leaks from ambitious traders, power-thrilled Wall Street lawyers, jealous investment bankers; it had been a simple matter of seeing through corporate balance sheets and profit statements fixed up and glossied by financial publicists and self-protecting accountants. These had been the ingredients which blended to pay her $75,000 a year. Nickels and dimes against the value of the scams she wrote about.

But this was different.

When Sol had finished telling her the story, she'd been stunned silent.

"Jesus, Sol, how can I write this?"

"Because it's the story of a lifetime, sweetheart."

"Sol, you're telling me that Gudge is a fraud? That he's faked all of this? That Gudge Universal Technology and Gudge Oil Development are just pieces of paper? Jesus Christ!"

"I didn't say he was a fraud. He's a rich man; very, very rich, in fact. As far as I know. As far as everyone knows—and there's the rub. All I'm telling you is that I've got information, really good information, that GUT and GOD exist only on paper, that he's put one over on Seaco, on the Street. On Winstead; on the lawyers, all of them; on every one of those anxious people who wanted God Himself to bail out the bond market; on Homer, who wants to save his job so badly that any savior looks acceptable, no questions asked. Believe me."

"And if you're wrong?"

"If I'm wrong, young lady, the sun won't rise tomorrow."

Her mind went spinning through the logic of what she was hearing. What was in it for Sol for him to bear this kind of tale? What was in it for a billionaire like Gudge for him to spring something like this? Where was the sense in it all?

"Can I call you back, Sol?"

"If you want; but don't miss your deadline." He hung up.

Jill sat staring at her typewriter. If Sol was telling the truth, he was giving her a shot at predicting an earthquake. Earthquake-predicting made Pulitzers, and she was a reporter. But . . . motives? Sol's first. Well, Sol had been shabbily treated by the Gudges. So much for him. Homer Seabury had been sweating his job until Gudge came along. So much for him—and it wouldn't be the first time a big business had been put on the line to save the jobs of the guys at the top; so . . . so much for Homer. And Gudge? How the hell did that fit in? It didn't make sense for him, and it was his money. Except the way Sol told it, she suddenly saw, Gudge's money wasn't on the line. He'd put nothing on the line except a lot of paper—no more than he'd ever really said it was. He was really rich: at least, that's what everybody knew. Or thought.

She jumped up and went quickly across her office to scrabble through her files.

Of course, she said to herself, thumbing furiously through the two Gudge prospectuses. There isn't any proof in here about what Gudge owns. Just a lot of representations and indemnities. Every expert's in Gudge's pocket. Gudge says this is here and that's there, and they're worth X and earn Y or Z; he indemnifies his representations, and that's all. Jesus, she thought; it's like being a kid in the park: maybe his fingers are crossed behind his back? She read through them again. There aren't any independent accountants here, she said. She knew the way the Street worked. If Seaco said it bought Gudge's story, then the rest of the Street would; just as Seaco would if Gilbert, Gale had put its name on a prospectus. Except that Gilbert, Gale hadn't had Granada or Bogle breathing down its neck, to color its judgment with the urge to survive, to put personal status ahead of the safety of the business.

She saw it all—or at least enough to take Sol at his word.

What the hell should I do now? she asked herself. My motives are clean. There's nothing in it for me. Just the opposite. She had $20,000 of her own savings at Seaco. There must be thousands like her. Maybe she should tip off the SEC, or someone somewhere; get Seaco closed down; get the Securities Investor Protection people in. Cry Uncle.

She made herself a cup of tea and thought. Abstract decency whined in her mind against the damage she could make by writing the piece Sol wanted her to write.

The hell with it, she said to herself. You're a writer. A truth-teller. She took a long look out the kitchen window. Gray as the day was, Central Park was full of people trying to make the best of Saturday: kids and sinuous men on roller skates, lovers jogging hand in hand, hot dogs, Good Humors, kites jumping in the bleary sky. She sipped her tea, thinking of all the people who would be involved—involved and hurt—and what they were to her. Thought of Caryn Gudge, and Granada, and Hugo Winstead, and Homer Seabury. Poor, sappy Homer. The hell with all of you, she finally said to herself; what've you done for me? With that, she went back to her office, flicked on the terminal that connected her to *Pritchett's* and began to type, steadily, although her hands shook so with the import of what she was writing that she could barely get it done.

> Over the weekend, *Pritchett's* has learned of a possible investigation by the Securities and Exchange Commission of grave irregularities, possibly involving massive fraud, of two of the hottest new stock issues of the last decade: Gudge Universal Technology and Gudge Oil Development,

Creighton's piece began. It had been printed within black borders in the upper center of the front page of a special edition.

Dynamite, thought Sol Greschner, as he continued to read the article aloud. It was three short paragraphs in length.

> . . . Among the areas expected to be investigated are undisclosed transfers of substantial assets and falsification and misrepresentation of corporate records, including financial statements. Since the Commission and the companies' offices are closed until Monday morning, it has proved impossible to obtain confirmation or denial of the report.

"Excellent," said Katagira on the other end of the phone. "Very astute of you to direct attention to the SEC."

"It had to be written that way. It gives weight to the story—and complicates it, which we agreed was desirable. Complexity leads easily to confusion, and confusion is what we want."

"I understand. You'll be ready with your denial when the companies refer any inquiries to us and we pass them on to your office?"

"Of course."

"And Creighton is fully briefed?"

"Fully."

"So that everything should proceed in sequence, beginning tomorrow morning?"

"At a very fast clip, I should expect."

"Excellent. I trust you can receive Mr. Gudge?"

"Certainly."

"I'd think you'll be seeing him around Thursday, then."

"It will be my pleasure." They hung up.

A fast clip indeed, Sol thought. The hounds would be onto both the SEC and GUT and GOD tomorrow. And after Creighton, too. The SEC wouldn't know anything, of course; and GUT and GOD would pass the interrogators on to Number 17, where Sol, speaking for his client, would deny everything and challenge Creighton. That would take an injunction.

And Gudge would be unavailable. Nowhere to be found. Secure in the impenetrable fastness of Number 17.

Very satisfactory. Sol smiled and picked up the latest issue of *That Woman!* There were six pages of pictures and smartass captions to do with the Gudge party. He flipped to Jill's column:

> . . . Although the Administration in Washington has made tireless ostentation the benchmark of IN America, leave it to Texans CARYN AND BUBBER GUDGE to show us folks up East how it oughter be done. Their weekend wingding for four hundred of the INNEST folks we know has surely established CARYN GUDGE, the mistress of the fabulous Lazy G Ranch and the no-less-fabulous Gudge Art Collection soon to be housed in their own li'l museum right there on the ranch among the cows, as the hostess with the mostest. What next, CARYN? Washington? . . .

He read through the list of names. The diadem of society was rhinestones and paste these days, he thought. Just as well these days were about running out.

By Tuesday night, Homer Seabury hadn't slept for forty-eight hours. He was drowning in confusion and fear. No one seemed to know anything; calls to the Lazy G only reached a Mexican who said Gudge and Katagira were traveling. Surely it was a ruse, he thought, but it troubled him so to think it might be—the implications were so ominous if it was a pretext—that he talked himself into accepting José's story. His Washington contacts—he'd even called Lassiter—had come up dry on the SEC angle. Nobody at the Commission seemed to know anything about an investigation. Winstead and his minions had struck out too.

The bond market had continued to fall, although its headlong velocity had been slowed by the fact that there were few bids to be found anywhere. The market now consisted of traders grousing to each other over their hot lines, waiting for some signal—from God, the White House, the Federal Reserve—that would tell them to do something.

The story about GUT and GOD had beaten up the equity market, though. Trading in the two issues had been immediately suspended, so the stocks never opened; if they had, according to the specialists in the stocks, they looked 25 to 30 percent lower. This was a market that panicked as a matter of reflex. So the GUT-GOD rumors spread through the rest of the market like malignant fire. The Dow had dropped 23 points on Monday; today, Tuesday, a halfhearted rally had been snuffed out in the first hour of trading; when the body count had finally been completed, 73 million shares had changed hands and the Dow was off another 18.

Ninety percent of the trouble was related to Seaco. Everybody knew that Seaco was on the edge to begin with, and had been since the bond market had turned definitively lower a month earlier; everybody knew that Seaco was hanging on thanks to Gudge; the professionals in the trading rooms varied in their estimate of Seaco's problem, but everybody knew that if the Gudge-Seaco partnership collapsed, Seaco was looking at an unhedged liability of over $200 million on its own account, against a total capital that its trading losses had reduced to $140 million. And that was at market; if Seaco should, God help anyone from using the word, *liquidate*, and its bond positions had to be sold out, nobody could calculate how great the losses would be. About midday, the rumor had flowered that it looked as if Seaco's customers' free-credit balances, said to be in the neighborhood of $750 million, could be down the drain.

Already the firm was hemorrhaging accounts. Seabury's day had been spent fruitlessly trying to assure one of his partners after another that everything was okay. The parade had begun in midmorning when his equity sales manager had reported that requests for the immediate mailing-out of over $23 million in customer balances, both cash and securities, had come in overnight on the wire. Mostly Europe and Asia. The Old Worlds were always more alert to trouble and never hesitated to act on instinct. They weren't encumbered with that innate optimism which led Americans to sit hopefully as the canoe plunged toward unseen rapids. The sales manager helpfully reappeared later in the day to report that 6,892 customer accounts had fallen below 30-percent equity and that a total of $50 million in margin calls was going out.

Financial Engineering had put in a sanctimonious cameo appearance just before lunch.

"Now that the animals downstairs have got us in this mess, what am I supposed to tell our banking clients? I just had a call from the treasurer of Amalgamated. He wants to know whether we'll be able to go forward with this offer we're handling for them."

"Tell them what you want!" Homer had exploded. "You're the smart boys with your MBAs and your law degrees who worked up those GUT and GOD prospectuses. You tell me. These rumors in *Pritchett's* that may kill this firm. Can they be true? What in tarnation could be wrong at those companies?"

"Nothing," the young man replied, looking more assuredly rodentlike than ever. "I went over the figures myself. I went down and looked at their rigs. Talked to the people on the line. We did our diligence."

"Well I don't know." Homer shook his head. He just didn't understand.

"So my information is that the two Gudge stock issues, Gudge Universal Technology and Gudge Oil Development, are complete fabrications. They're just pieces of paper which investors have been led to believe represent ownership of companies controlled by the Gudge interests that have significant industrial and oil and gas operations. No one doubts that the Gudge interests do themselves control such assets. Billions of dollars' worth. What my source, who I believe to be completely reliable, asserts is that none of these assets is in fact the legal property of either of the two companies. Which means, Chuck, that none of the figures released up to now by the two Gudge companies, including the figures in the original prospectus, is anything but a complete fiction. A figment, probably, of someone's imagination. Or some computer's."

This was the most that the Network's New York and Washington bureaus had been able to come up with.

"Are you saying, then, Bruce, that Wall Street has been taken for a four-hundred-and-ninety-million-dollar ride? Is Wall Street saying that the richest man in America has possibly put over a half-billion-dollar fraud?"

A strange eruptive sound back of the cameras told the anchorman that his voicing a supposition and an opinion over the air had sent the network's lawyer running to the men's room.

"I'm not saying or claiming anything, Chuck," said the Network business analyst. "All we know is that Wall Street, and one large firm in particular, are being battered by rumors that two companies, which have a lot of investor capital tied up in them, are not all they seem."

"Do you think, Bruce, that this could be a planted rumor, to turn the general market down for the benefit, say, of a few short-sellers? Wasn't it last fall that a gold trader started a rumor about a presidential heart attack?"

"Chuck, we just don't know. Anything could be true."

As the anchorman thanked the analyst, Harvey Bogle got up and turned off the television set.

"I'll be a sonofabitch," he said to Nick. They were sitting in Bogle's apartment in the Tennyson, having spent the afternoon at the Fuller, inspecting a traveling exhibition of small Dutch landscapes the Institute was hosting.

What an irony, Nick thought. He had helped Max sell Gudge $400 million of pictures, most of which were fakes—and Frodo had made off with the real ones—and it turned out that Gudge himself might have been doing a billion-dollar fraud of his own. Nick wondered if Gudge had used the money from the stock sales to buy the fakes. Fraud on fraud.

"Sonofabitch," Bogle repeated. "That Gudge must hate Wall Street. Or someone on Wall Street."

"What do you mean, Harvey?"

"Figure it out. Gudge doesn't need the money. I got friends in Texas who've laid a few Gudge numbers on me, and they are very, very big. And he's not one of these financial psychopaths who never have enough. You know the kind: not happy with ten million, got to have twenty; not happy with twenty, got to have thirty. That's not Gudge. I kind of wondered when he first started playing in the bond market. I thought all that stuff in the papers about faith in the new economics, the new program, was a lot of crap. Guys like Gudge put their big dough in the ground—in things they can see, taste, touch or smell. Not paper. And suddenly here's this guy becomes the biggest paper merchant of them all. It didn't make sense. I figure it's Granada Masterman. And poor old Seabury's balls are going to get cut off in the process."

"Granada?"

"Why not? I don't know anything except she and Gudge are half-related. Same mother. But look at it. Granada was getting into Seabury's pants, to take over his firm and hand it to Lassiter, who is a grade-A phony if there ever was one. Homer's busted his butt doing a not-very-good job, but at least his name's on the door, and it's all he's got, so he's damned if he's gonna lose it if he can help it. But Granada has the votes, until out of the blue this cowboy rides up and starts throwing the bucks at Homer, including a safety net. And before you know it, things are moving so fast around Seaco that the only thing Homer knows is that he's safe from Granada. But he's a pawn.

"And look at the rest of it. Suddenly Mrs. Gudge appears on the scene, chaperoned by Sol Greschner, and behaving as if she's under close orders to rain on Granada's parade. Which she has. And, incidentally, who made the introduction of Gudge to Seabury? S. Greschner. And who is masterminding Mrs. Gudge? S. Greschner. And who was the spokesman denying all just after the close on behalf of Gudge? S. Greschner. It figures, Nick."

Nick too thought it did.

"Anyway, what I think's gonna happen is that it's gonna turn out that these two stocks are phonies. Copies of companies. What you got to blame is Seabury betting his company to save his own skin. That's why I don't feel sorry for the sonofabitch. He bet Seaco to save his ass; it's only fair that it's his ass gets burnt worst if the thing goes down the tube."

And as far as Nick could judge from everything he'd read or heard, down the tube was exactly where Seaco was heading.

Thursday morning, the moral hyenas rushed onto the scene in full howling hindsight: "It is the height of irresponsibility," thundered *The New York Times*, "for the management of a major investment firm to permit itself to get into a position where a drastic price move in a single market segment can endanger the firm, the assets of its customers, the jobs of its employees and public confidence in the integrity, intelligence and stewardship of the financial markets." By then, however, it was clear that only a miracle could prevent Seaco's convulsions from becoming fatal. A miracle: namely, the appearance of Gudge to set things straight.

But Gudge could not be found. Nor could anyone else who could speak convincingly about GUT and GOD. The companies' directors claimed lamely that all they'd been given was the same figures as everyone else and hastened to consult their lawyers. In Houston and Amarillo, London and Atlanta, the men who ran the satellites of the Lazy G could state only that they worked for Mr. Gudge, and however he chose to arrange the chess pieces was his business. The operations they ran were doing well, thank you, and they had been supplied with more than adequate capital to support and expand their operations. No, Mr. Gudge didn't believe in leaving a whole lot of cash lying around. No, they didn't have consolidated figures on the complexes of which their operations were components; they believed that those figures could be found in Houston. Or New Orleans. Or London. Or Kuala Lumpur. No one seemed to know.

The hands of the Securities and Exchange Commission were tied. Market hysteria based on a rumor did not exactly constitute evidence that a malfeasance had been committed. While plans were being made to subpoena *Pritchett's*, the Commission received an anonymous letter, postmarked Fort Worth, typed on the letterhead of a GUT subsidiary in Burleson which made drilling plugs. It said simply that Gudge Undersurface Technology had never taken legal title to this subsidiary, which was listed in the GUT prospectus as 100 percent owned by GUT, and that this was true, the writer knew, of at least the nine other GUT companies that made up GUT's so-called "Industrial Components Group." The writer had also been in touch with sources in other Lazy G companies, and the figures looked funny. Attached to the letter was a rough, hand-penciled work sheet showing the first quarter's composite sales and profits for the group. Together, the ten companies had done $67 million in sales and showed an operating profit of $8.2 million. The newly published quarterly report of Gudge Undersurface Technology, of which a copy was also appended, with the relevant figures circled in red marker pen, showed the Industrial Components Group as having sales of $126 million and operating profits of $17.6 million. The back of the report showed the Industrial Components Group as composed of exactly the ten companies from which the writer's figures derived.

The letter had been Katagira's inspiration. It had been typed on a rented IBM Selectric by Katagira himself, who had also made up the work sheet, disguising his own writing.

Katagira was extremely happy with the way things were going. Gudge was holed up at Number 17. Stumpy had headed off to Amarillo to dispatch the three dozen letters that would set the seal on the whole business. If Federal Express did its job, they should be at their destinations early Friday morning. All inquiries were being referred to the Lazy G's Houston law firm, which had been instructed to deflect any queries pending Mr. Gudge's return from overseas.

In the Big House, Mrs. Gudge was preoccupied with her Vietnamese architect and the plans for the gallery. She had once or twice asked Katagira or José when she might expect her husband back, but Katagira had thought her eagerness for Gudge's return seemed, at best, muted. He had his meals brought to his house, or ate in the kitchen with José—an arrangement that suited the lady of the manor, and didn't bother him. That evening he telephoned New York and spoke first to Greschner.

"How is he?"

"Tired—very tired, Mr. Katagira. But we've made him comfortable, and I've gotten him some very strong painkiller—morphine, in fact—from a doctor friend of mine. Frankly, I wouldn't guess he's going to last much longer. He's very weak. We got him one of those TV tape things and a lot of films of football games, and that keeps him content."

"Could I speak with him?"

"I don't think right now would be opportune. Incidentally, I think you should watch the evening news."

"Really? Why?"

"I've just had a call from Winstead's firm. The SEC got to Wilmington first. Apparently they got the Delaware Secretary of State to open the office. After hours; the first time that's ever happened. But be that as it may, it's been confirmed in Washington and to Seabury that of the thirty-five Delaware corporations which the Street thinks make up Gudge Undersurface Technology, thirty-four seem to have been transferred, perfectly legitimately, to a group of trusts established for the benefit of their employees. Apparently there are planeloads of Commission lawyers headed at this moment for every state of incorporation of any of your companies. The game is most assuredly afoot."

Of course, Greschner wasn't telling Katagira anything they didn't already both know; he spoke in the tone of a man reporting facts over a wire that might be tapped, but with something in his voice which undeniably mocked any eavesdropper.

"I expect they'll be backtracking through the oil company now, too," said Katagira. "That should provide an additional measure of excitement." The Lazy G owned close to $150 million in shares of seven swap funds. Those transactions had been legitimate; the leases swapped had been in good title. These would be distributed to Gudge employees around the world, who were also now the employee-owners of the operating companies. That had been his final inspiration; Stumpy's trip to Federal Express had put the documents in the mail. Systematically, Buford Gudge IV was giving the Lazy G away.

More than $30 million in cash was earmarked for the people at the ranch, over half for Katagira. His share had already been directed to a series of sixty accounts at scattered banks and brokerages in five countries, including one at Seaco—a small account, but a nice touch; Katagira admired himself for that one. And of course there was the gold in the Tulsa miniwarehouse.

As Gudge had instructed, wire transfers for $50 million on Mrs. Gudge's account had been completed, through the Lazy G's Netherlands Antilles, Cayman Island and Bermuda intermediaries, to newly opened accounts in the name of Caryn Gudge in Switzerland.

"She's just gonna have to live real poor," Gudge had observed philosophically as he put his hand on the rail of the steps of the Gulfstream. In that moment, he and Katagira both sensed that this was possibly goodbye. The momentum of events they had acknowledged a lifetime ago, when what was now tearing cracks and crevasses in Wall Street had been a wish and an idea, was now beyond their control.

"Well . . ." Gudge had started to say something, and had stopped halfway through. "Well . . ." Then, hesitant, he'd stuck out his hand; the eyes behind the thick glasses had blinked—perhaps they had—as he turned away.

"See you."

"Yes, indeed. Goodbye, sir."

And that was that.

CHAPTER TWENTY-EIGHT

Now, Katagira thought: should we do something about Seabury? The man was, in his shallow way, as decent as he was foolish. Perhaps he should be thrown a bone. No, he decided, it was Seabury's blind, inexcusable self-centeredness that had made these things possible; he deserved to be torn apart by all those whose interests he had put so far behind his own. Clerks and customers; salesmen, investors, traders and clients. No sops for Seabury. To pity him would compromise the point of it all.

Katagira did find occasion to reflect on what Mr. Gudge's grandfather would have thought about the dismemberment of the empire that had weathered almost a hundred years. Well, he thought, we must live in the present, mustn't we? He noted that with the onset of summer, the light stayed on; smiling, seeing that there was time for at least a good half-hour's casting, he took up his rod and went outside. From upstairs in the Main House came a sound, a female squeal—part pain, part thrill—that slid into a high moan; it sounded obscene in the clean, watery twilight.

"I'm afraid it's true, Homer." Winstead was evidently as shaken as he was. His voice came over the telephone thin and quivery. "What in the world are we going to do?"

Thus had begun the longest and worst twenty-four hours in Homer Seabury's life, Solomon Greschner's feelings about his father notwithstanding. He had spent the night in his office, worrying at sleep like a terrier. Everything that had happened was so utterly incomprehensible. Oh, he might have been more cautious in getting the firm so deep into the bond market; but Gudge had been right there with him shoulder to shoulder, and it had gone really well for a long time. And how could he have second-guessed himself on Gudge? The man was Buford Gudge IV. Everybody knew how rich he was. Rich enough to buy a small nation and put it on his hotel bill. And how could he, Homer, have ever picked up on the fraud? It was axiomatic that a dishonest man could keep it going until somebody squealed on him, or he pyramided too much, or got careless. Then, like Equity Funding, or Tino DeAngelis, or Billy Sol Estes, or Westec, or those computer guys on the West Coast that beat the Bank of America and Security Pacific out of millions . . .

Homer knew that his fate and that of Seaco were in hands other than his. All he could do was try to hold things together and play for time. Somewhere in the back of his mind, he believed that Gudge would turn up and fix everything; prove it was just a big bookkeeping mistake, a few reversible legal details that could be worked out with a couple of calls and a telex or two. If I can make a mistake in the checkbook, Seabury thought, can't a billionaire make a hundred-million error? By then, of course, his mind was in such a state that the distinction between hope and probability, like a line toed in the desert during a sandstorm, was completely obliterated.

The first locust, a harbinger of plague, a lawyer representing one of Seaco's former partners who had been prevailed upon to leave some capital in the firm as a subordinated lender, arrived shortly after nine mouthing threats of action upon action for malfeasance unless his client was immediately paid off. The litigious trickle soon became a stream, then a creek, then a torrent. By three o'clock, the firm's auditorium had been sequestered as a roosting place for the phalanx of attorneys who sipped coffee and doughnuts furnished by Seaco. These mostly represented customers, associates and debenture-holders and unaffiliated stockholders. The heavy artillery had not yet been rolled up. But six blocks north, the banking consortium that had over $11 billion of credit—loans, repurchase agreements, Eurodollar lines—tied up in Seaco and its affiliation with Gudge was known to be meeting, its white-knuckled collective hand grasping the cord attached to the plug. When that meeting recessed, and Seabury had been notified of its outcome, he realized—finally, but for the first time—that he was down to twenty-four hours in which to find his miracle. It would have been a job and a half for a certified genius; for a man of Homer's equipment, it came down to prayer, mostly, and hopes which more skeptical men would have scoffed at. It was all he had, though, even if it meant trying to plead his case with his mouth stuffed full of crow. At least there was one small mercy: things were spinning so fast now that he scarcely had time to pause, to realize what an awful fool he had been.

Nick was ignorant of all of this. And would remain so until *Pritchett's,* not wishing to wait out its normal publication schedule, had taken the plunge and spent several hundred thousand dollars in press overtime to get out another special edition carrying Creighton's scoop detailing the whole Gudge-Seaco mess. But that was still a day off, as he sat alone in Central Park, under a brilliant June sky that seemed to have been scrubbed to the gleam and transparency of crystal.

He was tired and he had a lot of things on his mind. He was on the verge of committing nearly $18 million—everything he had and everything he could borrow—to buy a collection of paintings that had been presented to him by a scout in Mexico. They were the property of a wealthy French family who had emigrated to Cuernavaca after the First World War, taking their pictures with them. Now the inevitable quarrel had developed among the third generation, a dispute that only the dispersal of the collection *en bloc* could resolve, although none of the disputants—heirs and heiresses to a substantial fortune in coffee, sulfur and cotton—needed the money. The suicidal moral stubbornness implicit in French quarrels had made it impossible to adjudicate a division of the paintings.

There were several things that Harvey would go for, he felt. Harvey would move quickly, too. The thing that made Harvey a dealer's dream, Nick had grown to realize, was not that he didn't haggle. Hell, he didn't need to. That stony frown and the ice in the eyes intimidated a man into quoting the right, the fair price. What made Harvey click was that he liked interesting pictures. There were three that Nick had reserved in his mind to give Bogle first crack at. The small Goya—one of the savage, pessimistic, enigmatic "black pictures" of the artist's last years; *Let the Fools Beware* was its title; it suited Bogle. The Altdorfer portrait of a man, a wealthy burgher, captured Germany for all time; monogrammed and dated 1526, the painting captured that special assurance, that material self-satisfaction which was a matter of divine right, which thrived fanatically under Gestapo black, under the polished steel of medieval armor or behind the wheel of a $30,000 Mercedes.

And there was a Parmigianino, a psychologically incisive study of Judas depicted as a money changer, painted barely a decade later than the Altdorfer, which gave off essences of duplicity and spiritual twistedness, in aura as well as attenuated, nervous form, and which looked forward to the deeper confusions of modern times. The picture was said to be a portrait of Giovanni Buonamico, a North Italian prince who had betrayed his city to the German troops of the imperial army of Charles V.

The remaining works would find suitable homes, Nick felt sure, but it would take time. And time, these days, thanks to the collapsed bond market, carried an annual cost of close to 22 percent. It would be a coup to swing this one all by himself—a coup he badly wanted; not that he needed it: the last year had handed him more than his fair share of triumphs.

Maybe he ought to cut Sandler in, he thought. He'd talk to Jill about it if he could ever get her on the phone. Or ever see her again. Christ, that big-deal reunion he'd gotten all heated up about in Texas seemed to have been postponed for the duration. He'd talked to her only once in the last ten days. She was working on something; probably this Seabury thing.

Of course he'd offer the deal to Sandler. What the hell could he have been thinking, to hesitate even for an instant? Bears got something, Bogle had once told him, and bulls got something, but pigs got nothing. Maybe this world I've been involved in for the past year came close to getting me, he reflected. Getting me to think only of Number One, like the rest of them; making me just another thread in that ridiculous tapestry of parties and chest-thumping and name-dropping. What could I have been thinking? he wondered. Eighteen million dollars! Of my money! Jesus H. Christ!

Ten minutes later he turned from Fifth Avenue onto Seventy-eighth Street. In the bright sun, the stainless steel facade of Sandler Contemporary Art glistened down the block, shining like a lighthouse identifying a safe haven.

The same sun, under the same bright, but warmer sky, spread its warmth over Washington. West of the Mall, lines of Southern schoolchildren, early vacationers, assembled dutifully in lines snaking up the walkways to the Washington Monument.

The light seemed sucked through the high windows of Senator Rufus Lassiter's office in the Everett M. Dirksen Building, brightening the polished paneling on which was displayed the full range of appurtenances and evidences of senatorial power! Enlarged photographs, framed in wood silver-gilt or dark, with golden-edged mats, of the incumbent shaking hands with the repositories of influence and might. Within the frames three Presidents shook hands with Rufus Lassiter; four Majority Leaders slung carelessly comforting arms over his faultlessly tailored shoulders; labor magnates and titans of industry bumped frames; culture was there too: the favored tenors, dress designers and purveyors of good taste to three Administrations smirked lovingly out into the office from walls and the broad ledge under the windows; and mandatory ethnics: here the Senator conducted spirituals at a picnic on Lenox Avenue; there he hugged a withered Hispanic, fully a hundred years old, while in the background a rubbled South Bronx lot glared like a curse; a half-dozen photographs captured Lassiter's open gullet devouring knishes, watermelon, zeppole, won ton; or, jaws closed tight in a skull's clench, in a symbolic hunger strike. The light through the window threw genial highlights on the wings of plastic aircraft, the conning towers of plastic submarines, the embroidered emblems of a scattering of National Guard units.

On the heavy oak desk, which had belonged to Warren Harding's accountant, once the Comptroller of the Currency, three photographs in heavy sterling silver frames took pride of place. They were artfully arranged, Homer Seabury saw, so that visitors to the Senator's office could appreciate fully the reach of the Senator, in whom the very daily sight of these images presumably inspired rededication to the America of every carefully edited, approved schoolboy textbook. On a counter behind the desk were more photographs, presumably of greater importance. One was of the Senator's wife; Homer glanced at his sister's broad, portentous face frowning approvingly at the world behind the portraitist's camera. Another showed Lassiter embracing Granada Masterman on the stage at St. Willoughby's after announcing his candidacy to the New York Women's Conference. The last showed the *Peconic* dead in the water. For an instant, Homer worried how

Hugo Winstead, in the chair to his left, might respond to that picture. He needed Hugo's articulateness; that Hugo had been secure on Palau, making love to nurses in spite of his ankle cast, while he and Rufus had plunged into a sea filled with sharks and the steaming spill of wreckage from the carrier was not a helpful memory at this moment.

"Homer, there's just nothing I can do." Rufus grinned. It was reflexive. He would have smiled bringing the news of Thermopylae to the Persian encampment. "It's policy.

"And a darn good policy, too," he added. "Just the thing for these times. Restores the spirit of the free market. Gets the government out of our pockets." Lassiter had the habit of nursing a platitude for an extra second, the way a golfer held his preening follow-through after a good shot. With advancing age, his head and profile were acquiring the nobility of Warren Harding. It was a good effect, well presented, but of no consolation to the supplicants who sat across the desk from him.

Senator Lassiter had no taste for becoming the captain of a sinking ship. Old friends or not, shipmates, partners, whatever, the game was over for the men facing him. The man at 1600 Pennsylvania Avenue had taken the government out of the bail-out business. Lassiter's lines into the White House had fairly screamed with the message that the Old Man had been convinced that the next one of these business crises would have to be left uncured. Especially a paper merchant like Seaco. The word from the Oval Office was that the boys close to the throne were secretly gleeful at the turn of events in Seaco; the Administration mistrusted Wall Street as violently as any nineteenth-century anarchist; Wall Street herded no sacred cows like Defense, or Energy, or Big Labor; its collapse wouldn't cream the little guy too badly, and for once the goddamn poor couldn't be raised as an issue. The deals with Big Oil to cut up the Gudge assets and make the banks whole were already on the drafting table at the Treasury; Lassiter had gotten his hat in the ring on that one. And, of course, this Seaco mess had diverted the eyes of the nation from the real mess that an economic philosophy described by one observer as "half rape, half theory" had made out of the country's finances.

All this Lassiter knew; it would have been nice to run Seaco for Granada, he'd thought briefly, but his extreme pragmatism never let him linger too long on what was over and dead. A corpse was a corpse.

"Look, Rufus," Seabury pleaded, "if Gudge gets back, it'll get squared away. You know it will."

"Of course I do," said Lassiter, his voice freighted with riskless consolation. "Of course; but damn it, Homer, where the hell is he?"

Which Homer couldn't answer. All he knew, from what Hugo Winstead had managed to find out, was that a Gudge jet had unloaded a stretcher at LaGuardia three days earlier.

"Look, Rufus"—Hugo now—"Jesus, think about the three of us. I mean, for God's sake, you bailed out everything before this, goddammit! You bailed out Chrysler—which a bunch of accountants busted—and you bailed out the Hunts; Jesus, Rufus, you know you did; and Poland! Why the hell not Homer? Rufus, you've got the influence on the Hill to swing this thing! If Seaco goes, Rufus, nearly five thousand people will lose their jobs, for God's sake. An important channel of capital movement will be closed. And think who got you here, Rufus. Don't the Seaburys mean a damn thing to you?" Hugo's voice was rising. Seabury sat watching. Lassiter grinned.

"Jesus, Rufus, what the hell'd we fight the war for?"

The Senator maintained his smile: the ivory earnest of easy self-confidence that had taken him to wealth and adulation; the caring it-won't-hurt-that-much flashed by the hangman to his victim. He let Winstead continue.

"I mean, Rufus, dammit, after all we've been through together. All we need are some loan guarantees until this Gudge mess gets sorted out. There was a time—you know there was—when we'd have gone to the wall for each other."

When Lassiter next spoke, his voice was sharp.

"Cut it out, Hugo. Then was then. Now is now."

Winstead exploded. "Bullshit, Rufus. Bullshit! Morgan Seabury made you, man. This is Homer Seabury sitting here, Rufus. Your old partner. Son of the man who made you. God almighty, Rufus, what the hell is going on?" It would be Hugo's only fine moment.

Lassiter smiled the photogenic, caring smile he used at slain policemen's funerals. "Hugo, I know what you must think. But that's the way it is. Goodness, Hugo, I don't make the rules. The old boy up the street's made up his mind and that's that. It's been in the wind for months now; something you boys might've thought about before you let this Gudge lead you down the garden path." He looked reproachfully at his visitors.

Homer could find nothing to say. Articulateness, never his strongest asset, was smothered by a disappointment that made him shiver. It was beyond his understanding, this attitude of Lassiter's: as if comradeship, old favors, the agreed and preached values and virtues of his childhood, school days, life in the Navy—as if all these were so much tattered currency consigned to the Furnace at the Bureau of Engraving and Printing. The world and he were on different orbits now.

"No hope, is there, Rufus?" he said finally. "At least, not from you, I guess."

Rufus smiled. In Seabury's eyes the expression melded with all the other Lassiter smiles beaming out from the frames around the room until he felt that he was alone under a mocking sky of infinite blackness in which all the stars and constellations had been replaced by the shiny white points of grinning teeth.

Hugo Winstead stared at the walls of his Greenwich Village apartment, vexed out of reason. Whatever in his world hadn't collapsed had now been snatched from him, and all he could think about was revenge.

There had been no point in hanging around Washington, so he and

Seabury had caught the three-o'clock shuttle back to LaGuardia. It had been a silent trip; each man was caught up in the engulfing crisis. Characteristically, Seabury was trying to calculate how to mitigate the damage to the people who had looked to him for responsible, patriarchal leadership, just as he himself had looked to Gudge for security. Winstead, on the other hand, was mapping escape routes in his head: which way led to disinvolvement with Seaco; which way would let him keep his place with Granada; what could be done to prevent Calypso from finding out what the failure of Seaco, as well as the bond-market collapse it had played so great a part in precipitating, had done to the Fuller Endowment; how to evade discovery of his own sales of Seaco on the eve of the market break.

And each of his schemes crumpled like tissue in the three hours following his return to New York. He was no sooner back in the office than the firm's comptroller called him. He'd been contacted by his opposite number at Masterman United, he reported to Winstead, and asked for an updated, final—he repeated "final"—billing. What was that about? And, while he had Mr. Winstead on the phone, he felt obliged to report that he'd done some figuring and, well, if Seaco went under, as it looked as if it might, the firm's pension fund was going to be underfunded by a couple of million because of the loss on the Seaco stock and the bonds. He just thought Mr. Winstead ought to know.

There had been a message from Granada. She'd tried fruitlessly to reach him and now was gone for the weekend. Her message said: be at her office at ten sharp Tuesday. And a message from an attorney in the local section of the SEC's Enforcement Division: could Mr. Winstead please call on Monday. And just before he left the office, there had been a call from the senior partner of the Houston firm that had handled Granada's Seaco tender. When the man speaking from Texas realized that Winstead had no idea of the reason for this courtesy call about picking up the Masterman files and making the transition as smooth as possible for the client, he huffed apologetically and waffled the uneasy conversation to an end.

The other shoe had dropped when he arrived home to find Calypso in the living room, sitting between two men he had never seen before.

When he came in, she paled for an instant. When she spoke, her voice trembled faintly with the effort at restraint.

"Hugo, this is Mr. Peter Bromberg, an attorney. He will represent me in my divorce action." She turned to the beefier of the two men, on her left. "This is Mr. Shaughnessy of the International Security Bureau. He's here to throw you out of this apartment. Your bags have been packed and are in the back parlor."

When he started to say something, Calypso put her face in her hands, stifling a tiny sob; when she raised her face to him, there was a fury in her eyes more terrifying than anything he had ever seen. Her expression stuffed his excuses down his throat. All he could say was "Why?"—a single word that broke the dam.

Calypso could have tolerated almost anything of Hugo: infidelity, pretentiousness, callowness. Almost anything, except that he should put the Institute, which was all she had left of her father, at risk.

"Why?" Her voice was as small as ever, but it had a new, steely edge. "*Why!* Hugo, how can you ask me that? *Why!* Oh, Hugo, it's not enough that I've known about your apartment and your girlfriends and the dirtiness that you are at bottom. I could take that easily enough; after all, I never liked you from the minute I found out what you really were. Which is why I never wanted your children. Sol warned me about you, Hugo. He said that he'd misjudged you terribly, that you were smallness incarnate, despite the good looks and the smooth talk. And so you proved to be, you awful man; but by then it was too late, because you were by then in the center of all that I really ever loved. The Institute. You were lodged there, Hugo, like some vile worm at an apple's core. And now you've wrecked it. I talked to the accountant. Yes. This morning. There's enough in the Endowment to pay the mortgage on the Annex that I never wanted but you talked everyone into. But we'll have to let some of the guards go. And close at least two days a week. And my father wanted it to be open every day; it was his present to his city. And you've wrecked it with your opportunism and your cleverness and your ego. Sometimes, Hugo, I wonder that there's an institution left in this city, or anywhere, that people like you haven't wrecked or put in peril with your egos. Well, you can get out of my life now."

"Calypso, listen . . ." He stepped toward her.

"Easy, handsome." The big man got to his feet. "Why not just go along easy, huh?"

"Yes," said Calypso. "Why not?"

Now he sat in the Village apartment, raging at everything that had been forced upon him. He made himself a drink, picking his way with disgust through the unpacked bags stationed in the living room. His mind was full and fixed on revenge; someone else, the guilty party, must be hurt. Gudge. In his whirling mind, the names came forward as if out of some murk and muck. Greschner. Gudge. Greschner had never liked him. That's what Calypso had said. Gudge. An animal. Angry about the wife, maybe. Gudge and Greschner. The animal and the Kike. Both out to get me, because I've gotten to be bigger than either of them; I fuck one's wife and run the other's Sheeny ass out of the Fuller. So they're out to get me. Well, I will get them. He turned on his tape machine.

CHAPTER TWENTY-NINE

"He didn't say anything else, sir." Vosper handed Greschner the manila envelope with the name of Winstead's law firm printed in an upper corner. It was addressed to Buford Gudge IV in care of Solomon Greschner, Esq. "No, sir; he just said he assumed you'd know where to find Mr. Gudge."

Greschner turned over the envelope slowly.

"Well, I think we'll have to assume that it's not a bomb. Why not take it up to him? How's he feeling this evening?"

"It's very difficult to say, sir. He's very weak and in great pain, it appears, although Dr. Sartorian's medication appears to help."

"Well, he's a terribly sick man. Might as well give him this. I can't imagine what Winstead—you say it was Winstead himself? Surprising, that. Have we had any more reporters?" Greschner handed the package to Vosper.

"Not since you issued the release that Mr. Gudge was believed to be visiting certain installations in the Arctic, sir."

"Very good."

Vosper made his momentous way upstairs to the rooms in which Gudge had been installed. He was thankful Mr. Gudge was not bedridden. Nor did he seem to require any extraordinary care, apart from Dr. Sartorian's inoculations. None of the bodily functions had failed yet, although that was sure to come, Vosper guessed. It seemed to him that Mr. Gudge had husbanded all his remaining strength in an effort to stay together for one final, consummating effort in the next few days.

He found Gudge sitting in an armchair, watching one of the football games he observed with the same patient avidity Vosper himself dedicated to cricket.

"This came for you, sir."

Vosper handed over the envelope, took a careful look around to satisfy himself that Mr. Gudge had everything he might require and withdrew.

Gudge weighed the packet in hands made nearly transparent by his disease. As weak as he was, it took some effort on his part to tear it open. He took out a videocassette. Crossing the room as painfully as if the rug were a bed of smoldering coals, he changed cassettes and went back to his chair.

The electronic gurry on the TV screen was succeeded by the image of a nondescript room dominated by a king-size double bed which virtually filled the screen. As Bubber watched, his wife, Caryn, appeared, her hands behind her undoing the catch of her skirt; another figure, already stripped down to his underpants, slid onto the bed. Gudge recognized him as the lawyer fellow who'd been around with Seabury; the one who was the head of that museum or whatever Caryn was always talking about.

An apprehension that even his disease had been unable to create made itself felt, like small icy wires jabbing at his marrow. He watched Caryn slide out of her clothes as the lawyer fellow's mouth came down on her breast; his tongue danced around her nipple while she reached for the visible bulge under his shorts. Gudge looked away. Tears came and ran onto the lenses of his glasses, smearing his surroundings into a blur of damask and chintz.

He guessed he passed out for a spell. When he came to his senses, the TV screen was a dancing mess of blips. As he pulled his mind together, he found lingering there an image that receded even as he grasped for it, to lock it in memory. Maybe it was from the tape, maybe it was from a kind of dream, or whatever, that had come while he was out, but as it faded away, he caught just enough of it—a trace picture, two bodies on a bed—before it plipped away into the shadows from which it had come.

Downstairs, Solomon Greschner was nodding by the unlit fire, trying to keep his attention on the book he was reading, when he noticed that one of the buttons on the telephone at his elbow had suddenly come alight. Gudge is on the phone, he thought. A good sign. His vitality must be returning. Excellent. The week to come should be quite a week.

Katagira listened carefully, nodding in consonance to Gudge's words as they poured over the telephone. When he had finished, he handed the receiver to Stumpy, who listened for a minute before murmuring acknowledgment and hanging up.

They made an odd pair, standing in the half-darkened kitchen of the Main House—the runty, grizzled little ranch hand and the solemn Japanese, austere and slender, whose skin seemed as polished as a statue.

There was no question in Stumpy's mind about what he was supposed to do. The orders were clear; hell, history repeated itself all the time. The story'd come down in backstairs gossip over the last forty years. It was part of the land. And he figured the Jap'd hold his end up; that Jap was one mean sonofabitch, Stumpy figured, when he had to be.

"See you tomorrow, then." He extended his hand to Katagira without quite knowing why. Far as he could remember, it was the first time they'd shaken hands.

Stumpy went into the hall and flicked on a switch. The lights in the memorabilia cabinets went on. Over his head the old boards of the house creaked; a high scream, thin and tenuous as a nail scratch, came from upstairs. Good thing, thought Stumpy, turning the key he kept on the chain around his neck. They ain't paying attention to nothing, he thought, hearing the old glass doors' whispering creak as he opened them and reached in to get what he wanted.

Seaco finally expired around cocktail time on Sunday. A squadron of Exchange officials, SEC representatives and interested members of the financial community had worked through the weekend, along with Homer Seabury and a team of his people and a congeries of lawyers representing every shade and tint of altruism, desperation and cupidity; but they had failed to produce a solution that would save the firm. Seaco's capital had been destroyed; public confidence in the entire market system brought to the brink; a ready reckoning of the financial damages indicated that close to $400 million of obliterated equity, impaired customer balances and defaulted bank loans—might be the price to be paid for Seaco's insolvency. Not to mention the jobs of close to four thousand employees. Although Wall Street stood ready to contribute $100 million of its own to recompense Seaco's smaller brokerage customers for any losses, the financial shortfall was beyond resolving, unless a miracle occurred. And no miracles were in view. Gudge could not be found; the bond market was a wreck; questions were being asked, at the board level, in the stratospheres of Seaco's principal banks. Sadly, because it still liked to think of itself as a sort of gentlemen's club, particularly when the world's gaze was elsewhere, Wall Street was now convinced that it had no option but to mete out its cruelest punishment: to turn its back on one of its own.

An anxious crowd of Seaco employees, mostly back-office people, along with a few investors, had gathered at the main entrance to the downtown skyscraper that housed Seaco's offices. Television news crews passed among them, soliciting suitably anguished reactions. The crowd obliged.

Bogle and Nick were sitting, watching, in the penthouse at the Tennyson. Bogle had been interested in a couple of things in Grundy's July Old Masters Sale and had asked Nick to come by to brainstorm a bidding strategy.

"I doubt we'll get away with another number like the Giotto bid last fall," he'd remarked. "I hear the boys in London have stopped playing cute with their reserves. I also hear, on quite another front, that the banks are sighting in on Gudge, including the pictures he bought from Max Lefcourt. Put them up at auction against his guarantee. Are they ever in for a surprise! I know," he said, smiling at Nick's noncommittal expression: "you're not talking. But if those pictures I saw in Texas are the real McCoy, then my wife's Charlotte Brontë."

Onscreen, the cameras' scrutiny shifted from the anxious crowd to the bulky figure of Homer Seabury coming through the glass doors of his building; at his back were the groomed silver thatch of Hugo Winstead and a posse of other men Nick didn't recognize. Lawyers, he guessed; always lawyers.

He watched Seabury brush his way awkwardly past the extended microphones and forward-pressing reporters. Inaudible under the buzz of questions, his mouth shaped "No comment" repeatedly; then, seemingly propelled by Winstead, who looked as pale as death to Nick, he was through the throng, tracked by the camera, until his broad, flanneled back vanished into a waiting limousine. Even in disaster, limousines, thought Nick.

"Jesus, Harvey, he looks terrible."

"No shit," said Bogle. "For most guys this'd be trouble. For Homer, this's a tragedy, poor bastard.

"He came to see me day before yesterday, you know," Bogle continued, "him and Greschner. Wanted to know would I help. Would I? Hell, *could I; could* who? We're talking four hundred big ones. Banks, mom-and-pop investors, widows and orphans, stockholders, Uncle Sam, the goddamn works! This's gonna make Penn Central look like peanuts by the time everyone gets his oar in. Or his knife. Which is exactly the way somebody wanted it; which is what I told Homer."

"What did he say?"

"What'd he say? Hell, he cried. Guys like that, they can't believe there are other guys out there who want to do a number on them. Which is what this Gudge has done on Homer. But you think Homer understands that, poor shmuck that he is? Christ, no! Decent guys like Homer never get the message: which is that somebody out there wants 'em dead—for whatever reason; it doesn't make a shit's worth of difference, Nick. Anyway, I learned a long time ago that dollars don't have tear ducts."

"How about Sol?" asked Nick.

"Hard to say. Homer's old man really put Greschner on the map, you know. He kind of let Sol show around a picture of himself with old Seabury's arm around his shoulders. Sol got rich off that. That picture opened doors."

Bogle sipped his drink.

"See, Nick, these guys all want to make a lot of money without using any of their own. Get rich without risk. We're living in the golden age of the middleman: brokers, agents, consultants, lawyers, non-risk-takers; guys who use words instead of money. Sol's one of those."

Bogle looked at Nick reflectively.

"The reason I do business with you is your guts are on the line. You sell me something, and I don't like it, I can shove it right back to you. You can't afford to be scared."

"Scared?"

"Scared. You and I deal just between you and me; what you're selling and I'm buying. The deal's on the table. Nobody's looking over your shoulder, like Homer's old man. There isn't any room in the deal for ghosts."

"Homer's father's dead, I thought."

"Those guys never die. They got shadows that'd stretch from here to Pluto. Guys like Homer wear their last names like chains. I mean, Homer's sixty, and I bet half the time he still gets called 'Morgan Seabury's son.' Guys like Homer, their fathers clank around in their heads like Hamlet's ghost. That's their immortality. Fucking their kids' heads from beyond the grave. I'll bet Homer doesn't get much sleep these days.

"I think Gudge was after Homer's father's ghost—and Granada.

"Anyhow, Granada figured all this out about six weeks ago and reached for the ripcord. That's when she 'surrendered'—as the papers, which don't understand a goddamn thing about business except that columnist in *Pritchett's*, put it. Well, Granada figured a white flag was easier to swallow than a fast ticket back to the perfume counter at Bloomingdale's. She's out maybe twenty-five million bottom line, but that business of hers can stand that kind of trouble, whereas if she'd stayed in all the way it would've been touch-and-go. Touch-and-go is too close for Granada, you know. Everybody's got one thing they're really scared of. I don't know what yours is, but Granada's is going back to Larchmont, on the wrong side of the tracks, and selling perfume to Stamford."

On the television screen a newscaster was describing Washington reactions to Seaco's collapse. It struck Nick, listening with half an ear, that Gudge wasn't mentioned. He asked Bogle about that.

"Shit, they can't chase after Gudge on the tube until they've got him good and nailed down. From what the papers say, they can't even get a look-see at the corporate records, which are scattered to hell and gone around the world. Inferences, which are all they've got on Gudge so far, are sure as hell enough to cash in Seaco's stake, but they won't do for Bubber, even if they can find him. Anyway, as you can gather, and just as well for our business together, I had to turn Homer and Sol down. Now, what about this Brueghel drawing; you think I can really get it for seven hundred thousand?"

It was less than ten blocks from the Tennyson to Nick's maisonette, but he took what he called "the great circle route": across Fifth into the park; around the lake where lingering couples held hands and watched their children frolic in the early-summer sun; up the hill and across the Park Drive embouching on Seventy-second Street—a bedlam of cyclists, joggers, skaters, food vendors and strollers weaving cheerfully in and around each other; past the playground—more gaily shouting children and, to his right, a small crowded field, its momentary spring grass already worn away to dust by weeks of softball, school games, Frisbee chasing; then down the hill, under trees freshly green and shiny; left up the slight rise past another playground and out among the strolling crowds on Fifth Avenue. As he went, it hit him how incongruous it was that only half an hour earlier, not five miles from this pleasant Sunday melee, Homer Seabury, a not inconsiderable, if a limited, man, had been seen to fall and shatter, soundlessly for all this part of the island cared, like a heavy statue in the desert toppled by the uncontrollably shifting sands. A casualty of an inferior age. A plastic Ozymandias.

Later that night he was talking to Jill on the phone. They spoke almost daily now—a habit they had slipped into more or less unconsciously over the last two weeks. Nick kept his fingers crossed.

"What happens to Homer?" he asked Jill. "In the Middle Ages he'd have had his hands cut off or his entrails run out on a windlass."

"Nothing much. Homer's only crime was believing he was as capable as Gudge told him he was. Nothing unusual about that. Big egos come cheap in business these days—except to the stockholders and employees and customers of the companies that get bankrupted. So Homer's no big deal that way. I've been doing a little nosing around. Seaco's a corporation, and Homer can hide behind that. His personal assets are okay—except, of course, he loses his Seaco stock. Against which, I gather, he had no personal loans. And he'll take a loss on his own account—I gather somewhere between thirty and forty percent in Homer's bracket. They're going to try to make the minnows whole. I hear that SIPC, the Securities Investor Protection Corporation, which is Uncle Sam's safety net for the securities markets, is going to play hardball on this one, alleging fraud. According to my sources, the Seaco pensions were insured outside, which means Homer'll get one hundred seventy-five thousand dollars a year for life. Nobody fired him, after all; his firm just vanished."

"That doesn't seem fair. How about all those people who lost their jobs?"

" 'Fair' is not a word used in big business, sweetie. Fair is for the other fellow. The unwritten rule is, you take care of your own. The clerks in the back offices and the traders who hustle bonds aren't your own."

"Well, whose the hell are they?"

"Nobody's quite figured that out. Somebody else's. So Homer's going to be all right. How are you?"

"Without you, no better than fair. You?"

"About the usual. Tired. This has been a tough story, getting it all down without blowing my cover. Sol's been a peach, keeping me fed."

"I'll bet he has. Jill, where the hell does he fit into all this, do you think? Wherever Gudge's heavy foot has been, all hell has broken loose. Take Florence. He wanted Max's pictures and he got 'em; and Max and Frank are dead. He ties up with Seabury and appears to have put something over and that firm's dead. And wherever Gudge has been, Sol's been right there too, smiling, making introductions. And you and me. What do you think?"

"Nick, what can I say? If there's a fraud case on Gudge, it'll take five years in the courts."

"I hear Gudge may have tried to get at Mrs. Masterman by blowing up Seabury."

"I heard that too. There may be something to it. But there are a lot of other things. The Street's saying right now that Gudge blew all his money in some secret nuclear-technology deal in Pakistan and needed to make a big hit to get even. I heard from a very respected analyst that Gudge was short the gross national product of Germany in Deutschmark foreign exchange and needed to blow dollar interest rates out of sight to even up his futures position. They're saying he's raised a secret mercenary strike force in the wilds of New Mexico, outfitted with 747s he bought cheap from the airlines, to descend on Washington and take it over in the panic he figures will happen. They say he's under the influence of some guru his wife found in Paris—all doped up and doing a Howard Hughes. Nick, they say he's up to this, up to that, and the only one who's not saying what he's up to is Mr. Buford Gudge IV. God, no one even knows where he is."

"Sol?"

"Not Sol. I made him swear on the head of my child. He did. Nick, he doesn't know."

"Well, so where's it all come out?"

"Just another overnight sensation, love; another ten days' wonder—like Penn Central, like Equity Funding, like TWA, like Hayden Stone. Like Chrysler. Just another big name. Another door sign to be repainted. Who cares, after all? The Street will wake up in a couple of weeks; discover it's still in business, and that all that's been lost is a lot of other people's money and other people's jobs. And so it goes."

Despite the casual, too contrivedly offhanded way she put it, Nick was pleased to hear a note of caring in Jill's voice. He asked after Jenny, was pleased to hear she was well and told Jill maybe they could talk tomorrow. No point in pressing; when she was ready to see him again, she'd say. At least they could talk; that was something. And it was nice to detect that she found a margin for caring in this Seaco mess, because he did, and he grasped at anything they appeared to have in common as if it were the staff of life.

Monday, in New York an ugly day which repudiated the sunny pleasantness of the previous evening, had been hot and dry in the Panhandle. Katagira had spent the day making his final preparations. Each of the vaqueros had been given $100,000 in cash; they and their families, and the few possessions they found worth keeping, had been driven off in the chartered bus which would take them south to Mexico. The cattle had been consigned to the Blue Ribbon All-American Sale later in the year and had been trucked to a custom feeder up near Dalhart. José and his wife had left after dinner on the first leg of a trip that would take them to relatives in California. In the back of their dusty old Plymouth was an old suitcase of Gudge's with $300,000 in it.

It was darkening rapidly. Standing on the porch of his little house, Katagira looked, as he so often had, at the lights of the Main House glowing in the twilight. Not a happy place, he thought. A shadow moved across one of the upper windows. Mrs. Gudge. She had returned just after six from her trip up to see the Palo Duro with the Vietnamese architect; he would be leaving early next morning, she'd advised Katagira.

It was time for a reckoning, he knew.

On the surface, everything had gone more or less smoothly; the immediate objectives had been achieved. That morning—as the evening's network news had confirmed—the governors of six states, the comptrollers or mayors of a dozen cities and the presidents or principal administrators of eleven universities and hospitals, as well as the Secretary of Health and Human Services, had received parcels delivered by Federal Express. Each parcel contained the conveyance of proved fee title to one significant portion of the Lazy G's remaining oil and gas assets. Thus the Chancellor of the University of Texas found himself the delighted beneficiary of a gift of 15,000 acres in the Yates Field; the mayors of New York and Philadelphia each now ruled over not merely acres of slums, but thousands of acres of major producing and prospective leases in East Texas and South Louisiana, which Gudge had given those cities as public benefactions. The administrator of the largest hospital in Chicago, who had agonized through the weekend over a federal cutoff that threatened to close his doors, could now command the revenue flow from fifty wells and six gas plants in Colorado and Wyoming. And the Secretary of Health and Human Services, compelled, in spite of himself, to prepare a plan for the extinction of his department's humane functions, now had nearly $100 million a year earmarked for food stamps, flowing steadily from production platforms in the North Sea and the Sabine Pass. Title was in every case good and legal; in most cases, moreover, title was to assets the banks had thought they were holding as collateral, not to mention what the investors in GOD had thought they were buying.

It was a public benefaction beyond recall. It was celebrated from pulpits, on television, in the slums and ghettos. And in the courts.

Across the nation, attorneys representing nearly a thousand firms and ten times that number of claimants filed actions on behalf of investors in GUT and GOD, for citizens' groups, for the Internal Revenue Service, the Securities and Exchange Commission, the Federal Communications Commission, the Coalition for Less Government, the Coalition for More Government and no fewer than twenty-three womens'-rights groups.

Katagira's ultimate plan had been to turn the Lazy G into carrion for lawyers by establishing endless competing claims to its properties. In New York the mayor and his principal banks were at each other's throats; in Kansas City, the gala lunch celebrating the marriage of the public and private sectors had ended in a fistfight on the dais. Wrapping up the network news that evening, NBC's legal expert had opined that on the basis of litigation filed during the day, it appeared that at current legal billing rates, "the total ten-billion-dollars-plus value of the assets given by Mr. Gudge will be exhausted in legal fees within five years." He added that because the courts were still open in California, which was expected to be a critical venue of Gudge-oriented litigation, viewers should not jump to an early conclusion as to the final figure.

And they had badly wounded Mrs. Masterman, even if she had slipped the whole noose. She had, after all, been a principal target. Yet Mr. Gudge hadn't seemed to mind, not really, when Katagira had spoken with him an hour earlier. He'd sounded as if his mind were on something else.

"Oh, let her go, K," he'd said, wearily; "she ain't worth any more trouble." It was as if Gudge were saying nothing was worth any more trouble. The time must be getting close now. Stumpy had said as much; he'd gotten back from New York earlier.

"Boss's about done with, seems to me."

"You gave him what he wanted."

"Yessir. He's all set; leastways, that's what he said." Stumpy looked abashed; he had something on his tongue he didn't much want to have to say. Katagira had noticed.

"Is there something else?"

"Well, sir, yessir, there is, I guess." Stumpy dropped his gaze to his boot tops and gathered his voice so as to be able to say it out all at once and get it done with. "Well, sir, he said to say goodbye, and thanks. I guess he won't be coming back."

"I feared as much. But thank you for telling me."

They had discussed what had to be done. Stumpy was clearly up to it, Katagira saw. Which pleased him—he was not much of a samurai himself, more a thinker, although his revered ancestor's blade stood in the corner of his room.

It was dark now. Katagira could hear a riffle on the surface of his fishpond. As he thought of his trout, he regretted not having had time to catch them all. Absently he wondered what would become of them. In time, he expected, without him to winnow them, they would grow fat as pigs on the hatches that would come with the murmuring evenings of July and August.

There was little enough for him to pack. His books—De Tocqueville, Emerson, Thoreau, *The Federalist*—those shards of the old America of his heart. A few clothes. He changed into a business suit. His papers were in order. The gold had been sold in Mexico earlier in the week.

He reached to turn out the lights, letting his eyes drift around the room that had been his home so long. There was no souvenir for him here; all he took with him was an early map of the Lazy G which Stumpy had picked from the case near the dining room. Another remembrance of a time when everything was simpler—and because simpler, better.

He turned out the light. Standing on the porch, looking toward the Big House, he waited for the downstairs lights to go out. When they did, and the lights in the upper bedroom flashed on, it was time to go. He picked up his bag and walked quickly around to the back of the bunkhouse; under his feet, the gravel made a barely audible sigh. The rental car was there, just as Stumpy, who'd come back from New York on a commercial flight, had said. He started it up and pulled out and down the driveway, a familiar white crescent in the moonlight. As he passed out the gates of the Lazy G, down the long road that led to the highway, he didn't look back. His mind was already on Hong Kong, where he was bound. He'd spend the night in Amarillo, at a motel near the airport; then on to Dallas/Fort Worth for the morning flight to Honolulu. No one would notice him. No one would think a second thought. Hell, as he'd heard Texans say, these days there were Japs everywhere a man looked.

Stumpy heard the door of the rental car chunk shut; he heard the engine whir into life and the swish of gravel as it pulled out. Then he was alone, looking out the window of the unlit bunkhouse, up at the Big House looming a hundred yards away.

After a while, he guessed it was time. He picked up his hat and set it on the back of his head and quietly opened the door and went out into the moonlight. He crossed the strip of lawn and dirt silently, and let himself in through the kitchen door. Upstairs, he heard the ruckus he'd been expecting and waiting for. His hand heavy with the weight it held, he slid into the hall and started up the stairs.

Caryn Gudge had never had such good fooling around; she hoped her husband would never come home. This was one thing you never got up East, never had time for, 'cause nobody up there ever just seemed to want to screw just for the sake of screwing. Everybody wanted something; or tricked it all up with drugs or drinking; although there were a couple of times that old Gratiane, bless her, had done things to her that had made her just squeal like a little pig, and she had to admit that those little red pills of Sartorian's made her all shivery till she was like to bust. It was a strain keeping up in New York and Paris, and this week down here had given her a good rest. She could get back on the old round as soon as Buford came back and gave his permission for the new Gudge Museum.

Caryn's mind and attention were a jumble of recently lived ecstasy; anticipation of Monte Carlo and a rented house in Southampton, which meant a whole mess of new summer clothes, and the plans for the Gudge Museum, and a party to open it and maybe another party in New York when she went on the Fuller Board, together with her wonderment that a little brown man with a little brown thing could get the job done so all-fired good when she'd always thought you had to get hold of a man with a pizzle like a buck mule. Next to her lay the Vietnamese architect, who had just demonstrated the Flower of the Sixth Orifice, which took out of the man all it gave to the woman. Like Caryn, he was suspended in that netherworld of unfocused exhaustion, sinking free-fall through drowsiness, barely able to move.

When the door to the bedroom slammed open, it was all he could do to raise his head and squint at the figure in the doorway. He thought he recognized it as that cowboy who was around the house, a weird, squat, uncouth little figure with legs bowed and gnarled like mesquite branches. As his vision sharpened, he saw that the cowboy was holding something; then he saw it was a rifle; then he heard Caryn scream something; then Stumpy blew off the top of his head.

Caryn felt the breath of the bullet and the mucuslike rainy burst of his blood spatter her face. Instinctively, she covered her breasts and groin with her hands; at the same time she started to scream, as her horrified eyes saw the barrel of Stumpy's .30-30 come around as he levered another shell into the chamber. His eyes appeared to blaze bright as fire.

In the doorway, Stumpy watched the bodies twitch and subside. Instinctively, he brought up the muzzle of the gun and blew the smoke from it as unconcernedly as he might cool his soup.

Time to get to work. He went downstairs, into the basement room, among the silent machines that Katagira had ruled, and set the fuse timers. In the kitchen closet, he found the gasoline cans he'd placed there earlier. Working methodically, conscious of the time allowed him by the incendiaries downstairs, he sloshed the kerosene mixture throughout the house—over the flatboard dining-room table; into the cabinets that held the maps and deeds; through the kitchen; then up the stairs and through the bedrooms, dropping each can as he emptied it, finally soaking the bodies stiffening on the blood-drenched bed.

He felt real tired all of a sudden. At the head of the stairs, he sat down heavily, not thinking much about anything, just flatass beat. From the basement came a dull thump, which shook the house, and tongues of flame licked up through the burst floorboards and ignited the kerosene. It jumped like a jackrabbit, he thought, watching it spread, leaping across the roof beams. As the fire started up the stairs, as malevolent and purposeful as a snake after a bird, he watched it, feeling the first wisps of smoke in the air. From outside came the sounds of other explosions. That would be Katagira's house and the bunkhouse and the new building where all them pictures were hanging. Pity about the pictures, Stumpy thought; but then, there weren't gonna be no one around to look at them anyway, so what was the point?

The fire kept climbing the stairs. This was an old house; the wood burned fast. He thought he could smell a strange, acrid odor; probably the plastic wires melting that room downstairs, and the tapes. He'd done like Katagira said: opened all the file drawers before he set the fuses.

A light breeze from the open bedroom window behind him reminded him that he'd better get going. Out over the roof and down the rope ladder that hung from its edge.

Time to get going, he said to himself. I'm real, real tired. And where to go? This was his land; the Gudges was his people—the only people he'd ever really had. He took his strength from the Lazy G; his blood was in its roots; he knew its skies, its seasons, its gullies and washes and wallows, its trees and bushes and creeks and every star in the sky overhead, which on nights like this seemed like a black tent roof as wide and far as the world could stretch. He knew all this, and it was all he knew. Where could he go? Where else was there? Who would take him?

The fire was up the stairs now and hot on his boots, starting to hurt. Stumpy was home, and that was where a man belonged. He picked up the rifle; the fire-hot barrel seared his hand. Without a thought, he put the muzzle in his mouth and pulled the trigger.

A quarter-mile away, a lone coyote heard the report and looked briefly toward the sound, incurious but wary. He returned then to his howling, baying at a moon that poured its light on the earth with such intensity and plenitude that it seemed to blend in a single flare with the lonely fire devouring the ranch buildings.

CHAPTER THIRTY

The first of what would become an epidemic of food-stamp riots broke out before dawn in Harlem. Nick was awakened at six-thirty by a raging of sirens such as he had never in his life heard. It sounded as if every police car, ambulance and fire engine in Manhattan were on Park Avenue. When he opened the front door of the maisonette and looked up the avenue, it seemed all he could see was flashing lights. As he watched, more official traffic racketed north.

What the hell was going on? he wondered. In the kitchen, as the water heated, he clicked around the dial of the radio, trying to find a focused report. Bits and pieces of reportage made up a mosaic: ". . . *every supermarket in Harlem and the Bronx reported to be ransacked and burned . . . marauding groups moving south through Central Park and along major north–south arteries in Manhattan . . . police lines being established across the West Side at One-hundredth Street and the East Side at Ninety-sixth . . . residents north of Ninetieth Street advised to stay indoors . . . subway operations shut down north of Eighty-sixth Street . . .*"

Christ, he thought.

But by late morning, the activity on Park Avenue had slowed down. He guessed that the riots had subsided. The avenue was still dominated by the flashing lights of police cars, but a trickle of conventional traffic had appeared. It was an ugly day, he saw. Damp, under a foul gray sky tinged with orange smoke that seemed to press down and suffocate the city with its fetid weight. The atmosphere seemed touched with the dismal stink with which hot summer days would soon mantle the streets. A day for tempers and violence.

Across the park, Jill had heard the sirens on Central Park West. She rose from her typewriter, where she had been working since five that morning, when her anxiousness to get going on the story had driven her from a restless sleep. Looking from her living-room window, she watched in mystification as flashing light after flashing light rushed north. The sky was the color of sweat-stained flannel; on the far side of the park the concrete peaks of the East Side seemed blurred and anonymous, varieties of stone reduced by the bitter morning to a dreary aggregate of yellowish gray.

She returned to her workroom. Switching from the classical-music station to which she habitually did her late-hour writing, she heard the same news Nick had.

Ironic, she thought, turning back to the text in her typewriter. All hell has finally broken loose. The sky looked like brimstone. The radio reported that Wall Street was a paralyzed wreck. And here she was, holding the key to one large piece of everyone's puzzlement, trying to get it exactly as Sol had told it to her when he'd called around midnight. He'd sounded oddly valedictory. Something in his words and tone of voice had insisted, over what she wanted to be hearing, that this was Solomon Greschner's last public relations hurrah. But it was the story he'd promised her; all she'd had to give over in return was the promise not to print it until *Pritchett's* next regular weekly number.

"Sources close to Buford Gudge IV," she'd begun the column,

> have revealed the multibillionaire's mysterious motives in perpetrating what appears now to have been a massive fraud on Wall Street and the United States investment community at large, coupled with a series of public and private benefactions, including billion-dollar subventions to departments of the Federal Government itself.
>
> As announced through Solomon Greschner Associates, Gudge's public relations counsel, what Mr. Gudge's actions amount to is a massive personal sacrifice, which this writer estimates to be in excess of $10 billion, of the Gudge empire to teach a lesson to the country.

The column went on to describe an ideology that Jill, on the basis of her sense of the man and what she'd seen and read, was absolutely unconvinced was Gudge's. An ideology that deplored the nation's economic divisiveness; that despised the speculative fads and furies developed and unleashed by Wall Street's marketing geniuses, paper storms which had deflected the nation's creative fiscal energies and resources into eddying, useless channels; that loathed the publicized and emulated effete, ninny-boy values orchestrated by New York homosexuals and poseurs which poisoned the spiritual well of solid middle-class ethics; that sorrowed at an egocentricized, elitist, foolish, unpatriotic collection of managers and oligarchs perched like starlings on the Washington–New York axis. Keeping to Sol's description, she presented Gudge's self-induced financial immolation, this suttee he'd performed on the flaming pyre of the values he'd been raised to love, as a crusade, a Texas *jihad*, a war of conscience.

That was the way she wrote it, knowing its effect would be redoubled. But Jill wasn't convinced. Not that she didn't share some of the sentiments which Sol had passed along, claiming to speak for Gudge. The noble motives attributed to Gudge, irreproachable as they might sound, were, she felt, more noise than conviction. It might be, she figured, another example of Sol's handling a client like a ventriloquist's dummy. But who could say? As long as Gudge remained hidden away, unwilling to speak for himself, the Greschner version was going to be the accepted version, and what a hell of a story it was. Man bites country.

After she finished, she took a short nap and then read until the radio news suggested all was probably clear outside. This story wasn't going to be transmitted to *Pritchett's* in the usual way; too risky that someone might decide to push up the deadline, and she had her word to Sol to keep. She left and walked over to the Ansonia post office; next-day delivery would be plenty time enough. Later, she could telephone Sol.

Nick had phoned Jill to make sure she was okay. Her answering machine informed him she'd be back by one. You dumbbell, he thought, to be on the street—consoling himself with the knowledge that at least Jenny was out of school, and hopefully in the country.

Figuring he had the day to himself, since few pictures were likely to be sold on a day discolored by the lingering smoke of social unrest, he put *Die Walküre* on the stereo and reread the papers. The *Times* was full of Seaco and Gudge. The trouble was spreading. A judge in Philadelphia had enjoined any distribution of Seaco assets in response to a motion filed in connection with a $500-million class-action suit on behalf of any and all purchasers of GUT and GOD. Something like $4 billion of Seaco's customers' securities was effectively locked by litigation into the wounded firm. A similar suit had been entered against Granada Masterman, Masterman United Corporation, the directors of MUD and Hugo Winstead, Esq., specifically, alleging the misuse of inside information in MUD's selling Seaco shares prior to the firm's collapse. The Attorney General of the State of New York, as well as the Securities and Exchange Commission and the city bar association, had announced an investigation of Winstead's role in various transactions. On other pages, the controversies and litigation surrounding Gudge's cataclysmic benefactions were detailed.

A professor of law at Harvard had calculated that if all the lawsuits so far filed or brought in connection with Seaco-Gudge were consolidated into a single enterprise, the result would be the forty-sixth-largest business in America. The dean of a well-known Midwestern law school, who had only days before publicly bemoaned what he saw as a declining demand for lawyers by a society sick of attorneys and disgusted with litigation, was quoted as declaring, "The collapse of Seaco marks a red-letter day for the annals of American legal education."

All the numbers and claims and counterclaims made Nick feel ill. At Jill's suggestion, he'd been trying to read *Bleak House*. It was the same now as then. Human interests buried under the billions and the trillions and the whereases and the wherefores. Shoveled under by lawyers.

He was making a sandwich when Sol called.

"How are you, Nicholas? Isn't this a mess? How is it uptown?"

There seemed to be an echo behind Sol's voice.

"Where are you?"

"At the airport. I'm taking an extended vacation in Sta. Marta. I just wanted to call and say goodbye. My plane will be off shortly."

Running away, are you? Nick wanted to ask. Instead he said, "When will you be back?"

"Oh, sometime, Nicholas, sometime. You see, I've sold Number Seventeen. And its contents, including Vosper. To Mr. Gudge. A big house like that is too much of a job for an old man like me. I crave the air of the mountains and the company of my friend Frucht."

Nick was speechless.

"Nicholas . . ." Sol's voice had turned serious. "You know how fond I am of Jill and you. I also think you know what sort of people you are. At least, now you know it. Do try to take care of each other. I doubt you'll do better with others."

"Sol, I'm trying."

There was something strange in Sol's voice, something Nick had never heard. He searched for the right word: apprehensive, apologetic, valedictory. Something of each of those, jumbled together in a way for which he knew no exact word.

"Well, I'm afraid they're calling my plane. Nicholas, there are one or two little favors I'd like you to do. I've left a letter with Vosper for you. Goodbye now, Nicholas; take care of my two ladies."

Greschner hung up.

Nick spent the next hour and a half wandering aimlessly around his office. He felt a mysterious need to stay by the telephone. True to his forebodings, it rang. The voice on the other end was shaken, trembled down to a hoarse whisper. Nick recognized the voice.

"Mr. Reverey. It's Vosper. Can you come at once, please, sir? Oh, sir, such trouble." Vosper's voice broke.

Nick asked no further questions. If Greschner's imperturbable butler was shaken, a man who had been among the last taken off the beach at Dunkirk, when the Stukas swarmed like flies, it must be bad. He slammed down the phone, grabbed his jacket and raced downstairs.

The commotion uptown had confused traffic, so Nick had to run nearly to Sixtieth Street before he found a taxi. Then it was another fifteen minutes snaking downtown before the cab turned off Fifth toward Rostval Place. It halted short of Madison Avenue, where a policeman was waving traffic away. Nick paid off the driver; as he climbed out of the taxi, he saw lights flashing on the far side of the arch joining the Fuller buildings. He threaded his way across Madison Avenue and entered the square. Three flashing police cruisers were pulled up in front of Number 17, where a small, curious crowd was starting to gather. The entrance to the house was blocked by two policemen, standing stiff and immovable as the guards at

Buckingham Palace. To one side, surrounded by rubberneckers, a TV newswoman was interviewing a police officer.

There was no way in, Nick saw; even if there had been, he wasn't sure he wanted to go in. Always, Number 17 had been friendly, a second home, a place to be sought out. Now, on this ugly afternoon, it seemed hunched on the edge of the square, a charnel house.

He saw an authoritative-looking policeman standing to one side, so he edged through the growing crowd to his side.

"Excuse me, Officer." Nick found himself speaking with the slightly guilty tone in which even the most unblemished citizen addresses the police. "Can you tell me what happened? I'm a friend of the owner of this house." He thought a small lie might induce some information. "I had an appointment later this afternoon."

The officer eyed him.

"Hard to say. Got two D.O.A.s in there. One shot the other, then hisself; the M.E.'s in there now. The deceased's pending a positive identification."

"How'd it happen?"

"Dunno."

Over the officer's shoulder Nick saw a plainclothes detective come out of Number 17; from his left hand dangled a handkerchief knotted through the trigger guard of what Nick took to be an old-fashioned six-shooter. In his left, he carried what appeared to be a wooden case; something in its lid caught the light as the detective crossed to his car. A plaque of some kind, Nick guessed, of brass or polished copper.

Nick returned his whole concentration to the policeman. "They got the butler in there now, but it don't look like he done it." The officer rumbled crudely at his own joke. "Funny thing. The guy could shoot. Hit the other guy twice. First one right in the balls with what looks like a .44 Soft Point. Found his dick on the far side of the room." The officer lowered his voice in exaggerated gentility. "The next one did the job: blew him away right between the eyes. Then hisself."

Nick walked over to the freshly painted black fence surrounding Rostval Park and leaned against it, waiting for some cue. He let his eyes wander around the square. Christ, had it really been little more than a year ago that he'd come under that arch—then fresh steel gleaming in the twilight, now pitted by a city year, aged a dozen years in one, the way this city wore out everything?

"Mr. Reverey, sir."

"Are you all right, Vosper?"

"Thank you, sir: shaken but alive." Vosper tried a faint smile and gave up halfway through. "It's terrible, sir . . ." He started to choke up, but generations of inbred professional poise stiffened him. "Mr. Winstead. Mr. Gudge . . ."

"Tell me what happened, Vosper."

As Vosper told it, Winstead had been telephoned by Greschner, first thing in the morning, to come to the house at three. Vosper hadn't overheard Mr. Greschner's conversation with Winstead, as he was packing for his master, but doubtless a strong inducement had been offered. Vosper had gotten the impression that the invitation to Winstead was made at Mr. Gudge's request. Yes, Mr. Gudge had been staying in the house last week, since Thursday. Mr. Gudge had only had one visitor, Vosper had told the detective; a little rough-looking man, who'd rung the bell Sunday night and given Mr. Gudge some kind of wooden box. Vosper had seen it in Mr. Gudge's room; it had a little brass plate set in its top with a date on it. That was where the gun had been.

Anyway, Winstead had arrived promptly, and Vosper had shown him into the drawing room, where Mr. Gudge, whom Vosper had brought downstairs in his wheelchair in the elevator, was waiting. Then Vosper had withdrawn. About ten minutes later, there had been a terrible booming noise—a gunshot—and a scream worse than anything Vosper had ever heard, even when the beaches had been strafed, and then a second shot and then, after a pause, a third, and then nothing. He'd rushed upstairs, he had, to find Mr. Winstead lying all bloody and dead across the sofa, not four feet from where Mr. Gudge was in his wheelchair, dead too, the gun on his lap.

"So I called the police first, sir. Then you. And Mr. Greschner's lawyer. And Mr. Winstead's firm. There're a lot of people up there now. I tried to call Mr. Gudge's ranch, but it seems there's trouble on the line. It's out of my hands now."

Vosper looked grave. He reached into the pocket of his striped waistcoat and took out what Nick saw was a coat check.

"Mr. Greschner knew there was going to be some trouble, I think, sir. Just after he spoke with Mr. Winstead, he put some things in an envelope for you and asked that I carry them across to the Institute and leave them in the cloakroom. Then he left."

Vosper handed over the ticket.

"Listen, Vosper, you've been wonderful. You've done Mr. Greschner proud. I'd better run and get this now. See what it's about. Call me tomorrow."

He walked quickly over to the Institute and exchanged the ticket for a large manila envelope. Too impatient and nervous to wait until he got home, he walked around to the other side of Rostval Place, away from the commotion in front of Number 17, and sat down on a bench. He blinked in the light; he hadn't noticed that a fresh breeze had pushed the clouds across the East River and let the sun come through.

He opened the envelope and took out its contents. The largest item was a cardboard mat covered in tissue paper, about the size of a typewritten sheet. He removed the tissue carefully. The center of the mat had been cut out, leaving a square about five inches on a side, edged in bands of gold leaf and blue. In the middle of the lower border a watercolor cartouche bore the printed name "INGRES." Centered in the cutout was a drawing of a young and sickly man, obviously English, fair and long-nosed. Nick knew this too. It was supposed to be a drawing Ingres had made of Keats, when the mortally ill poet and the artist on the brink of fame and recognition had both been in Rome in 1819. He contemplated the drawing. The artist had caught, with a pencil's edge, the shadow of death under the transparent, stretched skin of his subject. Looking at it, Nick found at last the answer to something that had bothered him from the first moment he had laid eyes on Bubber Gudge; there had been something about Gudge that seemed familiar—some essence that Nick had caught the sight or scent of elsewhere. Now he knew where. Too late. Assuming he could have done anything. About anything. For anyone.

Two envelopes addressed in Sol's handwriting remained. The first was to Jill; in the Anglo-gentrified fashion Sol favored, its front was marked "*By Hand/Courtesy Mr. Nicholas Reverey*" and the flap left unsealed. Without thinking, Nick took out the folded sheet and read:

> *Darling Jill:*
> *If you receive this please call my attorney as below. He will fix things up. My love to Jenny; may she grow tall and happy. Take care of Nicholas and he will take care of you in a way that the Greschners owe you.*
> *Love,*
> *Sol*

The name and phone number of Sol's personal attorney were written across the bottom.

Nick looked at the last envelope, turning it in his hands as if to open it might release some fearsome demon. What could be worse than what had already happened? What demons could possibly be left?

> *Dear Nicholas:*
> *Things are moving too rapidly for this old head. Some of them of my own mischief, I fear. As I will by now have told you, I am going away. There are some things that need to be done. They are the sort of things a man should have a son to do, but you are the closest I have to that, so bear with me. First, keep the Ingres drawing. I really think it is of Keats. I want you to have something; I flattered myself to believe that you found me at least as enjoyable and interesting as any of the objects my money bought me.*
> *Second, please give the enclosed letter personally to Jill. And keep after her. And don't be foolish.*
> *Finally, and this may sound strange, would you go down to Little Italy, to the old St. Patrick's church on Mulberry Street, and light a candle. You'll wonder why, but it doesn't matter. Just do this one favor.*
> *As for me, if you can find a cock for Asclepius, I'd be grateful.*
> *Yours,*
> *Sol*

Nick's chest felt as if his whole being had sucked in around his heart and dropped into some fathomless, pointless emptiness. Follow instructions, he told himself; pick up your cues. He hoped he could make Jill see that in a world where everyone was alone, two were better than one. He felt unendurably alone.

There was a pay phone on the corner of Rostval Place. He dialed Jill, relieved to hear her answer on the second ring. He explained as best and as quickly as he could what had happened—hearing her exclaim in fright succeeded by horror succeeded by tears.

"Come up," she said. It might be a new beginning, he thought, hanging up.

Gazing at Number 17, he felt no loss, no sense of tragedy. His tragedy was buried in Florence, he knew. He thought of Max's collection slumbering in its secret mountain fastness, a goddess in a gown of endless colors, waiting to be reborn. That was where the value was stored up against the day it would be needed. Not under these tawdry banners for which so much blood and unhappiness had been spilled. How cheesy it was, this world which revolved around money and the kinds of things that could be priced and possessed because of it. He thought of that morning, of the squad cars racing up Park Avenue to beat back the rage of the hungry and disadvantaged; next to that, who the hell needs the troubles of the rich? he thought, suddenly angry.

Another police car bleated up to Number 17. Standing under the Fuller arch, a few steps from Madison Avenue, Nick looked at Greschner's house, perhaps for the last time; its parlor windows reflected the west-moving sun like the eyes of a blind man. Behind and beyond, glowing pale gold in the deepening light, clouds scudded over the East River, pushed along by the freshening afternoon wind. They look like galleons, Nick thought: treasure ships to be cursed, and all that sailed in them.

The vividness of his anger startled him. Then he realized it had been brought on by nothing more than confections of light and moisture. Tricks, as all of this had been.

He looked back at Number 17, feeling his eyes fill in rage and sorrow. Then he turned into Madison Avenue, hailed a cab and let it carry him away uptown.

AFTERWORD

The premise of *Someone Else's Money* was first suggested, offhandedly, by Donald H. Loomis, then general counsel of Lehman Brothers, in a conversation which took place longer ago than any vain man might care to remember. It was a discussion to which the late Raymond S. Rusmisel added that quantum of positiveness which embeds things in memory.

David Halberstam made a characteristically generous and insightful suggestion, when the book was still in the thinking stage, that served as an important point of departure. Likewise Douglas Lamont, Dean of the Walter Heller School of Business Administration, to which grown men and women come for the answers, but only after they have figured out the questions.

I hope this book reverberates with a love of art history. Messrs. John Hutchins and Glen Krause started me off. More than twenty-five years ago, John Spencer, then an instructor at Yale, since a distinguished teacher, scholar and arts administrator, opened my eyes to the enduring magic of Renaissance painting. I have been lucky since then to have shared the company and thoughts of a galaxy of art dealers, art historians, art critics and art collectors: William and Nicholas Acquavella; Julian and Geoffrey Agnew; Brooke Alexander; John Baskett; Harry Bober; Harry Brooks; Carter Brown; Jonathan Brown; David Carritt (unarguably the greatest "eye" of our time); Desmond and Gerald Corcoran; Richard Day; Anthony d'Offay and Caroline Cuthbert; James Deely; Gilbert Edelson; Colin Eisler; Everett Fahy; Sidney Freedberg and John Pope-Hennessy (*maestri fra maestri*); Marco Grassi and Mario Modestini (*miti nella storia dell' restauro*, along with John Brealey); Egbert Havekamp-Begemann; Lore and Rudolph Heinemann; my old colleague Tom Hoving; H. W. Janson; Irving Lavin; John Jay Mortimer; Clyde Newhouse; Donald Posner; Olga Raggio; James Rorimer; Theodore Rousseau; Charles Ryskamp; Margaretta Salinger; Charles Seymour; Craig Smyth; Hubert von Sonnenburg; Martin Summers; Eugene V. Thaw; A. Richard Turner. And particularly Elizabeth Gardner and Robert Lehman. There is something from them all somewhere in this book. Not to mention Julius S. Held, whose definitive catalogue of Rubens' oil sketches might as well be a character in this novel.

If this book "works," it is due to my editors: Larry Freundlich, who wrote the good parts; Lynn Chalmers, who gave me the text I couldn't give myself; Paul Sidey, who understands (with Housman) that malt does at least as much as Fowler can to justify man's words to man. And John Saumarez Smith. And Ned Leavitt. And, especially, Paula Schwartz.

could go back in history and walk into a Corinthian church service, everybody would be speaking in tongues at the same time. So-called prophets would be trying to prophesy over the top of one another. Can you imagine? Chaos and disorder everywhere.

When Paul heard these things, he told the church that people coming in would conclude they were mad! Paul said, "I would rather speak five words with my understanding, that I may teach others also, than ten thousand words in a tongue" (1 Cor. 14:19, *NKJV*). He reminded the Corinthians that they were not to use the giftings for themselves but rather for the purpose of edifying others.

For the past 15 or so years, the Western world has experienced what was supposed to be a charismatic revival. I want to suggest that it has been a Corinthian moment—nothing but confusion. People have been flying all over the world, saying, "What is in it for me? I want one more touch for myself. I want one more thing, one more gift! More for me!" The unsaved have looked at it and concluded, "These people are crazy."

Confusion is the result of self-exaltation. It is a simple principle: Hey, look at me! Look at me to the exclusion of the outsider, to the exclusion of the man or woman who is coming in and looking for God, looking for help, looking for hope. The end result is just a hodgepodge of spiritual nonsense.

We must remember that "God is not the author of confusion, but of peace" (1 Cor. 14:33). The moment in our hearts that we use what we have for others, the confusion dissipates and divine order comes into the house of God.

From Chaos to Calm

So many believers today remain confused and have trouble hearing the voice of God. It is typically due to the fact that they are merely looking to confirm the direction of their own flesh, and all the while they are holding back something that God has specifically asked them to lay down. God wants something deeper from us—He wants us to walk where He walks, to do what He does, to see people through His eyes. He wants our hands to become His hands and our voice to speak His heart. That is when He can give us a life that we can only dream about. But first we must let go of whatever we are holding on to so tightly.

I once knew a young lady who came to Christ and was so alive in God; an extraordinary worshipper in fact. She also happened to be part of one of the Broadway shows in New York City. One Sunday she came to me and said, "It can't be that God is asking me to give this up. I have lived my whole life for this career!" She was waiting for me to reassure her that it couldn't be God.

I simply replied, "Well, I don't know what the Holy Spirit is asking of you, but all I can tell you is that when God speaks to you, you should obey Him. Something greater for your life awaits you—far greater than what you think your life should be."

Aware of this struggle, I watched her over the next few weeks. I noticed her sitting closer and closer to the back of the church each service. She did come back to see me again three times or so, each time shaking her head, concluding,

"It can't be." Then one day she came and asserted, "The Lord has told me that I can keep my career."

She left the church shortly after that.

In the same way, the Corinthian church was looking for something to confirm its self-image. Yet all along the Lord was saying, "No, if you want to hear My voice, you must walk with Me."

Once you decide to get up and move toward the work of Christ, things in your life will begin to fall into order. You can be assured that every half-hearted Christian you meet along the way will try to turn you back. But don't be discouraged, just keep moving towards what God is speaking in your life.

For some, the move will start across the dinner table. If you are alienated from your family, moving toward Christ means walking humbly, asking for forgiveness and trusting God. Denying self is where it starts. Then it moves across the hall to the struggling family, and then out into the neighborhood.

You will not always know exactly where God is going to lead you, but the true Christian life is found in looking outside of oneself to other people. It is the toughest battle you will ever fight. You thought it was tough when you first came to Christ. You thought giving up smoking, drinking and gossiping was tough. It is true that some of these things are tough for many people. But the final step in the Christian journey is to give yourself for people, even those who hate you.

If the Lord is speaking to you to let go of something and move toward the work of Christ, wherever that starts, obey

Him. And as you choose to walk in obedience to the will of God, you will have peace in the storm, much like Paul when he found himself on a sinking ship.

From Captive to Captain

The apostle Paul was clearly someone who was God-gripped for the souls of men. This is what defined his life and what he longed to impart to the Corinthian church. Yet the people of Corinth, like many people today, continued to embrace Christ solely for what they could get from Him. They were led by whatever wind seemed the softest, and away they went—even if it ended up carrying them far away from the heart of God.

Paul, on the other hand, deliberately chose to go on what he knew would prove to be a journey of hardship—one that no natural man would willingly undertake. Yet rather than disregarding a society headed for peril, Paul chose to follow the pathway that God had for his life, knowing that it would be for the benefit of many. Paul had an inner assurance that God was in full control, and that there was a purpose for everything He allowed. We will return to Paul's story later. But first, let's follow the journey of two Old Testament prophets.

A Journey All the Way to the Jordan

The Lord has called each of us on a journey with Him. You and I will always have a choice—we can either stay the full course of the journey, no matter what difficulties arise along the way, or we can choose to opt out. The prophet Elisha was presented with this choice when the Lord was ready to take Elijah to heaven.

> And Elijah said unto Elisha, Tarry here, I pray thee; for the LORD hath sent me to Bethel. And Elisha said unto

> him, As the LORD liveth, and as thy soul liveth, I will not leave thee. So they went down to Bethel (2 Kings 2:2).

Many biblical scholars believe that Elijah was a type of Christ. If you study his life, you will be able to draw countless parallels to the Messiah. In this passage, however, Elijah can also be seen as a type of man who has known the anointing of God and has come to the final steps of his journey where he is ready to pass on the baton to someone coming after him. But Elisha said, "As the LORD lives, and as your soul lives, I will not leave you!" (v. 2, *NKJV*).

It would do us well today to emulate Elisha's importunity, saying, "Lord, I am not leaving this journey. I am not opting out; I am not going to look for the easy way out." Sadly, I believe many will get to the throne of grace one day only to find out what they could have been—what God would have done through their life had they not chosen to stop short of the full journey.

So Elijah and Elisha set out, first toward Bethel—home to many young prophets and scholars. As they saw Elijah coming with Elisha on his coattails, they warned Elisha, "Do you not know that you are going to lose your master this day?" In other words, "This journey you are on will result in loss; we are not willing to undertake this journey with you. There is going to be hardship, and your heart is going to be broken." So speak the scholars who study the journey—they historically know all about it, but they will not go to where the blessing of God really is.

After Bethel, Elijah and Elisha passed by Jericho, a place where there had once been a great victory. You remember the story in Joshua 6. Now Jericho represents a people who do not go any further; they live on the laurels of a past victory. If asked for a testimony, they would stand up and share what happened back in 1971. It may be a wonderful testimony indeed. However, we are not called to camp on past successes. We are not to build a wall around an experience and stay there.

The prophets from Jericho came out and taunted Elisha with the same words: "Do you not know that on this journey you are going to lose your master? Do you not know that there is going to be loss? Do you not know that there is going to be heartache?"

How many people hear words like these and decide to turn back? God calls them to keep pressing on, but they refuse. They may instead go to an altar or to their Bibles to study some more, and there may even be a stirring in them. The Holy Spirit continues to bring to the forefront the very purpose for which they were created. Nevertheless, they refuse to make the journey—they simply will not go. They choose to stay and camp around a past experience. "This is enough. I have gone farther than others, so I do not need to go any farther."

Elijah and Elisha persisted on the journey and finally came to the Jordan, a place which typifies dying to oneself to live again in Christ. When they arrived, 50 of the students of the prophets came out to view them from afar—those who were willing to watch and examine the life of others, but w unwilling to join them. They stayed back a distance, for the did not want to make it too obvious that they were unwilling to cross over into the life of God through Christ.

They watched as Elijah parted the waters of death and the two of them crossed over on dry ground. When Elijah was lifted up into the air in the chariot and horses of fire, his mantle fell to Elisha. This is a picture of when Christ ascended to heaven and, shortly after, the Holy Spirit descended on the day of Pentecost. This "mantle" of God's life, God's grace and Christ's suffering was picked up by the original 120 disciples that were in the Upper Room (see Acts 2).

As Elisha struck the waters with the mantle of Elijah, they parted once again and he crossed back over. On his way back into Jericho, he encountered the prophets who would not make the journey with him. These prophets of Jericho said to Elisha, "Behold, I pray thee, the situation of this city is pleasant, as my lord seeth: but the water is naught, and the ground barren" (2 Kings 2:19). Historians say that there was something in the water that was causing trees to bear fruit, but the fruit would be cast off the tree before anybody could pick and eat it. Other scholars go a step further and say there was evidence of miscarrying wombs as well.

In Jericho, they blamed it on the water. Yet here we have a picture of a place where people are offered hope, but before anyone can eat of that hope, it falls to the ground. People are made to feel that new life is within them, but before the new life comes forth, it dies in the womb. How much of this is just as commonly seen in our generation? How much of what is spoken in God's name are just empty promises?

Elisha, the one who was willing to make the journey, was able to enter this place and usher in healing (see 2 Kings 2:19-22). There was salt in the vessel that he used to heal the waters, and that salt is a symbol of bringing not only healing but also thirst. If you are truly in Christ, you will create a thirst in people's lives for what you have. There is something in those who know God that creates a thirst for God in others.

On his way back to Bethel, Elisha ran into a group of youths who ridiculed him (It is a good sign when a backslidden society begins to ridicule you, for Jesus Himself said it is evidence that His life is in you). They called to him, "Go up, thou bald head; go up, thou bald head" (2 Kings 2:23). In other words, if you have the power of God on you now, let us see you go up to heaven like Elijah just went up. Of course, God took care of this mockery.

Despite constant ridicule and everything else that tried to hinder him along the way, Elisha did not hesitate to go on the full journey that God called him to. And over the course of his life, God did not hesitate to release the miraculous.

A Journey Through the Storm

Clearly aware that the ship was headed for destruction, the apostle Paul nevertheless chose to obey God's call and make the journey to Rome. He was a prisoner at the time, but he certainly still could have opted out. He could have used his influence, perhaps sending a note to a leader in the Sanhedrin. But for the sake of Christ and for the sake of the will of God for his life, Paul chose to finish his course alongside people who refused to heed his warnings. So off they went, the south wind blowing softly, everyone perceiving it to be a favorable voyage.

Perhaps lately you have found yourself in a similar situation. You have been trying to speak to your family, urging them to be prepared for the difficult days to come. You have been warning your children not to hang around with bad company. But nobody will listen to you because the wind is blowing softly and all appears to be smooth sailing. They have a vision of endless joy awaiting them in the coming days.

> But not long after there arose against it a tempestuous wind, called Euroclydon. And when the ship was caught, and could not bear up into the wind, we let her drive (Acts 27:14-15).

One minute it was a south wind blowing softly, and the next it was a violent windstorm! Can you imagine how miserable it must have been in the bottom of that ship? Paul was chained up in the belly of that ship along with the other prisoners, forced to endure what must have been a putrid stench from the excrement and other refuse floating in the water that seeped into the ship by that point. All around him the slaves were most likely ranting and raving about the fact that they were not guilty, that they did not deserve to be there.

Don't you think Paul was tempted to be at least slightly bitter? It would have been easy for him to join the chorus of discontentment down in the belly of unspeakable hardship.

When you find yourself in such a place, or perhaps if you are there right now, beware! Beware that this type of spirit does not poison you along with every bitter soul around you. I can picture Paul beginning instead to pray—the only one down there who makes a right choice and begins to seek God. Remember, he would not have even been in this place if it weren't for the ignorance of these men. Even so, Paul was praying for deliverance—for the slaves, for the sinners, for the spiritually ignorant and for those who had brought him into such hardship. God had shown Paul that this journey was going to end in disaster, so Paul was praying for mercy. Jesus said to pray for your enemies, pray for those who despitefully use you, pray for those who are on a journey that is going to cost them.

So how did God answer Paul's prayer? The storm got worse! More precisely, it was a storm unbeatable except by the power of God. Quite often the Lord will answer prayer in a way that you and I never anticipated. The mariners were now trying to hold the ship together with ropes and every other strategy known to the natural mind. But it was all falling apart, and everybody knew it.

> And we being exceedingly tossed with a tempest, the next day they lightened the ship; and the third day we cast out with our own hands the tackling of the

> ship. And when neither sun nor stars in many days appeared, and no small tempest lay on us, all hope that we should be saved was then taken away (Acts 27:18-20).

All human effort and capabilities were clearly inadequate to save this ship. It was at this point of sheer hopelessness that I can picture the captain crying, "Get me that man who said we should not be taking this journey—the one who warned us that we would find ourselves in great peril very soon. I want to hear what that man has to say!"

Suddenly Paul finds himself on the deck, standing with a word of exhortation, standing there giving the orders. This time people were listening. He was no longer captive but captain of the ship!

Around midnight of the fourteenth night, they sensed that they were approaching land, and they began to drop anchors for fear of running into the rocks. A few sailors headed to the front of the ship, pretending that they were going to put down some more anchors. But Paul, aware that they were actually intending to lower the lifeboat and head for shore on their own, strictly admonished the centurion and soldiers, "Except these abide in the ship, ye cannot be saved" (v. 31).

What that really meant was: cut off the lifeboat! And that is exactly what the soldiers did—they cut the ropes and off went the lifeboat! You see, there is no back door to this journey, no easy way out. It is solely faith in the Word of God that will see you through the storm. All schemes, all plans, all natural abilities and instincts must be abandoned. Only the power of God is going to get you through your journey. You must listen to what God is speaking.

Then Paul does something incredible:

> And while the day was coming on, Paul besought them all to take meat, saying, This day is the fourteenth day that ye have tarried and continued fasting, having taken nothing. Wherefore I pray you to take some meat: for this is for your health: for there shall not an hair fall from the head of any of you. And when he had thus spoken, he took bread, and gave thanks to God in presence of them all: and when he had broken it, he began to eat. Then were they all of good cheer, and they also took some meat (vv. 33-36).

Can you feel it? The waves are crashing, the ship is being tossed to and fro, and the tackling is gone. All hope, except for what God offers, is overboard. And here is Paul, initiating a communion service! He begins to break bread and give thanks. I imagine the prayer of his heart was, "God, thank you for your faithfulness. Thank you that not only am I still on the journey, but you have given me all these souls sailing with me!" They were all promised to come through to victory–all who had abused Paul, who had mocked him, who hated him, who refused to listen to him. And now Paul is thanking God, keenly aware that all of this had to happen, all of this had to be endured, in order for these 276 people to be able to hear the Word of God.

I wonder if in these last days God has a Church—one to whom He can point to and say to this generation, "Look! This is My Body which is broken for you. This is My Body that has endured your ridicule and suffered abuse at your hands. But this Body allowed her own strength and her own ambitions to be broken on this journey for a society living in spiritual ignorance. This Body allowed herself to be broken for you."

Where did Paul learn some of the most profound truths that he later penned? It was in situations like being chained in the belly of a ship, that's where! It was in the dark, difficult places that he got to know God's sustaining power, and this is why Paul could stand in the midst of a raging storm and give thanks. He heard God's call and went. And throughout the difficult journey of his life, Paul wrote. How could he have known that a divine hand was over his hand? How could Paul have known that he was writing most of what we would know to be our New Testament? How could he have known that he was writing into your life and mine?

Enough Wood to Go Around

We are living in a time very similar to Paul's situation on the ship. As a society, we have employed every device we could think of in attempts to keep everything together, yet all this has done is drive us further away from God. Now everything is starting to fall apart all around us.

All the while, you find yourself caught in the belly of this society that is traveling so far away from God. You go to work and face the most unspeakable evil—dirty jokes, reviling remarks about your Savior and Lord. You rub shoulders with people who seem to be such God haters and who are moving in a direction you know is going to bring about disaster.

There is a great storm brewing that is about to break out over this world, yet not everyone recognizes it. We are coming into the last days in the very way that Christ spoke about them. He said we will be led to a place where men's hearts are going to fail them for fear of what will come.

And suddenly when the storm hits, when all hell breaks out in this world, those who once rejected you will finally be ready to listen, just like those on the ship were ready to heed the words of Paul. Neighbors who have laughed at you, and your kids who thought you were old-fashioned will suddenly come to you and say, "Listen, I would like to hear again what you have to say."

Notice that when Paul and the crew had nearly reached land and the ship was breaking up, the instructions essentially were, "Those of you who can swim, throw yourselves overboard and make for shore. For those of you who cannot swim, there will be lots of wood to go around very soon. Grab a piece of wood and kick with your feet. Everyone will make it safely to shore!" (see Acts 27:43-44).

Just as the non-swimmers were told that there would be plenty of wood to save them, the message to this last generation is going to be that the cross is big enough! There is plenty of wood from the cross! Those who lay hold of it, throwing their complete dependence on it, will find the fullness of God's redemption. Jesus was crucified on that cross, rose from the dead, and now He sits at the right hand of God—far above every name that is named and above all power and authority (see Eph. 1:20-21). He is above fear, every disaster, every concern about the future. And so we are to implore this generation to lay hold of the cross in the midst of the storm, and they will surely make it safely to the other side.

Strength for the Days Ahead

Do you know where you learn that you can do all things through Christ? *In the storm.* Just like Paul, you come to know the strength of Christ when you are led into places where natural abilities can no longer sustain you. Your natural love, natural skills and natural wisdom cannot sustain you in the storm. It is a journey that is too hard—it is something that has to come from God.

Paul broke bread on that ship and told everyone to eat, for they would need strength to go on. I believe this is what the Lord is telling us today as well: Go and get your strength now! You will surely need it in the coming days, for this journey is going to be tough. Dig in and eat—get your strength from the Word of God.

As you choose to seek to know God and find His strength now, very soon the knocks will be coming to your door. People in your office who are desperately afraid of losing their jobs are going to come over to your desk and ask the reason for the hope that is in you. Soon you, too, will no longer be the captive, but the captain! You will be able to tell others, "This is the way out—here is what you need to do. This is what God says!"

Remember, there is always a divine purpose for everything that you have to go through. If you were wondering why you have been in the midst of a personal storm lately, it is because the Lord is about to bring people your way. He has allowed the suffering and the trials in your life for the sake of others, just like He did in Paul's life. So learn to trust God now. Take the full journey. Don't opt out; He has designed it specifically for you!

Grinding in the Prison House

Satan's plan to make the Church ineffective has always been to turn the supernatural into the natural—to have the power of God, which is most clearly understood through the preaching of the cross, fade into the background. The enemy does this by attempting to take away the spiritual vision of every true believer in Christ and instead moving him or her into profitless labor—a place where there is no outflow of the supernatural and therefore little threat to his kingdom.

Now Paul knew biblical history, and he was familiar with the patterns and plans of the devil. After all, it was Paul himself who wrote, "We are not ignorant of Satan's devices" (see 2 Cor. 2:11). I am sure he must have considered these things when he wrote to the church of Corinth: "But I fear, lest somehow, as the serpent deceived Eve by his craftiness, so your minds may be corrupted from the simplicity that is in Christ" (2 Cor. 11:3, *NKJV*).

As a spiritual father, Paul was desperately concerned about the spiritual condition of the Corinthian church. He knew that they were being drawn away from the simplicity of Christ and had instead opened their heart to deception. He essentially told them, "I brought something of the Savior to you. I brought you to an understanding of where true power in the Christian life lies. It is not in gathering to yourself, it is in allowing the life of God to flow through you to others. But if you turn from this simplicity in Christ and open your heart to another way, you will be left powerless."

How many of us need this same reminder today? There is a simplicity that is in Christ. Incredible power is available when we surrender to God. Now, Satan knows this. He knows we have the power of God at our disposal—a strength far superior to his own with the potential to take his kingdom down. In fact, he lives in fear of the day when somebody realizes this and rises up out of complacency. He knows what can happen to his kingdom when a boy like D. L. Moody, a young prankster who could barely read or write, comes to Christ through a Sunday School teacher and decides to give his all to God. Thousands of people in the years after Moody came to Christ would have their lives transformed through the message of this bumbling, stumbling preacher who could hardly pronounce the word "Jerusalem."

Satan knows that he must do something in order to hold the people of God captive and render them powerless. Therefore he goes after the one thing that he knows will make believers as weak as other men if they yield to it. It is what he is after in you and me today. And if he can get it, we will end up just as powerless as every other person in society. Let's look at a classic example of his strategy in action.

Samson's Story

In the Book of Judges, we find the story of Samson—a mighty, anointed man of God who was called to bring deliverance to the people of Israel. When the angel of God initially appeared to Samson's mother, he told her, "For, lo, thou shalt conceive, and bear a son; and no razor shall come on his head: for the child shall be a Nazarite unto God from the womb: and he shall begin to deliver Israel out of the hand of the Philistines" (Judg. 13:5).

Samson was set apart to God from birth. Throughout the story of Samson, at least three times the Bible says "the Spirit of the Lord came upon him in power." His mighty physical strength came straight from God! Yet despite the incredible call on his life and the demonstration of God's power that he experienced time and again, Samson eventually allowed himself to be seduced. Proverbs 5:7-10 speaks of the spiritual condition to which Samson succumbed:

> Hear me now therefore, O ye children, and depart not from the words of my mouth. Remove thy way far from her, and come not nigh the door of her house: lest thou give thine honour unto others, and thy years unto the cruel: lest strangers be filled with thy wealth; and thy labours be in the house of a stranger.

The "her" in these passages speaks about a seductive religion. In the case of Samson, her name was Delilah, and he fell in love with her.

Now Samson was anointed with such great strength that he could not be held with any form of cord that this world could produce. Delilah sought to discover his secret in order that she might reveal it to the Philistines in exchange for silver. "And Delilah said to Samson, Tell me, I pray thee, wherein thy great strength lieth, and wherewith thou mightest be bound to afflict thee" (Judg. 16:6).

Samson knew the source—He knew that he was set apart to God from the moment of his birth. Nevertheless, he began to play a very dangerous game with Delilah. Samson said to her, "If I were tied up with seven new bowstrings that have not yet been dried, I would become as weak as anyone else" (Judg. 16:7, *NLT*). Now Samson had an inner knowledge that he could not be bound by any multitude of new devices. This represents any new battles, new trials or strategies that one has not faced before.

Today the devil will try to tell you that he has you bound. He will send you a battle that you have never faced before and tell you that you will not get through it. But Christ has already triumphed! He has broken all the cords of sin; He has broken every power of hell. There is no new struggle, there is no new battle that can bind you and take away the strength of God in you.

The seven bow strings did not keep Samson bound, so Delilah persisted and asked him again about the source of his strength. Samson said to her, "If I were tied up with brand-new ropes that had never been used, I would become as weak as anyone else" (v. 11, *NLT*). However, he knew that even the greatest of the proven strengths of this world would not work, for with the anointing of God on him, he could not be kept bound.

The third time she asked, Samson told Delilah, "If you were to weave the seven braids of my hair into the fabric on your loom and tighten it with the loom shuttle, I would become as weak as anyone else" (v. 13, *NLT*). The Philistines could try to tie his head down, but Samson knew that this, too, would be to no avail. This alludes to the fact that we as believers cannot be defeated in our mind. That is where the arguments come, and that is where the devil would try to tie us down. But as we stay in the Word of truth and know our identity in Christ, we will not be defeated.

Delilah pressed Samson daily with her words, urging and vexing him until he finally divulged the truth.

> That he told her all his heart, and said unto her, There hath not come a razor upon mine head; for I have been a Nazarite unto God from my mother's womb: if I be shaven, then my strength will go from me, and I shall become weak, and be like any other man (v. 17).

Here was what the devil was after all along—what Samson finally revealed to this seductive spirit in the form of Delilah: "If my separation to God for the purpose of freeing others from oppression is willfully or unwittingly forfeited, then I will become as weak as any other man." And that is exactly what happened to him.

When we lose our separation to God and begin to use God's anointing for ourselves, we lose the power of God. When our whole focus of coming to church is "What can I get out of God today," we are more like the world than separate from it. We have lost the understanding that we are not called to be and think like a world that is living for itself. We are called to be separated to God and empowered by His Spirit.

The apostle Paul fought hard for the Corinthians to maintain their separation to God, but many refused. As the Lord said to the prophet Ezekiel, "They come, they listen, you are like a sweet song being played on a trumpet, but they will not do it. They will not walk there, although they know it is truth" (see Ezek. 33:32). In other words, as long as we know where truth is, we can go out and play our games for another week, another two weeks; we can live for ourselves. But if things get really tough, we know where to find truth. We know where we can come back to; we know how to get it right someday. But for now, we go out and lose our separation to God. That is the game Samson played, and it ultimately cost him everything. Judges 16:18-21 tells us what happened next:

> And when Delilah saw that he had told her all his heart, she sent and called for the lords of the Philistines, saying, Come up this once, for he hath shewed me all his heart. Then the lords of the Philistines came up unto her, and brought money in their hand. And she made him sleep upon her knees; and she called for a man, and she caused him to shave off the seven locks of his head; and she began to afflict him, and his strength went from him. And she said, The Philistines be upon thee, Samson. And he awoke out of his sleep, and said, I will go out as at other times before, and shake myself. And he wist not that the LORD was departed from

> him. But the Philistines took him, and put out his eyes, and brought him down to Gaza, and bound him with fetters of brass; and he did grind in the prison house.

Samson lost his separation unto God, and the anointing was taken away. He ended up blind, grinding in the prison house. A classic snapshot of spiritual blindness and profitless labor . . . Satan had him right where he wanted him!

A Seductive Religion

It is our separation to God that the enemy is after, and to a large extent he has succeeded. That is why we are living in a weak and emaciated Church age. No wonder society can pass by the doors of most churches in America today and not even give a second thought as to what is going on inside. They recognize that the value system is the same inside that door as it is outside. There is nothing in the church that confronts the ungodliness of the surrounding society.

In attempts to take away this separation to God, Satan will always send a form of seductive and enticing religion. Think about Delilah coming to Samson, pleading with him until his soul was vexed. What amazes me is that it was not even hidden—she overtly said, "Show me the source of your strength. I want to take it away!" And although Samson knew that she was ratting him out to the Philistines, he still continued to play this dangerous game. Similarly, how many of us say, "Just once more," or "I'll start tomorrow?" We know what truth is, but we still go home and turn on Delilah one more time because it makes us feel good. We are usually aware that it is a seductive spirit in pursuit of us. We know it is going after the source of the life of Christ in us, yet we play this dangerous game anyway.

Let's look at another picture of this seductive religion that comes to take away the anointing of God from the Church of Jesus Christ. The book of Proverbs describes this spirit as a harlot who seduces a young man:

> Passing through the street near her corner; and he went the way to her house. . . . And, behold, there met him a woman with the attire of an harlot, and subtil of heart. . . . So she caught him, and kissed him, and with an impudent face said unto him, I have peace offerings with me; this day have I payed my vows. . . . I have decked my bed with coverings of tapestry, with carved works, with fine linen of Egypt. I have perfumed my bed with myrrh, aloes, and cinnamon. Come, let us take our fill of love until the morning: let us solace ourselves with loves (Prov. 7:8-18).

This seductive spirit catches the man and says she has peace offerings; she has paid her vows. In other words, "I have a relationship with God. I know the way to peace." She further entices him and says, "Let's just focus on ourselves and do the things we love to do." That is the basic theology of the seductive spirit.

> Hearken unto me now therefore, O ye children, and attend to the words of my mouth. Let not thine heart decline to her ways, go not astray in her paths. For she hath cast down many wounded: yea, many strong men have been slain by her. Her house is the way to hell, going down to the chambers of death (vv. 24-27).

Today there are thousands sitting in churches under a seductive spirit—one that is using the name of Jesus Christ yet causing the people to turn from a focus on God to a focus on themselves. These are people who should be strong and mighty in God, but instead they have been slain by this seductive spirit. Everything that God intended them to be is now forfeited. Instead they sit there glassy-eyed, watching star-spangled preachers stand before them with a theological perspective that is entirely contrary to that which is found in Christ. Their strength has been depleted, but they do not know it. They are simply grinding grain in a prison house, going around and around with profitless works. There is no spiritual vision and no outflow of the supernatural.

What a tragedy! These are people who were destined to do something for God. They should be on the mission field; they should be walking with God; they should be living in the supernatural. But they have been deceived. They have no discernment, for they have walked into a house of a spiritual harlot and are now focused on themselves. This is exactly where the church of Corinth was headed, and that is why Paul battled desperately to get the Corinthians to see exactly what was at stake.

Rise Up, O Church!

Fortunately, that does not have to be the end of the story. Consider Samson once more. After Samson's eyes were gouged out and he was confined to grinding in the prison house, Scripture says that the hair of his head began to grow again.

The devil had been having a party over Samson's head. He was enjoying this triumph, gathering together the hordes of Philistines that were given to darkness, and laughing over the balcony as he looked down at Samson who was supposed to be the deliverer with the anointing to bring the people of God out of captivity. Satan was thoroughly enjoying Samson's vulnerability. The Philistine lords even called together 3,000 people who were of like spirit to watch Samson in his defeat as they praised their god Dagon.

> And when the people saw him, they praised their god: for they said, Our god hath delivered into our hands our enemy, and the destroyer of our country, which slew many of us. And it came to pass, when their hearts were merry, that they said, Call for Samson, that he may make us sport. And they called for Samson out of the prison house; and he made them

sport: and they set him between the pillars (Judg. 16:24-25).

But all the while, not only was Samson's hair growing, he was growing tired of the mockery. I believe a similar thing is happening in our generation today. People are tired—tired of the conferences and seminars. They are tired of hearing about the power of God yet never attaining it. Tired of going nowhere, tired of grinding, tired of the devil mocking them at every turn. But just as Samson's hair was growing, I see a people coming back—returning to their separation unto God.

When blind Samson came into the house, he said to the lad that held him by the hand, "Suffer me that I may feel the pillars whereupon the house standeth, that I may lean upon them" (v. 26). There were two pillars that held this house up: *worship of the false* and *mockery of the true*. As the 3,000 Philistines on the roof of the house praised their god who delivered Samson into their hands, Samson called to the Lord one more time and said, "Let me die with the Philistines!" (v. 30). Samson had grown tired of the mockery and sacrificed his life in order for the power of God to be revealed through him one more time!

Pull Down the Pillars

There is a generation rising up today that is doing the same thing as Samson. They are asking, "Where are the pillars of this mockery that allow what is evil to exalt itself above that which is good—the pillars that allow ungodly people to make fun of the Church of Jesus Christ as if we had no power; to laugh as if there is no consequence to living in sin; to live as if they will never stand before a holy God to be judged? Show me the pillars of this house that I might bring them down!"

Abandoning oneself to the purposes of God is where the power of God lies. That is where the anointing of the Holy Spirit is found and where the glory of God is manifested. When Samson finally refocused on the true source of his power, he called out to God to enable him to bring down the pillars and destroy what had been given over to Satan. No more grinding in the prison house for Samson; no more walking around without spiritual vision. The moment he pulled down the pillars, Samson died to himself and lived for the honor and purposes of God.

This is what we as a church age must do. We have to realize where the power of God really lies. It is not manifested in people who live for themselves, but in those who die to themselves. Jesus said, unless the seed falls into the ground and dies, it will abide alone; but if it dies, it will bear much fruit (see John 12:24). Jesus also said, If you seek to gain your life, you are going to lose it (see Luke 9:24). He is not talking about physical life; He is talking about what He has for you. He is talking about the glory of God, the power of God, the ability that God gives you to reach out in the supernatural and do things you cannot do in your own strength.

The Party Is Over

Hell may be having a party over your head right now. The devil may be laughing. He may be trying to bind you with new battles or by bringing back old struggles.

Just as it was with Samson, it is time for you to cancel that party! That is what Samson did. He grabbed hold of those pillars and brought them down, saying, "The party is over. You have laughed at my God long enough!"

The only way we can do this is by laying hold of God's purposes for our life. Jesus Christ did not come to this world and die so that we, through Him, could fulfill our own desires. He bought us with the price of His blood. We are no longer our own; we are rightfully owned by the Son of God. He has the right to use our lives as He sees fit.

Like Samson, we must make the choice to be willing to die to self and live for the honor of God. It is the only way we can bring down the powerless mockery that abounds today. We are called to bring freedom and victory to other people. It is time for us to stop grinding in the prison house. It is time once again to be separated to the purposes of God that we might live in the supernatural!

The Tabernacle of David

The incredible sense of heaviness enshrouding our world today has sent many in search of something to lighten their hearts. Unfortunately the majority, even among Christians, are looking in the wrong places. If only they knew that the Lord is speaking something in this hour that offers His people absolute freedom . . . a freedom that can only be found as they embrace the truth. It is not good feeling that sets the church of Jesus Christ free; it is the truth. Truth digs; truth challenges; truth goes underneath foundations that are not built in Christ and tears them down, and then truth builds. Truth gives an anointing and brings strength. "And ye shall know the truth, and the truth shall make you free" (John 8:32). Paul longed to bring the Corinthian church into this freedom. That is why he spoke to them as a spiritual father, constantly showing them a picture of their true spiritual condition.

> Moreover, brethren, I would not that ye should be ignorant, how that all our fathers were under the cloud, and all passed through the sea. . . . And did all eat the same spiritual meat; and did all drink the same spiritual drink: for they drank of that spiritual Rock that followed them: and that Rock was Christ. But with many of them God was not well pleased: for they were overthrown in the wilderness. Now these things were our examples, to the intent we should not lust after evil things, as they also lusted. Neither be ye idolaters, as were some of them; as it is written, The people sat down to eat and drink, and rose up to play. Neither let us com-

> mit fornication, as some of them committed, and fell in one day three and twenty thousand. Neither let us tempt Christ, as some of them also tempted, and were destroyed of serpents. Neither murmur ye, as some of them also murmured, and were destroyed of the destroyer. Now all these things happened unto them for examples: and they are written for our admonition, upon whom the ends of the world are come (1 Cor. 10:1-11).

Although they had a clear revelation of God, we see that the Children of Israel still chose to embrace certain types of destructive behavior. The Scripture indicates that all the while, Christ followed them. They were able to drink of that life that Paul said was Christ. Yet they tempted Christ, bringing upon themselves not only weakness but a great and encroaching judgment. Just as Paul set this story before the Corinthians as an example to them, it equally serves as an example to us today. Remember, such accounts were recorded in the Scriptures for our admonition, upon whom the end of the world will come.

> Wherefore let him that thinketh he standeth take heed lest he fall. There hath no temptation taken you but such as is common to man: but God is faithful, who will not suffer you to be tempted above that ye are able; but will with the temptation also make a way to escape, that ye may be able to bear it. Wherefore, my dearly beloved, flee from idolatry (1 Cor. 10:12-14).

Paul told the Corinthians that they, too, would be tempted to do the very same things that the Children of Israel did. It is an inherent flaw in all of fallen humanity; a condition of the human heart that departs from the simplicity of living for God in Christ. But, he told them, your spiritual condition is not such that you cannot escape it. You cannot be overcome if it is in your heart to walk in truth.

Christ triumphed over all of these failings and sins, and He will be faithful to keep you from that which brought others in the past to spiritual defeat. You have a resident power within you, and God will not allow you to be tempted or tested above what you can bear. The devil will come and say, "Try this," or "Complain against these people," or "Reach out and grab this." He may come at you with a theology straight from hell to try to lure you away from the simplicity that is in your life in Christ. But Paul says that if you will turn to God, He will make a way for you to escape it.

Notice that in verse 14, Paul says, "Wherefore, my beloved, flee from idolatry." The word "idolatry" in this verse refers to everything that has its roots in setting your own judgment and thoughts above that which God has already clearly spoken. So in other words, flee from making yourself God! Flee from exalting your knowledge above the knowledge of God. Flee from trying to reason everything, from creating another Christ that makes an easier way for you. Flee from all of this idolatry, and trust God to bring you through. You and I will need to have this trust to get through the days we are living in and the days yet to come.

Perhaps it would be helpful to take a look at another account in the Old Testament—this, too, recorded to serve as an example . . . a type and shadow of where the Body of Christ has come to in this generation.

Don't Prophesy Here!

The book of Amos (eighth-century B.C.) shows us the spiritual condition of a people just prior to the judgment of God that was coming to their nation. God raised up an ordinary man, a shepherd from Tekoa, to warn His people.

> And he [the Lord] said, Amos, what seest thou? And I said, A basket of summer fruit. Then said the LORD unto me, The end is come upon my people of Israel; I will not again pass by them any more (Amos 8:2).

The Lord said, "I have tried, I have sent voices, I have warned." Of course there comes a time when we do not expect the nation to hear; we do not expect the ungodly to listen. After all, it is the Church that God speaks to. However, it often seems to be the case that when society has degenerated to a certain point, even those who claim to believe in God are no longer willing to listen. Instead, they have settled into a form of worship they find very satisfying and pleasing, and so they will not be moved, even if Christ Himself were to stand and preach in their midst.

It was during such a season that God raised up Amos to speak to the people. Now first of all, why would anybody even listen to Amos? He was just an ordinary man. He had no pedigree or list of degrees behind his name; he had no litany of successes. He was just an ordinary shepherd sent by God to speak to the people. As expected, the people were highly offended that this man would come in and begin to challenge their spiritual bankruptcy.

All through history this has been the pattern. So God said, "I will not pass by them again anymore." To me, that is the most fearsome statement; it is the most tragic place that a person who claims to know God could ever find himself or herself—when God says, "I am not coming to you anymore. I am not speaking to you anymore. You have hardened your heart to the point that you don't want to hear, so I will no longer speak to you. I will give you only what you want to hear."

> And the songs of the temple shall be howlings in that day, saith the Lord God: there shall be many dead bodies in every place; they shall cast them forth with silence (Amos 8:3).

The Lord says there is going to be a stunned silence that will come to these people. Suddenly all the voices that were not speaking for God will be at a loss for what to say. The songs that were purported to be praise to God will be gone. Only that which cannot be shaken will remain.

However, in such a season, the true follower of Christ can take comfort in the promise: "You will have a song in the night," (see Isa. 30:29). We must realize that this song does not come when the trial starts and the darkness has already set in; it is born long before. The Hebrew boys in the fiery furnace had that song before they were thrust into a time of difficulty. In the same way, you have to get the song now; you cannot get it in the day of trouble. You must determine in your heart that no matter what happens, you are going to learn who God is. You are going to walk with Christ; you are going to praise Him with all your heart. You are not going to hold back or close your heart to the Lord, settling in at some halfway place to salvation. You are going to seek God now, and you are going to find His will for your life and your generation.

> Hear this, O ye that swallow up the needy, even to make the poor of the land to fail, saying, When will the new moon be gone, that we may sell corn? And the sabbath, that we may set forth wheat, making the ephah small, and the shekel great, and falsifying the balances by deceit? (Amos 8:4-5).

These people were anxious to leave the presence of the Lord so that they could continue in commerce. They wanted to get back to what their lives were really all about—getting gain by any means, including that which was against the law of the nation and the law of God. They justified living a life all for self, no matter what had to be done. Today it would be like those who sit in church on Sunday, yet all the while they are watching the time, counting down until the service is over so they can get back to what is really gripping their hearts.

> That we may buy the poor for silver, and the needy for a pair of shoes; yea, and sell the refuse of the wheat (v. 6).

Here we see the indictment of God against this people. He said, "You are using every man for personal advantage. As a matter of fact, you are trampling on the heads of the poor and needy in your quest to pursue things that are not even lasting!"

> Woe to them that are at ease in Zion, and trust in the mountain of Samaria, which are named chief of the nations, to whom the house of Israel came! Ye that put far away the evil day, and cause the seat of violence to come near (Amos 6:1,3).

This is a spiritual climate that puts the righteous judgment of God far away—one marked by scoffers walking after their own lusts, challenging the idea of the soon return of Christ. They will continue to buy, sell and get gain, living like they did in the days of Noah—as if Christ were not coming. But the Scripture says that He comes suddenly, like a thief in the night (see 2 Pet. 3:4-10).

> That lie upon beds of ivory, and stretch themselves upon their couches, and eat the lambs out of the flock, and the calves out of the midst of the stall; that chant to

> the sound of the viol, and invent to themselves instruments of musick, like David (Amos 6:4-5).

In other words, they focus on personal ease and the incomplete worship that accompanies it. Notice that it says they have to invent worship for themselves—a type of worship that does not confront their spiritual bankruptcy. Haven't you heard some of this in our own generation? In certain places, some of the songs are completely devoid of any spiritual, doctrinal or musical sense—not to mention rather annoying as well! This worship is merely an invention of hearts that do not really want to go with God. Living a Christ-centered life requires more, and so worship is invented.

> That drink wine in bowls, and anoint themselves with the chief ointments: but they are not grieved for the affliction of Joseph (v. 6).

They were preoccupied with personal joy and anointing. Sure, they didn't mind lying on a couch and singing beautiful songs about how much they loved God. But as for entering into the work of God? No, thank you. These people were not at all grieved for the affliction of Joseph—for the brother sold off into slavery and suffering unjustly. They put this out of their conscience, and subsequently their whole sense of worship was a fraud.

> Therefore now shall they go captive with the first that go captive, and the banquet of them that stretched themselves shall be removed (v. 7).

They were completely unaware of their true spiritual position. The Lord says, when judgment comes, these are going first. I am going to remove them. I have to take them out of my house because they are an abomination to truth.

> Also Amaziah said unto Amos, O thou seer, go, flee thee away into the land of Judah, and there eat bread, and prophesy there: But prophesy not again any more at Bethel: for it is the king's chapel, and it is the king's court (Amos 7:12-13).

God did all that He could to warn the people through Amos, but the end result was a multitude of voices raised against Amos, saying, "Don't prophesy here at Bethel. This is where we worship; this is where truth is; we have the history. We are on a spiritual journey to be blessed and we do not want you interrupting us!"

So what happens when people choose to ignore the warnings that God sends? The Lord paints a picture for us in the following chapter of Amos.

> And I will turn your feasts into mourning, and all your songs into lamentation; and I will bring up sackcloth upon all loins, and baldness upon every head; and I will make it as the mourning of an only son, and the end thereof as a bitter day. Behold, the days come, saith the Lord GOD, that I will send a famine in the land, not a famine of bread, nor a thirst

> for water, but of hearing the words of the LORD: And they shall wander from sea to sea, and from the north even to the east, they shall run to and fro to seek the word of the LORD, and shall not find it. In that day shall the fair virgins and young men faint for thirst. They that swear by the sin of Samaria, and say, Thy god, O Dan, liveth; and, The manner of Beersheba liveth; even they shall fall, and never rise up again (Amos 8:10-14).

God said He would take away their song, for they had chosen to worship at a place that fell short of the truth. There would be a famine, not of food but of hearing the true words of God. He also said that in that day the fair virgins and strong young men would faint from thirst. In other words, there was going to be a loss to the next generation.

Worship in Spirit and in Truth

Although we read all these prophesies of coming judgment and see that the response of the people ultimately resulted in their captivity, we can still take heart, for the last chapter of Amos contains an incredible promise from God:

> In that day will I raise up the tabernacle of David that is fallen, and close up the breaches thereof; and I will raise up his ruins, and I will build it as in the days of old (Amos 9:11).

The Lord was saying that He will raise up the tabernacle of David again—where His people once again seek Him in the way He ordained, in the manner that is written in His Word. What does this look like? Let's go back to a scene in the book of 2 Samuel to find out.

> So David went and brought up the ark of God from the house of Obededom into the city of David with gladness. And David danced before the LORD with all his might; and David was girded with a linen ephod (2 Sam. 6:12, 14).

Here we see David worshiping God with a worship so pure, so clean—filled with the joy of the Lord. But Michal, the daughter of the fallen kingdom of Saul, despised David's worship when she saw it. In her heart she hated the purity of the worship. It was almost as if she could endure anything except for a man truly worshiping God in spirit and in truth.

What brought David to a place of such pure worship before the Lord? Recall that David had tried to bring back the Ark of the Covenant once before, but along the procession, God had killed a man named Uzzah. David was grieved by this and said, "I was trying to bring this ark of God's presence into the center of Jerusalem, but Lord, you killed the parade. Why did you do it?"

God spoke to David, giving him a valuable revelation that he would need in order to continue walking with the

Lord. David took the truth to heart and was later able to explain the reason to the Levites, as recorded for us in 1 Chronicles 15:13: "For because ye did it not at the first, the LORD our God made a breach upon us, for that we sought him not after the due order." In other words, "There is a way that we were supposed to move the ark, a way to honor His presence, a way to walk in obedience to His Word. But we chose to operate outside of the Word of God—incorrectly and carelessly handling the truth we were given."

Maybe they felt they had a revelation or some extrabiblical knowledge that would add to the parade. But the Lord stretched forth His hand and stopped the whole thing, saying, "No, this is not spirit and truth; this is not coming into the center of Jerusalem. You will never know the fullness of My joy until you do it the way I have called you to worship Me."

Jesus said that the Father seeks people to worship Him in spirit and truth (see John 4:23). You cannot have one without the other. Now there are many who speak from the Word, which is indeed truth, but it is evident that there is no revelation, no life, no anointing of the Holy Spirit on it. Instead, what they speak is merely the product of human logic and reasoning, leaving the listeners dry. On the other hand, many others have tried to have the spirit without the truth. They have turned aside to extra-biblical revelation—a hodge-podge of false prophecy that purports to be revelation from God yet is found nowhere in the Bible. What a dangerous parade to march in.

Where God Dwells

When we read the Bible and we believe it; when we see the claims of Christ and do not shy away—this is the tabernacle of David. We see what we should be as followers of Jesus Christ, and we do not try to change or alter anything; we do not attempt to make it more palatable. To truly follow Christ means to seek first the kingdom of God and His righteousness. And the Lord says, "You go that way and I will add everything that you need. You begin to move to the needs around you, and I will open your prison doors and put clothes on your back. I will put food in your belly and a roof over your head. No matter what, just move in the direction I show you in the Word."

First Chronicles 21 gives us even further insight into this tabernacle of David. Here we find David in a place where he had to deal with the consequences of his own foolishness. He had taken a census of the number of Israelites in order to ascertain his power, resulting in the outbreak of a plague among the people. After 70,000 men of Israel had died, David saw the angel, standing by the threshing floor of Ornan the Jebusite with his sword drawn over Jerusalem.

Ornan, an ordinary man, was threshing wheat with his four sons when he looked up and saw this angel and then looked down and saw the king coming toward him. What a picture of Christ coming to his church again, coming to the ordinary man!

King David humbly came to Ornan and said, "I need what you have, but I will not take it from you for free. I will pay the full price for it." In a similar way, God comes to His Church in this hour and says, "I need what you have, and I already paid the full price for it. I paid with My blood that I might dwell within you and have you as a physical body on this side of eternity—that I may walk through you, flow through you, speak through you and touch others through you."

Now when Ornan looked up and saw judgment hanging over the city of Jerusalem and also saw David coming in humility toward him, he said, "You can have everything I have—I give it to you. I do not ask you for a thing. I see the need, and it is all yours."

Immediately, David was given a revelation. As soon as this man gave everything, David declared, "This is the house of the LORD God, and this is the altar of the burnt offering for Israel" (1 Chron. 22:1). Finally David's eyes were opened, and he realized this was what it was all about. God dwells with ordinary men like Ornan and his family—those who see the depth of the need and give the little they have in order to meet that need.

This is the tabernacle of David; this is the house of God—ordinary people like you and me. We do not have an army or military skills; we do not have the means to stop what we see as an encroaching judgment in our society today. But we also do not see ourselves the way God sees us. The Lord says, "You have exactly what I need. Just give me the little you have and watch what I am going to do with it."

Later, in David's praise to the Lord, we see what happened as a result:

> I know also, my God, that thou triest the heart, and hast pleasure in uprightness. As for me, in the uprightness of mine heart I have willingly offered all these things: and now have I seen with joy thy people, which are present here, to offer willingly unto thee (1 Chron. 29:17).

David and the people entered into a willingness to give of themselves. David was preparing to build a temple—a dwelling place for God. And as he freely gave of himself for a higher purpose, he was able to witness with joy as the people did likewise. David told them, "This is where God dwells. He dwells among a people who are willing to give to His work, not necessarily expecting anything in return. His presence is sufficient for them." David knew it was at this place that God's judgment for his sin was averted. Death was turned to life and darkness was made light again.

David then said, "O LORD God of Abraham, Isaac, and of Israel, our fathers, keep this for ever in the imagination of the thoughts of the heart of thy people, and prepare their heart unto thee" (v. 18). In other words, "Oh, God, I see this is where Your power is; this is how the plague of judgment is stopped. Please, God, keep this in the hearts of the people, not just in Israel, but in Your people forever." Perhaps David saw, in the Spirit, into our day—a day when God's people would need to be reminded that God does not dwell in a place where Christ is used for selfish gain. That is not where God's power is found, nor will it ever help to avert the encroaching darkness and judgment upon a society.

A Harvest of Souls

Jesus Christ spoke about His own life in John 10:18, "No man taketh it from me, but I lay it down of myself." Nobody takes My life—it is a free choice I am making to lay it down for the betterment of others. This same selflessness is what the Lord requires of His church, and it is the Lord Himself who will secure this in the hearts of those who are willing.

> "On that day I will raise up the tabernacle of David . . . that they may possess the remnant of Edom, and all the Gentiles who are called by My name," says the LORD who does this thing. "Behold, the days are coming," says the LORD, "When the plowman shall overtake the reaper, and the treader of grapes him who sows seed; the mountains shall drip with sweet wine, and all the hills shall flow *with* it" (Amos 9:11-13, *NKJV*).

The Lord was essentially saying that when He raises up the tabernacle of David, selfishness will finally be overcome. Edom is Esau, the one who sold his birthright for a bowl of soup. But in place of Edom will be a selfless people who will lead others into the abundance of the life of God. I see a day coming when those who disciple new converts will not be able to keep up with the people who are preaching. There will be such a harvest that we will not be able to handle the volumes of people coming into the true Church.

God says, "When I have a people who understand this tabernacle of David, who understand what it means to be in

Christ and have Christ in them; when once again I have a people who possess My heart and are able to take that heart to fallen humanity, there will be an influx and an abundance of souls coming into the kingdom of God."

All we need to do is get up and move towards the work of God, and He will raise up the tabernacle of David that is fallen—rebuilding this life and testimony of Christ, beginning in our hearts.

7

My Preaching Is Good for Nothing

Paul would have said so. And as a pastor, I gladly come to the same conclusion: *My preaching is good for nothing.* Certainly by the end of this chapter, you, too, will be in agreement.

In 1 Corinthians 2:1-5, Paul wrote to the church:

> And I, brethren, when I came to you, came not with excellency of speech or of wisdom, declaring unto you the testimony of God. For I determined not to know any thing among you, save Jesus Christ, and him crucified. And I was with you in weakness, and in fear, and in much trembling. And my speech and my preaching was not with enticing words of man's wisdom, but in demonstration of the Spirit and of power: That your faith should not stand in the wisdom of men, but in the power of God.

As we have previously concluded, the Corinthian church continued to be largely influenced by the worldly mindset of the surrounding society. It is always the case that when a church begins to be led primarily by thoughts that originate from the hearts of men, it becomes in great danger of losing the supernatural and beginning to walk only in the natural. Paul reminded the Corinthian church that their faith should not be in this human wisdom but in the power of God. It should not be possible to figure everything out, and it is not through methodologies that the life of Christ would be made manifest in them—it is through faith in what God has spoken.

> Howbeit we speak wisdom among them that are perfect: yet not the wisdom of this world. . . . But we speak the wisdom of God in a mystery, even the hidden wisdom, which God ordained before the world unto our glory (1 Cor. 2:6-7).

Paul was speaking of a wisdom that is not of this world. It is a hidden wisdom—not hidden to those who know Christ, but hidden to those who walk outside of this realm of God's life in Christ. It is a hidden wisdom that God ordained before the foundation of the world.

Did you know that God was thinking and speaking about you before the world was even formed? He was speaking things about your life—who you were going to be, how you were going to bring Him glory. The word "glory," in the Greek means that God may be brought to reputation through us. So, God was already speaking things that you cannot hear with the natural ear, but you can hear when the Holy Spirit comes into your life. He was thinking about how He would draw you and what He would make you into; where you would go and how His name would be brought to glory through your life—all before the creation of the world.

In 1 Corinthians 3:19, Paul says, "For the wisdom of this world is foolishness with God." As wise as this world can get, its wisdom is still foolishness; it still falls short of the glory of God. We cannot reason ourselves into this life that God has already bought for us through Christ. The worldly wise, Paul says, are taken in their own craftiness. That means that they are duped! It means they are sold something of significantly inferior quality.

Have you ever seen a tourist in New York City who buys a watch from someone on a street corner? The tourist walks away and brags that he bought this watch for $25. We all know you can get that watch for $8. Actually, if you hang around long enough, you can get it for $6. And, of course, the street vendor only paid $3.50 for the watch that will turn wrists green and last a month if you're lucky. But the tourist saunters down the street with his new $25 watch, talking about what a great deal he got and how smart he is.

That is what Paul says about those who come into the kingdom of God and bring this worldly mindset with them—they are duped by their own craftiness. They are walking away with a fraudulent product; they are walking out of the house of God with all these steps that have been formulated in their own minds of how to live a godly life and how to do this and how to do that. They bought something of inferior quality because they were not willing to surrender their thinking and let the Holy Spirit guide them. Listen to what Paul says in 1 Corinthians 4:19-20:

> But I will come to you shortly, if the Lord will, and will know, not the speech of them which are puffed up, but the power. For the kingdom of God is not in word, but in power.

Paul was saying that true wisdom does not come with puffed-up speech but with power. The word "power" in the

Greek means divine enablement. There is a divine enablement that accompanies the wisdom from God.

When God speaks to us and faith arises in our hearts—when we begin to agree with God no matter how impossible it may seem—we are given a divine enablement. In other words, we are made into something by God's grace and power that we could never hope to be in ourselves. Paul said it is not found in fine speech. Remember, the Corinthian church was falling prey to very charismatic, gifted speakers, but these speakers preached empty words. All they could do was lead the people into a deeper naturalness—a deeper pathway of human reasoning that would prove to be powerless.

Paul said that he would rather come to them in weakness. He was aware of the fact that God chose him not for his eloquence, but for his willingness to stand before the Corinthians in fear and trembling. He did not need letters of commendation from men. He knew that the power of God was being perfected in his weakness, and therefore something supernatural was happening in the hearts of those who listened. The pen of God was engraving things that would become part of the character of the church members. That was all that Paul needed—to know that lives were transformed by the glorious power of almighty God. The kingdom of God is not in word but in power—in the divine enablement of God.

"Now if Christ be preached that he rose from the dead, how say some among you that there is no resurrection of the dead?" (1 Cor. 15:12). The Corinthians began to doubt the miracles of God. How did this happen? Why were they speaking these things? It actually further reveals the depth of the problem in Corinth. When the natural mind begins to lead the church, there is a resulting powerlessness in the present that leads to hopelessness for the future. That is exactly where this theology was coming from. They had to figure it all out now, which meant they would have to figure it all out in the days ahead. Because they were not living in the resurrected life, there was a loss of hope for the future.

God Needs Plenty of Nothing

Whenever I go anywhere to hear the Word of God, I do not want to hear from the mind of man. I do not want people's opinions about God. I want to hear what God is saying through the Holy Spirit.

"For as in Adam all die . . ." meaning, if what I am listening to is emanating from the natural wisdom given to a man, I will die spiritually. I will not be able to finish this journey. I will lose heart in the present; I will lose hope for the future. ". . . even so in Christ shall all be made alive" (1 Cor. 15:22). This implies that there has to be the life of another lived in me. There has to be something other than what I possess that takes me on this journey. We see this truth from the very beginning of the biblical record.

> In the beginning God created the heaven and the earth. And the earth was without form, and void; and dark-

> ness was upon the face of the deep. And the Spirit of God moved upon the face of the waters (Gen. 1:1-2).

The word "darkness" in the Hebrew means "falsehood, ignorance or blindness." When God created the world, it was as if everything were under judgment or in the grave. Darkness was on the face of the earth. Darkness is also on the man without God, the one who fails to surrender to the wisdom of God in Christ.

"The Spirit of God moved upon the face of the waters. And God said, Let there be light: and there was light" (Gen. 1:2-3). In the same way, when we let the Spirit of God come upon us and we listen to what God speaks, everything begins to change.

Notice that when God spoke, suddenly out of nothing, light appeared. You see, God doesn't need anything to make something. All He needs to make something is nothing! Our problem is that we think we are something. We think we have something to bring to God. We think we have something good in us that we are not willing to let go of. And because we are unwilling to admit that we are nothing without God, we sell ourselves short of what God wants to do in our lives. Unfortunately, many churches today are walking in the natural because everybody is so focused on being something. Yet all the while God says, "I cannot work with something—I need nothing to work with!"

Remember how God gave Abraham a promise that he would be the father of many nations? Even when he and his wife were both clearly past child-bearing age, Abraham "believed, even God, who quickeneth the dead, and calleth those things which be not as though they were" (Romans 4:17). He believed that God was able to perform what He had spoken. Abraham did not consider his own body, which the Scripture says was as good as dead. He believed in the God who calls things out of nothing.

In Genesis 2:7, we are told that the Lord God formed man of the dust of the ground. What did He have to work with? Nothing. He looked down at the ground, and Scripture says He breathed into the nostrils of dust, and man became a living soul.

God breathed into nothing, and it became alive! Think about the creative power of God manifested so perfectly. Out of this nothingness came the miracle of man who, by the power of the reasoning that God gave him, walked away from the very one who gave him life. By God's voice, man became something. And in his something-ness, he started to think that he was smarter than God, and so he turned and walked his own way. Man has been doing this now for thousands of years—circling the globe, trying to gather what he knows was lost.

When we are living apart from God, we instinctively know that we have lost something. We come up with every fad, pick up every self-help book, embrace every new theory that comes along. Yet there is still an inherent emptiness that will not go away because we were created in the image of God and for God.

A Disappointing Form of Wisdom

We cannot come back to God until we know that we are nothing without Him. However, instead of humbling themselves before Him, many people choose instead to grip tenaciously to a limited and disappointing form of wisdom.

Paul said that this worldly wisdom stands as foolishness in comparison to that which rests in the mind of God (see 1 Cor. 3:19). Man can only see the circumstance, and when the solution is too great for his own reasoning, he concludes that his situation is also beyond the power of God. The natural man does not see a way out, and so he convinces himself that God does not know how to get him out either.

This is the exact conclusion that the Children of Israel came to, even after the Lord had supernaturally delivered them from the hand of the Egyptians. They spoke against God, and in their limited human reasoning, asked, "Can God furnish a table in the wilderness?" (see Ps. 78). And when they reached the shores of incredible promise and sent spies into Canaan, finding the land to be everything God said it was, they still limited the Holy One of Israel. They concluded, "No, God cannot do this. There are giants in the land, and we do not have the power to defeat them." So the Children of Israel turned back and died in the wilderness of their limited human reasoning.

If only the Church would learn to forsake man's wisdom and embrace the wisdom of God, even at the cost of having to admit they are nothing. The possibilities would be endless! In fact, I have personally witnessed what can happen when we choose not to limit God with our own natural thinking.

When I was a young Christian, I had a secret prayer. I used to pray it all the time, and I was very specific about it. At the time I was not a pastor and had never even been a speaker anywhere. I didn't have the gifting to stand before anybody. In fact, all through college I had to take pills just to be able to stay in the classroom, for if I were singled out, I would panic and either collapse or run out of the room. But after I came to Christ, I began to pray, "God, I want to win 100,000 people to You before I die. And I don't want these people to simply come to an altar. I want these to be people who are truly converted and will live for You for the rest of their lives." Of course I knew I was the least likely candidate to even think of praying this kind of prayer. It was completely out of the realm of my human reasoning, far beyond anything I could ever hope to achieve in order to see this happen.

It was a few years ago in Nigeria that I was reminded of this prayer. A team from our church was holding nightly services where an estimated range of 400,000-700,000 people gathered. From my vantage point, I just could not see the end of this crowd in any direction—it was a giant sea of people. And I remember one night speaking an evangelistic message where I gave a very definitive altar call at the end. Of course I could not ask the people to come forward, for they would be killed in a crowd of that size. So I asked them to raise their hands. However, I made it very restrictive. "If you have no intention to stop stealing or beating your wives or drinking and fornicating, don't even think of disgracing the name of God by raising your hand. You are deceiving yourself. But if you want to live for Christ, go to heaven when you die and know the supernatural while you live on this earth, please raise your hand." There had to be at least 100,000 hands that were raised in that particular service.

I went back to my hotel room that night, and kneeling beside my bed, it finally dawned on me—God had answered that prayer I prayed as a young Christian! In one service He answered what seemed to me to be impossible. If I were to try to reason it with my own wisdom, it would have taken me a lifetime to ever get there. But in one service, God did it!

As I was down on my knees beside that bed, the Holy Spirit spoke to me and said, "Carter, don't limit me. Don't limit what I can do through a surrendered life." I believe that this is what the Holy Spirit is reminding His Church today as well. Don't limit God. Don't retreat to the confines of man's wisdom, trying to figure your own way out because you concluded that God cannot furnish a table in the wilderness.

When the Barren Cry

In 1 Samuel 1–2, there is a story of a woman named Hannah who came up to the temple every year to worship. Hannah was barren; the Scripture says that God had closed her womb. In other words, there was no life within her. It was an incredible disgrace in that society for a woman not to have a child—a mark of failure, a complete and total lack of accomplishment. To make things even more difficult, Hannah had an adversary living in her own house who constantly provoked her, pointing out her barrenness: "There is no life in you; you have no power to bring forth life. You go year after year, and God does not answer you" (see 1 Sam. 1:6-7).

Hannah became so provoked by this adversary that a bout of weeping came on her spirit. This is actually quite often a precursor to a special move of God. He produces a weeping in you, an inability to be satisfied by all of the things that go on around you. You come to the house of God and say, "Lord, I am just not satisfied until something is born in my life. I am tired of being empty."

The Bible says that Hannah prayed in the bitterness of her soul. Some people think that we always have to be happy when we pray—that there can be no question in our hearts; that it is like a formula we have to somehow get right before God will answer. No, the Scripture says that Hannah was so grieved that she could only move her lips in a whisper. I imagine she prayed a simple prayer: "God, I am empty. I have no power to bring forth life. This area of my life is hopeless; it is barren. But if You will put life there, I will bring it to you for

Your service. I will give You glory." That was just what the Lord was waiting for.

Hannah's prayer is the story of the birth of Samuel. God answered her prayer by giving not only her but also the nation of Israel a great prophet. During that time in Israel, natural men—carnal men—had been running a natural kingdom. God's answer to this was the supernatural. God's answer to every generation is always supernatural. He takes the nothings, the nobodies, and does a work.

Remember the dust that became a man? Hannah was a type of dust; a type of nothing who cried out to a holy, powerful, compassionate God. Paul said that God has chosen those who realize their nothingness (see 1 Cor. 1:27). They realize their need for the miraculous intervention of God. He does this so that no flesh should glory in His presence. Nobody will be able to say, "I knew how to do this. I knew how to arrive where I needed to be by my own power and my own reasoning."

So, thank God if you are a nothing today. If you are something, you have a long way to go. But if you are nothing, what you hear from God will transform your life—and not only your life, but also your family, your neighborhood, your city, your country, the world. If you know that you are nothing without God, and if you, like Hannah, are willing to say, "Lord, put something into my life, and I will bring it back to You for Your glory," then you will no doubt experience the supernatural power of God.

We must never be content to settle into any place until the whole world has come to the knowledge of Jesus Christ. God has a wisdom that was ordained before the foundation of the world, and it was for us and for God's glory. Our part is to come to Him in humility. The proud will never understand this. The people whose whole sense of worth is built on their ministry, position, appearance or achievements cannot hear this. They will never understand until they admit that God is all and they are nothing. Until then, these people will carry on writing books and espousing theories about godliness, never personally experiencing the supernatural power of God. But the lame will press through, the blind will cry from the side of the road, and the lepers will appear—the nothings and the nobodies of society will bypass all of the religion and say, "God, I would like to see, I would like to behold, I would like to walk with You!"

In essence, Paul told the church in Corinth, "My preaching is good for nothing." Today God is calling every nothing to astound this world with a demonstration of His power. One more time, God is going to pour out His Spirit on all flesh. He is going to do something supernatural in the lives of those who want to know Him—those who are willing to come to Him and acknowledge their nothingness. He will utterly confound the wisdom of the wise as He uses the nothings to bring glory to His name in this generation.

Now isn't that something?

When Carnal Men Claim the Throne

If it could be at all possible to fast-forward oneself to the throne of God, then the Corinthians had surely done it. Paul told the church, "Now ye are full, now ye are rich, ye have reigned as kings without us" (1 Cor. 4:8). In other words, you have left us behind. We led you to Christ, and then you allowed into your midst a theological perspective that somehow advanced you to the throne of God where you are supposedly ruling and reigning. You have moved to what you think is the victory; you abandoned the journey of faith and you have left us all behind—those of us who have led you to Christ. You have been led into theological error.

He added, "I write not these things to shame you, but as my beloved sons I warn you. For though ye have ten thousand instructors in Christ, yet have ye not many fathers: for in Christ Jesus I have begotten you through the gospel. Wherefore I beseech you, be ye followers of me" (vv. 14-16).

Paul was saying, "Christ bought you, but I, like a father, brought you into the kingdom. It was the gospel that I preached that engraved something of God on your hearts, and you started out so well. What happened to you? Who threw this curve to you? Who brought you on this journey where you sped ahead and are now reigning without us? Now you are accepted, knowledgeable and popular. But we, those of us who are walking as apostles, are not." Paul pleaded, "Be followers of me."

What Paul was trying to get through to the Corinthians was that they had been bought with the blood of Christ and had been given a righteousness in Him. But now they were a righteous people in the wrong place. If you are righteous but in the wrong place, it can launch you into a blindness that is so deep, an error that is so wrong, a Christ that is so other than the Christ of the Bible—which in the end will sow spiritual confusion into a generation looking for truth.

Go Up and Prosper!

We see a similar case in 2 Chronicles 18 with the story of Jehoshaphat, king of Judah. Jehoshaphat was a righteous man, but he, too, was found in the wrong place. He had allied himself with Ahab, king of Israel. Ahab was the type of man who surrounded himself with ministry voices telling him what he wanted to hear about himself. He wanted a form of God, but he did not want the power of God that would lead him into something other than what he envisioned himself to be. So he surrounded himself with spiritual "yes men." There is never a shortage of such men—those who find their gratification by getting close to power, influence and money. The Bible says there were 400 of them around Ahab's throne, willing to tell the king anything he wanted to hear.

If this is what you are looking for today, without a doubt you will find it. There are a multitude of preachers today who are willing to tell you anything you want to hear about yourself—as long as they can get close to your finances. They don't care what they have to speak in order to please you, even if it sends you to destruction. Listen to what the Lord said in another portion of Old Testament Scripture:

> I have not sent these prophets, yet they ran: I have not spoken to them, yet they prophesied. But if they had stood in my counsel, and had caused my people to hear my words, then they should have turned them from their evil way, and from the evil of their doings (Jer. 23:21-22).

This was yet another time and season where God's people were going into captivity. All kinds of prophets were preaching about the wonderful times in which they were living. "What prosperity awaits us!" Yet God said, "I have not spoken to these prophets, but they ran. If they had stood in My presence, they would turn you from that which is going to destroy you. They would bring you in line with My heart and My ways."

I have no doubt that the ministry of the 400 prophets around Ahab was positive and encouraging. "And all the prophets prophesied so, saying, Go up to Ramothgilead, and prosper: for the LORD shall deliver it into the king's hand" (1 Kings 22:12). That was their message—go up and prosper, do whatever you want, live however you want to live, you are going to prosper.

Jehoshaphat was sitting there with Ahab, listening to the advice of the 400 prophets. But because Jehoshaphat was a righteous man, a troubling began to stir within his heart. So he asked Ahab, "Is there anyone else you can ask about what to do?" Ahab replied, "Well there is one other man, but I never call him because he never has anything good to say to me." Nevertheless, Jehoshaphat urged him to call this man, so Ahab sent an emissary to fetch Micaiah. When he found him, the emissary told Micaiah, "For once in your life, please just say what the rest are saying." Micaiah replied, "I can only say what God tells me to say."

So Micaiah went to the king's throne, looked at Ahab and already knew he would not listen to truth. Therefore Micaiah said, "Go up and prosper, and God is going to deliver it into your hands."

Then an unusual thing happened. Although Micaiah had just said what the 400 false prophets had been saying all along, Ahab rebuked him and told him to speak only the truth. Perhaps it was the way he said it? In any event, Micaiah then delivered the true word of the Lord:

> Again he said, Therefore hear the word of the LORD; I saw the LORD sitting upon his throne, and all the host of heaven standing on his right hand and on his left. And the LORD said, Who shall entice Ahab king of Israel, that he may go up and fall at Ramothgilead? And one spake saying after this manner, and another saying after that manner. Then there came out a spirit, and stood before the LORD, and said, I will entice him. And the LORD said unto him, Wherewith? And he said, I will go out, and be a lying spirit in the mouth of all his prophets. And the LORD said, Thou shalt entice him, and thou shalt also prevail: go out, and do even so (2 Chron. 18:18-21).

Micaiah stood in the court and said, "Listen, God has allowed this lying spirit to come, and it has manifested as a lying spirit in the mouths of all these prophets. The Lord has declared disaster against you." As he shared the truth, one of the lying prophets slapped his face and said, "How did the Spirit of the Lord leave me and go to you?" Micaiah looked at this very zealous false prophet and said, "There is a day coming when you are going to go into an inner chamber and hide yourself" (see vv. 22-24).

A day is coming in our generation when all the false prophets and everybody who has robbed the people of God are going to seek seclusion. They are going to hide because suddenly something will happen. The people will know they have not been sitting under truth.

After Micaiah warned the king, Ahab responded, "Feed this man with the bread of affliction." That is what a carnal church will always do to a man who speaks for God. Slander him, cause him heartache, write articles about him, call him bitter, call him divisive. And Micaiah, as he was being led out, said, "If God has spoken by me, you will know it." Micaiah knew he had heard a word from the Lord, but he was trying to speak to a king who was completely given over to carnality. Ahab had been given awakenings and opportunities to follow truth, but his heart was ultimately seduced back into living for himself.

Remember, Ahab was the one who had been with Elijah the prophet and had witnessed the fire of God come down on Mount Carmel. He had seen the Spirit of the Lord come on

Elijah and watched as this prophet outran his own chariot back into the city. Ahab had been stirred, and he had had these stirrings before. People who are given to wrong theology did not always start there, nor did they become blind overnight. It is a blindness that comes on gradually. They can recognize truth along the way, but ultimately they are given to carnality.

Aren't You the King?

In 1 Kings 21:1-4, we see a season shortly before King Ahab's death where he was lying on his bed pouting—he would not even eat. Do you know why he was so sullen? Because his neighbor had a garden, and he wanted it! Ahab had gone to his neighbor and asked for the garden, but the neighbor told him the garden was something that had been set apart for his family. Ahab was so grieved over being denied this garden that he went into his bedroom, laid down and turned his head toward the wall.

I see all the Christians in our generation who go home pouting. "I don't have a new car. I didn't get that promotion. Everyone else seems to be doing so well, but look at how hard my life is!" And as Ahab lay on his bed feeling sorry for himself, in comes his wife, Jezebel. She represents yet another type of a seductive spirit that comes to those who are spiritually asleep and whose hearts are still gripped with a longing for carnal things. Jezebel approaches him and says, "Aren't you the king?" (Remember what Paul said to Corinth? You are reigning as kings now without us.) "Do not be sad, I'll get you what you want." A seductive spirit always says, "I'll get you what you want. I'll give you your heart's desire. Not God's heart's desire for you, but yours. You can have whatever you want."

So Jezebel took the owner of the garden, threw him a party, and hired false witnesses to stand up in the midst of the celebration and say they had heard him blaspheme God. They ended up stoning this man and killing him. You see, Jezebel is an employer of false reasoning and false witnesses who take reward against the innocent. I cannot help but think of all the people today who, in God's name, are taking for themselves what rightfully belongs to someone else. The Scriptures warn us that the right of the fatherless and the widow must never be taken away. Under the Old Testament law, the people were commanded not to harvest everything for themselves. There should always be a portion left for the widow; the fatherless should always be cared for.

However, selfishness will take it all. The Corinthian church was eating their meals by themselves. They were pushing away the poor and those who had nothing, regarding them as insignificant. But when this happens, God says, "I must rise up and set this right. I have to bring it all down to show the world this is not who I am."

Ahab was killed in battle.

Now in Revelation chapter 2, there was a church called Thyatira—a church whose good deeds were actually increasing in measure, and the Lord had even commended them. But at the same time, He also said to this church:

> Notwithstanding I have a few things against thee, because thou sufferest that woman Jezebel, which calleth herself a prophetess, to teach and to seduce my servants to commit fornication, and to eat things sacrificed unto idols (Rev. 2:20).

They had allowed the same spirit of Jezebel—a different person, but the same spirit—into their midst. The Lord acknowledged them to be a good church, a working church, yet they were also giving part of their reasoning over to this seductive spirit. Christ issued this message of warning to the church at Thyatira because He knew what destruction this pathway would bring. It was the same message that Paul was speaking to the Corinthian church. Could it be the same word of warning that the Lord is trying to speak to us as well?

Come Out from Among Them

In 2 Corinthians 5:15, Paul preached, "And that he died for all, that they which live should not henceforth live unto themselves, but unto him which died for them, and rose again." They should not be motivated by self, but by Him who died for them and rose again. However, there was a problem in the church that prevented this:

> O ye Corinthians, our mouth is open unto you, our heart is enlarged. Ye are not straitened in us, but ye are straitened in your own bowels (2 Cor. 6:11-12).

The word "straitened" means "knit together" in the Greek text. Paul was saying, "Listen, we are completely given for you. God has enlarged our hearts for you, and we have this vision of God because our hearts are opened to you. We are not here to take from you; we are here to give to you. We are here to nurture you and see you grow in the grace and knowledge of Christ. But you are not knit together with us, with this new nature in Christ. You are knit with the interior desires of your own nature. You still have a bond to your old nature."

Paul then pleaded, "Be ye not unequally yoked together with unbelievers: for what fellowship hath righteousness with unrighteousness? and what communion hath light with darkness?" (2 Cor. 6:14-18). Paul was talking about being yoked to these theological unbelievers and the selfish theology that had so interwoven itself in Corinth. It was taking them away from Christ, and Paul was saying, "Come out from among them!"

Notice that although Ahab was killed in the battle, the Scripture says that Jehoshaphat cried out to the Lord, and the Lord heard and saved him. And when Jehoshaphat went back to Jerusalem, a prophet of God came to him and asked, "Shouldest thou help the ungodly, and love them that hate the LORD?" (2 Chron. 19:2). In other words, "Why are you yoked to the ungodly? Why are you listening to the very reasoning they use to lead themselves and others away from Christ? What are you doing helping men who are taking away the fear of the Lord, the covenant promises of God, the atonement of Christ's blood, and the awesome reverence that is due a holy God?"

This same voice of the Lord is calling out to all the Jehoshaphats of our generation—those righteous people who are found in an unrighteous place, who are intermixed with something ungodly. He is speaking to those who know where truth is found, yet ignore it in exchange for something that might provide personal gain—even if it means supporting thieves who take from them and smite their simplicity in Christ. And God is asking, "What are you doing helping these men? What are you doing helping the enemies of the Lord? Should you help the ungodly?"

Oh, that the church of Jesus Christ in this generation would ask God for an eye salve once again—that we may recognize what we are listening to and escape from the theology of this selfish generation! There is nothing in this inward focus that can represent God, and the pathway leads only to destruction. Come out from among them!

Back to the Heart of God

Jehoshaphat did come out. He was not crushed by the words of the prophet; rather, the Scripture indicates that he became a true servant of the Lord. He went back to Jerusalem and dwelt there.

Jerusalem represents the very center of God's heart, the very center of where He desires to dwell among His people. Jerusalem is where the Lord's feet are going to come down when He returns again; where He is going to rule and reign. Jerusalem is also where David brought in the Ark of God, where

Solomon's temple was built, where Abraham offered up Isaac, where the Jebusite gave all he had to stop the plague of death that was over that society. Jerusalem! Jehoshaphat went back to Jerusalem!

That is what we have to do in this generation—get back to where God's heart is. We need to get back to where truth is; get back to what it means to be a Bible-believing follower of Jesus Christ.

> And Jehoshaphat dwelt at Jerusalem: and he went out again through the people from Beersheba to mount Ephraim, and brought them back unto the LORD God of their fathers. And he set judges in the land. . . . And said to the judges, Take heed what ye do: for ye judge not for man, but for the LORD, who is with you in the judgment. Wherefore now let the fear of the LORD be upon you; take heed and do it: for there is no iniquity with the LORD our God, nor respect of persons, nor taking of gifts (2 Chron. 19:4-7).

Jehoshaphat taught the fear of the Lord; he taught the people to walk righteously and truly represent God. He told them not to flatter people, not to allow any bribery to come in and take the Word of God out of their mouths. They were not to be a respecter of persons, not to be given over to self-gratification or to the taking of gifts. Jehoshaphat had seen it all firsthand; he had walked in the consequences of doing these things. He knew exactly where those voices lead.

> And he charged them, saying, Thus shall ye do in the fear of the LORD, faithfully, and with a perfect heart (2 Chron. 19:9).

Jehoshaphat learned what kind of heart would please God. He inspired courage in others as they faced their own decision to give their all for the purposes of God. Later, when an incredible army came in against the kingdom he was leading, Jehoshaphat was able to hear the voice of God again, and he proclaimed a fast throughout all Judah. People came out of all the cities of Judah to gather and seek the Lord. Jehoshaphat knew that human strategy was powerless. So under his leadership, the people learned to stand still until the voice of God came through.

Second Chronicles 20:15 contains a great promise: "Be not afraid nor dismayed by reason of this great multitude; for the battle is not yours, but God's." Jehoshaphat said, "You will not need to fight in this battle. It is God's battle! Stand still and see His salvation. There is no need to fear, for the Lord is with you!" (see v. 17). It is time once again for us to move into the miraculous—to see the salvation of God. It is time to seek Him in fasting and prayer; it is time to deal with righteousness one more time. Jehoshaphat said, "Believe in the LORD your God, so shall ye be established; believe his prophets, so shall ye prosper" (v. 20).

What a difference! Jehoshaphat heard 400 self-seeking voices and saw the destruction they brought. Only one man stood and spoke for God—only one knew true prosperity.

It is not found in a larger house, a more prominent position, or a bigger slice of the socioeconomic pie. That is not biblical prosperity. Biblical prosperity is defined by being given to the purposes of God and for the need of humanity around us. Christ said, "Therefore I say unto you, Take no thought for your life, what ye shall eat, or what ye shall drink; nor yet for your body, what ye shall put on. . . . But seek ye first the kingdom of God, and his righteousness; and all these things shall be added unto you" (Matt. 6:25,33).

We cannot receive God's revelation, nor can we truly know His power and provision until we seek first His Kingdom. Of course this is not the natural inclination of our flesh. However, I believe that we are living in an hour when God is blessing His people—blessing us by turning us away from ourselves, which is really the greatest blessing of all. And as we are faithful to heed His promptings, to take to heart the examples He has graciously laid before us, the Lord will bring us back to Jerusalem . . . back to His heart where we belong.

When Prophets Return to the Gate

You can probably remember when your last visit to the doctor's office was. Perhaps you were exhibiting symptoms that needed to be checked out, or it was time for your annual physical exam. But can you remember the last time you had a *spiritual* exam? If it has been a while, it is time to make an appointment . . . with yourself. That is exactly what Paul told the Corinthian church to do.

> Examine yourselves, whether ye be in the faith; prove your own selves. Know ye not your own selves, how that Jesus Christ is in you, except ye be reprobates? But I trust that ye shall know that we are not reprobates (2 Cor. 13:5-6).

When Paul speaks about "reprobates" in verse 5, he is referring to "something that is unapproved, undiscerning, empty of judgment; it possesses a mindset that is abhorred by God and should be abhorred by man." A reprobate is basically one who allows the natural mind to take control. Remember, the natural mind is opposed to the spiritual mind—the new mind given to us in Jesus Christ. And when the natural mind (undiscerning, empty of judgment) takes control among believers, the end result is eventually fashioning and embracing an image of God that is not true. Not an uncommon phenomenon these days. In fact, much of the gospel that is on our airways today is the preaching of another Christ—one fashioned out of the minds of men.

Paul instructs the Corinthian church, "Examine yourselves and take a look at what image you are following. Who is the

Christ you are serving?" He had tried to get the Corinthian church to do this all throughout his writings to them. He is at the end now, and he says, "Examine yourself in the light of all I have written to you, being mindful of what I have shown your ministry to be. Examine yourselves and see if the Jesus that you fashioned is the Christ of the Scriptures, the Christ that has been revealed to me."

The reprobate that Paul mentions is a person who blocks out of his mind the image of God he doesn't want to follow and creates a new image that better fits his liking. Isn't that precisely what happened in the story of the Exodus?

Finding Satisfaction in Christ

When the Children of Israel came out of Egypt, they had traveled only a short distance before they wanted to go back to what they had left behind. They said, "We remember the flesh pots and we remember the vegetables and the bread. We could fill our bellies with these things" (see Exod. 16:3). Self-consumption still very much remained at the core of the people. They wanted to go back, but in order to do that they had to block out the image of God through Moses' leadership—the image that was leading them in a direction that their natural minds found very unappealing.

In Exodus 15:22, the Scripture says:

> So Moses brought Israel from the Red sea, and they went out into the Wilderness of Shur; and they went three days in the wilderness and found no water.

The Israelites had just witnessed the miraculous. They had watched God part the Red Sea and destroy their enemies. But once they reached the wilderness, they started to complain.

> And when they came to Marah, they could not drink of the waters of Marah, for they were bitter: therefore the name of it was called Marah. And the people murmured against Moses, saying, What shall we drink? And he cried unto the LORD; and the LORD shewed him a tree, which when he had cast into the waters, the waters were made sweet: there he made for them a statute and an ordinance, and there he proved them (Exod. 15:23-25).

Only three days out, and they found no water that appealed to them.

Now remember, everything in the Bible speaks of Jesus Christ. If you read the Scriptures in this context, all of a sudden they begin to come alive. You see that God had one thing in mind before the foundation of the world. He had a Son who was going to come to this earth, and He had a Bride who was going to be redeemed out of a fallen condition. This Bride was going to be empowered by the Holy Spirit and cleansed by the blood of the Son, which would be shed on Calvary. And this Bride would bring the name of God to reputation and honor in the earth. God saw all this in the deliverance of the Israelites and their journey in the desert.

So here were the Israelites coming out of Egypt, just like you and I came out of sin when we came to Christ. They were walking in the wilderness and found the waters bitter, so they refused to drink what was before them. Then God showed Moses a tree—a staff of wood. When Moses cast this tree, a type of the cross of Christ, into the water, the tree made the bitter waters sweet.

Now think about it for a moment. Why are so many people, even those who have come to Christ, still dissatisfied today? Why do they still find that none of the water appeals to them? Why are so many people running from pillar to post all through the Christian community, looking for a word, a touch, something from someone, somewhere?

It is because a self-focused people—whether they are the children delivered from Egypt, the sensual Corinthian church or the Church in our generation—will never be satisfied on their Christian journey until the core of why they are walking with God is to live for others, just as Christ did. They will travel from church to church, conference to conference, place to place and complain about the waters. They will look in the Scriptures, but what they read will seem too hard, too remote, and too bitter to swallow. They will not like what they find until the giving of themselves is the very core of why they walk with God.

An Image of Gold

Consider the multitudes who were following Jesus when suddenly He turns to them and says, "Verily, verily, I say unto you,

Except ye eat the flesh of the Son of man, and drink his blood, ye have no life in you. . . . As the living Father hath sent me, and I live by the Father: so he that eateth me, even he shall live by me" (John 6:53,57). Christ was saying, "You need the power of My life within you to finish this journey. You need My power to put away your old life; you need a new mind, a new heart, a new spirit."

However, at that point many of His disciples turned back and walked with Him no more. Scripture does not imply that they ceased from religion. In fact, they probably became even more "religious." But they stopped walking with Jesus. The bottom line was that they turned from the image of God manifested in the flesh. Hebrews 1:3 says that Jesus is the express image of God's person. Yet they did not want to follow this common man who was not using His power for Himself. He was not gathering an army they could see with their natural eye, nor was He pressing in to the hallways of political power and using His influence the way they thought it should be used. When the crowds gathered, He seemed to get in a boat and go somewhere else. Everywhere they thought He should go, He didn't go; and everything they thought He should do, He didn't do. They looked at Him but saw nothing in Him that they should desire him. So they walked away!

The Israelites who were delivered from slavery said the same thing. In Exodus 32:1, we read that the people said, "As for this Moses, the man that brought us up out of the land of Egypt, we wot not what is become of him." In other words, "We don't know what has become of him—he is too distant, too hard to understand, too hard to follow. Everything we hoped he would lead us to is taking too long to happen." They knew what they wanted God to look like, so they made a god of gold. They made him a god of personal advantage and wealth, and they pointed him in the direction they wanted to go.

Whenever a society turns away from the true image of God, they will recreate a god in the image of gold. This god doesn't lead them; they begin to lead him because they are now free to fashion this god any way they want. They are free to make him say whatever they think he should be saying, although they don't have to listen to him anyway. But this is not the God of the Bible. This is a god of personal advantage, a god of gold.

Jesus warned, "If therefore the light that is in there be darkness, how great is that darkness" (Matt. 6:23). If you know biblical truth and it is turning you away from the image of God, there is a darkness that will enter your soul—much deeper than the darkness of sin. The deepest darkness that you will ever find in this world is a religious darkness. Bear in mind that Jesus was speaking to many people who were seeing the express image of God in human form yet were the very ones who would soon call out for His death. "We do not want this image of God; this is not who we think God is. Crucify this image of God!" Likewise, we are living in a generation where many are saying, "Get rid of the blood. Get the cross out of what we preach. Get rid of this God, put this image to death!" It is as deep as darkness will get.

Proverbs 29:18 says that where there is no vision, the people perish. *The Living Bible* says it this way: "Where there is ignorance of God, the people run wild." Where there is no vision, no image, the people run wild. Have you ever stopped to consider why people are running wild in our generation? Could it be due to the fact that much of the Church of Jesus Christ is not a reflection of the true image of God? Is it possible that people walk by church after church in our society because nothing there represents God; nothing brings Him to reputation and honor?

I am sure Paul would have preferred to share a comforting, loving message with the Corinthian church. But he would not spare them the tough message. He said, "If I come again I will not spare" (2 Cor. 13:2). He was jealous over the Corinthans with a godly jealousy. He wanted them to know the real Jesus and to be a reflection of the true image of Christ. He wanted them to know that the power of God could never be found in any image that the natural mind fashions or embraces. Paul would not spare them this message!

Neither would Moses spare the Israelites. When he came down the mountain and saw what the Israelites had done, a righteous indignation filled his heart. He took the calf they made, burned it, ground it into powder, threw it in the river and then made the people drink it (see Exod. 32:20). He made them drink of their error and taste of the spiritual foolishness they had created! He saw that they were naked before their enemies—that they had been made spiritually bankrupt by this god of gold they had created. They would have no influence, no military power against their enemies, no ability to enter the land of promise. Moses essentially said, "I would like to ignore what you have done, but I can't; you have to taste the bitterness of this. You have to be able to taste what this has done to you, to your families, to this entire nation that has come out of captivity."

God help us in this generation to understand the bitterness of this error before it's too late.

Whose Side Are You On?

After he made the Israelites drink of their error, Moses stood in the gate of the camp and said, "Who is on the Lord's side? let him come unto me" (Exod. 32:26). That is the cry of my heart—God, give us prophets who will once again stand in the gate. The gate was where the battle plans were formed, where business was transacted. The gate was actually the entranceway into where God dwelt. And that is where Moses stood and asked the question that everyone will have to reckon with sooner or later.

Consider the words of Malachi, the last prophetic voice for 400 years until John the Baptist appeared:

> The Lord, whom ye seek, shall suddenly come to his temple, even the messenger of the covenant, whom ye delight in: behold, he shall come, saith the Lord of hosts. But who may abide the day of his coming? and who shall stand when he appeareth? for he is like a

> refiner's fire, and like fullers' soap: And he shall sit as a refiner and purifier of silver: and he shall purify the sons of Levi (Mal. 3:1-3).

Remember, it was the sons of Levi, the true worshipers, who made the break and came back to stand where Moses was. Worshipers are caught in midstream even in our generation. But the true children of God recognize His voice. They recognize when the Holy Spirit is speaking, and they step out and make the break to return to His side. And the Lord shall purify them.

I believe there will be prophets again, men and women of God raised up all through the world, calling the sons of Levi back again. They will be standing in the gate just like Moses did, asking, "Who is on the Lord's side?" It is time that the dividing line, or the plumb line as in Amos' day, fall once again and voices be raised saying, "Enough of this foolishness, enough dancing around a golden calf, enough self and sensual religion! Who is on the Lord's side? Who is going to walk with the Christ of the Bible?"

True Christ-followers

Continuing in the book of Malachi, we see a picture of those who make the definitive choice to be on the Lord's side.

> "Then they that feared the Lord spake often one to another: and the Lord hearkened, and heard it, and a

> book of remembrance was written before him for them that feared the Lord, and that thought upon his name" (Mal. 3:16).

There will be a people who are concerned about the glory of the Lord, who "think upon His name." What is happening to God's name today? What are men saying about Him in the world? Churches will stop and consider: How is God's name being glorified as we meet? Is the conviction of God found in the meeting places where we gather together? Do sinners come in? Are their lives changed? Can people find the true image of Christ here? And more personally, individuals will ask: Is God's name being glorified in my life? In the workplace, am I bringing Christ to reputation? Am I honest in my dealings? Do I speak well of other people when most are tearing them to pieces? Do people know that I am a godly person by the way I govern my life?

Have you thought about His name lately? Have you thought about His image? Or is it all about *your* name and *your* image?

> And they shall be mine, saith the Lord of hosts, in that day when I make up my jewels; and I will spare them. . . . Then shall ye return, and discern between the righteous and the wicked, between him that serveth God and him that serveth him not (Mal. 3:17-18).

When you come back and embrace the true image of Christ, the very first thing that happens is that you will have discernment again. You know immediately who is speaking for God and who is not; who is serving Him and who is pretending to serve Him.

> For, behold, the day cometh, that shall burn as an oven; and all the proud, yea, and all that do wickedly, shall be stubble. . . . But unto you that fear my name shall the Sun of righteousness arise with healing in his wings; and ye shall go forth, and grow up as calves of the stall (Mal. 4:1-2).

This is a promise in the last days for those who come to the image of Christ—the true Christ. God promises to come with healing for those who fear His name. It will be a time when everything that people thought would give them safety and security will be failing. Men will be casting their gold and silver to moles and bats, looking for places to hide. But as you embrace the true image of Christ, you will be going in a completely different direction. You will be growing in knowledge and grace by the Holy Spirit, expanding your borders on every side.

The Lord also says that you will "grow up as calves of the stall." Something of God will be birthed in your heart. It will be a new freedom, a new joy, and you will bring Christ to reputation everywhere you go. I used to live next to a dairy farm, so I have witnessed the incredible sight of a new calf coming out of the stall for its first appearance. The calf bursts forth, leaping and dancing for joy all over the field! It is amazing, considering how sedate cows end up, to actually see them when they are young, finding their first taste of freedom.

> And ye shall tread down the wicked; for they shall be ashes under the soles of your feet in the day that I shall do this, saith the Lord of hosts (v. 3).

In other words, you will have spiritual victory when everyone else is being triumphed over. They will find that they have put their trust in the wrong Jesus. They will be left naked and bankrupt before their enemies; but you will be walking in the righteousness of Christ, in the purposes of God. The strength and power of the Holy Spirit will be on you, and you will put the serpent under your feet where he belongs.

> Behold, I will send you Elijah [that's the voice of Elijah; the spirit of Elijah] the prophet before the coming of the great and dreadful day of the Lord: And he shall turn the heart of the fathers to the children, and the heart of the children to their fathers, lest I come and smite the earth with a curse (vv. 5-6).

Remember, Elijah was the one who confronted the religious wickedness of his day. He built another altar, the glory of God came down, and the hearts of the people were turned back to God again. This is what the Lord will do once again in these last days. He will destroy the selfishness of fallen humanity and turn hearts back to Him, back to His purposes. Fathers will suddenly look at coming generations with care and compassion. Children will again be looking to their spiritual fathers.

I see revival in the midst of whatever is coming our way. I see a glorious visitation of God. The Lord knows that selfishness is what is bringing the curse of sin to its full fruition. That is why He is essentially saying, "I will come and turn hearts—I will turn this selfishness lest the earth be smitten with the curse."

Is it possible that *we* are this generation? Could it be that we are the ones who God is calling to return and discern—to grow again in the grace of Christ, to embrace the Jesus of the Bible, to have His heart for other people?

Paul said, "But we all, with open face beholding as in a glass the glory of the Lord, are changed into the same image from glory to glory, even as by the Spirit of the Lord" (2 Cor. 3:18). In other words, if you are looking at the true image of God, if in your heart you choose to be on the Lord's side, saying, "Yes, this is the Christ, this is the Son of God; these are His words and these are His ways—this is what I want. If You call me to take up my cross, to be abandoned all the days of my life for the good of others in this world, then so be it"—as you behold *this* image, you will be changed from glory to glory. The word for "glory" in the Greek is "doxo" which refers to the inward life of Christ that brings the person of God to reputation in the earth.

We may very well be the generation that Malachi spoke about—the generation that is going to bring Christ to reputation again. Even so, it all begins with a personal choice. You still must decide for yourself–are you in, or are you out? Which image will you follow? Will you follow a Christ that allows you to be sensual and self-indulgent, or will you follow the Christ who Moses did, giving himself to lead millions into freedom? Paul told the Corinthian church, "Examine yourselves." Moses asked, "Who is on the Lord's side?" I urge you to stop and consider today where you stand.

When God Is Exalted in Judgment

History has proven that there are times and seasons when judgment is inevitable. However, God is not in the habit of bringing it about unannounced. We see, for example, that the Lord spoke through the prophet Isaiah not only to warn the people of impending judgment, but also to reveal to them the reasons why this judgment was necessary. In light of the times we are living in, this is no doubt worth some serious consideration on our part. Remember, the Corinthian church was primed for God's judgment . . . so, too, are we in this generation.

In Isaiah 5, the prophet Isaiah told the people of God that they were headed into judgment, and he told them what the judgment was going to look like.

> Woe unto them that join house to house, that lay field to field, till there be no place, that they may be placed alone in the midst of the earth! In mine ears said the LORD of hosts, of a truth many houses shall be desolate, even great and fair, without inhabitant (Isa. 5:8-9).

In other words, woe to them who are thinking only of their own good. They are reaching out and making allegiances, joining fields and houses until they are the only ones who will be able to find any place of security. Little do they know that soon some of the finest and wealthiest houses will be left empty.

> Woe unto them that rise up early in the morning, that they may follow strong drink; that continue until night, till wine inflame them! (v. 11).

In other words, they are led by the intoxicating foolishness of their own human spirit. Woe to them, because all they are doing is seeking one new high after another, one new place of self-satisfaction after another.

> They do not regard the work of the Lord, nor consider the operation of His hands. Therefore my people have gone into captivity . . . . Sheol has enlarged itself and opened its mouth beyond measure; their glory and their multitude and their pomp, and he who is jubilant, shall descend into it (vv. 12-14, *NKJV*).

Remember, this is not written to a heathen nation, this is written to the people of God—those who are supposed to know Him and walk in His promises. Unfortunately, they remained oblivious to the judgment that historically came. Isaiah knew it was coming, but the people refused to believe it.

> And the mean man shall be brought down, and the mighty man shall be humbled, and the eyes of the lofty shall be humbled: But the Lord of hosts shall be exalted in judgment, and God that is holy shall be sanctified in righteousness (vv. 15-16).

God was basically saying, "If you will not exalt Me, I will be exalted anyway." If you will not judge this behavior and heart attitude, God said to Israel, I will judge you. One way or another, I will be exalted. One way or another, people will know that I am a righteous God, a God of truth.

There is a season where the selfishness of those who are God's own people is so consuming that it obscures His glory. We are called to be representatives of God in the earth. We are called to stand for Him. The Holy Spirit should be able to point to us and say, "This is My Church, and this represents Christ. If you want to know what Jesus Christ was like, look at My Church." Yet there comes a point when the only way that Christ can be brought to reputation is to bring divine judgment so that others will know the behavior of "His people" is not a true manifestation of who is the real Christ. It is when God says, "Enough! I can no longer walk with this. I can no longer allow My Name to be proclaimed through the nations like this and let people think this represents Me!"

There was no delight in the heart of the Lord when He allowed Assyria to swallow up the northern part of Israel and Babylon to conquer Judah. It grieved Him to see Jerusalem time and again overrun by heathen nations; the temple where His glory once appeared later completely obliterated. There is no secret delight in the heart of God to bring about judgment. He just finally comes to a point where He says, "I cannot allow this anymore. This is such a gross misrepresentation of My name."

You would not allow it either. Think about those who have been victims of identity theft. These victims use every legal means possible to protect and rightfully reclaim their identity. How much more when we take the identity of God and walk through the nations, completely misrepresenting Him? Of course this occurs in small measure everyday, but the Holy Spirit faithfully comes with conviction. He might say to us, "That was rather selfish of you" or "You should not be walking in that direction." Genuine followers of Jesus Christ walk in humility before God and heed His rebuke, and they are brought back into line. But there is a point when God's people become so religiously stubborn that He has no choice but to bring all of it down. Psalm 46:10 says, "Be still, and know that I am God: I will be exalted among the heathen, I will be exalted in the earth."

Past and Future Seasons of Judgment

In Luke 17, Jesus Himself described the day when judgment must come. His description can very well fit the days we are living in now. Or if we are not there yet, we are very, very close.

> And as it was in the days of Noe, so shall it be also in the days of the Son of man. They did eat, they drank, they married wives, they were given in marriage, until the day that Noe entered into the ark, and the flood came, and destroyed them all (Luke 17:26-27).

None of these things Jesus mentioned are wrong in themselves. It doesn't make you holy if you do not eat. They married wives, they were given in marriage; these things are fine. All of these things have to happen, but that is not what Jesus was talking about.

Jesus was talking about a coming season when self-preoccupation will so blind the people that they will not be aware of the hour they are living in. Amazing! Christ is about to return, and people will just be out there carrying on business as usual. They will put far from their minds any thoughts of the day that is coming—that "great and terrible" Day of the Lord (see Joel 2:31). If you look in the Scriptures and study them carefully, you will see that the Day of the Lord is going to be an extremely difficult time on the whole earth.

The Handwriting Is on the Wall

The story in the book of Daniel gives us another example of a season when judgment was at hand but the people were unaware. In Daniel 5, King Belteshazzar threw a great feast for a thousand of his lords. He took the vessels that were captured out of Solomon's temple in Jerusalem and they all began drinking and eating out of what were supposed to be set apart and holy. Suddenly interrupting the party, a hand appeared in mid-air and began to write on the wall. Scripture tells us that the king became so terrified that his knees were literally knocking together. He immediately called for the magicians, astrologers and soothsayers who were all attending this religious party, but none of them could decipher what the writing meant.

Finally, the king called in Daniel, a man who knew God. From the time of his youth, Daniel had never compromised his walk with God. He had deliberately chosen not to partake of the things that had produced this form of spiritual blindness in that particular society.

Daniel explained to them the message from the Lord. “God has looked upon this kingdom and has used it for a season and for a purpose. But there is wantonness in it now. You are playing with holy things, and you have crossed the line.” That is where the line is always crossed. God will endure a lot of things, for He is a God of mercy. We saw God’s mercy to the wicked city of Ninevah, to the ungodly who were sailing with Paul. However, there is a flashpoint with God. The line gets crossed when holy things are played with—when there is no longer any reverence for the person of God nor for anything that represents godliness.

Daniel told King Belteshazzar, “You knew that God is holy, but yet you chose to play the fool and party with all of these holy things. And because of this party mentality that has come into your court, the hand of God has appeared, and the writing is on the wall. God has numbered your kingdom and has finished it. Another nation is going to take over the place that God Himself had destined you to occupy.”

Picture this. Daniel has just told King Belteshazzar, “It’s over—the writing says it’s over.” Nevertheless, Belteshazzar and the people in that room remained spiritually blind. What did they do? The king commanded, “Put a fine robe on Daniel, and put a golden chain around his neck.” And he has his herald come out and pronounce Daniel “Sir Ruler” in the kingdom! Daniel has just told Belteshazzar it’s over, yet the king proceeded to decorate Daniel, appointing him third ruler in his kingdom . . . the kingdom that Daniel had just said was finished!

That very same night, Belteshazzar was killed. The enemy was already at the gate. While the enemy was pounding at the gate, the people at the religious party had become so blind and deaf that they could neither see nor hear anymore.

Just as Belteshazzar decorated Daniel, we are living in a day when we are decorating Jesus Christ all over the world. Rather than actually heeding His words of warning, we are dressing Him as we please, making Him into an image that we like (and one that would be palatable for others as well), calling Him "ruler" over a life that we still insist on living our own way. We are decorating the very God whose hand has written a message on the wall. Oh, that this church age would wake up and take notice of the manifold warnings we have been given of God! And that we would do it very quickly, for just as the end came for Belteshazzar that same night, time may be shorter than we think.

Escape to the Mountain

No doubt there will be a myriad of voices in these last days saying, "Don't listen to those who are talking of justice and the coming judgment of God. These things have been talked about for thousands of years, and everything carries on just as it always has. Instead, join us and find some entertainment and satisfaction in the things that you see all around you. Look at us; we are being blessed. Look at us; we are moving forward in influence and power and anointing and authority. Don't listen to the voices that are telling you the enemy is at the gate." But Jesus said:

> Likewise also as it was in the days of Lot; they did eat, they drank, they bought, they sold, they planted, they builded; but the same day that Lot went out of Sodom it rained fire and brimstone from heaven, and destroyed them all. Even thus shall it be in the day when the Son of man is revealed. . . . Whosoever shall seek to save his life shall lose it; and whosoever shall lose his life shall preserve it. I tell you, in that night there shall be two men in one bed; the one shall be taken, and the other shall be left. Two women shall be grinding together; the one shall be taken, and the other left. Two men shall be in the field; the one shall be taken, and the other left. And they answered and said unto him, Where, Lord? And he said unto them, Wheresoever the body is, thither will the eagles be gathered together (Luke 17:28-37).

"Where, Lord?" they asked Him. There are different ways to look at this question. It is possible that they were asking, "Where will they be taken?" It is also possible they were asking, "Where will they be left?" The third possibility is that they were asking for both answers.

If the question is referring to where they will be left, verse 37 says, "Wherever the body is, there the eagles will be gathered together." When you look this up in the original text, it means that wherever the carcass is, there will the vultures be gathered. Those who are left are going to be left in a place where self-indulgence feeds on death. People in our generation are going to be caught unaware. They are in a place where they are feeding on death and, in many cases, they believe that somehow this is the provision of God. They do not realize it is taking away their spiritual vision.

Now, if the question is regarding where they will be taken, remember that Jesus was speaking in the context of what happened to Lot in Sodom (see Gen. 19). When the city was being destroyed, Lot, his wife and his two daughters were taken by the mercy of God. The angels took them by the hand, outside of the city, and gave them the message in Genesis 19:17: "Escape for thy life; look not behind thee, neither stay thou in all the plain; escape to the mountain, lest thou be consumed."

In our generation, just as in the days of Sodom and Gomorrah, there will be some left to suffer the judgment of God. But if you can hear what the Holy Spirit is saying, God in His mercy is taking you by the hand in this hour, leading you outside of Corinth—outside of the value system of a city that is going to be nothing more in the years to come. There is nothing lasting, nothing eternal in any city in this world. But God's mercy is taking people now by the hand, saying, "Get out of the thinking of this city! Get out of the self-consumption, the lust for money and fame. Get out of looking for satisfaction in the things of this life. Get out of the theology that is blinding thousands of people and sending them to a place that will not survive the justice of God in the day of Christ's coming. Escape to the mountain!"

Where will they be taken? To the mountain—and the mountain of safety is Calvary! Paul was telling the Corinthian church that this mountain, this place of escape, is in a place being given for others. It is that simple. That is what Paul was trying to get through to the Corinthians. We are not called to live for ourselves, taking the holy things and bringing them into a banquet hall of self-indulgence. God has already put the writing on the wall against this form of religion!

The Soup-bowl Believer

Knowing that seasons of judgment must come, and that God will be exalted in judgment, we ought to carefully consider the words of Paul:

> For if we would judge ourselves, we should not be judged. But when we are judged, we are chastened of the Lord, that we should not be condemned with the world (1 Cor. 11:31-32).

Paul said that if we would judge ourselves, we would not be judged. How do we do that, you ask? We judge ourselves when we allow the Word of God to be a mirror to us—when we allow it to try and prove us, to examine our hearts and make sure that the pathway we are on is truly bringing honor to God. Let me give you an example of someone who chose to judge himself.

Consider the two brothers, Jacob and Esau, whose story is in the book of Genesis. Both of these brothers had access at some point to the blessing of God. Their lineage continued on right through to Jesus Christ. Remember that Jacob had stolen the firstborn's blessing from his brother, Esau. Many years later, when Jacob returned to see his brother, he was afraid of what was going to happen. Esau met him with 400 men, which makes for quite an intimidating welcoming committee, especially when they were coming in at full gallop! So Jacob tried to appease Esau by giving him gifts.

What was Esau's testimony? He essentially said, "I have enough. I have achieved. I have gathered power, 400 men, influence, and I have provision." Remember, Esau sold his birthright for a bowl of stew. His birthright was that the lineage of Christ would flow through him, but he didn't want that birthright. Perhaps it didn't look attractive to him at some point. *Why would I want this? Look at my father, all he does is wander all over the place and talk about this God I can't see, about this day of visitation that is going to come, about the land of promise that one day we are going to occupy.* Scripture bears witness to the fact that Esau began to disdain his birthright.

One day he comes in from hunting in the field, and his brother, Jacob, is making stew. Esau says, "Listen, give me a bowl of that. I'm starving." And Jacob, says, "Well, I will trade you your birthright for the soup." So Esau trades it. That's how much he valued it.

I see a generation that is trading this birthright in Christ for soup. They have their face stuck in the soup bowl. They're thinking, *As long as my belly is full, as long as I am happy, as long as I don't have any personal lack, this is the blessing of God, and that's all I want. As for the truth where this is supposed to lead, I am not interested in it.*

We can liken this choice to the many people who say, "Don't talk to me about the cross; I don't want to hear about the blood. Don't talk to me about sacrifice, about judgment, about personal commitment. I want to hear about soup in the house of God. I want to know what is on the menu today. I want to walk out of here and be satisfied, and I want to pursue power and influence and achievement and provision. I want to be recognized!" That's a soup-bowl Christian!

Paul wrote about the consequences in Romans 9:13: "As it is written, Jacob have I loved, but Esau have I hated." There is a great difference between these two brothers. When they meet many years after the birthright incident, they are momentarily reconciled. In Genesis 33:12, Esau says to Jacob, "And he said, Let us take our journey, and let us go, and I will go before thee." You see, being first is still in Esau's heart: "I will go before you." But Jacob says to him, "No, you go ahead, I will only travel as fast as the youngest and weakest among us can go."

Now Jacob is an example of one who had judged himself. Before going back into that place of God's blessing, Jacob had an encounter with God. It was during this encounter that he came to the end of his scheming and pushing and promoting of himself. He said, "God, I want your blessing" and the Lord said, "What is thy name?" (Gen. 32:27).

Now his name Jacob means supplanter. "Supplanter" basically means "I want to be first." Jacob was the second-born son, but he wanted to be first. Now, the very root of human sin is a desire to be first. Satan wanted to be first, and when he fell, he brought that self-promotion into the Garden of Eden with him. That selfishness was sown in the hearts of fallen men, and it led Jacob into a life of lying and scheming.

But when God asked his name, He simply said, "Jacob." He agreed with God. That is what it means to judge ourselves. Paul said to the Corinthian church, "You are pushing the poor to the sides of the temple. You are indulging yourselves and using this relationship with God for personal gain." But he added, "If we would judge ourselves, we would not be judged." In other words, we must get to the point where we freely admit, "It is in me to want to be first. I want to be seen, I want to be known and loved. I want preeminence, even in the church."

Jacob had to realize his very nature was wrong, for God says, "Can two walk together, except they be agreed?" (Amos 3:3). There had to be something in Jacob at that very moment that wanted everything to change. He needed something supernatural to happen in order to put God first; to put others first and himself last. How does it happen? Jacob simply said, "Look, this is my name. I want the blessing, but I acknowledge that my name is 'I want to be first'." Something in his heart finally agreed with God and recognized the error of his selfish ways.

The Mark of God

What did God do in response? God physically touches Jacob and puts in his body an inability to outrun the weak. And so here comes Esau stampeding out, saying, "I've got what I feel the blessing of God is. I have money and influence and power. But I'm out to get more." But Jacob stands there and says, "No, you go on ahead, I'm not going any faster than the youngest and weakest among us can travel. You go ahead, Esau—fill your belly. Have a great time. I am going to travel with these people. I'm not leaving behind those who God has given to me!"

Jacob could no longer outrun anybody, for he was now walking with a limp. That is how God responded to him! I can picture him walking with a little kid saying, "Hey, wait up for me!" because he can hardly keep up. You see, Jacob now had something in him that gave him compassion for the old and the withered and those who had a hard time keeping up, for he himself had tasted it.

Today, the mark that God puts on His people is compassion. God places compassion in our hearts that will not allow us to walk away from those who need us to be there for them. It becomes simply impossible for us to embrace a religion of selfishness. We cannot walk a walk, in God's name, where the central focus of what we are doing is about ourselves. No! All of a sudden it is not about us.

Once you start wondering, *What can I get out of this Christian life? How can I have a better security, a greater future?* you come dangerously close to being like Esau. But if in your heart you are saying, *God, there has to be somebody who needs me. There has to be somebody who needs an encouraging word; somebody who is walking slowly and needs somebody just as slow to walk alongside him or her as a reminder that nobody gets left behind,* that is a baptism of God's compassion!

In his encounter with God, Jacob could have agreed with the Lord, and then just easily added, "Well, I don't care. I want to be first, and that is just my nature. I can't help it." The Lord would have responded, "No, don't stop there, Jacob. Let Me touch you. Let Me give you a new name. You will no longer be called Jacob—you will be called Israel. I am going to change you and bring you to a place where you cannot be first anymore."

If we judge ourselves, we will not be judged. But don't stop at this place of realizing that you fall short of the glory of God. It may be true that compassion is something we cannot produce in our own hearts, but God says, "I can, if you will let Me put that mark on you. We will walk together, and you will enter into something of My life that you have only dreamed you could have." If it takes a limp, then it takes a limp. But if you allow Him, God will do whatever is necessary in order to bring you to the point where you say, "No, you go first. Are you doing okay? Can I help you with that? You look sad, is everything alright?" It is a spirit entirely other than what you will find in this world today. That's compassion. It is the true mark of God.

Judging Angels

We all want the blessing of God, don't we? The Corinthian church certainly wanted it. We saw that Jacob wrestled to attain it. And as a believer in Jesus Christ today, surely you long to be blessed as well. There is nothing wrong with that, for it is God's desire to bless us. In fact, that was the covenant promise that the Lord made to our forefather Abraham: "I will bless thee, and make thy name great" (Gen. 12:2). The problem arises, however, when we neglect the second half of that promise: "And thou shalt be a blessing."

The blessing is not something to be consumed upon ourselves. In fact, the true blessing of God will ultimately lead us to other people—to the poor, to the despairing, to those who are captive in their minds, to those who have no helper. That is where the anointing of God will always lead. Unfortunately, the Corinthian church did not seem to be able to grasp this concept, and that is why the true blessing of God eluded them. Likewise, many people today wonder why they are not blessed. Even if they are able to move past this desire for material and temporal "blessings," they still wonder why they do not see the giftings of God operating in their life; why there is so little joy, so little revelation, so little anointing. But the real question is, what are they currently investing the majority of their time and their lives in? Does it really require the true blessing of God?

Let's return for a moment to the story of Jacob. Remember, we saw that Jacob wanted the blessing of God, and he tried to get it by deception; he tried to press his way into the blessing without a changed nature. Yet because of the virtue of his name, "I want to be first," he could never fully know it. God was certainly willing to give the blessing to him, but first He had to take Jacob on a journey. And of course, as we saw in the lives of Paul, Elijah and Elisha, the journey did not necessarily lead to an easy place.

> And Jacob went out from Beersheba, and went toward Haran. And he lighted upon a certain place, and tarried there all night, because the sun was set; and he took of the stones of that place, and put them for his pillows, and lay down in that place to sleep. And he dreamed, and behold a ladder set up on the earth, and the top of it reached to heaven: and behold the angels of God ascending and descending on it. And, behold, the LORD stood above it, and said, I am the LORD God of Abraham thy father, and the God of Isaac: the land whereon thou liest, to thee will I give it, and to thy seed; and thy seed shall be as the dust of the earth, and thou shalt spread abroad to the west, and to the east, and to the north, and to the south: and in thee and in thy seed shall all the families of the earth be blessed (Gen. 28:10-14).

After Jacob had taken the blessing from his brother Esau, we see him in this next season of life heading out to a hard place. In fact, he had to resort to using stones for pillows. Yet it was in this difficult place that God gave him a vision in which he was able to witness something of how God operates.

In the vision, God was standing at the top of what Jacob described to be a ladder—some kind of a causeway between earth and heaven. He saw angels coming down to the earth and going back up—a picture of the strength of God being released from heaven to the earth. It is God coming and touching people like you and me, giving us strength so that we can become what He has destined us to be. Along with this vision of angels, Jacob heard incredible promises: "I will give you places that are not yours right now. I will multiply your seed as the dust of the earth. You will spread abroad in every direction, and all the families of the earth are going to be blessed."

What remarkable promises of God, all given to a man who was lying there with his head on a stone—a tough place to be indeed! You see, it is often in the toughest places that you will find revelation of God, not where the pillows are soft and the way is easy. We ought also to take notice of something particular about Jacob's journey: perhaps for the very first time, Jacob got a true glimpse of where the blessing of God in his life might be leading him, for verse 17 says, "And he was afraid, and said, How dreadful is this place! this is none other but the house of God, and this is the gate of heaven."

The word "dreadful" in the Hebrew text means "a very positive feeling of awe and reverence toward God." But it also means "an emotional and intellectual anticipation of personal harm; what one feels may go wrong." Have you ever been in a "dreadful" place defined by both of these meanings? Have you ever been in a church when an altar call was given, or the gospel was preached, and you heard these words: "Give your life fully to Jesus Christ, and God will use you! Great glory will be brought through your life, and much good will come to people around you"? In your heart you said, *This is a dreadful place. On one hand I know that the awesomeness of God is calling me to something that is far beyond myself. But on the other hand, look at all the things that could go wrong. How difficult might it be?*

"And he called the name of that place Bethel" (v. 19), or in other words, Jacob called this place "the house of God." It is where our all is given for the cause of Christ. Remember, we saw that David had this same revelation when Ornan the Jebusite gave of all he had to stop the plague that was on the nation of Israel (see 1 Chron. 21). He, too, called it the house of the Lord—this place where ordinary people give everything they have, not for themselves, but for the sake of others.

Now, many people today claim to have an open heaven and visions of God just like Jacob did. However, most of these visions are from the wrong perspective. These people see God, they see the angels, they see His provision—but they see this whole connection to heaven as a means for the angels to come down simply to provide them with everything they want for themselves. They mistakenly believe that God has opened the heavens and is sending provision so that they might be first.

By contrast, in the book of John we meet a man named Nathaniel—a man who would be given a true vision from God. Jesus Himself came to him and said, "Hereafter ye shall see heaven open, and the angels of God ascending and descending upon the Son of man" (John 1:51). He did not mean that Nathaniel was going to have the same vision as Jacob; rather, he was going to see what Jacob's vision was all about.

Ultimately, it is all about Christ. Everything that happened to Abraham, Isaac and Jacob led to Jesus Christ. It is all about God ordaining before the foundation of the world that His Son would come down from heaven to supply the need we have for redemption—to have in the earth a church body that He could indwell, showing the world His willingness to forgive the ignorance of man and the folly of men's sin. He moves through the earth doing good to men even though the majority of society may oppose their own salvation. Jesus said, "You will see this, Nathaniel. Because you are a man in whom there is no deceit, you are going to be given this revelation. You are going to see that all of God's provision has come down and is being made available now to you and to all who choose to walk with God."

An Angel's Resume

As we look at this ladder and are given a picture of the provision of God being released from heaven to earth through angels, the next logical question would be, "What exactly can angels do?" Let's see what the Scriptures tell us.

> And [Satan] saith unto him, If thou be the Son of God, cast thyself down: for it is written, He shall give his angels charge concerning thee: and in their hands

> they shall bear thee up, lest at any time thou dash thy foot against a stone (Matt. 4:6).

Here we see that even Satan himself knew what angels could do. He knew the Scriptures, as distorted as his mind may have been, so he was aware that the angels could have prevented Jesus from suffering any personal pain. Angels still have the ability to do so today. God could have ordained a Church in the world in which He charged the angels to prevent all suffering from coming our way. He could have used this to create a very clear distinction between the saved and the lost. For example, He could make it so that the lost lose their jobs but the saved do not. Only the lost would suffer, never the saved. But of course that is not the case. The saved have to walk through the same world as everyone else.

> And he shall send his angels with a great sound of a trumpet, and they shall gather together his elect from the four winds, from one end of heaven to the other (Matt. 24:31).

Angels could come at the command of God. The Lord could command them even right now, and they would immediately gather the whole Church, taking us all to a place of safety and protecting us from the difficult days that are to come.

> When the Son of man shall come in his glory, and all the holy angels with him, then shall he sit upon the throne of his glory (Matt. 25:31).

Angels could be the agents of God, establishing Christ and His Church in a place of reigning and authority right now. They could push aside every argument, settle every issue, and set us in a place of ruling and reigning, just as is promised to those who belong to Christ. But remember Paul said to Corinth, "You are reigning just a little too soon."

> Thinkest thou that I cannot now pray to my Father, and he shall presently give me more than twelve legions of angels? But how then shall the scriptures be fulfilled, that thus it must be? (Matt. 26:53-54).

Angels could be dispatched in legions to immediately judge and destroy every power that sets itself up against truth. All it would take is a simple prayer to the Father.

Now these are just some of the things that angels are able to do. And in the context of Jacob's vision, this is what many people picture to be the provision that God *should* be sending down to the earth. They consider the power of God to be for the sole purpose of preventing all suffering, all personal discomfort and pain—for keeping them from difficult days that are destined to come to everyone on earth.

Jesus made it very clear that angels *could* do these things. So why don't they? Why didn't the angels come in rescue mode while Jesus was being tempted in the wilderness? We read in Matthew 4:11 that angels came to strengthen Jesus after Satan left. Was there a reason why they were fashionably late, showing up *after* the devil had already thrown his best shots at trying to undermine Jesus' confidence in His Father and divert Him from the will of God?

Of course we know God is never late. You see, the devil had tried one of his all-time favorite arguments on Jesus: "You don't have to suffer hardship, there is an easier way to do all this." Now Jesus could have bowed to the enemy's logic. Or He could have asked His Father to send a legion of angels to deliver Him from that moment of trial and testing, as opposed to having the angels show up later. But Jesus refused, and here's why (He explained it best Himself): "How then could the Scriptures be fulfilled?" (Matt. 26:54, *NKJV*). He chose instead to fully obey the will of His Father.

Angels in the Wings

If you look back in church history at generations prior, you will see that many saints had to endure times of immense difficulty, suffering and persecution. Yet suddenly, in our generation, we have arrived at a place where suffering is no longer part of the theology of the Church. We are no longer a people called to suffer for the sake of Christ—everybody is supposed to be happy and trouble-free until the day Jesus comes to take us home. However, angels don't show up in this kind of place. In other words, the provision of God does not come for this kind of theological thinking. The ministering angels came to Jesus after Satan fought against Him and He still refused to be turned from the will of His Father.

Satan will also fight against you—against what you are reading right now. He will fight against the life that is willing to be sacrificed for the cause of others and for that which is in the heart of God. Satan does not care if you are a selfish Christian. As a matter of fact, he wants you to be a selfish Christian because that would render you no threat to his kingdom whatsoever. You will have the same spirit as the world around you. You might go in God's name, but you will have the same pursuits as the world and therefore no influence. The devil knows that you will not be bringing the real Savior anywhere you go, so he will likely even get behind you and encourage you in your mediocrity.

However, the moment you rise up and conclude, "I am not content to live a life of ease while this generation is dying," Satan will oppose you with everything he's got! Yet that is when you will find angels coming down to strengthen you. The Word of God will come alive in you and the Holy Spirit will become your best friend in this whole world. You will be given resources and wisdom, compassion and giftings of the Spirit that do not come to the natural man but only to those who are willing to walk in the supernatural. You will find delight in things that do not delight the hearts of carnal men. You will be heading out and doing the will of God. At times, you will have to walk through the gauntlet of even Christian opposition—those who have stopped along the way because they do not want to walk with God or lay their lives down for the cause of Christ. But angels will come and strengthen you.

Luke 22 tells us that right before He went to the cross, Jesus went into the Garden of Gethsemane and an intense agony came upon Him—one that we will never be able to fully understand until we get to heaven. Jesus was about to be momentarily separated from His Father, something that had never occurred in all of eternity past. God is one, and now God the Father was going to turn His back on the Son and put the full weight of your and my sin upon Him. Thankfully, Jesus did not turn around and change His mind. He did not call for the legions of angels to rescue Him, though they would have surely come. Instead, He was willing to pay the full price of obedience that would take Him all the way to Calvary. Had he chosen not to, there would be no freedom, no testimony, no tomorrow and no heaven. It would all be just a religious illusion. There would be no power in it whatsoever if He had turned around and called for the help that could have been given Him. Instead Jesus knelt in the Garden and prayed:

> Father, if thou be willing, remove this cup from me: nevertheless not my will, but thine, be done. And there appeared an angel unto him from heaven, strengthening him (see Luke 22:42-43).

If only Jesus' prayer would become ours in this generation. "Not my will but thine." If only we would look the cross square in the eye and say, "God, if that is what You have for my life, then that is where I am going. If that is my future, I trust

You for the strength to follow the path." When you set your eye to living for God and even to going to the four corners of the earth, if necessary, you will begin to see heaven opened. You will see the angels of God ascending and descending, and you will begin to experience the supernatural power of God in your life.

If You Want an Open Heaven

As we have seen, angels have the potential to bring the very strength of heaven to God's people here on earth. This might evoke an image of a mighty angel like Gabriel who appeared to Daniel and also to Zechariah, both of whom fell down in fear before him . . . or perhaps Michael and the other angels fighting against the dragon as we read in Revelation. But do you realize what our relationship to angels will one day be? Paul reveals it in the midst of his rebuke to the Corinthian church:

> Dare any of you, having a matter against another, go to law before the unjust, and not before the saints? Do ye not know that the saints shall judge the world? and if the world shall be judged by you, are ye unworthy to judge the smallest matters? Know ye not that we shall judge angels? how much more things that pertain to this life (1 Cor. 6:1-3)?

One day we will judge angels! But first Paul was saying to the Corinthians, "Look at the direct contrast between who Christ is and where you still are. Christ lived for the salvation of others, enduring opposition to the point of shedding His blood for them. That is why He had an open heaven and angels came to minister to Him. Yet how many of you are holding on to petty grievances, refusing to forgive past wrongs? You are even looking to unsaved men, to a court of public opinion, to agree with you. Now if you cannot even judge insignificant matters, and you remain unwilling to let go of these petty grievances, how do you expect to one day judge angels?"

Once again, do we not bear an uncanny resemblance to the Corinthian church? How many people are going nowhere in the Church of Jesus Christ today because they simply will not forgive? Culture will not forgive culture, race will not forgive race, and country will not forgive country. Many are holding to grievances of the past, and at the same time they wonder why heaven seems closed and why the angels are not descending Jacob's ladder with their personal provision. At the very core of this problem is an unforgiving spirit—an unwillingness to be the blessing of God to all men. They are unwilling to be sacrificed as Christ was so that people—even those who spit in His face, mocked Him, beat Him and betrayed Him—might come to the saving knowledge of God through the shedding of His blood. This is the pathway to the power of God. Only when you and I are willing to let go of all grievances can we share in the provision of Christ.

Paul said in 1 Corinthians 6:9, "Do you not know that the unrighteous will not inherit the kingdom of God?"

In other words, "Do you not know that this power which is given to those who are called to be a blessing in the earth does not come to those who hold grievances in their heart?" Think about all the useless religion that goes on and has gone on for years in the name of God—all the shouting and running around that actually has at its core a deep unforgiveness toward man, yet still portrays itself as that which represents Christ. How can we claim that the life of Christ is flowing through us, that the provision of God is ours, if in our heart we are not willing to forgive all who have ever wronged us?

If the devil can keep us from forgiving others, he knows he has neutralized the whole message of the gospel. We will sing and shout and preach without power. I am sure he was chuckling when the Corinthian church was taking each other to court for petty grievances that could have been settled in the Spirit. There was simply an unwillingness to forgive. I fear that if we do not get this one truth right, it will swallow much of the Church in our generation. Churches will start preaching hate instead of reconciliation, division instead of unity.

Paul reminded the Corinthians, "Where the Spirit of the Lord is, there is liberty" (2 Cor. 3:17). The word "liberty" means generosity. Paul is saying, "As we behold Christ, whatever is in Christ becomes ours." Think of Jacob as he beheld God. He was willing to walk with God, so the strength of God became His. As we behold Christ and His Spirit comes to us, the generosity of God in Christ toward all men becomes ours.

We have the power to forgive all men and to desire that all men be forgiven. That is when hell begins to tremble and the kingdom of God begins to move forward with power.

After you and I acknowledged our need of a Savior and came to Him, why did God leave us here? Did He leave us to sing songs and make noise and run the aisles at our conventions? Or did He leave us here to bring the message to all men that Christ died so that none should perish in their sins, but that all should come to the saving knowledge of what Christ has done on Calvary? Consider what Jesus once told His disciples:

> For verily I say unto you, That whosoever shall say unto this mountain, Be thou removed, and be thou cast into the sea; and shall not doubt in his heart, but shall believe that those things which he saith shall come to pass; he shall have whatsoever he saith. Therefore I say unto you, What things soever ye desire, when ye pray, believe that ye receive them, and ye shall have them (Mark 11:23-24).

In our generation, I believe the "mountain" is this inability to want to do the will of God. It is where we consider full obedience to God and living as He did to be a hard place; a dreadful place. Yet Jesus says that we can speak to this mountain and tell it to move, and it will get out of the way. And then whatever we ask for, whatever provision of God we need, will come down from heaven and will be ours.

Jesus then says something in the next verse that seems almost unrelated. "And when ye stand praying, forgive" (v. 25). In other words, forgiveness is the very bedrock of this life of the blessing of God. We must be willing to forgive all who have wronged us, just as God was. That is where it all begins.

So how do you know you have truly forgiven someone? When you forgive somebody, you let the debt go. You say, "You don't owe me anything anymore. I am ripping up the list of grievances and not picking it up again. It is gone." Then, if God leads you to be a blessing to that person, you are willing to do that for the sake of Christ.

Forgiveness is in no way an easy call. In fact, it is a difficult place, a dreadful place. Many people have been sexually abused, others have lived through genocides, some have had family members killed. Having to let go of these things may feel like laying your head on a stone just like Jacob did. It is an incredibly hard place to think that God is calling you to be a blessing to the very people who have inflicted such pain, perhaps not only to you but maybe even to people of your own culture.

However, total forgiveness is what God requires. That is when we are given an open heaven. We begin to see angels ascending and descending—the provision of God being sent down. Jesus came down and loved the very people who He knew would ultimately reject and hurt Him. But He endured, for in His heart was this bedrock of seeing us forgiven. Now He sits above the angels where we will one day be.

Do you not know, Paul says, that one day you will judge angels? However, you must first follow in the footsteps of your

Master, which may mean retiring your feather pillow for now. But think about what Jacob did: he took all of the stones—all of the hard places—and made an altar out of them. He poured oil on them and worshiped God! I challenge you to do as Jacob did, and one day, when you realize how many people were led to the forgiveness of God; when you find yourself in a position of authority higher than even the angels, you will count it all worth it.

The Broken Body of Christ

Brokenness is by no means a popular concept today. In fact, you rarely hear very much about it in church anymore. People tend to come to Jesus in order to be made whole again out of every kind of fallen human condition, so the concept of being broken after being made whole can be both confusing as well as unappealing.

In 1 Corinthians 11:23-25, Paul said:

> For I have received of the Lord that which also I delivered unto you, that the Lord Jesus the same night in which he was betrayed took bread: and when he had given thanks, he brake it, and said, Take, eat: this is my body, which is broken for you: this do in remembrance of me. After the same manner also he took the cup, when he had supped, saying, this cup is the new testament in my blood: this do ye, as oft as ye drink it, in remembrance of me.

In speaking about the broken body of Christ, Paul was not merely giving the Corinthian church a formula for communion; he was drawing a direct contrast to the self-seeking attitudes still very much embedded in their value system. He told them, "*This* is the Christ I received; this is the revelation that was given to me and that I passed on to you. It was a Christ who was broken for you."

Paul was once again reminding them that Christ had come to do the will of His Father, which is that none should perish, but all should come to this saving knowledge of

Christ. And because of this, He was willing to give His life as a sacrifice—not just His body, but His blood was poured out to pay the price for their sin. Christ did this because He saw they had a need, a debt they could not repay.

> For as often as ye eat this bread, and drink this cup, ye do shew the Lord's death till he come (v. 26).

In other words, you show the reason for the sacrifice of Christ. Paul was plainly describing to the Corinthians the call on their lives as part of the Church of Jesus Christ: They were to become a physical demonstration, as a body, of why God came to the earth in human form as the Son of God—of why He went to a cross and endured the ridicule and scorn of all men who were walking in another direction. They were to be witnesses of the fact that sins are forgiven in Christ and that God does come in the power of the Holy Spirit, offering freedom from the power of death.

But how do self-seeking people become such a witness? It is not possible. Paul was telling this church that as long as they were coming together only for their own good, they were far from being witnesses of Christ's sacrifice. Instead, they fell right in line with the selfish, me-first-and-everyone-else-last world, blending in with a society that was going in a completely different direction from where Christ's life, death and resurrection lead. That is why Paul warned them, "Wherefore whosoever shall eat this bread, and drink this cup of the Lord, unworthily, shall be guilty of the body and blood of the

Lord. . . . For this cause many are weak and sickly among you, and many sleep" (1 Cor. 11:27, 30).

Today we find ourselves in a state that would likely warrant the same rebuke from Paul. A weakness, a spiritual slumber has come upon the Body of Christ in our generation. Many are gathering in the name of Christ but see so little fruit. It is because there is an overriding spiritual death at work here, for they have failed to discern what it really means to be part of the Lord's broken body.

The Human Dilemma

In Matthew 27, we see an example of where this life of brokenness is clearly rejected. In this scene, Jesus Christ is standing before Pilate just before going to the cross. Here we actually have a picture of the dilemma that confronts all men in their fallen condition—the choice of whether or not to cling to a fallen value system even as they come face-to-face with the visible image of God in Christ Jesus. It is the irony of ironies.

Pilate was governor, a man who had schemed and manipulated. He had made his way into what he regarded as power and achievement. Pilate had an image of himself as successful, but now he was confronted with the image of God in Christ Jesus. So ironically, there stood Pilate, who appeared to be in a place of strength, control, achievement and authority, but it was all temporary. And before him stood Jesus, a man who seemed to be weak, captive, a failure and at the mercy of others, yet His authority was in truth. It is the ultimate irony: *The man who seems to be permanent is temporary, and the man who seems to be temporary is permanent.* Everything becomes inverted, flipped upside down when you consider things from the perspective of how the world sees spiritual truth.

When Pilate looked at Jesus, even he must have sensed the irony. He asked Jesus, "Are You the King of the Jews?" Jesus replied, "Thou sayest" (Matt. 27:11), which means, "Yes, it is just as you say." Although we read nothing that would attest to Pilate's being a righteous man, Scripture bears witness that he became troubled. There was something confronting him that he had to deal with, whether or not he wanted to. Even Pilate's wife, an unsaved, possibly heathen woman, came to him and said, "Listen, don't have anything to do with this man; he conforms to what is right. I have suffered many things in a dream because of him" (see Matt 27:19). The word "suffered" means to have experienced something evil. I believe Pilate's wife had been given a premonition that there was something about this man that they had better not touch. Tragically, even many Christians do not have this kind of revelation. Arrogant men have touched the glory and the image of God in our generation. Now, you and I regard it as utterly foolish when somebody refuses to trade what is temporary for what is eternal. Yet how many people today are doing this very same thing—clinging desperately to what is temporary and pushing away this image of Christ, this eternal image, which is actually the image of God?

Pilate was stirred in his heart, and although He sought to release Jesus, there was something inside him saying, "Yes, this is a righteous man, a just man. But I'll pass on this life of brokenness and being yielded for others. No sir, not for me! After all, some king this is! Who would want to reign with Him? And for that matter, who would want to be under His authority?" Verse 24 tells us that Pilate then took water and made the clear choice to wash his hands of this image of Christ standing before him. This is a type of those who, even through the use of Scriptures, create another image of God. Remember, the Bible talks about the Word of God as living water. In Ezekiel 36:25, God says, "I will sprinkle clean water on you, and ye shall be clean." But people who do not want this image of Christ will take this Word, put their hands on it and actually wash their hands of the image of God that is portrayed in the Scriptures.

What happens to those who do so? In the case of Pilate, history and tradition tell us that he became a troubled man for the rest of his life. Some say he even became a compulsive washer of his hands. It reminds me of people today who are always running—always looking for some image, some new corner on God. They even go so far as to applaud themselves for being students of the Word, yet all along they are actually washing their hands of the true image of God. As a result, there is a troubling that never goes away. They are left with an inner itch that cannot seem to be scratched; a sense that the Lord is just a foot away, yet always out of their grasp.

Loss Is Gain

One of the problems today is that our concept of brokenness is not the same as that which the Bible speaks. We understand brokenness to be loss, not gain—an impediment or a barrier to our journey. We simply cannot see brokenness from a scriptural point of view.

In 1 Corinthians 11, Paul conveys the brokenness of Christ as the fulfillment and the completeness of the work which God ordained before the world was fashioned. From God's perspective, brokenness is not loss; it is actually the beginning of something. Paul had a personal revelation of this, as evidenced in his words to the Philippians:

> But what things were gain to me, those I counted loss for Christ. Yea doubtless, and I count all things but loss for the excellency of the knowledge of Christ Jesus my Lord: for whom I have suffered the loss of all things, and do count them but dung, that I may win Christ (Phil. 3:7-8).

A brilliant theologian, Paul certainly had a reputation in the synagogue. He had a righteousness that he claimed exceeded the righteousness of most everyone around him, for he carefully kept all of the 600-plus laws in Judaism at the time. He had a level of authority that even permitted him to persecute believers in Jesus Christ. And yet he said, I counted these things loss; I counted them but dung that I may win Christ.

Paul must have seen something greater than all that he had accomplished over his lifetime. Unfortunately, this is not the perspective of many people today. They go to what are supposed to be houses of worship, but they don't see anything greater than what they already have. As a result, they simply try to add Christ to an existing value system, attempting to employ some formula that will allow the continued pursuit of old values that should have passed away when they came to Christ.

Reaching the place where Paul regarded everything as loss in order to win Christ requires the spiritual principle of brokenness. In actuality, brokenness is an incredible trading in of something old for something new—for something that was formerly hidden, but now we understand to be of great value.

A Grain of Truth

Jesus said in Matthew 13:45-46, "Again, the kingdom of heaven is like unto a merchant man, seeking goodly pearls: Who, when he had found one pearl of great price, went and sold all that he had, and bought it." Of course Christ was referring to Himself as this pearl of great price.

Did you know that inside of every pearl there is a tiny grain around which all of its exterior beauty is formed? That is how a pearl is created—it begins when an oyster ingests a grain of sand. Because the oyster has a soft interior, this grain of sand becomes an irritation.

You and I are like oysters—we don't like irritation. That is why many people gravitate to a soft gospel. Remember Jesus said, "Except ye eat the flesh of the Son of man, and drink his blood, ye have no life in you" (John 6:53). Jesus had just flicked a grain (of truth, so to speak) into the center of all the Christian oysters following Him, and it was an irritation to all the religious. That is why many of them turned back from following Him at that point.

Now, we can look at a pearl as a reflection of a new value system; the embracing of a new way of living. The "irritation" at the center of softness is this idea of giving oneself for the purposes of God and people. And just as the oyster begins to cover this hard, irritating grain with layers of a substance that eventually form the pearl, as we embrace the cross, layers of the beauty of Christ begin to wrap around this grain within us and form the pearl of His beauty.

We adorn ourselves with pearls, and that is exactly what God is going to do in the last moments of time. He is going to claim a people who are willing to embrace what irritates the world and who allow the glory of God to cover them layer upon layer, until they become a manifestation of the image of God in the earth. And in the end, He will call them His jewels, His crown for all eternity.

It is in the midst of this whole process that ambition is broken and the beauty of surrender begins to form in us. Self-will dies and following the will of God begins to live. Self-seeking turns into the seeking of God for others' sake. However, if we are truly going to have an impact in our cities and our generation, it is possible that there is something else that needs to be broken as well.

Beauty for Ashes

Isaiah 61 talks about the anointing of God coming on the Savior, and subsequently on His Church.

> The Spirit of the Lord GOD is upon Me . . . to comfort all that mourn . . . to give unto them beauty for ashes (Isa. 61:1-3).

Perhaps today you are among the many people who have concluded that their life is a mess. You just do not see much hope of living up to all that Christ has called His people to be. When you look in the mirror, all you see is failure. You wonder, *What can I give to God? I have only ashes!*

God says, "I have come to break that image you have of yourself." You see, it is not just what we give to God, it is what God has given to us through Christ. He says, "I have come to give you beauty, and that beauty is Christ. I have come to take the life that you may consider a waste, and the beauty of My life is going to start unfolding through you." You might be an angry person, but you are going to become loving. You might be selfish, but you are going to become generous. If you let God take the ashes of your life, you will begin to witness this unfolding of the beauty of Christ within you. He has come to give joy instead of mourning over what could have been, what should have been.

Some people get so used to mourning that they become professional wailers over their lives. But that brings no glory to God's name. He calls us to turn away from what brought sorrow into our hearts. "I have come to take away the spirit of heaviness and to give you a garment of praise. I am going to take away the heaviness of your own sin, the heaviness of trying to live a godly life without the power of God in you, and bring you into a place of praise" (see Isa. 61:3).

True praise does not come from anything of this world. It is not choreographed, and it is not produced just because of a musical or singing ability. True praise comes from the life of God lived inside of people who have made the choice to let Christ be glorified. Perhaps in the past, the only time you would ever break out into praise was if you got a promotion or raise in the workplace—when things in the world went your way. But God is going to change your value system, and you will go to bed saying, "Thank You, Lord, that I had enough to get an extra box of groceries for that single mother and her kids down the hall. Oh, God, thank You that I can be an extension of Christ to this generation. You have taken away from me a selfish heart and given me the ability to be used for the glory of God in the earth!"

It all begins with the prayer, "Lord, break me!"

After all that you have gleaned from the previous chapters, I trust that you have a better understanding of what this prayer entails as well as an idea of what specific things may need to be broken in your life. If you find today that you still have an inner desire to be first, a habit of focusing on the enjoyment of your own life at the cost of indifference to others, confess it before God and let Him break the power of self. If you find that you are afraid to embrace the fullness of the cross, to go the full journey, to truly step over onto the Lord's side where your life is given for the sake of others . . . let God break all of those fears. Whatever the Lord has put His finger on, lay it at His feet and allow Him to bring you to a place of brokenness. You know that you will not be suffering the loss of anything that would do you any good if it is part of the value system of this world.

As you allow the Lord to do this deep work in your heart, you will soon notice that as everyone else is becoming increasingly afraid, you will be filled with a boldness and a confidence. When everyone else's hands are clutched, trying to grasp whatever provision they can find for themselves, your hands will be open in giving. When everyone else is shaking their fist, looking for someone to blame, your hands will be raised in adoration and thanksgiving to God. It will all be because you have been broken to something of this world and have been made alive to something of God. It is this that will keep you in the coming days.

Conclusion

Despite the foreboding times in which we live, I remain an optimist at heart. The times have no power to dishearten the true follower of Jesus Christ. As the apostle Peter wrote, "Beloved, think it not strange concerning the fiery trial which is to try you, as though some strange thing happened to you" (1 Pet. 4:12).

The book of Hebrews also tells us of a coming time that will thoroughly test the very genuineness of that which we have declared to be a representation of the life and love of God within us on this earth:

> Whose voice then shook the earth: but now He hath promised, saying, Yet once more I shake not the earth only, but also heaven. And this word, Yet once more, signifieth the removing of those things that are shaken, as of things that are made [which have neither divine origin nor ability to withstand the fire], that those things which cannot be shaken may remain. Wherefore we receiving a kingdom which cannot be moved, let us have grace, whereby we may serve God acceptably with reverence and godly fear: For our God is a consuming fire (Heb. 12:26-29).

Fire and trial often seem to be synonymous with darkness. It was at the darkest hour, midnight, when death to the hope and future of families caused sorrow and fear to reign in the majority of homes in Egypt: "There was a great cry in Egypt, for there was not a house where there was not one dead" (Exod. 12:30).

Paul the apostle also speaks of a time of darkness, describing a season of unspeakable lawlessness among people as this world as we know it draws to a close (see 2 Tim. 3). Long-held values will shift with such rapidity that even the most optimistic among us will be tempted to fear. Truth, integrity, loyalty, honor and family will, as Isaiah once said, "fall in the street" (see Isa. 59:14). A type of religiosity will gain a foothold over the people of this generation. It will not come upon them suddenly but rather by stealth, creeping into houses and leading people astray through unsurrendered inner lusts. These will be people who go to church or at least attend church through some form of media, yet their conversion experience is incomplete. The direction and spiritual expression of their lives will have little or no resemblance to the Christ who gave His all to save people who were lost.

It was also at midnight during the shipwreck which we spoke about previously (see chapter 4) that "the shipmen deemed that they drew near to some country" (Acts 27:27). Fearing for their safety, they cast anchors from the rear of the ship to slow it down and wished for the day to come. We find ourselves as a society in the same situation—perilously and speedily heading to an unfamiliar place. We are trying our best to halt the inevitable. Yet this world is on a collision course with Christ. We must deal with the One whom we have largely ignored.

> For by him were all things created, that are in heaven, and that are in earth, visible and invisible, whether

> they be thrones, or dominions, or principalities, or powers: all things were created by him and for him: And he is before all things, and by him all things consist (Col. 1:16-17).

Again, it was the hour of midnight that Jesus used to illustrate the foolishness of those who will be unprepared to meet Him at His sudden return (see Matt. 25). Jesus preceded this parable by warning His disciples of a season of wars, deceptions, false Christs and calamities upon the earth as well as in the heavens. He then went on to speak of a certain wisdom indwelling those who will be prepared for His coming in such a darkened hour. "But the wise took oil in their vessels with their lamps . . . and at midnight there was a cry made, Behold the bridegroom cometh; go ye out to meet him" (Matt. 25:4,6).

There have been many theories about this oil. However, I would like to suggest that it simply speaks of the inner life of a people who have taken the time and initiative to cultivate an honest relationship with God. They have wanted to make a difference in the earth. As we saw in the example of Elisha (see chapter 4), they had to be willing to go beyond the advice and theories of those who were filled with opinions about a journey which they themselves were unprepared to take: "And the sons of the prophets that were at Bethel came forth to Elisha, and said unto him, Knowest thou that the LORD will take away thy master from thy head today? And he said, Yea, I know it; hold you your peace" (2 Kings 2:3).

Loss . . . loss . . . loss was all that these supposed students of the Scriptures could perceive of this journey. It was as if they were saying, "Think of what you could lose if you persist in following the One who has given His all for the glory of God and the souls of men. All we can see is hardship and sorrow ahead for you. Won't you stop here and join us in our study? There is so much yet to be learned here!" Oh yes, my friend, everything hell and earth has will be thrown at you to stop you on the journey of living a life for the benefit of others.

Religion offers a soft pillow for the conscience and presents a wonderful substitute for the heart that has declined to undertake its personal journey with Christ. "And who is my neighbor?" asked the scholarly lawyer when confronted with his pretended love for God that manifested itself in unconcern for his fellow man (see Luke 10:25-37). Although arguing an indefensible position, he nevertheless was trying to infer that he was studying the concept and was perhaps willing to move in such a direction when it was clearly defined to him. After all, what if he's an Amalekite? Didn't God Himself declare that He had an ongoing controversy with these people? Should I help the enemies of God?

I remember this argument being used one time by Christians who didn't want to be involved in feeding some of the poor families in the community where I once pastored. "After all, the father is a drunk," they said, "and if we provide food, we will be enabling him to use his money to buy more liquor." And so some went home with their Bibles tucked firmly under their arms (usually the side closest to the heart), satisfied that right had been done. How sad it is when children go to bed hungry when we could have helped them.

And now, as we become increasingly aware that we draw nearer to the midnight hour with each passing day, let us strive to be like those wise virgins Jesus spoke about—those who were able to see the Bridegroom at His return. Could it be that, from the beginning, His life was theirs and theirs was His? Were they perhaps a people who walked so closely and intimately with Him that He had become a very real moment-by-moment friend as opposed to a soon-coming stranger? I believe they had seen Him everyday—every time His hands reached out through theirs, and every time a smile came to a stranger's face because of a kind word He had enabled them to speak. They were simply doing His work on the earth. It is as if Jesus had a people to whom He could say, "I'll be here to get you at midnight tonight."

That has been the whole focus of this book. It is all about a people who are prepared, undeceived, focused, in love with the work of God. John the apostle described Jesus as "the true light which lighteth every man that cometh into the world" (John 1:9). His life within us is light. We truly begin to see when we allow Him to continue His redemptive work on the earth through us. That simply means that the way Jesus interacted with people, His focus, and His deeds of love and kindness become the pattern of our lives as well. It means that we are being given for the sake of others. Paul warned the Corinthian church of all the perils of not heeding this great truth, just as the Lord is graciously warning us in this hour.

I began this final chapter by saying that I'm an optimist. I know that in those places where I have failed and I am willing to meet God on honest ground, He is more than willing and able to help me change. He has promised to be the light of my life and of the lives of all those who walk with Him in truth, regardless of the darkness of the hour.

> Is not this the fast that I have chosen? to loose the bands of wickedness, to undo the heavy burdens, and to let the oppressed go free, and that ye break every yoke? Is it not to deal thy bread to the hungry, and that thou bring the poor that are cast out to thy house? When thou seest the naked, that thou cover him; and that thou hide not thyself from thine own flesh? Then shall thy light break forth as the morning, and thine health shall spring forth speedily: and thy righteousness shall go before thee; the glory of the LORD shall be thy reward (Isa. 58:6-8).

At the end of this journey, I want to be among the multitudes who have an inner knowledge that they have lived in a manner that truly represents the love and compassion of God for all people. I am optimistic that many who read these thoughts will join us on this journey. And although there are many voices with even more opinions about what the focus of the Christian life should be, ultimately it will all come down to One before whom we will all have to stand. At that time, all will be clear and every argument will be settled.

> Then shall the King say unto them on his right hand, Come, ye blessed of my Father, inherit the kingdom prepared for you from the foundation of the world: For I was an hungred, and ye gave me meat: I was thirsty, and ye gave me drink: I was a stranger, and ye took me in: Naked, and ye clothed me: I was sick, and ye visited me: I was in prison, and ye came unto me (Matt. 25:34-36).

If these ways of giving yourself are not the focus of your Christian life, beginning with those in the house of God, I implore you to make the 180-degree turn now. We are living in a critical hour when we must be found close to His heart, kept by His power, moved with His compassion, and fulfilling all that He has purposed for His Church to be in these last days.

I believe that the sincere seeker will know that the words in this book are true. And I am optimistic that you and I, having gone the full journey, will one day meet at the throne of grace, hug each other and shout with joy unspeakable and full of glory.

Acknowledgments

Special thanks are in order for those who have tirelessly given of themselves so that this series of messages might be put into print. To Neil, Tammy, Luly, Leslie and Eileen, and to the late Pastor David Wilkerson, who insisted that the thoughts in this book be recorded, my deepest appreciation. To all the staff at Regal Books . . . you have been such a pleasure to work with. You are truly dedicated to the cause of Christ. My hope, as yours, is that this book will strengthen the Church of Jesus Christ. In addition, we believe that the proceeds of it will be used in an honorable way to alleviate much human suffering.

TIMES SQUARE ■ CHURCH

Visit Times Square Church at:

1657 Broadway
New York, New York 10019

(212) 541-6300

www.tscnyc.org

MORE TITLES BY
CARTER CONLON

Quiet Times
Music CD

Where Christmas Never Ends
Music CD

Day by Day
Music CD

Clunky of Maryborough
Children's Book

Katie & the Dogs Are Gone
Children's Book

Every Good House Needs a Mouse
Children's Book

Petey Yikes!
Children's Book

Buy a Book, Feed a Child!
100% of the net proceeds from the sale of these children's books will benefit ChildCry, a ministry of Times Square Church (NYC) that feeds hungry children throughout the world. For more information visit: **childcrynyc.org**

o purchase or learn more
bout these titles visit our web store at: **tscnyc.org**